1950

Shadows of Aggar

Chris Anne Wolfe

Published by Pride Publications
Radnor, Ohio

Pride books by Chris Anne Wolfe
Shadows of Aggar
Fires of Aggar
Roses and Thorns: Beauty and the Beast Retold (Bitter Thorns)
Annabel and I

Shadows of Aggar
Copyright 1991 by Chris Anne Wolfe
Published by Pride Publications

ISBN 1-886383-30-8

First Pride edition November 1997
9 8 7 6 5 4 3 2

Original cover art by Ginger Brown.
Cover color and interior design by Pride Publications.

Printed in the United States of America.

Pride Publications is a four imprint, international organization involved in publishing books in all genres including electronic publications, producing games, toys, video and audio cassettes as well as representing authors and artists through syndication and as literary agents. The lion and cradled inverted triangle logo are trademarks of Pride Publications. Logo design by Adam Gage and Daniel Gilman.

Pride Publications
Post Office Box 148
Radnor, Ohio 43066-0148.

PridePblsh@aol.com

http://members.aol.com/pridepblsh/pride.html

T-shirts, cloth patches, mouse pads and other products are available featuring the full-color cover of *Shadows of Aggar.* Send a SASE for a complete listing.

This book was originally published by
New Victoria Publishers, POB 27, Norwich, Vermont 05055

Dedication

For M.A. and Laurel, who launched me from home
with orders to "Fight Fiercely!"
For Susan B. and Susan S. who kept encouraging.
For Carrie who kept reassuring.
For Elizabeth who kept asking for more
and especially for Miz who helped make this all possible.

Acknowledgments

My special thanks for the aid of Merlin Stone's *Ancient Mirrors of Womanhood*, published by Beacon Press (Boston, 1984), and the consolidation of reference materials the book provided.

Julia Franklin's assistance with the geological and geographical development of Aggar was invaluable.

Lastly, my appreciation to my sister muse and publisher, Jennifer DiMarco, who is the heart of Pride.

— C.A. Wolfe

About the Author

Chris Anne Wolfe, Ph.D., published four novels and completed numerous short stories and novellas before her death on July 2, 1997 from cancer. She found home and friends in Germany, New York, California, Florida, Indiana and Ohio — to name just a few locales — but she also treasured her champions met through letters as more and more readers discovered her books.

She will be missed.

A Note from the Publisher

Unlike readers all over the world, I came to know Blue Sighted Elana and the Amazon Diana quite late. *Shadows of Aggar* was published and nominated for a Lambda Literary Award in 1991, but I didn't pick up my copy until 1993 — the year I met Chris Anne while touring with my own science fiction tale. To say the least, I found *Shadows of Aggar,* with its *eitteh* flying-cats, powerful women and magic-and-mayhem adventure unforgettable.

Before her death on July 2nd, Chris Anne — one of Pride's first authors and a dear friend — had published four novels: *Shadows of Aggar, Fires of Aggar, Annabel and I* and *Bitter Thorns* (soon to be reprinted as *Roses and Thorns*). Each novel is unique but all have one thing in common — they give us the stories we long for. Chris Anne's gift was to reach into the hearts of women and find the words we most want for our own. Her books begin with timeless foundations, familiar plots and archetypal characters, but examined in a different light they reflect and reveal the lives, desires, and strengths of women everywhere.

With *Shadows of Aggar*, Chris Anne recreated the classic warrior/mage adventure, and in *Fires of Aggar* she brought us a tale of culture clash and political intrigue through the eyes of two couples. *Annabel and I* has been called a *Somewhere in Time* for lesbians, and *Roses and Thorns* retold the *Beauty and the Beast* myth with two heroines. Chris Anne's novels are what she gave back to the community she loved.

Because of Chris Anne's clarity of vision, she resisted any changes to her work that might alter her intent — from shortening a scene to removing an ellipse. Luckily, the staff here at Pride understand the vital importance of an author's input. It seemed only fitting that when Chris Anne's previous publisher decided they no longer wanted to reprint the *Aggar* books, Chris Anne asked Pride to release author-approved editions. We're honored by the opportunity.

Purchasing the rights to and re-releasing books is a monumental task, demanding hard work. Our thanks go to Pride intern Daniel Gilman who translated the *Aggar* disks from Macintosh to PC, and to Cris Newport and Amy E. Fuchs for proof-reading the book. Special thanks to our loyal readers who purchased instead of borrowing our titles, especially *At the Edge* which was inspired by my friendship with Chris Anne. All of the proceeds from *At the Edge* were used to help republish *Shadows of Aggar.*

As many of you already know, Chris Anne was diagnosed with cancer the same year *Shadows of Aggar* was initially published. Though her health did not always allow her to respond, all letters from readers were forwarded, and she assured us that they were read and treasured. Thank you for writing.

In closing, please know that Pride will continue to donate a portion of the proceeds from the sale of Chris Anne's books to cancer research. We will also insure that her work is never allowed to go out of print. Chris Anne's gifts will always be there for new readers to discover and old friends to treasure.

Sincerely,

Jennifer DiMarco
President of Pride Publications & Imprints

Shadows of Aggar

Chris Anne Wolfe

Published by Pride Publications
Radnor, Ohio

Part One

Dreams Yield, Awake!

Chapter One

The night was bright with thickly scattered stars and the first moon was nearly full. From the eastern peaks, white and crescent-like, the midnight moon came to join her sister and beneath their care the mountain stronghold slept.

A breeze flitted down from the peaks above, dancing along the upper edges of one stony wall until it found a small, arched window with the shutters tied open. Slender strands of moonlight slipped in with the breeze and the dry, bitter chill in the dormitory room stirred.

It was a long, stark room with rows of heavily framed beds and leather-hinged chests. Slumbering figures huddled beneath furred skins and woolen blankets, safe from the late autumn cold.

The night breezes whispered again. The woman nearest the arching window stirred and wakened. Ice blue eyes, blurred by sleep, looked to a stone slated hearth. Flickering, dancing orange flames leapt high, and the subtle smell of smoke drifted to her nostrils. An insistent knock drew her drowsy attention to the door beside the hearth and to the torch-light that pushed through the ill-fitted planks. Urgency clenched her stomach and adrenaline surged through her blood.

At the door the banging began again.

What door? The icy clear eyes blinked as the woman remembered there was no door to the left of their fireplace. The vision began to swim, drifting into pieces, until the flames were swallowed by the empty cavern of the hearth. The wall stood dark now before her inquisitive gaze. She blinked again, and the remnants of the smoky smell were sent away, but the vision left a restlessness, a taunting lure of urgency, that would not leave.

She should not be surprised. The haunting dreams had come all too often. Through warm summer eves and harsh winter darkness, the teasing glimpses of that unnamable person had followed her across more than two tenmoons. Now, the call strengthened, and nearly every night she found herself wakened.

Several beds away someone shifted, then settled back into sleep and the woman realized that her Blue Gift would soon project her uneasiness to everyone in the room if she was not careful. She would have to leave or concentrate on containing herself. She was not prepared to do the latter; she needed to think. With a stern calm clamped across her restless feelings, she tossed back the thick covers.

Her skin was pale in the moons' light, and her small breasts grew hard in the coldness. Unmindful of the chilled stones underfoot, she hurried to her clothes chest. Soft tights of brown wool were donned, and an undyed linen tunic slipped over her head. A wooden comb tamed the length of her dark, curling hair and the strands about her face were caught and drawn back to be bound by a leather thong. The soft hide of the indoor shoes slipped on easily and the ankle laces were knotted.

She noted the moonlight shimmering as it slid through the small window. The Twin Moons tempted her to use her gift more consciously and to send her Blue Sight soaring through that window in search of the one who so persistently wakened her with these murky, indecipherable dreams. She resisted the temptation, knowing it would be in vain. She was a Blue Sight, but she was not trained as a Seer. Her impatience grew. She snatched the light cloak from her chest and marched past the drapes hanging in the archway.

The upper windows in the hall were open as usual, and beneath the moons' light her cloak twirled, settling about her shoulders as she fastened it. The fabric was useless against a winter's cold, but the snows were still many ten-days away. For now, it broke the occasional draft of the Keep's passageways.

She made her way through the maze of gray stone walls and tomb-like silence. Her stride was long and quick. Though she was tall for a woman of this planet, her tread was noiseless as she crossed the polished wood balcony above the hall. Then again the stone closed in around her. With a faint frown, she quickened her pace.

Few of her world would call her an exceptionally pretty woman, her features were neither fashionably plump nor delicately chiseled. Except for her height and the striking, almost translucent blue of her eyes, she was typical of countless young women of her planet. And the unusual color of her eyes could easily be hidden from a stranger by a trick of the cloak and Sight, a special skill practiced by any who aspired to be a Shadow — and who was also gifted with the Blue Sight.

The tension in her expression eased as her own feelings usurped the urgent beckoning of the dream. Her own anger and frustration she could manage, but emotions of dreamspun visions were quite another matter. In truth she was more annoyed by her inability to decipher the visions than upset by their constant appearance.

It did not appease her to remind herself that confusion was often the price of the Blue Sight. The Gift that allowed her to glimpse the amarin — the flowing, hidden patterns of each life — often prevented her from understanding the reasons compelling such life into motion. It was as if she was so acutely aware of each glossy, green-barked tree that the edges of her mind could not define the forest as a whole.

Still, after so many tenmoons of hauntings, she could have hoped for a breath more of understanding.

Ahead the glow of fires and torches sent huge, wavering shadows against the walls, and suddenly she hesitated as the Grand Hall opened below. Dozens of the Keep's scribes, traders and historians filled the Hall. Scattered among them stood the robed figures of both the Blue-Sighted Seers and the revered Council Masters. Kitchen pages darted about with hastily prepared platters of meats and day-old sweets. In the far hearth the mulled Wine of Decisions simmered and the herbal, fruity scent of the liquor made her nostrils flare. She wondered if the Wine's touch had somehow called up her own blurred Sight while these Seers drank and sought visions.

She hovered at the balcony above, searching the crowd for one robed figure in particular.

"Here!" a voice snapped from behind. A woman, grown gray by

countless tenmoons, closed a heavy door. Her black robe shifted as she adjusted its wide, rope belt with fingers gnarled by age. "It always amazes me that so few hear when your mind shouts like that," the Old Mistress snorted. Then she relented some as she started down the steps. "What brings you from bed, Elana?"

The younger woman glanced up quickly. Her full, given name...e-lah ´-na...was rarely spoken here.

"I have decided that you are growing too old for such childishness as Ona," the Mistress continued. "You have been with us for nine of the tenmoon seasons. You are the Eldest Prepared." A dry laugh came. "If you had stayed with your parents, you would already be married to a smithy and have borne three children."

"Two," Elana corrected fondly. "My parents would have waited until I was of age at eight tenmoons."

A disbelieving humpf came from the elder. "Elana will be more fitting, use it."

"Yes, Mistress."

"Why are you up?" she repeated, leading the way to an empty seat beside a smaller hearth. "Surely this did not waken you so far away in the dormitories?" A piercing gray eye suddenly examined the young face, "Unless you do not sleep these nights in your own bed?"

Elana assured her mentor, "I am still in my bed — alone."

"Then?"

"I was awakened...." Elana hesitated, wondering if her personal matters shouldn't wait until the dealings of the Council were finished.

"Vision-stirred," the Mistress murmured knowingly. A boy pushed by with a tray, and she halted him to confiscate drink for both of them.

Elana refused the food, and he left them as the old one sighed again. "Certainly you were touched," she continued almost to herself. "Why am I always so amazed?" She smiled and patted the strong, smooth hand. "You are the oldest of our trainees now. You have a maturity matching the best of any we have chosen as Shadows. And you have the Blue Sight with a basic skill that surpasses most of the Seers' apprentices. I would be more surprised if you were not disturbed by your Sight tonight." She nodded toward the figures gathered at the far hearth. "I fear this crisis our Seers now speak of may involve more than the peoples of Aggar."

The elder's amarin were strong, drawing Elana's gaze to her face. Elana asked, "The off-worlders? How could aliens be threatened by us?"

"Humans, child. Not aliens. These Terrans are as like us as our apprentices are like Council Masters."

A cynical smile turned Elana's lips. "That is sometimes very little, no?"

The Mistress chuckled appreciatively. "Sometimes." Then more somberly she said, "We do not threaten the off-worlders. It seems they threaten themselves. But we of Aggar, I fear, are again being drawn in as pawns in their interstellar game."

As pawns? Or as the Mother's own players? Elana's heart pounded faster. Imagine a chance to turn the fates of whole planets! The magnitude of the idea enticed Elana's very soul.

But then her haunting vision surfaced again and she knew the off-worlders' technology had not built the plank door she had seen. "The off-worlders' games are not what I saw, Mistress."

A thin brow lifted skeptically. "What did you see?"

"The same woman I have always spoken of." Elana gazed down into her wine cup. A face appeared in the ruby depths of the liquid...the face of the woman she had seen in so many dreams. "Only I did not see her. I saw with her tonight. Through her eyes I saw a hearth. Through her body I moved to reach the door. I felt her need for haste." The vision of the face dissolved in her wine, and she looked to the Mistress again.

With a warm clasp she took Elana's hand. "So, perhaps your destiny prepares to meet you? For you, this is more important than all the off-worlders' politics."

"Such self-importance." Elana laughed.

"No," the Old Mistress corrected her quietly, "it is neither selfishness nor pride. It merely is."

Elana absorbed the words slowly, and then with a nod, she accepted them.

The elder turned to the murmuring crowd around them. "In the meanwhile, as Eldest of the Prepared you should stay for this. Even if you truly are not to play a part in their interstellar game, you may know of another trainee who should."

"Perhaps so," Elana agreed as a shadow fell across them.

"I'm glad you have deemed it fit to join us again, Mistress." The Master bowed, but there was a glint of humor in his dark eyes. He pulled a stool nearer the hearth and nodded to Elana. "It is good to see you here as well."

Elana returned her teacher's nod, studying him with concern. He was tired. Lines were etched deeply around his eyes. His balding head drooped with fatigue.

He and the Mistress shared the duties of instructing Elana and her peers in the Preparations; the lure of the challenge — the striving for the undoable was a desire he deliberately cultivated in all the trainees who sought to become a Shadow. But tonight, he merely looked old. Despite his beliefs and his commitment to his planet's survival, he, like the Mistress, had seen too many challenges from Fates' Jests. He clearly did not relish yet another one.

"Have they learned more?" the Mistress prodded, nodding to the Seers that gathered about the far hearth where the Wine of Decisions brewed.

"Some," he admitted and straightened. "The man is indeed an off-worlder. His craft fell somewhere in the Maltar's vast realm. Where he comes from exactly — why the crash...?" The Master shrugged. "The Seers' visions do not say. But of the man himself, it becomes clearer. His name is Garrison. He is skilled as an engineer as well as a pilot. His craft crashed at darkfall this afternoon. He is alone. Some three tenmoons ago, it seems he was assigned to the Terran base, although he worked above on their refueling station. He never actually set foot to Aggar's soil."

The Mistress spoke suddenly. "Do we know what sort of work the off-worlders were doing the season he was here? Perhaps he returned to complete something?"

"The Master Historian has mentioned nothing, but the thought is intriguing. Perhaps we should send a runner to the vaults, the records should tell us."

The Mistress sighed as he wandered off on his task, and Elana turned as the old woman grasped her hand. "I fear," the Mistress muttered, "it will be a long night."

❊ ❊ ❊

Chapter Two

With one hand Diana n'Athena tossed a log into the already blazing fire. In her other she held a metal chalice of the local version of mead. It was certainly not her first cup for the evening, but she was beyond caring. That imbecile Baily had refused her request for the last of the monarc off, claiming she had so little time left to work that she wasn't entitled to disappear off to some god-forsaken village for weeks on end. It would never occur to him that he could send to Colmar for her if anything so urgent came up. The problem was — Diana drained her cup — he knew this was probably the last thing he could order her to do, and Thomas Baily was certainly petty enough not to pass it up.

Terran men! She poured the last of the mead from the clay jug and swallowed deeply. He'd be nowhere without Cleis and herself — or rather, he'd be nowhere without Tad Liest and Tad Di'nay. That was how Aggar's folk knew them, as two men. Could Thomas have any idea how aggravating it was for an Amazon to use her strength and bearing to disguise herself as a man of any race?! No, no, he resented the fact that they could do it at all! Never mind that Aggar's society didn't give much freedom to women so they would be rather useless agents if she and Cleis couldn't pass! His little ego was just too threatened!!

And all this changed nothing. Which went to prove, Diana thought dryly, that it was time to go home. Dear Goddess, after two-and-a-half tenmoons on Aggar and an odd assortment of years and planets before then, it was definitely time for this Sister to go home.

Loneliness grew to an ache, and regretful, Diana dropped down on the large bed. She wondered for a moment where her Sister, Cleis, was this monarc. Friends by circumstances and pillowmates by isolation, they had joined and nurtured their strength to stand against Thomas Baily and his imperial hierarchy. But Diana knew that even if Cleis was here, Thomas wouldn't have been swayed.

Despairingly Diana emptied the chalice and set it on the floor beside her feet. As the fire and mead warmed her body to a fine sweat, she drew the sleeping shirt off over her head, and her thoughts turned back to Maryl in Colmar. Maryl had made the simple linen nightshirt for her, and the bed had been welcoming even in its celibacy because of Maryl's companionship.

Maryl had been good to her, even if she had never truly returned the love Diana had given her. Be honest! Diana snorted cynically. She had never been in love with Maryl. She had been infatuated, but Maryl had not returned the sentiment, so they had settled into an odd charade. To outsiders they appeared as man-and-mistress; with desperate fervor Maryl had always played that part for any audience. Alone, Diana had respected Maryl's silent boundaries and they had become friends.

Actually, she would have suffocated under Maryl's wifely presence, if it had been a lifetime arrangement. Maryl's apprenticeship in Mattee's kitchen had been the one saving grace. The brusque, barrel-chested innkeeper had been downright eager to accept an apprentice whom he could work-a-moon and not pay to support. Although to be fair, he had always been an honest manager in his inn.

He'd been pleased that Maryl roomed with Diana; it saved him the difficulties of finding Maryl accommodations. Maryl had saved him the trouble of looking after Diana's belongings when she was away on her frequent excursions. As for Diana, Maryl's working had saved her own peace of mind more than once.

Yes, it had been fine for a tenmoon, but it couldn't have lasted. Maryl had been too subservient for Diana, despite all the Amazon had tried to teach her of self-esteem. Diana wasn't a man, and that was difficult for Maryl, difficult and shameful despite Diana's male guise for outsiders. The strain had begun to show. It had been luck that Diana had run into the young baker again in Colmar. She had known his father and had been saddened to hear of his death, but the young man had been dealing with more pressing troubles. He had inherited his father's establishment and was despairing of finding a wife with any desire or skill to work in a public kitchen. Unfortunately, the business had been suffering with the lack of his father's hands. This meant he was not able to obtain an appropriately skilled mate either. That he would even consider a free bride – a woman without dowry or unblemished background – had impressed Diana and eventually Maryl.

In the end, and at Maryl's request, Diana had arranged for their marriage and Maryl's settlement in Colmar. She had also promised to visit frequently which had been Maryl's only real assurance that if the young stranger was not as caring as he appeared, she could change her mind. But she had not, and Diana's visits had lessened with the news of the expected arrival of their firstborn.

Wistfully her brown eyes turned to the naked pillow, and Diana slid her arm across the quilt beside her. The young man had never known Diana was a woman, and Maryl knew not to enlighten him.

No, as far as Colmar was concerned – or Gronday for that matter – Tad Di'nay the Southern Trader was a barterer for rare trinkets, a carrier of town messages and very much a man. It was not surprising. At six foot two without her boots, who on Aggar would doubt it? Add that little piece of anatomical fact to her swordsmanship, and there were very few of Colmar who would believe in her womanhood. Even – she laughed at the thought – even if she stood naked in the town square, she'd probably not convince everyone.

Not that she would want to. She sobered with a shiver, noticing the night chill was seeping in through the bottle-glass windows. Begrudgingly she rolled under the bedcovers. She wondered why she missed the woman anyway. Still, to leave planet and not say good-bye would be rather unkind. She could always send a note; the baker read. She snuggled down into the downy quilts; yes, that was what she would do. She would send it with Cleis. It would take a while, but at least Cleis would be sure the good-bye was a proper one. She could send an inheritance of sorts too. Some of the pay Thomas was holding for her could easily be converted into tin and pewter dishware — perhaps cooking sheets for the bakery?

Yes — she burrowed into a pillow — that was exactly what she would do... and Thomas wouldn't have a thing to say about it!

❋ ❋ ❋

An infernal pounding shook her mead-drugged sleep. Blurrily, Diana focused on leaping flames. Cold, she thought as she smelled the curling smoke. Soon she would have to stack up a few more logs. The banging began again, and she looked to the loose-fitted door beside the fireplace. The light from a hand held torch flickered through gaps at the edges of the door planks and she pushed herself upright.

Damn, now what? But her head was clearing rapidly, and she could feel her heart begin to quicken as she threw on a night shirt. There was trouble or Mattee would have waited for dawn.

She pulled the door open under the thundering fist. Wordlessly the lumbering male stared at her. Then he grunted and, holding the torch high, pushed into the room. As the door shut, he turned to eye the fire, probably wondered how the Southerner didn't suffocate in the room's heat, but he only said, "There's one of your southways folk just in."

Diana nodded curtly and waited.

"He's in the commons." Mattee ran a palm, callused from the hot kitchen cauldron, across his beard. "There's no one 'bout this time of night. He'll not be seen."

"Good." She took her breeches from the chair and pulled a glass coin from the pocket. With her thumb she flipped it across the room, and Mattee grabbed it neatly from the air. "See he gets what he needs and I'll be down soon. If he's tired, he'll sleep in here."

"Aye." He nodded. "You're off again, I figured. Already have my woman parceling food. Boy's set to ready your horse. Do you have a care to which mount? Or don't you know yet?"

"I'll know when I see the man," she replied.

He moved back towards the door. At the latch he paused, and with a merry glint in his eye, ventured, "Was the mead to your liking, Di'nay?"

A shout of laughter escaped Diana as she sat back on the rough table and retorted lightly, "The whole of it's gone, Mattee. Judge what you will."

A grin split his grizzled face and he mumbled, "I judge lucky you waken'd."

He left and Diana turned quickly to her locked chest. Within were laid an assortment of mechanical gadgets, but these were ignored as she pulled one of her fieldsuits from the corner. Made from an ultra-light fiber, it fit her body as comfortably as a second skin; more important, the white jumpsuit was thermal controlled by the power cells sewn into the cuffs and low collar. Gratefully she slid her feet into the suit and pulled the fabric over her strong thighs. As she put her arms in the sleeves and fastened the velcro seam, her toes tingled warmly. She thought that the only time she'd been warm on this planet was when she was suited or in a lover's arms.

Her dark hide boots were slipped on and laced up to her knees. She found she had to concentrate to keep from lacing the ankle joint too tight. How the local men ever managed to tie themselves together after holiday festivals she'd never understand. But then, she wasn't in the habit of drinking quite that much either, so she hadn't had the practice. And on that irritable thought, Diana shouldered her small, ever-ready bag of mechanical tricks and grabbed for her fur-lined cloak.

Commander Baily had sent Stevens, one of the three men who shared the dubious job of planetary cultural liaisons with Diana and Cleis. Stevens looked decidedly uncomfortable standing there in his locally made sword and cloak. Clumsy, she noted and wondered how many years it took Terrans to acclimate culturally? No doubt a good many more than an Amazon.

Her bag and wrap landed with a thump on one of the tables. Stevens jumped but hid it well. Mud was thick on his boots, and his cloak was still wrapped around his shoulders and clenched in his hands. With a touch of satisfaction, Diana realized he was as cold as she had been; there were some things no one was meant to adapt to.

"There's a fire in my room," Diana reassured him. "Mattee will send the food that way if you ask him to."

"No need. I've edible supplies with me." Stevens had not taken time to shave. His mission must be considered urgent. Normally he was smooth shaven like local travelers; it made their expressions of peaceful tidings easier to read.

She suppressed a sigh. How could one be a cultural expert if one wouldn't even eat the food? "Suit yourself. Now what can't wait for daybreak?"

He shrugged. "Honestly, Diana, I don't know the details. I was told to send you back immediately. Baily swore there are 'interplanetary repercussions,' but he wouldn't say what. Cleis is a hundred leagues out, in some healer's cave with broken ribs. Baily is sure this is beyond me — or Jörges and Cedros for that matter."

Broken ribs? Diana hid her frown. Her friend had undoubtedly been caught championing some poor soul again; she hoped Cleis was all right. A resigned knot settled into her stomach. She would obviously not be going off-planet as planned. Her dark eyes met his levelly. "What else?"

"Be at HQ come sunrise?" Both of them smiled at Baily's apparent panic.

"Well, this may be a valid disaster. But he'll have to settle for darkfall — sundown," she said quickly. Stevens raised a brow. They had been speaking

Imperial Common, yet her unconscious time reference had long ago adopted the cycles of Aggar's sun and twin moons, and her language reflected the shift. "And you?"

"I'll stay here for a day, then come on after you. Although I don't expect to make it back as quickly as I came out."

"Fine.... Mattee!"

The innkeeper appeared in the kitchen doorway.

"My red stallion and saddle bags only...no pack horse." Her voice was clipped as she used the local dialect. "I travel fast."

Mattee grunted and gave Stevens a dubious scowl. He paused in leaving as she added, "Sword and long bow too."

"Aye," he said by way of reassurance and departed.

"Do you know where my chamber is?" she asked Stevens, switching smoothly back into Common.

Stevens nodded. "Furthest window still unlatch to let you out onto the roof?"

"Out over the kitchen, yes."

The Amazon threw on her heavy cape, the hood falling naturally to the back as she fastened the peg-like button. Beside the awkward Terran she looked comfortable and every bit the green-garbed Southern Trader. Her brown hair was short and parted in the middle. There was strength and hard won experience in the lines of her face, although the touch of sun and wind had long ago snatched the feminine softness from her skin. But then Amazons were not women to be measured by the standards of Aggar or the Empire.

"Is there anything else?" Diana asked abruptly, and Stevens shook his head. "Certain you have what you need here?"

He shrugged. "A fire, a drink — a warm bed and I'll do just fine."

"You should try their mead." A wry grin lifted the edge of her mouth as she thought of the empty bottle upstairs. "It really is a very good brew."

And then she left him.

Chapter Three

Elana was aware that outside the Great Hall the moons drifted lower as the Seers sipped their wine and mumbled, adding small pieces to the growing matrix. Even with the roaring fire, the Council shivered with foreboding at the scattered words and sent runners in search of translations and ancient symbols.

Slowly, the gameboard became clearer. The risks to Aggar and to the Terran Empire grew more evident. But the Council's responsibility was not so easily defined. They could react in their own subtle, respectful way or they could stand by patiently and hope that those involved would successfully navigate through the rising chaos. Either path seemed pitifully inadequate in this venture. Yet the time for decisions had come, and the Council of Ten would face that responsibility alone.

Tradesmen, scribes and then finally the Seers drifted away as their roles were finished. Dawn was coming, the Great Hall was nearly emptied, and Elana rose to leave with the last of the guests. But the Old Mistress laid a hand to her arm and drew the young woman along with her to the circle of benches and chairs at the central hearth. The Mistresses and Masters of the Council were gathering there with a handful of their prized apprentices. Elana felt the weight of responsibility more keenly than any elation at the honor of being included. She settled herself solemnly at the feet of her mentor to listen as information was reviewed by the Council.

It appeared that the Terrans had sent this spy, Garrison, into the star systems of their enemy, the Alliance. The Terrans had nearly lost this Garrison. On his return his ship had been pursued, and he had barely managed to cross the galactic border back into the Empire's zone. His craft had been so seriously damaged that it had reached Aggar only to tumble into the planet's atmosphere. He had crashed in the Maltar's realm. Somewhere amidst the northern ice ranges and the great forests of blackpines, the Terran spy and all his information were lost. But the exact location even the best of the Council's Seers could not determine.

"It may well be a matter of Aggar's survival," the elderly Historian finished wearily. "The information this pilot-spy carries may prevent the Empire's Chairman from being assassinated. As tedious as we find this Terran Empire to be, it is their strength which guards the neighboring galactic border — and us. If their Chairman should be assassinated by the Alliance, interstellar war would certainly follow, and Aggar would ultimately be destroyed."

"For our own sake this off-worlder pilot must not remain in Maltar territory." The Council Speaker sighed heavily, surveying the somber faces about him. He was a younger Master than many, his hair still jet black and his skin just beginning to crease around his eyes. "The cultural risks we face should the tribes of Aggar discover the Terran Empire's continued presence here are enormous. Not only would our autonomy from Terran rule be threatened, but petty disputes over Terran favors, for their technology and metals would arise. The effects would be catastrophic. Aggar barely managed to survive that battle of two hundred tenmoons past. I think we are clear that we do not want such disaster again."

"Yet we must move cautiously or we will be inviting the Empire's so-called 'protective' guardianship back," the Old Master said.

The Council Speaker nodded. "True. The fact that the present Terran base commander is somewhat inexperienced may allow us to guide him into our own plans... if we choose to deal with him."

"This base commander, Baily," a younger member said, "is an organizer by nature, not a leader. Once he learns of this crash — and undoubtedly the Terrans will soon know their pilot is missing regardless of our reports — Commander Baily will wish to dispatch a low flying craft to retrieve his pilot. The question is, do we need to dissuade Baily?"

"From flying across our continent? We must," the Mistress said quickly. "Permit him such free flight and we give him an aerial map of our Northern Continent. That is a gift the Terran strategists would dearly love."

"The Unseen Wall would still be in place."

"Around the Terran Quadrant, but not around the planet. Our Seers haven't the power to sustain that kind of wall! Not with everything they do." The Mistress snorted impatiently. "No, we can't risk providing the Terrans with such a map. Give them that and they might finally be able to make sense of their jumbled satellite pictures. And that would give them the ability to pick and choose a number of landing points beyond their base quadrant."

"Yet if this pilot's information is too long delayed, their Chairman may be lost," responded the Master. "Which could mean we've no planet left to protect."

"Perhaps we should merely inform the Terrans of the plot?" A young Mistress folded her hood back from her face as she spoke, but her voice held little conviction. "It is unfortunate that we still do not know which border parsec is in question in the assassination attempt. Without the planned location, I admit the warning would be vague. Perhaps too vague to be helpful?"

"It continues to be the problem. Our Seers have failed in that search. As for the rest of us...?" The Historian paused, glancing about almost hoping someone would contradict him. "We can do nothing without the pilot's star maps."

The Council Speaker looked at each of them. "There is no question then that we must participate in the rescue? The Maltar's realm is a large one."

"Actually there is time." The Historian straightened. "It is fully a quarter tenmoon — almost six Terran months — before the Chairman begins his border tour."

"Then help them, yes, but within our traditional restrictions," the Old Mistress cautioned. "Let the Terrans use their agents, not their flying technology."

"An overland search then."

"With a Shadow," Elana whispered, and in the licking tongues of the fire she again saw the brown eyes of her vision-maker.

"Exactly." The Speaker smiled with satisfaction, tolerant of whom the words had come from. "If we do not permit a rescue flight, Baily will send one of his cultural liaisons north to find this pilot-spy. We will match one of our Shadows with the agent he sends." The others nodded consideringly, and the Council Speaker went on. "At present the Terrans have five of their cultural liaisons here on Aggar. Three are too clumsy for our purposes. However, the two women the Terrans identify as Amazons are quite skilled — they have a reputation for accomplishing difficult feats. They are also uncannily astute."

The Mistress frowned. "The Amazons have always learned more about us than we intend them to."

"It does make them dangerous," another warned.

"But they are different from other Terran peoples," the Historian pointed out. "Much of what they learn never makes its way into the Terran Imperial records."

"They do seem to answer to a higher ethic," observed the Master.

"Trust?" the Mistress suggested, almost with surprise.

"In truth," the Council Speaker said, nodding. "It is the reason that one of them may very well succeed."

The dawn had passed when the Council adjourned. They withdrew, assembling into smaller groups as they went, and gradually the Grand Hall grew almost empty.

Sighing, the Master stood, helping the Mistress to her feet. Elana touched the elder woman's shoulder, nodding towards a few that had gathered at a far door.

The Speaker left the others and returned to them. "Would either of you care to greet this Terran Commander Baily this morning?"

The Master chuckled and shook his head. "I'll leave that to you, my boy. My diplomatic ways have been long frayed into cynical sneers."

"As your numerous students have noted," the Speaker rejoined with a smile. "And you, Mistress? Will you hear this man today?"

"Certainly not!" she snapped, indignant at the thought. "When you have decided who you will entrust to our Shadow's care, then I will meet, if necessary, with this Baily, but at no point do I intend to be diplomatic. That, my boy, is why you are the Council's Speaker."

"A born arbitrator," the Master chuckled. "He does a good job of it too."

"Thank you." The younger man smiled broadly and then his gaze came to Elana. "And you are the Eldest Prepared?"

Elana affirmed it with a tip of her head, careful as always to avoid meeting another's gaze because of her Blue Sight.

"It was wise of your Mistress to summon you. Do you think you'll be Shadow to this Amazon's adventure, Elana?"

"Perhaps." She noted that he had addressed her by her full name and wondered just when the Mistress had decided upon the change.

"Well enough." He turned back to her mentors with more pressing matters. "I have sent the runners to retrieve the details we have on these Amazons. They are ordered to present everything to you for inspection before passing it on to us."

The Mistress nodded. "We can meet later — when you have finished with Baily."

"Yes, that will be the time for more decisions." The Council Speaker bowed slightly and, returning to other responsibilities, he took his leave of them.

The Master muttered as they mounted the stairs, "I do not envy this Shadow. The risks to Aggar and the Terran Empire demand the lifebond. We need a Shadow to place his or her life between success and failure. But the lifebonding...it becomes a painful risk in itself in the case of an off-worlder."

Elana glanced at him, confused. Shadows were always lifebound...why would it be any different with an off-worlder? Then abruptly she realized she had answered her own question; the off-worlder would eventually return to the stars, and lifebound — the separation would mean the Shadow's death.

Together the three paused at the top of the steps; the somber knowledge hung between them. The old man turned slowly to face his two dearest companions. "There are some pairs which separate, and yet the Shadow lives."

"Yes, in our years, three have survived the loss of their companions," the Old Mistress confirmed quietly. "In each case there was great distance between the companion and the Shadow. And the actual death of the companion was sudden."

The Master considered it. "The space craft would put great distance between them too. It would do it quickly — suddenly. Would it be similar to such a death?"

"But the Amazon would still live. There has been no instance of surviving the separation, if the companion still lives."

"But such distances...to another star? A distance greater than such separations."

"At speed greater than any before."

Elana's icy gaze went from one to the other. These two were the mentors who knew most about the intricacies and knottings of the Shadowmate. Theirs was the sum of all written, remembered — suspected — knowledge of the Preparations, and here, for the first time in her life, Elana saw them uncertain of answers.

"All three Shadows that survived were young — strong," the Master said. "Each had a purpose to live for."

The Mistress nodded. "Each was consumed by their mission and adventure. Emotionally, none were committed absolutely — irrevocably — to their companion."

"Should we hope then that this Amazon is not charismatic?"

"No," Elana interjected flatly, grimly.

"Speak your mind, child," the Master prompted.

"If it were I selected as Shadowmate, I would choose death to perpetual frailty and insanity," she said evenly.

The quiet stretched for a moment, then the Mistress said, "The Amazon may ask to be accompanied off-world."

The Master suggested, "Some Shadows would find that just as undesirable."

"And some would be enthusiastic," the Mistress countered, a gleam in her eye.

"Let us hope," the Master ended, "that one will be appointed by the Fates. This choosing will be complex — and painful."

The Mistress grasped Elana's hand. "Speak to no one until we've heard from the meeting with the Terran Commander. When we know more, then your thoughts will be most needed — and your words of discouragement to the less prepared."

Elana's eyes dropped to the flagstone floor. She understood; for the few who would meet the qualifications, one or two would be too rash to grasp the situation fully. She would dissuade these even if it meant a change in their amarin.

The Master half-bowed in his parting. "I will see to the vault's findings."

The Mistress absently patted Elana's hand once more as they found themselves alone. Neither was sure whom the reassuring touch was for. "Carry on with the tumbling this morning, Elana. See to it that those lazy newcomers fall on their shoulders and not their stupid necks. I am in need of an hour's sleep."

"Yes Mistress." Gently the slender woman bent and placed a kiss on the thinning gray hair.

Without another word the old woman left her. Resolutely, the evening's happenings were set aside, and Elana turned for the still sleeping dormitories.

❋ ❋ ❋

With a sudden burst of speed Elana bounded over the rocky crest of the trail to finish her run. The south wind met her with a refreshing if chilly touch; the yellow sun's warmth was faint in this late autumn. A deep, satisfied breath came from her lungs, and with hands on hips she walked in a slow circle waiting for her pounding heart to settle. A small bit of pride stirred as she noticed the healthy caramel blush to her skin; she was in the best shape of her life. She wiped the salty water from her brow and enjoyed the feeling of sheer aliveness in her body. She felt her balance — eager but tempered with patience, strong but clever under the Old Mistress' tutoring. She was ripe, but for what destiny? She stilled to stare out across the forest below.

As usual for trainees running or tumbling, she wore her thigh-length tunic and short knits beneath, not woolen tights, and the strength of her thighs glistened with perspiration as she stepped off of the trail. The hides of her soft leather boots protected her calves and knees as she pushed through the thorny scrub. Her expression grew more serious as she scaled the side of a mammoth weathered stone that jutted from the mountain's slope. She gained the top of it and settled, dangling her feet above the treeline.

So much needed to be clearer, Elana thought as she gazed out across the endless green and black of the forests below. The air pressed and swirled past her, blowing hair into her face. Impatiently she pushed the tousled braid over her shoulder and out of her way. And then she grew bold in her impatience.

"By your Twin Moons, Mother! What have you planned for me?!"

The stillness of the heights echoed only the wind, and the clouds above were scattered fingers. There was no answer. She hesitated, a moment of doubting her readiness, yet she felt her being centered and knew — not with youthful arrogance or exuberant pride, but with calm certainty — she knew her right as the Eldest Prepared. Again, deliberately pitching her voice low to carry far in the dancing winds, Elana cried with open arms, "Mother! Hear me!"

A shrill eagle's call pierced the wind, and quickly Elana turned left to spot its flight. It banked. From high in the sky it crashed into the forest's depths, and suddenly she was one with the bird. The shadows felt cool. Dappled sunlight streamed down to touch a well-trodden road below. And on the road a figure appeared, riding hard on a tall chestnut. The horse was sweating white, but willingly it pushed on for its rider. Briefly the weathered, angular lines of the woman's face were clear, then she was gone.

From her distant perch Elana blinked and found herself alone again. On the horizon, the eagle swooped then lifted, soaring through the blueness until it too was nothing. Grim and clear that her destiny was this vision woman and not the Terrans' crisis, Elana stood. In her depths she warred with the desire to discard her endless waiting, for it was obvious that the rider was some distance from the Keep and worse, traveling in the wrong direction.

After two tenmoons of visions, she was tired of waiting. This new venture with the off-worlders was sorely tempting. An adventure that promised great challenge — where the jesting Fates would gather the frayed ends of history and seal the chapter with wax and death or begin an intricate reweaving of tomorrow's stories.

But, sullenly, Elana admitted she knew that to play in the destruction or winning of this Terran game — would likely ensure complete failure. This temptation was only one door of many that could court failure. She knew her destiny was bound to that woman on the chestnut stallion — whether it was by the Mother's Hand or by Fates' Jest. Her Blue-Sighted visions had shown her enough to know that she must wait for this woman.

But this Terran challenge — seldom in the history of Aggar were the Shadows' stakes so weighty! More often it was the countless smaller efforts that were scattered through the centuries that brought Aggar safely through crises.

She remembered the Empire's history that she had studied. A terrifying number of civilizations had not slipped past self-destruction. It was amazing Aggar had not been lost as well.

Elana sighed and returned to the trail. Her lust was not and never would be for power or politics. Her desire to join this mission was not from pride or a drive for fame. Shadows were not to be noted in written histories; they were silent, unnamed partners to those humans whose efforts would determine the future. Shadows were the extra throw of the dice when the Fates seemed to be the least friendly. No, for Shadows, the need was much simpler and much more compelling in its simplicity. It was the urge to adventure...to dare the undoable.

And just which Shadow was to attempt the impossible this time? She had not been appointed Eldest by mere age or agility. Others were older. Many of the younger trainees could even best her on individual tasks, except for the sprint. But her maturity — that tempered stamina and continual, patient attention to details which was so crucial to survival — was a less conspicuous skill. It was, however, the very skill which might most be needed on this venture.

Elana began to review the talents of their more experienced trainees who paced themselves naturally. She knew the selection could not be based on a single ability. It would be best if the Shadow could compliment the off-worlder's own training. The chosen one would need a firm grasp of the northern terrain of both the Maltar's realms and the Ramains districts, as well as a thorough understanding of the people and languages. A hunter? She wondered if off-worlders ate meats or plants. She would need to review the vault records before she spoke with the Mistress about candidates.

Unless the unwitting soul had already been chosen by the Fates? Then all the records in the Keep would be worth naught — and with that ironic thought, Elana smiled faintly and ducked back into the forest's shadows.

✿ ✿ ✿
Chapter Four

The lazy crescent of a midnight moon hung above a wooded mountain peak, and the Old Mistress sighed, shifting her chilled joints. The stone of the garden bench was cold. Dawn was nearing, and the night's vigil had been a long one. The dampness of the air crept into her lungs, and wearily she forced a cough. She was becoming too old for this, her breathing more often labored now. Yet the shadows cast by the Twin Moons had always been generous to her; they had never denied her their wizened powers...until tonight.

A bird trilled, and a gray finger of light touched the clouds. Another's song broke, and beyond the garden wall, the birds' clear notes began to wrestle amongst the shimmering grey-green leaves and silverpine needles.

The old woman sighed heavily. The fumblings of these Terrans demanded much, and yet she could find no reason for her Ona to be excluded. In the past an impending crisis would draw so much attention that the smaller threads of Aggar's tapestry went forgotten until they slipped from the Council's careful grasp. Always in the silence of night, meditation would bring an awareness of the carelessness and steps could be taken to address the near-forgotten needs. She had hoped that this vision was such a task, something vital and yet less spectacular, that had been overlooked...something to concern her Ona and the vision-woman of those Blue-Sighted dreams. But she had found nothing.

It was possible, that this vision-woman was not of this time. It was rare even for a Seer to possess the talent of out-of-time seeing – but not unheard of.

But Elana was a Shadow trainee, she was to be protector and guide. She was not a Seer's apprentice; she was not one to be seduced and absorbed by that pulsing amarin of Aggar's very fiber. Indeed she had never held an interest in that dreadful lure of consuming power. No, Elana had not so finely mastered her Blue Sight that she could have seen beyond, to tomorrows.

Still in those dreamspun visions...Ona had witnessed something. Was it about this current adventure?

Or perhaps this confusion was from her own ambitions, the Old Mistress ruefully allowed. It was true, she did sorely want the Eldest Prepared to join the Terrans' excursion – a challenge worthy of Elana's talents. It was a challenge with stakes of awing proportions. And the treasures beyond – the travels and mysteries in the stars that might come too? Oh yes, despite all risks, she did want this task for Elana.

Her eyes fixed on the reddening, cloud-streaked sky as she remembered how she had watched the girl grow and mature. She had sternly reprimanded and disciplined the unthinking risks, the rashness...the stupidities of youth, but as the ignorance lessened and the stubborn childishness came under control, she had seen the emergence of a measured confidence – how it mixed with steely determination, harnessing a passion for conquering the unsurpassable. She had seen that lust for adventure tempered by Training as a sword's blade was tempered by red hot coals – to unique strength – found so seldom. This time she, as Mistress, had guided that forging. With honesty and with pride the old woman acknowledged the part she had played shaping Elana's life. But her part would be ending now. Grimly the Old Mistress shifted on her bench, knowing it was not just the cold that caused her discomfort.

"Mistress...?"

The old woman pushed her gnarled hands deep into the pockets of her robe. She knew her apprehension would be apparent to the young woman with her ability to read feelings as amarin — as would her annoyance at being caught by surprise.

Elana hesitated beside a tree, still half-hidden by its curtain of green-grey leaves. Unconsciously her left hand reached out to press against the green bark. She waited, absorbing the stoic strength of the tree's amarin.

"Thank you for speaking. It's unnerving to have you appear so."

A fond smile touched Elana's lips as she stepped forward. "I move only as you taught me, Mistress."

The woman relinquished her irritation. "Have you been searching for me long?"

"No."

The Mistress turned sharp eyes on her Eldest as the young woman sat down. There were bluish hollows beneath Elana's eyes and lines pulled at the corners of her full mouth. "You are tired. You have not slept...again."

Elana shrugged, her gaze fixed on the glistening golden-cast clouds above. "I've been answering questions."

"You have needed patience this night. Have any shown a responsible interest?"

"Two perhaps. Although, more did demand details."

"Few are appropriate for such a venture," the Mistress agreed calmly. "Did you dissuade any?"

"Some — their eagerness is admirable, but I feel their sheer persuasiveness might be too attractive to the Council Master. They simply are not prepared enough. One in particular, Najda, is too young — and sexually naive. It would have been an awkward match with the Amazon's cultural differences."

"Your judgment is sound. I'd not doubt your reasons. Did you show the woman the ramifications of her curiosities?"

Elana shifted uncomfortably, interlacing her fingers. "In truth, I did not."

"You didn't tamper with her amarin? Then she may well be drumming on my door this morning!"

"No, Mistress. I reflected the differences of the Terrans as I know of them. I simply reflected the end — if the Amazon departs Aggar."

"So you did not address the sexuality?"

"I could not," she repeated quietly.

A smile played across the elder's face. Elana felt an impish one of her own grow. "You are a bright child," the woman teased gently. "I know you could imagine such a joining if you put your mind to it."

Elana laughed a little. "With so many around me, I did not dare reflect it! If I'd succeeded — think of the scores of brown blushing faces we'd have this morning!"

"Truth." The Mistress could not resist the chuckle before she continued with, "Is your Sighted friend, Telias, curious?"

Elana responded with a regretful shake of her head.

The elder sighed. "Today I could wish more of our trainees had the Blue Sight. It would have been useful on this journey." Abruptly she tossed the thought aside. "Who are the two of your choice?"

"Miam or Lenial."

"Yes, they may do." The old woman pushed stiffly to her feet. The chattering menagerie of birds was growing as the sun climbed; the evening's peace had turned into a disruptive dawn. "I will talk with both of them after this morning's meeting."

"I asked them to be present at the observation."

"By all means, they should be. This Amazon promises to be quite an interesting woman." The Old Mistress went still, almost hearing an echo of her own words. A lingering thread from her night's musings tugged at her gently.

"Mistress?"

"I expect," she murmured absently, "that you will be present too?"

"As arranged." Elana rose, smiling tenderly at her mentor. A drifting concentration attuned to other matters shrouded the older figure. Elana knew it was time to leave.

"You should sleep!" the Mistress suddenly called after her. But even as Elana turned to acknowledge the instructions, the elder's thoughts had moved elsewhere, and the younger woman left the garden unnoticed.

❋ ❋ ❋

Chapter Five

The waiting hall echoed the impatient footsteps of Commander Baily. Irritably his palm clapped at his thigh as he turned heel and started across the hard wood floor again. His shining black synthetic boots struck hard with a double-clack.

He was a military man, not a diplomat, and he had a general distaste for "dealing with the natives." Skinny and nervous, he looked as out of place as he felt pacing beneath the great vaulted ceiling. Above him, the yellow sunlight streamed through the small, southeastern windows, and the colors glittered and shone in the stained glass mural opposite. But the Commander had no appreciation for that brilliant display that hung so far overhead.

With a bang his fist hit the desk. He paused abruptly, distracted by the resounding echo, then turned. The doors remained shut; there was no recognition of his childishness. His wide brow creased in frustration, and the thin, blond mustache twitched. How dare they make him wait?!

"Patience. I'm sure the Council of Ten hasn't forgotten us. After all, they did invite us," his companion offered. Diana was sprawled on a bench beneath the glass mural. Unlike Baily, she was comfortably dressed in the clothes of Aggar's men. She avoided the Empire's costumes whenever possible.

"You're not here to give orders," he grumbled and resumed his jittery pacing. "You just do what you're told."

"Always," she drawled sarcastically and folded her arms.

"They're watching us," he muttered, glancing suspiciously at the doors spread about the room.

Diana crossed her ankles and said nothing.

"And they say we're as inhospitable as Ait Skellor!"

An eyebrow quirked upwards. "As who?"

"As, as...well, you know. That thing they keep calling my – uh, our base."

"Oh, Fates' Cellar!"

"That's what I said." There was the note of childish stubbornness in his voice.

"No, Thomas. Fates' Cellar." He appeared thoroughly confused which didn't surprise Diana; his mastery of language and accent were exceptionally poor. "The Fates are their evil male deities. And Cellar is their term for an underground storage or dwelling."

"Deities? What deities?"

"The Fates." She studied his baffled face with fatigued disbelief. After all his years on Aggar, he should have known more. Diana tipped her head back against the wall and gazed at the arches above as she elaborated. "The two greater powers, if I remember correctly, are attributed to Malice and Ambition. Then there is a score or two of lessor minions such as Greed, Arrogance and War. The lot of them usually work together to cause grief with sadistic little plots like, say...," Diana kept a bland face and stared down at a boot, "...losing a pilot?"

"Humpf." Her commander returned to his pacing with a pinched, pained look.

The Amazon sighed, wearily remembering how apt it could be to refer to Baily's base as 'Hell.' Mae n'Pour, Goddess above, lend Your sweet strength!

The heavy door opened, squealing on its hinges as it admitted the Council Speaker, his gaze on the Commander. Someone outside shut the door for them. The Terran fidgeted beneath the Speaker's scrutiny. A deliberately bland, almost innocent expression settled across the Speaker's handsome face. With a lift of an eyebrow, he inquired, "Are we ready to proceed?"

The Terran's thin jaw clenched and his chin leveled. "We are."

The master looked past the Terran male to the relaxed, silent figure beyond.

For a moment, Diana returned the man's quiet appraisal, and then she smiled. She had not missed his quick glance overhead to the glass mural; she realized she had inadvertently placed herself beneath the hidden observers and well out of their view. Slowly her long legs unfolded, and amused, Diana stepped to the center of the room before approaching him.

The Speaker's smile broadened knowingly, and he extended his hands, palms upwards, in greeting.

"Aa — may I introduce my Cultural Liaison?"

"I know who your companion is, Commander."

"Then I am most honored." Diana bowed, clasping her hands over his. "No, Min."

Diana's amusement faded with the formality. A somber cloak seemed to descend about the Council Speaker as he said, "No. It is I that am honored, Diana N'Athena of Amazons. Perhaps, you will be able to help my people."

❁ ❁ ❁

Elana hid her smile as she entered the hidden observation room above. The three of them were standing at the wall of stained glass and looking down on the Council Master's conference. She heard Miam, the youngest of the two trainees, question the Old Master with a blatantly awed tone. "That is a woman?" She is so tall — look at her clothing."

"Does she always travel as man?" Lenial asked. "Never tights or skirts?"

The Old Master half-nodded to both of them. "Even as you often do here in the Keep. Now, study the dress closely. The make must be perfectly matched."

The Old Mistress raised an intolerant brow at Elana's tardiness, and the young woman hurried to the far corner of the window to join her.

"Beg patience," Elana murmured. "We had a slight riding accident on the woods' course today."

"The new boy, I'd suppose. What's his name, Thaden?"

Elana nodded with a rueful grin. "I took pity on him and didn't remind him of your warnings about taking a horse for granted."

The old woman smiled and nodded towards the figures below them.

"These Amazons seem much more respectful of our Council Speaker than the Terran Commander, don't they?" Lenial's distaste was clear in her voice, and the Mistress spared the others a glance. Lenial's perceptiveness pleased her. But as she turned back to question Elana's reactions, her shrewd gaze suddenly narrowed.

The Eldest Prepared stood with white knuckles clenching at the safety bar as emotions surged, darkening her skin. Triumph lit the old one's gaze and she knew, without glancing below, what had stolen such rapt attention from her student. The old woman watched for the tell-tale reaction of a protector's bonding as she baited, "You can control your repulsion to Terrans better than that, Elana."

Elana's blue-white eyes blinked and jerked from the figures below. Disoriented, her eyes locked with the elder's. A gnarled hand grabbed as the Mistress reeled with shock. Images of fires, stallions and riders — the power of that Amazon's angular face exploded through her mind as Elana's consciousness invaded hers. And then abruptly, it all stopped. "Mistress!" Young hands held the old one upright.

"Careless fool!" The Master seized the Mistress as she threatened to collapse.

Elana flinched, releasing the woman as she was struck by the Master's anger. His face flushed dark, nearly the shade of the stained wood panels of the room, and his fury pushed Elana's intuitive awareness into oblivion.

"It was not meant...." She was stricken. How could it have been? The Mistress was more dear to her than her own mother. Never could she seek to harm her — never! "I...was startled," she stammered and looked desperately to the darkened faces of her mentors. "Truly! I did not...I would not...."

"Hush, Elana." The Old Mistress placed an unsteady hand over Elana's own. "He was not speaking to you. At least if he has any intelligence at all, he was not!"

A grimness settled about the Master as he allowed the old woman to shrug off his aid. With a rumble in his throat, he declared, "Youth can only be foolish — not enough experience to be careless."

The Mistress snorted, smoothing her robes into more comfortable order.

Elana felt the Master's anger begin to dissolve. Slowly the presence of the Amazon began to seep into her awareness once more. Unobtrusively she forced the tension in her shoulders to ease and steadied her breathing. She felt her responses cautiously, already stretching to incorporate the patterns of this new amarin into her being. This time the connection with the others was not obliterated. Satisfied, she released a breath.

"What absorbed you so that this one could surprise you, Elana?"

"Foolish indeed. It is the one below."

"The Amazon?" Lenial ventured hesitantly.

"Certainly. It appears that this off-worlder is the woman Elana has been seeing in her dreams all these tenmoons."

"You knew!" Elana gasped, outraged and astonished. "And said nothing?!"

"I suspected," the old woman corrected firmly. But she was careful to avoid returning that blue gaze directly. "And only since this morning."

"It could be an admirable match." The Old Master wandered nearer the glass.

"She must choose it," Elana asserted suddenly as a protectiveness sprang up in her. She did not wish her Trainers to move for mere expediency's sake.

A delighted grin lit the Old Mistress' face. She squeezed Elana's hand reassuringly and winked. "You will be a fine protector."

"Nevertheless," the Master turned to their younger trainees, "Elana speaks truth. The final choice of who will accompany her must be the Amazon's. Destiny is — "

"Destiny, bah! The Mother is no fool," the old woman scoffed, moving towards the door. "Do not raise their hopes."

"Hopes?" Miam echoed with a relief that Elana could feel was genuine. "I would have named it fear," and the Old Master chuckled deeply, giving her a kind smile and a hug.

✻ ✻ ✻

Chapter Six

Wearily, Diana turned and half-sat against the low stone wall, crossing her arms. The garden was a luscious, thick collection of leafy brush and towering, green-barked trees. The peacefulness of the place touched her. She shifted slightly, resting one ankle over the other as she wondered what Thomas was still doing in the shuttlecraft. Probably avoiding her until their next meeting with the Council Speaker. Still, it might be for the best. She was fatigued from sleepless nights and hard riding, and she was not in the most tolerant of moods. And with Thomas, she admitted wryly, she needed a tolerant mood.

Silently Diana peered past the garden's edge to the wooded canyons below. The afternoon sun was warm even to her, and she welcomed the breezeless air selfishly. How long would it be now, she wondered, before she left planet? Before she glimpsed the topaz mountains of home? The lavender skies? The warmth of the near red sun? She had been gone too long. Rarely were any off-world so long as she had been — unless one counted the few who elected to work at the Sisters' moonbase on Shekina or the handful who left for a man's marriage. But they were scarce indeed.

To be rid of the games! She drew in the sun-warmed air smelling of tart silverpine resin and damp autumn leaves. That was all of her present ambition — just to be rid of the games! Just to be home! She could barely reconstruct her reasons for electing a second term of duty. Almost twenty years all together — five of them here on Aggar. It was a long time. Diana smiled at a passing gray cloud. Hadn't somebody promised her a little wisdom along the way?

Well, the universe was to be saved one more time. Her sarcasm faded, and she turned her back to the mountain canyons — unfortunately, this time it truly was important. Unfortunately, it always appeared to be.

There seemed to be an endless array of paths to civilized destruction. Diana wondered if those ancient travelers who had planted the human seeds across the universe ever regretted their sowing. Or perhaps those ancient ones had also gone the way of self-destruction? In all the stars, the Terrans had yet to find traces of them. Maybe they truly had ceased to exist.

She sighed, returning to the task at hand. Unlike Thomas, Diana did not particularly begrudge the Council's involvement. Thomas wouldn't care that Aggar could be invaded...or even destroyed should war come. Considering what was at risk, the "natives," as Thomas sneeringly referred to them, had just as much concern in this project as the Empire did. She respected the Council's insistence in being involved. Diana truthfully hoped that this pilot, Garrison, did have information that could forestall this disaster — if she could just get to him in time.

But what the Council was actually suggesting did bother her. To impose a partner on her? Now? That didn't seem wise. After twenty years of working alone, now was not the time to take on a partner!

A breeze descended from the mountain heights and out of habit Diana reached for the edges of her cloak, drawing it close. Her eye caught an odd stillness off to her right, and Diana became aware of a figure standing beneath the feathery, green-grey canopy of a tree. Barely a shadow — the thought flitted through her mind. Her body tensed. They train them well, Diana observed, appearing to stare at her own toes — very, very few people could move so near and remain so unknown to her. Unless she was much more fatigued than she was aware. She frowned very faintly. That could be dangerous. If she was that ready to be shipped home, it could get her killed. It could get a great many people killed.

"I can leave..."

Diana's dark head tipped sideways as she looked to where the stranger stood. The voice was low, but clearly a woman's. And surprisingly she spoke Imperial Common — hesitantly, with a faint accent, but undeniably it was Common.

"...if you wish to be alone?"

"No," Diana responded in the local tongue. With a rueful shake of her head, she added, "After all, I am your guest."

"I should not be here," Elana admitted as she stepped through the shimmering, leafy curtain. Without a sound her soft booted heels took her across the autumn twigs to stand before the Amazon.

She was tall for a woman of Aggar, Diana noted. Her waist was small, but not tiny, and her stomach was flat; the woolen tights displayed a runner's legs. She had dark, unruly hair that was longer than most. It lent her a youthful appearance that Diana thought might not be far from the truth. She was certainly beyond the usual age of marriage, judging by the taut stretch of the laced jerkin. Although that didn't narrow the seasons by much on Aggar, it was obvious to Diana that this woman did not spend her time solely tending babies.

"I am Di'nay," Diana offered finally. She watched the other closely, intensely aware that she was in turn being scrutinized, but differently. Blue eyes scanned her face, never meeting her own gaze directly, but there was no driving nervousness in the searching. Blue — Diana's gaze narrowed almost imperceptibly. She had not known the people of Aggar could genetically produce blue eyes.

"You prefer this name to..." Elana hesitated and then, "...Diana n'Athena?"

"Di'nay is how I am known on Aggar."

The faintest of nods and then, "I am Elana." Slowly she extended her right hand, and Diana had the distinct impression that the deliberateness of the action was so that Elana would not startle her. Just as slow, Diana uncrossed her arms and accepted the hand. She found the grip was neither soft nor dainty. She had been right; this woman was not typical of Aggar.

"As Eldest of the Prepared, I welcome you to this Keep, Di'nay."

Diana, as was the local custom, presented both her palms up. Quietly and formally, she answered, "I am honored in the greeting."

Two warm hands lay atop Diana's and squeezed briefly before parting — a gesture of intimacy. Diana's dark brows raised and she waited expectantly.

"You are to be given a Shadow," Elana responded to the woman's questioning amarin. "I do not know if they explained to you that it is your choice to name the companion. You need not choose the first presented. If you would rather select another, do so."

"I would rather go alone," Diana admitted cautiously, pulling her cloak around herself again as the wind shifted a bit. "But I'm told this will not be allowed."

"Should your Shadow become a burden and not an aid, you would be expected to leave her behind."

The mission comes first. Diana didn't know if that was good or bad, although it would certainly reassure Thomas.

"Are all Shadows women?" Diana asked abruptly.

"You will not be given a man," Elana reassured her, and baffled, Diana wondered just how the woman had known it would be a reassurance.

"You would be their first choice?"

Mutely Elana confirmed it with a nod.

"Have you come to ask that I not choose you?"

"No." Her voice was steady, her gaze resting squarely at eye level on the other's chest. "I would be honored. I would like this challenge, and...," she hesitated, "...I would like to work with you."

"You don't know me," Diana said bluntly, and Elana's startled eyes lifted to dart across the Amazon's face.

"I have the Blue Sight," Elana responded as if to remind her of something.

"I have noticed your eyes are blue," Diana said slowly, and then, tentatively, she reached out a hand. The younger woman went completely still as a single finger touched her, gently tipping her face up. But the icy gaze refused contact and rested instead on Diana's weathered brow.

"I travel with no one who will not look at me," Diana threatened softly and suddenly she found she did indeed want to travel with this woman.

Elana swallowed hard and guardedly lowered her gaze. Amazed by the courage of the Amazon, she tightly concentrated on reading Di'nay's amarin and wrestled against imposing the thoughts and images that raced through her own mind. And yes, there was courage — Elana grasped — courage mingled with an impenetrable strength. But there was also an uneasiness. Elana understood then that this woman did not know about the Sight and that Di'nay was only aware of some unnamable risk. Quickly Elana blinked and pulled free from the other's hand; it was too much like reading a diary without permission.

"The Blue Sight is a gift — or a curse," Elana began abruptly. "It is a genetic combination that is extremely rare. The strength of the powers vary with individuals, but has always been accompanied by bluish irises."

"Hence the name," Diana nodded. The cultural anthropologist in her was already preparing to sift apart facts and superstitions.

Elana stepped backwards a few paces, acutely aware of the skepticism that she was striking. "Some generations never see the blue eyes except for those born to the Seers of this Keep. Others may see a dozen or more, although they then come to join us here. I have been told that we are becoming somewhat more common in the last centuries, but just slightly so."

Di'nay said nothing, and Elana felt defensive at the silence. A natural reaction, she reminded herself, when someone was standing there judging you. "I can show you something of my own ability," Elana offered as a way of breaching the growing wariness. "You have a right to know these things before—" She stopped, suddenly remembering who she was speaking to and instead finished quietly, "If you have decided I am unsuitable, do not make me betray my people further."

"I haven't decided anything of the kind," Diana murmured, and then at the silence offered a formal oath, "In truth, I have not."

"I know." A faint smile touched Elana's full lips. "I have the Sight."

"This tells you if I'm lying?"

Elana shook her head, her dark hair rustling. "A Seer could tell, but I've not been trained as a Seer. I know only your outward amarin. They...it...has little to do with your words." Elana paused, aware that the tension between them had lessened as Di'nay suspended that skeptical corner within herself. This was not an easily explainable thing; it was more simply an experience. Struggling, she searched for the words to continue. "All things living – or once living – have an essence, an impression." She faltered, then tried again. "It is like a cloak. It enfolds a person or a...or a plant...all of us."

"I understand," Diana said quickly, and she did. At home the House n'Shea had witch healers who could see the life auras at will and who could touch and mold the flowing energies to repair damaged tissues and blood vessels. This was merely a non-mechanical technology that the Empire had never found the time for.

"With a person, the thoughts and feelings, they leave patterns. I read these. I see the...emotions." Elana glanced across the sun-bronzed face again and found the Amazon's amarin was reassuring. "It is sometimes helpful to know if a stranger is a friend or foe; this I can do. Also, I can change these patterns for a time. In that way I create illusions." She paused. "I could show you?"

Diana nodded, but oddly she was thinking of how disconcerting it was going to be to always be looking at the top of that dark head.

Elana's concentration dropped to her small, cupped hands. For a moment her gaze intentionally became unfocused. Abruptly – with a whoosh – a flame leapt from her palms and swept around the hollow of her cradled grasp. Elana smiled, feeling an unexpected delight in the Amazon's amazement.

Fascinated, the older woman stepped near and cautiously held a hand over the dancing flames. "It's cool."

Elana nodded her faint tip-of-the-head nod and then said, "Now it is hot."

She swept her hand through the flames again. Carelessly she passed too close and when Elana pulled the cupped fire away, it was not quickly enough. In pain and angered at her own foolishness, Diana sucked the air in through clenched teeth.

"I beg your patience, Di'nay," Elana murmured apologetically.

"My fault," Diana said with a strained smile, gripping her wrist. The side of her hand and little finger were scorched pink, and she glanced around. "Is there any water about?"

"It is only an illusion," Elana interjected quickly. "Watch."

The flames flickered suddenly into empty air, and just as rapidly the reddened skin faded into the familiar weathered brown. Within, Diana's hand still felt roasted and throbbing, but as she felt this, the evidence of her eyes began to reassert the scrambled neural messages.

"How long the illusion lasts once I have finished is a trick of the mind," explained the younger woman gently. "If you concentrated — focused well enough, the skin would not scorch at all."

"How is it that it was cool then hot?"

"As my intentions change, so does the...illusion."

"Can you project your intentions into another's mind then?"

"An illusion is my projection onto external things."

She had not answered the question, Diana realized immediately. Again she noticed the restless, avoiding gaze. "You can influence another's mind only by locking eyes, can't you?"

Elana grew very still. "It also allows me to — read one's amarin more clearly."

"How clearly?"

Elana answered steadily, "Very clearly."

It certainly gave Diana something to think about, especially considering she was the spy here — alias Cultural Liaison.

Elana turned on her heel, her attention rippling outward — startled. Diana watched curiously as she stood there motionless. "I must go," Elana whispered and glanced upwards at the woman beside her.

Diana nodded, remembering that she was not to have been there at all. She watched as Elana slipped back off into the feathery, leafed trees. There was grace in her fluid motion that reminded Diana of a wild Terran deer. Now where had that thought come from?

A gravely crunch told her of approaching company. A figure cowled in heavy robes paused at the sight of Diana. The hood was tossed back, and with a voice that crackled with imperious authority, the woman called, "Your Commander would talk with you, Amazon. He awaits you in his shuttlecraft. I wonder, do you mistrust listening walls as much as he?"

Diana smiled, reminded by this old woman of home and the crone witches in the House n'Shea. With a shrug of her lean frame she stepped forward. "No more than whispering trees."

A dry smile passed between them. "I am called Mistress here. I welcome you to this Keep."

"I am honored in the greeting. I am — "

"N'Athena, or the so-called Southern Trader, Tad Di'nay." The Old Mistress gave her a speculative glance. "In truth, I've seldom thought favorably of off-worlders, Amazon. You and your Sisters, however, have an admirable reputation. I admit I am impressed." She turned, leaving no room for comment. "This way."

Diana followed. Did everyone know of her then? Neither she nor Cleis had ever presumed they warranted more than the passing attentions of the Council of Ten. And the Empire had always harbored the fantasy that their cultural liaisons here were seldom watched and frequently forgotten. Although the Seers that Elana had mentioned as Blue Sights could certainly have supplied a few puzzle pieces, especially if they were as gifted as she suspected Elana to be. Actually, the fact that Elana was not a Seer might indicate she was not skilled enough — or perhaps still too young? Diana grinned wickedly. If she ever told Thomas, it would certainly give him something to fret about.

✳ ✳ ✳

Elana slid the jerkin on over the tunic with a sigh. Between the black knit underclothes, the thick tunic, and the leather trappings she was almost unbearably hot. But the warmth would be welcomed later when the snows threatened.

She suppressed another sigh, fastened the belt and stood quietly as the seamstress continued to fuss. "This will do," Teena nodded, beaming happily. "This will do very nicely."

The dividing curtain swished aside to admit the Old Master. Elana turned to face her teacher, standing her tallest as he approached her with a scowl. "Too stiff." She released the taut muscles, losing a fraction of height. "Better. The illusion's in the confidence, not the bulk."

He walked about her, shaking his head, mindful of an obtuse flaw that he was needing to identify. "There!" The back of a finger slapped against the leather belt.

Teena's quick hands tugged and loosened the offender, pulling it from Elana's waist. Puzzled she turned the wide band over, seeking the error.

"The Amazon wears a soft suede belt," the old man explained. "I suspect it may encase a hollow tube. It is three finger wide, I believe — "

"Less."

His bushy brows lifted, but he stared thoughtfully at the belt. He knew by habit not to challenge by meeting those eyes.

"A lesser width may be best," Teena said, hastening to bridge the silence. "The Amazon has a much greater stature. The belt would best be made to the Eldest's proportions. Or the misfitted style may reveal her as an impostor."

"Yes, certainly. Tend to it. Is the fit comfortable?" the Old Master asked Elana suddenly.

It was not what he wanted to know, Elana thought as she nodded slightly.

The Old Master turned a fretting gaze to his pupil. For a moment he simply stared at her while she calmly rested her eyes on his bony chin. His lips pursed then as he fingered a wispy black wave of her hair. It was decidedly different from the Amazon's cut. "It perhaps should be shortened," he suggested, but it was clearly an idea and not an order. "The Amazon wears it close cut as a man traveling would."

"It suits her well as guise," Elana agreed, glad to feel his intentions were not to force an immediate decision. She had a small, vain hope within her heart that Di'nay would approve of her long tresses.

"Would you pass more as a man with it short, you think?"

"Most likely not," she allowed reluctantly. "It would still curl over-much."

"Yes," he grunted, remembering a hearth accident she had suffered as a newly arrived youngster. A kettle of oil for frying bread had spilled and caught fire in the kitchen. The girl's loose hair had singed and flamed. Thereafter her hair had been cropped close, the resulting tousle of short curls reminding him of the bushy tail of a pripper. It had been an enchanting sight combined with her blue-white eyes but not masculine.

"You have often said," Elana reminded him gingerly, "that the disguise is in the bravado. I could never match her height without resorting to my Sight, but at night or from a distance perspective is often blurred. Clad in trousers and a cloak, my hair covered by a hood, I would mislead many."

He grunted, pleased with her insight and nodded, sliding his hands into the sleeves of his robe. "So we will let the length be. Also, your lover of women may find it pleasing that you do not look too mannish."

"It will be as she requests." If this Amazon preferred shorter hair, it would be less of a hardship to comply.

"So, make yourself ready for this formality of choosing." He startled her from her thoughts and she nodded. It would feel good to remove the warm underclothes.

"We'll wait for you in the anteroom. The off-worlders are already in the Hall."

As he left her to change she felt the insides of her stomach flutter and her shoulders tensed. Her control clamped down sternly and calmed the tremors. She had the Blue Sight; her wayward anxiety would not be welcomed by the others. Yet beneath the rational wall, her uneasiness persisted. Di'nay had not actually named her as Shadowmate nor promised such naming, although she expected it. Yet afterwards?

Absently she exchanged the trader's clothing for her familiar garb, finally facing the issue of what followed if she was chosen. Bonding was simultaneously the goal and the dread of all the trainees. It was painful. But more important, it was the last moment in destiny to question their path. It was their final opportunity to reject the luring seduction of the wanderlust.

For many it was a time of soul-searching. There were those who had grown old in desire while waiting to be chosen or those who swayed between two mistresses of fate — for these, some withdrew and the task of Shadow was reappointed. Always they would have places in the Keep as teachers or Council advisors, or they were free, as her parents had been, to follow a way separate from the stone walls.

But for those that remained unswayed, it meant an end to the life — and the rule of the Council and Keep. It meant adventure and commitment with the appointed other. It meant the unknown.

Elana unrolled the soft suede of her boot as she drew it up and over her calf. She fastened the thongs as her blue gaze unfocused. The vividness of those brown eyes had stared at her for more than two tenmoon seasons now; it had been a haunting that had surged to the intensity of obsession on occasion. And today in the garden they had finally met. Yet as she had stared into that dark gaze to touch that familiar strength so tempered with kindness...she had also found a weariness, a desire for home. A desire that warred with a sense of duty and responsibility towards all life.

A frown of resolve hardened Elana's conviction. She would not hold this woman to Aggar by unbidden chains of the lifebond. Di'nay had not requested interference. Inconsiderate ploys of the Fates would not darken the rest of this Amazon's life — she would not be exiled from her place of birth. Elana would not permit it!

No! Di'nay's choice must be freely made. Just as she was now choosing her own path with this Amazon, Di'nay must choose if they were to remain together. She must not be coerced. She would not be told of the fatal consequences of their final parting.

A faint smile twisted Elana's lips. Such noble intentions...the unspoken assumption that she would live to deal with such consequences? The Maltar would chuckle that she, a mere woman of twelve tenmoons, would deem to challenge any of his strongholds with so little concern for the task. Yes, it would amuse him greatly. In truth then, it was better to attend to the coming trials; the future mists would clear at their own leisure.

❋ ❋ ❋

Chapter Seven

The Council Speaker and the aged Mistress escorted Diana and Commander Baily along the stone corridors in silence. The upper windows showed that the sun had set in a sparsely clouded sky, and the early moon had already risen high enough to cast her reflected light, sparing Aggar from the fall of dense night. For once Colonel Thomas Baily was appropriately mute.

The fiasco of naming her Shadowmate had unnerved Diana more than she would admit. Baily's display of temper at discovering the Council's three prospects were all women had been singularly insulting to both Diana and their hosts. The sole redeeming grace had been his poor command of the language and only Diana had borne the brunt of his stupidity. The Council Speaker had been unbending, however; these three were the most qualified candidates for this mission, and in the end, necessity had silenced Thomas. But any tolerance for him that Diana had allowed to develop as she anticipated her retirement had been obliterated.

It made her no less uncomfortable to know that Elana had grasped something of their exchange.

The procession halted. The wooden bolt lifted easily under the Speaker's hand, and the four of them entered a small foyer. At the sound of the latch a woman near Diana's age appeared from behind a curtain. She smiled warmly at the Amazon but extended her hands only to the Mistress. Her sleeveless mantle shimmered over the long gown — a satin mantle. The fabric registered vaguely with Diana; it was a rare material in this region.

"Your gracious escort is honorably acknowledged," the woman addressed the men, her words ringing with a ritualistic resonance. "May your parting be without worry and your thoughts of blessing hasten the bonding."

"Parting — as in leaving?" The nervous Terran plucked at Diana's arm, uncertain of his own translation of the woman's phrase. "They're not leaving us with...?"

Diana smiled stiffly for the sake of their hosts and said in a deadly, quiet tone, "No, you are leaving me. And if you don't behave yourself, you may explain to your superior why I quit the field assignment on the date of my official retirement."

His small eyes blinked and his thin nostrils almost shut with his tense intake of breath. But Thomas said nothing.

Stiffly, Diana nodded to the Council Speaker. He returned her smile almost encouragingly, and with a firm hand escorted the Colonel away.

"Please." The satin-mantled figure smiled again. "Take a moment to wash." She gestured to the stone trough of steaming water beside her, then disappeared through the curtain again.

The Old Mistress moved and Diana started, glancing over her shoulder as the elder laid out a snow-white tunic and a sash of shimmering black. Surprised to find her agitation with Thomas had turned into apprehension, Diana sighed and removed her cloak. "Who is that woman, Mistress?"

The Mistress produced a cake of soap and a towel from a stone shelf. "She is called Jezebet. It is her title and name here even as Mistress is mine."

"What is her role?"

"She is...a priestess of sorts. She or one of hers has always guided the Shadowmates to meet their destiny. With her, they pass the walls that separate us all. She weaves the lifebonding."

Diana's breath caught and her teeth clenched in anger. "Mistress, I have no need for life-long anything. When this pilot is safely returned, I will be leaving for home. As I said at the Choosing, I will tolerate no ties that bind me to this planet."

"It is the custom...."

"It's barbaric!"

"You know nothing of it."

The quiet truth silenced her, and in frustrated defeat, Diana slumped forward over the steaming water trough.

"Your Shadow, Amazon, is a remarkable one," the Old Mistress began quietly. "There are many reasons why she is favored for this journey — not the least of which is that she's Eldest Prepared. I suspect, from all my seasons, that she is the finest of our trainees. But you — Diana n'Athena Amazon...you, I have not seen to prepare her for. How will you come to her? When you hurt, will you reach for her — you who are so self-sufficient? If you are lost, will you cry out for her? Certainly the lifebond will call her to you, but what welcome will you give — now or later? Will you offer her patience as she fumbles to learn your ways? Can you offer a safe haven of any sort?"

But why must it be she who learns my ways? Diana's soul protested. She shut her eyes against the image of the beautiful woman bowed in submission. The thought of Maryl rose suddenly. Diana knew what she could offer this Shadow — freedom. At least, freedom of a sort...a role of her own choosing. Just as Maryl had chosen the baker's life, perhaps this young woman too had a dream to be followed.

Diana straightened, nodding faintly. "There will be time for learning, Mistress."

"Would you care for her already, Amazon?"

Elana was a woman in her own right, why would she not care? But Diana's heart did not believe it was a mere question of ethics. She sighed, "It changes nothing. I will still leave her when we are finished — sooner if necessity beckons."

The Old Mistress studied her for a long moment, mindful of the brittle fatigue that wrapped itself around this woman. There was strength here, she saw, but she worried for her Ona too — there was much that these two could share, but their paths would not be easily entwined. Finally, tentatively, she ventured, "Ponder compassion, young Amazon. For her struggles...and for your own."

"My own?"

The Mistress nodded slowly. "Your own. She will guide you — guard you — befriend you...cherish you if you allow it. You must ask yourself, if you still dare to trust...you who have been so long alone. Perhaps it is time to find compassion for yourself. Learn of the bonding. There can be much to treasure, I promise you."

Too much to risk, Diana added silently and felt the faint stirrings of panic in her stomach. Was she so very exposed before this old Crone then?

"Enough," the Mistress ended gently. "You need washing. Give me your tunic."

Mutely Diana stripped the travel-worn jerkin and shirt from her skin, wishing that this awkward vulnerability would dissolve in the soap and water with the dirt. She dried herself and turned to don the new tunic. Shimmering white, it lay open in the front, barely concealing her slight breasts. The softness of the material was disconcerting too; it drew memories from her body — memories of satin-skinned lovers...of safe places. But this was not home — she needed her defenses here.

The Mistress knotted a black belt about Diana's waist, ignoring the Amazon's stiffness. I must look odd to her with such a browned face and white chest, Diana thought suddenly, ushering her more practical self forward. She felt some of the tension leave her shoulders then, and she drew an easier breath. This was merely a local ritual of title — a necessary evil in this insanity.

But it went against every fiber of her being — against the struggle of the Sisterhood's dreams. They had fought so hard, for so long over that treasured dream of personal dignity! Somehow she would have to find a way to share some of that dream with this Shadow — with this woman.

As she was an Amazon, z'ki Sak, Diana! She would not betray that dream!

"It is time," the Old Mistress ordered, and she lifted the curtain aside.

Within, the shadowed room was warm and humid, the air heavy with scented oils. Fire filled a gaping hearth, its yellow-white flames leaping easily the height of a man. Motionless, a silhouette of black stood before that fire. With a flutter of fabric, Jezebet appeared again, carrying a tiny jar to the hearth.

Diana nodded tentatively at the woman's calm smile of greeting. At a slight push from the Mistress, Diana went forward.

Jezebet stood between the fire and the dark, cloaked form. The figure shrugged slightly, pushing long hair over her shoulder. It was Elana, Diana realized, and it was no cloak but her hair loosened. Impulsively, she touched Elana's bare shoulder. Smiling, Elana looked at her expectantly.

Breath caught in Diana's throat. Elana's skin glistened from the perfumed oil, and the heat had tinged her coloring to a light, even caramel. She wore no tunic or mantel, and Diana realized her breeches and boots were the same cut as Diana's own. The gentle slopes of her breasts were too slight, the smoothness of her waist too taut for Aggar's childbearers. Diana's pulse raced at the shimmering, oiled beauty of the young woman. There was nothing objective in that response.

A moment of panic whipped through her body as Diana remembered Elana's Blue Sight, but if the woman had read her breathless scrutiny, she was not saying. Mutely she let Elana's hand guide her to the far side of the small pedestal so that they stood facing each other across it.

At Diana's entry the stone pedestal had been hidden by Elana's form. Now she saw that it was filled to the wide-lipped brim with reddened coals. Heat shimmered in waves and the threads in Jezebet's gray mantle sparkled orange with reflecting light. The rest of the room was in flickering blackness. Cases of books, tables with oil jars danced in and out of vision as the fire leapt and retreated. Deep in the darkness behind Elana, Diana made out a stillness that must be the Old Mistress.

"You may choose a cloth to bind your eyes, Child," Jezebet's soft voice said to Elana. Diana felt a sudden rush of fury in her blood at the request for submission.

"No," Elana said calmly, but her tongue nervously passed over her lips. She had felt the anger rise in the woman across from her. With suddenness she grasped the amarin, seeing the blindfolding and ritual as they must seem to the Amazon — barbaric. "It is my Sight," Elana whispered quickly as Jezebet turned to the hearth. "It is not to hide anything from me, but to protect you — and the others."

Only half reassured, Diana nodded and resolved to bear whatever was coming with a little more detachment. Elana was obviously sensitive to her anger. It was perhaps not the time to be careless with distractions.

Jezebet returned with the small urn that had been warming at the fire's edge. She lifted the close-fitted lid, and the fragrance of the hot oil grew stronger. Careful, without a word, the woman tipped a little into Elana's cupped hands. Then, she stayed the trickling flow; not a drop tainted the outer edge of the jar.

With hands held over the glowing coals, Elana began to smooth the thick liquid into her skin. Her shimmering body was already covered, but the ritual was to serve as instruction for the adopting person. Deliberately Elana's fingers spread the oil along her wrists and forearms. Her skin tingled, awakening, and she smiled. It was not an unpleasant sensation.

When she finished, Elana held out her hands to Di'nay. "Your hands," she said, almost inaudibly. Di'nay presented them and Elana turned them palm up and cupped them together.

Again with care Jezebet poured the oil, this time into the Amazon's hands. The warm oil began to pool in the cup of her palms. Elana's hands slipped beneath Di'nay's long fingers, catching the elusive droplets that would have slipped free. It was not yet time for the oil to feed the embers.

Uncertain, Diana began to spread oil across her skin. It was almost hot to her touch and little darts of electricity seemed to skip through her senses. It felt a little like a bubbling wine on the roof of one's mouth, Diana thought, amused, then noted with a blurring blink that the heavy scent seemed to be just as intoxicating.

Elana's fingers gently separated her rubbing hands and began to smooth the oil more evenly into the weathered skin. With an effort Diana attempted to concentrate and clear her head. But the tracing fingertips that slipped between her own slender fingers distracted...the brush of thumbs across that tender point on her wrists...the hot skin of palms against her forearms.

She blinked again to force her vision clear as deftly, with one hand to each of Diana's, Elana worked the oil into the Amazon's skin, softening the calluses of travel and the toughened shell of time. Diana forced a breath, her nostrils flaring, as her senses stirred, and she began to melt just a little.

She felt panic rise and then fade again. This stirring, shivering touch was so much like making love. She should have protested, but that little edge of panic merely disappeared as if soothed away by a chalice or two of wine.

Elana seemed untouched by it all, Diana noticed as she obediently cupped her hands again. Perhaps it is my alien biology, Diana wondered and watched as the oil was poured first into Elana's grasp and then her own. There was little difference — physiologically — between them. Maybe she should tell Jezebet — or the Mistress — that something was wrong; she wasn't responsible for these hands any more. But her voice remained still as she imitated Elana's movements.

Together the women spread the aged oils across their breasts and the smooth center hollow. Over my pounding heart, Diana realized as she finished and held out her hands with Elana for more oil.

Diana's fingers slid richly, warmly against her face, and the heady scent conjured fleeting images of gentle lovers. The scent of women seemed to fill her nose and lungs as she rubbed the oil into her skin...it was like burying herself into the warm, moist well of a treasured lover. She felt her stomach ease and turn liquid. She paused to breathe the thick fragrance from her fingers.

Her hands dropped slowly as she faced Elana across the pedestal. Diana saw that the other woman did not go entirely unaffected; her skin had darkened ever so slightly into a deeper caramel. No, she decided, floating in her unbidden cloud, she was not being affected because she was an alien. This was a powerful combination of tranquilizer and stimulant. Her brain felt disengaged from the reality around her but she felt safe, as if she was wrapped in cotton puff or...no — she smiled with the thoughts — she felt wrapped in a woman's womb. Her senses floated. Her body surged with life and power.

Elana returned Di'nay's smile, watching the Amazon closely. Their eyes met in passing and the image of the woman's safety...of softened, caring places danced through Elana's mind. The calm stayed as their glances separated, lingering reassuringly. Elana's mind slowed as it turned the pictures over and over again. Even as Jezebet moved near again, she released the last of her fears, letting her body respond to the inevitable.

A leather chamois slowly unfolded in Jezebet's hands to reveal a stone. An opal, Diana thought at once, watching the way color sparkled and fired within the milky white depths. But it was not an opal. As Jezebet held it, the duller whites asserted their prowess, smothering the colors imperiously. It seemed innocuously opaque then and rather small. It would fit in the palm of anyone's hand; Diana guessed it was perhaps four centimeters long, three at its widest.

Carefully Jezebet slipped the rock onto a bronzed plate. It slid, but the woman tilted the saucer and settled the stone back into the shallow basin. With barely a scratch of metal to coal, she laid it upon the burning embers.

Diana's detachment rippled at the thought of the heat the stone and plate were absorbing. Then the moistened, scented air reached into her mind, and the addicting calm engulfed her. Jezebet deftly plucked the stone from its warming place. Diana noticed no hesitancy in her movement and wondered if it hadn't grown hot after all.

"Take the stone," Elana instructed quietly, and Diana thought she sounded as if she were very far away. Acceptingly, the Amazon opened her hands. As it fell into her palms the whiteness flashed, and she shut her eyes for an instant against the sudden glare. The oval looked strangely small in the center of her hand. It was smooth and warm, yet it was not uncomfortably hot. Its brightness faded then into a subtle sparkle that danced and darted in the murky depths.

It must be an odd quartz, Diana thought as she rubbed it between her palms, marveling at the polished smoothness. She looked questioningly to Jezebet but the quiet smile directed her towards Elana.

Elana's gaze was fixed intently on the stone as she pointed to her own wrist. "Place it here on your left arm."

Diana wondered if it was possible to balance it so with its fine polish and oil. She extended her forearm and cautiously attempted to place it on her flattened wrist. Elana's hand reached across the coals, demonstrating how Diana should curl her fingers and bend her hand back downward. Surprised to see the tendons disappear with such a simple movement, Diana did the same and found the stone sat more securely.

With a single finger Jezebet centered the stone so that the length of the oval followed the line of the forearm. The electrical tingle that surged through her body suddenly found its way to her wrist. The tender skin inside of her upper arm prickled and felt raw as the energy rushed downward to converge on the small stone. A curious ache centered beneath the warmed rock — as if she had bent her wrist too far and had slightly strained it — as if the stone carried much more weight than it possibly could.

The stone's sparkling depths caught Diana's attention and the dull throb was forgotten. Fluttering strands of crimson and purple struggled to flow within the milkiness. As she watched the colors fused and separated again into smaller tributaries. An oddly familiar definition of line and flow sharpened and settled into an unchanging pattern. Then she recognized her own wrist — a kind of diagram of the pulsing blood beneath.

Jezebet moved, interrupting Diana's thoughts. Careful to handle only the very edges of the stone, her fingers lifted it from the bent wrist and pressed it lightly against Diana's breast. The warmth of the stone had faded to a coolness. Fascinated she again felt the stone focus her skin's senses.

Her heart seemed to be pounding in her ears, though not faster than normal — that sound and feeling through the mist of the stone was just stronger, louder. The stone demanded it louder yet. She ached beneath her ribs at the force of each pumping contraction. The steady lines in the stone shivered and awakened to the thudding beat. Alive — the ruby-blue tracings pulsed and surged through the white mire.

Her lungs gasped for breath as Jezebet pulled the stone from her skin. But the rite was not done, and silently Jezebet held the stone inches from Diana's forehead. The fizzling charges made the hair on the back of her neck stand on end. The skin beneath the stone felt unbearably sensitive, vulnerable. Almost unwillingly, her eyes closed at the stone's touch. Suspended, her breath stayed — muscles tightened, not able to stir — her thoughts were frozen, blocked in frenzied fright.

The stone left her and her teeth grated as she sucked in the scented air, her spine releasing its iron-rod straightness. Amazed at the intensity of her responses, Diana found the shock had freed her from the oil's scented stupor.

She forced air into her lungs more slowly, concentrating on the quivering jelly that seemed to be her nerves and muscles. This was no longer acceptable to her — she was frightened, Diana admitted to herself, and that was a feeling she did not care for at all.

A soft clack brought her attention back to the others. Jezebet had returned the stone to the plate atop the coals; the pulsing pattern in its depths was still alive. Again, it rested but a moment before Jezebet reached for it.

As she stepped to Elana's side Diana heard her mutter and watched Elana nod before those intense blue eyes slipped shut. She is beautiful, Diana thought in that brief second before Jezebet placed the stone against the brown-skinned forehead.

Elana's body stiffened almost violently and her teeth snapped shut. Diana felt the pit of her stomach harden and her own hands clench tight, her short nails biting her palms. The woman shivered and a thin sweat broke to mingle with the oil. Anger swelled, shortening Diana's breath.

A touch at her elbow made her start, and she looked to find the Old Mistress. "Patience," the woman bid and turned to Elana.

As stone was lifted from Elana's skin, her eyes were still shut tightly, the muscles of her neck taut, and her hands stretched open at her sides. Elana's fingers curled compulsively, then stiffly were thrown open again.

It was not over; Diana trembled with her growing fury. It was not over. Elana knew each step of what was to come — knew and stood there doing nothing!

The oval touched Elana's breast, above her heart, and her stillness broke with a shudder. A ragged breath was pulled in between her teeth as her head jerked forward, the dark hair hiding her face from Diana. Her lungs seemed to pull and push at the same time as if she had forgotten the sequence of inhale-exhale.

Jezebet removed the stone and returned it to the plate.

Straining, Elana forced her body to straighten, and with an effort relaxed her jaw enough to gasp for air. The Mistress, careful not to touch the oiled, brown-flushed skin, gingerly lifted the dark hair over Elana's shoulders.

The tension in Diana eased as Elana's eyes flickered and finally opened. She tipped her head back and allowed the Mistress to arrange long tresses behind her. She had not been hiding tears, Diana decided, and suddenly, harshly, she wondered, why she was so concerned anyway? Elana did not meekly submit to anything, if their forbidden exchange in the garden was any example. Yet Diana did care. It proved nothing that Elana was a willing participant — nothing except that the woman believed in the rite.

That was not good enough, Diana admitted. Beliefs in customs did not make them right. It often merely condoned the barbarism.

The small jar reappeared and Jezebet began to drizzle the perfumed oil around the embers, circling the bronze plate. The liquid crackled, re-lighting the charred fragments; incense sputtered into smoke. The flames danced about the glittering plate, and Diana felt her throat grow parched and raw from the thickening fumes. Their touch no longer induced the balmy fog for her. Looking to Elana, she saw that blue gaze fastened, unblinking, on the fiery depths. Elana was obviously still bound beneath that scented spell.

Jezebet reached again for the stone amidst the flames. Off-center, between the dark caramel breasts, the skin reddened — scorched. Diana frowned as Elana extended her left hand low over the dwindling flames to warm the oil of her wrist.

Slowly Elana rotated her palm upwards, clenching her fingers, arching her wrist flat. The bluish veins were barely distinguishable under the brown flesh. The stone hovered above the exposed skin, and Elana was held bewitched by its white depths.

"Your eyes, Child," Jezebet prompted gently. The warm, almost loving tone of her voice angered Diana as Elana's eyes closed obediently. It was the voice of a mother sending a trusting child off to dreams — off to nightmares!

"If you stop this now," the Mistress said, reading her thoughts, "she will not live through the hour. It is too late to alter the course."

Diana's furious gaze locked with the elder's, but it was too late. Jezebet's fingers dropped the white stone, perfectly centered, onto the small wrist.

A cry tore from Elana's lips and her free hand grasped her arm, forcing it level. Her head flung back. Desperately her body struggled to stand upright — fighting her knees from buckling — her stomach from cramping. The whiteness of the stone was gone; a chaos of scarlet, blue and lavender streaked across the polished surface. Oil poured thick over the rock and wrist, down to the blazing coals below. The stench of burnt flesh tainted the air as skin blackened and crisped at the stone's edge.

A hand clamped against Diana's arm. Her glaring rage stared the old woman down, but in this moment of distraction, it was finished.

The leaping fire atop the coals retreated into nothing but orange embers. Incense and the sickening reek of flesh evaporated; only the wood smoke from the hearthfire touched the air.

The coolness of a night's breeze seemed to whip through the small chamber, bringing a freshness. Diana shuddered at the sudden cold. Confused, she looked to Elana's bent form. Her arm was still supported by her hand; her shoulders huddled low, but she was breathing again — ragged, uneven breaths, and her cheeks were scarred with tears — but she was breathing.

Jezebet spread a pasty salve around the stone on Elana's wrist. Diana stepped nearer to stare.

"Don't touch me!" Elana pleaded in a strangled whisper. "Not...yet...."

Diana nodded, moved by the tear-stricken face. Elana's eyes were still closed, but from exhaustion now, not pain. Diana's gaze was drawn back to the stone. The rock had paled to a dull white with the pattern of pulsing veins still ruby-blue within. But it no longer rested atop her wrist; it fit flush with the brown skin. Jezebet wrapped the arm in a soft dressing to heal, hiding the stone from her probing stare.

"You will be fine?" Diana asked in Common. A piece of her urgently needed reassurance independent from the Mistress.

The blue eyes opened and blinked as Elana nodded. "I need rest. That is all...."

"She must sleep," Jezebet said quietly, wrapping a warm cloak around her charge. "Her body must adapt to your rhythms. She will be with you for eventide."

How could anyone think of food now? Diana thought with irritation.

"I must go," Elana murmured.

"Yes." Diana desperately wanted to carry her to her bed if she wasn't to lie down here. Anything to get her off her feet quickly.

A serving man appeared from the black curtained entrance in the chamber's back. He hesitated at the sight of Diana. Jezebet signaled him forward.

"Until eventide." The Mistress smiled, and Elana gratefully, wearily, nodded.

The burly servant lifted her carefully, touching only the cloak, not her bare skin.

Jezebet led him from the room and Diana watched with a feeling of frustration and helplessness. The Mistress would not let her be. With a tug on her tunic, the woman summoned Diana along. "I have a warm bath prepared, young Amazon. Let us not dawdle until it cools."

"Yes." With an effort she took her eyes from the curtained exit and followed.

❊ ❊ ❊

Chapter Eight

The long table was spread with everything from a smoked fowl lexion to an assortment of peeled fruits. The sweet aroma of mulled wine drifted across the chamber, and Diana's mouth watered. It was her habit to forget about her stomach when food was not readily available. A convenient mental trick, often resulting in mild headaches — and a voracious appetite when there finally was an opportunity to eat. Diana anticipated the food as she half-listened to the Council Speaker prattle on about weather projections and supplies. There were only seven of the high-backed chairs pulled forward from their places along the tapestry-hung walls, although judging by the quantity of food laid, they easily could have been expecting fifteen or so guests.

The Council Speaker excused himself and crossed the room as a dark-cowled Seer appeared, leaving Diana to her own devices. She wondered if the robed one was the same Seer she had been presented to after her bath. It had been a rather unnerving experience, considering her earlier conversation with Elana. Although her Imperial loyalty had not been strained in the least, her concerns for her own Sisterhood had been another matter entirely.

To the outsiders, dey Sorormin was a society of highly aggressive women who were technologically sophisticated — and very dangerous. The risk in challenging their planetary rights had always seemed too great, and so since the colonization of their solar system, Amazons had been warily respected and their rights seldom disputed. But like Aggar, the Sisterhood was relatively independent of the Empire. Amazons did hold chairs on the Imperial Senate and they did contribute the minimal monies and personnel to the Imperial Government that their Senate membership required. However, they were isolationists at heart, just like Aggar's Council of Ten. The Sisterhood believed in their own path and control of their own destiny even more than the Imperial governing males liked to admit. The fact that their society was based on a balance of ecology and technology and not on hi-tech bravado was something that no outsider knew. It was something the Sisterhood dearly hoped none ever would. It was the sheer reputation of the Amazons' strength that had averted so many disasters, and so it was a mythical reputation that the Sisterhood dearly guarded.

So faced with the Council's Seer, Diana had desperately sifted through Elana's warning words and sought to weave some kind of defense. Patterns of thoughts and feelings, Elana had said. Diana had resurrected her anger from the life-bonding ceremony, drawing upon the very intensity of her hostility and hoping to blur those patterns which would have sprung from mere thoughts. And

Elana had admitted to the importance of locking gazes. Diana had completely refused to look at the Seer. She did not know if the interview had proven as fruitless as she'd intended, but she had been fairly confident that it had not been as profitable as the Council expected.

The door opposite Diana opened, and she grimaced as Baily reappeared. She'd thought he might have returned to the base and to his regular military duties, but it seemed such hopes were futile.

He charged across the room in a nervous fury, "What are you doing dressed like that!? N'Athena, it's positively indecent — "

A single eyebrow lifted and her silence made Baily falter. The man pressed his lips together as his mustache twitched. They both knew that he had no idea whether she was inappropriately clothed or not. He should know that tights and belted tunics were as commonplace indoors as jerkins and britches were outdoors.

After a moment, Diana said, "They generously offered to clean my traveling gear. I took them up on it."

Baily cleared his throat and glanced around, attempting to reclaim his authority as he tugged on the waist of his short jacket. "That was considerate of them."

"Is the equipment I requested unloaded?"

"Your pack and small saddle bag. Everything is locked in a rather insecure looking trunk in some bedchamber."

"It'll be left alone." At his dubious stare, Diana attempted to put it in terms he'd understand. "They need our cooperation, Thomas. They'll not jeopardize that for a five minute look, and they know we'll pull out completely if they actually steal anything. They have an investment in this mission too, you know."

"Yes, I suppose you're right. Still...I worry."

She gave up, folded her arms, and consoled herself with the promise of eventide. Even Thomas could not spoil her appetite.

"That partner of yours. Damn but she's a pretty one!" Baily's sudden smile grew into a leer. "Someone ought to warn her how long you've been away from home."

"Terran!" Glaring eyes cut him off as Diana turned on him with a hiss. "You will not subject her to your crudeness!"

"Now look here. I'm still your commander — "

"Persist in your sordid insinuations and you'll be hard pressed to be one again!"

"You...don't have that kind of authority!" But his voice wavered, betraying him.

"I have Sisters who do."

The blond mustache twitched twice. "I won't be intimidated."

"You have already behaved badly enough. Your conduct at the Choosing was unbefitting any commander!"

"Yes, well." With an obvious effort he turned, straightening his shoulders stiffly. "There is no cause to discuss this further...given your cooperation...and propriety. It would certainly discourage our tenuous relations with their Elders to press the matter."

Slowly Diana recognized his need to save face and controlled her temper. But she did not trust this man, and it always bothered her to remember just how much she disliked him too.

Baily coughed loudly as the others approached. "Gentlemen...," he bent his stiffest, most courteous bow to the Speaker and Old Master, "...it is kind of you to extend your hospitality to the evening meal. The table is well set, I compliment you both." He paused and the Council Speaker translated briefly for the Master.

The man acknowledged the Commander's words with a patently formal smile, but Baily had already turned as Elana slid around the others and joined Diana. "It's Elana, yes? A lovely name, almost as lovely as the girl that carries it."

Startled at his over-anxious, over-enthusiastic approach, Elana halted as the man grasped her hand in both of his. Deliberately she kept her eyes downcast and her amarin hazy. This was not someone she wished to notice her blue eyes.

"May I say how prettily you are dressed tonight? Your tan is most becoming against the blue of your blouse."

Diana flexed upwards on her toes as her hands clenched and unclenched at his tactlessness. It was a rude breech of privacy on Aggar to comment on another's change of skin color. Emotions were not openly discussed even among many families — and certainly never with strangers.

Elana smiled hesitantly, confused by her lack of Common vocabulary. His amarin was obviously intent on flattering her, but equally blatant was Di'nay's fury. Carefully she returned in his tongue, "Your compliment is accepted, Commander."

Taken aback by her use of his language, the man blinked and his smile broadened. But Elana moved quickly aside, allowing the Council Speaker to escort Baily diplomatically off towards the table. The Old Master followed with an evident reluctance with which Elana empathized .

In concern Diana touched Elana's shoulder. "Are you well?"

"Yes." Elana smiled with reassurance.

Then abruptly, as if suddenly burnt, Diana's hand dropped. She found herself acutely conscious of the cool blueness of Elana's tunic and the thin, matching ribbons that were braided into the dark hair. Dismayed, Diana realized that she was attracted to this woman — to this child?! There must be fourteen — fifteen years difference between them? She was reacting just as Thomas said!

Z'ki Sak, Diana. Diana bit off a short breath. She didn't need this!

"They wait for you," Elana murmured hesitantly, nodding towards the table. Another pair of robed figures had joined them and everyone was being seated.

"Yes, I know." Diana scowled, making no move towards them.

Curiously Elana watched her. The aura of anger and impatience was apparent to her, but there was no target she understood. "May I help?" Elana offered finally.

"No," Diana said flatly, spinning on her heel. "They've waited long enough."

Elana followed quickly.

For Elana the evening that followed passed much too quickly. Di'nay was introduced to the Master Steward who'd arrived with the Mistress, and the discussion launched into the most recent news regarding trading routes and way stations.

As the night progressed, a very bored Baily excused himself and returned to his base and the tables were cleared. Maps appeared and the conversation shifted away from supplies to dependable local contacts. As the parchments of Aggar's terrain were unrolled, Elana felt the startled confusion in Di'nay's amarin. The Amazon was keenly aware of the fact that she was the first off-worlder ever to see such drawings — and Elana was proud that her shadowmate was grasping the dangers the Terran pilot Garrison presented to this delicately balanced world.

Elana's pride grew into astonished respect as the Amazon listened, challenging assumptions and memorizing routes. Di'nay focused on each task, intently piecing questions and answers together almost faster than Elana could fathom the need to ask. Seldom, perhaps never, had Elana seen such quickness, such absorption by a person. And as her admiration grew, so did her attraction to this handsome woman.

Elana watched the idle tracings of those long fingers as they played with the stem of a goblet. Tonight Di'nay was her work, not the planning of the trek. The details of her world were already as familiar as her own room, but Di'nay....

With an almost religious ferocity Elana bent her attention to this woman's complexities. She read the intensity of that dark stare as it absorbed details, as it darted warily from the face of one council member to another. That mouth...Elana noticed the faint, controlled motion of lips as Di'nay spoke; the corners tightened slightly and drew downwards as her brow furrowed with concentration — the angular plains of her face would smooth and the mouth thin when she was displeased.

As the evening wore on, Elana became more and more aware of a mounting displeasure in the woman she studied.

There was a small lull in the session as one map was exchanged for another. And with confusion, Elana paused in filling Di'nay's water goblet. Alarm suddenly gripped her shadowmate, and hesitantly Elana placed the glass before the woman, subtly calling Di'nay's attention to her with both action and Sight.

An expression of smoldering fury answered her. Elana frowned in silent inquiry.

The Council Speaker made some sound to continue and Diana turned swiftly. The man grew still, stunned by the sudden anger of his guest.

"There is...something amiss?" The Speaker waved his hand in open query.

Coldly her dark gaze met his. "Why me?"

He looked confused and glanced to the Old Master and Mistress for some hint of the problem. They shook their heads in unison, acutely attending to the Amazon.

"Why me?" Diana repeated more distinctly, rising slowly to lean across the broad table. And she took a moment to deliberately eye each Council member present. "There are hundreds of places in the Maltar's realm for this pilot to be lost. There are hundreds of subtle, cultural disasters awaiting your world by his sheer presence. And yet you do not send a legion of your best scouts. You do not usher your trusted traders in a mass search. Instead you choose me, a lone agent of the Empire, to send in search of him. You show me scrolls the Terrans should never see. You speak of political factions that you have always hidden. What game are you playing with me?"

The Speaker bowed his head. For a long moment he said nothing, then with a sorrowful smile, he met her angry gaze. "I had hoped you of all Imperial Peoples — as an Amazon — would understand. We are a Council. We are guides, Min Di'nay. We have no legions to send. Force — even the mere show of such potential — has never wrought the greater good in the end. Yes, there are dangers this pilot presents to our world, but the disasters of calling attention to this search are just as great. His strangeness may do us harm, yet let it be known that we, the Council, are interested in him and that strangeness will be magnified and the harm multiplied. As for yourself...do you scorn information that we might unearth and give you? Is it not to all our best interests to work together, if only for this one occasion?"

He met no response in her. He tried again. "Min, your Empire would have sent you on this quest regardless of our involvement. It is not our way to interfere with the decisions of others. Our only intent is to lend aid to those who have already been appointed by the Fates and by the Mother — "

"Not to interfere?!" Diana rasped, stunned. "Then what do you call such a thing as lifebonding?"

Elana flinched, stepping back as Di'nay's hand swung in a wide gesture to point at her. The intensity of that amarin was startling.

"You demand I not travel alone! Then you bind me to a woman only to ignore her very presence until it suits you to call on her for whatever purpose?! Explain to me how that is not interfering?"

"It is our way — "

"But it is not mine!"

The Council Speaker drew a chilly mantel about himself. His words were uttered slowly and very distinctly. "You will fail if you attempt this alone. Now, do we return to the study or do we merely entrust you to your Shadow's care and be done?"

Elana swallowed hard, watching Di'nay waver between suspicions and necessities. The intensity defied Elana's ability to decipher the Amazon's amarin. The woman's chair squeaked and Elana felt herself breathe a sigh of relief as Di'nay abruptly sat back. A hand flicked towards the waiting parchments. "Continue — "

❋ ❋ ❋

"We are here tonight. Your gear is there." Elana pointed to the chest beneath the shuttered windows, leaving the taller woman to swing the door shut.

Frowning, Elana hurried to the hearth and picked up the flint. The wood needed only for the tinder to be lit, but she was displeased that her orders had not been carried through to completion. The room should have been warmed long before Di'nay's arrival.

The back of her neck prickled and she felt more than heard Di'nay's approach. Self-consciously she rearranged the kindling before reaching for the strike stone.

"Here." Diana's sharpness shattered the silence.

Elana glanced upwards and saw the small, straight dagger the other offered. Mutely she accepted it, and Di'nay left her. Half-wishing that she could put more than air space between herself and her companion, Elana turned back to the hearth. She turned the sheathed dagger and used the steel knotted hilt to strike the flint. There was no need to dull the blade. The tinder caught the sparks and tiny flames licked out. Sitting back on her heels, she watched the wood catch. She needed a second or two before she faced the cold anger of the woman behind her. An icy touch radiated from Di'nay just as heat did from the fire. This woman was much too complicated, Elana realized, to be understood by merely deciphering her amarin. But the power within Di'nay seemed to heighten her own sensitivities. It would take practice to learn to think clearly around those bombarding forces.

Concentrating, Elana mentally eased herself away from Di'nay's anger and wrapped herself in the warmth of the fire. The living forces that had once flowed through this crackling wood were still tangible to her — still welcoming to her; if she could but relax and reach out for that calming strength. Her eyes unfocused a bit, and she felt herself immersed in the warmth....

After a moment, she sighed and gently retreated from the calm. There was still the stony displeasure to face. She rose and moved to the bed where Di'nay sat rummaging through a leather pack. She extended the small knife, hilt first.

"Keep it." Diana waved ungraciously. "I've got another."

It startled Elana to be reminded of the older woman's wealth, although she vaguely remembered that other worlds were not as metal-poor as Aggar. Still, the thrill to actually own a hand dagger of steels! She pulled the small blade from its sheath almost reverently. Swords of varying quality were common enough with travelers and soldiers, but such a small item was indeed a luxury. Most knives were of finely honed stone or kiln-fired black glass. They were certainly cutting and lethal enough, but they were easily worn past sharpening within a tenmoon or so.

"Thank you," she whispered somewhat belatedly, once again intensely aware of Di'nay's brooding stare.

"Will you answer me something?" Diana asked abruptly, setting her pack aside.

Elana nodded, placing her new treasure carefully on the chest.

"Why you? What makes you so well-equipped for this mission?" Even sitting on the bed Diana was not eye level with the young woman; she found it exasperating.

"My Sight — and I am — was the Eldest Prepared." It was strange to remember that she was not any longer.

"Have you ever been out of the Keep?" Diana fired.

"Seldom. I was not born here."

"But you have been to Maltar's lands?"

"I have not."

"Yet you know the way well enough that the Speaker can't be bothered to share his precious maps with you?" The sarcasm was thick in her voice and an ironic, disbelieving twist curled her lips.

"I did not learn the routes by studying maps," Elana agreed, quietly serious.

That unspoken assurance eased the taunt from Diana's expression. "How did you learn them?"

"The Seers taught me."

"Then would it have been redundant to have added a comment or two? Since you know so much?" The accusation was meant to sting, but Diana couldn't tell if it had. Damn it, was the girl as boneless as a dishrag after all?

"It was not expected, Di'nay."

"Not expected!" she rasped and felt her Amazon blood boil at the servitude in the answer. "By who? The Council Speaker?"

"Nor by you."

Diana swallowed some of her fury. It was true. She too had forgotten Elana's presence for much of that meeting. "And so you said nothing?"

Elana frowned slightly. "I said nothing, because I had nothing to say."

She took a short bite of air and after a moment asked more quietly, "Could you tell me, Elana, just what should I expect from you?"

"I am your Shadow," Elana returned with a faintly puzzled shrug. "I am an extra set of ears and eyes for you. With my Sight, some might say I am better qualified than most because I can literally fade into the shadows of a room...."

Diana remembered their meeting in the garden.

"I am charged with your life, Di'nay."

"In what way?" Diana's teeth clamped tight again.

"With your safety and your comfort. I am guide when you request...guard or companion as you need. You are to survive and strongly if you are to deal with Fates' tasks. I am expected to see that you do. I am to be cook, bedfellow, protector — whatever you need, I am to provide it."

"In short, your life," she grunted.

"If need be, certainly."

"Mae n'Pour!" Diana gasped in her own tongue, cursing the wastes — grappling for the Goddess' sweet strength. She wanted to smash something. Anything! "Tell me, child! How much did they pay your parents to buy you?"

Elana held silent at the insult. Her gaze dropped.

Diana shut her mouth, scolding herself. Elana was not responsible for her anger. She was angry at the Council, at Baily, at the demeaning societies she had become so disenchanted with. It was not permissible to take her temper out on this woman.

Diana rose and paced to the hearth, gripping the mantel with white-knuckled tension. She was becoming too old for this sort of thing. Her detachment was fraying. She needed to quit, not because she was tired of saving this world or that from eternal crisis, but because she was tired of the senselessness of so many societies — such wasted, useless customs of power and slavery.

Okay, she acknowledged almost with defeat, I am again a disillusioned sociologist. I can't change this world, but dear Goddess why can't I stop acting as if I agreeably belong to it — like some insensitive male cad! Where was her respect for the woman's being? A slow, deep breath gathered in her lungs. The anger and tension finally receded. Yes, she was a Sister — this world — it was not hers. Relief flooded her suddenly as she remembered that truth. With surprise, Diana wondered when she had last been without that tension. Had it been even before Maryl's departure? She hadn't known she'd resented the woman's leaving so much. No, not leaving, she knew, but the choice of the man over her — an Amazon.

Diana turned wearily from the hearth. "I beg your patience. I spoke out of turn."

"I...I find no grudge," Elana stammered quickly, again finding the intensity of Di'nay's amarin blurred any ability to anticipate action. She had not expected a formal apology.

Diana gestured helplessly. "It's just...I don't want to own you, but I feel I do."

Gently Elana shook her dark head. "I am here by choice." She hesitated, then added, "Perhaps more so than you are."

So Elana had guessed something of this struggle. Diana nodded. She found a half-hearted grin. "I'm glad one of us wants to be here."

The soft, full lips smiled. Disconcerted, Diana was reminded of the woman's beauty. Stubbornly, she pushed the thought away. "How old are you, Elana?"

"Twelve and more tenmoons."

"You look barely past ten seasons," Diana said flatly, moving back to the bed and to her pack.

"And you do not seem forty years," Elana said quietly, slipping into Common.

Diana hid a smile as she produced a leather package and began to unlace it. "Thank you. I'm not quite twenty seasons, actually. But it's nice to know that the job hasn't aged me too much.

"This is not an ordinary set," Diana said, shifting their attention to the array of cookware she'd laid out. The pieces had been well-fitted and packed, one inside the other with a lid securing the lot together. She handed the largest pot to Elana; it wasn't more than twenty centimeters in diameter.

The texture of the piece felt like well-fired ceramic, and the discolored glaze looked like any typical travel dish. Elana turned the pot over curiously. The amarin was wrong, almost absent, and it was much too light for clay or stone. Suddenly she turned to the chest and picked up the small knife. She tapped the hilt to the pot. It gave a nice, satisfying tinny clack. She smiled. It was the alien alloy again.

Diana was impressed. Few of Aggar had ever noticed the weight discrepancy, and none had ever guessed it was not ceramic. "You'll find it heats more rapidly, but it's the weight that's important."

"It's less than a third of what a clay set would be," Elana noted, finding it surprisingly practical for Terran equipment. "And there are more pieces."

"I like fire brewed tea," Diana confessed. "It takes too long to brew it and heat the wash water unless I've got separate containers. Anyway," she slid the set back into its bag and handed the lot to Elana, "this is for you. So's the blanket."

"It too is not — ordinary?"

"It's a synthetic thermal," Diana struggled with how to translate into non-tech language. She wondered just how much Common Elana really knew. "It becomes hot — or cold as you decide what you need."

Somberly Elana lifted her face and with great care took Di'nay's chin between her fingers. From habit the Amazon shifted her eyes down to meet the blue-white gaze for an instant — and then the contact was broken. "It is synthetic," Elana said quietly, easily tonguing the new word. "Neither wool nor linen."

Diana blinked. Those depths of shimmering sapphire no longer mesmerized her soul.

"It creates heat as one needs it, yes?"

Diana mentally shook herself and turned the tightly stitched edging over at the corner. "Here is the control." She guided Elana's fingers over the small, embedded rectangle. "Squeeze this way...on the flattened side...and it will heat. Press the edge so...yes and it will cool."

"And how do you turn it off?"

"Bend it in half." She pinched the fabric. "The only drawback is it's thin." She folded the blanket loosely and gave it to Elana. "And the ground does get terribly hard sometimes."

The woman smiled. "Thank you. It will save much room."

Diana pulled a short rod from her bag and bent it in the middle with a crack. A light burst forth and the two of them blinked in the brightness before she twisted the end and reduced it to a narrow beam. She cracked it again, off, and tossed it on the bed muttering, "One flashlight."

Elana's tongue moistened her lips slightly before she said, "I see...differently at night. Perhaps we need take only yours?"

Diana hesitated, eyeing her companion suspiciously, but in the end she merely shrugged. "There is only the one."

"Also — matches." She gave Elana a small box of blue-tipped sticks. "They're for starting fires when it's too damp to catch a spark easily." Deftly she struck one against the box and it flared. She blew it out and tossed it into the hearth. "They work even when they're wet, but they're hard to come by at the base, so I try not to use them unless it's an emergency. We should both carry a box."

Elana nodded.

"What do you usually carry?" Diana asked then, finishing with the pack and settling herself down on the edge of the bed.

"Three days' dried food and waterskin, a bedroll, an extra set of clothing, cookery, spices and salt, my medicine purse, a hunting knife, a sheath of bolts and my crossbow."

"Knife!" Diana quickly dove back into the pack and returned with a hunting knife. She slid the tie loop free and pulled it from the black sheath. It was smooth, sharp and curved along one side. The other was straight and lined with biting, serrated teeth. Grinning at the thought of Baily's outrage, Diana re-sheathed it, presenting it to Elana, "A hunting knife — one for each of us."

"Thank you." Another knife — a metal knife! Elana wondered if this woman had ever even used the black glass knives of Aggar's design.

"You said a crossbow? Do you carry any other weapons?"

A little self-derisively Elana admitted that, "I've been trained to carry full gear ...from leather breast plates to long sword...if I must."

"How long of a sword can you manage?"

"I'm most comfortable with a twenty-eight length."

"No longer?"

She shrugged. "I do not have the reach to take advantage of a longer piece."

"Is it the weight or the length you have trouble with?"

"Length," Elana admitted. "A blade made with your metals would be easier to wield, but we are taught with wooden pieces from a young age. They were light enough. I am more than adequate defensively." She allowed a small smile of satisfaction. "I know where the other strikes even as he does it. I am not quite so effective offensively, especially against men. There is six inches and more difference in our reach. And it is clumsy to wear."

"And the long bow?"

She shook her head. "I have not the strength to be reliable in extended use."

Diana nodded. She knew Terran women also had to work particularly hard and with focus to develop upper body strength. "You don't have trouble loading the crossbow then?"

"I can load it quickly by force when I must," Elana assured her, "but it is seldom necessary. I have made several adjustments in mine. I've a small crank that re-sets the two strings, and a pulley system that multiplies the throw force."

Diana raised an eyebrow with interest. She was impressed. "Your own design?"

"We are expected to adapt our gear to our individual needs."

"Others have similar crossbows then?"

Elana thought a moment, then half-shook her head. "Few have given it much use here at the Keep. I believe I'm the only one proficient in it for many years now."

"How much more force do you get with the modifications?"

"Equivalent to one-and-a-half that of a standard long bow."

Diana whistled silently. It was a very deadly weapon. She drew a deep breath. "You do better to carry more bolts than worry about swords and leathers."

"I'll do as you think best."

"No," Diana turned to her, "I want us to talk. We make joint decisions as long as both of our lives are at stake."

Elana's eyes were blue-white as they skirted across the woman's face, noting her gravity. She remembered the lingering unease of the evening's meeting. Quietly she asserted, "You talk of being partners. That requires some trust, Di'nay."

The Amazon paused, and her fingers pressed tiredly against the bridge of her nose. Reluctantly her hand dropped as she nodded. "Yes, I suppose it does."

Elana felt her heart ache at the loneliness she felt from the woman. In a desperate answer to that emptiness she ventured, "Perhaps...in time we might find it?"

Diana found herself wanting that so much it hurt. She despaired of ever trusting one so young with so much. "I expect we will...eventually."

For a long moment, Elana stood saying nothing; then at Diana's glance she turned slowly for the hearth to bank the fire.

With weariness, Diana found herself staring at the single, mammoth bed. She sighed. Most people of Aggar enforced strong bans on sexual relations, and she had too long experienced Maryl's discomfort to believe that her new companion was going to relish sharing the blankets. "Elana...?" The woman glanced at her expectantly. "I haven't slept in almost two days. I'm completely exhausted. If I promise I wish only to sleep, do you believe we could share the bed?"

A small laugh escaped her as Elana half-turned, still kneeling at the hearth. "Where else would we be?"

"I could be on the floor," Diana responded flatly.

Elana dropped her jesting at Di'nay's solemnness. "This Keep does not hold to customs that either permit or ban bedfellows. You have no need to protect me here. Beyond these walls, it will be assumed that we are wed or that you own me. Neither appearance distresses me." For a long moment they looked at one another, until finally Elana prompted, "There is something more."

Her mouth felt dry as Diana asked, "What do you think on sharing this bed?"

"You are my Shadowmate, whether here or traveling I may share your bed."

Diana found herself disbelieving the response. Then the thought flitted through her mind that the rarity of her kind here might be to blame. The girl might simply not know. She swallowed uncomfortably. Amazons were such common knowledge in the Empire that she did not have much practice in this. "Elana, you know I am from another world...?"

"You are an Amazon."

"Do you know what that means?"

Di'nay's amarin were so overwhelmingly clear that Elana did not hesitate. "You are a woman who loves women."

"You're not frightened by this?"

Her heart jumped in her chest and her breath shortened, but Elana was old enough to know it was not from fear. "Why should I fear you, Di'nay?"

With amusement Diana admitted, "In bed, many would fear what I would do instead of sleeping."

Elana turned back to the fire. "With you, I would not fear that either."

Despite her weariness the adrenaline shot through her veins. Spoken like a true Shadow, Diana thought with an icy sarcasm. In the end patience and fatigue won over her temper, and she promised herself that she'd face that problem when and if it materialized. She sighed and reached down to pull off the flimsy, indoor boots.

Elana brightened the lamp centered in the wall above their bed to compensate for the dampened fire, asking, "Will you be warm enough?"

"...be fine," Diana mumbled as she drew her tunic over her head. And tomorrow she would be. Tomorrow she'd climb into her fieldsuit to stay warm and toasty, and she'd be fine all day long. Beyond that she refused to think right now. She tugged on her nightshirt.

What was it that had brought her here anyway? Travel — fly — see the Universe — if they'd only told her then, that she'd still be here....

And Elana? As she slipped under the linen sheets, Diana wondered what the local propaganda was about Shadows. She rolled over to find Elana naked, sitting cross-legged on the bed. A lump closed her throat. The woman was struggling with the knotted hair ribbons, her braid already undone. Unbidden, despite her fatigue, Diana felt desire stir again. She swallowed, quietly managing, "Do you need help?"

"No thank you." Elana tossed a smile at her absently. A ribbon slipped and then finally gave. Elana sighed in victory. "It seems each woman ties a different sort of knot. And on every occasion I find someone new is helping."

"A problem I've never had." Diana chuckled despite herself. Elana picked up a comb and Diana noticed the wide bands that were still laced around the woman's wrists. Gently she reached out, tapping a wrist piece. "These are pretty." A finger traced the floral pattern at the edges of the black leather. "You always wear them?"

With a half-nod Elana moved reluctantly from the curious touch to comb out her hair. "Now I do. The lifestone is hidden under the left one. It is still healing. After tomorrow it will be well, but — "

"But?"

"It's less conspicuous to wear these than display the stone."

Diana nodded.Then she smiled suddenly. "And how about you?"

"Me?" Elana fastened her hair back with a leather band that was very like her wristbands.

"I seem to have been asking a great many things this night. What about yourself? Do you have any questions for me?"

Thoughtfully the young woman tightened the laces of the hair band and considered the evening. Finally, seriously, she turned and asked, "What is tan?"

Surprised, Diana laughed. Of all things, it was the last she had expected. She sat upright in bed and opened a few more buttons on her nightshirt, pointing to her neck where it had been browned by the wind and sun, "This is tan." She pointed to her breast and sternum. "This is the color my skin usually is. White Terrans change color after the skin is exposed to the sun. The rays change the pigments color."

"But you are not Terran. Or no?"

"No," she repeated slowly. "But my people's ancestors were Terrans. A very long time ago."

Elana digested that before: "Terrans are not all pale?"

"No. Many are brown — as dark as your people become from excitement or exertion. I'm told the skin substance of both your folk and ours is similar chemically, with the one exception that yours responds to emotion."

"Then you have dark Amazons as well?"

"Definitely."

"Your Commander Baily wished to honor me by saying that I was tan. He doesn't know we of Aggar do not brown from the sun but when — aroused?"

"In some parts, tanned Terrans are considered fashionable and the reference is considered a compliment. He is from one of those places."

"But it is in your records that we of Aggar brown due to emotion and exertion. Has Commander Baily not seen these reports?"

Diana dimmed the oil lamp above their bed to a low, warm glow, saying, "Thomas is a fool, Elana. He knows but persists in his Terran customs. He's not worth understanding."

"Perhaps so," Elana agreed, settling down into the linens and furs, "if he has been here more than four tenmoons and is still so poorly informed."

That Elana knew what the records held about how long Thomas had been assigned to Aggar was a surprising bit of information, Diana thought. But right now she was much too tired to worry and the bed was surprisingly comfortable.

"May your dreams be smiling, Di'nay," Elana wished her softly and turned to her side.

"And yours," Diana murmured, a fond curve suddenly touching her lips. She had never truly enjoyed sleeping alone.

❈ ❈ ❈

Chapter Nine

Unsettled, Elana blinked and awoke from a deep sleep. She was annoyed at her sluggishness as she forced herself to full awareness until she remembered the bonding and the woman that lay next to her. It was to be expected that she would sleep heavier for a day or two. Steeling herself against the necessity of moving, Elana slid sideways. As her feet hit the floor her hands hastily sought the knitted undergarments. Something was not as planned.

Without disturbing her companion, Elana pulled on her soft suede breeches and left.

She moved soundlessly down the corridors, her feet bare except for the stirrups of her knit tights. The stone beneath her toes was cold — a barren cold, so she quickened her steps until she came to the walkway above the vast Entrance Hall. She halted, still in the shadows. The wood underfoot greeted her with its familiar strength of aged life. Unconsciously she absorbed its touch and her body relaxed, drinking in the sweetened power. She took in the scene below — a traveler stood within arm's reach of the entry way. The massive doors were still open behind him.

Dropping to a crouch, she crossed the width of the balcony. The visitor glanced about apprehensively, but Blue Sight and training were well meshed in the woman; the man literally looked right through her.

Her senses strained to hear the curt exchanges between the two boys on watch and the stranger. Abruptly the man shouted an obscenity, silencing them both. His muddied, gloved hands pushed the youngest towards the inner doors, and Elana glimpsed a thick scroll in the boy's clasp as he darted off.

As the man turned to leave, Elana saw a flash of the maroon and gold of the vest beneath his cloak — Maltar's man. He paused as the older boy rushed forward to say something. To do him credit, the lad adroitly placed himself between the stranger and the door, desperately buying time, Elana knew, until a Master and Seer could arrive. She suddenly realized that this was exactly what the soldier was fearing. He turned again, searching the hall. She frowned, irritated. The distance was too great to lock eyes and wrest the anxious secrets from him. There was something of paramount importance that he knew and that the Council was not to know.

Her second glance at his face burned its details into her memory as he struck the boy from his path. The door shut with a reverberating thud that made the wood she crouched upon ache with a pain equal to that in the boy's thin frame. Elana straightened, disappearing into the stone hallways. This time she headed for the stables.

There would be time enough to report to the Mistress and Council Speaker. Her first duties now were to Di'nay, and they were to leave before dawn.

The black mud caking the clothing of the soldier she had just observed had held the amarin of the river. That meant he had ridden hard this very night or he would have had the time to brush the garments clean. The short, black beard that had lined only the edges of his jaw and mouth had been too immaculately trimmed to suggest the man would have uncaringly cantered about the countryside muddied. Beneath the anxiety, his own amarin had shimmered of exhaustion. That meant if she and Di'nay hurried, the trail would be fresh to follow. She quickened her pace; they would need their mounts and supplies sooner than dawn.

The Keep was much more active now than when Elana had descended into the stables. The Seers were already gathering, and the spiced wine was brewing again. It had been strange that no one had known of the soldier's coming, Elana thought, yet she knew that the Wine of Decision often rendered its users impotent in more ways than one. The Council was assembling in full too, but Elana was not prepared to meet them. She made herself unnoticeable and moved across the open balcony.

"A little chilly to the bootless," Diana commented matter-of-factly as Elana stepped into their room.

"Not too bad." Elana's tone was also matter-of fact as she settled on the side of the bed to pull on her stockings and boots. She noticed Di'nay was already dressed.

"What's everyone concerned about?" Diana asked, tying her pack together.

"The Council is reviewing a newly-delivered scroll. I do not know what they intend to do other than inform us of the contents — eventually."

"Eventually?" Diana repeated with a lift of her brow. She thought she'd detected a hint of disapproval.

Elana donned her tunic, smiling. "They have been known to deliberate overly long on minor points."

With an amused chuckle, Diana folded her arms and leaned against the bedpost. "Do you know what this 'minor point' is?"

"No." Elana wrapped the soft belt about the waist of her jerkin. "The messenger, however, was from Maltar. He'd been riding hard and was anxious not to meet a Seer. I suspect that he knows about the crash."

"You saw this messenger?"

"Briefly. He was too far away for me to catch his eye."

Inwardly Diana balked at the implications indicating Elana's power, but said only, "Wager metal to rock his errand is about Garrison. It seems our worst fear is about to be realized. Garrison's been found by the Maltar sovereign."

"So it appears."

Complications already, Diana groaned inwardly. "Yet this fellow you saw couldn't have come from the Maltar's court. Garrison only crashed at darkfall two days ago. It would have taken the man ten-days of travel to reach here."

Elana nodded, pulling the last of her pack together. "Most likely he's from one of Maltar's spy rings here in the Ramains. The Maltar probably sent orders by messenger hawk to these men."

"He was not alone?"

"He was wearing the maroon and gold colors. He would not travel alone here in the Ramains in such a uniform. The Ramains King is not quite that tolerant." Elana shook her head slightly. "But what he was hiding...?"

"Garrison is being held," Diana said abruptly. "Either the man knows or he's certain he has a comrade who does."

"But how would he know? The Council doesn't even know, Di'nay. There are a dozen and a half military outposts in the Maltar's realm and — "

"By the hawk and the hawker's colors."

"In truth...," Elana breathed, the pieces suddenly falling into place. The ownership tag on the messenger hawk would mark the region where the Maltar issued his orders. Even if it was a secretive clan, the hawkers within the group would recognize their own tags. Although it was unlikely that Garrison had actually crashed in the Maltar's lap, it was also unlikely that the ruling gentleman would go to Garrison. Garrison would have been brought to the Maltar — to the region the monarc had dispatched his message from — to the region designated by the hawker's colors.

"There is no assurance," Elana murmured, "that the Maltar will not move the pilot once he has seen him."

"But it is a place to start." Diana nodded with a grim satisfaction. "And I would rather search every military stronghold in Maltar on the premise that he's been found than search every league of wilderness. So — it would appear we have a choice."

Elana looked at her quizzically.

"Either we can snatch this messenger fellow you glimpsed tonight and find what he knows, or we can be a little more subtle and follow him back to his own roost. There we'd locate his trusted hawker and know for certain the hawker will have the information we want."

"If we overtake the messenger on the trail, he will have comrades."

"The more people that guess we're looking for the hawk's roost, the more warnings the Maltar might get." Diana shrugged. "Personally, I usually prefer quiet stealth and patience to a frontal assault. But then, I've always worked alone."

"And I am a Shadow," Elana reminded her quietly. "I know very well the value of patience and stealth."

"Good enough — we'll trail him to his hawker." Diana straightened. "Shall we go see if this Maltar's message truly does concern our Garrison?"

Diana's eyes flickered over Elana as she shouldered her pack. The cascading length of her bound hair was caught under the shoulder strap, its dark color gleaming in the lamplight. The green jerkin matched the laced suede of Elana's boots; and although the green-brown leather of her breeches was loose, to Diana's practiced eye the fit still very much bespoke the woman's figure beneath it.

"I see we're going as twins." Diana half-smiled. Did anyone really believe she looked like that?

Elana returned the smile. "I am a little short."

"And your hair's a little too long." Diana pulled wryly at her own brown strands. "No — won't stretch."

She was rewarded with a laugh. Elana assured her, "I'd not expected it would."

Diana turned somewhat abruptly on the pretense of fetching her pack and cloak. Something was suddenly feeling very wrong. It was not her place to be entertaining this woman. But her pleasure at... Diana suddenly saw just how much she had wanted to bring forth that smile.

Don't get hooked, Diana n'Athena. Don't you dare get hooked!

"My hair can be cut," Elana offered, hastily, breaking the stretching silence. Di'nay's sudden abruptness alarmed her. "If you think the length is inappropriate? Or find it displeasing?"

"What?" Diana snapped from her thoughts and shouldered her pack. "No, it's fine the way it is. Let's find your Council Speaker and get out of here."

Elana pulled her cloak from the door peg and sighed at the retreating figure. Somehow Di'nay's words had not been so very reassuring.

❀ ❀ ❀

"It means the scoundrel does not know what he holds," the Mistress muttered as she walked beside Diana. She and the young Council Speaker were escorting the two women to their horses.

"There is the possibility," the Speaker mused, "that Maltar may never understand this pilot is an off-worlder."

"Then he obviously wouldn't have seen his craft," Diana said. "With luck it was burned up in the atmosphere or it disintegrated on contact."

"He 'descended from the sky on a cloud of white cloth' or so the parchment reports," the Speaker agreed.

Diana wondered if it had been a parachute.

"The Maltar is assuming Garrison is one of our more 'supernatural' spies. I expect he thinks his magician rooted out the poor fellow. Maltar's asking for forty load of refined iron and twenty of bronze."

A low whistle pushed between Diana's teeth. It was a small fortune they were demanding. "Are you certain they don't know who he is?"

"For now. You could pay it outright."

"Certainly," Diana scoffed, "and have the lot of us shot in the back as we leave his outpost?"

"Not to mention the Empire's standing edict forbidding ransom negotiations," murmured the Council Speaker.

"Yes," the Old Mistress nodded, "and the threat this pilot presents Aggar will not be eased if he should elude the Maltar's assassins only to become a captive within another tribe or fortress."

Diana glanced behind her, searching for Elana. The woman lengthened her step to draw abreast, remembering the Amazon preferred her to be more prominent.

"What do you suggest?" Diana asked her.

"My thoughts have not changed. Find the messenger's hawker. From him find from where in Maltar's lands the bird came; then search for your pilot in that area."

"The ransom request changes nothing?"

A faint shrug rippled the green cloak and shifted the pack beneath it. "Maltar has seldom honored such bribes in his family's history."

"What are the chances of him sitting on his prize and not questioning Garrison too closely?" Diana asked, turning again to the Mistress.

"It is more likely that he will inadvertently kill your pilot in an interrogation. He does not truly expect us to bargain. We never have in the past. In telling us of his new captive, he merely gloats over his prize."

"I'm liking this fellow less and less."

"You are still biased," the elder bit out grimly. "When you know him better, you'll loath him. Loath him...yet beware of him."

Diana glanced at her sharply. "Have you a personal grudge against this king, Mistress?"

"Very personal, child. He executed my husband."

The small group crossed the court in silence, and Elana felt the stillness in her bones. Sorrow...bitterness had always been sharp in the Old Mistress when the Maltar's name surfaced, but over the years she had kept her own counsel. Even Elana had not known of this grudging secret, only of the anguished amarin.

Elana swallowed the surging anger before it slipped past her and touched the others of the party. The Mistress had seen her through too much — separations, growing pains — there was little she would not hate that had painted the aged one's life with so much pain.

She moved to her horse then, letting her hands distract her heart as she secured her pack amidst the bundled food supplies. She finished and turned to Di'nay's; her tension finally had begun to ease a little.

I will miss her, Elana admitted and an awareness of the other's amarin followed closely — the Mistress would miss her too. She and the old woman had been inseparable for so many seasons that she could not gauge the void from leaving now. But the time for leaving had been coming for a long while. They both had known it.

Blindly she mounted the blood bay. She took comfort from the warm, solid feel of the mare beneath her. Leggings and she went way back too.

She glanced quickly at the black gelding that tossed his head in impatience. He was a graceful but broad-chested horse of seventeen hands. Restlessly he shifted at the Amazon's approach, and Elana had to resist the impulse to soothe his wariness with her Sight. He needed to meet his new rider on his own terms.

The Amazon leapt easily into the stirrup-less saddle, sliding her sword sheath and bow into a more comfortable angle at her right knee. When her calves closed firmly about the horse, the animal chaffed less. Elana noted that the confidence in Di'nay's seat and her light touch on the bit were effectively calming the black even more quickly than she would have hoped.

"Ona — "

She glanced down quickly. "Yes, Mistress?"

Hands reached high to cover Elana's own as they lay on the cloth pommel. The smooth thinness of the old skin felt glossy to Elana, and again she was amazed at the age of this woman. Often she forgot that there were generations between them.

The Old Mistress looked upon her favorite proudly. "Care for yourself — as well as your proud Amazon."

A smile hovered on her lips. "I will."

"The Mother will ride your winds. Take heed of Her signs."

"Yes," she whispered, her throat tight. "And may you walk with Her blessings."

"May we both." The stiff fingers patted her hands with a final tap, and the Old Mistress walked back to the Council Speaker.

"Take this Amazon away, Ona!" the stern voice crackled. "Or this young chatterbox will have you here 'til dawn breaks!"

With a nod Elana reined Leggings for the bridge and the open gate beyond.

Diana brought her horse nearer the robed figure and leaned low. "I will ponder on how to be compassionate, Mistress."

"May Her blessings ride your winds, Amazon."

"And may they walk with you, Mistress." Diana's heels closed and the black steed leapt forward. Cantering hooves rang in the stillness as the two crossed the bridge. Above, the midnight moon began to wind her way down into the slumbering cliffs.

❀ ❀ ❀

"What was it that the Mistress called you as we left the Keep?" Diana asked quietly as the sun finally began to break through the gray ceiling above them. They'd ridden for nearly half the morning in silence.

"Ona, you mean?"

"Anna?" and she pressed the black closer to the bay, straining to hear.

"Ahh-na," Elana repeated distinctly. "It is a shortening of Elana, usually reserved for children of two or three — or for slaves."

"Ona," Diana glanced sideways, thinking she certainly looked young enough for the nickname, but in the same moment she saw the woman. "She continues to call you this?"

"She nearly always has, since I came to the Keep when I was four or more seasons — about age nine by your Imperial reckoning." The green cloaked shoulders shrugged. "By comparison to her moons, I am still very young."

Diana was not reassured, and she fell quiet again. Confidence not born of experience was something Diana had learned to be wary of. But perhaps that wasn't being fair to Elana. If she had been at the Keep since she was four seasons, then that roughly figured to be eight or so tenmoons of training. It certainly outdid Diana's own brief months of instruction before the Empire dropped her here on Aggar. Inwardly she sighed, wondering if it was Elana's youth or her own age that she was being so sensitive about.

The birds and prippers darted about noisily in the trees above, and Elana drew her thoughts away from Di'nay's brooding amarin, concentrating on the riders they followed. She suspected the men would set camp early today — beyond the Council's borders most likely, as the man she'd seen had obviously been riding for the better part of the night. She and Diana would need to be careful or they'd overtake the messenger's party before it arrived at its destination. Her glance dropped to the packed ground under hoof and the men's tracks.

"Still there?" Diana asked suddenly, attempting a smile.

Recognizing the peace offering, Elana smiled and said, "Yes."

Hesitating, Diana cast about for something else to say as they rode on. "Your horses, at the Keep, they're a fine lot. Do you breed them yourselves?"

"Some. The majority we trade for. But these are home bred."

"Does the black have a name? Or is that beneath the Council's stables?"

Elana chuckled at that. "He's called Nightstorm. This mare is Leggings."

"For her black stockings, uh-hm. Is Nightstorm foreboding of something I should know about? He's not scared of shadows? Or shy of thunder, is he?" Diana had been on several idiosyncratic beasts in the past, and despite her levity, her concern was genuine.

"He certainly is not frightened by me nor by storms." Elana laughed, and the Amazon blinked at the reminder of Elana's Council-imposed role. "He was born in a cloudburst at midnight, that is all."

"He seems well trained." Diana ran a gloved hand admiringly over the arched neck before her. "Spirited, but very workable."

"I thank you." Elana was unexpectedly shy and pleased at the compliment until she felt Di'nay's caution.

"Are you saying you trained him?"

"Yes. Leggings too, but she's special." Elana stroked the glossy red hide of her mare's neck. "I raised her, despite her mother's death. No one could coax her to feed, but then I am the only Blue Sight this generation who has the animal sense. For me...I remember her trying to suckle off my fingers as often as from the bottles."

For a long moment Diana was silent. She was finding that she didn't like that she had assumed to know so much about Elana's abilities. When she spoke again her voice had grown softer. "You said he was gelded. I would have thought he'd make good breeding stock?"

"We could not afford another stallion exclusively for breeding, and I couldn't get anyone else near enough to ride him." Elana's voice lowered with the pain of regrets. "There was a day, I wasn't there — he killed one man and nearly a second."

Diana nodded in sympathy, but she felt a sudden panic that the life lost might have been Elana's own. Then she reminded herself rationally, the accident had happened because Elana hadn't been there, not because of carelessness; there were a great many things that one could learn in twenty-four years. Still, her picture of this quiet woman did not mesh with the image of her breaking violent horses to saddle.

Diana was beginning to believe that there were a great many things about Elana that could be surprising.

❄ ❄ ❄

"We should camp here," Elana announced quietly.

Diana looked up from refilling her waterskin. Nightstorm snorted playfully, blowing bubbles in the small creek beside her. Elana's back was to her, standing at the clearing's edge; her eyes searched the trees along the road ahead.

"We've still three hours of daylight, at least," Diana said.

"They have been stopping too frequently. There is only one more place to stop this side of the river's gorge, and only one within short reach across it. If they are wary of followers, they will surely leave a scout at the next point — if they don't decide to actually camp there. They did travel overly hard yesterday. They may have no errand for returning home as quickly."

"If they're going home," Diana muttered. "All right then. We camp here." She slipped her packs and saddle bags to the ground, but long bow and sword stayed. "You set things up. I'll ride ahead and see if I can get a look at the next site. If the three of them do decide to stop before the gorge, we can be certain one of them will be circling back later. It would be nice to know if we should post watch or not."

"Beneath my Sight I could...." Elana faltered in the face of Di'nay's sudden coldness. The Amazon's trust was not so easily given, she reminded herself.

"I would rather do this myself."

Elana nodded awkwardly. "Certainly. I'll see if I can catch us something for eventide."

Diana mounted quickly, frowning as she realized Elana had been hurt by her curtness. She toyed with the reins, hesitating uncomfortably.

"I understand, Di'nay," Elana murmured gently.

Diana sighed. She didn't know if that made it better or not. She glanced down at Elana. "I'll be back by darkfall." Her heels closed and Nightstorm jumped forward into a canter.

The lifestone warmed faintly beneath the black leather. With a sad smile, Elana raised her arm in Di'nay's direction as the Amazon disappeared. The rhythmic pulse of the stone steadied in perfect harmonics. This was lifebonding — to the person and not the cause. She could only wish Di'nay would come to feel the same.

❋ ❋ ❋

With concern Diana approached the campsite where she had left Elana. Even across the short distance between road and clearing, there was no flickering fire to call welcome. She drew Nightstorm to a cautious halt.

"Here."

Diana started at the soft voice and suddenly the dimness lifted.

A small blaze was cheerfully dancing within the fire pit where a pair of small fowl were skewered and roasting. The bedding was spread beneath the frayed roof of the three-sided traveler's hut, and Leggings was munching contentedly near the stream. Elana rose slowly from the fireside, brushing her hands clean along the sides of her breeches.

Diana slipped out of the saddle, grimly deciding that there was more to this Blue Sighted gift than she wished to know.

"You found them."

"A single scout. The others moved beyond the gorge." She shrugged and stalked past the fire with the gelding in tow. "The man was drinking rather heavily. I doubt we need worry about him riding out again tonight."

Elana nodded, but she lingered instead of turning back to the fire, watching Di'nay unsaddle Nightstorm. The strength and grace of the Amazon's movements caught the breath in her throat, and Elana remembered the countless nights she had glimpsed those same hands — those same movements in her dreamspun visions.

"Eventide smells good," Diana offered a sudden peace with a faint grin. "What did you catch?"

"Jumier — a fairly plump set."

"My birds never smelled like that." Diana took a brush to Nightstorm's dusty hide and the animal grunted with appreciation. "Mine barely seemed edible."

Elana laughed. "I'll take that as a compliment."

"Will it be ready soon? Or do I have time to wash a little when I'm through here?"

"You have time." Elana felt her stomach flutter at the thought of Di'nay bathing.

"Good." Diana glanced at the still figure again and paused in grooming the black.

Elana attempted to gather herself together. "You said last night that — that you like fire brewed tea. I thought you might have your own? Or — there is the blend from the Keep's stocks?"

Diana's smallest saddle bag still lay next to the fire. The odd knot she habitually used to tie it was in place; the bag had not been touched. It surprised her to realize that she had not really believed it would be disturbed. She smiled with a sudden warmth and answered, "I have my own. I'll fetch it when I'm through, Elana."

Elana turned back to Di'nay.

"I do not expect you to do all the cooking, whatever the Council's instructions."

"Our personal arrangements are left to us." Elana shrugged, unconcerned. "But it is something I enjoy doing that — "

"I would not enjoy having you do it for me."

For a long moment, Elana faced the Amazon's stony grimness. Then suddenly Di'nay's own words came back to mind, and Elana found herself prompted by a faint bit of humor. "What you say might be taken as a threat, Di'nay, if your jumier is barely edible?"

Despite herself, Diana found she was laughing. "I suppose I could be content with the wash-up."

"All right." With a tip of her head, Elana moved away slowly, savoring the growing warmth in the Amazon's amarin. She felt as if she'd been given a present.

❋ ❋ ❋

Chapter Ten

"Is breakfast mobile?" Diana asked, drawing near the fire. The horses had been saddled and packed except for the last of Elana's cookery.

"Very." The woman passed a trio of leaf-wrapped bundles to the Amazon before tipping the small pan of boiling water into the fire.

"What is it? If I may ask?" Diana sniffed cautiously. Each bundle was about the size of an ear of corn but much softer.

"Boko." The suede booted toes kicked at the dirt, burying the coals.

"Which is?" Diana could not suppress a smile. At times she was reminded just how new she was to this world and just how much she could never hope to learn.

Elana smiled faintly, taking her own breakfast and the pan in hand. "It is a little this, a little that, depending on what's available — wrapped in a steamed torin leaf. Did you like the stuffing last night?"

"Hm-hmm."

"This is similar."

"Do I peel it or eat it whole?"

"Whole." She laced her saddlebag closed, and they mounted and left as the sun finally found a crack somewhere in the eastern wall of the mountains and the sky lightened gray over the treetops. There was slim chance of the clouds breaking up as the day progressed.

Diana munched on her breakfast, wondering if it was going to rain. It was too early in the tenmoon for snow. She tried to be optimistic, but then again, there was always the odd season. The young woman was being very quiet. That quietness went too well with the image of a Shadow. Diana glanced at Elana again, noticing the single, half-eaten boko and asked, "Is that going to be enough for you?"

Elana dipped her head absently. Her concentration was focused outward, seeking confirmation that the scout had also broken camp early.

Let her take care of herself, Diana reminded herself grumpily. Just because the people of Aggar had a higher metabolism didn't mean they ate more. The woman probably didn't ever eat much breakfast.

"Something is wrong...!" Elana kicked her mare into a gallop.

Alarmed, Diana reined Nightstorm in, keeping him to a trot as he followed. Her gloved hand reached for the long sword at her knee and slid it soundlessly from the sheath. She swallowed the curse on her lips. She had no idea what that old woman had been teaching this child, but it obviously did not include caution.

As the road turned sharply right Diana's ears strained to decipher the unusual from the morning sounds. Nightstorm stepped quietly and refrained from tossing his head. Gingerly she edged him around the corner.

Before her the road opened onto a dusty clearing where she had spied the scout last night. At the far end there was a rushing stream whose faint roar hinted that further on it dropped into the gorge to join the main river.

But the clearing had changed since last night's visit. The sparse grass had become scarred black from a careless fire; it still smoldered in places. The wicked pattern looked like the gnarled veins on the back of a dry leaf. With a frown Diana urged her mount forward. What in Fates' Cellars had happened?

Near the stream, partly hidden by higher brush she spotted Leggings. The blood bay was motionless, her head low. Nightstorm approached, carefully stepping clear of the black soot, and the mare looked up quickly, snorting in recognition. There was a stench here that made Diana's stomach tighten.

Elana was kneeling at the stream's bank. Her body was rigidly still amidst the thick brambles. Diana swallowed heavily as her horse halted. Almost hidden by the woman's frame, an animal corpse, baked black with a shard of white bone, lay caught between branch and rock, almost submerged by the laughing waters. The creature had been fifteen, maybe twenty pounds. What kind of animal it had been was an unanswerable question.

A rasping hiss startled her, and she glanced back to Elana's bent figure.

"Put your sword away," Elana murmured steadily. The Amazon hesitated and Elana said, "Please, Di'nay. You are frightening her."

Mutely, Diana complied.

"Thank you." Slowly but smoothly Elana stood. With equal deliberateness she turned and Diana's breath caught. In Elana's arms was a cat-like beast, but winged. Its golden body was half-held by, half-clutching to its rescuer. Small ears lay flat as the wide chest heaved with its panting; fine furred wings opened partially, hiding Elana's shoulder and half of the beast itself. A long, twitching tail snaked out from beneath the cloaking wingspan. The emerald-lime eyes fastened warningly on the black steed and rider, and Diana forced a steadying breath. Those eyes reminded her of another pair; they held the same intensity in a different color.

"Isn't that an eitteh?" Diana whispered faintly. "A men-cat?"

"Ee´-tah," Elana corrected her pronunciation automatically, and yet her voice was low and calm. "The males are men-cats. This is a female, a winged-cat."

She certainly was. The fully opened wingspan must be eight or nine feet. "I thought they killed on sight?" Diana said.

"So it is said," Elana murmured, bending her concentration to the animal. "In truth, they kill when sighted."

"Fine distinction." Diana was still unable to tear her gaze from the creature.

"Men tend to pursue them. They have learned not to leave witnesses."

"They are sentient then?"

"They are," she echoed softly. A deep throated purr began in the depths of the eitteh and its eyelids drooped lazily. "They are so near the intelligence of humans that the males are called men-cats. They live high in the mountains and do not fly, so humans rarely see them. In the spring the females go there to mate, but they do not stay. Their flight frees the females to create a very separatist society."

That certainly has its advantages, Diana thought but held her tongue. She glanced at the charred corpse again. "Was that also an eitteh?" She took care in her pronunciation this time.

Elana nodded. The animal voiced an ambiguous rumble and scrambled from Elana's grasp, jumping to the ground. With a rippling shudder the wings folded tightly as it sat. A forepaw shook distastefully at a leaf bit that had the audacity to cling, and then, with an air of painfully polite patience, the animal turned her green gaze onto the two humans. Haughtily her tail swished and she waited.

Diana again found it an effort to tear her eyes from that magnetic green stare. "Do you know what happened here?"

"That one," Elana's hand waved toward the stream, "was her mother. She was old and ill. This one is the last of her litter."

"I don't understand."

"Eitteh are familial. The youngest stays with the mother until the next litter or until the mother's death." She gave the barest of sighs. "This one expected her to die, but not like…. she left her mother to hunt. When she returned the drunken scout was playing his fire games." A shudder rippled across Elana's shoulders.

Diana ran a tongue over dry lips, realizing that in some blue-sighted way this woman had seen the beast's torment as clearly as if she had been there. In another culture, on another planet, Diana had once seen some boys playing. They had tied a burning branch to an animal's tail and sent it running. Of all the things that the Universe would choose to reproduce again and again across the stars….

Elana broke into her thoughts. "She is young. She attacked emotionally, without preparations, without stalking and she was flung into the trees. Her wing was dislocated and her head hit. It was the Mother's blessing that she went unconscious or she'd have been killed too. He left in a panic after she disappeared."

The animal blinked calmly, watching the younger woman. Experimentally it stretched its wings, ushering the fine hairs into a more comfortable order before folding them away again.

"Her wing seems better." Diana glanced back to Elana. "That's your doing?"

"I could not leave her so."

"There's no reason you should," she acknowledged softly. Nightstorm shifted restlessly beneath her, reminding Diana of Elana's breakneck departure. Her face darkening with fury. "I would appreciate it, however, if you'd say something before you go gallivanting off into nowhere like that."

Elana felt Di'nay's emotional leap to anger and grew confused. The Amazon was upset by more than Elana's seemingly rash actions, but Elana could not decipher what else was at play in that tangle of amarin. Cautiously she offered a tentative nod. "Next time I will explain first."

Diana swallowed her temper, uncomfortable. She wasn't one to lose her temper so easily. "It's just — when you said trouble I assumed it was Maltar's party."

"I beg patience then." Elana stepped through the high brush to mount Leggings. From her seat the blue eyes addressed the winged cat, who voiced a very human sound of agreement and got to its feet. With little effort the eitteh sprang atop the mare's flanks. She nosed the strange packs carefully, circled once and then settled herself, comfortably stretching prone across the lot.

"Is she safe to travel with?" Diana asked warily.

"She is less safe stalking us."

Diana shifted stiffly in her saddle. Dearest Goddess, what did she think about when she was traveling alone? The rain had begun to drizzle shortly after they crossed the river gorge, and the gray clouds had darkened almost to black in the subsequent hour. Her cloak was well oiled and shed water easily, but the dampness still found a way to chill her bones. One thing was certain, if she were riding alone she wouldn't be worrying about that animal. She wouldn't be jealous either.

Since the rain had begun, the eitteh had been curled up snugly under Elana's cloak, huddled in her lap. It was disconcerting for Diana to glance across and be greeted from those shadowy depths by that regal green gaze and a lazy blink. She felt the distance between herself and Elana grow. But that was for the best. Didn't frustration build character? "I'll be forty end of this year," she grumbled. "I don't need any more character."

She knew the same problem existed on all missions on non-tech worlds — travel. Distance was covered so slowly that a person had too much time to think. The trouble with cold, clammy, wet travel was that everything you thought about was morbid.

All right then, what could she mull over that was constructive? How about extracting Garrison from his prison? Assuming this was not some strange game the Council was playing with her, it would take some doing to free Garrison, especially considering how out of practice she was in the art of breaking-and-entering — a talent she hadn't used since coming to Aggar. That would make it Ruethun...before that even! It had been that mess on Cyrol II — a high tech planet. Why wasn't she finding that reassuring? Because machines were always much more predictable than people and she had yet to meet a locking device that could not be countered with another gadget. She would rather destroy machines than kill people. She breathed a short prayer; she knew death was a probable part of this venture, and how careful they'd have to be not to become victims themselves.

They? She absently chewed on her lower lip. It was just possible that one person really could go where two couldn't. Too soon — she cautioned herself. The Council of Ten had a legitimate stake; it was not something to be decided hastily.

Elana reined in and Diana stiffened, suddenly alert. Without a downward glance, the young woman pulled her crossbow free. Her wrist jerked; there was a sharp snap, and the twin bows were locked into place. Silently she began to set the bolts, the stock balanced against her thigh.

"What is it?" Diana whispered, her hand hovering between long bow and sword.

"I am not certain." Elana's blue eyes scanned the heavily wooded slope to their right. The road had narrowed to grudgingly allow two abreast. Above, the trees had been thinned at unexpected intervals by the mountain's rock slides, and small rivulets of mud were cutting across the road into the lower woods.

Diana slid her sword from its sheath and pushed the bulky hood back from her head. She was soaking inside of a minute, but there was nothing to be done.

The rain splattered and pitted across the thick leaves and into sloppy puddles. It was foggy; the air smelt of damp moss and horses' sweat. Annoyed at the drafty parting of Elana's cloak, the eitteh shook its golden head. It dropped to the ground, choosing to be wet rather than insulted.

"I don't see anything," Diana said slowly, her brown gaze searching the forest above them.

"Neither do I — directly," Elana mumbled. "Still...."

Diana nodded slowly, watching. "Hang back a little. Give us room to maneuver." Her heels touched the black flanks and Nightstorm stepped forward uneasily.

Their hooves sucked and plopped. Each step echoed in Elana's awareness. Her mind stretched and clutched at every nuance her Sight provided — dim bumps high in the trees that became miserably damp, little birds, nearly hidden. The tail tip of the wood mouse quivered; the amarin of the great silverpine monoliths shimmered. Everywhere there was an oddness of auras; the disturbance of the interwoven patterns was unmistakable. Like a lakefly riding the swelling ripples of a pond, Elana could only grasp the broad direction of the intruder. Whether the ripples came from a descending pebble or rising fish, she could not see.

Movement caught her eye — the eitteh. Slunk low to the ground, she too was stalking. The tension of the humans was contagious.

Nightstorm side-stepped a rotting tree.

Tension!?

Elana looked sharply to the hillside above.

Gut string drew taut on a long bow. A single arrow flew. Elana's Sight reached to Nightstorm as her crossbow fired. With a hyper-awareness she felt the muscles of the great steed stretch and twist — rearing high to strike with his ebony hooves at the unseen foe. Elana felt the pressure of Di'nay's knees as she clung to his back — felt the fired wood of her dart splitting the misty swells, traveling at almost twice the speed of the feathered quill. And she felt the tearing — the burning agony of her black colt as the shaft parted his glossy hide, sinking deeply through his chest even as her bolt struck the burly form of their attacker.

Crashing downwards man and beast each met earth. The fine black legs folded, knees smashing and splintering. Above mud and shale crushed and slithered under the man's rolling body.

Diana pushed clear of her own wounded mount as he threatened to pin her. Rounding, sword in hand, she was up, rushing to seize the assailant as he tumbled to the road.

Nervously, Leggings pranced into the rubbled clearing as Elana scanned the dimness around them. There was no sign of comrades. She turned in the saddle, stretching her gaze into the misty distance.

"Are there others?" Diana asked abruptly, barely glancing towards Elana. Her sword tip played at the edge of the maroon and gold vest of their prisoner. Roughly her gloved hand clutched his collar. Her feet were planted wide for balance; she wasn't prepared to take chances.

"He is alone," Elana said finally and slid from her saddle.

With a grunt Diana half-pushed, half-dragged Maltar's man to the rotting, downed tree. He bent double and slid into the mud again as she dropped him. He was thoroughly coated, almost to the point of hiding the scratches and cuts in his bearded face. But there was no hiding the blood that spread slowly beneath his clenched, browned fist.

Mutely Elana turned to Nightstorm. Pushing back her thick cloak, she knelt at his head. She lifted his soft muzzle gently into her lap and eased the bone bit from his mouth. With a deep-throated snort, he recognized her and made the effort to push his nose into her stomach. She held his head and looked into his white-laced eye. Slowly her mind wrapped itself around his consciousness and removed, first, the brittle pain of the broken bones and, then, the searing fire within his chest. Under the tender stroking of her hands his breathing steadied and grew more and more shallow. His shredded heart relaxed, until finally — peacefully, it stopped altogether. With the gentlest of motions Elana touched his forehead, and her fingers closed his fluid brown eye against the rain. Swallowing hard, she lowered his head back onto the muddied road and numbly took up her crossbow to leave him.

Beside Di'nay she halted, her gaze falling to their captive. The rain was coming harder, and the man's grubby face was soaked as he gasped for air against the pain in his side. Elana stared at him, her brow wrinkled in bewilderment.

Diana asked finally, "Do you know him? He's the scout I saw last night."

"No, I don't." Only half-attending, Elana shook her head, and then, with a more decisive shake, she drew back. "I do not understand why he is surprised by us."

"Surprised?" Diana grunted in disbelief. "Tell me if I've missed something, but didn't he just ambush us?"

"I do not mean the attack," Elana mumbled quietly. Wrapping her cloak around her waist she squatted. The crossbow rested haphazardly across a knee, but a finger curled about the trigger and the shaft pointed at him. Elana addressed him in an innocent, child-like manner. "It seems like you might have meant to kill us?"

Diana was astonished at the woman's approach.

The wariness in his expression melted into a contemptuous sneer. His head turned with a raspy laugh. "I was merely hunting for my eventide." His mocking words died abruptly in the icy blue lock of her eyes.

Diana's weight shifted back to her heels. With grim satisfaction she chided herself for doubting Elana's ploy to disarm his defenses. Now Maltar's man resembled a statue of frozen terror. And even despite the drenching rain, Diana granted wryly that Elana's still beauty was accentuated by the contrast.

Diana checked his wound; the man was going to die. She watched as his bloodied fingers were washed clean by the rain almost as quickly as the crimson stained them. It was necessary, she told herself harshly. Her teeth clenched until they hurt. Even if they could tend him, there was no horse to take him with them.

"Bitch!"

"Enough!" Diana's sword swung closer, the steel edge pressing menacingly against the ragged beard.

He glowered with hatred but held his tongue.

The sword point dropped. With half an eye on the man, Diana's gloved hand hooked under Elana's elbow and brought the woman to her feet.

"Are you all right?" Diana prodded, speaking slowly in Common.

A weak nod, then Elana drew herself together. With an unsteady smile she glanced at her companion's face. "In truth."

Only partly satisfied, Diana released her.

Elana forced a breath into her lungs and turned for her saddlebag. "His side needs tending."

Diana hesitated, glancing at the muddied heap and then at the woman's retreating back. Damn it! She stepped over the man's feet. "Elana!"

The woman spun with a cry. Diana twisted as something gold flashed by. An awful crack resounded through the misty depths of the forest; then a hush descended. Diana blinked the rain from her eyes and met the gem-cold gaze of the eitteh. The creature crouched beyond the scout, its mighty wings half-lifted for flight. The man's head lolled opened-eyed against his shoulder, his neck snapped.

"No...."

Elana's eyes were shut. The crossbow hung limply at her side. Diana drove her sword into the earth and left it standing. Gently she pried Elana's fingers from the wooden hilt and set the crossbow aside. With compassion she gathered her near. She didn't need any Sight to tell her that the woman had never been part of a man's killing before. That and Nightstorm....

"I'm fine," Elana murmured, stiffening suddenly.

"I don't believe that," the older woman returned softly, not releasing her.

A moment of indecision passed, then the young body relaxed, almost slumping into the tall frame. With a shaking breath Elana amended, "I will be."

With a grim smile hidden against the wet hair, Diana said, "I know you will be."

"I should have known she would attack...." Her voice was muffled against the heavy cloak and jerkin. "I let my attention wander. She was waiting for that."

Diana's hold tightened with Elana's tremor. "You could not have stopped it."

"No," she insisted, "I could have!"

"It was necessary. We could not take him with us."

Elana didn't respond, and it seemed as if she stopped breathing. Diana waited, vaguely wondering how she herself was to be judged. She found the warmth of the slender body comforting. She only hoped Elana found strength in their clasp too.

Elana straightened reluctantly, stepping away. "I beg your patience, I did— "

"I find no grudge to hold," Diana interrupted softly with formal traditional words. Impulsively she pulled her hand free of its glove and placed her cool fingers against Elana's cheek, urging that blue gaze upwards. Their eyes met, and Elana read the gentle support. She blinked deliberately, and they separated.

"We need to strip the supplies and saddle from Nightstorm," Elana murmured, but she made no move towards the animal.

Diana's tongue wet her lips. The crisis past, her mind suddenly realized what had happened. "It was you — you sent Nightstorm high to take the arrow."

The dark head nodded silently.

"Thank you...." The words sounded so terribly hollow to her own ears. Abruptly she pulled her thick hood forward and turned aside. "Come then."

They worked mutely. The dull drumming of the rain echoed their grim spirits. The ice of death would not be easily shrugged aside.

Diana began to unlace the packs from the freed saddle. "Perhaps his horse is hidden near somewhere?"

"No, he was left behind to wait for us. His plan was to go overland on foot and meet his comrades in the Inn at Colmar."

Diana glanced back at her, "What else did you learn?"

"He is from Colmar himself."

"But he wears the maroon and gold?"

Elana wrapped the green cloak about her as a tent. "The Maltar owns the allegiance of many who dwell outside of his lands. Some he has sent outwards to settle. Others he has bought. A few he has claimed kin as hostage."

"Charming. Dare I ask how far Colmar is from here?" She had the vague recollection of this road meeting up with the track from Gronday.

"By foot and if we stay to the road, we would make the Crossroad Inn by darkfall, and Colmar two days after — in time for eventide."

"That means if they ride hard tonight, they'll arrive by darkfall tomorrow."

Elana nodded. Then hesitantly she offered, "There is a mountain trail."

"This fellow was going to use it, yes?"

Again a nod.

"It's that much shorter?"

A faint shrug stirred the green cloak. "We could not take the horse."

Diana felt a knot in the pit of her stomach as her suspicions of the Council's ploys rose again. "If we released your mount, would she return to the Keep?"

"If freed in the very court of the Maltar himself, Leggings would find her way back to the Council's Keep."

"And tell them by her very appearance the route that we've chosen."

Elana faced her solemnly in the drenching rains. "The Council did not do this."

The quiet, unfaltering assurance forced Diana still. Elana spoke with the steadiness of a Woman's Vow. Despairingly she felt the answering chord of belief rise within her heart. But this was not home, she pleaded with herself. This woman was not a Sister. Why did she want so desperately to trust — despite caution, experience — despite all reason! Diana spun on her heel, savagely throwing aside her traitorous instincts. "We stay to the road."

"Then the packs will need to be lightened. Especially if we ride double."

"There is much I can leave behind," Diana returned curtly. It would not be the first time she had buried the heavier bulk of her Imperial equipment. She would radio Thomas to send someone to retrieve it — and she would bury it a good ways down the road from here. "We'll strip the scout of his weapons and vest too. I'd rather we left it looking more like a thieves' raid than an assassin's ambush."

Elana bowed her head in mute consent.

❀ ❀ ❀

The rain had given way to a damp mist and twilight lent the woods an eerie gray gloom. But the mud-blanketed road belied the myths of forest terrors with the very dreariness of its reality. Leggings plodded along unconcerned, head hanging low near her mistress's shoulder as Elana walked. They had been alternating between riding and walking, and Diana had grudgingly admitted to herself that somewhere she had acquired a certain degree of Imperial chauvinism. It had not been easy for her to accept the saddle when her companion was trudging through the ankle deep muck. But then, as Elana admitted, it was no less easy for her to ride when her Shadowmate walked. Perhaps they were more alike in some ways than she'd credited.

Leggings snorted, pulling up as Elana halted in her tracks. Sword drawn, Diana slipped to the ground in a silent, easy motion. Fleetingly she thought of the eitteh that had left them after the ambush. Her eyes searched the murky forests around them, but she could find nothing.

Concerned, she joined Elana. Diana recognized in Elana's faint, unfocused stare her deep state of concentration. Elana had looked that way when she held the fire in the gardens. The Amazon glanced about again; still it seemed all was in its place.

"Alone...! Alone!" Elana returned to the present.

"What is?"

"The scout." Elana gripped Di'nay's arms in excitement. "He thought there would be one alone! "

"What?"

"Remember, I said he was surprised, and I did not understand why."

"Yes, but — "

"He was startled because there were two of us! He was expecting only one. He expected a single green-garbed rider, not two!"

"Green-garbed...?"

"Very specifically, yes."

Diana's brow creased in bewilderment, and she turned to sheathe her sword. It was not a secret that Di'nay, Courier of the Southlands — trader of news and small trinkets — usually rode alone. And the green cloak and jerkin were the standard garb of all the Southern Traders...and, of Baily's crew. But why would Maltar's men connect her so quickly with their errand? She had taken great pains to insure her reputation concerning politics was one of aloof disinterest.

"It is possible," Elana murmured, as they began walking again, "that you are not truly seen as a visitor from the Desert Peoples."

"No one has ever questioned my history. The position was established shortly after the appearance of the Unseen Wall around the Terran Base. We have simply rotated new Amazons into Mattee's family inn. Why should my presence be seen as anything different now?"

"Perhaps it has always been seen differently? That you come from the Southlands may not be challenged, but that you are a trader for the Desert Peoples may be less credible. Perhaps you are suspected of being one of the Council's men."

"That would explain why Maltar's spies would expect the Southern Trader's appearance, especially if they generally trail my whereabouts. My midnight departure from Gronday would have been suspiciously well-timed with Garrison's crash. But, it does not explain why he was waiting for us — me, on this specific trail. How would they have known that they were being followed? To the best of our knowledge, they never circled back to sight us. Yet he was certain enough to abandon his horse and commit to a thirty league trek over the mountains."

"I know you were not seen. That scout did not recognize you, but — there is another way."

"Somebody in your precious Keep talked!" Diana said bitterly.

"Not of the Keep, Di'nay. The Seers would have apprehended the person long ago. But it could be someone from the village where you stayed. Someone tending the animals or the kitchen. Otherwise they would have known you were assigned a Shadow, Di'nay. They would have known there were two of us."

"Or to be fair," Diana amended tiredly, "it could have been my people who inadvertently gave away my destination. The man Baily sent to fetch me at Mattee's would have left word for our colleague since I wouldn't be keeping our usual schedule. The message could easily have been intercepted."

"Such a message would be understood?"

"They're in the local tongue. Certainly...it would be why the attack was not made in the night. A rider from Gronday would have come from the Crossroads. Their rear escort would not have known until after his tangle with the two eitteh."

"But word from their spies or hawkers would've had to come from Gronday or Colmar too, so it tells us nothing about who was the informer!"

With a disgusted sigh, Diana said, "Facts suggest there's extra help from somewhere; knowing who is little help for now."

"Yet, if their information says one person trails them," Elana ventured, "might we not be able to use that?"

"Perhaps. The obvious response would be to openly travel as a pair." Elana was beginning to seem indispensable...Diana didn't like that. She said, "I am known at this Inn, and further on, in Colmar. Whether I travel alone or not, I will be recognized. Perhaps it would still be best for me to follow my usual solitary routine and keep you relatively hidden."

"There is more?" Elana prodded, sensitive to Di'nay's shifting amarin.

Leggings snorted, her withers shuddering as a silverpine dripped on her from the heights above. Diana eyed the bay mare. "I am also known to be quite partial to red horses. My favorite is a chestnut stallion, Kaing."

She should have known that, Elana realized with surprise. Her visions had never shown Di'nay riding anything other than a bay or a chestnut. Elana sighed, resigned to the stony displeasure she was about to face. "I know you are wary of the Council's motives, Di'nay, but if Leggings is going to place you at risk, perhaps we should send her back to the Keep? Or... sell her."

The silence stretched between them as they went. Hesitantly Elana opened herself a little more to the impressions of Di'nay's amarin. But there was no surging anger to weather this time. There was only that sense of tightly reined turmoil. No, it was not anger, Elana reflected, it was some sort of confusion that was churning within her Amazon. "Di'nay...?"

Diana drew a measured breath and shook her head, a steely set to her mouth. "When you speak of the Council, I almost find myself believing in them."

Patiently, Elana said nothing.

"Experience has taught me much of the ambitions and of the senseless games of men. To trust them...," she glanced apologetically at Elana, "...or their agents has never been wise. Your Council sits so serenely in its little Keep, watching and toying with the lives of these people... yet, it is not that simple here, is it? The Council is autonomous from the Empire by what means? I do not understand them, but I begin to suspect the ways of the Terrans — their covetous ways of power — do not quite apply to this Council of Ten."

Elana quietly answered, "Their goals are ambitious, Di'nay, but not in the way of your Empire."

"Not my Empire," Diana said brusquely.

"I beg your patience. You are not wrong; the Council is not to be judged by the Terrans' accomplishments."

Diana studied her curiously. "How should they be judged?"

Elana took a long time in considering that. "Perhaps as parent? Think of them as parents who stand behind their child. They watch, they intervene to protect but mostly — they are simply there. They offer a bit of wisdom if asked, but, in truth, most children are often not prepared to listen. Children would rather make their own mistakes, grow and find their own strengths — their own faults. For all their patience, the Council members are quite human. They make mistakes as parents will. Sometimes they should have stepped in sooner, perhaps a bit more forcefully — sometimes they move too quickly when they are not truly needed and they have made the situation worse."

"What are their ambitions for this — child then?"

"What does any good parent wish? To see their child grow and mature — that adulthood may be one of kindness and gentleness. That they may know the difference between pettiness and forgiveness — that they will value peace and fairness. But the evolution of a society — of an entire world, Di'nay! That requires patience, and a respect for the child's potential that spans across eons."

Diana's respect for this woman grew even if her uncertainty could not be completely banished. "You believe in their way?"

"Perhaps." Elana's laugh was tinged with irony. "Sometimes I question their methods. Aggar suffers from senseless slavery and greed. There are times I wonder at the Council's seeming passiveness. But, yes, I do believe in their dream."

❃ ❃ ❃

Chapter Eleven

The Crossroads Inn had grown in the generations since its founding. Even with the thinning trade of the late autumn, the stables were well-filled and the rooms well-frequented. Although the establishment was called inn, it resembled a small village rather than a single roadhouse. It was an assortment of large manor houses made of fine stained silverpine with porches and suspended walkways which interconnected sprawling buildings much like the branches that interweave a forest's roof. A place where a trader could announce his latest success and sponsor the finest of celebrations, it was also where a quieter traveler could go unnoticed.

The latter was something Diana decided might be particularly helpful now. They arrived after darkfall and well after the more boisterous patrons had settled into the commons for drinks and food. They took care not to be seen together after their initial passage through the gates. With a trick of the cloak and Elana's Sight, only the most alert of the patrons would notice the green-garbed Southern Trader occasionally appeared to be in two places at once. While Elana tended to the stabling, Diana sought out the manager. Due to their long acquaintance from her travels between Gronday and Colmar, she quickly procured a room and private bath without a public announcement.

She cautiously inquired if a pair of riders from the East had been seen that day. The manager regretfully reported that he knew of no parties out of the Keep for several days. It did not surprise her. Elana had been fairly confident that the messenger and his companion had avoided the Inn and continued on towards Colmar; despite the rain, Elana found that a few of their tracks had lingered, along with the glimmering edges of their horses' amarin.

Between the cold and damp, Elana was more than willing to allow the Amazon to go in search of the odd bits of news and gossip in the crowded commons. With her own muddy breeches and bedraggled hair, Elana was not looking in the least like any man's flirtatious young mala´, and she was tired enough to be relieved at not needing to bother with illusions. There was, she decided, a certain advantage in having a Shadowmate who could take care of herself.

Sighing with weary pleasure, Elana slipped into the private bathing room. Steam was rising from the stone encased pool, turning the air hot and humid. Wood slatted benches lined the walls, glass lamps burned brightly from above, and a plentiful supply of towels had been stacked to the side. A faint, musky scent like incense surrounded her, and she felt a prickle of apprehension along the suddenly exposed edge of her nerves. The memory of the lifebonding stirred, and Elana smiled at herself, gently accepting the place that jumbled corner of anxiety had within her. It had been a taxing few days.

She stripped the clothes from her body and slid into that inviting, steamy pool. Her skin was already deepening its color, and the languid warmth relaxed her chilled muscles. The taut, ragged knots inside her finally began to unwind. Her arms extended out as she laid back, floating upwards. She liked this room. The heavy stone was well laid with earthen mortar and the water was fresh. The wooden fixtures were soothing and protective. The stone insulated her from much of the throbbing world outside while the hot water cradled her near as if in a mother's womb. She wondered if the Seers had a similar retreat hidden near the Keep. Surely they must?

Taking some soft soap from the corner, she dunked her hair again and with a cup, began to wash it. Her long tresses were thick, and Elana patiently, methodically worked the lather through, although her mind was only half on her task. The uneasiness that was still rising within her was reminiscent of childhood insecurities, and it turned her thoughts inward for the moment.

There had been so much that had happened in such a short time, yet, after so many tenmoons of waiting to meet this woman, there was an odd lack as well. The nervous, unsettled feelings persisted as she thought of Di'nay. Elana suddenly worried that the Mistress' training was not enough, given the restless eons of waiting — given the way her heart rose to her throat at the sight of this Amazon. It was as if her physical attraction to Di'nay could draw in her Sight — narrow her vision until nothing else was clear. It frightened her to think of their attacker this afternoon. It had taken her such an inordinate amount of time to decipher the amarin of that...that? Her thoughts faltered and her blue eyes squeezed shut. Yes, that man — and Elana had her answer. The pieces had come together slowly because of his death and because of her role in it — not because of any charming distractions from Di'nay.

The hot tears stung as they slipped from her closed lids, and she sank down into the water, arching back to rinse her hair. Absently her hands moved as the tears thickened, and then she remembered Nightstorm's liquid gaze — such a trusting touch. A sob escaped and she gave up on her hair. It had been too much — too much death. The detached corner of herself was losing its struggle, and with wet hands she wiped her tears aside as another sob broke from her.

Perhaps it had been necessary, but none of it had been right!

A foot shuffled, and her training cued danger. The pain hid; her eyes flew open as her hands clenched, hitting the water with a splash.

"Me — Di'nay."

Unmoving they faced one another. The inner door had been bolted, Di'nay's cloak and packages were thrown on the bench, and the Amazon stood within a step of the bathing pool. Seldom could anyone approach so near — then the pain came rushing back, and Elana barely managed to contain it. Her eyes flickered closed and then opened; an almost motionless battle of will, until the trembling began.

Diana shuddered as the aching wave brushed past her. Impulsively she reached for Elana, pulling her out of the water and into her arms as she sank down onto the broad edge of the bath.

"Cry," Diana ordered softly, pressing the damp head to her shoulder. "It's all right. Cry."

And the strong arms held her as, with legs still dangling in the pool, Elana's struggle ended. Her body shook with the sobbing and her skin grew flushed. For the first time in her adult life, Elana's emotions overtook her completely.

"Cry — just cry," and blinking back her own tears, Diana rocked her, protectively huddling her body around Elana's as the anguish engulfed them both. She buried her face in the wet hair, realizing only that these tears sprang from loss. But she knew, it was going to be all right; somehow they would make it turn out right. Yet she still felt her helplessness rise as Elana crumpled almost in half with the tears.

Images came, flooding Diana with that blue-sighted grief. She saw the black colt tossing his head in his first halter...the Mistress nodding approval...Nightstorm grown, a muddied victim of death. She saw an old woman come to hold Elana, the newly come child...frightened, already regretting her choices. She saw the years of weapons practice with crossbow and bolts...the falling form of the Maltar's soldier...the visions drifted apart only to form and tumble again into oblivion; and through it all, Diana's sheltering arms held strong. It was all she could do.

Slowly the intensity began to subside. Elana's hands loosened their bruising grip on Diana's arms. Her body unbent slightly as her head lay against the linen clad shoulder. Still Diana kept her close, a gentle hand soothing as it stroked the damp, tangled hair.

A broken laugh weakly asserted itself as Elana noticed her companion was soaking wet. With effort she jested, "You did want a bath, yes?"

Diana chuckled faintly, saying, "Yes."

Gingerly Elana moved then, exploring her body's ability to respond to her commands. Without looking up she slipped back into the water, and Diana let her go. Elana splashed the tears from her face and found the water felt good. It seemed to help calm the ragged breathing that hurt her chest so much.

"It's all right." Diana spoke quietly, unmoving.

Elana turned to her. The amarin she found offered no pity, only care and concern. She nodded stiffly — thankfully.

"Do you want to tell me about it?" Diana's voice was so gentle that Elana felt enfolded by her arms once more.

She sniffled, wiping the remains of her tears away. "It's not one thing. Perhaps, a little of everything? Missing people, Nightstorm...I have never killed anyone."

Diana nodded slowly, painfully. "That part may not grow easier."

"Yes, I know."

The Amazon studied the woman standing waist deep in the water.

Then she said, "Is there anything I can do?"

Elana looked blank for a moment, then her humor rose. She tugged on a wet strand of hair, suggesting, "Help me get the soap out?"

Diana smiled at that. "Certainly." She crossed the room to strip off her dripping garments and deposit them on the bench.

Gulping air, Elana quickly averted her eyes as Di'nay returned to her. She realized that she had never seen Di'nay naked, neither in vision nor in person, and she was totally unprepared for the fluttering attack of her stomach. It was not an overwhelming response, but it felt inappropriate somehow. She was ashamed of it and fearful that Di'nay would discover it. She had not meant to arrange anything!

"Having second thoughts?" Diana slipped over the side and into the water with a graceful, fluid motion.

Guiltily Elana looked anywhere but at her and stammered, "I did not mean to — to stare."

"You weren't." Diana suppressed her smile and for a moment dropped low enough to let the water cover her shoulders. Then standing again she said, "It's your not looking that's noticeable."

There was no response.

"I could leave?" she suggested, but not quite seriously.

That raised a smile and a shake of Elana's head.

"I do not bite — "

"It's not you I worry about," Elana admitted quietly. She pressed her hands to her face briefly, then pushed the wet strands back and straightening, added, "I've never seen — all of you before."

"I'm just like any other woman, a little taller...skinnier perhaps." Diana smiled kindly, but she found she was enjoying Elana's trepidation. It was reassuring to see the humanness.

"No." Elana shook her head decisively. "You're much...prettier."

Flattered and very disbelieving, Diana grinned outright. "Thank you. You're pretty too."

Elana laughed and it was a full, bright sound that delighted Diana. Very pleased and resisting the urge to rebuke herself for teasing the woman, Diana reached out and spun Elana around to face the wall. "Now down." and she pushed Elana's shoulders under the water.

Obediently, Elana tipped her head back with her arms floating out for balance as Di'nay guided her. With a tender firmness, Di'nay began to massage her scalp, moving the water through the thick masses. One hand cradled her neck for support as the other worked rhythmically. Elana's ears echoed with the faint crackle of soap suds, and her body relaxed with the water's warmth.

The sound brought a memory of Elana's earlier days. The Mistress had found her crying in the gardens, hiding from the supervised baths. It must have been within the first ten-day or two of her arrival. She had been afraid of the older trainees and their impatience in baby-sitting the newest arrival. At the time Elana had not understood that their short-tempered amarin had also stemmed from their fear of her Sight, but the Mistress had not been daunted in the least.

Elana had long, unruly hair even then, that had been the focal point of her distress. Before coming to the Keep her mother had always helped her wash and patiently comb out the snarls. It had hurt unbearably when the trainees hurriedly tugged through the tangles.

The Old Mistress had not been angered at all in finding the intruder in her quiet retreat. Instead she had taken the child by the hand and led her to the more private baths of the mistresses. The stern but kindly manner that later came to characterize most of her dealings with the young Ona had been uncovered that day as the old woman washed, combed, and finally braided the dark length. After that they had met regularly — often feeling like thieves, sneaking about in the moons' light.

Even after an accident had forced Elana's hair to be cut for a time, the two had continued the tradition. She had learned so much during those stolen hours, Elana recalled. How often had the old woman spoken of the extra cautions of the Sight or the ways to decipher the deceits of cornered men? The nuances of molding children into Masters, dreamers into Shadows — all the knowledge she could condense into those too short hours, all the compassion that was needed to bring the gifted child to womanhood — strong and proud of her uniqueness, not ashamed...all of herself that she could and did share in those nights.

Diana quietly broke into their silence. "You're drifting a long way off."

Eyes fluttered open, and Elana smiled at the face above her.

"Tell me if it feels clean enough?"

Reluctantly Elana moved away. Her hair seemed squeaky beneath her probing fingers, and she dunked her head back once to straighten her hair — as much as would ever be possible. "Thank you. It feels good."

"May I ask where you were?" Diana reached for the soap. "I think it must have been a very special place."

Elana smiled. "Perhaps your people with brown eyes are Sighted? I was remembering a time when the Mistress would help me with my hair."

"You don't mean the old woman I met?"

"Certainly, I do." She smiled. The soap lathered on her body, releasing its full, musky scent. "But how did you guess?"

"How does anyone ever know what another means?" She stopped herself with an apologetic shrug as she remembered Elana was not just anyone. "I noticed she was concerned about your welfare — in a very personal way. You mean a great deal to her. I suppose I assumed you thought similarly of her."

"I do." Elana sank into the pool until her chin broke the surface. She swirled the water about her body, reluctant to touch her skin again. There was a growing yearning to know how differently Di'nay's hands would feel. "She is more than my guardian or teacher. She is my guide — my mentor, perhaps?" Elana remembered the glow of eagerness in the Mistress that even weariness had not covered on the dawn of that last Council meeting. "I believe she would have sought this place beside you if she'd been younger."

"Oh?" Diana looked at her with interest.

"This deed kindled a lost spark in her. The adventure, the opportunity of knowing you — every sense of purpose and every curious fiber within her responded to your arrival."

"So she settled for sending you, her favorite?" Diana thought she understood. Dreams fulfilled vicariously could be such dangerous things. Aloud she only wondered, "And if she were younger, would she really have come?"

"No!" Elana spoke quickly, aggressively. "You are mine. She could not have changed that — even had she been Eldest Prepared, I would not have let her."

Diana pondered the strange mixture of youth and strength that stood before her. Elana was beautiful. Her skin had browned to the color of dark, rich cocoa and shimmered in the reflecting light of the pool. The blueness of her eyes sparkled like sapphires set in mahogany.

A pale light drew Diana's gaze into the water — the opal-white of her wrist's stone. Perhaps I have been the naive one, Diana wondered and slowly reached for more soap. "So your Mistress was excited about my arrival? Did you share her enthusiasm?"

Elana relaxed, smiling as her thoughts went to those vision-haunted nights. She turned to pull herself up out of the water. "It was not the same for me."

"What did you think then?" Diana was oddly undisturbed by the pleasure she was feeling as she watched Elana cross the room to fetch her comb.

"Me? I was shocked!" She laughed then as she sat on the pool's edge to comb out her wet hair. "I had not expected you to be an off-worlder."

"Did you expect a woman?"

Elana took a moment to consider. It was true that since her visions had drifted into her dreams, she had known Di'nay to be a woman. Yet before then? Indirectly she responded, "I've been prepared to shadow for man, woman or child."

The evasion was not unnoticed, but Diana said nothing. She stretched out along the submerged bench, leaning against the wall as she listened.

"I was taught to join a man in arms or be his companion in bed. I can tend a child with croup or calm a nightmare. I can counsel a woman or guide her through a desert safely. But you — " Elana broke off, shaking her head.

"An Amazon is neither woman nor man by your world's standards."

"I first thought of you as a woman," Elana protested. "But as an off-worlder...?"

"An Amazon," Diana interjected firmly. At home the word was very specific and most of her Sisters rarely used the term; its only relevance was to the Empire, but it was a distinction that most of the galaxy recognized. An off-worlder named Amazon would be insulted, but for a Sister to be carelessly called an off-worlder — to be assumed to hold with the Imperial Terran values — that was an outrage.

"I believe I understand some of the difference," Elana returned carefully, acutely attuned to the passionate amarin. "But it was my prejudice against the off-worlders that initially shocked me. It is the fact that you are an Amazon that attracts me."

Diana deliberately ignored the choice of adjectives and repeated her original question. "Did you expect your assignment would be with a woman?"

"I did not expect a man," Elana answered slowly, gradually realizing how true she spoke. She gave up with a shrug. "Is it so important?"

"No." But wasn't it? Wasn't it instinctively part of her assessment? No, just curiosity, Diana insisted. But Elana was satisfied with the curt reply and busy weaving her hair into a single braid.

"You're amazingly — relaxed, Di'nay."

Diana grinned. "I'm on my best behavior."

Intrigued, Elana's fingers paused. "Do you need to be?"

"Perhaps." She sat up quickly, wrapping her arms about her knees, and the water splashed against the stone. "It feels as if I've been overly... sensitive? I'm beginning to suspect... if we're to be partners, a little basic trust is in order. Isn't it?"

Elana felt the breath catch in her throat, and her glance dropped. "I am honored you see me deserving."

Diana laughed, lifting herself and a goodly amount of water onto the edge beside Elana. "I don't know if I'd say it quite that way."

Elana smiled as she finished her braid. "Dare I ask what you do see in me?"

"Very honest," Diana responded, suddenly serious again. "Young. Very capable, but still — young."

Elana shook her head in a faint gesture of denial. What Di'nay's amarin so clearly implied was that something about youth was not to be trusted. But what was equally clear was Di'nay's own confusion about that feeling, and Elana didn't know how to answer such ambivalence.

Diana shifted restlessly, growing uncomfortable in their silence. Changing the subject, she bent her head towards a paper-bound parcel that lay near her clean clothes. "I stopped at the mercantile above. I got you some things...."

"Me?" Elana almost gasped, she was so surprised.

"Why don't you take a look? You did say it might be helpful — if you need to look less like a man. I hope you like...."

"A skirt!" Elana pulled the dark cloth from the top of the bundle. She held it up against her waist and spread the fabric wide. "So much of it!"

"There's kirtle and — and a blue tunic there for you too. I grabbed a rather flimsy pair of shoes to match. I thought they'd travel light. They're upstairs." She watched as Elana drew the tunic out.

Pleased, Elana's mouth formed a silent 'oh'. She slipped on the thickly woven tunic. It hung below her hips with a subtle tuck at her waist to set off the curves of breast and thigh. The string-like weave was done in blues and grays. An undyed yoke framed her collarbones and dove modestly between her breasts. She tied the sash and smoothed the cloth down over her hips in pleasure.

"The blue isn't quite as pale as your eyes," Diana murmured softly, wondering at the disappearance of the muscular lines beneath the bulky fabric. The youthful girlishness seemed to evaporate as the curves grew fuller. Her throat tightened; she had not expected the color to go so beautifully with Elana's richer skin tones. At this moment, she couldn't imagine a lovelier sight.

"It's so pretty," Elana whispered, "thank you."

"It fits well enough?" Diana said anxiously. "I was unsure of your size."

"Yes, it fits," Elana assured her, smiling happily. "And yes — I like it. I don't think I've ever had anything so wonderful before."

Diana forced a breath to calm her nervous jitters. It was an alarming bit of insecurity she had about giving women presents; it always disturbed her.

"Here." Elana startled her. She had come nearer and stood offering a towel. "It really is beautiful, Di'nay. Thank you."

"It was the least I could do after marching you through all that mud."

"Odd," the younger woman teased, "I thought I'd been the guide."

A laugh escaped her and Diana felt at ease again.

"Was there news in the commons?" Elana asked, exchanging the tunic for kirtle.

"Very little," Diana admitted. "May I borrow your comb?"

"Certainly."

"Apparently the topic for the evening was hoofmoss and shattered shells. There was no mention of anything out of the ordinary, but my education on Aggar's horse trading and, in particular, sound hooves, was expanded."

"Judging by the way you ride, Di'nay, I would not have suspected you needed the tutorage."

"Well, I have a fondness for horses. And I pity the poor creature that frays its hooves for a careless rider. Z'ki Sak, Diana!" she said in her own tongue. "How I wish your people had horseshoes!"

Elana watched her quizzically. Her quick ears had caught Di'nay's true name in the strange speech. "Put shoes on horses?"

"No, not shoe shoes," Diana amended quickly as she began to dress. "At home we have metal — well, half-moons. They're fitted to the shape of each hoof and tapped in with metal spikes. It doesn't hurt the animal, but it protects the hoof from splintering and the tender spot from so many jagged stones and such."

"What does it mean when you say 'zah kihs ahk, Diana'?"

Diana concentrated on deciphering the syllables. Then grinning, she said, "Z'ki...Sak...Diana."

"Z'ki Sak, Diana," Elana repeated, fluently this time, and Di'nay glanced at her in surprise at the mastered accent. "And it means?"

"Oh." Diana brought herself back and, settling on the bench, reached for her boots. "It's an idiom — like by the Mother's Hand or something."

"You are named for the Mother?" Elana asked in astonishment.

"No — well, after one of them...almost." Diana sighed, realizing she was being rather confusing. "Diana was an ancient Terran goddess. The Terran legends didn't have a single Mother, they had many — "

"As different tribes call her different names?"

"More than that. Some tribes had a family of spirits, gods and goddesses and each represented different powers. Some of them more just than others."

With sudden insight, Elana dropped to the seat beside her and asked, "Did they embody both the Fates' and the Mother's roles?"

"Yes." The Amazon smiled wryly at the obvious simplification. "Diana was one of those goddesses. N'Athena, the name of my mother's house, also recalls such a goddess."

"Do all your — " Elana paused, searching for the right word, and Di'nay looked at her expectantly. In frustration Elana turned her gaze directly on Di'nay. In an instant their gazes blended and Elana murmured, "Do all the Houses of your Sisters recall such Terran powers?"

Suspended in the magic of that utter blueness Diana remembered a fragment of the Mother's litany, and softly she spoke:

N'Awehai bin n'Shea
corae' mae...
n'Cee, n'Puor, n'Minmee.
Z'Sor felan m'Sheaz.

Kusak n'Sappho ann
vu neh' sueht.
Kum' m'be Mauen z'Quinn,
Kamak dey Sorormin.

Silently Elana absorbed the words, placing them into something nearer her own understanding:

From Awehai to the Shea
hold them dear,
their ways, their strength, their very birth,
for Woman began as earth.

By clever hand of Sappho
were few lost.
Bring all whose heart peace has sought
to One, for Sisterhood is wrought.

...and Elana grasped a little of Di'nay's past in those cherished verses. Finally, and gently, she released the Amazon to her solitude.

"We are dey Soromin...the Sisterhood," Diana mumbled, feeling adrift without that gentle bond — and resenting it. "We are made of seven Sisters...seven Houses. Six houses are memorials to the ancient goddess-women...Awehai, Athena, Huitaca, Minona, Hina, and Shea — the seventh House names a single woman of lost times, Sappho. She was a poet, a scholar, a lawmaker; she was wise...shrewd. Our Founding Mothers desperately needed her every skill in their bartering and building of our world."

"You're very proud of your people," Elana observed quietly.

"And you are not?"

"Not in the same way, I think." Elana studied her hands folded in her lap. Then quickly she said, "Have you eaten?"

Diana shook her head, eyeing the woman, curious at the sudden change in tone. "I thought I'd raid the kitchens before bed. The noise in the commons was growing a bit loud for my tastes."

Elana smiled faintly, reaching for their soiled clothes. "I did arrange for a tray of meat and cheese to be sent up. If you'd like, it should be waiting for us."

Diana snatched Elana's hand from the muddied discards. "You are not my servant. It's not your place to tend my clothes or wait on my meals!"

"I act by choice, Di'nay," Elana returned evenly, though she was very aware of the fingers that now clasped her lifestone.

"You are not my servant."

"At times, yes! I am," Elana retorted. Her equilibrium was slipping beneath the stone's feeling of taunting sweetness. "I am what is needed, Di'nay. Sometimes servant — a soldier if need be. I am whoever is needed so that we can safely be in whatever situation arises. That is what I do! By my choice, that is why I am here."

"And I have no say at all in the matter?!"

"No — yes." She shook her head helplessly, feeling her knees begin to melt. "Certainly you do. I didn't mean to imply...but there are times when neither of us will have much say in — "

"And there are times," Diana bit out sharply, "like now, when there is no need for you to play any role!"

"Like now? When I want to do something for you only because I — care?"

"Or because the Council — Ouch!" Diana pulled back, her hand scalded. Her fingertips glowed bright pink. Argument forgotten, she looked at the pulsing, vibrant colors of the stone. "Mae n'Pour — are you all right?"

Bereft and heart in throat, Elana snatched up her leather cuffs quickly.

"Why did it do that?" Diana's voice was suddenly gentle with her concern.

"Imprinting..." Elana faltered hoarsely — on my very soul. "As in the Keep."

"Will it do that all the time?"

"Well," Elana jested unconvincingly, "when you think about it, how often do you hold my uncovered wrist?" She swallowed painfully. "If there's nothing more you need, I'll go up. Sleep sounds like a wonderful idea just now."

"Certainly, whatever you like." Baffled, Diana watched Elana collect her new clothes and leave. There were still some things that were not being said.

❊ ❊ ❊

Diana paused to stretch. She found her neck was getting stiff from hunching over as she cleaned her long sword and knife. She started, finding Elana had appeared at the clearing's edge.

"...beg patience," Elana murmured, but they shared a tentative smile before Elana turned to fold away her soap and comb in her pack. She was well aware of the fact that Di'nay was becoming accustomed to her silent comings and goings, and, in truth, the Amazon respected her blue-sighted stealth more than feared it. That growing, almost matter-of-fact acceptance that Di'nay held for her Sight was something that Elana found pleasantly surprising; it was not an acceptance many of Aggar extended even after tenmoons of acquaintance.

"Your eitteh," Diana pointed at the sleek, golden creature that stretched out before the fire, "seems to have an inordinate amount of interest in our eventide."

With a chuckle Elana settled herself next to the winged cat. "I thought you had already eaten?"

The eitteh gave a low growl as she quickly bounded onto Elana's shoulders and wrapped herself around the woman's neck. As Elana slumped forward beneath the sudden weight, a deep throated rumble began. Despite herself Elana was laughing.

Diana's eyes narrowed, finding a faint stir of envy within herself as the animal rubbed against Elana's pale cheek. The young woman's smile grew tender and she rubbed the furry ears with a quiet murmur of something.

"It seems you have acquired a devoted friend," Diana observed, finally able to push her selfish discomfort aside. "Will she follow you into Colmar, do you think?"

"Oh no." Elana shook her head, carefully offering a hand for the eitteh's inspection now that the creature had drawn back from the petting. "She might appear again when we leave it as she did this morning when we left the Crossroads, but...she is young. Her curiosity may be caught by something new, and then she'll be gone. As I have said, eitteh are not usually fond of humans."

"Save for the Blue-Sighted ones?"

Elana smiled at Diana then said, "Perhaps."

The animal shook its head disdainfully, disagreeing that her taste in companions could be quite so limited. Disgruntled, it dropped from Elana's shoulders and padded off a few steps before pausing to glance back. Its emerald eyes sought Elana's and after the shortest of breaths, they both blinked and broke the contact. It eyed Diana for an equally brief moment and then with a ripple of its golden hide, opened its wings and leapt into the air.

"She has decided she is hungry after all," Elana said, watching the creature disappear above the trees.

"Will she be back tonight?"

"I don't know." Elana looked back from the moons' lit sky. "She must go deep into the mountains, away from the road before it will be safe for her to hunt."

A snuffling grunt from the small stream bed reminded Diana of another animal she was concerned with. She looked across the campsite, beyond the small, worn structure of the traveler's shelter to the dim outline of their horse. Leggings snorted, stepping away from the water as she returned to her contented munching.

Elana paused from turning their skewered dinner, following Diana's gaze.

"In Colmar, did the Steward not say the King's Dracoon was a Council friend?"

"Yes," Elana said, curious.

"Perhaps he might return Leggings to the Keep for us." Diana quietly faced Elana. "I have been thinking about what you said. It might be better if — after Colmar — we were to travel more openly as a pair without my accustomed red mount."

Slowly Elana crumbled the leaves into the tea water, taking care as she chose her words. "I had wondered why we did not purchase another at the Crossroads."

Diana shrugged. "I did not want to call more attention to us than necessary. Horse thieves are common, but the road between Gronday and the Crossroads is too well traveled and the route takes less than a day. The risk is too high for thieves in such a short stretch — and I'm known to handle a sword well. There would have been too many questions. Someone might have guessed that I'd not come from my usual place."

"What will they say if you purchase two mounts while giving Leggings away?"

"Well — shall we say, she was never mine to sell, and we are simply surrendering her to the Dracoon's care as would any honorable trader who has found an abandoned steed?"

Elana smiled at that. "I had forgotten your unblemished reputation, Di'nay."

Diana laughed and finished with her weapons. "Certainly Maryl will not find it out-of-character...nor will half of Colmar, I'd wager."

"Maryl? That's the baker's wife who we'll stay with in Colmar?" Elana handed Di'nay some tea.

Diana grinned suddenly at an old memory. "Do you know she abhorred this drink?"

"Your tea?" Confused, Elana, sniffed at her own cup curiously. "It is a strange blend, but certainly not unpleasant."

"You like it then?" and there was something in the stillness of Di'nay's anticipation that caused Elana to pause. "You have never really said if you do or do not," Diana pointed out.

"I do — very much," she admitted, suspicious of that faint humor in her companion. "Is there a reason I should not?"

"It is not of Aggar...?"

Elana smiled quickly. "Neither are you, Di'nay. And I like you well enough. Now...," she pulled a roasted jumier from the fire, "...see how you like my latest concoctions. There's a different set of spices to this one — "

Willingly Diana stabbed the crisp bird with her knife and carefully bit into it. "It's as good as it smells."

Delighted, Elana hugged the praise to herself, reaching for her own dinner.

For a time they each ate in silence, content with the food and the growing warmth of their company. But Di'nay's teasing words returned, and as she chewed Elana asked curiously, "Who is this Maryl — aside from the baker's wife?"

"She is the woman who shared my house for a tenmoon."

"But she is not an Amazon?"

"No. Maryl is like you...a woman of Aggar." Diana's face was somber as she remembered Maryl's choice. "She preferred...to marry the baker. She helps him run a public kitchen now. Actually, they were doing quite well, last I saw, and expecting their first born." Diana paused in licking her fingers as she figured the monarcs. "I think she will be birthing...this monarc even."

Elana stared across their campfire in silence. Outwardly Di'nay seemed unconcerned. Her feelings, however, were not so lukewarm.

"I wish it could have been different for you, Di'nay."

"Hmm, no." Diana shook off her melancholy. "Maryl's happy and everything's worked out for the best."

Somehow, Elana thought as she dug the vegetable stuffing out with her fingers, Di'nay was not wholly certain of that. Hoping to turn the subject to less difficult thoughts, Elana questioned, "Do you have an Amazon such as Maryl waiting for you at home?"

"Home-home, you mean? No." Diana chuckled. "My attraction for Maryl was mostly born of pity, I think. I would be hard pressed to find any Sister back home that I would feel that over-protective of...and have it tolerated."

"There is no one at home then? Or there is no one like Maryl?"

"Both."

Was that good or bad? Elana wondered, her stomach fluttering nervously. But she was relieved to find that no one was anxiously awaiting this Amazon's return.

"And you? Do you have anyone special?"

Elana smiled with sudden, impish honesty. "You." Laughing at Di'nay's surprise, she leaned near to squeeze the leather clad knee in reassurance. "Only if you want me, Di'nay. Please, do not look so thunderstruck! I do not bite!"

Disconcerted, Diana laughed, but, strangely, she found she rather liked being teased. That sort of camaraderie had been largely missing in her life on Aggar. A smile settled across her weathered features...this was not the time for debates — nor for complaints. Her stomach was full, the tea warm and she had a whole night's sleep to look forward to; she found she did not want to spoil any of it with self-reflection. "Myself aside then, have you someone at the Keep?"

Elana shook her head. The day's travels and the wind had loosened a few dark strands of hair and, looking to the fire, she brushed them back from her face. "Shadow trainees are generally unattached...by choice. It would make it very hard for any of us to pick up and leave at a moment's notice if we had families."

"Leaving friends can be just as hard," Diana pointed out.

"But not as hard as lovers."

"That sounds as if you've had the experience. "

"Me? I have not had a lover." Elana tossed her left-over bones into the fire. "But I have watched...and felt...friends in their separations."

Diana stared as the flames danced and crackled in the darkness. She remembered when she'd had to say good-bye to her first love. "Most of us only have to struggle through that pain when it's our own. Must be Fates' Jest to deal with it as often as each friend faces it."

"Fates' Jest — sometimes, yes." Elana's voice was not bitter, but it was sad. "Some say the Blue Sight is a curse of the Fates. They fear it...knowing only of our childhood accidents. To them, it seems that the Council must intervene or the Sight would be used to invade or control the unsuspecting. Too easily, they come to believe that the malice of our Fates...that the twisted games of those demi-gods must be behind the Sight's making."

"Yet could you not also say, it is the Mother's Gift?"

Tenderness softened Elana's expression. "Yes, some do. Perhaps you will?"

"Did you want more tea?"

Elana found she had been staring into her empty cup. "Is there enough?"

"Certainly, help yourself."

Her throat tightened as Diana watched Elana lean nearer the fire, careful in pouring from the hot bowl. She possessed such a rare beauty — the strength in her hands — her body so easily showing the confidence of her movements. Diana was so tired of the Maryls — the chattel-like women of this planet who exhausted so much energy in hiding their physical prowess or in actively destroying their muscular abilities. She mourned the beauty they lost in the slackening of their body tone. It wasn't that she couldn't appreciate vivaciousness in soft curves and the lack of protruding, angular bones — but to see no balance of pride in those with lithe, powerful motions...?

It was perhaps what she had most missed since leaving home. On Aggar it was worse, though throughout most of the Terran Empire such denial was still there in its subtler forms. But at home a woman such as Elana was cherished — a woman of strength and power — such bewitching power. Would they think her a mystic, a witch perhaps? One of N'Shea?

Suddenly Diana saw this dark-haired shea in a different setting — amidst the white-blond wheat and the pale lavender skies. Yes, this woman moved as one of them — Diana caught herself. This line of thinking was wrong. It was not her job to recruit young women in vulnerable positions of trust to...to what? To a better way? To a gentler way? To a more self-confident, less oppressive, less hypocritical way of life? No, hypocritical was the operative word — exactly what she'd be if she took advantage of this situation. It was time to admit to herself just how attractive...yes! disarmingly, alluringly — enchantingly attractive...she found Elana to be. And anything else that was flitting through her mind stemmed from that, she told herself...so she shouldn't get on any high-and-mighty horse about better ways of freedom or what-not!

But she could look — and the image of Elana's beauty from the baths last night drifted through her mind. A dull ache rose in her womb, and regretfully, Diana let go of her thoughts, unknotting a leg from its scissor-like crisscross.

It was then that she found Elana's pale eyes were resting squarely on her chin. Diana tossed the last of her jumier bones into the fire, wrestling with chagrin. The woman was probably attuned to every sexual nuance in this poor old body! And then she wondered just how old — no, ancient! fourteen — or was it fifteen? — years difference made her seem to this young woman of Aggar. By ages and planets — such worlds apart! Diana sighed, swirling the last of her tea around in her cup, and reluctantly she rose to her feet. "I think it is a good time for bed."

"Certainly." Elana reflected the tentative smile with a warm, full one of her own. But inside her heart was pounding. She was acutely aware of Di'nay's attraction — and to her own stirring responses.

"I don't think I ever asked you," Diana paused, turning back, "do you mind my habit of using my saddle for a headrest? No objections to the horsy smell?"

"None...but tonight...would you not find my shoulder a softer pillow, Di'nay?"

Air was sucked sharply through her teeth, then, abruptly Diana grinned. She had that coming. It served her right for dwelling on those feelings. "Thanks anyway, but you are a little short."

What did that have to do with it? Elana wondered, remembering the way Di'nay slept — so still and curled tight. She followed the woman quickly.

"Is it your custom," Elana probed curiously and Di'nay stopped in lifting her saddle, "that the taller may not lay her head on the smaller woman's breast?"

This was not teasing, Diana realized. She was serious...tenderly serious. Maybe I should kiss her and be done with it. Probably scare her to death. Disgusted with herself, she heaved up her saddle and moved for the shelter, saying, "Sometimes."

"There are occasions when it is appropriate then?"

Mae n'Pour, this was exactly why she'd been glad to be rid of Maryl. This unquestioning acceptance of the way things ought to be! And this woman is a Council's Shadow, prepared to be companion and even bedfellow to her assigned person...her own feelings in the matter dutifully thrust aside!

"Di'nay — " Anger smacked her between the eyes and Elana half-stumbled back a step, stunned. She blinked at the almost physical pain and gasped as if the wind had been knocked from her lungs. The words barely managed to come. "What have I done?"

"Nothing," Diana assured her wearily.

The softening tone did not match the jumbled fury that pressed against Elana.

"It is just..., " Diana's voice grew even gentler, "...we are not lovers."

"We are as...," Elana choked the words silent. She had been so certain. It had not been possible to mistake Di'nay's intentions. Or had this all been some odd product of lifebonding within an alien biology?

"Have I...misunderstood your amarin?" Elana whispered, seeking that small piece of gentleness amidst the stormy rage that hung about Di'nay. "I had thought...?"

"Wanting is not the same thing as loving," Diana said slowly. But inwardly she was cursing; sexuality was so hard in and of itself without imposed directives from some formidable Council member!

"For you, wanting is not enough?" Elana dared, her whisper growing more faint. Somewhat guiltily, Diana's thoughts were abruptly brought back to her own transgressions. She swallowed hard. "I try not to let it be. Sometimes I do not succeed."

"Those times...you find them regrettable?"

Diana frowned grimly — especially those since leaving home. "Very regrettable."

Elana retreated. The fire needed tending, her rational mind directed. Thankfully her hands took up the task of banking the glowing embers for morning.

The Council had been wrong this time. Perhaps they had not known enough of the off-worlder customs or biology — their decisions had been based primarily on their knowledge of Aggar's needs — too narrow a foundation, Elana thought, suddenly bitter. Lifebonding had tied this woman to her — a woman whose physical feelings did not match her personal ethics or her emotional reluctance. Only now did Elana begin to understand the difficulties. Yet how could the lifebonding have awakened Di'nay's desire but not her heart? Elana struggled to comprehend. In one breath Di'nay wanted her, in the next moment rejected her for that same attraction. The Council should have sent a man so that there would not have been this question of attractions — or there should not have been a lifestone. It was going to threaten the very fiber of their working relationship.

And what of her own hopes? Gifted with Sight, Elana could seldom keep secrets from herself; the Sight presented the depths of her own amarin more clearly than any other's. Aching, Elana feared that she had lost any chance of touching...of sharing the closeness of their bodies. Of loving her, she admitted silently, and she closed her eyes as the tears scalded her browned cheeks. All those nights of watching Di'nay move, seeing her laugh — ride...all that time of waiting, seeking patience against impatient excitement...poised so tightly for her coming. So sweet and so long in coming, and the denial hurt so now.

The wind blew chilly against her face, and Elana rebelliously rubbed her cheeks dry, taking herself in hand. But she resisted the temptation to open her eyes just yet. The Amazon did not need the added pressures of knowing exactly how she felt; if she opened her eyes now, every living creature for a league would know it.

Slowly Elana drew in the evening air and began to concentrate. Beneath the suede cloth on her knees she could feel the rich dampness of the earth and the faint warmth of flowing amarin. The sapling branch in her hand whispered of a still tangible strength. Outward, her reach ebbed through the close-cropped stems that had known the blunted teeth of too many horses...through the briar and brush near the clearing's edge. Purposefully she skirted around the shelter and horse to the bubbling creek beyond and then finally into the towering heights of the trees...those silver, smooth-barked giants of such aged strength. Elana stretched her awareness to meet the brooding, massive stance of the ageless Mother and her children. The calm depths of the trees rushed back along the living lines, flooding her being with their strength. Somehow the emotional fuss of her humanness could always be tamed when entwined with the sheer force and sheer beauty of the living cycles.

Her blue eyes fluttered open. Abruptly she was aware of the horse dozing behind her and of Di'nay standing within arm's reach at her back.

"I'm all right," Elana said softly, breaking the evening's subtle whispering with reluctance. She did not have to turn around to feel the indecision and concern with which Di'nay was struggling.

"You have been still for a very long time," Diana ventured cautiously.

Elana looked down to find the branch still in her hand. She tossed it away, saying, "I've been talking to the trees."

Diana did not try to understand that remark. Slowly she stepped around to squat low beside Elana's kneeling figure. "Would you like to talk?"

"I don't need to," Elana reassured her truthfully. Then impulsively she opened her palms to the woman. Without hesitation the Amazon placed her hands atop the smaller ones and returned the strength of the grip.

"I beg your patience for the Council," Elana said in earnest, gazing across the beautifully strong face before her. "I fear they've made life very difficult for you, Di'nay."

"No less for you," Diana returned quietly.

"Perhaps," Elana forced a smile, "but it was by my own choosing. You were somewhat more cajoled by the Fates, I think."

"Let us call a truce? Agree to disagree. Tolerance for our...contrived circumstances?"

Hesitantly Elana nodded, her tongue moistening her lips before she took courage to rush on. "And if I am too forward, you will tell me? Yes? I don't wish to create discomfort — or regret. I do not know your ways as well as the Council would have you believe. It is Aggar I understand. But I would like to understand...to know you. If I tread off the proper path, you must tell me, please?"

"I will tell you," Diana assured her, growing solemn in response to the urgency and plea in her companion. Then she breathed, "In return for an answer."

The tension that flowed between them warned Elana to be cautious. She nodded, uncertainly.

"Are you afraid of me?"

Her nervous qualms vanished. She smiled but managed not to laugh. "No. How could you think such a thing?"

Diana studied her mutely. It was so difficult to tell without meeting her gaze in the evening's dimness.

"What have I done that you suspect I fear you, Di'nay?" Elana questioned more seriously.

"There are times, when you seem afraid that I will strike you."

"But I am not." Elana frowned. "When do I look that way?"

"Our first night together in the Keep — when I handed you the dagger at the hearth. And this evening, when you left me at the shelter."

Her dark head shook somberly. She lifted Di'nay's hands, curling them in her clasp and she stared at the slender strength in their lines. Again her head shook. "No, Di'nay. You would not strike me. This I know. When you have seen me 'afraid' as you say, I am not frightened as much as I am concentrating — attempting to separate myself from your amarin. When you become abruptly angry, it is difficult for me...not from fear, but...your amarin are very powerful and it is those that I must deal with."

"Are you that way whenever anyone is angered?"

Elana smiled then. "Oh no. I would go mad, I think, if that were so. It is just that I am more sensitive to some persons than to others. And then, the lifestone magnifies sensitivity to you."

"It's a wonder that you don't lose your mind." It was staggering to realize just how many levels and sorts of feelings this woman could be forced to juggle inside a normal day.

"I do not," she assured Diana, calmly. "Sometimes it requires more concentration not to be eclipsed, that's all."

"What happens when we're — if we're forced into a sword fight?"

"That is entirely different," Elana said quickly. "My attention won't be centered on you, and my defenses will be as intact as usual. But when we are alone — I don't know how to explain it. I am open to you...overly aware perhaps? It becomes easier as I come to know you. It is already easier than the first night I — " Elana bit off the end of the sentence. She was not prepared to disclose that the first restless evening had not been during Diana's brief stay at the Keep. "But no, I am not afraid of you."

This was not all of it, Diana knew, yet there was no reason why Elana should share her life's story. Diana found herself amused then, realizing she did want to know everything there was to know about Elana and her life before they'd met.

"There is something else?" Elana pressed softly.

Diana shook her head, unwilling to voice that particular desire. Instead she asked, "Could you explain about talking to the trees?"

Elana felt the strength of the neighboring silverpines and soil reach out to embrace them both. Gently she released Di'nay's grasp and took the Amazon's face in her hands.

Diana felt Elana's pale gaze more than she actually saw it in the moon's light, but she found herself growing very still. Slowly the sparkling depths...like falling into the shimmering facets of a blue gem...absorbed her. Light grew amidst the swirling scents of pine and wood and leaf...the length of her body relaxed — the dampness of the earth crept into an all-consuming awareness. The touch of silver-rooted tendrils steadied her pounding heart. The stir of the topmost needled wisps calmed the rushing flow of her thoughts, and the power of the immortal, cycling life of tree and soil and Goddess engulfed her.

Diana blinked and, vision still blurred, saw a low, slanted roof above

her. The smell of hard ridden leather touched her nostrils and she placed herself
— the shelter. She was warm beneath the thermal blanket, her boots off. And
Elana?

"Here," a soft voice murmured from somewhere beyond her head and
outside. A moment later the woman crawled in, stripped to the soft, black
undergarments. She was almost invisible as the moons' light was dimmed by the
wooden slats.

"Is your tea good cold?"

Diana nodded, realizing her throat was parched. She half-sat and took
the offered drink. It was delightfully fresh, and her mind drew images of frothing
streams dancing over the roots of a willow.

"Is that a tree you know at home?" Elana queried almost too softly to
hear.

"Yes." She returned the cup and sank down again. "What did you do to
me?"

There was only curiosity in the question, and stretching out beneath the
blanket beside her, Elana said, "I showed you how to talk to the trees...through
me. You began telling them about home, I think. Or perhaps they were merely
talking to you in ways that fit your mind's own pictures? I will have to be careful
with you, Di'nay. I did not think you were so easily ensnared by the non-
scientific. You did not want to leave them."

Diana could almost hear the laughter the other suppressed and she
grinned. "My Sisters are often disagreeing there. We of n'Athena are supposed
to be too technically minded, especially after working off-world."

"N'Athena? That is your mother's name, yes?"

"My mother's House — and mine."

"Do you hurt anywhere?" Elana stroked the soft hair from the woman's
brow. "Your head, does it ache?"

"No, not at all."

"Good. Then you must tell your Sisters that they are wrong. At least
about you."

"It was...nice." The words seemed so trite when she voiced them. Not
at all the right ones. "I thank you for — sharing that with me. It was...peaceful,"
she fumbled. There simply were no words.

"Nourishing," Elana supplied, still speaking very low. "I am pleased that
you liked it."

"It was — beautiful. Do you do that often?"

Elana breathed, feeling that poignant sweetness even here from the
rough walls of the shelter. "It is less a matter of doing. Every piece of wood I
touch or blade of grass I bend sends me a piece of this. Always I can draw from
its strength. There are times, however, when I chose to do nothing else."

"Can all of Aggar do that? Or only you of the Blue Sight?"

"Only those with the Sight." Elana traced a finger in an unseen pattern
on the blanket before she said, "Not all of us are so strongly connected, I am
told. But — "

Diana reached out a hand to find the softness of her face. "But?"

Elana drew her chin away from the tender touch and clasped Di'nay's hand in her own. "Sometimes it feels like I am isolated because of these eyes. But then, it seems that to live so alone, never — or rarely — touching this flowing strength of life...that seems perhaps to be more lonely and desolate than any imposed social distance could ever be."

To know your place in the universe, Diana thought, nodding slowly.

"Now — you must sleep, Di'nay," Elana ordered solemnly. "We have far to go tomorrow."

"Agreed," Diana said as she shifted into a more comfortable position. Sleep would feel good; she did not begrudge it. But the calm Elana had shared with her had done more than any number of night's slumber. Beneath that caressing ebb of life, she found some of her cynical fatigue fading. With a warm sense of belonging, she slipped into dreams of home.

❀ ❀ ❀

Chapter Twelve

The sun had become a white, heatless glare as the noon hour approached, and the woman stepped gratefully clear of the sweltering kitchen into the outdoors. For a moment she stood shading her eyes, unaccustomed to the brightness after the dim interiors. Her face was rounded and dark, glistening with sweat from the morning's baking and exertion. A late autumn breeze arrived in a gusty puff, swirling the dry leaves, but winter was still a ways off and the leaf dancers soon skittered back to the ground.

The woman smiled with satisfaction at the line of mill and yard that stretched outwards from the stone buildings. Her small garden had yielded well with vegetables and a few fruits. Now the soil was dark and rich, turned and fertilized, already blanketed for the winter. Her husband's field beyond had been harvested too; the sturdy bunt grain had long since been separated and ground at their mill. It had been a good season not only for them, but for the entire district. For a time, they had even taken on extra hands to work the mill. Today, however, the stone hut was shuttered; it too was ready for winter.

A gray eagle cried and the woman looked skyward. The creature soared and dipped and was lost in the dark silverpines of the foothills. Two rather chubby, pale ponies munched contentedly on the husks in the emptied field, and she chuckled. The animals undoubtedly felt quite accomplished at their escape from the mill's corral, but they were doing no harm and saving feed besides, so she let them be. She gave a sigh of pleasure and lifted her apron to wipe her brow, but the white flour encrusted there stopped her. The child she carried often resulted in more flour settling across her protruding waist than across the kneading board. Cheerfully reminded of her charge, the woman shook out her apron and brushed dark, bound hair back with a sleeve. Her hands were still sticky from the last batch of breads.

With a hand to sturdy her aching back, she took up the wooden pail and went to the well. Its roof had been newly thatched and gave a sweet smell of damp and dry straw, and it was cool there in the shade with the dampness rising from the waters. An almost disbelieving smile came to her as she attached the bucket and cranked it below. It was still very hard to believe she was here — part of this.

"Maryl!"

She glanced over her shoulder without a pause in the cranking. The husky young man that ran from the kitchen reminded her of an excited colt. His face was clean-shaven and easily kept so, and his black, straight hair was freeing itself from the thong at the back of his neck. She caught her breath again at the sight of him. It was clear that she was his senior by at least the eight seasons that actually separated them, but the devotion in his handsome, boyish face assured Maryl of a different sort of youth.

"Yes, Bowgyn?"

"I've done it! Settled! This very hour in fact."

"The arrangement with the commons?"

With a massive hug from behind, he wrapped himself about her voluptuous curves, half-lifting her from the ground. "On the next morrow we begin delivery. Two weight of the seasoned loaves and half again of the dumpling bits!"

"And the price?"

Bowgyn stood before her proudly. "I held exactly to what we spoke on."

"And he took it?"

"Aye!" He held his arms wide, saying, "Just as you knew he would!"

"Oh Bowgyn!" Maryl laughed and collapsed gleefully into his embrace. "I knew ye wou' do et! I knew — "

"Ah...careful," he whispered wickedly into her ear, "your accent is slipping."

She forced a laugh and hugged him quickly, "We Southerners are allowed our moments too."

Bowgyn's teasing gentled, and he placed a tender kiss to his wife's mouth. "Your past does not concern me. Our home, our child — does."

Maryl blinked back her tears and pushed her young ruffian aside. "But I am proud of you, Bowgyn. So very proud. You've done so well."

"I have, haven't I?" He brightened even more, if that was possible. He bounded to the well side, still talking as she went to wind the bucket up. "You know what this means, do you not, Maryl? We'll be able to keep the extra kitchen help."

"And the housegirl?" she asked anxiously. With the child coming she was poignantly aware of the work that needed to be done at the public tables as well as in their own house.

"She's yours, her time bought and papered! It was the only place I stopped at on my way 'cross city."

"Not rented?" Maryl breathed in amazement. It had never occurred to her that their home would come before the business.

"You do not mind?" Bowgyn leaned across the well suddenly. The awful thought struck him. "You did not want another? She works hard enough, yes? She minds manners and all?"

"It's a beautiful gift!" Maryl cried, shaking her head, and the bucket sloshed onto the stone ledge. "There's not a thing wrong with her. Not a thing!"

He rounded the well and awkwardly put his arms around her. "Maryl, you're cryin'?"

"I'm pregnant, foolish boy!" she wailed and slapped him across the chest. "I'm allowed to cry when I'm expecting."

Bowgyn grinned and kissed her. "Then I wish you years of tears, pretty wife."

She choked on her laughter and pulled out of his hold. "Don't you have duties in the bakery, Tad? The books haven't been tended since the milling stopped."

"Such a scolding." He laughed and kissed her again. "Then I'm to be a good lad!" And with a backward skip and a wave of the hand, he disappeared into the shadowy kitchen.

Maryl leaned herself back against the gray stone of the well and stretched her aching muscles. The contract had been signed. After all his hard work and planning, it had happened. She glanced down at her swelling body. The time couldn't have been more blessed if the Mother had decreed it Herself.

Pride filled her and with a sudden burst of energy she pulled the bucket to her. Startled to find it almost empty, she laughed at herself and lowered it again.

A nervous neigh carried across the field from their ponies. Her dark eyes lifted. Worriedly she spied the two figures and horse emerging from the outlying forest.

"Min!"

Maryl twisted to catch sight of a slender girl, who was barely seven, disappearing from the upstairs window. Less than a moment later the girl was racing down the outdoor steps. Her auburn hair was streaming behind her, covered only with a tattered kerchief. She was their responsibility now, Maryl thought. She wondered if they could afford a few new clothes for the lass. It was a disgrace to see her filling form bursting through the old linen kirtle, and she did work so hard and honestly.

She saw the freckled face was smudged with soot, and Maryl remembered casually mentioning that the firehearth in the guest room badly needed attention. She smiled warmly as the girl skidded to a stop, grabbing her mistress's arms frantically.

"Calm yourself, Szori. Nothing can be so distressing."

"But...but there!" She pulled her mistress away from the well, pointing across the barren fields. "Strangers, Min!"

Maryl's hands rubbed the lass's arms reassuringly as her eyes again sought the visitors. Their steady pace continued towards the house, yet the distance allowed few details to be discerned. The taller one wore a cloak that swirled with the lifting wind; the smaller one — it was not a cloak but hair. It was a woman with her hair blowing behind. Maryl's gaze returned to the taller form. Her heart thudded painfully, fear and pleasure springing alive as she recognized the ghost from her past.

"Not strangers," she said calmly for the girl's benefit. "A friend of this house for many seasons." Her smile was quick to reassure as she said to Szori, "The Master is in the kitchens. Run and tell him we have guests tonight – his father's Southern friend. Then be quick and make up the guest room." Maryl paused, gently wiping the dust from the young face. "I'm afraid we shall need to spoil your fine work. This one journeys from a different climate and will need extra firewood tonight."

Szori shrugged, pleased and shy that the woman had noticed her efforts. "The room will be ready, Min."

"Tell Bowgyn first," Maryl warned and at her hasty nod, let the girl go.

Thoughtfully Maryl turned to watch them then. Di'nay raised an arm in greeting and Maryl answered with the same. Slowly she went back to the well and drew up the water. This time little was spilled as she pulled the pail onto the stone rim, unhitching the bulky rope handle.

It had been so long that she had come to believe Di'nay would not return. She had understood that the Southerners were rotated regularly and that Di'nay's tour of duty was soon to end. She should have known better, Maryl rebuked herself. Di'nay had always kept a promise, and on their last meeting one final visit had been pledged. One last safeguard, Maryl remembered guiltily. She had even been pregnant then, and still Di'nay had unquestioningly accepted that she could return if she needed to – no, if she had even merely wished to.

The clatter of wood-soled shoes caught her attention, and she glanced back to watch Szori dash up the stairs. The situation had not been without its difficulties. But she had learned much from Di'nay...much about patience, responsibilities...much about learning. For all her tavern-hardened years, there was so much she had not guessed at, and the mere polishing of her uneducated drawl would never have changed her as Di'nay had.

She moved forward slowly as the two led their horse around the corner of the split rail fencing. Maryl reluctantly admitted that whatever regrets – whatever the doubts, she had shared much...owed much to this – person.

Her mind still refused to be comfortable with Di'nay's gender, but their odd friendship had made allowances for even that. Many allowances had passed between them, Maryl thought. And as she waited, watching the long, smooth strides devour the distance between them, a very real smile of welcome grew on her lips.

"Min Bowg." Diana reached for the outstretched hands of her friend and bowed, left foot stretched back, in the most formal, most honorable of greetings.

"As Mistress here," Maryl spoke just as formally...and sincerely, "I welcome you and yours to this place."

"We are honored," Diana tenderly released the soft hands. She had not changed, Diana thought, taking in the full, rounded body made fuller by the child. Seeing her now, Diana rejoiced for her. She was indeed blossoming under this Bowgyn's attentions; the anticipation of their child was only giving her a humble way to boast of her good fortune. And no one, Diana believed fervently, could have worked harder and been more deserving of receiving a dream's wish than this woman.

Diana turned to Elana. "This is Ona." She gallantly suppressed a wince, but few slaves carried a full name. And Elana had staunchly announced that she would rather play that role and dodge the servants' orders than their curiosity for new gossip.

"Welcome," Maryl said, quickly stepping forward to grasp Elana's hands when she appeared reluctant. "You're newly acquainted with Di'nay, are you?"

Elana nodded deferentially. It was obvious that Maryl thought her a servant, and it was equally as blatant in her amarin that there was an acknowledged approval of the distance between their stations. But there were a great many conflicting amarin within this small circle. Elana glanced at Di'nay. She would gamble that this handsome Amazon was the root of the confusion.

"Ona has been with me for less than a monarc," Diana's smile was charming.

"I've acquired a new girl to help with the household too, although she's a bit younger." Then directing her words to Elana, she said, "But the two of you may find comfort in discovering you not so very different, being new in strange places."

Elana was surprised at the sincerity of the woman's thoughtful wish to ease any homesickness. She began to see why Di'nay hoped that life would treat this woman well, and again she wondered what had separated them. But as she watched Maryl, the answer became clear. This woman was ambivalent in her feelings towards the Amazon. Tenderness and compassion were certainly there, but no less so was a repulsion and hint of panic.

"You have but one horse. Your fine chestnut has not come to harm, I trust?"

"No, he's doing quite well. I believe he was contentedly munching in the clover patch last I saw," Diana said tersely as Maryl stepped back to the well to retrieve the heavy bucket. It would have been socially insulting her hostess to help. "We were riding new mounts this time, and unfortunately, others thought them much too handsome of stock and confiscated them. As for this poor soul, we found her wandering with only a tattered bridle. I thought it best to bring her in for the Dracoon. There is undoubtedly a family somewhere that is wondering about her rider."

"Thieves took you, Di'nay?!" Maryl looked shocked. She had seen Di'nay wield a sword and was not so easily convinced.

"It was at night," Diana returned slowly, distinctly. She knew the words that would silence the matter. "My attention was elsewhere, Maryl."

"May I take this, Min?" Elana asked, deftly sliding the bucket's handle from the already loosened fingers. With measured control she bent Maryl's amarin so it seemed she was merely redeeming herself for an inattention to duty. Maryl was not in the least offended at what would have been assertiveness from another servant. Elana had not missed the sudden wincing spasms in Maryl's lower back.

"Put the pail by the door for now." Maryl pointed absently. "I'm grieved to hear you lost your animals. I know you chose them well."

"At least it was not Kaing."

"Yes, thank the Mother for small favors."

"There you are!" Bowgyn appeared in the wooden door frame. The leather-bound parchment and quill were still in his hand. "I could not believe it when Szori descended with a tale of the Southerner arriving on foot!"

"Szori?"

"Our new girl."

"Ah — " Diana grinned as Bowgyn awkwardly, book under arm, extended his palms to meet her greeting. "There are many such tales of horse thieves, I fear. So, tell me, are there any decent animal traders presently about?"

He snorted derisively. "Nattersu is always around."

"But not always so decent."

"Naturally, he is a horse trader." They laughed together. Then Bowgyn asked seriously, "Do you need them today? Or are you staying a time this visit?"

"I cannot stay long," Diana answered truthfully, "although this will be the last time I'm to see you, my friends."

"You're going South then?" Bowgyn inquired and unconsciously settled his arm around Maryl's shoulders as she moved nearer to him.

"Yes, it seems after this tour of the countryside I am to be replaced."

"Oh, but...," Maryl glanced over her shoulder at the woman near the kitchen door, "...what of your girl, Di'nay?"

"Much is undecided. It is likely she will need to stay behind."

Impulsively Maryl clutched her husband's tunic, asking and offering in the same breath, "We may always find a place for her, Di'nay, if you'd need. Someone of your house is known to be dependable...."

Surprised, Bowgyn turned away from his wife's pleading, and said, "Certainly. There'd be room for her."

Somewhat startled, Elana watched the couple closely. From the young man's amarin, it was obvious that the idea was a little unsettling. They were not so affluent that feeding another mouth was easily done.

"Thank you, I'll keep it in mind." Diana smiled, then abruptly changed the subject. "I do need to see about those horses, Bowgyn. Would you have time to do some bartering with me? I also have some financial arrangements for you. Maryl here has vested interests that have unexpectedly produced some good fortune."

"Investments?" Bowgyn looked questioningly at his wife.

"I'd forgotten." Maryl shrugged weakly.

"Actually, I don't think I ever mentioned the thing after the start." Diana grinned sheepishly. "For some time it appeared the sea merchant had absconded with the lot, and I tried to forget the whole muddle. But I've received word that his ships were run aground and his goods re-routed by caravan. Apparently his profits were still most handsome."

"But I don't understand," he said, looking as confused as ever. "What does Maryl have to do with a sea merchant?"

"She had nothing to do with it," Diana assured him, sensing his discomfort that his wife might have been involved in any sort of risky venture. She removed her pack and stretched. "The small pittance — aside from her dowry — that her uncle left in my care was part of my investment in the man's tradings. I had sent it South for my family's bargaining, and as I said, for a while I assumed it had soured. It has been a most pleasant discovery to find otherwise."

Elana found it puzzling; she was very aware of the fact that Di'nay had concocted the entire story.

"Our good fortune is scarce believed!" Bowgyn hugged his bemused wife close before turning to the bakery. "Come in now. Let me put these away and we'll see to the horses. I can't spare the entire afternoon for you, but I can certainly walk you over. I must tell you what we've been bargaining...I'll be right with you...." His exuberant voice was carried off into the kitchens.

Diana paused beside Elana as Maryl stepped near. "Settle us in with the Min and then see the bay 'cross city to the Dracoon."

Elana nodded quickly, eyes downcast and very aware of Maryl's scrutiny.

"Min — " Diana bowed as Maryl forced a smile. Reluctantly, she joined Bowgyn.

The low-set ceiling and the dark finished wood reminded Elana of the Old Mistress' room. For a fleeting moment she wondered if Di'nay would not hit her head on the beams, but the uncomfortable amarin of her hostess demanded her attention.

"Szori...," Maryl drew the girl away from laying out the quilted bedding, "...go see to the tables. We've both been away too long."

Obediently the girl nodded, but she couldn't help casting a half-curious, half-fearful glance back at the newcomer.

Maryl followed Szori's look to Elana's inquiring expression. Mistaking Elana's query for misunderstanding, Maryl elaborated, "We run a public kitchen next to our bakery. The fare is plain, little competition for the Inn's commons 'cross city, but we do well enough. We're not open for eventide, just breakfast and mid-day."

Elana nodded, setting down her pack beside Di'nay's at the foot of the bed. Vaguely she wondered what Maryl was waiting to say. The woman was finding it decidedly difficult to begin, and cautiously Elana said, "Min Di'nay told me of — "

"Tad!" Maryl cried out the term for a male's address with strangled panic. Abruptly she caught herself. She took in some air and managed more calmly, "Here he is known as Tad Di'nay. You will remember this."

It was a plea, an almost desperate plea. Elana nodded mutely. But knowing of the woman's fear did not explain its origins. Again Elana wondered if the Sight made things clearer or if it just showed the depths of the muddle.

"The habit, in general, is a good one to cultivate," Maryl explained lamely. "One never knows if you're truly alone. What...what else has Di'nay spoken of?"

This woman was ashamed Elana knew then, and wearily, she bowed her head. "I've been told to speak of nothing, Min."

Maryl accepted the reassurance, but had a feeling that things were out of sorts. There was something too complacent about this Ona. Di'nay was not an owner of servants as Maryl herself knew only too well. If this one had come to Di'nay, it had been for a very good reason. And Di'nay would never have been content to simply remove her from an abusive clan. No, the Southerner would have begun with first names and proceeded from there. Yet the woman before her, by every appearance, was a slave — and a meek one at that. Unless this was assertive compared to where she had been? Maryl shuddered at the image of a place that could have produced such emptiness. Determinedly she straightened her aching back. The worst was done, the best thing for it was to address the present.

"I expect you're tired after the journey," Maryl began briskly. "If you like, when you return from your errand you may use the bath hall. It is perfectly safe," she added hurriedly, remembering well how fearful a concern that could be. "The door bolts...and our two kitchen men are respectable. If you'd like, Szori could join you. The men know her and her tongue's quick enough with them for all her youth."

"Thank you, Min. I can manage fine alone."

So mild, Maryl's brow wrinkled. She must talk to Di'nay. The irony of that, she thought, then said, "You're welcomed to foods in the kitchen too. The bath hall is just the other side of the kitchen. The ovens warm the waters some. It's quite pleasant. Mind you," she teased slightly, "no sleeping down there. You'll end up drowning." Absolutely no response. Maryl felt her concern rise; the girl must have been very severely abused before Di'nay's care.

"You may use the indoor steps." She pointed to the half-open door leading to the rest of the house. "Through there, left, and its the steps at the very end that go to the bath hall. The narrow ones. The main staircase in front of that will take you to the kitchen."

"Yes, Min."

Maryl's dark eyes passed uncertainly over her again. By the Mother's Hand, how was Di'nay tolerating her? Di'nay — who despised servitude of any kind — what was she doing with this woman?! Her stomach tightened, remembering her fleeting glimpses of Di'nay and that Southern friend, Liest. Something akin to revulsion but uncomfortably close to jealousy made Maryl feel ill. Her eyes turned to the sprawling bed as she remembered Di'nay's earlier comment about the horse thieves catching them by surprise. But Di'nay would not have if...would she?

Gingerly Maryl crossed the room. She placed a tentative hand on the young woman's shoulder. She could have sworn the girl had ducked her head even more. "I have no power over the doings outside of this house, Ona. But if you'd like, you may sleep with Szori while here. It can be arranged."

"No thank you, Min."

"There'd be no repercussions, I promise you." Maryl dropped her hand, already knowing the obligatory response. "I know Di'nay well. It would not be a problem."

"Thank you, Min." Elana's stomach trembled at the thought of the precious time this woman had wasted with Di'nay, and her voice slipped from its submissive echo. "I would choose to stay, Min."

The inflection was not lost on Maryl and she retreated respectfully. Whatever her reasons, the girl would remain. It was not so very long ago, she reminded herself, that she would have offered such loyalty too.

"Very well." Maryl turned for the doorway. "Should you or Tad Di'nay require anything, simply ask Szori. I'll leave you to your errand now — "

"Thank you, Min." Elana was careful of her tone again.

For the briefest of moments, Maryl paused at the door, then with a sigh she shook her maternal instincts aside. What was done, was done. There were other things to be attended.

❀ ❀ ❀

Chapter Thirteen

Diana stretched reluctantly and rubbed her blurry eyes. The bed beside her was still vacant, she noticed — with regret? She frowned faintly and stared at the feather pillow almost accusingly. Why shouldn't the girl choose to nap elsewhere? Maryl had probably arranged for her to share Szori's room. After all, there was nothing in her pack that Elana couldn't have easily borrowed.

The thought was not mollifying. She pushed the heavy quilt aside and snatched her new tunic from the stool. It was not Elana's absence, Diana told herself as she dressed quickly, but the hour. Darkfall had come and gone. Eventide was finished in most houses, and it was time for her to join the rabble 'cross city at the commons. No, she told herself sternly and laced up the boot, it wasn't Elana's absence; it was just that she hated to be rushed.

A gust of wind rattled through the open shutter slats and almost hid the faint scuff of the door bolt. Diana glanced at the entering figure. Stubbornly she refused to acknowledge Elana and picked up her other boot.

Disconcerted, Elana slipped the hood back from her head and shut the door. Whatever softened rapport they had struck during their day's travel had obviously been bedded with the day's sun. Dear Mother, would a spoiled child have been any more irascible? Repressing a sigh, she went to stoke up the fire.

"I was worried," Diana muttered, finally, without turning.

"I beg your patience, it was not my intention."

"I had expected to find you somewhere about when I returned from the horse trader's — or at least soon to come?"

Elana's stomach tightened at the intensity of the sullen assault of Di'nay's amarin. "I would have." She moistened her dry lips and knelt beside the fire to prod it with a stick. "Maryl broke water and I was ordered to fetch the mid-wife — "

"Ordered!?" Diana stood abruptly, forgetting her own childishness. "By who?"

"Bowgyn." Elana glanced up with a growing tenderness.

"You are not his to order!"

"Maryl is in labor," Elana said patiently. "Protocol is easily lost at such times."

"How is she?" and in the same breath, "Where was Szori?"

"Maryl is doing well. There's much time before she will birth the pair, I fear. And Szori is with her. Tad Bowgyn did not wish to leave his Min but neither was he comfortable tending her without a woman's — "

"Cursed Fates' Jest!" Diana muttered savagely, grabbing the mantle with white-knuckled hands. "He was comfortable enough bedding her alone, wasn't he?!"

Elana eyed her in concern, rising to her feet. "Are you jealous, Di'nay?"

"No!" Guiltily Diana realized she had shouted. More calmly she repeated, "No, just frightened." She drew a slow breath, but the anxiety still knotted her stomach. "Do you know how old she is, Elana? Almost twenty-three seasons...and this is her first — Mother help her!" It was a strangled plea and her eyes burned with unshed tears. "I had truly hoped not to be on this planet when...."

Consolingly Elana touched her shoulder, "She is strong, Di'nay. I do not know if the children will survive, but if the mid-wife is adequate, there's no reason Maryl should not live. She will be all right."

"Children?" Diana looked at her quickly.

"She bears a pair," Elana announced softly, and worried, she squeezed Diana's arm as the woman paled. "I do not need the Sight to see her walk — her shape. They have said nothing of this to you?"

Diana shook her head dully. Stillborn twins were all too common on Aggar. She had lived long enough in Gronday to know this. "You said the mid-wife is here?"

"I believe so. I spoke with her at eventide, and she set out at once. I returned by way of the South Gate — "

"Yes...Leggings." Diana forced herself to concentrate. "The King's Dracoon. Did you learn anything about the Maltar's pair? Or news of Garrison?"

"Perhaps." Reluctantly Elana accepted the fact that Di'nay did not want her comfort and her hand fell from the Amazon's arm as she explained, "This morning one of the Dracoon's hunting birds brought down a courier hawk. The bird was marked with a Black Falls band, but which handler it belonged to, he could not tell. The note merely acknowledged instructions had been received."

"Odd...no handler tag." Diana stared into the flames. "Black Falls, you say?"

She said, "North and northwest of here."

"Right direction. You know something of it then?"

"A little more than the Seers perhaps. I was born there."

Just yesterday probably. Diana winced at her own cynicism. What had happened to their truce? The one she herself had extended the other night in the baths?

"I beg patience," Diana muttered, aware that Elana would be

uncomfortable beneath this disjointed anger. Diana finally saw — really saw — the woman before her; she looked exhausted. She pushed an unruly strand of hair from Elana's face, saying, "You deserve a bath and some sleep."

Beneath the embracing warmth of Di'nay's amarin Elana smiled too. "That sounds wonderful. I'll look in on Maryl first. Then I promise to tend to myself."

"Tell her I asked after her."

"Certainly. Di'nay..." Elana hesitated, feeling a little foolish, but she went on, "Take care tonight? Please?"

Diana remembered the black horse as it lay in the mud. "Yes. I will."

❀ ❀ ❀

The stale floral scent of tobacco greeted Diana as she stepped through the low door. The room was already crowded, the air gray with smoke. She took a breath reluctantly, blinking to adjust to the dim light. Usually, she knew, she was quite capable of enjoying an evening in the commons. The boisterous lot was generally cheerful, and the local musicians might be sober enough to start with a few dancing tunes later. The Inn's commons were the best entertainment available. Certainly a more efficient news service than any of the King's messengers.

She waved to the innkeeper across the room. Taks lifted his good hand with a hearty shout that died in the midst of everyone else's commotion. She and Taks went back a ways — to her first monarc of arrival. Cleis had been riding with her that summer day. It had been Diana's initial trek out into Aggar, and they had interrupted a band of thieves waylaying a brewer's wagon. The driver was dead and his companion unconscious when the scuffle ended. They had tended Taks' wounds the best they could, but his left arm had had tendons severed.

All in all Taks had taken the crippling well. Being the Inn's owner, his livelihood had not been as threatened by the loss of his arm's use as it would have been by the loss of the wagon's contents...at least, that was how he told it.

"Aye, it's the time to be seeing Tad Di'nay again," he greeted her cheerfully. "I was just speaking to Min yesterday about it. And how are you?"

Atop the bar she clasped the upraised palm, laughing, "I'm never so good as you're looking, my friend. How's business?"

"Picking up after the end of harvest slump," he chuckled and pulled a gray stein from the stack. Taks was a tall man and bulky. Even with his left arm tucked against his apron string, he rarely seemed clumsy. Deftly he sidled the stein against the lower counter as he twisted the tap closed, and with a flourish, Taks presented her with a mug of mead. "As always, Tad, the first for you is by my pleasure — "

"But the rest takes coin well measur'd!" she finished for him and lifted the toast. "May the Fates forget you, Tad Taks, and may the Mother hold you near."

He was silent while she drank, then said, "You're here for the lass's birthing?"

She set her mug down before removing her cloak. "I was surprised to find she's bearing so soon. I'd come to bring my farewells. I'm off for m'

Homeland."

"You're saying?" His thin black eyebrows arched worriedly. "You've not done anything displeasing to your king now, have you?"

"Not at all." She grinned reassuringly, touched by his concern. "My duty is served, and my family awaits me. No more and no less."

"Aye," he nodded thoughtfully. "You've been a long time gone for a son to be missed. You're saying you're looking forward to the journey then?"

She nodded but with all truth added, "But I'll be missing a lot of these Northern peoples. You not the least, Tad."

His small black eyes lifted, staring at her mutely. There was too much he owed this Southern Trader; it was a debt he had barely begun to repay. Tad Di'nay would never know how much that single wagon of ale and whiskey had meant to this business. His family would have been ruined, if it had been lost. As it was, he now claimed the best cellars in the regions, personally supplying the Dracoon with all his needs. This alone had doubled his life's fortune in a single tenmoon. He looked down at the counter and rubbed a drop of moisture dry with his finger. "Tonight your money's not welcome. Your drink is from me."

It was clear to Diana how much this meant to him. She nodded. "I'm honored."

He straightened pulling the rag free from his apron, not glancing at her. "I'm the one honored." He left her on the pretense of wiping the far end of the counter.

Diana drew a long drink from her stein, watching him go. These were odd sorts of good-byes. Emotional openness was strictly relegated to the woman's role here. She was not sure if she should be thankful that this forced her into such casual farewells. After so many years of guarded, superficial relationships, was she truly aware of what she was saying good-bye to?

Home would be difficult after this practiced hiding. For the first time, she glimpsed the more personal reasons for the moonbound time on Shekhina...reasons aside from the vague risks of cultural sabotage. Perhaps she had forgotten how to relate openly — vulnerably — even to women. Perhaps especially to women. Her thoughts drew pictures of a blue-eyed shea.

"So the day's trek did not tire you over much!" A booming voice and a hefty slap across her back harshly broke her solitude.

Diana grinned with practiced effort at the round tub of lard that plunked his tankard down beside hers. "Tad Nattersu, a good evening to you. I'd have thought you weary of my company after the day's bartering?"

One of the bartenders refreshed Nattersu's draught. He smiled his broadest and best, raising his mug to her. She groaned inwardly. One of the browns he'd sold her was probably colicky.

Wiping his frothy mouth with his sleeve, he gasped, "A proposition for you, Tad Di'nay!" He pointed to an empty bench beside the roaring hearth, "Shall we talk?"

She tipped her head and waved him on first, following him through the tables and crowd. The empty bench was usually the last to fill because of the heat of the hearthstones, but Diana had always been fairly partial to it herself.

"Now tell me of this proposition, Tad Nattersu? Have you not taken enough of my monies already?" and she dropped her cloak down before sitting on top of it. To date it had been her best method of not losing it in a brawl or rowdy dance.

"Well, Tad, I remember your dissatisfaction of this day when my animals were not up to spring stock."

"Aye," she said politely, cocking an ear towards him, but her eyes skimmed across the crowd. She paid particular attention to the brawny twosome that were so noisy behind the band; the slender one had a trim little beard, an anomaly in this region, but they were being treated like regulars.

"And I had promised myself, Tad, that should a better animal grace my stables before delivery of your strong pair — "

"That naturally you would think to allow me first honors?"

"Yes, my point precisely." He beamed cheerfully, his eyes rolling to look at her as his sweaty, round face was lost in his tankard once more.

"Well indeed I'm honored." Diana raised her mead with a slightly sarcastic gesture. They both knew she had the readiest money and the best need of a good horse and that Nattersu wasn't fool enough to let the opportunity slip by.

"It's a fine steed we're speaking about now." Nattersu pulled his arm across his jowl again. "He's very much to your liking — along the lines of your chestnut in Gronday I'm describing."

"So handsome?" Diana challenged good-naturedly. Gratefully, she suddenly sighted Pel, one of the tavern maids. The plump, brown-haired girl squealed and tossed a laugh in their direction. Diana raised her mug in salute, and with a saucy tug to her hair's kerchief, the girl disappeared into the kitchens.

"Now do not let the pretty thing cloud your mind!" Nattersu hastened on, knowing his time had just grown considerably shorter. He was no match for the wench's charms. "This is a fine animal. Fifteen hands and not a popped knee or swollen joint in his body!"

"Fifteen your saying?"

"Fit for the Dracoon's stables. Sleek, good grooming and sound in hoof— "

"Do tell, Tad, where did you come by such a beast?" Despite her friendly tone, Diana felt a strong suspicion creeping to mind. "Was he promised to another this afternoon and so you forgot to show him to me?"

"No, no," he said, laughing in relief at having captured her attention again. "He was sold to me just today — not so long after you'd left us."

"Do say?"

"Aye!" He nodded emphatically. "Two of the south county farmers brought him in. They raise some handsome horses right here in the region, you know."

She waited as he took another drink.

"And they come by with this fine gelding. A sorrel with sound legs, Tad. Very sound. It seems they'd run into the same marauder you may have..."

Best bet said they were friends of her marauder.

"...and their comrade then was cut down."

Diana grimaced. "Makes me thankful for the midnight stealth of my thieves."

"Aye. A deep slumber has saved many men's lives, I'd wager." Nattersu drank to that and then continued, "They saw the raider, you know? Shortish to middling man, garbed in green, they're saying. And riding a red horse."

"Not much of a description," Diana observed dryly. Her suspicions appeared to be correct. Someone was obviously intent on framing the Southern Trader. What a shame she'd left her chestnut stallion at the base. "Now back to this horse...?"

"Aye, aye. Fine animal as I was saying."

"It's just the one sorrel then?" She wasn't about to ride anything remotely 'red' at this point. "I need the other to keep pace with me, you rightly know now."

"Still — "

"And it's not that much of a journey back to Gronday, Tad." She looked considering into her half-empty mug but off to the side she saw Pel appear with a heaping tray of bread and steaming stew. "No, I think not, Tad. I consider myself honored by your attentions, but you were speaking true this day. You pointed out the pair is just right for my purposes. I believe I stand with your first advice."

"Oh, but — " he sputtered. "Tad Di'nay, surely...?"

"Di'nay!" Pel launched herself the last few feet, landing adroitly in Diana's lap without spilling a drop of mead. "You didn't send word you'd be coming tonight!"

Diana patently ignored Nattersu and charmingly played to the maid on her lap. "I couldn't stay away any longer, and to send word?" She lifted the woman's hand to her lips. "Why, Pel? I thought to tell you myself. Can you forgive me?"

Nattersu made a disgruntled snort, taking himself off for another tankard of ale.

"Naturally, you're forgiven," Pel giggled and, still balancing the plate, kissed Di'nay soundly. "Aye Tad...," she whispered softly, "you're still the best to kiss in the whole of these parts."

Diana grinned at her pleasure and offered her the seat that was so recently freed by Nattersu. Pel took the mead and kept Di'nay's arm snugly wrapped around her shoulders as she began to catch Di'nay up on the recent gossip.

With genuine pleasure Diana listened and started to work on the plate of food. Practice had taught her well how to eat in this particular one-handed fashion. Most of the inns that she'd come to frequent in the last tenmoons had a Pel or Atten or some maid waiting for her — it avoided the embarrassing moments that being single and available aroused when fathers were husband-shopping for their daughters, or innkeepers were marketing their tavern maids for the evening. It was an odd arrangement from Pel's perspective since the Southerner always looked for her, always coveted her for the evening, but never

— despite the affectionate, enthusiastic public displays like their greeting — never made the slightest of demands on her in private. Often she was carted off to the overhead lofts or occasionally even to a paid room, but it was for the peace and quiet of the place and not for sex. It had confused her. Even when she was doing the inviting, Di'nay was not buying — or more to the truth, not taking advantage of the purchase since the Southerner always paid very well. Although, Pel wasn't fool enough (nor were any of her counterparts in other taverns) to announce their activity to the whole of the commons. On the contrary, the money always suggested a variety of feats. Diana had been amazed at the stories that drifted back to her regarding the Southerner's prowess.

"I suppose you need to be leaving early tonight?" Pel said. "Since your ward — the bakery Min — she's birthing?"

Diana smiled reassuringly. "But I did have to see you before disappearing." With a gentle hand Diana brushed a curly lock back into place.

"Taks — he's saying you're to be gone. Your people are wanting you home?"

She sidled closer to the girl, grasping the small hand. "Will you miss me, Pel?"

She laughed awkwardly. Diana realized the girl had stopped playing their game.

"Pel?" Diana tipped the round, young face up to her.

"You're going away, that's all." She sniffled and her voice faltered. "You're going to have to train a new maid about liking your stew extra hot, now you hear? Don't expect to settle for just the cold dish when you're really wanting it hot!"

Diana nodded solemnly. She was touched at the very real concern beneath the simple order. "I promise you. I'll not be too quiet — "

"Too quiet you are! Come now, Trader. Share her some with the rest of us!"

Diana's arm intercepted the massive hand that grabbed for Pel. Steadily she met the half-drunken stare of the man standing over them. "You're not welcome here, Tad. Move along — "

"What for!? She's not too cursing good for the lot of us! It's time to share her for the dancing!" the drunkard bellowed, and with a sudden lurch he snatched Pel's wrist and pulled her to her feet. The half-empty mug tipped and threw the mead in an arc, dousing both Diana and the intruder.

Diana launched herself to her feet with a solid left to the ruffian's chin, and he toppled backwards, crashing table, chairs, and patrons on his way. The ring of the sword leaving its sheath sent Pel slipping off and customers scrambling aside.

The music hushed, and the man shook his head before it registered that he was staring up at a sword point. The scowl deepened, and the glaze in his eyes sobered to dark fury. He scrambled backwards, gaining his feet and jerking his blade from its tattered scabbard. He inched away slowly into the clearing of the dance floor, and Diana followed him, sword circling.

"Taks!" Nattersu whispered harshly. "Stop them — Jekin'll kill the scrawny likes of the Southerner!"

"Hmm, you weren't in the last time, were you?" The barkeeper paused in drying a mug to watch the wary figures. The Dracoon's stable-hand was a good head taller than Di'nay and twice the bulk, but Taks remembered other fights and other swordsmen. He shrugged and put away the mug. "Di'nay is short-tempered but just. Obvious Tad Jekin's to fault."

"But Di'nay — "

"Can handle himself well enough," Taks said firmly and glanced at the empty stein in Nattersu's grasp. "Do you need a bit more there, Tad?"

Nattersu's eyes still followed the tensed pair. "Why don't they do something?"

"Jekin will soon," Taks replied matter-of-factly and handed him a full tankard.

Jekin did. With a gruesome cry and two hands to the hilt, the sword arched high and down. It deflected easily with a singing clash. Again it sliced from the left, but Diana stepped quick and parried, sword in her left hand. Bewildered, the bigger man circled, uneasily keeping his sword to the front.

"I want your apology, Tad," Diana muttered tersely, her gaze riveted to the man's black eyes. He was watching her sword tip.

With a growl and yell the blade came down, literally bouncing in his grasp as Diana met force with force. A booted foot hooked out and his knee folded, the sword clattering to the floor ahead of his thudding body. Diana stomped on his chest, sending the air out with a whoosh and then wedged her boot between his chin and Adam's apple. Her silver blade danced within inches of his eyes.

"I asked for an apology," Diana repeated coldly.

"Aye Tad," he wheezed, "you and your maid there...beg your patience."

The foot left his neck and the blade lifted. She strode around his gasping bulk, her sword still between them, to where his weapon lay. She stooped to retrieve it and passed it across the bar to Taks. As house rules in Colmar stood, the man would get it back an hour after Di'nay's departure — no sooner.

"Your apology is accepted," Diana replied formally and sheathed her blade. "I stand assured it was our misunderstanding."

He nodded blankly, trying to roll to his feet, and a couple of friends moved to help him. The music began again, and there was a general scuffle as furniture was righted. There was no sign of the bearded fellow and his bulky companion now.

It was time to go. Nattersu had told Diana enough and the men she sought were unlikely to try a brawl with her tonight. It was too uncommon a thing, tempting the Fates by challenging a swordsman already known as the evening's victor.

"We'll be missing your temper," Taks remarked blandly.

"Now I'm not so bad," Diana returned good-naturedly, dabbing the mead from her new jerkin with the rag he offered. "I haven't been fighting in here since — since last harvest! A full tenmoon, Taks!"

He rubbed his nose thoughtfully. "We could do with a little more excitement."

She laughed and threw the rag on the counter.

Nattersu grunted. "Your maid is gone. So much for your gallant efforts." And he stumbled off bemoaning the lack of loyalty in womenfolk.

"Pel always runs off when you fight," Taks grumbled by way of a reassurance.

Diana dug into her pocket for her money. "I once had her promise me so."

"Now that's a strange sort of promise."

"Is it?" She jingled the money thoughtfully. "If I died, I'd not want her to see it."

He scoffed with a grunt.

"See she gets this?" Diana handed him the money. As owner of the inn's maids, he'd get half, but Diana knew the rest would make its way to Pel.

He raised his eyebrows at the amount. "A pretty piece for spoiled service."

"A going off present," Diana retorted and covered his closed fist with her hand. "May the Mother hold you, Tad Taks."

"Aye," he nodded soberly, "and you, Southerner."

Diana grinned and released him. She claimed her cloak and at the tavern door paused to don it, glancing behind. The innkeeper had become engrossed with his duties and other patrons, the smoke curled thickly, and the hub-bub had risen to a steady din. There was not a soul who actually watched her leave and she knew it.

Chapter Fourteen

Elana jerked upright, waking from her half-slumber, and jumped off the hall chest. Someone was coming. She squinted to see through the wavy glass panel that framed the door and made out the amarin of the approaching figure. For a brief moment, she allowed herself to slump in relief, then hurriedly she attacked the door's bulky lock and latch.

Diana was surprised to find her companion waiting in the threshold. "I had thought to find you in bed!" She ducked quickly to enter, but did not stoop low enough and the door frame snagged at her hood before allowing passage. Annoyed, she glanced over her shoulder. It had been centuries since the city had actually been attacked, but the small, easily defensible doorways had only grown more ornate, not taller, and they were generally too low for Diana's liking.

"It's Maryl, Tad," Elana answered in a hushed whisper, careful of the servants in the neighboring room as she helped Di'nay off with her cloak and sword.

"Tell me."

"The mid-wife left shortly after you. Min Maryl would not let her take the pair to save herself." Elana moistened her dry lips and continued, "She has not told Tad Bowgyn. He believes the woman will return at dawn when most needed."

"He knows she carries twins?"

Elana shook her downcast head as one of the servants crossed the hall behind her and disappeared into the kitchen. Then she hurried on. "Maryl was adamant that he not know. Szori says she speaks of dying before denying him a child."

"Stupid little fool — "

"Please Tad!" Elana quieted her urgently, glancing over her shoulder with mute warning. "Szori was sworn to silence, but — she was scared."

"And by rights to be," Diana sighed wearily. Now what to do? She straightened slightly, asking, "Can you get the mid-wife back?"

"Certainly, but — "

"I'll deal with Maryl and Bowgyn."

"But... Di'nay!" Elana's hand clutched at her arm as the Amazon started down the hall. "It's too late for...she's been in labor so long. Her muscles — are fighting against her now. This mid-wife...I fear her skill is no longer enough."

Diana felt very cold. It couldn't be that simple. "Have you seen Maryl?" she asked quietly. "Are you certain it is too late?"

"No, I have not seen her." Elana spoke bluntly. "That's part of the problem." Di'nay looked at her then and Elana's voice softened. "Maryl demands solitude until the mid-wife's mythical return — except for Szori. Tad Bowgyn will honor the request. He will not let me see her."

"Could you help if he did?"

Elana hesitated, both confident and despairing. "I could save her, but the children...? She would learn of my Sight. I could keep the bondstone from her, I think."

"She has kept darker secrets," Diana said abruptly. "What do you need?"

"I have everything upstairs in my medicine purse, but I need to tend her alone."

Diana nodded steadily. "Get your purse. I'll deal with Bowgyn."

❋ ❋ ❋

"In'erfering bitch — " Maryl hissed at the ceiling. Her knuckles were white, her skin dark as she clenched at the loosened sheets. "She never could keep to her own business!"

Elana smiled consolingly from her place at the firehearth. She stirred the warming brew in the small cauldron and sniffed the spooned contents. Not quite satisfied, she elected to leave it a few more minutes.

"Where in Fates' Cellars did she find you anyway?"

Elana's hand cautiously stole over her lifestone. Even after several hours, the intermittent refocus of Maryl's amarin was unpredictable. The pain and strain in the woman's body were steadily overwhelming all Elana's awareness.

"In the mountains," Elana replied finally. The liquid threatened to bubble, and she quickly turned to pull it clear of the flames.

"The Council's people?" Maryl's sweating face glistened in the firelight. "Does the fire have to be so hot? Wood could be scarce come winter...?"

"It must be hot," Elana reassured her softly, mixing her brew with fresh water. It must be hot, she thought — weary of it herself — or the woman's muscles would tense without control and the infants would not be able to deal with the new environment. But it was excruciatingly hot in this room. The fire leapt the full height of the hearth, and both women were dark skinned and soaking wet in their kirtles.

"I am right." Maryl restlessly rolled her head back to face the younger woman. "You're Council's people."

"Yes, I am." Elana approached her bed and gently eased down beside her. "Now you must drink this."

"What is it?" she snapped suspiciously, but she was too weak to protest more. Elana's arm slid beneath her, lifting her upright, and she found the touch seemed strangely comforting.

"Sip it," Elana commanded softly, gently bending the amarin around the woman.

Breathing with difficulty, Maryl finished the small cup. It seemed to take forever even for such a little bit, and exhausted, she let her head sag into Elana's shoulder. "What is it?"

"Herb tea," Elana allowed, and after setting aside the cup, she began gathering up the discarded pillows with her free hand.

"Worse than her southways tea," Maryl muttered. "What was Di'nay doing with the Council's people?"

Elana chuckled quietly and lowered Maryl back into the pillows so that she continued to sit almost upright. "Where did she find you?"

"Tavern," Maryl closed her eyes against the tired aching of her body. "A little place to Gronday an' south... Ramains' south, not Deserts south. She and that Southern friend of hers were downstairs in the commons. Mother, she couldn't even speak the language. But the other could — Liest. You met Tad Liest?"

"No."

"Nice...woman like Di'nay though...two of them get together every so often. She always treated me real nice. Never let on where they found me. Couple other southerners came through now and then, but she never looked forward to them. Always meant work and traveling off. But not Liest. That one would come an' sometimes just visit."

"Sounds like a good friend."

"Wouldn't know," Maryl mumbled. That was too close to the truth. She tried to slide further down under the sheets.

Gently, Elana stayed her movement. "You can't have a baby flat on your back, Min. It will hurt too much."

"Mother — you even sound like her...wretched calm tone — never upset, not her!" Maybe that was why Maryl could believe in this young woman's touch?

"Why're you with her?" Please, Maryl thought, talk about anything but this loathsome body right now.

"I choose to be." Elana wiped her own forehead with the hem of the ragged, borrowed kirtle she wore. She had tied her hair back, but wisps of it were damp and clinging about her face. She pushed them aside with a sigh.

"Mother! You'd think the Council's village wouldn't have to be like all the rest...with the poor and the beatings." Maryl's mouth felt cottony and dry and the words came out sluggishly. "Is there any water?"

"Only tea for you," Elana returned firmly and diluted another cup for her.

"I was like you once," Maryl began again when she'd finished the drink. "Thought it was better than what was before."

"Wasn't it?" Elana asked quietly, only half-listening as she pulled a small knife of black glass from her purse and slipped it into the coals.

"She and Liest found me in a brawl, you know?" Maryl rattled on as her mind slipped back to the dampness and darkness of that night. "A prospective buyer was trying me on," she quipped with leering sarcasm. "I was too old for Mit'et — sell for what bit a'profits could be made. Mit'et didn't much care what was buying me." She blinked back the tears. Funny, she had thought that done with. "Brute finally finished with me, but I decided — only thing in my life I'd ever thought I could decide — I decided it'd be better dying than seeing more moons with that sort of man. So I grabbed for his knife."

Elana watched her curiously from the hearth. So much made sense now.

"Only the idiot thought I meant to hurt him and started hitting me around some more. Didn't work out just like Mit'et wanted." She laughed without much humor, remembering her skinny innkeeper's outrage as his buyer threw her and the door across the common's balcony. Di'nay and Liest had drawn swords and ended the fiasco in a matter of minutes. "You see, Tad Di'nay laid the monies out then. But Mit'et was no fool — not really such. He asked a better price and got it. He sent me off then and figured good rid'nce."

"And you?" Elana asked again. "Was it not better to be with Di'nay?"

She wheezed a very tired sigh. "She taught me manners...taught me maybe how to think. Sometimes I still...who'd have dreamed it? A slave with ideas? Then maybe that's how you stop being a slave — one way or the other...."

"You're not going to die," Elana responded to her silent panic. She clasped the damp hand in her own two. "At least not tonight."

She clutched at Elana, gritting her teeth to stifle a cry of pain as a contraction hit. It passed in a moment, and then Elana gently loosened a hand to grab a towel from the water basin. Carefully she cooled Maryl's browning face with the cloth.

"I thought no more," Maryl whispered limply, her eyes still shut. "You worked so hard to...to stop them?"

"It's time for them to start again," Elana explained quietly. "The tea you drank will hurry you along now."

"It's almost over?"

"Yes. It's almost over." Elana dabbed her hot face tenderly and nodded, unable to voice how much worse it would be before... but it would soon be done. The first child had crowned — finally. After so many hours of enforced relaxation, of gentle massaging... of patient blue bonding through Maryl's frightened gaze, the child had finally turned, and now the herb would prompt the rest.

And prompt her it did. With a fury, almost doubled from the hypnotic denial, the contractions returned. Maryl clung to the calm voice so far away... following orders... following orders, that's what she knew how to do... could do that well... had been raised doing it... following orders... but her age was battling with the Fates' guise and she pushed when Elana called not to. She sobbed as she tried to control her body... push or wait? Which was what? Dear Mother help...!

Elana locked her blue gaze into Maryl's tear-blurred vision and joined her pain. Her fingers worked frantically, spreading the white salve around the small neck and straining vagina... easing the friction... stretching tissues... slowly inching the life-giving cord free from its strangling hold, and all the time clenching teeth with the straining woman... holding muscles still... praying with her silent screams... and the child slipped free... shoulders... an arm... hips... all toes accounted for. Dear Mother not so quickly... but the cord had knotted and another small foot appeared... or had both cords tangled? There was too little tissue — too little time to follow the rhythms of Maryl's tiring body — to trace the flowing energies and unknot the mangle. Maryl's screams silenced again under her Sight and again they strained for the strength to pause and turn it. Then breach it must be... salved fingers slid deep — grasping for the other foot... pushing... pulling... pray, Mother, for speed now... and finally... finally... finally done.

Maryl sobbed hard and stilled in the pain. She sagged with the Sight's touch gone, her eyes closing, but Elana hurried... racing against the mocking Fates. So long, so tight the cords had been wrapped... how long had the pulsing flow been restricted? How long completely halted for both of them? They stirred, barely striving... and concentrating, with a delicate gentleness that she had rarely ever called upon, she reached out to them with her blue touch — coaxing their hearts into that pulsing rhythm of life... their lungs to draw and breathe. Wishing desperately that she had more hands, but not daring to pause, she rubbed them with the warmed salve — touched them... kept reminding them that they were alive, and all the while she kept that fragile blue bond with them, urging them to live. Gradually each began to respond — a kick... a jerking arm — and she almost laughed with relief as they convulsively stretched and tightened their small limbs. They were far from crying, far from eating, she knew, but they were breathing.

Tenderly she wrapped them snug and placed them in the bundled quilts on the floor nearer the fire. Her Blue Sight stretched to keep the sheltering calm over the small bodies — still attuned to their pulse and breath — still prompting, guiding their way to life as she turned her attention to Maryl. The contractions continued less violently, and gently she pulled at the last of the placenta. It came away cleanly, no infections — no evidence of hemorrhaging either, she noted gratefully. She thought the Mother had finally interceded to temper the games of the Fates. Hurriedly she washed the woman, fixing the dressings before changing the sheets.

"Are they dead?" Maryl asked finally, only dimly aware of being settled into the clean linens. "Was it all for Fates' Jest?"

"You are alive. Tad Bowgyn will not think poorly of that." Elana murmured reassuringly. She glanced at the children – her Sight again steadying their faltering rhythms.

"But the children?"

"They live – for the moment." She did not hesitate in her honesty. "It's too soon, Min. I do not know if they will survive to see dawn."

Absorbing the thought, Maryl nodded. Yet there was more hope to be had than the darkfall had promised. "May I hold them? I would know them each before they leave, if they must."

Elana smiled gently and squeezed her shoulder. She had seen mothers reject a struggling infant, fearing to look at it because the Fates might snatch it away. It would do these two well to hear their mother's heart again. Gently she eased each within an open arm, propping pillows and quilts to keep them close despite Maryl's weakness.

"What are they, Ona?" Maryl asked with difficulty. Her throat constricted and her eyes blurred with tears from a different kind of pain now. "Do they 'ave all their limbs? All their fingers?...toes?"

"Yes Min, each has everything. They are beautiful sons."

"Sons?" she sobbed in surprise and the pain deepened. She had not thought the Mother would give Bowgyn a son – not after her past. "Both of them?"

"Yes." Elana nodded and curled up on the foot of the bed, her back against the footboard. It saddened her faintly that both were sons, but then she realized she'd been thinking of Di'nay as their guardian – not Bowgyn. Vaguely she wondered how Sisters had babies, but it was a very distant thought, and her head lulled against the bedpost. Daybreak was still long in coming...the vigil was not yet over. Slowly, her attention narrowed as her eyes grew unfocused. She slipped into a hazy blue place where nothing existed but the bond between her and the children – and her struggle to teach them to breathe.

Shortly before the first light the second born failed. He died without ever tasting his mother's milk; he had been too weak. But the arrival of day saw the first born summon his father with a shrill wail.

✽ ✽ ✽

Diana joined the small family for a moment, extending sympathies and admiration. But as Szori departed to prepare the littlest for burial, Diana turned to where Elana sat quietly in the far corner of the room. She was nestled into the windowseat with her head tipped back against the wall. Her arms were wrapped wearily about her knees, and the old, borrowed kirtle was soiled with dried blood. Despite the fact that her skin had grown pale again, she looked exhausted.

Eyes half-closed, Elana turned her head as her Shadowmate came to squat beside her. Di'nay's intentions radiated a concern mixed with a shining pride, and like a child hugging in the warmth of a fire, Elana squeezed her knees to her chest. In truth she was too drained to have tended to much save the baby, but Di'nay's subtle strength was releasing her from even that chore now.

"The lad is suckling happily...and Bowgyn will stay until Szori returns," Diana murmured. Gently she brushed the hair from the corner of a blue eye. "Will you come sleep now?"

Fuzzily Elana nodded but moving was the last thing her body wanted to do. Her fingers loosened and painfully her knees unbent a fraction of an inch. Between the foot of the bed and this windowseat, she realized that she'd spent close to four hours knotted tight.

"Let me," Diana said. Elana didn't think to protest as arms encircled her and lifted. With a single bounce Diana shifted the woman's weight for balance and carried her from the room. Elana's arms wrapped around her neck, and she snuggled into the cool fabric of the Amazon's tunic.

"You smell good," Elana mumbled as she recognized a faint, clean scent that had nothing to do with the soap and water of the earlier bath. A deep-throated chuckle echoed kindly in her ears as they climbed the stairs.

A booted foot swung the door closed with something of a rattle, and Diana hesitated, turning to glance around the room.

"You're strong too," Elana muttered, still in that same half-drugged tone.

"I'm an Amazon," Diana reminded her with a grin, and her warm brown gaze rested on her sleepy charge. "Where's your clean kirtle, Darling?"

The faintly rational piece of her mind was still struggling with the fact that Di'nay was so completely unperturbed by her weight, but the endearment finally registered. Somewhat startled she roused herself and lifted her head, wondering if she had heard the word or if the soft amarin had triggered a mental echo.

"A...my pack," she managed. "Why do I need my kirtle? Are we leaving?"

"You're sleeping," Diana corrected firmly. "But not in this old thing."

"But I don't sleep in anything." That was right, she thought, confused. Perhaps she was supposed to...no, she knew her own habits, didn't she? Why was it so hard to think around this Amazon? She did smell good.

"Then nothing it is," Diana agreed easily. She withheld a teasing comment.

"Is that your tea?" Elana asked, suddenly aware of another scent in the air.

Di'nay deposited her carefully on the large bed. Her fingers pulled patiently at the laces in the kirtle's bodice. "Would you like some?"

That sounded delightful, Elana thought. "Mhmm, please."

She stripped the old garment off over her head as Di'nay fetched her the drink. It felt good to slide between the cool layers of the sheets, and the cobwebs in her head seemed to lessen. Somehow just knowing the luxury of sleep was near made the urgency for it fade. The change of the rooms — in the tensions — it felt so good.

The tea was delicious and not too hot. It eased the ache of her parched throat. She smiled as Di'nay produced her comb and almost eagerly wiggled to the center of the bed to make room for the Amazon.

The long, tempered strokes pulled through her hair and the weariness was freed with the tangles. The tea refreshed and soothed. The gentle hands calmed. As the comb finally slid without catching time and again, a long, low purr passed through her lips. She was content.

"Done with your tea?" Diana queried softly.

Elana nodded, smiling gratefully over her shoulder as Di'nay took the cup away. "Thank you," she said suddenly, remembering her manners.

"Thank you," Diana said softly. She dropped another log into the flames, and starting to undress, she came to bed. "You saved Maryl's life — and the little one's."

Elana sighed in regret. "The second was so close — "

"The Mother will hold him near," Diana murmured softly. She shed the last of her garments and snuffed out the candle. Beside the bed she paused, silently considering the young woman. "You did more than the Fates had thought possible, Elana. There was nothing else that could have been done."

Elana smiled faintly, eyes fixed on the fire beyond the footboard. "It was the Mother's doing that they were even alive so late in carrying. We of Aggar are such poor bearers of twins."

"It is simply the way you are built." Diana climbed into bed cautiously. Every nurturing instinct she possessed was crying out for her to gather this woman near to hold and sleep. But she also knew herself well enough to know that compassion was not the sole motivator in such desires.

Elana looked at Di'nay, and for a long moment they were still as the flickering shadows danced about them. A small voice in the corner of Elana's mind asked if she had learned nothing from last night, but she was achingly tired — and lonely. She moistened her lips and ventured, "I see something of your amarin...would I be unwelcome if — if I asked that you hold me?" She looked at her hands. "I would like you to, I think."

Startled, Diana realized it was the first such statement from Elana she believed. The knot in her own stomach began to unwind. This woman — with her shining dark hair cloaking her back — the ivory of her face and shoulders shimmering in the firelight — was beautiful.

"You'd be very welcomed," Diana murmured. Her touch on Elana's shoulder was gentle as she drew her down and into her arms. The coolness of their skins warmed quickly...just as quickly their unease melted.

The softness of the shoulder under her cheek amazed her, and Elana wondered if women were always so soft — so incredibly soft. Her hand slid tentatively across the arched ribs before Di'nay pulled it higher to rest between her breasts. The tender clasp stayed, coveting Elana's hand.

The clean scent that Elana was beginning to associate with Di'nay warmed with the heat of their closeness and gradually enveloped her senses. Her body relaxed in the languid grasp of Di'nay's amarin, and with contentment she slipped off to sleep.

❄ ❄ ❄

Chapter Fifteen

At the faint knock, Diana looked up from her seat beside the fire. Her eyes sought the still figure huddled beneath the covers, hoping Elana was undisturbed. Satisfied, Diana quietly shrugged off the heavy blanket, slid on her tunic, and crossed the room. Maryl had instructed the girl well, Diana thought with relief. She cracked the door to find Szori leaning patiently against the far wall. But then Maryl was even more wary of others discovering Di'nay's sex than Diana herself was.

"Tad...." The girl half-bobbed a curtsy in greeting. "My Master would have you know the horses arrived."

"Fine," Diana whispered, "send them to the stables. I am not prepared to travel today."

The girl nodded nervously, eyes fixed on the bare toes visible below the blanket's edges. "Will you be needing your breakfast fetched up for you, Tad?"

Diana suppressed a smile; it was almost mid-day. "Enough for two. Knock and leave it at the door."

"Aye, Tad." She bobbed again and scampered away.

Did she really look as if she ate unsuspecting housemaids for breakfast? Diana grinned and shut the door carefully to turn and dress. Actually, she doubted that she looked as imposing as most men would in the morning, considering her lack of whiskers. It was fortunate that in reality the Southern Desert Peoples rarely could grow heavy beards.

Diana cinched her belt loosely and settled down into her fireside chair again with the blanket wrapped around her. She really was getting too finicky about clean clothes and weather and such.

Thunder rumbled somewhere. Winter was threatening early this season. Outside rain splattered heavily against the shuttered windows, dimming the already gray light. She shifted, returning her gaze to the hearthstones as memories descended.

Heavy rain can be the Goddess' blessing, Terri had often said. "You warm the fires and gather your family. It's a time to remember your children and to spin stories. And when you're older, it's an extra moment to treasure with your lover...."

Diana blinked as the tears stung the backs of her eyes unexpectedly. She had been ten, maybe eleven years old when Terri had taken her up on her lap and talked of rains and things. Barely a season later her Aunt Ivory, Terri's mate, had died in the spring flood. It had never changed the way Terri spoke of the seasons' cycles or of the Goddess, but it changed her smile. It tempered the teasing mirth — the careless laughter that her family had always known from her. She still laughed and she was still very loving, giving and even happy — especially since she'd joined with Bess. But the reckless abandon had been washed away in those foaming waters.

Odd, she hadn't thought about Terri's loss in a long, long time.

Diana remembered Terri's arrival had coincided with the birth of her cousin, Rosa. The two additions had brought the family's total to eleven...three

couples, four children, and Oma Hanna. Hanna had taken the summer in stride
and welcomed all with plans for a new wing. By fall the adobe house had fairly
doubled in size, Aunt Ivory was again on Shekhina for Moonbase duty, and
Terri was proving herself invaluable to the family's sanity.

Smiling, Diana remembered climbing into Terri's lap and those strong
arms holding tight. That particular stormy day had only been one of many. For
whatever unfathomable reasons children choose, Terri had become her idol,
and the loving woman had done her best never to disillusion her small niece.
Diana chuckled. The entire family had probably recognized the girlish crush.

Diana could remember her mother, Kate, smiling as she would
seriously cite Terri's opinion or advice. She half-suspected that on many
occasions, Terri had merely re-iterated Kate's words.

And on that day? When she had spoken of lovers' stolen moments?
What had she been saying?

Diana remembered the gray-blue eyes and the shaggy, dark hair that
tousled across Terri's pale forehead and tapered down between her shoulders.
Diana had been asking about what lovers did and why sex was not always spoken
of as lovemaking. Very weighty questions for a ten-year-old, Diana mused. But
Morgan, the eldest of the four — no five, by then Jasmin had been born —
Morgan for the first time was dating someone seriously, and Diana had been
hearing Oma Hanna and the adults worrying about her. Diana hadn't quite
understood why seeing a friend frequently could suddenly result in so much
crying and hurt. It had seemed as if Morgan was terribly unhappy one day and
joyously excited the next.

Her mother had tried to explain. But Diana had only vaguely grasped
that it had something to do with the difference between making love and having
sex. So she had trotted off to the living room to ask Terri.

Diana smiled wryly. Couldn't really say that she had learned a lot from
Terri either, considering the string of disasters she'd muddled through since
going off-world. But she doubted that Terri had been at fault there.

"Sometimes you feel all wound up and ready to skip and dance," she
had said, "just like a top before you set it spinning. Then sometimes it feels
mellow and warm like late at night when you're sitting around the hearthstones
listening to Gum Lin sing...or Oma Hanna chant.

"If you meet someone and you're thinking about them just about all of
the time — and you're feeling like a top ready to spin, then she might become
your friend or maybe even your lover. If you meet someone that always makes
you feel warm and safe, then she may become your very dear friend...and well,
maybe your lover after a very long time. But when you find someone who makes
you feel one way sometimes and the other way other times, then you've found
someone who could be very, very special to you. And you may want to be her
friend or become her lover. But then you have to be careful, Diana, because you
may — deep down inside — truly want her to be your mate, and it can hurt a
whole lot if you really want to spend a lifetime with her and she just wants to be
friends for a little while."

They had talked more about what Morgan or her friend might be feeling, and about how Diana might act differently someday, but Diana didn't remember much else from that talk. There were days she doubted she remembered any of Terri's wisdom, but today was not one of them.

Diana turned sideways in her chair and rested her head against the back as she looked towards the bed. Elana was buried deeply under the quilts, curled tight in a fetal position, not even her dark hair visible. She wondered if Elana had been re-living the birthing in her dreams.

Diana hadn't felt that wound-up top feeling in ages. What she had felt briefly with Maryl resembled it, but with this dark-haired little shea...? Her own sexual awareness had a much different pull to it — much less urgent with her. The woman was beautiful; few Sisters — Amazons or not — would not find her attractive....

But that other kind of love...that had been missing in her life. That warming, home-hearth kinship that bound friends together for a lifetime. Was that what she was so constantly on guard against now? Given that they did not have the possibility of a lifetime together, was it the pain at their parting that she feared? Being lonely had made Diana doubly vulnerable and even less trusting of her judgment as well as weary of losses and good-byes.

But what would be their parting be like if she truly kept Elana at arms' length?

If she drew back and remained on the logical but companionable footing she had originally intended, in a monarc what would be missing at their parting? Did she really want to leave Elana without ever knowing her? Had she grown so cynical that she would not cherish the beauty of an early bud simply because the frost would not let it open?

And their attraction?

Diana sighed. She had desired and declined before, and seldom regretted it. At times it had been difficult, at other times easily ignored.

But last night she had tempered her feelings rather than flatly rejecting them and it had felt good. Diana smiled very faintly; perhaps the Goddess was beginning to prepare her for Home?

❄ ❄ ❄

Circling, swirling, her fingers slid through the lush moisture...the woman's hips arched and pushed upwards into her grasp...trembling, fluttering downward, then exploding with a deep-throated moan. The touch eased — playing...soothing...her mouth kissed the darkened skin tenderly, nuzzling the heavy, soft breast aside — burying kisses in the warm valley.

"Beautiful...," Diana purred, half-drugged in the softness beneath her, "so very beautiful — "

A sob of pure anguish escaped the woman and, alarmed, Diana paused, lifting her head as she said, "It's what I do!"

Diana jumped, bolting upright from her dream.

"Di'nay?" Elana's hand questioningly touched her arm.

"It's all right," Diana mumbled quickly. "Just a dream. Go back to sleep."

"For certain?"

Diana said stiffly, "I'll get up and get some tea." She forced herself to throw back the thin blanket. She slid on her boots, refusing to acknowledge the cold, and crawled out from beneath the low branches of the silverwood pine where they had camped for the night.

She built the fire up brighter than she needed to, to chase the darkness back. She desperately wished the dream images would flee with it. Cruelly she pinched the bridge of her nose, but that pain did not free her. She set the water to heat and squatted, her fingers tucked under her armpits, rather than getting her gloves and cloak which lay with her bedding.

She shivered again, but it was not from the frosty night. She squeezed her eyes shut and faced that dream — that dream of the event which Maryl had so feared might happen. That fear had surfaced during their third monarc together, after Cleis' visit. Maryl had finally understood the relationship Leist and Di'nay shared.

Maryl had been too much a creature of the punishing restrictions of her upbringing not to have been shaken and terrified by that understanding. The world she lived in was a very different one from that of the Council. Once again Diana wondered at the tolerance of that Council for the barbaric customs of the peoples they tried to guide. She did not have Elana's faith.

Her dream had been a muddle of desires and — shame. Initially she had cared for the woman, and in the back of her mind she had hoped one day to become closer. But during the monarc following Cleis' visit, they had lived with Maryl's silent terror, and Diana had been at a loss for what to do.

She had never thought of herself as a threat to another woman's safety. But the frightened silence that had struck if she glanced up and the shuffling gait that had hurried Maryl away had been brutal testimony to the contrary. She did not even dare ask Maryl what violence she feared.

Her personal experience on other planets with homophobia had been limited to silent distaste or ludicrous, loud hypocrisy. There had been some ugliness, but never this utter fear. She felt guilt because of her attraction to the woman and shame in being attracted when Maryl's unwillingness was so blatantly evident.

And so the caring dreams had changed...had become stories of insensitivity and abused power fueled by her fears of inadequacy. In their life she had searched for covert pressures...persuasions with which she might be intimidating her new friend; she found none. She grasped for ways to affirm Maryl's control in their day-to-day living, and finally — slowly, she had seen the trust return. Yet the dreams had stayed.

Diana had finally realized that the dreams sprang from the fact that she 'owned' the woman. The tradition which allowed her to own a malá and her services combined with Diana's desires created a situation in which Maryl had no options, just as if Diana had truly been a man of Maryl's society. If Diana pressed, Maryl would have had no recourse.

Diana's shame at creating the situation — maintaining the situation — had haunted her while her rational mind spoke of the social limits with which they both struggled. The truth was that Diana n'Athena had stepped so close to her personal line of integrity that she feared she had crossed it.

Diana opened her eyes. Dear Goddess, had she unwittingly walked into that situation again? Or this time had she arrogantly assumed she could master the nuances and prevent the terror, and all the while she was forgetting that there were so many ways to abuse power.

Mechanically she added the tea to the boiling water. She sat down with a bump and crossed her legs wearily. Had she truly broken her pledge never to put another in that position?

Covering her eyes, Diana sighed. They had been up with the sun, were averaging twenty-six leagues a day, and they hadn't crossed a sign of humans — all too much time for thinking.

"Di'nay...?" Dressed in black underknits, Elana stood barefooted behind her.

Diana shook her head clear, pulling the tea from the fire. "I did not mean to wake you. Why don't you go back to sleep? Daybreak won't be long in coming."

Then, stepping nearer, Elana knelt behind the Amazon and wrapped her bare arms around the woman's shoulders, hugging her protectively. She murmured, her mouth near Di'nay's ear, "We both need sleep. That doesn't mean we can."

Diana surrendered with a sigh and leaned her head back into the welcoming shoulder. If the Goddess could only let some things be simple. The trembling in her body faded gradually as Elana's breath warmed her cheek and her arms cradled her.

"Tell me of this ghost that haunts you."

Diana's head lifted, and her hands covered the hugging arms almost as if to ensure their embrace. She drew a breath, staring into the depths of the night. Not far off the hill dropped away, and the stars shimmered, silhouetting the mountains' wall that rose in the North. She felt very close to the Mother here, if she would just let go of her fears and high-handed expectations.

"Have you ever seen a woman attacked?" Diana murmured softly.

"Through the Seers," Elana replied just as quietly.

"Have you ever seen her intimidated by the threat of it?"

Elana's arms tightened. She was not deceived by the use of pronouns. "You speak of Maryl."

A disbelieving laugh died shortly. "Do you ever miss anything?"

Elana smiled and pressed a kiss against the feathered brown hair.

"I created a situation — it wasn't right."

"You did not attack her," Elana reminded her. "We are not always responsible for the situations we find ourselves in — only for what we do once there."

"I paid money for her. I was responsible for that exchange."

"You did what was necessary," Elana countered softly. "If you had not paid, the Dracoon's men would have followed you."

"It was not right."

"It was unfortunate," Elana murmured, remembering much of Maryl's disclosure before and during the birthing...and much more that the Sight had shown her. "You can not change the ways of Aggar, Di'nay. Even the Council must work across generations and generations of people for change."

"But," her head lowered as she breathed her fears, "was that why I bought her?"

Gently Elana's cheek pressed Di'nay's as she quietly, distinctly prodded, "The question is, Diana n'Athena, if you had known of her reluctance, would you still have paid?"

"I couldn't — leave her there," Diana stammered brokenly. "She — they — she was almost beaten to death."

"The Fates set the game in motion and the players choose their alliance."

Diana's brow knit in confusion, but she was listening.

"You did what was necessary," Elana repeated. "There was no evil in your choice. And desires?" She shrugged, thinking again of Maryl. "You hid them well. Maryl feared you might be attracted to her, but your respect for her limits led her to have faith in your friendship...and in her own worth."

"In truth?" Diana's breath caught in her throat.

She hugged the Amazon nearer, their cheeks touching as she said, "In truth."

Diana's brown eyes closed as she leant back in Elana's grasp, the aching in her head soothed and her body warmed. Perhaps now the nightmares would finally leave her?

She recognized the scent the night breeze stirred as the subtle fragrance of the woman holding her. Perhaps not.

"I am not Maryl," Elana whispered fiercely, courageous in her outrage. Releasing Di'nay to face her, she said, "I am Elana, Shadow of Council and Keep, here by choice." Tenderly her hand touched the wind-bronzed cheek of the Amazon. "I do not shy from your grasp, Di'nay. Please — do not see another in me...."

She would have to be blind to do that, Diana thought, cherishing the sight of her as her skin was touched by gold from the fire's light and her dark tresses were unruly wisps about her face. The shimmering, dancing blueness of her eyes was spellbinding. The soft angles of her face...the almost upward lift of her nose...dear Goddess, she was beautiful. Diana's eyes rested, mesmerized by the full, half-parted lips that were tensed just slightly at their corners. She could almost taste their softness. A warning bell clamored somewhere — far off in her mind, but drawn by the beauty, Diana leaned nearer — slowly. Aware of every nuance of the woman before her, she gave her every chance to withdraw. She was amazed; the light fingers against her cheek were steady and Elana did not retreat.

Her amazement was eclipsed as her eyes shut...their lips met...molding perfectly...the melting warmth reaching. Subtly she moved...skin rubbing skin...igniting a satiny friction — begging a response.

Frightened that the sensitive sharing might halt — Elana dared to return the exploring touch. Skimming...grasping...meeting Di'nay's every move, she leaned into the kiss — and lost her partner.

Questioningly her blue eyes flew open. Di'nay studied her with an intensity that obliterated her Sight's decipherings.

"I can't tell if you've done this," Diana said cautiously. Her heart pounded with a ferocity that she had forgotten it could possess. This feeling could not be hers only, could it?

"Never this," Elana breathed. Oh Mother, no one had ever spoken of this....

She's not Maryl, Diana's mind echoed. In one fluid, careful motion she gathered Elana into her arms and lowered her to the ground. There was not a single protest uttered. Elana's hands slid about her. The warmth of her arms penetrated Diana's tunic — a fiery touch — a possessive pull that dissolved the distance between Diana and the soft body.

With infinite tenderness Diana kissed her again. Her soft, brushing lips tingling nerves as she held her breath.

Elana gasped. Di'nay's mouth paused, hovering so near. Elana's arms tightened, urging, and the subtle touch returned. So light...so fine...so attuned to the other they shared the sweet, breathless intensity.

What was she doing?! Diana's mouth pulled free. Goddess no!

"No...!!" Elana cried, clutching Di'nay as her world tore apart, "...nooo!" Anguished, retched in disbelief, eyes squeezed shut as Elana buried her face against the woman she held so tightly.

Diana rolled quickly, pulling Elana with her. "Hush. It's all right." With gentle strokes she smoothed the tousled hair.

"What — is — wrong?!" Elana pleaded, choking through her tears. She didn't understand. She just didn't understand!

"Nothing," Diana soothed, misinterpreting her cry. "You didn't do anything — nothing happened. It's all right — "

Elana shook her head, protesting, her body racking with this utter coldness. "Please...what...?"

"Shh." Diana held her, aching inside with her own hurt — her own stupidity. "It's my fault — not yours, little one. Shhh...it's all right. It's over — it won't happen again. Hush...."

Elana's eyes shut tighter against the cruelty as her body shook. Di'nay's words from an earlier night rose unbidden. "...Wanting is not the same thing as loving." Even if one of you is loving? She questioned herself desperately. Even then?

Stop it! Stop it, Elana commanded her body. This was not acceptable of Blue Sight or Shadow. She was not a little girl with time for such selfish indulgences. If she loved this woman, then allow her respect and support for her values. Neither Mistress nor Seer had ever said the path would be easy; it was truly time to stop expecting it to be so! "...beg your patience." Elana rolled away and sat upright.

Diana sat up. She was careful not to touch the woman as she repeated, "You did nothing, Ona."

Elana laughed bitterly at the childhood name. It certainly seemed appropriate, and then another fear came rushing in. "We still have our truce, yes?"

"Yes — certainly."

She was lying, Elana realized. It shot through her like a fiery dart. The wall was back. For three — four days, it had been banished into some oblivion. But now it was back. She ached, feeling the emptiness.

"It will be light soon," Elana asserted, glancing at the moonless sky. "If you would bring some fresh water, I'll start breakfast. We can be in Black Falls before eventide, if we push."

Diana stared at the tear-streaked face in silence. She had no idea where they went from here. Breakfast sounded somewhat anti-climatic, but it was the best proposal available. She got to her feet.

Part Two

Finding the Way

Chapter One

Morning drifted into afternoon as the two women rode on to Black Falls. A winged figure caught Elana's eye and she looked overhead, not really hopeful. She hadn't seen the eitteh since the day they had parted at Colmar. She suspected the animal had satisfied its curiosity concerning humans and had returned to the forest's depths. It would not change things if she were here, Elana regretfully admitted — not what she truly wished changed.

"When did you last see Black Falls?" Diana asked quietly.

Elana thought sadly that after so many hours of bleak silence the mundane question was not much of a peace-offering. "I have not seen Black Falls or my parents since I was four and more tenmoons — at age nine years by Imperial reckoning?"

Diana nodded, frowning. "Would you be more comfortable staying at the Inn?"

"No, it would insult their hospitality. Besides, my parents will be eager to meet you. It's a rare chance for them. Most Shadows never return home after lifebonding. They will be most curious to see who I protect."

"It sounds as if they're very proud of you." Diana could not make sense of a family that sent a nine-year-old child away.

"I expect so." Elana smiled with genuine fondness. "Last letter invited me to Alonz' wedding next spring. So I know I'm still very much thought of."

"And who is Alonz?"

"My foster brother. I've never actually met him. They took him in five — no, six seasons after I left. He's celebrating his ninth tenmoon this winter. Mother writes that Papa is very pleased with him, but I suspect she is just as proud considering it was her doing they adopted him. I understand he's very capable in the smithy."

Diana raised an eyebrow. "Your father too is a smithy?"

"Did you really think my parents too poor to raise me, Di'nay?"

Diana shrugged uncomfortably.

Elana laughed and Diana could not help smiling. The cheerful sound eased some of her silent aching. "My father owns the Smith Shop in Black Falls. He deals in both glass and metals. Mother is a sorceress when it comes to molding glass — the colors she binds! The King even commissioned a piece for his last son's blessing."

"A little before my time. How many brothers and sisters have you, Elana?"

Elana's dark head moved regretfully. "None. I was first born. Mother's second was a complicated miscarriage. As hard as they tried, she never conceived again."

Something didn't fit. "Why did they give you up then?"

"They had little choice." Her blue eyes sparkled as she glanced at her puzzled companion. She took pity. "I am the eldest child of two trainees, Di'nay."

Trainees became Shadows, didn't they? "I still don't understand."

"My parents were training at the Keep. When they fell in love, they decided upon a different course and came to Black Falls."

"The Council did not demand you from them, did they?"

"No!" She chuckled at the outrageousness of the idea. "They were both lovers of adventure, Di'nay. They both dreamed and desired to wander. Certainly that desire was finally tempered by age. Perhaps, it was less strong in them than some, since they did come so to love each other and their life in Black Falls. But their children would be born with the same desire for adventure. That is why I'm not a Seer — I could never be content to sit and watch...to live vicariously."

She spoke as if adventuring were a genetic trait, Diana thought sourly. "Surely one could travel, could explore without giving up your identity? Or your family?"

Elana repeated softly, "Giving away my identity?" Was that what Di'nay saw? She shook her head slowly, "No, I have not done that. There are many who dream of wandering — of strange peoples and new things; there are just as many lost in the responsibilities and ties of home. Most wait and hope, looking for the single opportunity that may never come. But being a Shadow...to train for that time...to be in that moment when the Fates choose the players...to grasp destiny! This has always been my identity. Truly, to stay with my parents would have been to rob me of it."

Diana looked down, rearranging the reins. So much of what Elana said was true for herself too — described her driving need to qualify, so many years ago, as an Amazon. None of that made it any more sane, she thought miserably. It just made the flashing blue eyes and the wind-tousled hair more attractive — dangerously more attractive. There was so much that could be shared — so much that such kindred souls could grasp. Even at home few would embrace such — freedom. It was a spirit, not an understanding. She is of Aggar, Diana rebuked herself sternly. I am of another, infinitely more different culture than any she has ever dreamed of.

I could not leave her, if I became involved. Diana blinked suddenly against tears. Never to see Home again? Her soul would die; it was so weary now. And her heart would shred if she left alone...unless she left soon.

"Di'nay?" Elana spoke with quiet concern, her hand reaching across to cover a gloved one. Silent agony wrapped around Elana like a mourning cloak. Anxiously she studied the tense profile. "Are you all right?"

"I was just thinking of home," Diana finally managed. It was partly true.

"When did you last see your family?" Elana asked gently, withdrawing her hand. The wall was securely in place again; she honored the insistence of distance.

"Briefly, just before coming to Aggar. This is the longest I've been away."

"When did you first leave?"

"I became an Amazon not quite two seasons before you left Black Falls."

"Tell me about your choice?" Elana was worried about this melancholy air of Di'nay's. "You said you 'became' an Amazon. Are not all your Sisters Amazons?"

"No." Diana glanced at her, smiling wryly. Somehow she knew that she could trust Elana with her Sisters' secrets. "Not at all, although it's not common knowledge in the Empire. An Amazon is a bit different from most Sisters. We wish to protect our world by venturing forth into the Imperial Realm. In doing this, we preserve our galactic treaty by visibly mingling with and dutifully serving with the militia, usually as cultural liaisons. We personify the stereotype."

"I do not understand."

"We are exactly what the Terrans expect of us — tall, strong, somewhat imposing — more handsome than beautiful...and always short haired." Diana chuckled. "There are a few on record who are slender, ravishing beauties, but very few."

"But why?"

"Defense. Your Council does not publicize those with the Blue Sight?" Elana nodded attentively.

"My Sisters do not choose to publicize our variations either."

"But the outward appearance is not what we hide. It is the power of the Seers that we are shielding, not the color of their eyes."

Diana said, "We protect ourselves by presenting power. You've met Thomas — who would intimidate him more? An army of women like myself? Or a mixed lot of women like your Mistress and — oh, Szori?"

Elana laughed. "You, naturally."

"If we are seen as aggressive and strong, our planetary rights are not so often challenged. It also helps our Sisters who work secretly within the Terran Empire. They are less apt to be discovered merely because they do not look like Amazons."

"What do your Sisters typically look like then?"

Diana shrugged. "What does any woman look like? Tall, small, slender, voluptuous, long hair — short hair...we're no different. Well, maybe sometimes a little stronger or perhaps intellectually quicker, because of the environment and the gene selection. But we are simply women."

"Do I...," Elana moistened her lips nervously, "...do I look like one of you?"

A soft smile touched Diana's face. "You would easily pass as one of us. You have a walk of confidence and an inner pride that we seek. You would do well."

"Do you think your...your family would like me?"

Diana paused. Some things hurt when examined too closely. "Perhaps. I don't think they would dislike you."

"You..." Elana hesitated, knowing this question might be sensitive, but she was curious — and she did not understand. "...You don't have a father, do you?"

"No," Diana answered quietly, "no men. My mother does have a mate — Estelle. A very beautiful, sensitive woman with brown skin and black, curling hair."

"Like my hair?" Elana felt unexpectedly anxious about the comparison.

"Not quite. Hers isn't as long, and the texture is — crisper." Diana's eyes grew wistful. It had been a long time since she'd sat in Estelle's lap, learning to read. "It was graying some last I saw." Yes, she would be sixty by now.

"Do you look like her at all?"

She smiled at that. "No, not at all. I don't have her genes. My sister, Teresa, looks very much like her though."

"Teresa carries her genes?"

Diana nodded. "Before my mother met Estelle, she was lovers with an Amazon, Jes. They spent several years seeing each other often but never living together. Jes went off-world with the Sisterhood; when she returned Mother had met Estelle."

"That's very sad," Elana murmured quietly.

"In truth, no. They were not mated. They never had plans to be. It was several years between Jes' departure and her return. I seriously doubt if either of them were expecting Mother to wait. I think Teresa was already walking when—"

Elana stopped her in confusion, asking, "How old were you?"

Diana laughed. "I wasn't born yet. Teresa is a season-and-a-half older than I am. Mother and Estelle contributed the genes for her. Jes and Mother made me."

"Estelle did not object?" This was one custom Elana would never accept.

"No." Diana's laughter quieted, sensitive again to their differences. "With my people, making love has nothing to do with reproduction, Elana."

Not if they were of Terran descent. They would require men if it did.

"We conceive in one of two ways. A medical procedure — it joins the genetic material from two women and replaces the embryo into the womb of one mother. The other is spontaneous. For whatever reason, a woman's egg..." Diana stopped. So much for her language fluency. "Well, it fertilizes itself."

"Is it common for — for the egg to do that?" Elana was pulling at fuzzy memories of her biology lectures. All she really remembered was being amazed at how much the Council physicians knew compared to most of Aggar.

"It is becoming more common among the Sisterhood, although I'm told it happens sporadically in some humans. The medical procedure is still the most common. It is reliable and mixes the gene pool well."

Elana returned to the subject that really interested her. "Why did your mother decide to have you?"

Diana bit back an embarrassed grin. "She and Estelle wanted another child and — well, everyone thought I'd be...pretty."

Beautiful, don't you mean? Elana corrected silently. Aloud she offered, "They made a good decision."

At that tactful answer Diana laughed, especially when she thought of Rosa and Jasmin angrily vying with her for the adults' attention. "I'm not so certain of their wisdom. By the time my younger cousins were born, we were quite a handful."

"Did they live with you?"

She nodded. It felt good to remember the family squabbles too. "Oma Hanna is our matriarch. My mother, Kate, is the middle daughter of her three. After joining, all three of her daughters and their mates moved in with Hanna. I think that always surprised Hanna as much as it delighted her. Usually someone moves away, but," she admitted quietly, "we made a good family."

"Did they all have children?" It was sounding very different from her early life and the undivided attention of her two parents.

"No. My mothers, Kate and Estelle, had the two of us. Martha and Gum Lin had Morgan, Rosa, and Jasmin, but Ivory and Terri never elected to have children. I suspect we were enough to handle, and we were as much Terri's as anyone's."

"Are you the only Amazon in your family?"

"No. Terri is — or rather, was. It was her stories of the Amazons and the off-worlders that drew me from home."

"She was very important to you."

"I believe she taught me how to think — at a younger age than most. It's saved my life more than once." Even before leaving home, Diana remembered grimly.

Elana absorbed that before she said, "Terri is your aunt?"

"Yes — no. I mean, she's not my mother's blood sister."

"But your mother, Jes, was an Amazon?"

"She's not my mother. I've rarely seen her. What are you thinking?"

Elana shrugged. "It would appear that your Sisters are as genetically predisposed to things as we of Aggar are."

Meaning you and I were destined to wander? Diana thought as she felt herself grow cold again, and the aching knot in her stomach returned. She wondered fleetingly if she would be afraid of this young woman in another place at another time.

❋ ❋ ❋

Chapter Two

"I'm surprised it's so big," Diana commented quietly. She shifted, stiff from the long ride, and her saddle creaked.

They sat high on a wooded crest in foothills, overlooking a narrow valley and its village. Mountainous in their own right, these southern foothills were an unyielding wilderness, but some of the lowlands between were held by people.

Black Falls was a cluster of low-roofed buildings and occasional two-tiered cottages that spread the width of the valley, crowding closely against the sheer face of a towering cliff wall to the north. She knew that there was a road rising to pierce that forbidding fortress, but she was at a loss to see it from this distance.

Her gaze drifted to the shimmering column of silver and white that severed the gray stone — a waterfall that began in the heights of the cliff and fell straight, a thousand feet, to the valley floor. From this distance the great, gaping black hole that swallowed the waters was barely visible, hidden in the shadow of the cliff; the thunderous turmoil rumbled through the ground to be felt even five leagues away.

"There is the road west to the river port and finally to the north sea road that travels around to the wastelands' plateau." Elana pointed left to where the valley followed the foothills around and out of sight. "Cellar's Gate is the faint trail that leaves the village nearer here."

The narrower road Elana called Cellar's Gate doubled back east along the base of the mountains. Their vantage point did not allow Diana to see where it began to climb. "Is it open, do you think?" It could save them two or three ten-days to cut due north, she knew, depending on where in Maltar's realm they were going. She sighed; if they took that trail they would have to leave the horses.

"When we left, the Seers reported that the first of the winter storms had yet to strike. If we were to be caught in a storm, we would be delayed, but we should still make it through — if we weathered it in one of the shelters."

They wouldn't survive if they did not, Diana knew. Discouraged, she looked again to Black Falls. It was a rather large place to search for one secretive hawker. "It looks bigger than Colmar."

Elana nodded. "It has less government, more people. Some call it 'the edge of eternity' because there is nothing north of here until Maltar's lands — except for the plateau. Yet the only known ore deposits in the Ramains' kingdom are in these mountains. There are the salt mines too. In the summer the plateau people, the Changlings, come through the pass to barter for weapons and clothes. Then there are also mountain people who come to trade furs and replenish supplies. Always, the King's men are here — to guard the pass and the mines."

"Sounds like the 'edge of eternity' is a busy place," Diana joked dryly.

Elana looked at her seriously. "I suspect it would be even in the Empire."

Point taken. Diana remembered Aggar's location and the string of events that had brought her to this forested knoll. "So, where is your family?"

Elana pointed towards the silver column. "Near the base. They house the cooperative that catches and filters a portion of the falls. They use the sand and such for the glass-making, and it's the town's chief source of fresh water. It is their glasswares that are traded to the south, sent on the summer caravans with the furs. Actually, it's because of the traders and because of the King's soldiers stationed here that you'll find the village's dialect is not so very splintered despite the location."

"The language is similar to Colmar then?"

"Yes...it is."

"Languages have never been my strong suit," Diana admitted. "At home we have only one; our Founding Mothers created it. We are too young a culture to have evolved actual dialects yet." The Amazon shrugged with a shake of her head. "On most Imperial planets I've relied on translating devices; they're so common that it's never been a problem. But here...here I am often lost."

Slowly Elana nodded. "You will have no trouble here, but further on? For once perhaps my talents may compliment your own, Di'nay. I am said to be quite fluent with foreign tongues — another gift of my Sight."

"Fluent? Or passable?"

"Passable as native born. Or so the Seers judge me."

Diana felt surprised — again — at this young woman's abilities. That nagging little voice within sought to remind her just how different Elana might be from others. She shut her mind against the rising uneasiness, and asked, "Do you know the dialect used in Maltar then?"

"Certainly." Again that small, self-derisive smile appeared as she said, "A requirement of the job." Elana shook her self-pity aside. "In Maltar, it is not a dialect. It is another tongue. The language descends from completely different tribes."

It would have been odd not to find such a variety, Diana reminded herself.

Puzzled at Di'nay's shifting amarin, Elana prodded, "You find it strange that a planet has more than one tongue?"

"No, I was just thinking of how spoiled I am. There is only one Sororian. We chose to construct a new language to separate ourselves from the prejudices and judgements of the past."

"And yet, if they must strive so hard to abandon ancient ways, Di'nay, are not your Sisters still being controlled by those ways?"

Sadness grew within Diana's dark eyes. "Yes." And then a touch of humor gentled the melancholy. "But even butterflies must crawl before they fly."

Diana felt the weighty failures of all her off-world years descend upon her again. There was so much left in the universe of the patriarchal ways that her Sisters had struggled to leave behind...Terrans who could not grasp the need to question, let alone the necessity to reject those ancient paths.

"It is not your Sisters you mourn, I think," Elana said gently.

"No." Diana's voice was hoarse with unshed tears. "As much as I have often hated them, Elana — those in power on the Terran worlds and their senseless games of control and ruin — I still find myself aching for them in their ignorance...for what they will never know."

"For what you cannot heal."

Diana frowned and roughly swung her horse around back to the road, scorning herself for that rising pity for Terrans. It was not a compassion she was always fond of acknowledging to herself. She nudged her mount into a quicker step, pushing the thoughts aside and refocusing on more practical matters. "Do we need to announce your presence to the whole village? I understand your parents will be welcoming, but I would rather the village not know you are my Shadow or that either of us come recently from the Council's Keep."

"It would give this hawker we seek a bit of warning. But it shouldn't be a problem, Di'nay. Many stay with my family when passing through Black Falls if the smithy is tending their weapons. We will simply be two — "

"And I do not need a slave. I will not repeat our guise from Colmar."

"All right." Elana twisted in her saddle to pull her cloak and gloves free. "Would you care for comrade-in-arms or for a wife?"

Her mouth thinned at her heart's erratic beating. They were not talking about the cherished moments with a mate, Diana reminded herself sternly.

"My dress is more appropriate to a man." Di'nay's coldness struck her.

Elana tugged on gloves and pulled her hood up. Disappearing into the cloak's depths, her posture altered slightly to take on more of a slouch. Except for height, Diana reluctantly granted, Elana looked every bit like a weary male traveler. Diana was seeing what she expected to see, and her brown eyes narrowed. The illusion was well-laid; bulk and height had been added. This companion, although built more squarely, was easily her own size.

Unexpectedly disgruntled, Diana jerked her own hood forward in like style and dug her heels into her horse. There were still five leagues to make before eventide.

❄ ❄ ❄

They halted before a low building of stone masonry. The side of it stretched back into the alley. Further along the main street, Diana saw the building's courtyard. Before them two massive wooden doors were flung open. The dull din of the unseen waterfall was intermittently disturbed by the rhythmic ping and bounce of a smithy's hammer. More than one hammer, Diana recognized as they dismounted. She knotted her reins to the hitching post, studying the dim interior. Three burly, grim-faced men were intent on their projects — their anvils positioned around the sweltering bellows and glowing coal bin. Deep in the distance she glimpsed clay furnaces of a different type, but the glass kilns were shut tight for the night.

"May we help you gentlemen?"

Diana was startled at the well-practiced accent of the young man. His dusty hair was neatly parted but hung low into his hazel eyes. He was a handsome lad, clean cut by youth and not by razor. His sleeveless jerkin was belted loosely and the thick muscles of his arms bulged as he rubbed his hands together.

He grinned a little less comfortably at their silence and gave an anxious half-laugh. "You can see we are preparing to close up with darkfall. But if your need is urgent, we can certainly arrange something?"

Diana wondered if Elana realized this must be her foster brother, Alonz.

"The master of this house is available?" Elana dropped her guise for Alonz, the illusion of the male bulk slipping away with the softness of her question, but the hood stayed low; Elana did not intend this foster-brother to see her face.

"Well — why yes, certainly." He waved them to the benches just inside the doors. "If you'll make yourselves comfortable?"

"You have another place," Elana asked him gently. "A garden seat?"

"This way." They followed him through the deserted glass workshops and down a small hallway. He opened the narrow door and bowed them through.

It was a small, pleasant area enclosed by high walls and an arching, frosted glass ceiling. The hanging lanterns had already been lit for the evening. Large potted ferns and small plots of frothy greenery were between the white stone benches. Beige and brown rock were laid in mortar forming the floor and a single, solid tree stood in the center of the court. Its willowy, green-grey tendrils reminded Diana of the tree Elana had once stood beneath at the Keep.

The young man said, "I could see that your horses are stabled, if you like?"

Elana's green hood nodded in assent. He bowed and hurriedly departed.

"You're set on keeping him in his place?" Diana asked quietly, shrugging from her wrap. The courtyard was reminiscent of Imperial solariums.

"No." Elana refused the half-teasing bait, tossing her hood back. "He is young — excitable. I don't know who my parents are with. It didn't seem appropriate to risk Alonz telling a neighbor or shop hand that I am home."

The matter-of-factness of the words did not match their mumbled delivery. For the first time in hours, Diana gave Elana her full attention, watching her nervously slip out of the green cloak. "They will like you."

Elana turned, startled. "They what?" She had been concentrating, trying to reach through the wooden doors to feel an approach.

"They will like you." Diana tenderly touched her cheek — the pale skin like satin under her fingers. Helpless to stop herself, she slid fingers into the dark, silken hair.

Elana gave a melting, relieved sigh and covered the gentle hand with her own, pressing her cheek into the open palm. She drank in the warmth and support of her friend. She did not question why the wall had evaporated again. "I didn't realize," she whispered hoarsely, "how anxious I would be about this meeting."

Diana smiled, feeling more certain of herself in this sisterly role. She drew Elana into a strong hug. "You're human. You're allowed to be nervous. Meeting one's parents after any separation can be a daunting thing."

"Even for you with nearly twenty seasons?"

"Especially at twenty."

Elana drew a steadying breath. It felt good to belong with this woman.

Diana waved a hand around the small court. "How did an Imperial design come to grace a Ramains' village house?"

Elana sat down on a center bench. "No, the question is — how did a design of the archipelagoes come to be here in the Ramains? The White Isles have used bleached stone for benches and flower troughs for centuries. They have precious little wood and became creative with their native rock."

"I wonder if that's how it originated on Terra." She took the bench opposite Elana. "Tell me more about these islands?"

"They're east of here beyond the Firecap Mountains — on the other side of the continent — and extend across the Qu'entar Sea. They're volcanic and...." There was the sound of a door bolt.

Diana rose slowly, stunned by the beauty of the woman who came through the door. She was breathtaking. A few tenmoons older than Diana, she was tall for Aggar but willowy slender with eyes of deep velvet brown — eyes so brown that they were almost as black as the hair that was swept high into a coiled braid.

The woman's dark gaze moved to Elana's still figure with her back to the doors. The unruly length of hair gathered by the leather band falling below Elana's waist seemed blacker than ever in this white stone setting.

"I would know those unmanageable tangles anywhere," the woman said adoringly and came forward, her arms opening.

Elana turned to hug her mother fiercely. "Mother!"

The older woman laughed gently, pressing Elana's head to her own. She kissed her daughter's temple briefly, only to hug her tightly again. "Let me see you!" she said at last, smiling through her tears. They parted just enough to face one another. "Oh but you've grown — "

"No taller than you."

"Yet so much more beautifully." She held her daughter's face between her hands. Her dark eyes darted quickly to the hands that held her own wrists and she freed herself to grasp the black leather bands. "Ona! I am so happy for you! I know you've worked hard." Her voice dropped low. "I am so very pleased for you."

Dark eyes lifted to the silent figure behind her daughter and then back to Elana questioningly. Elana nodded and slipped an arm through her mother's as she whispered, "Come meet Di'nay.

"Di'nay?" Elana smiled faintly, but Diana was not deceived by her calmness. "My mother, Rai Min Sym."

Rai's dark eyes were steady and her smile unfaltering. "As Mistress here I welcome you, Terran, to this place...and to Aggar."

"I am honored in your greeting," Diana took her hands and thought that this was exactly why formalities were created — to cover shock.

Elana desperately hoped Di'nay was not going to withdraw behind that cold wall again. "Mother, this is Diana n'Athena."

Her name sang across the woman's lips. Elana's inflections captured Diana's Sororian accent. Diana grinned, she hoped, charmingly. "Please, here I am Di'nay."

Graciously Rai nodded. "I am most honored, Di'nay."

"Forgive me if I seem awkward. Many have commented on my poor accent."

"It is your skin color," Rai explained softly. "The men of Aggar do not brown with the wind and sun as do your young men; a fact I am sure you have noticed. Or..." she directed her question to both daughter and guest, "am I still in error?"

Diana lifted a brow questioningly and looked to Elana. She remembered Elana saying her mother had also trained at the Keep.

In Common Elana murmured, "She does not wish to insult you by naming you man if you are woman."

Diana broke into a friendly laugh. "You daughter comes by her cleverness well, I see." Diana bowed. "I pose as such to move freely on Aggar."

Rai nodded. "Your secrets are safe here."

"Now, your father?" Rai turned, her excitement renewed. "We must tell him."

"Alonz has gone to fetch him."

"Yes, naturally, he showed you in. But come." Her arm encircled Elana's waist. "It will not be the first time I've stolen your father's guests from him." She paused, extending a hand to her new guest.

"We'll have you fed first, and then let you settle down for a nice long bath. I do remember how dreadfully dusty and tiresome traveling can be."

Diana was amazed at the spaciousness of the house. The kitchen area opened directly into the living room and was divided only by a heavy but beautifully crafted table. It was in some ways reminiscent of the sweeping lines and grand spaces of the Keep, she realized. But here the ceiling housed white glass skylights and the almost bare walls were lightened with whitewash. The corners held bushy ferns, and dark wood shelves and chests were sparsely set against the walls.

Rai motioned them to be seated at a table laid for two. The lack of servants did not go unnoticed by Diana as Rai went to fetch the extra settings — nor did the large, brick wall that housed the kitchen's two ovens, grill and hearth. Diana felt her toes curl in appreciation; the room was warm and toasty.

The aroma of sweet bread pudding drifted to her and Diana felt her hunger stir. In the last few days they had skipped their mid-day meal in order to speed travel.

"Mother!"

Diana recognized Alonz' voice. Rai put the stack of plates aside quickly as the she called in answer, "Coming!"

Rai said, hand on her daughter's shoulder, "A fine boy, but young. He is to share eventide with his betrothed and her family. Perhaps it would be best if he did?"

Elana read the wariness and excitement her mother struggled with. "Yes, if you fear he may talk of my return. We're on Council business."

Rai squeezed her shoulder reassuringly. "Then it is best he not know who you are until you depart. I'll be but a moment."

Diana's gaze returned to Elana as Rai left them. Why had she never noticed how beautiful the ivory tone of Elana's skin could be? It was the dark chair frame — the lighting and the contrast. Elana suddenly turned to her and Diana said, "I did say she would like you, didn't I?"

The soft laughter rang with joy as Elana said, "You are wise." Then more seriously, she asked, "And you? Do you like her?"

"She is an intelligent, beautiful woman."

"Yes." Those were terms endearingly apt for her Amazon too. "Yes, she is."

Elana changed the subject. "What do we do tonight? The commons?"

"I can manage well enough," Diana said. "Why don't you stay with your family. If I stumble across anything, we can follow it through in the morning."

"I was right, then? The language is not too strange for you?" She was disappointed. It would have been nice to include Di'nay in her family reunion.

"It won't be a problem," Diana assured her. "I need to call Thomas too." It made her head ache just to think about the man, although maybe the satellite com-link was still on the blink. She had tried twice since leaving Colmar. "Where would be the flattest ground around here, you think?"

"East on the road to Cellar's Gate. There are few trees, but the brush is thick enough to conceal you fairly well. I could easily show you the place."

"Sounds like I can find it myself. It'll be late and one of us should sleep — or at least, " she grinned encouragingly, "be enjoying a pleasant evening."

"You'll wait for the second moon's rising again?"

Diana nodded. "Satellite should be nearest then."

"You are certain you do not wish me to come?" Elana remembered all too well their bearded ambusher.

"Yes," Diana said firmly. "I'll get the radio around mid-night, take a cautious evening stroll, and be back before your Sight can warn you I'm near."

Elana fought a smile. It was irreverent to refer so off-handedly to the Blue Sight, but she was finding some of Di'nay's alien assumptions rather refreshing.

"We should ask my father if he has noticed anything unusual in the last ten-day. Between the odd assortment of patrons he attracts and his own crew, he often knows what goes on before it happens."

Rai returned, her proud, loving gaze on Elana. "Alonz is off and your father — "

"Comes!" A deep booming voice pounced into the room as its master bounded up the step to the kitchen. He was dressed much as Alonz had been in sleeveless jerkin and breeches, but he was broader of shoulder and shorter than most men of Aggar. His salt-and-pepper hair was still thick despite age, and his hazel-brown eyes latched onto his daughter hungrily.

For a long, silent moment the pair faced each other across the room, blue eyes stilled locked with her parent's. Then Elana was blinking.

The man laughed heartily, stretching his arms wide. "Aye! My lass!" She laughed with him as he picked her up in a bear hug, spinning about. "It is my Ona!" He set her down, hugging her near. "My Ona — "

"Papa!" She squeezed her eyes shut, struggling to calm her emotions, then looked into his grizzled old face. "It is good to be with you again, Papa."

His hand cupped her cheek tenderly. "Very good, child."

"There is another to greet, Husband." Rai spoke softly, proudly. "Our child has become a Shadow."

He moved quickly toward her. Diana suspected he spent a great deal of energy dampening his natural exuberance and wondered that he had ever aspired to anything so restrained as being a Shadow. She grinned; she liked this man.

"Welcome here, Terran!" his clasping hands were firm and strong. "Di'nay, is it? Yes — I am Symmum, supposedly master of this dubious establishment and household." He glanced playfully at Rai. "But most all name me Sy, and I'd be most honored if you would as well."

"Sy it is then," Diana agreed, returning the friendly squeeze of his hands.

"Please — sit?" He waved her back into her seat and, turning, helped Rai with the heavy meat platter.

Elana smiled as her parents wrestled over who could carry it to the table. She seated herself and leaned nearer Di'nay, whispering, "They argued so when I was young as well — "

Diana choked down her laughter as Sy stepped between them, sliding the plate of partially sliced meat on the table.

"There is more than enough now," interjected Rai hurriedly. Bowls of steaming greens and creamed finger spuds joined the meat.

"Ahh!" Sy rubbed his hands together in satisfaction as he eyed the table. "What can I offer you to drink? We have some excellent mead put up this last season? Or there's a southwestern wine that's arrived?"

"The mead will be fine." Her metabolism wasn't ready for Aggar's wines.

"And for me," Elana said.

"Mead it is!"

Rai began passing the food along. "Ona, how does the Old Mistress?"

"Well, I think. She grows stiffer with the winters, but she is healthy and still strong enough to throw a brash recruit."

Rai smiled faintly, remembering the woman with a special warmth. "She has raised you well, Daughter."

Elana paused in ladling out creamed spuds. "She said the same of you."

"Try this?" Sy reappeared and snatched Di'nay's goblet. "It's a bit sweet...?"

Di'nay accepted and shook her head after a sip. "Not at all. It's very good."

Sy poured for the others. "Has the Empire such a brew, Di'nay? Or is this new to your palate?"

Diana laughed, setting the last of the serving dishes near his empty plate. "No indeed. My mother's people have always preferred mead to wines."

Elana thought of the old soldiers' maxim, "Beware lips touched of honey and wetted by mead, she'll take all your money and depart with good speed." If it would only be my money, Elana despaired.

"Elana tells me you know much of the doings in this city?" Diana asked Sy as he sat down. "Have you noticed anything — anyone — peculiar in the last ten-day?"

Sy shrugged. "That is a broad sort of question, Di'nay. Is there nothing more specific I could think on?"

"News from Colmar, Papa? Or perhaps from the Maltar's realm?"

A slow breath was drawn by each and the parents exchanged worried glances. They both could have wished for a less dangerous target to attract their child.

Sy cut into his meat. "Of Maltar I am certain of no word. None have traveled through from the north since last monarc."

"We suspect," Diana explained between bites, "that they use messenger hawks. It is their hawker that we seek."

Rai's knife stilled suddenly. She looked at her husband. "Was there not a strange hawk found dead a ten-day back?"

Cautiously Sy's head bobbed in agreement. "Out in Putma's field, but no one claimed it. And we never found out where it came from. It's messenger ties were empty. Colmar now...." He pointed his knife at Di'nay, "Tartuk was just in this morning muttering something about some trouble down there. He was anxious, at least for him, he was. Yes, he was expecting some friends — a pair from Colmar."

Elana glanced at Di'nay. "Our ambushing friend's two companions?"

"Perhaps. But why would they leave Colmar?"

"If we had talked to their scout at length, their identity would be known. They might not think it safe for them to remain."

Diana nodded slowly. "Or they may be traveling on to see the Maltar after all."

"How did Tartuk know they were coming?" Elana asked her father.

"Sorry, Lass, I do not know. I suppose the King's men brought word. The winter garrison just arrived a while back."

"Anything else odd about this Tartuk?" Diana asked. Sy put down his fork and knife with a shout of laughter. Puzzled, Diana looked at Elana and Rai.

"Symmum! Do not be cruel," Rai rebuked him softly but firmly.

"No, yes — you're right." He swallowed his jest and wiped his watering eyes clear. "It is not his fault. And I beg your patience, my honored Terran." He snatched a full breath and, with a sip of mead, calmed himself. "Tartuk is entirely an odd sort of man, Di'nay — both inwardly and outwardly odd."

"He cannot help his appearance," Rai said and continued her meal.

"No, that he cannot." Sy turned pointedly to Di'nay. "But his character he cannot so easily excuse."

"So tell me of Tartuk."

"He is a tall man and gauntly thin. He would be better made if carved of wood than flesh. He looks as if his bones and skin is all he's made of. His face is not distorted so much as discolored with whitish-gray scars. I suspect he was burned as a child, but his beard grows and his eyebrows are bushy enough, so perhaps not. He's black haired and black eyed and rarely talkative."

"And his character?"

Sy shook his head in disgust and picked up his fork. "I would not trust him near lass or cash."

"You say he's not talkative. How did you come to know he expects visitors?"

"Not so much visitors as traveling companions. He came to collect forty of his metal-shafted arrows and to have his weapons sharpened. He was particularly anxious that we would be open tomorrow should his friends' lot need sharpening."

"You told him no, I trust?" Rai said.

"I most certainly did!" Sy set his goblet down with a bang. "It's not every day of the tenmoon that I celebrate my son's betrothal!"

Rai smiled. There had been times his memory had lapsed for greater things.

"Now as I was saying, Tartuk tried to barter me open for just the half-hour come morning. He was adamant that they would not be able to stay over past the night. He said he was worried to travel with men armed by blunted swords."

"Did he mention why he thought they would be blunted?" Diana asked.

"Aye, the man said a horse thief had been troubling the region and that the fellows had met up with him once already before making Colmar. Seems everyone riding out of the place feared on meeting this thief again."

Diana reached for her mead. "It's comforting to know I'm so notorious."

"You?" Rai's dark brows arched in surprise.

"The men we are tracking," Elana explained quietly, "would rather be tracking us. The single horse thief he has invented is Di'nay."

"So they do not know she is shadowed?" her father asked.

"At least, not to date," Diana agreed.

"It was by the Mother's Hand you did not meet them on the trail coming here, if they are to leave again on the morrow," Rai pointed out.

Elana shrugged. "They may very well believe Di'nay is still searching Colmar for them. There was no sign that they were ahead of us, and if they come after, the mark of two horses should have been reassuring, not distressing."

Diana nodded. "They would be more concerned with someone following."

Sy sighed. "I am sorry I can't give you more. It would not surprise me to find Tartuk was from the north. He has the manners befitting Maltar's court!"

"You really think so lowly of him, Papa?"

"Aye, he's tried to cheat me on one too many occasions, Ona. He's not just poor at bartering. He is a liar — and probably a thief too."

"And you, Mother? What do you think of him?"

Rai lifted a shoulder uncertainly and opened the sealed pudding crock. "I've seen him only a few times and never have spoken to him directly. I'll grant I have never been comfortable near him."

Troubled, Elana accepted the bowl of pudding in silence. It said a great deal that Rai even admitted to ill feelings regarding this man. Her mother was usually overly tolerant of others.

"Do you handle a sword, Di'nay?"

Diana glanced at Sy, startled by his abruptness. "Yes, why?"

Elana looked at him sharply. The sudden tension in his amarin was striking. "You have something important to share, Papa?"

"Not in your way, Ona." Rai reached across to squeeze her daughter's hand. "It is just very exciting for him."

"How would you know?" he challenged his wife stubbornly. "Have you taken to deciphering amarin of late?"

Rai laughed, replacing the pudding crock's lid. "Surely after so many tenmoons, Husband, your every amarin is clear to me."

He grunted and stabbed his spoon into his bread pudding.

"This is delicious." Diana smiled at Rai with all the charm she could muster. "As was the whole of the meal."

"Thank you." Rai tipped her head graciously. "There is more if you like."

Diana acknowledged that with a half-nod and turned to Sy. "You were inquiring about my sword?"

Elana was impressed with the smoothness of Di'nay's distracting tactic. Of course, she too could have done it — with anyone but her own parents.

"I was wondering if you were pleased with it?" Sy said cautiously. "My understanding of your people is limited, but am I correct in assuming Terrans rarely use such — primitive — weapons?"

"For better or worse, Tad, yes — Terrans rarely carry such sidearms."

"I have heard," Rai interjected quietly, without raising her dark eyes from her dish, "that Terrans prefer to kill without watching their enemies die. Does that not lead them to devalue life?"

"As I said, it may be for the better — or for the worse."

Sy glanced at her briefly. "And yourself?"

"Di'nay is from a planet much as ours," Elana said quickly. She was not prepared to have her Amazon compromise her Imperial or ethical responsibilities. "They frequently differ with the Empire's policies and value independence."

Sy nodded, apparently satisfied. "So you do handle a sword well?"

"Well enough."

His bushy brows raised at the non-committal response and he turned to his daughter. "And you? What do you think of her sword arm?"

Elana smiled proudly. "I have not seen Di'nay fight, Papa, only draw. Di'nay wields a full length with one arm and good balance. I am sure the rumor of the scuffle in Colmar the other night was not an exaggeration."

"And what was the rumor?" Sy prodded.

"Di'nay bested a man nearly twice the weight in short time. Di'nay has a reputation for being short-tempered."

"Naturally," Rai said from Elana's far side, "the brown skin would only add to that perception."

Diana had never thought of it in that light. She had often casually remarked it was 'just the way' of the southern people when asked by Maryl or Pel about her skin tone. But that may well have affirmed their opinions of her hot-headedness.

"What is your explanation?" Elana prompted Di'nay with a touch of mischief.

"I would prefer swords to a wrestling match." She glanced around the table self-consciously. "I would not want my tunic torn — "

"Aye!" Sy hit the table and rattled the dishes. "She uses her head! Have I got a gift for you, Lass!"

Astonished, Diana started to object, but Sy was already gone from the room. She could not afford to leave her own sword of Terran metals here or any place else.

Elana turned to her mother. "I do not understand. He surely knows of the Terran alloys?"

Rai patted her hand and met Di'nay's worried gaze. "He has worked hard on this piece, Di'nay. I would beg you to look before deciding. I suspect it will not compromise your allegiance."

"But if he has labored so, there must be a worthy buyer who — "

"No buyers!" he shouted sternly. He came with a long sword in hand. It was wrapped generously in soft chamois, its hilt barely visible. "There is not a man of Aggar I would sell, give or trade this to."

"But so valuable a piece — how could I — "

Elana's hand closed over hers. "Why Di'nay, Papa?"

"Because...." He drew a breath with effort and his skin flushed brown. "Because you are my daughter's Shadowmate." He gazed at them both proudly. "Long ago, before Rai and I departed the Keep, there was a Seer. A very old man, Ona, who died shortly before you were born, but he was gifted with future Sight. He warned of your Sight and your journey to a darkness." Sy forced another shaking breath. "Living so near the north, I should perhaps have guessed the Maltar would be involved. Still...he said the one you shadowed would be unique — exceptional, if you chose by the Mother. And then he said there would be a time when my skills would stand between you both — and Fates' Cellar." Hesitantly, Sy caressed the bundle before him. "I do not know if the old man meant my skill in this craft," his watery gaze searched his daughter's face, "or if he meant my skill in raising you so many years ago."

Carefully he began to unwrap his gift. "I know you do not carry such swords by choice, Daughter. Many years ago when I began this, I had thought it would be yours. As you grew and your letters came, I understood it would be for the one you shadowed, if he..." Sy paused, the last chamois still hiding the sheath beneath as he looked at Di'nay, "or she...would choose to carry it."

Diana already knew she could not deny this man his giving.

The chamois slid away to reveal the shimmering black of a well oiled scabbard; the length of it was plain, without a single etching. The thickly sewn edges were evenly cut and neatly secured. A gleam of high polished metal drew attention to the sword's hilt. The design was simple. A flattened three-leaf clover made the knob and single flattened curls were at either side of the blade guard, but the grip was neither leather nor silver.

Amazed, Diana touched a finger to the hilt. The opal-like stones were sunk into the black etched silver; three ovals for front and three for back. They were mounted at a slant, fitting perfectly across the diagonal of the grip. Subtle teasing colors flashed through the dazzling depths, and Diana remembered Elana's lifestone.

Cautiously Diana stood and grasped the hilt. It was warm, but there was none of the shivering sensation she'd experienced at Elana's bonding. It slid with deadly — utter — silence from its sheath; she held it upright before her.

The fine, broad blade glittered white-silver. The edges were smooth sharp, not a single nick or chip in the length. The very point was wide but tapered enough for an effective lunge. It was slightly longer, perhaps by an inch, than her own, but it was better balanced.

With disbelief she studied the length, her wrist twisting, weighing its bulk. The hilt encased a heavier metal, Diana realized, to compensate its balance for the long reach, but the rest of the sword — blade and hilt — was made of Terran alloy.

"You — made this?" Diana asked, astonished. The stones certainly denied an Imperial artisan.

"It is your alien metal...embedded with lifestones," Elana whispered in awe. She had never seen a polished lifestone bent to any will other than a Jezebet's for bonding. She had known it was possible since the Changlings used them occasionally, but she had never thought to see them used in her father's craft.

"There were Terran ships lost in these mountains during the battling years of our first contact," Sy explained somberly. "Most that was salvageable was collected by the Council and by the kings hundreds of years ago, but there are still scraps to be found — for those who know where to look."

Elana glanced at him sharply. "You chose Black Falls for this resource."

"Yes, the Council approved of the venture. For the most part I blend the Terran alloy with our own metals. It increases the strength of our weapons and controls the disbursement of the alloy. But this one..." Sy's hazel gaze returned to his crafted piece. "This one was to be different."

"Why the stones?" Diana asked. The grip seemed to mold to her hand's clasp, yet it was firm and smooth.

"Your alloy — it has a special property when joined with Aggar's lifestones." Sy glanced at his daughter. "The Council has known of this too. It is one of the ways they interfere with the satellite communications of the Terrans. The stone is energy without form — without purpose. It bonds and links life energies together — increasing or decreasing reserves, depending upon the task." His hand reached, palm open to the flat side of the blade.

Diana jumped. A flashing aura of powder-soft blue engulfed the blade.

"Here it blocks or bludgeons. Here..." his hand drew a little further away and moved to parallel the cutting edge. It sparkled an ember orange. "...it melts or slices. In theory you could half another man's sword, but I'm not convinced six rather imperfect stones could actually carry enough power to do that.

"If you are angered or more intent, it becomes more powerful."

Diana eyed him warily. She wasn't sure she wanted anything more powerful.

"It has other properties," Sy pointed out hurriedly, seeing the hesitancy in both his guest and daughter. "The lifestones will be sensitive to your own, Ona — through Di'nay. Should you become separated, Di'nay might be able to trace you."

He looked to Di'nay. "If you should ever lose it, the sword will eventually disintegrate. Unlike your own piece, you would not have to risk the alloy falling into local hands and announcing your people's continued presence on Aggar."

A very attractive point, although what of her own sword? Diana slid the precious blade back into the sheath. "If I left it with you, would you melt down my old blade and mix it with your metals?"

"Aye," he agreed solemnly.

Her fingers tapped the black leather. With this weapon she felt as if she would be taking unfair advantage of her enemies.

Sy interrupted her thoughts. "Few will suspect you are Council sent. The basic design of three stones and clover curls has been mine for many years. And the Changlings have used the lifestones in their slingshots for eons. Any witnesses will either be naming you magician or assuming that I have arranged a new kind of pact with the Changlings."

She forced a slow, deep breath, and her fingers closed around the grip. Aside from its use, it was beautifully crafted. And the advantage? Diana remembered what might truly be at stake here. Perhaps it was only right that the resources of both Aggar and the Empire be united in such a tool. Perhaps the Mother's Hand had guided this.

Diana glanced at Elana's still figure. Had her part been to bring them here to her father's house?

"It is a fine piece," Diana said finally. She extended her hands to Sy. "I thank you for the honor and for your aid." She looked to Rai. "Both of you."

She slipped the scabbard from the table and belted it about her hips. It hung well and fit comfortably. She had a fleeting wish that she might never need to use it.

Chapter Three

Elana stirred in her sleep. Fuzzily she opened her eyes; it was still very much night-time. Her lids slid shut again; she was reluctant to come fully awake.

A sensation persisted — an awkward, dull thudding in her ears that was not quite hidden by the slumberous roar of the waterfalls. She rolled over, realizing it was just the sound of her own blood pounding in her eardrum. Vaguely she wondered if Di'nay had managed to contact her commander. Even if she had not, she was undoubtedly on her way back here. Elana half-hoped that Di'nay had not stumbled onto anything at the Inn. She — they both — could benefit from a day's rest.

She rose on one elbow and punched the pillow. This was ridiculous.

Or was it?

She sat up abruptly, pressing the heels of her hands against her eyes, elbows on her knees. With measured breaths she forced her body to relax and concentrate. Two rhythms — two echoes in her ear. Her fingers tore open the black wristband. Steady as always the crimson and bluish lines coursed through it, but the white depths glowed intensely, brightly — almost as brightly as Di'nay's synthetic torch.

She threw the blanket aside and went to pull a shutter open. Gazing skyward at the almost full midnight moon, her Sight went soaring.

Beyond village streets, across fallow fields, her blue vision swept. She glimpsed three shadows, all men, in the rocky foothills marching to Cellar's Gate; she passed them by. A cloak stirred in the icy wind and her eyes narrowed — same road, hours behind the three — a lone figure moved. She would know that stride anywhere.

Elana shivered as she came back to her parents' home. She hastened to dress. For whatever reason, Di'nay must have retrieved her pack earlier and not just her green satchel. She knew better than to waste energy on self-pity in wondering why at just this moment. It was a good bet that the three figures she'd seen had something to do with either the hawker they sought or with Maltar's scouts from Colmar. Her stomach tightened at the thought of the last trio they'd trailed.

Rai knocked lightly as Elana was reaching for her boots. Her mother cracked the door without waiting for an answer. "I'm awake," Elana called.

Rai entered, holding a dim lantern high. She said nothing at the sight of her daughter lacing her boots tight. Instead she set the light down to turn up the wick.

"Something has happened." Elana said. "I must meet her in the foothills."

Rai nodded. "You're not coming back."

"Not tonight."

"Perhaps never," Rai admitted with more honesty.

Elana paused with cloak in hand. It was not to be denied. "Perhaps never."

For a long moment they looked at one another. Elana longed to lock eyes for their farewell. But she was too anxious and it would not be fair.

"I will send word, if I can," Elana offered finally.

"The Mistress will, if you cannot." Rai knew the way of it all too well.

"I will miss you. You and Papa...I always knew I could come back, but now — "

Rai tipped her head to hide her gathering tears. Too late she remembered her daughter's Sight; she also remembered that she had always hidden the tears anyway, even when the girl had been an infant.

"If your Terran wishes to settle on Aggar...," Rai smiled faintly, aware of that unlikelihood, "...you are both welcome here." The soft dark gaze searched her loved one's face. "And if she does not...I wish you happiness among her stars."

Elana wondered if that might ever be. "Traveling with her, I could be, Mother."

"That is more than most can say." Smiling sadly, Rai took Elana into her arms for a last hug. "I'll tell your father good-bye for you. He'll understand."

Elana squeezed tightly. "Tell him to do what he will with the horses...tell him...."

A curly strand had freed itself and Rai nodded as she tenderly tucked it behind her daughter's ear. "We both love you too, Ona..." She smiled. "...Elana."

Tears threatened and Elana's throat ached — the pain of missed seasons with them mingling with that of their parting. But she could find nothing more to say. Elana kissed her mother's cheek and left quickly.

✳ ✳ ✳

The dawn crept into the valley as Diana reached the northern foothills. Her eyes stung from lack of sleep and her stomach was tight from anticipating the monthly annoyance of her bleeding; at least she need not deal with it for a day or two. Reluctantly she rested beside a small creek, munching on a dry breakfast of wafers and jerky and just managing a bath. She suspected that the barren mountains ahead would not give her another chance to wash soon. Fires would be as unlikely: she couldn't risk the flames here, not so close to the crew ahead of her. She was equally uneasy about someone coming from behind.

She scrambled up a small rise, barely hidden by the brush, and peered through her tiny binoculars. The trio was moving again. She hurried back for her pack.

Elana should be waking about now, Diana decided. It was still early, but the young woman seldom seemed to wait for the sunrise. Diana glanced overhead; she had probably been up for awhile. She would be worried, Diana admitted guiltily. But at least Elana was safe. Safe with her family who obviously did care what became of her — safe from the wary men ahead and from the sadistic Maltar beyond.

And for herself? Diana frowned. The distraction — the preoccupations would be done with and she would be able to face herself each morning. She had done what she needed to do.

Elana was not Maryl, her heart whispered, but she set her mouth sternly. She knew that only too well. Perhaps it was truly the reason for her leaving.

Fates' Jests and Mother's Blessings — the beliefs of Aggar were in some ways too closely akin to those of her Sisters. She accepted the blame for her departure. The appearance of Tartuk and his two comrades had given her the opportunity — indeed, the necessity to move quickly. It had been her choice to move alone.

Choice? Diana glanced regretfully over her shoulder. Precious Goddess, what could she have done differently?

✳ ✳ ✳

Night fell as Elana calmly made camp. She knew this game of cat-and-mouse was superbly easy compared to what the coming trail would allow. She stirred her small fire, feeding it more wood as she worried about Di'nay. The Amazon would not light a fire tonight. Further on she would have to be doubly careful not to stumble into the trio's camp, since rocky caverns and wind breaks would be few and far between. At that moment, Elana wished the Amazon her

Blue Sight to veil the flickering firelight...to gauge the movements of those ahead and retreat into safety.

The wind rustled oddly and Elana's head jerked up. Her Sight rippled outwards, but there was no sign of danger — or men. A smile gentled her expression, and still squatting, she swiveled to stare into the darkness. A small shape appeared from the brush, dragging a furry carcass almost twice its size.

"Eitteh!"

Proudly the animal deposited her catch at the woman's knee with a swish of her tail, sat — yes, she was back.

Elana chuckled fondly and smoothed the fur back over its regal brow. The eitteh purred low and dipped its chin, encouraging the fingers to rub behind an ear.

"Have you missed me, Golden One?" Elana asked gaily and then picked up the fresh catch. "Or have you merely acquired a taste for roasted meats?"

An indignant purr rumbled from her, and the eitteh took itself off to the far side of the fire. With a plop it stretched full out, opening the fur-clad wings to absorb the toasty heat.

Laughing, Elana pulled her knife from its sheath and set about skinning their eventide.

❀ ❀ ❀

The two moons rose and one chased the other through their heavenly arc. The wind pushed the inky clouds and seemed to swirl the patterns of the stars, but the travelers below took heed only of the faint storm warnings. The winter was soon to begin in the heights above, spurring them on to the crest of the Gate. Elana noted the signs with more concern than those whom she followed; her Sight provided her with more than an educated guess — afternoon of the third day, eventide at best, before it would hit with full force. She did not doubt the trio would clear the pass and lodge in the shelter just over the summit. It was possible, although unlikely, that they might even miss the worst of the storm if they cleared the dividing ridge.

Di'nay would not have the luxury of reaching that way-station. If she did, she would meet with those she trailed. By the signs Elana guessed Di'nay was stalking with no desire to overtake the men. Her Amazon was gradually lengthening the distance between herself and the trio as the land permitted less and less cover.

Elana had almost overtaken Di'nay earlier that afternoon. Her concentration had been so intent on keeping pace and on the men further ahead that she had inadvertently come too near. She berated herself for her incompetence, although she realized she was probably just disgruntled and uncomfortable; her bleeding had begun earlier than usual and she hurt. Trekking across an increasingly barren and chilly countryside was not improving her mood. It had hurt more when she had come close enough to decipher Di'nay's amarin.

Elana sighed dejectedly, and the eitteh lifted its head from her shoulders. The animal had, as usual, elected to lay itself atop pack and shoulders to doze as Elana marched on. But the melancholy that wrapped its human worried the small creature. A downy soft paw touched the flushed cheek, and Elana smiled, glancing at her concerned friend. She stroked a finger across a paw top but could offer no more reassurance. Then, each understanding the limits of the other, they let their attentions return to their own thoughts.

It was clear to Elana that the Amazon had deliberately set out on her own. Still, a piece within her heart hoped that the woman half-expected to be followed and to be found. That Di'nay feared Elana's following had been evident in her amarin and frequent back glances when Elana had gotten close. It had been a harsh, forbidding expectancy that recalled the icy wall that so often rose between them. The steely set to Di'nay's anger foretold a verbal confrontation — an outright refusal of her company should Elana appear.

Elana had retreated unseen, allowing herself to stay only close enough to calm the throbbing lifestone at her wrist. She remembered telling Di'nay on their first meeting that a Shadow was dispensable if she became burdensome. She thought herself foolish now to have arrogantly assumed that she could never become a hindrance. She took little comfort in the notion that no trainee would have been properly prepared for this relationship. But she'd been chosen by the Mother's own hand — somewhere she had neglected something that would have resolved this rift.

Memories of sleepless nights in the dormitories drifted back to her…times when her Sight had been plagued by couples in adjoining chambers. Memories, fantasies, stolen moments of amarin from the trainees and kitchen maids — all stumbled by, but even the most innocent, most tender of first kisses did not compare to what Di'nay and she had shared.

It was the lack of a reference point. It was like comparing men-cat to human. They were so different that it was nonsensical even to try. She did not want to try; she knew that she wanted this woman…she loved this woman. And she wanted her any way Di'nay would have her.

❋ ❋ ❋

The sun was rising again. At least a pale disk was growing visible through the overcast sky. The wind continued to push the ever thickening front to the south at a surprising speed. There was a chilly breeze at ground level, but no evidence of the ferocity that one glimpsed in the sky.

Elana found it reassuring. She would worry when the clouds became more sluggish and the wind dropped to howl across the earth.

There was a change in patterns that did concern her, however. It involved those she followed. The road climbed abruptly a few leagues ahead of Di'nay and presented the trio with one last opportunity to send someone scouting behind for trackers. Beyond that point, direct confrontation was about all that was possible; the trail was carved into rock and cliff, and there was scant cover available for hiding. It wasn't surprising when the three sent someone circling back.

Elana forced herself to relax. There was no immediate danger and plenty of time to counter his maneuver. Yet knowing that he was moving did not tell her exactly where he was. That detail she could discern only about Di'nay;

she was not a Seer.

The eitteh stirred in its placid repose and stretched with a yawn. Giving a light push, it jumped from the green-clad shoulders. It was curious that her human was choosing to stop again. It had not been long since the last halt.

Elana shrugged off the pack and sat down with a bump. She would have taken any excuse to sit...at least the cramps had lessened slightly. Exhausted, she opened her waterskin. It was still icy from the night air and cool in her mouth. She offered the eitteh a sniff, but the animal shook its head with ruffled indignation – there was better to be had even in these hills.

"Eitteh," Elana called to her companion as she capped the water and set it aside. Agreeably the beast approached and allowed Elana to half-lift it under its forelegs. Silently the emerald and sapphire gazes locked, and Elana posed her problem.

Disdainful, but lacking any particular reason to decline, the eitteh blinked and wiggled out of the gentle grasp. It walked a few leisurely paces and then took to the air with a lunge.

Elana leaned back against the scruffy tree trunk, only half-noting its sluggish rhythms. She watched the soaring shape as it ascended to a faint dot, then she was one with the eitteh surveying the barren ripples and dust of the land below.

The top soil here had long ago been washed into the valley's center and the scrub that was gray-green in the best of times was a tired brown as it awaited the onslaught of winter. Against such monotony humans were easily discernable.

The pictures swung in a slow spiral. There, the green-clad one marched on. Ahead, two fainter forms had mounted the trail into the pass. There was another – somewhere. There – in a dusky brown cloak that meshed well with the land was a tall figure, sickly thin to the eitteh's predatory eye even from this height. The figure moved quickly. Bent low, almost in a permanent hunch, it loped across the empty terrain. It was armed with bow and arrow.

Quickly the eitteh circled higher, wary of that weapon. The figure moved too fast for mere scouting, seeming to follow a pre-laid plan. As the eitteh turned for a final pass the figure too turned, angling back. It would meet the road south of the green-cloaked One.

Elana blinked, breaking the contact with her winged friend. She pressed her fingertips against her eyes. That scout would be coming from the west and taking Di'nay from behind, but his path would put him ahead of herself.

She reached for her crossbow and the air cracked with the sound of its setting. Companion or not, she was still protector.

❀ ❀ ❀

The eitteh rumbled coldly, distastefully, but the sound was faint and barely reached Elana's own ears. The creature, too, was leery of this tall form they watched.

With the eitteh, Elana glimpsed a grizzled, scarred profile as he turned, searching for his best vantage point. His greasy, blue-black hair was stringy and poorly cut at collar length. His beard was nearly as scruffy and ill-kept. If this was Tartuk, she understood her father's disgust; the amarin were stomach-retching.

The foothills had become a shallow maze of bluffs. The climb and drop of the rock afforded some cover but not much. Hesitant to confront his prey openly, he scrambled back down into the ravine. Elana's gaze followed his movements, noting his lack of pack and sword. There were two knives at his belt, a full quiver and the long bow. She recognized the cylindrical metal rods of her father's special arrows. Indeed this must be Tartuk — bent on a kill from a safe distance. He was an expert on ambush. His soundless tread, the muted color of cloak, and his metallic arrows all attested to his lethalness. A man would not risk losing a small fortune with each arrow released; he knew — not expected — but knew he would retrieve each arrow he loosed.

The eitteh circled off, and under her Sight's cloak Elana crept after the man. She moved cautiously, wary of his skills as she bent the auras around her. Her own pack and cloak had long been discarded; she needed the mobility. Her crossbow was set with two bolts and her knife had been moved from belt to boot. She did not carry extra bolts; she had no illusions about a second chance with this man.

A rock clacked against another and both hunters froze. Di'nay, Elana realized. She watched as her quarry carefully straightened enough to see beyond the ravine's north side. Elana did not need to look to know the Amazon had risen from her short rest and was shouldering her pack to move on.

The man crouched again and hurried forward, setting an arrow as he went.

Elana glanced ahead as she broke into a run. He wanted that bluff just beyond the crevice. It would give him the most unimpeded view of Di'nay's hollow and a deadly vantage point.

She reached the place opposite as his string drew back. Her knee hit the dirt and the stock found her shoulder. Her finger squeezed, but beyond she felt Di'nay turn, and Tartuk dove from sight — the bolt struck the ground, pinning his cape above his elbow.

Black eyes widened, startled as they found Elana. Together they shot and rolled, instinctively protecting themselves as they fired. The crossbow dropped. She lunged across the gully before he could grasp another arrow, but his hand had reached for a knife as her own pulled free.

The lip of the gulch gave way as they tumbled and dropped a half dozen feet. His rib broke with a muffled crack as they landed, his quiver beneath his back. But the momentum carried them on. Knives hovered — swayed — each with a hand grasped to wrist to stay a plunging blade.

He twisted and gained the weight advantage atop her. With a half-human snarl he thought of triumph. But her body bucked as his arm pulled free enough to strike and she faced him fully — her blue eyes piercing his small brain with a distorted fury. A scream gurgled into silence as her blade sank between his ribs.

Her head dodged, but his precious chance had been spent. His knife struck stone.

She heaved his smelly frame from her body. The fleeting moments of life that were left to him held him immobile, eyes frozen to the gray skies.

Urgently she snatched his thin chin in hand and jerked his face to hers again. Eyes locked as she concentrated, absorbing, pulling — robbing him of every last struggling thought — searching for anything that might be valuable.

He died wide-eyed, enmeshed with her mind until the final half-breath when even she abandoned him to his solitude.

Elana gasped for air and dropped back against the earth. The eitteh grumbled from a rocky perch above, pleased her human had been successful, though doubting her efficiency. Still, if she had failed, the eitteh would not have.

Stiffly Elana pushed herself up to a sitting position. Her body ached from the fall, but she was in one piece. And Di'nay?

The eitteh rumbled again and shared a picture with her of Di'nay unsuspecting and traveling on.

Good enough, Elana thought, and gasped in a little more air. Her stomach turned over as she looked at her victim; it was a struggle to swallow. Di'nay was right, it did not get any easier. The man stared, unseeing, at her boots.

She rose and picked up her hunting knife. Still — it was different when Di'nay's very breath was at stake.

❁ ❁ ❁

Chapter Four

Elana added a few more sticks to her small fire. Unseen, the snow blew outside the cave, and she sighed. The only cheering thoughts of the day had been that she had stopped bleeding and she had fresh meat for eventide, but she sorely missed the company of her furry friend. The eitteh had traveled with her into the mountains for a full day following Tartuk's death, but the altitude and the cold had already begun to affect her. Elana knew that usually the females of the eitteh's species avoided the wintry regions — except when it was their time for hibernation. The elevation had dulled the eitteh's senses, and finally the animal had chosen to go her own way. Elana did not blame her. The eitteh was not fattened enough to survive a long sleep, and the type of men Elana tracked were too dangerous. The winged-cat was wiser than to depend on Elana to get her through the mountains.

The wind howled, and a whistling whine sang above her. Elana looked curiously at the cave's ceiling. Somewhere the crack that drew the fire's smoke up was also flirting with that wind. She frowned. She did wonder where Di'nay was. This was the last decent way-station this side of Cellar's Gate. Further on where the cliffs jigged and jagged enough to offer a windbreak, there were a few places, but they were not going to be sufficient for this storm.

The winds changed directions slightly and the howl subsided. The cave was well set into the rock, and the triangular crevice that opened to the trail twisted sharply, creating a narrow entrance tunnel. It was an effective wind block; what little breeze did manage to seep in was deflected along the walls. That feature combined with the natural hot springs and dribbling waterfall created a surprisingly warm haven, and a fairly large one too. Eight or so could sleep comfortably — a dozen or more by necessity — on the sandy floor. Given its size and strategic location, it had not gone unnoticed by the King's militia. The soldiers had long ago added latrines, dry food stocks, and fire rings and had stoned up some of the springs to create a bathing pool.

Elana added another pinch of seasoning to the simmering stew. She had downed a middling-sized bird at mid-day and had had to do some scrambling to retrieve it. She hadn't been sure how well supplied the cave would be. Travelers were not expected this close to winter, and the food stores were usually not replenished until the spring. She was glad of her caution now. The salted meats were all but gone and everything else had long been used. It would last a couple days, but the first break in the weather she needed to go hunting. Actually, she had seen fresh signs of migrating schefea in the area; they would probably be faced with a similar need for food. That would make them easier to find even if the weather broke for only a few hours. Elana dished out her eventide on a less quieting thought. How was Di'nay going to react when she found herself saddled with a Shadow again?

The wind whistled faintly. Night would be falling all to soon. Elana decided she'd rather have the Amazon stony and angry and here than out there somewhere.

The almost smooth stone ceiling of the cavern did not help calm her fears. The ancient, silent rock housed small wisps of lichen and the waters some faint traces of algae, but it was a stern fortress that severely limited her Sight's powers. The wooden latrine stalls, the discarded shards of crockery, and the coursing flow of fresh water all touched her awareness and belied her isolation, but it was frustrating not being able to sense Di'nay's path. She was tempted to step outside the warm sanctuary, but the driving snow would blind her, and without clearer vision, her gift was useless.

Not wholly, Elana realized with a start and looked at the tunnel entrance. The Amazon stood hidden, wary — not yet in position to glimpse the interior fully.

Elana self-consciously pushed her loosened hair over a shoulder. Her heart pounded as she waited, and she knew it was from fear as well was relief.

A flash of silver flipped through the air as Diana tossed her knife over and sheathed it, stepping clear of the shadows. Snow dusted her brown hair and dampened the cloak and pack. She stood silent, long bow in hand, staring at the woman. Elana's pack was undone, her blanket laid, and her stew smelled delicious. Her black underknits and linen tunic had been washed and set aside to dry.

Diana's dark gaze narrowed as it returned to the young woman. Elana's breeches and blue tunic hid the slenderness of her body but not the curves. Her long tousled hair was still damp from a washing and her skin was rich ivory in this dim light. Had it been possible to forget how beautiful she was? Diana thanked the Goddess that she had. Her own rather pitiful illusions had caused her heartache enough; she doubted she would have survived a truer image's haunting. With a short sigh Diana dropped her bow and pack. There was no place to go but here.

Silently Elana turned and retrieved another two bowls and a spoon from her cooking set. One bowl she filled with stew and set aside for Di'nay. The other she took to the wall's trickling spring to fill. As she placed the water on the fire to boil, she caught the sarcastic lift of Di'nay's lips, but Elana could not tell if Di'nay was disapproving of the tea water or of some internal thought. She wasn't about to ask and sat down to resume eating.

Diana stripped off her wet garments and opened the velcro seams that had begun to chafe her collarbone. She spread her boots and clothes out to dry a bit and then, clad in her white fieldsuit, sat herself down next to the waiting dinner.

Sighing, she ate. But it wasn't going to work — this silence. With an effort she cleared her throat and offered softly, "Would it help if I apologized?"

"I did say a Shadow should be left if she becomes a burden."

"That wasn't why — " Diana stopped. She did not really want to explain her muddled reasons for departing, but she also did not want Elana believing she had been incompetent either. She tried again. "I did not find you burdensome."

Elana studied the beautiful angles of that solemn face. "Not even emotionally?"

Diana shuddered at her perceptiveness. "I beg your patience. I simply did not want you hurt."

By whom? Tartuk or herself? Elana thought and held her tongue.

"This is good," Diana murmured, stirring her stew a little. "I have missed your cooking."

Elana smiled sadly. It was Di'nay's way of saying she had missed her. "I'm glad you like it."

"I don't expect you would consider going back?"

"No," Elana said firmly. "Especially since you've no idea where the Priory is and your guides will be lost to you in this storm."

"Priory?" Diana watched her closely. "What do you know of the men I follow?"

"Enough." Elana remembered Tartuk's body with regret. "They are Maltar's men. He has sent for them because he believes they know the ways of the Council since they live relatively close by in Colmar. I suspect they know little, though they live nearer than any others he commands. They were to deliver the ransom demands to the Keep first and then join his Court. They recruited Tartuk for a bodyguard when their bearded friend did not reappear in Colmar. Tartuk had apparently worked for the Maltar often and was considered — trustworthy." She couldn't help the faint echo of disbelief that invaded her voice. "Their destination is the Priory, a fortress that long ago belonged to a religious order. Now it is used by the Maltar. It defends the northeastern bank of the river gorge — the borders of his lands. He often holds summer court there. His task for these men is to identify the 'strange spirit' that he holds there now."

Diana's brooding eyes studied Elana for a long moment. There was only one way the woman could have known all of this: somehow she must have run across and read Tartuk. Diana had been playing a hunch from overheard tidbits from the Inn. She had known that these men were Maltar's crew, that they were hurrying to meet him — and hopefully, Garrison — and that the two were probably the men they'd followed from the Keep. But exactly where and why they were traveling so hastily, she could not have guessed. Worried, she finished her stew. For all her good intentions, Elana could have been killed.

"I do know they are going to the Priory," Elana assured her quickly, misreading Di'nay's concern.

"For the past two and a half days, I have been expecting Tartuk to appear behind me," Diana began tiredly. "May I ask if you found him or he you?"

"He was about to put an arrow into your back," Elana said almost inaudibly. "I — dissuaded him."

Again death. "I'm glad you were not hurt."

"And I that you were not."

Sweet Goddess! You could have died so easily — a coldness gripped her heart. She truly could do nothing right with this woman. She felt numb, her body cold, but she was too exhausted to care; it felt like a kind of defeat. Whatever reason the Goddess had for throwing this woman into her life, Diana was lost. She had failed to comprehend the purpose just as she had failed to strike a balance in their friendship — and generally failed in her judgment.

Too weary for tears, Diana struggled to her feet and fetched her pack. She fumbled for her blanket, then bleakly paused, finding the tea pouch in her palm.

She returned to the fire and gingerly extended the small bag to Elana. "I don't much feel like tea tonight," she murmured and turned to spread out her blanket, pinching the temperature tab too high. Maybe it was the altitude? "You're welcome to some if you like."

"Thank you." She watched anxiously as Di'nay rolled herself into the blanket. Emotional fatigue...but she did nothing. Had not she wished just to have the Amazon here safe? Still — Elana shivered with the intensity of that exhaustion as Di'nay slipped off into a restless slumber.

❊ ❊ ❊

Diana woke as painful memories crowded her — memories of Elana. Her body hurt, protesting as she rolled to her side and curled tight. She felt as if she'd been physically beaten. She'd slept too many hours, none of them good; the night had been spent in a cold, black void that had imprisoned both her mind and body.

The trickling echo of the running water inched into Diana's awareness — a familiar, innocent sound. Memories of home with rain drizzling through gutters and across window panes came to her. She grasped for that elusive serenity. The ache in her body relaxed somewhat. But this fragile composure was an uncertain respite, but one she needed for however few the moments.

Then, startled, Diana realized that Elana was not there. Swiftly she sat up, her gaze sweeping the shadowy interior. The woman's blanket was neatly spread. Her pack held the dent of her once slumbering head. The fur-lined cloak and blue tunic were tossed over the rock — but the crossbow was gone.

Diana scrambled to her feet, grabbing her sword. Outside, the wind whipped down from the hidden pass above, but the snow had stopped and the narrow trail had been blown clear. The clouds were still gray and gloomy, hovering low.

Diana walked to the edge of the trail and stared into the murky mists below. Visibility was barely ten meters. Icy pins stung her face as the swirling snow was picked up and hurled back again.

Damn. Her chilled fingers flexed and clenched about her sword's hilt. The sun churned faintly through the mire. It was near mid-day and the blizzard had passed at dawn, judging by the wind-swept trail. Precious hours had been lost.

Abruptly Diana twisted as, scuffling and sliding, Elana descended the embankment above the cavern. Amidst ice and gravel the woman skidded over the last few feet to the trail. Breeches and boots were stained damp. Her skin was flushed dark, and her braided hair was disheveled. She carried her crossbow in one hand, balanced a hoofed animal carcass across her shoulders with another, and had two rodents tied to her hip.

Elana deposited her prey on the more level ground. The hoofed beast was nearly a hundred pounds, Diana guessed. The circular tusks and protruding canine teeth did not look endearing.

"Morning," Elana offered flatly and disappeared inside. She returned after exchanging her crossbow for knife.

"Almost afternoon," Diana said gratingly. She pressed the seam closed at her collarbone against the cold.

"We'll not see it." Elana tugged the hoofed beast nearer the trail's edge. "I did not wake you because the storm will return soon — perhaps an hour."

"We could have been half-way to the Gate by now."

"There is no shelter between here and the summit," Elana said firmly, distinctly, as if she were instructing a child. "It is a full day's hike. We would not make it. We need food, not a death trek."

"What is that?" Diana pointed at the animal.

"Schefea."

Diana squinted against the wind and frowned. "They're poisonous."

"I intend to eat it, not be attacked by it. May I borrow your sword?"

"I was told their meat is toxic to humans."

"Only if you don't gut it properly. The venom is in its digestive track. Your sword?"

"Why?"

"To discard its head." The knife waved at the grotesquely snarling jaws. "The raw venom is acidic enough to burn bare skin. It is produced in the saliva glands. It is much easier to skin the thing if I do not have to deal with the head."

Diana stepped nearer, gripping both hands to the hilt. "Where?"

Elana pointed near the top of the neck. With a single, efficient swing that barely drew a spark, Diana severed the muscle and vertebra. Wordlessly Elana kicked the head over the cliff's side and squatted to dig her knife into the brown hide.

"And those two?"

"Grubbers," Elana returned without a glance. "They're relatively harmless root-diggers. But the meat is good roasted."

"Are we anticipating company or do you expect the storm to last that long?" It was a lot of meat for two people.

"It has the earmarks of a blizzard. We may be here a ten-day."

Diana glanced skyward as a few fresh snowflakes were thrown about. "In an hour, you say?"

"Yes."

Diana refused to recognize that it meant seclusion with this woman. Instead she set her mind to their practical needs. "I'll get my knife." She didn't know anything about schefea, but the smaller pair she could manage well enough.

❋ ❋ ❋

Elana sighed audibly and sank back into the soothing depths of the steaming pool. The storm had eased for a moment, and Di'nay had marched off with her miniature transmitter. She still had not been able to reach her commander; she needed to try again — weather permitting.

It was more like the pause between inhaling and exhaling than a break in a storming blizzard. But Elana understood Di'nay had needed the distance. All afternoon and evening she had kept busy — first with the skinning, then with the salting — then laundry, bathing, tending weapons, fire and finally roasting their dinner. And all the while the silence had stretched between them in longer and longer intervals. The tension was as tight as a wet leather knot shrunk dry — and as unmalleable.

Elana's gaze fell to the small box centered in the fire ring. Di'nay had pulled it from her green satchel of tricks when faced with the problem of their dwindling fuel supplies. It was a heating element that was not much larger than a thick slice of bread, but it radiated an amazing amount of heat and light. The wood that was left could be reserved for cooking now.

The small device reminded her of Di'nay's complexities and she shivered. In spite of the Amazon's personal discomfort, she had only chosen to use the heating element as a last resort. Her commitment to the delicate, non-technological balance of Aggar again impressed Elana. But the cultural differences between them were magnified.

No, Di'nay was not being overly conscientious for Commander Baily's sake. She was escaping.

Mother, ten days? Elana felt daunted by the prospect of spending — wasting — so much time and energy between them. They would begin to hate each other — especially snowbound and in such close quarters. There must be some sort of compromise that they could reach.

She climbed from the pool, brushing the clinging droplets from her skin before damply donning her clothes. All the while, she was wondering exactly what it was that Di'nay was struggling with. She could feel the Amazon's bitterness as well as her attraction, but the ambivalent faith Di'nay held for her own perceptions was not easily explained by deciphering amarin.

She simply had no answers, Elana admitted wearily as she settled by the fire, uncoiling the braid atop her head to shake her hair loose. Her sensitivity was probably clouding her judgment in this particular instance. Then again, perhaps it was simple...perhaps Di'nay herself did not know what she wanted? Amazons were human, Elana remembered, smiling faintly as her comb attacked her tangles. However seldom she tended to equate that mortal status with Di'nay, it was true. And, in reality, it was that mix of vulnerability and strength that drew her to the woman.

Elana hugged that knowledge inside so that even Di'nay's sullen return did not perturb her immediately. In many ways, just having the Amazon safe and near — knowing the Mother had granted a respite from the mission — was a gift to be treasured. At least now they had time to deal with the murky conflicts of this friendship.

"Is there any more tea?" Diana asked brusquely, shedding her green cloak. She had not bothered to don clothes over her fieldsuit.

"Certainly." Elana reached for Di'nay's cup.

"I can do that!"

Elana gritted her teeth and patiently handed the still-empty cup to her. So much for treasured gifts of togetherness.

Di'nay's tight-lipped frown reminded Elana of an irritated, pouting child — no, not irritated, Elana corrected, shifting her gaze away from the woman. Injured was a better description — injured and still hurting... "Di'nay — "

"Yes."

...and brittle. Elana suppressed a sigh. "Did you reach your people?"

"Thomas is not — " Diana forced a breath. Things were obviously not getting any better between them. She pinched the bridge of her nose, vaguely hoping to relieve the aching tension in her head. "I beg patience, I have no cause to be angry with you. The answer is no, I did not reach them."

As the amarin shifted Elana recognized that the silent cry for distance had lessened. There was a tentative desire to mend — to make peace. Elana turned the comb over in her hands, gathering her courage. Come what may, it was time to talk.

Diana glanced at her forcing half a grin, "I do apologize. Should we find a suitable penance for me? Perhaps the dishes for a ten-day?"

Elana moistened her lips. "Perhaps...just talking?"

There was a pause before a guarded, "Certainly. About what?"

"About us." Elana was acutely attuned to Di'nay's discomfort. "About what happened — what is happening."

Diana stared at her tea, thinking absurdly that she hated it lukewarm. "All right. What do you think is happening?"

Elana hesitated, biting her lip. Her blue eyes dropped to the comb again. "I'm not certain. Something changed when...when we were kissing that night." Her gaze sought Di'nay's face. She swallowed hard at the drawn, closed expression and the tightly leashed amarin. "We were so close...." Elana felt disbelief ripple through the Amazon, and she abruptly realized something. "I did enjoy your touch, Di'nay."

For a moment you did, Diana thought begrudgingly.

"But then it — it all came crashing apart again, and I felt...so lost?"

Diana began to tremble, caught somewhere between fear and anger. Blessed Goddess, why couldn't people just care for people? Why were expectations always so wound up into everything? Her throat ached with the pain she had caused Elana, and she barely managed to say, "As Daughter of Mothers, I beg your forgiveness!"

Elana stiffened, but held silent.

"It has never been my intention to hurt you — ever." Diana almost choked on the anguish but she forced the words, "It was never my intention to seduce you. I swear it by the Mother's Hand!"

"Perhaps it should have been."

Pain turned to bitter irony as Diana said, "Would it have been so easy to follow the Council's designs? Would you be any more comfortable with me right now?"

"I suggest," Elana murmured quietly, fearfully, "that we are having problems because you are not comfortable with yourself."

"Truth." Diana accepted the blame wholly. "You've done nothing wrong."

Elana's breath hissed in frustration. "You said that after we kissed! I do not understand it any better now than I did then." She shook her head, the long curls shimmering forward into a curtain that hid her face. She tried again. "You once said that — for you — making love required caring as well as attraction. I had come to believe that we cared for each other — that we were strong friends?"

"Friendship is different from...." Diana was not sure that it was so very different now.

"You have also said," Elana continued more firmly, her temper gathering, "that you are not demanding a commitment from anyone until you are home. Or has that changed?" At her pause there was no reply from the woman. She demanded, "At least tell me why we are so ill-suited as lovers, Di'nay? When we both desire the same thing, why is it so forbidden to you?"

The amarin of anguish washed through Di'nay and struck Elana harshly. A torrent of sarcasm and anger came tearing through the pain. Confused — hurt, Elana's eyes sought the wind-bronzed face.

But the Amazon's face was a mask of cold stone. "Can we spare enough wood for fresh tea? This stuff's getting bitter."

Elana felt her skin tone darken. "Like your temper?"

Diana grabbed the heater, jerking it from the fire ring. She would not be baited!

With a chilly silence Elana dropped the wood beside the Amazon, leaving the woman to start the fire herself. She stalked across the sand to her pack, suddenly — defiantly — dissatisfied with Di'nay's alien brew. She would drink her own tea!

"Why no answer to my question?" Elana spat bitterly, rummaging savagely through her pack. The sarcasm faded from her voice as she said, "Is there some rite of purification I have not done, Di'nay? Or that you have not?

Why is it not just that we want to be together for a while?"

Because I would want you for life! Diana shouted silently. The raging frustration strained her control to its very edges. "Simple! Woman — there is nothing simple about it!"

"Don't you think I know that!?!!" Elana shrieked, squeezing her eyes shut against the pummeling emotions and struggling to rein in her temper as her skin took on the dark richness of mahogany. "Mother, if it were simple I would not need you to explain it to me — !"

"No!" The stick cracked in Diana's grasp and pieces flew against the cavern wall, splintering with the force. Diana spun, crouched like a cornered animal. "Leave me alone! Because you're young and — and feel a bit of something — you think you know me, girl?! You think I want you to?! You? A little Council pawn with a...a reckless sense of duty and — ?"

Elana exploded with fury. Blue flashed and from across the cave she struck — and Diana saw no mere girl or Council pawn. Tall and lithe of limb — strong with a power of soul and body, a woman stood. So still she stood — skin shimmering with health — eyes blazing with defiance — a strong, supple figure of confidence and truth. Here was no child. Here was a woman of ability!

Diana's head split with the intensity, and a black schism shattered the picture in her mind. She reeled down into darkness.

❋ ❋ ❋

Diana awoke to the scent of freshly brewed tea. She found herself beneath her blanket. The back of her head felt as if it'd been struck by a rock. Her eyes shut again as she realized what had happened. No wonder the Council had never explained the Blue Sight to the Empire.

But — Mae n'Pour — how Elana must have resented her blindness! Council aside, cultures aside, she deserved more credit than Diana had granted — in all things.

"I beg your patience, Diana n'Athena."

Diana drew a deep breath, finding her head clearing. She tried sitting up and was pleased as the pain receded altogether. She was feeling more normal by the second.

"Are you all right?" Elana's whisper was almost inaudible.

She should have known that, Diana thought. Elana sat beside the dying embers of the fire, her arms hugged tightly around her knees. Her shoulders were hunched forward as her long hair hid her face.

"Yes, I am," Diana returned quietly, thinking those blue eyes must be shut.

A broken gasp caught in Elana's throat and she bit her lip to stay the tears.

"You owe me no apology," Diana said. She shifted the blanket aside. "We both lost our tempers. We'll know better next time."

There should not have been a first time. Elana buried her eyes against her knees.

"I'm all right," Diana repeated urgently. "You haven't hurt me."

"But I could have...."

"You didn't. And in truth, you wouldn't have. I'm certain of it."

Elana desperately wanting to believe that. She lifted her chin and said more clearly, "I have never struck anyone so hard."

"I should be honored," Diana whispered slowly, stunned by the depths of the emotions she had tapped in this woman.

"Honored?" Elana laughed weakly. "May the Mother spare you greater laurels."

Diana smiled at that, but her heart chilled as the dark head bowed again. The blue-clad shoulders shuddered, and she knew Elana was crying. She moved nearer and knelt, cautious not to touch her. "Please," Diana whispered, "don't do this on my account. I'm all right. Truly I am."

"We are not," Elana reminded her hoarsely.

"We — we will be."

"I try to understand, Di'nay. But each time I think I do, something happens and everything seems to change. First, before Colmar — then at Black Falls...am I truly so inexperienced? Inept at reading your advances or — or too clumsy in an embrace? Or is it because I am of Aggar and you are a Sister? Do you even know?!"

"It isn't you." Diana wearily pushed the hair back from her face. "Your inexperience is a factor, but mostly, it is my — differences. It's.... I'm the one who's afraid. I don't trust what I feel — what I see. I'm afraid of hurting you or — us. There is so little time left to me on Aggar. I don't know...what saying good-bye would mean."

"Would it be any more insane than what we live with now?" Elana asked.

"Perhaps...perhaps not." Diana's conviction was fading. Her eyes absorbed the rich brown of Elana's profile and the startling blue gaze that stared into oblivion. Diana moved slowly, pushing the heavy black curls aside and tucking the strands behind an ear. Elana's eyes slid shut, and regretfully Diana removed her hand.

Her chin dropped, but Elana could no longer hide behind her hair.

"I do worry about you," Diana said quietly.

"Me? In what way?"

"Even whores here do not know what a woman loving a woman is. It is so very uncommon. Yet you say you...want me. I am worried you think so merely because the Council says you should. You've spent your whole life doing their bidding — believing in them and what they say. Why shouldn't you now? I don't want you wanting me because of them. I could not. It wouldn't be right."

"No," Elana glanced up at Di'nay, "that would not be right."

For a very long moment, they looked at one another, then Elana's eyes blurred with tears again and her gaze dropped back to her hands. "Di'nay...I've said I am here because I have chosen to be. Yet you have never believed that. I can only say that I want to be with you...that I want you." She shook her head despairingly. "I do not know how to convince you. I have only my word to give — that my feelings are part of me...and not the Council's purpose. But my word has never been enough for you. I have nothing else for proof."

Diana clenched her teeth, fighting the frustration and confusion inside herself. Put so simply, could she still doubt the woman's pledge? "I beg patience, but...it is difficult to believe you're not afraid."

"I have never said I was not afraid. I am afraid — of losing you."

"Are you afraid of me?"

Elana laughed. "I would think you'd be more afraid of me — after what I have done to you."

She has not answered, Diana thought. Yet she too was still wary of Elana. Not because of what had happened, but because of what could happen. "I am not afraid of your Sight."

"No?" Elana challenged. She so desperately wanted to believe that.

"No." Diana's fingers gently turned Elana to face her. "As a matter of fact, I think you have the most beautiful blue eyes I've ever seen."

"Oh?" Elana smiled very faintly, her gaze lifting to Di'nay's.

"So incredibly lovely," Diana whispered, mesmerized by an awareness that had nothing to do with the Sight.

Blue eyes slipped away to rest on pale lips. Memory kindled desire, and quietly, simply, Elana said, "Kiss me?"

Her kiss was so sweet, melting into that subtle tingling warmth that Diana had dreamed of for so long. With a slowness born of utter abandon she absorbed the line, the shape, the silken texture of Elana's yielding mouth. Satiny touch parted their lips. Tongue stroked tongue, and her stomach quivered in her wanting.

Too much, she worried. Half-fearful of her own stirrings, Diana drew back, but Elana followed. Her mouth reclaimed Diana's as her fingers brushed the tanned cheek and her hand slipped about the nape of Diana's neck, preventing escape. Hungrily — desperately her tender assault coaxed and pleaded, and Diana released the reluctance. She did not want to go back; she wanted Elana as her lover.

Clothes parted, and fumbling fingers soon soothed as skin bared and shivered in dawning awareness. Franticness faded. Angles pressed into softer curves as bodies merged, and strands of silken hair wrapped around them, a shimmering ebony against the pale white and warming brown.

With lips and cheek and her own soft hair, Diana roamed across the satin-skinned softness of Elana's shoulders. Hands tugged, urging her return for the abandoned kisses. As she lifted herself she paused to look into a blue-jeweled gaze.

Elana's hands smoothed the pale, strong shoulders as she smiled up at Di'nay.

"Beautiful...," Diana's own smile grew slowly, "...so very beautiful."

Fingers slipped across Diana's breasts, and fascinated, Elana's gaze was drawn to the softness that filled her hands. Slight, yet so perfectly rounded, the small mounds yielded. With a moan Diana's eyes closed and she arched into Elana's touch. But the images within her head took new shapes and her mouth dried. She lowered herself again, her own mouth seeking the fuller curve of Elana's breast.

"So soft...," Diana whispered, lost in her Sisters' tongue as her lips circled the tender peak, "...so sweet — how could I not love you?"

Elana's fingers sank into Di'nay's hair as her lover's mouth claimed her. Softness of murmurs, of silken warm skin...always her voice...always her hands...arching, flying higher. Elana thought she could climb no higher...no touch could draw more. A tentative finger, a slender pressing touch amidst the moist heat, and then the cradling palm, cupped and rubbing...capturing her with such sweet aching. She breathed, "Please?" and wetness opened as she drew Di'nay within...spiraling higher...following...spinning...gathering with no end....

"Ti mae Elana." Diana lifted her head as she felt Elana's body still beneath her fingers' touch. The hands clenching her shoulders paused, frozen — the soft lips trembled. Diana called to her, "Ann n'Mee...z'ti Mau corae. Elana!"

Blue eyes opened as everything gave way, and Diana, locked in that sapphire gaze, fell with her. Tumbling, trembling...the waves shook apart and silver flashed white — like sunlight skimming water, it blinded. Scorching — burning it took them whole, and finally crumbling, dropped them through shards of light until they emerged, bound together. They drifted, their bodies melted, glowing. The blanket beneath them warmed the cavern's sands as the heater warmed the air, and slowly, they returned.

With effort Elana blinked and released Diana. Eyes fluttered closed as Diana arched, yielding a moan — so reluctant to leave that blueness. Exhausted then, she buried her face in the soft hair, and Elana's arms slipped around her.

For a long while they lay still as breathing steadied and hearts quieted. The friendly bubbling of the cavern's springs danced through the chambers, echoing their peace. For a guilty moment Diana was grateful for the raging blizzard outside.

She nuzzled deeper into the silky tresses and felt the guilt dissolve. The Mother allowed things in Her own good time — even this.

"I beg patience...," Elana murmured thickly, but there was a faint lisp of laughter in her low voice.

"Patience — why?" Diana pushed herself up an elbow unsteadily.

"You...." She moistened her dry lips, and Di'nay leaned forward to wet them with a gentle kiss. The softness lingered warmly.

"Why?" Diana asked again.

"You looked very — startled."

"It was not what I expected."

"Nor I." Elana brought Di'nay's fingers to her lips.

"What did you expect?" Had she ever truly sought to flee from this?

"Less." Elana felt Di'nay's hand, warm and still damp as it curled against her cheek. "It is so much more than what I — had observed with others."

Huskily, Diana said, "Does 'so much more' please you?"

"Yes...."

Diana's fingers sank in the thick, black hair. Her head moved almost in denial, amazed both at the silk beneath her touch and at the depths of her own feelings. "This...our attraction goes very deep."

"Perhaps there is more than...?" Elana did not quite dare to finish.

"Much more."

The words were answer enough. A faint smile touched Elana's lips as she drew Di'nay near again.

Diana sighed — a soft, warm sound as Elana drew a cloak over them. She found their bodies fit well together even in this languid peace, and the beat of Elana's heart was a steady pulse beneath her fingers. Strong — contented, its rhythm echoed her own heart's measure. Perfect harmonics, two and yet one....

Her mind drifted, the shadows of the cave whispering their reassurances. This was real. This was theirs. Slowly the subtle scent of their loving wrapped about them, and beneath the Mother's gentle hand, sleep descended.

❊ ❊ ❊

Chapter Five

Diana pushed herself away from the cavern wall and brushed the dust from her sleeve. She had been gazing down the short tunnel to the snowy whiteness beyond. The howl of the wind was fading, and reluctantly, the Amazon admitted that the time was coming to leave their mountain retreat. Now night was descending, granting them a last evening's reprieve, but tomorrow they must go. She wondered how much strength there was in this tentative bond they had forged.

A warmth with the strength of a blazing fire suddenly enveloped her. She turned, her dark gaze seeking Elana's once sleeping form. Tenderly the fire crept through her skin, easing her anxiety and filling her with a subtle peace.

Diana smiled ironically at her insecurities. She really did spend too much time thinking. "Here," she called finally and moved across the sandy floor.

Blue eyes met Diana's fully as she dropped down beside Elana. Like a tangible hug the amarin grew stronger, and Elana murmured, "I know...."

Diana gathered the woman into her arms, burying her face in the silky skin and hair. So much unsaid — stop thinking. Her lips sought Elana's — soft, welcoming.

❊ ❊ ❊

The women trudged through the loose gray stones, concentrating in silence as the path shifted and slid beneath their feet. The footing was uncertain at best. With each crunch and crystal-like clatter, their nerves tightened. They were crossing the remnants of the reef that guarded this ancient coast even before the mountains' upheaval. The once-sharp white and sandy pink columns were faded and worn to gray sand and mud. They still banked and climbed with an ugly foreboding, but the edges were not to be feared as much as the rubble into which it was disintegrating.

Elana paused uncertainly and pushed the wayward hair from her face. Although the wind was chilly, it lacked the icy touch of the alpine heights. She almost welcomed it after the exertion.

Several feet behind her Diana stopped, unwilling to crowd too close on this trail. She had never seen stuff as wicked as this. Her feet were bruised from the sharp thrusts and juts of it. For two days they had traveled through this — two days should have seen them through to the barren plateau of the exposed seabed. Yet, the twists and turns of the ancient reef allowed little glimpse ahead, and the cascading slopes of loose rock often eclipsed the trail-markings. It was thoroughly possible that they were lost, but there was nothing she could do about it. Sometime yesterday morning, she had lost her bearings; as long as Elana was willing to guide, she was willing to follow.

A light warmth surrounded her and Diana took her eyes from the crags above. It was odd how she was learning to heed the touch of Elana's blue gaze. The thought flickered through her mind that she would miss this intimacy — feel cheated almost, if ever there was another.

Elana pointed ahead. "If I am right that pass will drop down to the wastelands."

"And if you're not?"

"Then it will be another very uncomfortable night."

"All right then, let's go look."

Curious, Elana watched as Di'nay moved forward to take the lead. There was a trusting, matter-of-factness in her lover's amarin that surprised Elana. This calmness was no longer a mask. The fatigue and the homesickness were slowly melting away; the tightness about Di'nay's mouth had eased. She liked the fact that she had had a part in banishing that weariness. She was good for Di'nay, and it was beginning to show.

"You're thinking about me!" Diana's voice carried back over her shoulder.

Guiltily Elana pulled her eyes away. "You are awfully quiet. Good thoughts, I hope?"

"Very."

Diana laughed and trudged on.

✳ ✳ ✳

The sun brushed the amber of the sky with red and violet. Awed, Diana paused at the crest of the pass. Twilight had faded into gloom beneath dingy overcast clouds for so many days now that she had nearly forgotten Aggar's painted sunsets.

Elana reached her side, and Diana gestured to the orange tinted expanses below and the dance of light beyond. Silent, they stood together as the fiery bronzed orb shimmered and touched the line of the distant horizon. The wastelands glimmered with rose and gold...fingers of color stretching out from that glowing giant. Above, the blues darkened and indigoes emerged. With a slowness that hurt the eye, but with a rush that cheated souls, the sun sank, leaving the two women in twilight.

Elana broke their silence with a reluctant sigh. "We might make a league before darkfall. When the early moon rises, it will be near full tonight. We could easily reach the plateau in her light."

"How far?"

"Not quite six leagues."

Diana cast a more critical eye across the barrenness below. In the twilight the dry sea bed appeared unerringly flat from this height. Its evenness was broken only by stubby silhouettes of cacti-like trees. She looked at the exposed descent of the gravel trail and frowned. Its nakedness made her feel vulnerable.

Elana took half a step forward at her companion's show of concern. Her Sight swept the crags and slopes about them. She reached past the multitude of small reef dwellers, then out across the plains below. Plant — animal — all meshed into the expected patterns. Above, leagues away, a scavenger circled lazily, so far off that she could not distinguish its type nor the lure of its dead prey. She stretched further west, knowing there were Changling nomads and a few lone friends of the Council there. Distantly, so very distantly, were people. But none were near enough to identify. She turned to the north — to Maltar's black horizon. It was an indistinguishable dark haze, its hills of blackpines and plowfields hidden in dimness. "I see no one," she murmured.

Diana glanced at her sharply. "Where is the group we follow?"

That was puzzling to Elana. By the signs, the two men they had tracked into the Cellar's Gate had joined a small band of Maltar's militia at the pinnacle's shelter. Although they had not been snowbound quite as long as Di'nay and she, they certainly had not had time to cross the wastelands. "North." Elana pointed toward the Maltar's reign. She pulled her attention back from that shadowy horizon. She had not realized she was so exhausted. "To Maltar's realm, the only place they can be — along the reef edges — "

"But you can't see them?" Diana did not pretend to understand the nuances of the Blue Sight. It was Elana's uncertainty that unsettled her.

"No," Elana admitted with more assurance. She pointed again, outlining the crags to their right. "The reef is too dense there for me to see past. They must be following the edge around to Maltar. Several leagues out, it begins to break up and the foothills come down to the plateau. There is water and some small game. It is the more practical route to go, if one is not in a hurry."

Diana slowly breathed out. It didn't add up. The two out of Black Falls had been moving at an impossible pace. She didn't believe that their fear of a lone Southern Trader would have propelled such a flight. Since Elana's encounter with Tartuk, she had assumed that it was the Maltar's summons that spawned the men's urgency. Yet if the militia had revised their orders...? It was not comforting to think the Maltar's interest might have waned. That could mean he knew Garrison was Terran — or that Garrison was dead. She preferred to think that the Maltar had sent the soldiers as protective escorts, but she had no way to be certain of anything.

Still, as Elana had explained, crossing the wastelands was not lightly done. The upheaval of the mountains had driven the sea floor a thousand feet up. There were a few scattered water pockets here and there, but for the most part the sieve-like rock simply let the mountain waters seep down into oblivion. Perhaps the militia commander was a loyal, but doggedly practical sort of fellow.

"You worry they will be circling back?" Elana asked. It would be the first opportunity the land had presented in quite some time.

"I'm more worried about giving them the idea that they need to circle back because they know where we are now," Diana said, climbing back a few feet to look behind them. The cold canyons beyond the crest were already growing inky black.

"I could shadow our light. None would see then."

"And you wouldn't get any sleep," Diana pointed out practically. She sighed. She really hated the thought of another night on this stuff. A piece of her wanted to shelve the whole mission — just for one night. Be a little self-indulgent and have a hedonistically good night's sleep on some dusty, sandy grit. "It seems foolish to risk the exposure," Diana muttered, still weighing the decision.

Elana raised a tired grin. "I'll grant that it may be an unnecessary risk. I'm not so certain which is more foolish."

With a chuckle, Diana agreed. "Let's try over there, behind the reef, shall we?"

The early rest drew gratitude from every inch of their stiffened bodies. That, combined with the cold meat provisions and warmed toes from the compact heater, almost made them forget the rubble beneath them.

As the wind started to rise, Di'nay invited her nearer, and Elana admitted that they had chosen their nook rather well. At least the wind was well deflected.

They were literally dug into a natural cleft in the reef mountain that offered a wind break. The heater was pushed into the loose rock, a bit more secure than their packs. They sat back into the slope with the thermal blankets wrapped around them making a toasty cocoon. Diana had dug deep into the rubble, creating a form-fitting, if rather tenacious chair for them. As uncomfortable as the seating was, the view was more inspiring.

Above them the last of the overcast clouds had scattered and the clear black void of space was speckled with stars so vividly near that the red and blue tints of some were visible. The towering silhouettes of the rocky spirals ascended and met with the velvet dome — pillars holding a cathedral ceiling high.

"Where is your home?" Elana asked quietly. The peace of this evening was not something to be broken lightly.

"You can't see her from here," Diana said just as softly. She liked the feel of this woman cradled back against her body. She was undeniably in love. There was no other explanation for feeling quite so contented in such an impossible environment.

"Is it so far away?" The soft, curious voice called Diana back from her musings.

"Yes, and it's in the wrong direction."

"Nehna?"

Diana smiled at the Sororian. At Elana's insistence, she begrudgingly tutored her during their snowy retreat. "The nearest star cluster is only visible from your southern hemisphere. But even that marks only about the half-way point."

"Ann..." Careful, but secure in Di'nay's grasp, Elana turned, seeking Di'nay's face as she teased, "...you really are a Southerner?"

She had never thought of it that way. Diana asked, "Are you insulted?"

"Certainly not." Elana feigned disgust and settled back. Then after a moment she asked, "Is the disputed galactic border visible from here?"

"Yes." Diana's voice took on a somber tone. Her finger reached to trace a white haze on the black velvet and her head bent near to Elana's as she sighted for her. "That ribbon...that looks like a faint cloud. That's it."

"Is it as close as it seems?"

"Closer." Diana thought, Goddess, Garrison — don't you dare be dead!

"Are your Sisters far enough away to survive, if this brings war?" Elana asked, hoping Di'nay would have a safe haven.

"Possibly...probably. Many things would become uncertain."

Elana nodded. She knew from her Keep's studies that on Aggar the ramifications of war were eventually felt world-wide, although it might take generations. So much was interwoven. It would be the same across a galaxy as well.

"I would not leave here. My ship — the transport I would have to take — would never escape this quadrant safely, if war came."

Elana's heart thumped at that deadly forewarning. Slowly she shook her head. "I will send you home before war comes, Di'nay. This I promise."

"By the time we know, Darling, it will be too late."

The arms about Elana hugged her more tightly for a moment. But she again shook her head. "No, Di'nay, it will not be."

The Council had forbidden this disclosure, yet her allegiance, as Shadowmate, as lover — was not just to the Council but to this woman as well. "This pilot, Garrison, carries information regarding an assassination plot, Di'nay."

The figure behind her tensed.

"Your Imperial Chairman is to be the target. The Seers projected there is at least six of your Terran months before the attempt. The Seers could not tell exactly where or when the attempt would be made. The Council took that as a sign that — that an overland rescue would be the best response."

Reasonable, Diana granted. Much could happen in six months — no, five now. Plans changed. Spies were uncovered...the Chairman might be disposed of anyway. It would have risked too much to reveal such a vague threat to Thomas. The resulting military search for Garrison would have near destroyed Aggar's tentative autonomy — still, if the planet disintegrated, what use was independence?

"Thank you for telling me," Diana said finally, and consciously she released the tension from her body. She had always known there was urgency in this mission. It was almost like a reprieve to be given a realistic deadline of five months. Deadline...the ironic smile never got to her lips; it was a poor choice of words.

"I am sorry," Elana murmured in Sororian. Di'nay's amarin had become too indistinct for her to decipher.

"For what?"

"For not speaking sooner."

"It was the Council's decision not to tell Thomas, wasn't it?"

"Yes."

"Wise move," Diana admitted. "He would have summoned starblasters at the mere mention of the Chairman's involvement."

"Then you understand why he must not know now."

Diana nodded and tightened her embrace. Her lips brushed the bared neck, and she whispered, "And I find no grudge to hold."

Elana laughed with relief. "You seldom do, I think."

"Then why are you always so fearful?" Diana teased, but with a real interest.

That stilled her laughter with an emotional pain that was very real.

"Tell me?" Diana urged, sensitive to the fluttering that closed those bright eyes and quieted Elana's body.

"When I send you back there," Elana nodded toward the twinkling silver speck above, "I want you to have only the most beautiful of memories to take. And if I can keep you from discovering I'm human, perhaps you have a chance."

Yes, you will send me away, Diana thought, and what will you remember of me, dearest Elana? Will you remember my hands are easily cold with my alien blood? Or that I'm your elder by more than a decade and was blinded by your youth for too long? Or will you remember how my hands warmed against your body? — How soft the whiteness of my skin is against your deepening color? Will you remember our passion until another — a man? — is sent to your charge and you are touched again...?

I do not want you to forget, Diana thought and clasped Elana nearer, burying her face against the warm, soft skin of her neck. The woman arched as Diana's tongue traced the curve of bone, her hands spreading wide where they molded about the tunic-clad ribs.

The gravel beneath them shifted and Elana gave a startled shout. Rock and she so seldom got along.

A chuckle started deep as Diana recognized the riskiness of her intentions. "We're going to kill ourselves, aren't we?"

Elana began giggling at the same realization. She grabbed Di'nay's arms as their laughter moved them again.

"I've got you!" Diana said, only somewhat reassuring.

Elana gasped, leaning back into Diana's body. "You — I trust! But not this bed!"

❋ ❋ ❋

Chapter Six

"It doesn't look much more fun than what we've been through," Diana noted.

They were again standing in the pass overlooking the wastelands. The beige sandstone plain stretched monotonously north, a shimmering, glaring white further out that ended against a thin line of black. In the west, there were faint hues of orange and rust as the land began to break up into bluffs. Neither direction looked very inviting. "The fastest route is the straightest." Elana pointed to the faint black strip of the Maltar's lands. "It's roughly three-and-a-half days across."

"Is there water?"

She nodded tossing her braid over her shoulder. "A little...this far east it's always uncertain. The trail along the reef's edge is well marked. It has a few shelters and some of the mountain run-offs, but it is scouted by the Maltar's troops just as a matter of course. We'd have to be extremely careful not to be seen.

"West — it is a day-and-half to the bluffs. Many of the canyons can be followed the width of the plateau then. The Council has friends among the lone dwellers. They might have news of the Maltar's doings. By that route we would eventually have to double-back east — on this side of the river or in Maltar — if Tartuk's information is still correct and the Maltar is at the Priory." Elana hesitated a moment before adding, "You should know, the Changlings roam in the west. But most likely they've migrated toward the sea by this time, in preparation for winter."

Diana looked at her curiously. "Your father mentioned the Changlings. He does business with them, doesn't he?"

"The Council often needs their help and they need weapons, so my father becomes a natural mediator. They're not quite human. And they are mercenaries — although not particularly trustworthy ones. They have a tendency to sell information to any and all bidders. Tartuk would be considered saintly in comparison."

"Charming." Diana nodded ahead. "You have a preference?"

"If you believe your Garrison-pilot is still at the Priory, then I'd suggest cutting across the plateau."

"Do you think he's there?"

She shrugged. "I do not know. I am not a Seer."

"A wager?" Diana's dark eyes swept the dusty horizon. Hadn't she just been complaining about rain a few ten-day back? "What are the odds that Tartuk's friends would be following the eastern edge, if they were not going to the Priory?"

"Their route is the safer. Also once across the river they could make up a lot of time, if they have horses waiting. And they would not have the dangers of the Changlings' scouts in Maltar's country. They could ride openly and safely. Still..."

"Still," Diana continued, "marching straight across would save them precious time, and they would not be threatened by the Changlings, if they crossed the river before turning west again. But it seems odd that the patrol was sent all the way out here to meet the two from Colmar unless it was to update their instructions."

"Perhaps someone from Black Falls — the owner of that dead hawk Papa spoke of? Perhaps they found Tartuk's body?"

"Perhaps."

Elana looked at Di'nay. "If it were your prisoner, would you move him?"

"Not particularly — not unless I knew someone was coming. But then, if I was expecting only one or two, I'd be more apt to set a trap and use him for bait."

Elana felt her throat tighten. She had not thought of that possibility. It made her feel vulnerable to be so bound by her limitations when the stakes were so high.

"What would you do?" Di'nay turned to her again. "You know more of this Maltar than I do. What would you expect him to do?"

"I do not know," she repeated, nervously.

Diana's gaze narrowed. "What's wrong, Elana?"

"Nothing. Why do you ask?"

"Your hunches have been well played so far," Diana said. "The river trail, their rendezvous in Colmar...tracking Tartuk. Yet now?"

"Those were not hunches," Elana corrected her, matter-of-factly. "I read their signs and deciphered their amarin. As for Tartuk? I was following you, and they assumed you'd be following them. I merely ran into him first."

"You anticipated him well."

"No, I was being protectively cautious. I was covering the possibility that they would send someone back after you. I check and double-check because I do not double-guess my adversaries very well. It is something the Mistress taught me to do a long time ago. With luck, it will be enough to keep us alive." For an instant, her eyes caught Di'nay's. "I am an excellent guide, Diana n'Athena, but you would not enjoy a game of strategy with me...it would grow tedious with my clumsiness."

A hand brushed a wisp of hair from her cheek. "I've not found you clumsy. Perhaps you give yourself too little credit?"

Elana smiled softly before she shook her head. "My talents lie in many directions, but of the Maltar's plans — I have no inkling. The Blue Sight is notorious for its advantages and less renowned for its drawbacks. I can decipher cloudy amarin, anticipate imminent movement, and confound with illusion — but to unravel the scheming designs of men? That I rarely do well."

Diana's lips twisted cynically. "Whether fortunate or not, I seem to do that well enough. I suspect it's bred from a lack of trust."

"Because you are an Amazon? I wouldn't have you any other way." Then more seriously she asked, "Which way, Di'nay?"

"Across." Diana pointed into the sandy emptiness below. "I'll gamble this troop commander is a weary old career man who is trudging over the standard route. If any of them suspect Tartuk failed and the Southern Trader is following, then a bit of a detour will be to our advantage."

✿ ✿ ✿

The trail beneath their feet was firmer and less treacherous in the descent. Diana was still sliding a half-step here and there, but at least there was more solid ground beneath the gravel. The leagues steadily passed under them.

Rounding a bend, Diana called a halt. The path had twisted sharply into towering reefs, but below it angled back in a narrow ledge, finally dropping to the plateau. She glanced at the sun with satisfaction; it wasn't even mid-morning. They had made good time.

Elana offered her a waterskin, warning, "We need to be careful now. There will be one or two waterholes on our path, but they may be dry or polluted."

Diana returned the water after a single sip. "I don't know if your Council's records have it or not, but you should know — we Terran-types do very poorly after about three days without water."

"Yes, I know that." Elana laced the bag to her hip. "I won't let you die of thirst."

"I don't expect you would."

A wisp of breeze stirred the air. Puzzled, Elana turned to the path ahead of them. An odd breeze, she thought, her blue gaze searching, but the rock hid much. There were a few small creatures and a nest or two, but nothing seemed out of place.

"What do you see?" Diana asked quietly.

"I don't know." Elana looked above and then behind them. Perhaps a bird somewhere was hunting? But she should have been able to Sight that. "It's nothing...."

Diana watched her carefully. The woman's tone was too cautious for 'nothing.'

Elana moved down the trail. "I don't understand? It's different. But...."

"But?"

"There is nothing." Her blue gaze swung back to Di'nay. The Amazon stood, wary but patient. Her amarin's undertones of tenderness, respect — the passion — were all there — the woman she knew.

But this other...thing that was not? Elana studied the rock wall beside them, the crevice below...everything was there, yet...dormant? "There is...an emptiness."

Diana watched Elana struggle for words. The back of her neck prickled.

"Perhaps it is just the wastelands," Elana murmured, her gaze returning to that endless stretch of barrenness. "I've never actually stood beside a desert." But there was very little conviction in her voice.

Diana's gloved hand silently drew her sword. Her shoulders flexed beneath the pack and long bow, shifting in preparation — gaining mobility.

Elana pulled her crossbow free, snapping the twin bows into place.

"There is only one way down," Diana muttered grimly.

"It may truly be nothing."

"Then it will be nothing," Diana said quietly, stepping forward to take the lead.

"I am here to protect you!" Elana tried to stop her.

"Then protect my back!" Diana retorted and pushed past.

She was irritated, but Elana clamped it down firmly.

Their march was silent and tense. Diana's own senses grew uneasy with the passing of time, but Elana could only shake her head in puzzlement. There was still nothing specific to be named and so they went on.

The three came suddenly. Hoarse war cries rang as the soldiers sprang from the rocks above, jumping recklessly with knives drawn. The first finished his leap on Diana's blade. She slammed another into the cliff wall with her shoulder.

The crossbow swung like a club into the third giant, but Elana's footing slipped. She dropped the weapon and tumbled beneath his bulk, twisting his elbow as they fell. His knife folded between them, steel flat against her hand, and they rolled. Her glove slit as it guided the blade into his breast and his own weight pushed it deep.

Diana gasped as a knife's hilt pummeled into her shoulder blade. The soldier arched against the stone, using the leverage, and they both went to the ground. Her knife flew free from a solid punch to her wrist as her other hand deflected a downward thrust. Diana twisted, her leg locking about the man's knees as she sought to gain the top. Rubble gave way and suddenly their roll became a somersault.

A scream pierced the air as Elana grabbed and missed. A sharp crack rang up and echoed out into the steep canyon below as Di'nay's long bow broke with the impact. The soldier died when the two hit the bottom of the pit, his neck broken.

"Out! Get out!"

Diana blinked, disoriented. Her head cleared enough to let her feel the pain in her shoulder as it bathed everything in white. For an instant she lay stunned, gritting her teeth — fighting back unconsciousness. Something moved near her ear.

Her eyes flew open as Elana's voice penetrated the fog. "Climb! Di'nay! It is a cucarii nest! Climb!"

The adrenaline pumped as she heaved the soldier's body from her waist and scrambled to her feet. Her head was spinning, but she grabbed for rock and climbed toward that voice.

Stone and dirt slid loose, dumping her back into the hollow. She could see them now — small, shell-armored creatures scampering into the sunlight. Their mottled beige and gray bodies blended perfectly with the rock. Each looked like an odd flower, long petals grasping in and out of their centers as they clamored over the rubble in her direction.

She kicked the gravel and dust, burying a few and gaining precious seconds.

"Climb!" The order was imperious as Elana's cloak descended, but it reached only half-way.

The ground moved as her toes dug, the cucarii scrambling about her ankles. A blast of heat enveloped them as a roaring inferno leapt from the rocky pit. She clawed and reached for the blazing cloak as the creatures jerked spastically, dropping from their pursuit.

"It's not real...not real!" Diana muttered desperately, her hand blistering within its burning glove as she held tight to the cloak. The strained tendons in her shoulder shrieked with the pull.

It was done in a second, and Elana's hands were there, guiding her over the edge. Gasping, she sprawled limp. The roar of the flames died. Her gloves were unsinged. She concentrated, and slowly her body calmed, accepting the reality that there had been no burning.

Stiffly Diana rolled to her back and pushed herself up to sit against the cliff wall. Only vaguely aware, she watched as Elana unlaced and discarded her boots. She managed a faint "wait" as the woman drew her knife, intent on slicing through the fieldsuit's fabric.

Her shoulder protested as she slid the pack off beneath her cloak and leaned forward to pry open the velcro seams at her calves. Elana's fingers moved quickly, usurping her fumbling.

"Do you know if you were stung?" Elana asked.

Her head moved weakly in negation. She dropped back against her pack, wearily pushing the hair from her eyes. Goddess, she had wrenched that shoulder, and that tumble — between the bow shaft and the soldier she had taken quite a pummeling.

"I don't see any marks." Elana's voice softened with her relief, and she looked lovingly at Diana's drawn face. "Are you all right?"

A tired smile played across her lips, but Diana couldn't bring herself to open her eyes again. The warm concern radiated by that blue gaze enveloped her, and she tried a gallant nod.

"I am not sure if I should believe you?" Elana gently teased.

"Nothing is broken," Diana mumbled and tried to swallow. Elana produced the waterskin and guided her lips to it.

"Thank you." Her eyes fluttered open, and this time her smile was a little more convincing. "How about you?"

"A few bruises, nothing more."

"Good." Diana sat forward and felt her ears pound. Her stomach didn't feel queasy, though, that was good. She didn't particularly want to deal with a concussion this morning. "What about our friends?"

Elana glanced at the still figures that shared their ledge. "Dead. Have you hit your head badly? Or your shoulder?"

"I think my head's all right. My shoulder..." She rotated the arm slowly, stiffly. "It's not dislocated, but I strained the muscles pretty badly." It easily could have been worse. Diana took a deep breath and reached for her boots, grunting at the tenderness in her side where the bow had jammed before breaking. Still, everything seemed to work, although painfully. At least her eyes were feeling more normal in their sockets. "What are cucarii?"

Elana's fingers touched Di'nay's hair, straightening the tousled brown strands. "They're desert scavengers and quite deadly. They tend to hollow out nests in sandy or gravely terrain. They have few natural enemies because they are so poisonous."

Diana ventured a look over the trail's edge. The pit was littered with curled up cucarii — and the soldier. In a strange way, she had been lucky to land in their nest. A few meters to the left or right and she would have tumbled nearly a league to the ravine's floor. "They look dead, not...?"

"Those are," Elana confirmed. "Their nervous systems are too primitive to survive such a violent change in amarin — they can't discriminate between the illusion of change and the reality."

Diana laughed humorlessly. "For a moment, I wasn't so sure I could either." She forced herself to stand. Elana hovered near, but the world seemed to be behaving itself. Diana drew a deeper breath and mentally took inventory. Her ribs were sound, her legs steady, her head fairly clear... over all she was going to do fine. But more immediately, her hands felt a little too clammy in their gloves and the pain in that shoulder was enough to make her see stars.

"How are you?" Elana asked, concerned. "You are very white despite your tan."

Diana smiled weakly. "I have felt better." She gestured to her gear, unwilling to risk bending over quite yet. "In the green bag, there's a little box with a red cross."

Elana returned to find Diana looking around, somewhat confused. "What's missing, Di'nay?"

"My knife...I don't think we were so close to the edge that...?"

"It's there." Elana pointed up the trail a few feet to where it had fallen. "I'll get it. You take care of yourself."

Diana nodded. She was shaken. It had been a long time since a man had been able to wrestle her to the ground. She rummaged through the cluttered box and pulled the capsules free, swallowing two.

"What are those?" Elana asked, trading Di'nay's knife for the box.

"A great little drug that should keep me from going into shock." Diana winced as her shoulder reminded her not to shrug. "I think I'm all right. But I don't feel like leaving it to Fates' Jests."

Elana suspected Di'nay's shoulder was not their only cause for concern. She was very aware of their vulnerability on this trail. More soldiers could be stalking them soon. The brush with the death had been too close. She was not prepared to give up this beautiful woman to some Fates' whim — not yet.

Impulsively, Elana stood tip-toe and brushed Di'nay's lips with her own. A warm smile returned her uncertain look, and Di'nay gathered her close.

❋ ❋ ❋

The reefs parted and like towering sentinels stood back, rigidly frowning at the encrusted plain. The path tumbled out beyond their gravely feet and forked both east and west onto well-trodden roads. Elana paused to survey the deserted wilderness to the east as Di'nay rested.

Elana felt reassured. The dimness that had clouded her Sight before the ambush had lifted. The reef rock no longer shadowed either her body or her mind and the faint trace of Maltar's traveling band was readily visible in the mid-day sun. They had not sent others back yet; it was still too soon for them to guess the trio would not be returning. If luck held, the soldiers would not be missed before darkfall, and by then she and Di'nay would be well hidden in the rolling wastelands.

They pushed on.

Diana found her body less cooperative as the leagues passed. She had been hoping that she would do better once out of the reefs — once past the shifting, uncertain footing. The wastelands lent little improvement, however. The drifting sand and grit filled their path with small dunes that tugged at her toes and balance. She had to set her teeth with each jarring step when the ground was solid.

They rested and she forced another pair of capsules down her aching throat. She didn't protest as Elana opened the packs and began redistributing their gear. She was in no position to deny the help and long past hiding the pain from her lover.

Elana watched worriedly as Di'nay rose to continue. She did not know enough about Terran biology to disagree with the Amazon's own assessment. She had to trust Di'nay's judgment when she described the clammy, groggy ache as something that would wear off. The Blue Sight was a poor gift here; Elana recognized the pain and the quivering shakiness that told her of a weakening body, but the source was not clear. Her helplessness was as aggravating as Di'nay's distress was painful.

✹ ✹ ✹

The desert's sun was only half-way to the horizon as Elana called a prolonged halt. Di'nay's confidence in her ability to cross the wastelands was more uncertain with each league. Elana was loath to lead them to a point of no return. She compromised and set up a make-shift camp with her blanket creating a lean-to against the day's white glare. The chill of the faint wind negated any warmth from the sun, but Di'nay's relief in gaining refuge from the harsh light was tangible. Exhausted, she slipped into sleep — too quickly, Elana fretted. She hesitated, crossbow in hand as she surveyed the eastern land.

No one. Di'nay would be safe.

She was reluctant to leave her, but her reasons for stopping were only partially fulfilled. This close to the reefs, their tracks would need to be covered. With a final glance at Di'nay, Elana left to retrace their steps.

✹ ✹ ✹

Chapter Seven

"I'm not doing very well," Diana mumbled shakily, trying a sip of the weak tea. The admission was somewhat belated. Her skin was flushed pink and her temperature had risen drastically. Her eyes felt blurred, and she hadn't been able to focus on anything for very long since waking. Her throat was swollen — her whole body felt swollen, and her tongue felt like a roll of cotton.

Elana turned, watching the sun approach the horizon. There was no possibility that she could safely get Di'nay across this plateau in three days. She was past caring for their mission's urgency now. Survival was primary.

She came near and knelt beside the shivering woman. Even despite their metabolic differences, her fingers felt cool against Di'nay's forehead. "Well, n'Shea, what do you suggest?" Diana asked.

Elana pulled the cup and blanket from her grasp in quick decision. "I'm going to look at that shoulder and the rest of you — just as I should have in the beginning."

Diana winced as the vest and tunic were discarded. The hands seemed rough, but she kept silent. She knew any movement was too much, and at least the quickness meant it would be over soon.

"My guess would be that you've broken something and that the pain is from that," Elana murmured grimly. "The fever — I only hope you haven't injured something inside from the fall. There's so little I can do if you're bleeding internally...." Her fingers touched moisture and she stood, moving behind Di'nay. The fabric of the fieldsuit was shredded. Her shoulder was oozing blood.

"What is it?" Diana managed, gulping a dry swallow.

Elana said nothing and snatched up the discarded jerkin. The same ribbon tear was there. The fieldsuit had kept the blood from coming through to stain, but the semi-circled pattern was undeniable. "You must have fallen on one," Elana said quietly, pulling the white cloth away from Di'nay's back. The cuts were deep but almost swollen shut by the angry, red skin. The discolored swelling was easily twice the width of the wounds, with scarlet streaks extending further.

"I fell on my pack," Diana reminded her, trembling. She covered her eyes as she hunched forward, caring less about the pain than her increasingly blurred vision. "And I wrenched my shoulder even more than when I slammed into the cliff."

"I am certain you did," Elana agreed. The top of Di'nay's shoulder was bruised yellow-and-green in testimony. "But you have also been stung by a cucarae."

She didn't care anymore, Diana admitted as Elana moved off toward their dying fire. All she wanted to do was lie down and sleep.

She didn't, though. A piece of her realized how deadly such passivity might be, so she sat and watched as Elana brewed some unnamable concoction from her small bag of medicines. A poultice, her mind vaguely registered with relief. The smell had not been particularly unappealing, but her stomach was not entertained by the thought of accepting anything — not even more tea.

It was hot and numbed the pain, a relief that made Diana gasp, almost in tears. She had literally forgotten it could be so different.

"Take these."

She looked at the capsules from her medical kit and shook her head groggily. "I don't think I could keep them down."

Elana drew something from her bag and mixed it into the tea. She handed the capsules and tea to Di'nay. "This will help."

Still the Amazon hesitated.

"You must try, Di'nay."

A weak nod and she did. The tea was moist in her parched mouth but left a tingling sensation that relaxed the clenched muscles in her jaw. The capsules hit her stomach with a protestingly ill feeling. The feeling persisted but the knotted tightness lessened. She finished the tea.

"Better?" Elana asked, taking the empty cup.

Diana tried to nod. She suspected Elana's ministrations were only prolonging the process, not curing her. Her tongue touched her dry lips. "What now?"

"I am not certain," Elana replied honestly, wrapping the blanket more securely about Di'nay. Gently then she took her hands. "There is a healer, not quite a day's journey to the west of here. She will have what is needed for this kind of poison."

"Even though I am an alien?"

"It is your alien biology that has saved you so far, Diana n'Athena," Elana returned steadily. "If I had been stung, you would have buried me hours ago."

A dry laugh pushed out at that. "One of the few advantages to a less efficient metabolism?" The half-hearted smile faded. "I can't make a day's march anywhere, Elana. And I don't think my body is so inefficient that I will live another two days, so that you may bring help here."

"No," Elana brushed the hair from her clammy forehead, "I do not think you will." Her hand dropped and she drew a deeper breath. "But can you promise me a full day, Di'nay?" Her blue eyes captured Diana's blurring gaze and the Amazon felt the power of the woman's urgency. "I will get us there, but you must fight this poison. You must try to live — to breathe — to stay with me, Di'nay. You must try!"

To stay with you for always, Diana thought. For this woman of sapphire eyes and tender touch, she would try to move the very universe itself.

"Yes, I will try," Diana whispered. "But how will you...?"

"Shh, that is my concern."

The blueness of those eyes shut out the world about Diana. A softness of warmth surrounded her, lulling the groggy aching of her body into oblivion.

"I am going to ask you to sleep." Elana's voice drifted in from some distant place.

Concern stirred — a sleep that she might not awaken from.

"I will watch for you," Elana's voice answered soothingly. "Dream of me — Diana n'Athena — dream of me as you saw me in the mountain's cave..."

A tall, strong woman — Diana's mind reeled with the image and clutched to the strength of the woman.

"...strong enough to fight for you, Di'nay — strong enough to carry you west. Draw on this strength — our strength — as you fall weary. Don't let go of this life...don't let go — "

Elana lowered Diana gently, carefully preserving their contact. The sleep deepened, slowing her pulse and breath even more...slowing the poison's course even more. Elana only prayed to the Mother that it had slowed enough.

She worked quickly then, breaking camp. The packs were closed and buried along with their weapons. Water, knife, medicines, and a single cloak, she kept. Except for a few pieces, she scattered the dried meat. The scavengers would dispense with it. Left with the packs, the scent would have the creatures digging it up, and the Terran technology was to stay hidden, even if she was not to return for it. This way, the lifestones in the sword's hilt would eventually disintegrate the lot. She hoped to be back long before that happened.

The sun had set when she was done. The first moon would soon peer over the southeastern mountains. Her path would be brightly lit by the celestial pair tonight. Elana thanked the Mother for the small favor. She only hoped the healer, Melysa, was at home.

Elana stood, finishing her short meal as she gazed west. What she was about to do was against almost everything she had ever been taught as a Blue Sight. It was never needed by the Seers and seldom risked by others, but she didn't see an alternative. If Di'nay died, her time was certain to be short...a ten-day at the most.

She capped the waterskin and turned to the sleeping figure. It was not a question of being able to carry the woman; it was a question of time. If she kept a steady pace, she might make the journey in a two day march. If she ignored the natural exhaustion and fatigue of her body, she could match the pace of a normal pack's weight and reach Melysa's cellar by mid-day tomorrow. Mid-day — hopefully it would leave Di'nay enough hours of life to respond to the healer's touch.

She knelt beside her lover. That would be soon enough...if she didn't drop first.

There was little danger in projecting an intentionally exaggerated image to another as she had done with Di'nay. The risk came from deciphering the mythical image back and accepting it as reality. It created a hypnotic circle of illusion that prevented the Blue Sight from distinguishing illusion from reality. Elana would not feel the tiredness of her feet or the ache of strained muscles. If she stumbled and twisted an ankle, she would not feel the pain. The danger was that she truly would not know when she was past the point of exhaustion; she would merely drop into unconsciousness. If she was strong enough to push past that limit of endurance, she might simply drop into a coma. But if she did not try, Di'nay would not live.

She roused the Amazon just enough to lock eyes and share dreams. The power and freshness surged through her veins, and she let Di'nay slip back into sleep — pausing to be sure the Amazon's body rhythms were still slow and even.

Carefully then she pulled Di'nay up to her feet and swung an arm across her own shoulders. With an adroit dip, Elana grabbed Di'nay about the knees and lifted, saddling the woman across her lower back. She bounced her body quickly, settling Di'nay's weight more evenly on her hips. Her muscles barely protested the lift; her illusion of strength was so well entrenched. But Elana knew better than to waste her body's reserves with arrogance. The Old Master had taught her this carry, and in reality she could easily move a man three times her own size. Di'nay was considerably smaller than that, even if she was a good deal taller than Elana.

She glanced overhead. The first of the Twin Moons was just pushing past the hills. With the Mother's speed, her sister's rising would find them far to the west.

*** ***

Elana paused to rest, cautiously setting down her precious Amazon. It felt odd to drink when she was not thirsty and even stranger to methodically stretch muscles that still felt limber and loose. But she was taking no more chances than necessary.

Above, the sun had just cleared the southeastern hills and begun her long sail across the empty sky. There was still much time, Elana thought gratefully. There would be enough.

*** ***

The clouds were almost nonexistent. A few were scattered to the far south, seemingly caught on the mountain peaks, but the rest of the skies were clear. It was a harsh, glaring clear that hurt the eyes. It was too cold a sun to warm the wastelands and too bright to bring comfort.

Elana sipped the water and silently cursed her carelessness. She had lost track in her counting. Patiently, she began again. She had forgotten how many halts she had called; there had not been many. But it was important to wait the allotted time at each rest. There was no place here for carelessness today.

A lazy circling shadow caught her attention, and she had to concentrate not to immediately reach with her Sight to identify it. There was a limit to the number of things she could do at one time.

But she watched curiously as the spiral tightened and began to descend. There was a peculiar familiarity to its flight. Elana almost smiled as she recognized the eitteh's golden body. It registered faintly that she should have been more pleased, but her internal illusion had not been particularly fashioned for reunions — no more than it had been fashioned for counting.

The eitteh dropped to the ground a few feet away and warily approached, crouching lower with each step. Something was amiss. Her nostrils flared with a faint rumbling as she recognized the scent of failing life. She came closer then, sniffing Di'nay's still figure. The scruff of her neck ruffled and she stepped back, shaking her head.

Elana smiled grimly. So much for encouragement.

The animal turned to her, its emerald gaze narrowing.

Elana wondered briefly what the creature saw. But the thought was too close to testing the illusion, and hurriedly she dropped it.

The eitteh's purr rasped almost tenderly. Then the golden tail swished and it rose. With a parting snarl it trotted off, unfolding its finely furred wings. It caught the upward draft easily.

Elana was tempted to watch its majestic ascent, but time beckoned. She turned to lift Di'nay's limp form, wondering what obscure reasons had sent the eitteh around the mountain range and searching for them. The sun pushed higher; she doubted she would ever know.

*** ***

Mid-day approached and Elana heeded the stumbling step her feet produced. Her body felt no different from last night's beginning; but she noticed that her footing was less reliable now. It meant nothing, she promised herself harshly, shifting Di'nay's weight across her hips again.

They couldn't afford for it to mean anything.

✹ ✹ ✹

The green of Melysa's sheltering oasis grew steadily larger as the leagues passed, and Elana fought the illusion's arrogance to hurry her steps. She hoped she was not far from the healer's cellar, but distances were deceiving in this land.

Dear Mother give her the patience....

The prayer distracted her and the sand snatched at her toes; she went down to her knees with a startled cry. She concentrated, tightening her loosened hold about Di'nay's body. If she set her lover down here, Elana did not think she could pick her up again. The brief thought that she should leave and return with help was discarded. Di'nay had been locked to her mind for too long now; the unmingling would take time — and that they could not risk. Carefully she planted a foot, gathering her concentration to push up and stand again.

The braying whine of a burro broke the silence of the desolate plain. A second answered.

Elana's head snapped up, barely remembering not to search too distantly, but the animals were near. And not just them.

The breeze blew the loosened hair into her eyes, but it didn't matter. What she saw was no mirage.

Wispy sounds of a voice matter-of-factly urging on the harnessed burros was carried along on the stirring wind. A rickety creak heralded the two-wheeled cart.

Elana laughed weakly with joy. The tattered illusion of her self-image slipped from her to settle in Di'nay's faint consciousness. Gingerly she lowered Di'nay to the ground and laughed again — at her exhaustion, at her success — at the Mother's blessings that had sent the healer out in search of them.

✹ ✹ ✹

Chapter Eight

There was a bone rattling rumble vibrating through her weakened frame. Diana blinked fuzzily and forced her eyes to focus. An insolent emerald stare greeted her. She realized that the vibrations were the eitteh's purr; the creature was draped across her hips. Perhaps she should be just a little afraid, but that was too difficult to think about, and her eyes slipped shut again.

"Di'nay?" The soft voice reached to her over the purring, a warm tone that she thought she knew from somewhere. "Diana...?"

She opened her eyes again, to a welcoming blink from the eitteh. Its golden ears flicked back, and it turned, directing her to look to the side.

Elana smiled tenderly. She did not look well, Diana thought with muddled concern. Her face had an unhealthy tinge, and bruises edged her sapphire eyes. But she was smiling, and she was beautiful. Diana's eyes closed, and she remembered what had happened. The worst was over. "Was your healer...," Diana paused to swallow, "...surprised to see us?"

"No." Elana's fingers brushed across Di'nay's forehead. "It seems she was expecting us. Our eitteh brought her out to find us."

"Did she...?" Diana tried to to touch the cat's head, but the effort was too much.

"Are you thirsty?"

"Sae...."

Elana sat next to her, lifting her shoulders and supporting her head. The water tasted good — clean, and Diana drank thankfully.

"So she has returned to us." An aged woman padded to the bedside. Her worn robes were striped with the brown and grays of desert dwellers. She threw back her hood to expose her thinning, silver hair that tousled and strayed from its knot. Diana smiled. It reminded her of Elana's unruly wisps. "Greetings, young warrior." A cool grasp took her wrist and felt for her pulse. "It seems you are destined to live."

Diana did not feel destined to anything at the moment. She certainly did not feel young, although she felt battered enough for any battle-tried soldier.

"Di'nay, this is Melysa, mistress of this healer's cellar."

This was the woman who had saved her. Diana met the kindly gaze. "I am grateful, Mistress." Her words sounded so faint in comparison with the deed.

A compassionate chuckle and a warm pat on her hand reassured her. Melysa looked at the two of them, obviously proud of their struggle and her success in aiding them. "Save your words. You both have cheated Fates' death. That is thanks enough for me."

"Both...?" Diana's voice rasped weakly and her eyes sought Elana. "You...?"

"I've been telling her of the soldiers' attack." Elana said, avoiding the question. She ran her hand along Di'nay's forehead soothingly.

The fear in Diana's body eased and her eyes fluttered, finally closing. She had not just dreamed of Elana's arms holding her, carrying her so far...and again she felt the calm of that blue touch warm her. Diana stirred again. "How long...?"

"Sleep now," Elana murmured, stroking Di'nay's furrowed brow.

"But — "

"Hush." Fingers smoothed worries into oblivion and Diana drifted after them.

❊ ❊ ❊

The next time she woke it was to the scent of fresh baking bread and the prospect of food seemed appealing. The soft, worn quilt about her was cozy, and she found herself loath to open her eyes. If she concentrated, she could almost hear the low chant of Oma Hanna's morning prayers and Terri's patient voice quieting the children until Oma was done. Her youngest niece would be three now...what had they finally decided to name her? Tanya? Blond-streaked-brown hair, velvet brown eyes...yes, she remembered the last picture Rosa had sent. They called her something different for her honey-tan coloring...Tawney, that was it. The bed shifted gently. It couldn't be the three-year-old; they were much more rambunctious.

"I know you are awake," cool fingers touched her cheek, "but are you hungry?"

Diana started guiltily, her eyes flying open.

Elana smiled, "What were you dreaming of? Home?"

"Yes, Oma Hanna...my grandmother was saying morning prayers." Diana stared at the contrast of creamy skin and ebony hair; the bruised exhaustion was gone. What would Elana's child look like? She closed her eyes at the piercing sweetness of that image. "I dreamt of the children I have never seen — might never meet."

"You will see them," Elana returned firmly, and her lips pressed a gentle kiss to Di'nay's forehead. "I know you will."

Elana smiled sadly as Diana reminded her, "You are not future gifted."

"And neither are you."

Nor do I want to be, Diana thought. She wanted to live with the illusion that this would work out — that Oma Hanna would cherish this special addition and bless their bonds with the words of the ancient Houses. She looked at Elana, her heart in her eyes, and silently pleaded for a life together.

The small clasp enfolded her hand, squeezing tightly. "I am here."

It is when you will not be that I fear, Diana thought but held her tongue. Instead she asked more cheerfully, "Did you offer food?"

The broth was thin but gentle on her stomach, and the warm bread and honey satisfied her need to chew. Melysa appeared, frowning heavily as Diana asked for more, but she allowed more soup. "You are far too weak to devour a side of meat, young warrior," she admonished sternly. She settled her sturdy frame down onto a three-legged stool and watched her patient finish the second helping. "Even with your strange anatomy, you are not so hardy that after seven days of fasting you can bite into anything you like."

"Seven days?" Diana jerked upright against the headboard, muscles quivering with the sudden movement. "I have been ill for seven whole days?"

"Eight, if you count the day you were stung," Elana confirmed quietly.

"And you are still quite ill," Melysa pointed out, very aware that the Amazon's body was providing living, aching proof. "A few meals will not set you right. You will stay here for at least the rest of this ten-day." Diana opened her mouth to interrupt, but swallowed her words at Melysa's frown. "Most likely you will need several more. I will not tolerate anybody undoing my good work — especially after such dawdling as you two did getting here!" Melysa pushed her hands into her pockets. "You can not go gallivanting in Maltar's damp forests if you have pneumonia."

Diana's body did not feel capable of 'gallivanting' into the kitchen, let alone a forest. Elana's hands quickly guided her back into the pillows and under the quilt.

"You see that?" Melysa got up, waving a crooked finger. "You can't even tell which way is down without help! You're certainly not fit to sort out north from south!" Her glare pinned the Amazon to her pillows as Melysa said, "If I have to, I will hide your weapons and hire a local ruffian or two to stand guard...!"

"No need, Mistress," Elana said. "She is not going anywhere. I will see to it."

"Aye," Melysa grumbled and half-turned to leave, wondering if Elana was going to be any better at keeping the woman in bed than she'd been about keeping her out of the cucarii nest. She halted at the doorway, her lips pursed anxiously. "Perhaps I should not be leaving you so soon? This other may wait until — "

"We will be fine," Elana assured her, rising to guide Melysa through the curtain.

Diana watched them go with a sinking feeling. Time was too precious. Her own stupidity and clumsiness had not helped. That hulk never should have thrown her.

"She speaks truth," Elana said grimly. "You are not going anywhere today."

Diana wearily shook her head. "The time is so short — "

"By the Mother's own hand, Di'nay! You will listen!" Strong hands grabbed the Amazon's shoulders, and blue flashed as Elana angrily avoided Diana's gaze. "You were poisoned! You almost died! You don't know how close you slipped towards Fates' Cellars. You...." For an instant, she shook Di'nay in frustration. "I am not ready to lose you. Not yet, Diana n'Athena. Not yet!"

"You've not lost me." Diana said faintly. Her arms enfolded Elana's shuddering figure, remembering that it was not just her own heart involved. It was not that she was so certain that they both would live to see this mission completed, but she thought so seldom of those dangers. It was her departure from Aggar that her heart feared too well — to the exclusion of all else sometimes. She stroked the curling silk of Elana's hair and teased hesitantly, "Have I been such an unruly patient?"

Elana nodded, sitting up and brushing aside a tear. "In truth — yes." She smiled and said, "You have spent every moment arguing with that Terran Thomas or calling for Cleis to get you out of here. Given your love for Commander Baily, it was often difficult persuading you to stay in bed."

Diana grinned wryly. "Cleis usually runs interference for me when he grows too intolerable. Was there some place in particular I seemed to be going?"

"Home, I imagine." Elana put a hand to Di'nay's pale cheek.

Perhaps, Diana thought, and allowed her eyes to close. More likely a retreat — a few days away with Cleis — to tell her of this woman she had found — a few days tending the fire, sharing tea and philosophy, might preserve her soul. Diana wondered if her friend had returned to the base safely, and if her time at the southern healer's had been restful. Broken ribs, Stevens had said. More likely another sword's scar. Well, perhaps this time Cleis would earn her bonus points and think of resigning. That opened some interesting possibilities for the next Amazon pair assigned. It might be worthwhile suggesting that the next two be partners, preferably with a history of joint assignments — perhaps even mates.

Elana tentatively broke into her thoughts. "Can I get you anything?"

Diana smiled faintly. "Your company." Was she really thinking a partnership would have eased the long years on Aggar? Or was she realizing how very much she enjoyed Elana's part in her life now?

The younger woman squeezed her hand reassuringly. "I am here."

"And a bath," Diana voiced suddenly. Her body felt sticky and gritty. "Are you up to it?"

Diana stretched her legs experimentally. "Everything seems to work."

Her words may have been brash, Diana admitted as she sank into the water in the wooden tub. The hot water eased her shaking muscles, and the faint fragrance of the bath salts enveloped her senses. She could almost feel the layers of grime dissolve — which was good considering she couldn't imagine gripping, the soapy cloth long enough to use it.

Elana smiled at her lover's pleasure and lathered the soap. "Would you like your hair washed?"

"If you're offering, I would be eternally grateful."

A soft chuckle teased her as Elana's hands took up the task. "I would be careful of idle promises, Amazon. There are a great many nights in an eternity."

"Shea," Diana retorted without opening an eye.

Elana's laughter caught in her throat. She had been almost certain they would never laugh again — let alone touch.

Diana asked, "What have you been doing for the last ten-day — other than transporting stray Amazons and listening to my dubious opinions on Thomas?"

"Very little else," Elana said, remembering her struggle to keep Di'nay quiet and beneath the quilts. "I retrieved the packs, and Melysa had some news of Maltar." She paused to rinse the foam from Di'nay's hair. "It appears he has not moved his summer court from the Priory yet. There have been a few troops and women ushered west. But there has been no sign of his personal advisors or himself."

"I suppose we should be thankful for that."

Elana turned from replacing the kettle on the firehearth and knelt down beside the tub. "I have only one thing to thank the Mother for, Di'nay — and it has nothing to do with the Maltar."

Diana stared at the pensive young woman before her. Was she truly as old as twenty-five? At that moment, the soft line of her mouth and the smoothness of her skin made her seem far too vulnerable. "No," Diana murmured, "I have two things to be grateful for." How long had it been since she'd loved anyone so totally — if ever? Long before setting foot upon this world — much too long.

"I have news of your base also." Elana said. She rolled up her sleeves, retrieving the wash rag from the watery depths. "Your satellite has been repaired. You should be able to reach your Commander Baily now."

"He's not my Commander Baily," Diana reminded her, but she was grinning.

"I truly don't think of him as one of dey Sorormin, Di'nay."

Diana laughed. "A Sister? I should hope not! Now tell me of the satellite."

"Melysa received word by hawk message last eventide. Let me do your back..."

"A message? From Thomas? Since when has Thomas taken to hawking?"

"Nonsense. The Council sent word."

"But — how would anyone even know where to send word?"

"The Seers know," Elana returned sensibly, and she sat back on her heels. "Are you done? Or would you like more hot water to soak in?"

"But...is there more hot water?"

"Certainly." Elana got up to bring it.

"Don't — now." Caught between exhaustion and frustration, Diana subsided into silence.

"You are not done with your questions," Elana prodded quietly as she poured the steaming, fresh water into the tub.

"I am waiting for you to sit in one place, so that I can talk to you."

Elana hid her smile and pulled a stool close. "All right, Di'nay, I am sitting."

Diana realized how selfish and childish she was sounding. It wasn't particularly like her, except when she got sick. She tried to laugh at herself. "I really am a very poor patient, aren't I?"

"Very," Elana agreed without compunction. "Now ask your questions."

"What does the Council know about the satellite? And how — why do the Seers know where we are? I mean, aren't they usually attuned to disruptive events and anomalies — not to individuals?"

"The Council is always aware of your satellite. The Seers, in fact, are occasionally responsible for its sporadic behavior." Elana smiled, but did not give Diana a chance to interrupt. "It is true; the Seers are drawn to crises and struggles of Aggar first, but they follow our progress at will. They have known me a long time, Di'nay. My personal amarin is as familiar to them as your face is to your family. They met and spoke with you for the same reasons — to recognize your amarin. At the request of the Council, their Blue Sight finds us easily."

Wouldn't Thomas love that? "We should have had them pass on my reports. Could have saved Thomas from gnawing his fingernails to the bone!"

Elana shook her head. "Are all Terran supervisors so talented?"

Diana grew sober at the thought. "I wouldn't know. I haven't worked for all of them. I've worked with Thomas the longest. I suspect it's colored my judgment."

"How long do you usually work with someone?"

"Hmm...a tenmoon at most." She sighed and sank lower, slipping her shoulders into the water. Her knees were doomed to a chilly exposure.

"Why is it that you've spent more than twice that time on Aggar?"

"I was waiting to meet you," Diana answered flippantly.

"I am the Shadow here," Elana retorted in like tone. "I am the one who's been doing the waiting." And she knew just how long that waiting had been. She did not have to ask to know which day Di'nay had arrived on her planet. She looked at Diana now and almost wondered at the Mother's calling — that She had so clearly touched one of them and so completely kept the other in oblivion?

"You have drifted far away from me."

"Not very far," Elana assured her, her glance dancing lightly across Di'nay, "and you have yet to answer me."

"Do you mean the question, why five years with Thomas?...Aggar is a Charlie-Four planet. That required me to stay longer. Do you know what that is?"

"No." Should she? Elana frowned. The Sight should have told her in that first glimpse that Di'nay was an off-worlder. Then, at least, she could have taken the time to learn more of this.

"Charlie is a type C planet. It means Imperial relations are tentative, at best, and that there have been hostilities in the not-so-distant past. The Four designates a class of planets that is closed to trade and visitors. The restriction allows passengers and cargo crews access to the space station for refueling. But only military personnel are allowed planetfall. The base crew is typically assigned for a minimum of three Terran years, and anybody who has direct contact with your people must stay for five. It allows few to visit Aggar and none of your people to leave."

Elana felt her throat close painfully. She had known contact between the Empire and Aggar was limited, but it had always seemed to follow the Council's plans. She was reminded that there were real limitations to what the Council could do.

"Supposedly," Diana continued, "such a limited contact is to protect you. I suspect, in reality, it's that the Empire couldn't clearly win, so they keep you isolated."

Elana said sadly, "We have so little that they could want."

"Border defense," Diana reminded her solemnly. "Don't forget Aggar has the only breathable atmosphere in this quadrant. It would be most helpful to the Empire to freely build here."

"My understanding is that we are too close to the galactic borders for that. The Alliance would be eternally raiding. Aggar would be scorched beyond recognition in a matter of tenmoons — would it not?"

"The Empire would refortify and defend it again. Their strength could hold enough of the attackers off that the air would still sustain some life. The planet would still support their weapons."

"But not my people," Elana added grimly.

"No, not your people."

"Then I think," Elana said very quietly, staring into the murky white of her lifestone, "it is a good thing that Aggar is Charlie-Four." Her throat felt tight as she thought, even if I can never leave with you. She wondered if it might not be easier to die on their journey rather than face that day she must calmly send Di'nay away.

"Charlie-Four." Diana sighed deeply, feeling the weariness return. "They don't understand, so they classify. If they can label, then they think they understand — or that they have more control over you."

Diana wondered how this planet had escaped the Terran's patriarchal control and involvement with power and intrigue. But 'escape' was not quite the right word for Aggar. Perhaps the Council had succeeded in avoiding more involvement because they had not tried to eliminate the beast. Elana said they sought balance. Within their world's ecology, they tried to balance their various cultures' ways. They did not judge what should or should not be, as much as they balanced — technology and visions — borders and resources — futures and pasts. By Imperial standards the cultures seemed stagnated, but the peoples of Aggar were not subjugated to external forces, though individuals certainly were not free.

Balance? She wanted to believe with Elana that within this stagnation it was possible — that the Council meant to ignite an evolution of another sort. In the garden, Elana had said that the number of those gifted with the Blue Sight was increasing? Perhaps the fire was already lit?

❋ ❋ ❋

Chapter Nine

The night wind blew, tugging at the cloak about her, and Diana tucked an edge more securely under herself. She sat alone on the barren plain, not far from the yawning canyons that opened to the west. The air rushed and swirled from those grand depths, bringing faint scents of water and green.

She stirred again, seeking a more comfortable seat. The darkness above glittered imposingly with dusty star groups and the bright early moon. She was still feeling weakened after her bout with the cucarii. It had been six days before she felt stronger. Her sleep was still much too sound and long; Diana suspected the healer had been mixing potions into her evening drinks.

Tomorrow would be their last day with Melysa.

Diana had found herself growing restless and impatient. Jealousy perhaps? Had she grown so accustomed to having Elana to herself? Was it a kind of insecurity? In all honesty she was not so certain that Elana missed their private solitude.

She shook her thoughts aside, irritated at herself. Elana had done nothing — said nothing. She was always quick to give reassurance. To a point, Diana reminded herself. Elana had never spoken of love — but then neither of them had.

The wind tousled her freshly cut hair, and absently Diana's fingers brushed it back into order. Neither of them had talked of loving. She admitted it had been — still was — a deliberate silence on her part. Perhaps it was the same for Elana. Loving did not necessarily mean — I will change my life for you. And not only change it, Diana knew, but leave it — abandon people, customs, the very sky she had grown up calling her own.

Then why was she planning to talk to Cleis about Elana? Why was she waiting for Cleis to return her message? She wasn't assuming anything, she reassured herself. She would merely be creating options. In fact, it was because she was not assuming Elana would stay — or go — that she sat here waiting. The assumption of passivity — of unquestioning obedience to Aggar and the Council's will had clouded her judgment — her acceptance of Elana's desires before. Diana did not want to make that mistake a second time, not when a decision would be so final – even if she herself was uncertain of the woman's love.

Not true. Diana sighed, her eyes seeking the climbing half-moon as memories surrounded her. She had watched too many live without it, herself included, not to recognize love. She could worry that this love would not last – that their bond was too fragile for the strain of emigration, but her fears could not deny what was there – what they had already shared.

The amber lights flickered on the small display, warning of a forthcoming readout.

Shortly after the Empire's conflicts over Aggar had begun, the Imperial technicians had found the 'solar flares and turbulent atmosphere' precluded reliable voice communications. They had managed to redesign their transmitters and the satellite relay along the lines of their ancestors' antiques. Eventually they had produced their current system. Knowing what she did, Diana suspected it had been a decision of the Council's to allow this system to work.

A few numbers blinked across the screen, and Diana obediently reset the channel. She realized Cleis was using the back-up unit at Mattee's and wondered what she was doing in Gronday.

Greetings, the screen printed.

Diana wondered who might be listening. With Thomas' love of security, private communications were not always assured.

Greetings, Diana sent back. May have found an Amazon.

The screen was blank for an inordinate amount of time, and Diana was amused, thinking of Cleis' astonished reaction.

What House, the screen inquired.

Elana n'Sappho. Diana's amusement faded, her fingers trembling as they tapped the small keys. Her response was traditional, but its significance in this case caused her heart to race just a little faster. No matter who they would choose to become nor who sponsored their emigration, all new Sisters began as children of Sappho – gathering to her hearth just as the students of the ancient poet had.

Description.

Diana smiled at the image before her as she typed. She wondered if Cleis would be discharged and sent home soon. She realized just how much she was wishing to introduce Elana to her and to talk with her Sister about her muddled hopes.

Birth date.

Diana, disconcerted, realized she did not know. Uncertain.

Age.

Twenty-five. Diana did hope she had remembered that right.

Homebound date.

A slow breath gathered as she typed in, Uncertain.

Date or homebound?

Mission uncertain. Regardless of what Thomas may or may not have said to Cleis, that would certainly alert her Sister to the difficulties of this assignment.

The screen lit again. Maybe three of us then.

Diana blinked. It was a direct denial of Diana's suggestion that she might not be returning at all, but she stopped. It was nothing of the kind, she realized, and her fingers flew across the keys. Your ribs okay?

Fair.

Meaning not so fair, Diana guessed. In fact, fair was incredibly poor for Cleis to be admitting to on an open channel. It also told Diana that her friend was already concerned about this mission and was intent on staying on the active duty list until it was done — just in case. Yes, Cleis was trying to say she wasn't going to be finishing her full tour of duty and that after this mission, the three of them might very well be traveling together.

The lights flashed for her attention. Report said poison.

Past tense, Diana assured her.

Good. Careful.

Yes. Diana glanced at the digital clock in the corner of the transmitter and knew the base would be cutting in soon for higher priorities, but she was loath to let their contact break — guarded as it was. Why Gronday?

Horses and rent.

Good enough excuses, Diana thought. Thomas would have been thrilled to get rid of her red stallion and wouldn't guess that Mattee never raised a brow at the Southerner's erratic rent payments.

Take care yourself, Diana returned finally.

Will call n'Sappho. Usual eighteen days.

No hurry. Regretfully Diana thought there was still a lot of distance to cover on this journey.

The screen flashed an unintelligible array of amber and quieted. The base had noticed them.

Cleis regained the screen again. Goddess' blessings from gentle Helen.

Diana's ire at the interruption faded as a soft smile grew. She had almost forgotten. Goddess' blessings. Out.

The Feast of Helen — so far from calendars and home she had almost forgotten it. Diana felt the subtle strength of her Sisters, and her spirit calmed. Centered was the feeling, a feeling she had possessed only fleetingly for many years now. Perhaps — she turned her dark eyes to the eastern horizon — perhaps it would set deeper roots this season.

❋ ❋ ❋

Elana glanced up as the quick rhythm of Di'nay's step announced the Amazon's descent from the plateau. Elana could not help but smile as her lover appeared. Di'nay's limbs were sound again, carrying her tall frame with grace and self-confidence. The exhausted hunch to her shoulders had lifted and the pallor beneath her weathered brown skin had faded. Except for being leaner, she looked as strong as the day Elana had first met her.

The image of the still figure, ankles crossed as she leaned against the garden wall, drifted to mind. The fatigue and isolation of the Amazon colored the memory more vividly then the words they had exchanged. Watching her now, Elana wondered if perhaps Di'nay's spirit had healed as well as her body.

The weariness was gone — had been for some time. Perhaps the Mother had planned more for their meeting than this mission with the Maltar. That possibility warmed her inside, and Elana hugged the feeling. "I was missing you," Elana murmured as Di'nay joined her at the rough-hew table. "I was about to come searching."

For a long moment, Diana was content merely to feel the love that embraced their lives. The pleasure strengthened with the knowledge that Elana was acutely aware of her amarin. The Amazon reached a gentle hand forward to cover Elana's. "I beg your patience. I did not plan to be so long with Cleis."

"I worry overmuch." Elana recognized the inner turmoil, the bubbling confusion from which her emotions sprang. She squeezed Di'nay's long fingers briefly. "There is some southern tea I'd like you to try. It is not too dissimilar to your own. Melysa has offered us a package. If it suits you, perhaps we should take some. We've almost finished your own stock." Elana ladled the water into the mug and passed the drink to Di'nay. "You did reach your friend Cleis then?"

Diana sniffed the brew curiously. "She is looking forward to meeting you."

Cleis — was that it? Elana was almost shocked at her feelings. Jealousy? With what reason? She was not certain that their relationship had been so involved. Shadows are not quite spouses, she reminded herself firmly. The Mistress and Seers had all been quite clear on that. Possessiveness was acceptable only insofar as it aided you as a protector; beyond that it was inappropriate.

"You're very quiet," Diana prodded softly, and then teased, "Does the prospect of facing another off-worlder daunt you so?"

"No, I have found some off-worlders less objectionable than I would have imagined." Elana sipped her tea. "Cleis is more than your friend, is she not?"

"She is my Sister. We share much more than many might even want to."

Elana moistened her lips. "Physically...much more?"

Diana admitted, "At times. We have both been lonely, and we both care for each other deeply. I'm not certain we would be so close if we'd met at home, though I don't doubt that we'll remain close after we return. But we are not lovers."

Diana was suddenly sensitive to the insecurities that might have prompted the question. "We are dear friends, but there is no commitment beyond that friendship. And there is none that either of us would wish. I think, perhaps, we have something akin to what my mother and Jes had."

Jes — that was the Amazon who helped to mother Di'nay. Elana traced a finger around the mug's handle. "Would you have a child by Cleis?"

Barely audible, a sigh passed Diana's lips. A child — something she might regret. "I am perhaps too old to safely carry a baby now. The women in my family have not fared well with later year children."

With a sudden insight, Diana thought of Terri and Ivory. She had never really questioned why they'd not chosen to have children. It had been an assumption on her part that with Ivory on the moonbase so often, they had not considered it viable. But Terri had loved parenting the flock of them about the adobe, and Terri, like herself, had chosen a second tour of duty off-world. Ivory would not have wished them to risk that sort of pain. "And you?" Diana asked Elana. "Will you have children?"

She laughed. "It is doubtful."

"Oh?"

Drawing a deep breath, Elana tried to think about the question clearly. The inevitability of their parting aside, what did she want? "I don't know if I would want a child," she said honestly. "In another place, in another time, I think yes. But...."

"But?"

"I am a Shadow. My attention...my energy is so focused...separations so impossible...." She faltered, realizing what she had just said, but it was too late to interfere with Di'nay's amarin. She hurried on. "The role I've taken is so consuming that...that re-directing that purpose...is very difficult. It is difficult for me to imagine such a change." A very lame explanation, however true, she thought dismally.

But Di'nay did not appear to find anything odd in her stutterings. "There's nothing wrong with having no interest in motherhood."

"Actually," Elana admitted, relieved that the implications of her words had gone unnoticed, "there are many who would disapprove of me as a mother — aside from me shadowing an infant. It's not that I'm incapable. It's just that it is seldom done."

Diana reminded herself she was not supposed to be here to reorganize Aggar's society. "That position is a bit extreme, isn't it? I mean, when the assignment is done, why should your life continue to be so entangled with your partner's?"

"Many reasons," Elana returned warily.

Diana was acutely aware of the cautiousness and looked at Elana curiously, wondering if she had inadvertently tread upon one of Elana's personal convictions. More slowly she offered, "I don't mean to raise faults, only — only, I don't really understand your lifebonding."

"Few do. Taking a more rational direction, Di'nay. If the Fates or the Mother have marked an individual to sway destiny, who can say for certain which day — or which season of their life is the crucial one? Is it not more likely that it is their life, in its entirety, which will influence history?"

Diana turned her mug slowly, watching the crushed leaves collect in the middle. "So, after this assignment, will you accept another? A lifelong commitment?"

Elana studied her own tea. "I cannot tell you what will happen."

"If I had been of Aggar, would you have chosen to spend your life with me?"

"We are lifebound." Elana smiled. "My choice was made long ago, Di'nay."

Her long fingers massaged the bridge of her nose for a second as Diana

tried to interpret that cryptic remark. She hesitated, afraid to ask anything more
directly.

Elana was intensely aware of Di'nay's trepidation. Her heart melted at
the thought that Di'nay might regret having entered her life, and she reached
across the table to grasp both her lover's hands. "I do not need you to change
anything, Di'nay — not of the past or the future."

At the tenderness in her voice, Diana turned her gaze to meet those
blue eyes, and she felt the enfolding warmth strengthen.

"And I would not let you change anything, if it meant that I would miss
this time with you." Elana sighed, but she did not release her lover's hands.
"Once I said to you, I would be honored to work with you. But you have given
me far more. The friendship — the happiness you have shared with me will never
be measurable."

Diana uncomfortably withdrew her hands to pick up her tea. She was
embarrassed and unsettled that she was embarrassed. "I'm not a royal guard
mounted on a miraculous steed, Elana."

Elana's sweet laughter was infectious. Diana felt her tension ease as
Elana said, "Ann! You are not that." Then Elana said soberly, "No, you are an
extraordinary woman, at times very vulnerable, at times very strong. I would not
change you."

"But you have, you know. I am no longer so frustrated, so weary of my
inability to change... Thomas — his people — the people of Gronday — of your
world."

"Perhaps, it is more a matter of understanding your own part and less
of changing others?" Elana offered.

Wise words. Diana nodded faintly. "I knew that once, but it was
forgotten. I think you've retaught it to me."

"It was not deliberate, I assure you," Elana said, but she was smiling.

Diana returned the sparkling smile. "Would you like to learn
something more of my Sisters? Tomorrow is a sacred day to us. A day of
thanksgiving and blessings — and of rejoicing. Would you share the morning
rituals with me?" As if we were home, she added silently. As if we were Sisters —
and joined as mates.

"Sae, I would like that very much." Elana did not know if she was
breathless from Di'nay's urgency in asking or from her own pleasure at the
invitation.

That night they made love for the first time since the cucarii sting, and
it seemed to Elana as if her lover's touch was sweeter, more compelling than it
had yet been. It was almost as if by their very loving, Di'nay could transport them
the length of the universe to a haven that held no poisons, no crises, no
interruptions — whether they be human-made or cucarii-fashioned. Elana wove
sapphire and brown visions together, adding her own pleas for a haven without
tomorrows.

❋ ❋ ❋

The candle was lit and Elana held it steady, protecting the slender flame
from the canyon's wind. The rose and gold carpet of dawn unrolled across the

plateau. She repeated the chorus, and spellbound, she watched as the sun's rays danced amidst the tiny prisms of Di'nay's headband. She listened — single words unheard — as the rise and fall of Di'nay's voice carried her to a planet far away. She had never thought of her lover — of her Amazon — as singing, and the sheer beauty of it startled and awed her.

The last of Diana's native tea was scattered to the wind, a symbol of the first home harvest. The candle passed between them and back to Elana again, a sign of cares well shared — the dreams well woven — the circling exchange of hope and fear seen through the generations of dey Sorormin, generations of the Sisterhood, before Sappho, and in tomorrows yet to be spun.

The words of the songs blended with the morning's sun, a new birth — a remembrance of the first birth to the Sisterhood — the child that had greeted the rising alien sun who would never know it as alien. That child, Helen, had given her name to their star as she had given her hope — her virgin strength to her mothers. She had grown to lead them as only Sappho could have imagined. She had grown to unite them in balance, not in war against the outsiders. The day of her birth was honored as a day of blessings from the Highest Mother and as a day of proof that hope could be triumphant.

Words ended as the sun lifted herself clear of the mountains. Reverently, Elana lowered her hand to let the breeze sweep across the candle and douse the light.

For a moment Diana was silent, then her thoughts drew near Elana, yet not quite leaving that home so far away. Softly, across the lightspans, the Sisters embraced the two of them, and Diana began again — this time with the shortest of verses, one of Common — the verse meant to be shared with newfound kin:

"N'Awehai stood sound,
n'Sappho brought them
as n'Athena's hand guarded.

N'Shea 'came healer,
as n'Minona taught,
and n'Hina provided.

Now sowing is done,
with strength undivided.
N'Huitaca bring music!

Bright peace reigns
    Delighted —"

Elana turned to face the golden sun. So near — and still so distant. The Amazon's gaze left her, and Elana knew Di'nay did not see the dusty, muted tones of Aggar's heights; she was looking to that place much further away — to the rich amber and topaz hues of her native hills. "Thank you, Daughter of Mothers," Elana said softly. "Thank you very much."

Diana turned at the title, finding herself again on Aggar. She smiled sheepishly and guiltily pulled the headband off. "No, I thank you."

"You needn't remove it," Elana protested, touched by the woman's sudden shyness. "It's a beautiful crown."

Diana folded the band carefully. Each bead was the shape of a pyramid and the rows were laced together with a silvered filament. A midnight blue hue backed the inner flat of the beads, save for the centered symbols, and the small peaks caught and shimmered rainbows of light even as Diana closed her palm.

"The design." Elana pointed to the clear beads as Di'nay reopened her clasp. "Is there a meaning behind it?"

"It is an ancient Terran symbol for woman. Whenever two or three are entwined like these, it represents the unity of our Sisterhood. This was Terri's piece when she traveled off-world. It's made of much more durable stuff than the glass ones we have at home."

"Does each woman have her own then?"

Diana remembered the year Oma Hanna had presented hers. "A family fashions one for each of their daughters. Sometimes it will be similar to an elder's or sometimes it will symbolize something especially relevant to that daughter's life. Then when her menses begin, she is given the band and invited to share the Dawn Ritual and sing the Songs of Helen.

"Oh — it is a sight, Elana. The women of each community gather to greet the new day. They may number in tens or in thousands, depending upon the community's size, but their voices are always as one. The sun dances with our colors as the candles pass through our hands. It is so very beautiful.... I wish you could see it."

"In your home, does Terri's piece look like this one?"

Diana shook her head. She was not ready to leave the morning sun for the cellar below. "All Sisters traveling off-world carry this design or something similar. The color or the number of interlocked symbols may vary, but the subject is the same. We share very little of our home life with the Empire. Rationally, I suppose, it lessens the opportunities for spies to be assimilated into our culture. Emotionally, I know we hold our ways to be too precious. The struggle has been too long for us to be less greedy in our guardedness."

"And yet you invite me...here...this morning." Elana felt her eyes blur as again she recognized how much Di'nay's trust had come to mean to her. "What does your band look like?"

Elana looked at Di'nay, memorizing the way the early sun touched her face. She wanted to know what colors had shimmered across Di'nay's brow when she sang beside her family.

"I'm sorry." Diana drew her thoughts back. "You asked something?"

Elana repeated, "What does your band look like? You said this was Terri's."

Diana laughed at herself. "It's narrower than this, and the backing is woven gold of horsehair. Her voice softened as her memories took her again. "Most of the beads are clear...and it fairly glows like the sheen of corn silk in the sun. It's very plain. The only design in it is a thin copper cross. I suppose it's not really a cross, there's not a bottom half to it."

"Is it? Not really a cross?" Elana pressed. Then corrected herself, "I mean, why horsehair and copper in that design?"

Diana smiled mischievously. "You may not believe this, but before I went off-world, I trained horses."

"And I once worried if you could handle Nightstorm? Why did you not tell me?"

"I did not know you."

Elana smiled, her heart warmed by the fact that there had been changes since then. "Where does the copper come into it?"

"The half-cross?" Diana's eyes dropped as she recalled a less pleasant memory. "It's a geometric design. It represents an old mine with an air shaft slanting down into it. There was an accident when I was a child...in an abandoned copper mine. Oma Hanna wove the coil in as a reminder of my survival." A smile tugged at her lips. "I remember that before I went off-world, whenever I was particularly frightened or despairing, I would take the band out and run my fingers over those glassy ridges, remembering how hard it had been. And I'd think that no matter what was to come, I had dealt with that mine. I could deal with anything Fates' Jest might send on afterwards."

Elana glimpsed a piece of the fire that had gone into the forging of her lover's strength, but, then, Di'nay was laughing.

"I didn't escape completely unscathed," Diana admitted ruefully. "I still don't like the dark."

Elana gave a half-chuckle, soft in its compassion. "So I have noticed."

"Yes, certainly you would." Diana frowned, suddenly putting a few pieces together. "Below in Melysa's chambers, you have been pulling back the curtains at night. Has that been for my benefit? To let in the firelight?"

"That and the warmth. You do have a tendency to chill easily, you know."

"Thank you. It has helped."

"No need for thanks." Elana's voice was rich and low with her tenderness. "I am simply glad to be there."

❋ ❋ ❋

Chapter Ten

"I will miss your cooking, Shadow."

Elana was pleased at the healer's compliment, but she hid her amusement at Di'nay's wince. Her Amazon would never truly be comfortable with the Council's labels, Elana thought as she poured both women more tea and cleared the last of the earthenware dishes from the table.

Di'nay did not care much for that service, but Elana had claimed that she would be shamed if Di'nay insisted on usurping her caretaking duties in front of Melysa. The disapproval would have been easy enough for Elana to bear. It was common knowledge to those like Melysa who were from the Keep that each pair of shadowmates arranged things to their individual liking. But Elana enjoyed doing things for Di'nay, especially since the woman so seldom took advantage of her offers.

She had tried to explain that pleasure to Di'nay, but the Amazon was not one to sacrifice independence lightly — especially her own. Di'nay was still not ready to explore mutual dependency, so here at Melysa's Elana had guiltlessly seized her opportunity to do more. She understood Di'nay would respect her wishes for 'normalcy' just as she had respected Maryl's wishes to preserve outward appearances in Colmar. So, shameless, she enjoyed spoiling Di'nay in front of the healer.

"I trust that you've raided my larder adequately?" Melysa asked. "And did you find the field tent?" Diana ground her teeth tight and left it to Elana to answer. It seemed to be one of those 'duties' that they had spoken of.

"Yes, thank you. You've been very generous to us, Mistress." Elana smiled, turning from the low table near the hearth where she was washing dishes. "I can only apologize that we could not give you more in return."

The woman clucked her tongue. "Your warrior's quiver of arrows that you abandon here are overly handsome a payment. Do stop your fretting, child."

Diana eyed the sleeping eitteh draped about the slumped shoulders of the old woman. It was not the animal that Elana had found at the stream. This one was larger, with chocolate-furred boots and ears. Diana wondered if Melysa's bent frame had come from carrying such creatures throughout her lifetime. Diana nodded at the winged-cat. "I would have thought that your friends would disapprove of arrows. Or perhaps be insulted at the implication that they do not hunt well enough to serve you?"

The woman laughed, absently reaching up to stroke the satiny head. The animal did not stir from its sleep. "The arrows are not for me, young warrior. I will barter them as need arises for spices, fodder and such. They are well-made, 'tis clear to see, and will more than replace the meager stocks you've taken from me."

"But they do not replace your healing, Mistress," Diana said gratefully.

"Ah!" Her wrinkled hand pushed away the gratitude. She enjoyed tampering with the Fates in her own small ways, just as she enjoyed bemusing people by befriending injured eitteh. "It was not such a feat as you think. You are both strong and young, and there was time enough once you got here."

Elana cringed, her back to the two as she rinsed the last bowl. Melysa continued to refer to the fact that they both had needed her tending upon arrival. Elana could only ignore the remarks and hoped Di'nay was attributing them to some strangeness of the woman. She wished Melysa had been trained elsewhere than the Keep. Then her accent would have been thicker and the references more easily lost.

"Have you given much thought to your return journey?" Melysa's quick eyes darted back and forth between the two women, clearly expecting this to be an open matter for discussion.

Diana shrugged. "I have never seen the Maltar's lands, and I know of no other way back but around the mountains. It will be too late to cross."

"And you, Shadow?"

Elana dried her hands slowly as she took a seat beside Di'nay. "There is a third person involved, Mistress. Until we know how, or if, he can travel...."

Melysa's pale lips thinned. "If he can not travel, your effort and my work has truly been for naught."

Diana shook her head firmly. "Too many more would be dead if we fail. He will travel — somehow."

"Ahh, but in what direction will you take him?"

Diana said, "The Gate will be closed with the snows. I understand there is a road that forks to the west, however. It then travels around the mountains near the seashore. That road also has a southern fork which climbs through a less difficult pass which we might try. Or there is always the river that opens into the seas. We could take passage south and then eventually work our way northeast and across the Ramains plains again."

"A good enough way," Melysa said. "This early in winter, seafaring ships are still safe."

"They will look for us to sail home," Elana said quietly, and Di'nay glanced at her sharply.

"They will look for you in all three routes," Melysa said rather airily.

"The port is the easiest for them to watch," Elana said. "Maltar has a garrison there by treaty."

Diana remembered Elana's claim that she had difficulty in guessing how men plot. She wondered, suddenly, if this quiet, unassuming attitude was more than just the Shadow's training. What had Elana not told her? She turned back to Melysa. "Do you know of a path they will not be watching?"

But Melysa was not to be hurried. "One can never be certain of spying eyes." She looked at Elana as if waiting for permission to speak. Then as if she had somehow gained it she said, "There is a road through the mountains south of here. The Maltar very rarely considers its existence"

"The Wayward Path." Elana said sharply.

Melysa beamed. "In truth, it is an obvious solution to your dilemma, I think?"

"The Changlings guard it too well!" Elana protested. "They block one entrance, digging another so fast that finding a route is near impossible. Their sentries are well armed and well numbered. It is near suicide even to approach the Path!"

"Such nonsense," Melysa scoffed. "Compared with successfully entering any of Maltar's strongholds, Changlings will be easily dealt with."

Somehow that did not reassure Diana. But they were talking of saving a great deal of time, if they did not need to go around the mountains on the way back, and with Maltar's forces following them that might be essential.

"The entrance is easily enough found this season. They're just beginning at the next dig. They met with all sorts of delays trying to burrow in at the last place. So many foolish injuries and the like. Although, it was their own fault. The stuff was much too soft to be tunneling through safely, even I could see that." Melysa gave a disgusted snort. "You see — it was their foolish accidents that took me to them. They needed my skills and couldn't have cared less about letting an old witch discover the whereabouts of their precious tunnel."

"But then won't they suspect it was you who told us?" Diana asked with concern. "If you are the sole outsider with that knowledge, will we be endangering you by challenging the route?"

"Don't be a silly youth." Melysa straightened primly. "Even if they were smart enough to figure it out, which I doubt, the fact is that they need a healer and I'm the only one stubborn enough to live here. And, they would certainly rather brave the Council's wrath than my friends here."

"Your friends." Diana looked confused. She had seen no other humans in the vicinity. Elana hid her amusement behind her long hair.

"Eitteh, dear." Melysa tapped the little nose beside her cheek and the animal blinked, waking disgruntled, staring at the offending digit a moment, then rubbing its chin against her hand with a purr.

"Men — especially Council's men — reason and weigh the consequences of any action. My little eitteh friends here live by simpler rules. They would seek out the Changlings responsible for my death and the entire tribe would suffer, not just the individual assassins." She looked at the placid creature, scratching the dark furred ears on request. "Have no fear, young warrior. The Changlings have good reasons to leave me to my foolishness — reasons even their savage little minds can fathom."

✳ ✳ ✳

"Tell me more of the Wayward Path?" Diana asked. They were following the river through an echoing canyon. There was no real track, but rather a rocky shoulder that skirted the water's edge, supporting a scraggly array of trees and brush.

"What would you like to know?" Elana's soft step barely paused, her eyes fixed on the stream bed's smooth stones. She noticed Di'nay rarely spared a glance for her footing, and she fleetingly envied the confidence gained from a lifetime's experience of wandering across strange lands. The eitteh rumbled something that Elana pointedly ignored. If the animal did not like riding draped over a joggling pack, then she could take herself off to fly.

"Why did you agree to go this way if you are sure it is so dangerous?"

Elana frowned, dividing her attention between her feet and their discussion. "May I ask you something?"

"Certainly."

"Your amarin suggest that you find the Wayward Path route appealing. Why?"

"Less distance to travel, and, perhaps," Diana admitted matter-of-factly, "I do not fully understand the drawbacks."

"With me as guide the greatest difficulty is gaining entrance. I admit that it will save us several ten-days, if we are successful."

"With you as guide?"

Elana's voice softened, anticipating the anxiety her words might bring. "The Wayward Path is an ancient mine." She tried not to flinch at the strength of the fear that rushed through her lover. "Its tunnels twist and fold with both man-made and volcanic tunnels."

Diana's throat tightened with the press of childhood memories. She said, her voice controlled, "I thought you did poorly beneath stone — without some sort of organic contact? Wouldn't your Sight trouble you?"

"Mines trouble you more," Elana pointed out gently, halting to face her. "But these are different, Di'nay. They yield lifestones, not gems or metal ores. The Seers have shown me how many of the tunnel walls glitter with white dust and shimmering veins. They glisten with the very life energy of this planet." Her eyes returned from some far seen place and she smiled. "In truth, these tunnels are not all dark and dingy ore shafts."

"Why did not the Council mention the Path to me?"

"Aside from the fact that you are an off-worlder and they never intended you to see any lifestone apart from for our bondstone, the mines are not easily accessible. As Melysa said, the Changlings are very protective. They constantly seal caverns and tunnel new entrances to protect their ancient right to whatever trade in lifestones the Council still allows. The wastelands have little game and even less grazing. Each tribe manages a small herd and a few hunters, but the stones are their true treasure. The Council pays well. In their turn, the Changlings agree to limit trade and harvest little.

"So the Council has forbidden you to show me this Path."

Elana sighed. "You must see that the Council is right. If outsiders like Garrison should understand the power of the lifestones...? I know you would not betray the power of the stones to the Terrans. But the Council does not know you as I do. And I did wish to spare you that temptation."

Elana went on, "But if, as Melysa said, the current entrance is near the Changlings' settlement below the Dual Peaks, then it is a very viable route. Once inside I should have no trouble keeping to the Path. Undoubtedly there will be a few miners at work in the deeper caverns. There always are. But even if we can't avoid them, there will not be many in number, and my Sight will allow us to slip by them."

Elana did not describe the labyrinth of endless twisting tunnels, broken only by lava pits and seemingly bottomless crevices. Diana did not need to think about that. She did say, "On the southern side of the Divide, there are streams and underground channels that run to meet the Black River. The main tributary guides the Path only the last twenty leagues or so — as it leaves the mountains. Until then, the route is not clearly marked."

It did not sound like a terribly endearing place, Diana thought. But they were not talking about saving days. They were talking about several ten-days or even a monarc, if they could indeed travel under these mountains instead of around them. "Does your Sight allow you to follow this route despite its poor markings?"

"It will help." Elana touched her wrist where stone lay beneath the black leather band. "I wear the lifestone. The very walls of the caverns will speak to me. The Blue Sight will make me sensitive to their energies, but it is our lifebond that will allow me to guide us." Elana touched the sword that her father had wrought. "And your stones will let you feel the pull, perhaps too indistinctly to avail us much. But danger, dead ends, abrupt chasms, you might be aware of as we approach them."

Elana lifted her blue eyes to Di'nay's solemn gaze. "If we should become separated in the caverns, I might find you through this stone...but never Garrison."

Diana nodded. Elana's concerns bore thinking about. A picture of complete blackness, the coppermine of her childhood, flashed through her mind and she shivered. But there was so much at stake that she knew they had no alternative.

A light warmth reached out, slipping around her. Diana glanced up and found Elana's gentle gaze on her. She smiled, the fears inside easing a little as she remembered — this time, she wasn't alone.

❋ ❋ ❋

Diana sighed faintly, unobtrusively flexing the sore muscles in her back as she relinquished her armful of firewood. Considering how weak she still was, they had done very well today. But she had to admit that she was tired. The water tumbled through the late afternoon stillness as the riverbed twisted and ducked behind the brush and canyon rock, turning east again. A splash broke the tumbling rhythm, and Diana's head jerked towards the sound only to see the eitteh pounce on some unsuspecting river creature.

"...and I'll wager you'll still want some of ours." The Amazon couldn't help smiling as her gaze shifted to Elana. Nearer the shore, the woman stood beside the open packs with a string of eel-like fish at her feet. She too had paused to watch the river antics of the winged-cat.

Diana started down the slope as the eitteh lunged again. Water splayed and wings spread as the silver river creature twisted and turned beneath the batting paw. Elana laughed, shaking her head, and Diana's arms slid around her in a warm hug.

"You're looking very happy, Ona."

"And why shouldn't I?" Elana challenged softly, falling into Di'nay's Sororian as she leaned contentedly back into her Amazon's grasp. Her hands slipped beneath her lover's suede jerkin. "I have you healthy and whole — and all to myself. There is not a spy to be seen. We're far beyond even the searching blue eyes of the Seers in these rocky canyons...and it has been so very long since we've been alone. So tell me, why should I be anything but happy, n'Athena?"

A smile danced in Diana's brown eyes as she listened to Elana's rich warm voice. She liked the sound of Sororian when Elana spoke it, and the fit of Elana's hands.

"What makes you smile so?"

"Your accent — it reminds me of home."

"It should." Elana pretended to be indignant.

Diana's smile deepened. "Do you know what I think about when you speak?"

"No," her voice was soft now, "tell me."

"It seems as if we are home, out somewhere on an early autumn night, tending the yearlings or the cattle beasties. Tomorrow we'll be back down in the lowlands to find a warm meal in the adobe." A touch of reality crowded her image and she amended, "A warm meal and a clamoring clutch of children."

"A clutch you very much miss," Elana pointed out gently. "Perhaps, after all, you should find a mate who will bear you a child."

"Would you do that?" Diana asked, almost teasing. "If we were...home?"

"I would be most honored," Elana returned flippantly, but the direction of the conversation was becoming painful. She hugged Diana quickly, almost awkwardly. "I suppose you're going to insist on an equal share of the work again tonight?"

Off guard from the sudden withdrawal, Diana said, "Certainly, we're partners."

"Would you like to set up the tent or clean the catch?"

Diana's practical sense reasserted itself along with her humor. "I've never coped with one of your healer's field tents. I barely remember what they look like."

"Then this one would be a complete mystery to you. I trust you've seen silver fish before?"

That drew a suitable chuckle. "As a matter of fact, I have."

❀ ❀ ❀

The night breeze blew softly through the canyon. Elana breathed the rich scent of green and good earth that drifted with the folding air currents. It came from downstream somewhere.

By her side the water splashed and tumbled over itself in a pleasant monotony. It was strange to think that it would take them two days to reach the banks of the Ma'naur — two days of steady marching before they glimpsed the thick pine forests of Maltar's lands. Yet these jostling waters passing her now would find those vast rumbling depths before the sun had even risen.

And the green scents? She could not begin to guess what their journey had been like. But the tantalizing wisps of air were still vibrant and alive, so they could not have taken long in their travels.

A pair of wings rustled far overhead, and Elana scanned the bright stars, wondering if it was the eitteh. But the wind had tossed the sound into their canyon, leaving the creature beyond her Sight.

She poked the dying embers with a stick. There was little chance of seeing her furry friend before sunrise. The eitteh was a nocturnal creature and doubtless had far to go to hunt; if she was bothering to hunt at all. After so many days spent underground with the healer, the eitteh was as delighted to be out as Elana, and both were reveling in their freedom tonight.

Melysa's had not been so awful, Elana admitted. There had been timber, dry food stocks, and an abundance of medicinal herbs and roots, all reassuring in their amarin. Di'nay, too, had been there. Still....

Again Elana inhaled the wind's sweet scents; she had missed the unencumbered richness of the living things. She gazed downstream, her blue eyes drawn to the faint outlines of the thorny trees. Their dull brown twigs shone with a pale gray of life in the darkness. A glimpse of silver flashed under the water — a fish that vanished even as it came. The faintest of speckles dotted the streamside rocks — algae, and a misty outline of late autumn waterflys danced between the rocks and thorn trees.

So much in such a small world that even she took for granted. But how strange it would be, she thought, to be so isolated from those flowing cycles that you could blithely choose to live underground in stone.

The time spent at the healer's had helped. She was stronger for the rest and good diet — stronger in her love for Di'nay too. The time they had spent talking had been different from the snatches of conversation they had managed earlier — less plagued by the demands of their journey — less frequently interrupted by the desires of their bodies. Her story, Di'nay's Sisters called it, an accounting of past deeds, almost forgotten memories — of families and homes. They had shared much that neither would report to Council nor Sisterhood, but was part of their bond — a bond that went beyond the intimacy of a lifestone.

For those of Aggar, lifebonding was an intimacy few could cherish. Yet what she shared with this woman was only enhanced by their bondstone and her Sight — neither were the source of it. It seemed odd when she thought of how very different their worlds — their people. And yet it was Di'nay that always called her Sight a 'gift.' Her father had accepted the Sight as a sort of shorthand for expressing emotion, but Di'nay did more. It was Di'nay who cherished the images that she, Elana, had to share. Different was simply different to Di'nay — a piece of the whole — one characteristic of an individual. To Di'nay she was not just special because she was different, she was different because she was special.

Her heart warmed with the knowledge of their specialness — warmed and ached, remembering the stab of pain she had felt during their jesting about childbearing.

She closed her eyes and breathed deeply as those faint lines of life about her reached out and embraced her. She felt the tension ease, felt the cherished, precious place she held in Di'nay's heart — and the hurt faded to nothingness. Whatever parting would bring, she could not regret this sharing of theirs.

Content, she looked behind herself to where the tent stood. A smile curved softly across her lips as the amarin touched her; Di'nay was stirring within.

Time for sleeping. Elana aimlessly stirred the ashes. Tomorrow would present a long hike, but she still was not drowsy. The night air, the open space had roused her senses. No, she was feeling alive, alert, not at all sleepy. She would only keep Di'nay awake if she went to bed now. Still...Elana glanced at their tent again. Inside must be quite warm; their heating unit was set to a toasty temperature. She wondered if it was warm enough to coax Di'nay out of her fieldsuit.

Surprised by such thoughts, Elana jerked her attention back to the orange embers. She had been mixing the glowing bits with the ash in her mindless tracings. Hastily she used the stick to pull them together, and, banking the fire, she saved it for the morning's cooking. Determinedly, she tried to ignore the faint quaking in her hands; she felt rather like a trainee who was waiting for the Old Master to snap at some ineptness.

Inept? At what? Her heart thudded painfully as Elana suddenly realized that their loving had never been at her invitation, it had always been at Di'nay's. Since the repeated misunderstandings of their early days together, it seemed she had been content to follow Di'nay's inclinations.

Memories, images of Di'nay arching in that long, slow stretch as she was released from that magical blue bond — the feel of satin-skinned muscles dissolving beneath her hands as Di'nay fell against her, nearly lost beneath Elana's own black, black cape of silken hair. And Elana felt a new desire stir. She had never loved Di'nay without melding them together with the blue touch. She had never savored the trembling of that strong body against her own — held and felt her loving bring that beautiful woman pleasure — without that blue presence. Elana wanted that. Without the sharing of her Sight, she wanted Di'nay...to give to her alone...to slowly love her, and hold her, and selfishly know the pleasures she gave were hers alone to give.

Desire flamed, and shivering from that sweet ache, she pulled her cloak more closely around her. A soft smile touched her lips as she turned toward the tent and found the drowsy tenderness of Di'nay's amarin awaiting her. Her heart fluttered; she would be welcomed.

❋ ❋ ❋

Chapter Eleven

"Dear Mother and Goddess, what have these souls wrought?" Diana exclaimed.

"It is quite a fortress," Elana agreed quietly, a hand absently stroking the eitteh's silken head as the animal growled from atop her pack. "The dungeons are in the lower levels. The cavalry and main garrisons are quartered on the northern side. The main gate is east, but there are dozens of smaller entrances, but none by which an army could invade, however. Some are better guarded than others."

They stood against the face of southern cliffs that overshadowed the dark river, Ma'naur. Below, the swirling waters claimed eight hundred feet or more before meeting the north shore. Beyond that rocky beach extended a hundred leagues of blackpines. They were thick, towering evergreens with green-black needles and branches that pushed and meshed against their neighbors — aged mammoths that had starved off competing plants by exiling the sun. They had survived fires and battles and mercilessly swallowed lost travelers. But the Maltar had good use for them. If a man knew the forests, its shadows lent his militia cover, and the gaping barrenness beneath its roof allowed unhindered movement of horse and soldier. Further north and in the west, the trees were harvested for shipyards and builders, but here the jagged crests were unbroken except for that single hill.

Among hundreds of knolls, a slightly higher knoll rose from the blackpines, but shaved. Absurdly naked, it held the massive stone fortress above the dark sea.

The walls of the Priory were a barren, brown-beige color that matched the stone of the knoll — stripped of its topsoil after the trees had been rooted out. The age of the fortress and rock suggested that that rape had been eons ago. The walls had grown smooth in the seasons before the ancient monastery had fallen to more merciless hands, the winds polishing the stone. There were no graceful spiraling turrets nor arching palace gates. This place had been designed to hold the outer world at bay. The windows were small, angled slits; the doors deep set with double gates, and only the massive eastern entrance would allow a cavalry passage.

But the foreboding, austere front was not the cause of Diana's fear. Her gaze scanned the ancient fortress as she dug into a hidden pocket of her belt. She prayed she was mistaken as she opened accordion-style binoculars to look through them.

At the base of the embankment loomed a massive metal box with a laser gun atop it, casing flashing silver in the morning sun. Diana felt her chest tighten. Fifty meters to either side of it stood another. Grimly she noted a trail of them across the face of the hill. Undoubtedly the system extended around the entire fortress.

Z'ki Sak, Diana! What had Garrison been doing here?

"What are you looking at?" Elana asked suddenly, realizing it was not the Priory itself that drew Di'nay's attention.

"There," Diana pointed, offering the glasses to Elana, "at the base of the hill."

Elana's brow wrinkled slightly with perplexed concentration as she looked through the glass and queried, "The metal boxes worry you?"

"They're laser guns," Diana explained, folding her gadget away. "They control a narrow finger of light that eats through anything it touches. It strikes as fast as any snake but with the reach of a long bow."

"That does not sound promising," Elana muttered. The eitteh rumbled something. "She is right, Di'nay. We should go below. We are too exposed here."

✳ ✳ ✳

The next sunrise found them cloaked in the river's mists at the southern landing. Uneasily Diana walked across the dock and pulled the mallet off its hook. A dull clunk echoed out over the water as she struck the sounding tube.

"Three times," Elana called softly from the mists.

Diana waited, feeling vulnerable on that bare deck. Again she hit the three beats. This time there was an answering from the north shore. Diana returned the mallet to its place and stepped back into the fog.

"He comes alone," Elana muttered as Di'nay touched her shoulder.

"Good enough." But her stomach was tight; she felt like they were walking into a trap. This man's ferry was the nearest crossing to the Priory; he owed allegiance to the Maltar. They were, by necessity, using the Maltar's own front door — and using it with a weak bluff. They hoped that in brazenly announcing that they were destined for the Priory, the man would not find their presence too questionable.

"Where is he?" Diana muttered with impatience.

"Near the half-way mark." Elana's voice was quite calm.

Sarcasm laced Diana's voice as she said, "You haven't done this before?"

A flicker of a smile broke Elana's unreadable expression, but she made no reply.

The pulley system creaked as the river current dragged against the ferry. Diana sighed deeply to settle her nerves, straightening her shoulders. There was a point of no return that always produced a cold control deep in her. As the dim outline of the boatman and barge became visible, Diana realized that point had been reached.

Grimly she pulled off her cloak and folded it into her pack. She would not wear a green cloak just as she did not ride red horses into Maltar's backyard.

A few feet from the shore the man left his turn crank and sank his pole into the watery depths, guiding the ferry to the dock. "No heroics," Diana reminded her friend sternly. Elana nodded and, lifting the edge of her brown skirt, stepped carefully onto the dock. Her feet were bare and suitably muddy, but the boatman had not missed the flash of white calf. Elana had his full attention as they approached. He was not a stupid man, however, and the black scabbard at Diana's side had not gone unnoticed. But pretty wenches made much better pictures to contemplate.

"Good tidings to you, Sir," Elana said to the boatman in his native tongue, smiling hesitantly. "My Lord bids me ask, is the road, beyond, the Priory's way?"

"Your Lord?" The sidelong glance hovered between disrespect for a silent stranger and fear of a moody swordbearer.

This was more than a boatman, Elana suddenly understood. The scar along his right cheek had come from soldier's combat. She prayed he had not done too much port duty or he might question if Di'nay truly came from the southern continent.

"He too good to speak to freemen?"

Diana's dark eyes narrowed as she met the glowering challenge. The packs landed with a heavy thunk on his barge and obediently Elana boarded.

"Priory you said?" He looked around quickly at Elana, then back to the grim swordbearer with a nod. "True, this road goes that way."

Sullenly Diana stepped onto the barge and moved to the far corner. Elana hurried to get the packs — the good servant — dropping them near Di'nay, before settling herself against the railing. Folding her arms and crossing her ankles, Diana deliberately turned to face the north shore. Her message was clear — tolerance was scarce.

"May you pardon my Lord," Elana spoke hastily, as if unwilling to totally alienate their host quite yet. "It is a long journey from the lower continent that we have come. He is not accustomed to our climate — or our speech."

"South of Ramains, you say?"

"Desert Peoples, Sir."

"Then he's best excused. Never taught them manners." He squared his shoulders, pleased to be showing the lass how much more civilized he could be in comparison. His practicalities reasserted themselves abruptly. "Can he pay?"

She produced the standard number of glass shells from her purse and he grunted. Laboriously he dropped each into his palm counting the fare, but he eyed the figure in the corner. Worn, but quality clothing — he noted the stranger had money.

The last shell dropped and his palm stayed open. "It's not enough."

Fully aware of his amarin — that he could not count beyond six — Elana gasped and put a hand to her throat. "Oh please, Sir, do count them again!"

"What? You accuse me of cheating?!"

"No, oh please," she hushed him with a hurried look to Di'nay.

He grudgingly lowered his voice. "Do you accuse me then?"

"No, oh no." She pushed her hand into her small belt purse, finding nothing. "But I couldn't have lost any... oh please, do count it again, Sir. My Lord was quite specific when he counted out the pieces this morning — quite specific."

Warily his narrow eyes slid to the silent figure.

"He will be so angry with me!" Appealingly she bit her lip, gesturing to the shells in his hand. "Please...? How much more? Oh, he will beat me for certain...."

"There now, girl." He was not about to confront a swordbearing man who could count, and the chance to save face by sparing the girl a beating was almost a good deed. "I'll say it's the right price. There'll be no harm done to you over a bitty piece of glass now. Not while I can have a say about it."

"Oh but — oh, thank you. It's so kind of you."

"Not a word 'bout it." He unwrapped the mooring line and picked up the pole.

"But surely? I know. I will tell my Lord you have been very helpful — about the way to the Priory."

"Well that's not being much," he pointed out practically, enjoying her attention. With the pole in hand he guided the barge out into the river.

"And how you came out so quick and all, crossing the river just for us."

He grinned, flattered.

"I know my Lord will mention your kindness and service to those at the Priory."

That seemed to startle him. He looked at her blankly, then stalked off to the turn crank as his color rose. She followed him quickly. He frowned and cleared his throat. "Now where exactly did you say you're going to? At the Priory, I mean?"

"In truth, I'm not certain." She threw him a fluttering smile. "My Lord was summoned several monarcs ago. He is not even certain the Great One is still here — or if he has gone west for the winter by now?"

"Aye, well," the boatman said, looking pale. "He's still here all right. Lights flashing day and night around the place, burning trees." Elana did not miss the fear in his amarin. So the laser guns were not just decoration. She smiled demurely at him to distract him.

His face flushed darker. "Might you be staying in the cas'le proper then?"

"I would not know." Elana understood by this question that he'd rather they were as far away from the Priory's gossipy servants as possible, and that Malthar's guard and he were not on the best of terms.

He said, "Well, there's a couple of nice taverns on the road. Just inside the town wall there's a boarding house — some of the best food servings in these parts. Very little gossip too, girl. Might be a place for you — if your business is to be quiet."

"Oh yes, thank you." Elana beamed in delight and pushed her advantage. "Do you not see what I mean about yourself? Being so helpful and such?"

"Now what did I say?"

"But surely?"

"Are you deaf!" he interrupted flatly. He suddenly felt downright callused. This girl was getting to be too much trouble no matter how pretty her hair might be, and she was going to be getting him too much notice. "It's I who does the living around here. You keep your mouth shut. Understand? And I'll do likewise. Hear me?"

She nodded, backing up a step.

"Now off with you. Your Lord will be wondering if your affections is straying. And I got no need for trouble over a scrawny maid. Get!"

Elana turned on her heel and hurried to Di'nay.

When Elana's body was squarely between Diana and the boatman she broke into a broad grin. "I would love to have understood that exchange. You fluttered and danced like a tavern maid."

Elana made a scoffing sound. "He's shallow. I did not even have to tamper with his amarin."

"Did he notice your eyes?"

"What about them?"

Diana nodded. In the mist and with the Sight's guise, they looked quite gray. "So what did you learn? I gathered he was trying to demand a higher price from the crossing, but you lost me after that."

"The Maltar and his court is still here. And consequently this fellow does not want his name mentioned up on the hill."

"Friendly sort of place, isn't it?"

Elana shrugged. "I suspect he wouldn't be so cautious if they'd already moved west, but his beloved monarch is not one to seek favors from lightly."

"Why would he want something from the Maltar?"

"He would not, but I suggested we could call his good work to the Maltar's attention. From his amarin I gathered he'd rather go completely unnoticed."

"I take it he's not apt to say anything to anyone about us, even if they ask?"

"So we can hope. What he remembers will not help them in any case."

Their caution seemed prudent as they reached the northern shore. The militia's board carried a fresh poster. An exceptionally short man clad in a green cloak and traveling alone was being pursued. He spoke with a Ramainian accent and was to be considered a spy.

"I never particularly thought of myself as short," Diana commented dryly as they started up the road.

"Neither have I," Elana agreed as they exchanged smiles.

As the mist swallowed the boatman's cabin, Diana glanced over her shoulder uncertainly. The road ahead was rising, but the forest dimmed what little sunlight there was in this early morning.

"I can see through this," Elana reassured her, sensing her concern. "And it will clear a little when we reach higher ground as it warms."

"Warms? This is Aggar. Surely you jest?!"

But Elana surprised her by agreeing, "It is cold here. I only hope we leave before the snow sets in."

Not such an odd wish considering her bare feet and browning skin, Diana realized. But it wasn't safe to stop so close to the river. The creak of the barge ropes was still audible — a kind of haunting echo that urged them on.

"I refuse to suffer more than a league without boots," Elana announced flatly. "Sooner if you see some place safe."

The damp was seeping in through Diana's tunic and fieldsuit, but she did not call a halt either; this was not a day for foolishness.

❈ ❈ ❈

The rain had worsened when they made camp. Well hidden in the depths of the forest and away from the roads, they settled down to wait for darkfall and the sparse safety that the night would bring to their prowling.

With the descent of the first moon the icy drizzle lifted. Leaving the eitteh to guard their packs and camp, they started for the lasers. The forest felt cold and damp under their feet, a warning that before dawn there would be a thick frost and the pine needles of the forest's floor would freeze in thin sheets of ice.

Uncomfortable, Diana thought the air smelt like snow. She was loath to admit how uninviting the darkness had become. It was monarc's end, and the eighth single moon of the tenmoon season had long left the sky. Ten times a year, at regular intervals, one of the lunar sisters' was absent from the sky. The difference was imposing, foreboding black. A darkness unusual for a planet which seldom had a full hour or two of moonlessness on any night. Usually there was enough light from the Twins to allow even the poorest artisan to work by moons' light.

Diana grew more and more uneasy in the blackness. The forest's roof combined with the dense cloud cover to swallow whatever faint light the starry sky gave, and her flashlight was, by necessity, set on a very low, narrow beam.

That Elana moved confidently through the trees was only vaguely reassuring, and Diana had a brief image of herself as a child in that long, empty mine. She shook the picture aside and made herself focus on their task. Ahead — somewhere — stood the laser-guarded perimeter of the Priory's hill. They were approaching it through the woods, a good league west of the road that eventually wound around the rocky base to the Priory's eastern gates. The forest's paths were risky given the night's darkness; the Maltar might have assigned extra patrols in these woods.

Diana's plans were fairly simple — basic reconnaissance and the disarming of one laser gun for future passage across the perimeter. The guns Diana had seen through her binoculars had been old and varied in make and model. She knew from Terran history that a number of sky cruisers had been lost in this corner of Aggar during the Empire's initial invasions. Elana had added that the Maltar's ancestors had hoarded much of the wreckage from those turbulent days. The Council had never seen much to worry about, considering the imperial reactors that had powered the machines had long been destroyed. The rulers had been too greedy of their catch to allow the metal-smiths to melt their treasures down for alloy. The Council had seen no threat from the rulers possessing such a supply of the alien metal.

The presence of Garrison changed everything. With the power supply from his ship, he had the expertise to make these relics of an earlier age actually work.

The variety of machines meant the laser guns had not necessarily come from the same design; therefore, if they were working, they had to be jury-rigged with an individual control circuit for each. This also meant that the range and sweep diameter of each gun would be a little different. To prevent the cross-firing that would trigger an eternal firing sequence from the electric eyes of neighboring machines, there would be some fairly predictable gaps in the sweep patterns of each gun. It would be, supposedly, only a matter of dashing through the holes, attaching the decoder to the power cable below a gun's controlling circuit, and waiting until the proper command frequency was decoded. At that point, Diana could — independent of the other lasers — shut the gun down with a remote.

Although Diana had not come particularly prepared to disarm lasers, it was fairly simple to adapt the de-scrambler on her transmitter to suit her purposes. She was rather pleased with her ingenuity. What she was not pleased about was Elana's role in their little venture.

"You worry overmuch." Elana's tone was teasing as it drifted back to Diana. She gave an ambiguous 'humph' and held her tongue. Elana was perfectly justified in her insistence on being their runner. The woman had been the top sprinter amongst the trainees at the Keep — for several seasons. It made her the logical one to run the twenty or twenty-five meters across the perimeter. Diana had never been very good at the short race, but theoretically she should still be fast enough to slip through.

Theory alone was a rather weak argument, Elana had pointed out. Especially when one could strengthen the odds by adding a little speed.

Despite the simplicity of the plan, it seemed much less viable to Diana now that she wasn't going to be the one taking the risks.

❀ ❀ ❀

Elana blinked, suddenly feeling disoriented by the moonless sky. She shook her head, vaguely trying to rid herself of the blurred edges to her vision. The dense overcast above only worsened things. A heavy electrical charge seemed to hang in the air with the waiting storm clouds, and it distorted her Sight. She was fine for the first twenty meters or so, but beyond that, the individual boundaries of the trees blurred with sparkling, crackling shivers.

They squatted at the very edge of the forest, facing the barren perimeter with its ancient guns. They did not look ancient, just hulking and shadowy. Her Sight made out very few details since the guns were made of lifeless steel, but the ground stretching before them was littered with scarred soil and singed grass and trees. The path between the two machines was as clear to her as if a road had been laid.

"You are right," Diana muttered, closing the tiny computer she'd been bent over for so long. "The path you traced is true — unless they've reprogrammed the thing in the last few hours." That possibility, that Garrison had updated the firing program so the new tract was not yet visible, worried her. There had been sporadic firings of the laser. Elana had suffered from the death of the forest animals that got caught in the laser fire, but it meant that if the laser was activated the guard might assume it another animal caught.

"You know what to do?"

Elana nodded, turning the decoder over in her hand. "These points snap into the thick cylinder that climbs the base of the machine."

"Just beneath the gun box."

"You have shown me the place, Di'nay," Elana gently reminded her. Elana slipped from her cloak and made certain her hair was securely braided. Concentrating, she drew air into her lungs and her skin began to brown. She had shed her pale tunic before they left camp; the black undergarments provided a better camouflage. Her Sight might have shadowed her run, but that would have divided her attention and slowed her. At times, Elana knew, it was much better to use common sense.

"It may take some time for the decoder to unlock the system," Diana said, more for the sake of talking than for reminding. "It may be safer not to wait for it."

Elana blinked and her breath exhaled with a faint whoosh; her skin was a deep mahogany almost invisible in this darkness. She looked at Diana and suggested, "Let us wait and see how passable this field is before I decide when to return?"

Not able to see each other in the dark, they touched hands briefly. Then Elana tucked the decoder into her belt and crept closer to the perimeter. Balanced on toes and fingers, timing her breathing, she traced her route ahead. Then she was gone.

Yellow-white flashed once as a gun fired. The tracking hum ran and clicked — on and off — each gun aborting as the figure skirted in and out of its limits.

Diana held her breath, her eyes glued to the metal boxes. Almost — almost — her jaw clenched as the smallest of white lights appeared at the far gun's side.

Roll! her mind cried as her lips pressed, muting her scream.

Like a wave's push from behind Elana felt Di'nay's command and dove. The electric eyes broke with a flying wisp of hair and the light licked out into nothing — safely hitting its receptor on the neighboring gun.

Elana lay still behind the machines, watching the light from that line of defense flicker and die. For a moment she remained frozen, counting her heartbeats — reassuring herself that she was alive. The thought echoed in her mind that Di'nay would not have made it. She pushed herself up into a sitting position, automatically tossing her hair over a shoulder. She felt the singed edges of a few strands. Di'nay had been wrong; this laser thing struck much faster than a snake.

There was still much to be done. Standing, she pulled out the decoder. Her side felt bruised from rolling on the metal box, but the decoder did not seem the worse for wear. She stood behind the gun, carefully examining the cables and moorings. It was slightly different from the one Di'nay had mentally shown her, but the primary cable was obvious enough.

Elana knelt peering at the seam where it joined the upper box. She fleetingly wished Di'nay could have shared more than mental images with her; she was acutely aware of what a mistake would mean. It was a bit late to change things, so she set the decoder against the cable, and with the flat of her hand, she hit it squarely.

The small prongs penetrated the thin wrappings and held.

She looked at it uneasily, almost expecting it to explode or something, but the little box just sat there. Actually, it seemed quite at home beneath the bigger box, and Elana had a brief moment of satisfaction; even if Maltar's men stared straight at it, they would probably never see it.

With a quick glance about her Elana stood up. She did not like this place and the longer she was here, the more distinctly she felt the danger. But there was only darkness and rock — and across the perimeter, trees and Di'nay. Although, she admitted grimly, it was becoming more difficult to sense even Di'nay.

A vague hum followed by a slight click caught her attention, and she realized Di'nay had switched on the decoding sequence.

Elana rubbed her arms roughly; she was starting to get cold. She decided the worn folds of the bedrock behind her might be a little less exposed. Di'nay had said close to an hour — maybe less if they were lucky — before the combination unraveled. Apparently there were decoders that were much faster, but Di'nay did not have the proper equipment to make one of those. After seeing the likes of the laser gun, however, Elana was impressed that anything at all could be done to disarm it.

❄ ❄ ❄

Diana slipped off into the forest again. She couldn't fault Elana's decision to stay. It was virtually impossible to return through those horizontal lasers that connected the guns together. She should have considered that possibility when she first saw the machines. But it amazed her that Garrison would have been so thorough. Those machines had been taken from cruisers;

ships that had no need to string defensive electric eyes between their weaponry
because they were on board their ships. Even if Garrison had been coerced into
designing a defense system, there was no reason for such extremes. This was a
non-tech planet, not a science laboratory! Three guns strategically placed above
on the Priory's walls would have been sufficiently terrorizing. But this was insane!

Diana dropped to her stomach. The ring of sword and scabbard
startled her. Hidden by the depths of the forest and its brush, she strained her
eyes to see across the perimeter. Maroon and white tunics with gold-edged
cloaks of the Maltar's guards were suddenly visible in their lantern light. A patrol
of twenty seemed to have sprung from nowhere.... Diana shivered, as she looked
across to the base of the rising rock. Elana won't be seen — if she doesn't want to
be, she won't be — Elana!

❄ ❄ ❄

The sword tips clinked as the soldiers tapped blades — victory toasts
before the deed was even done — and Elana swallowed sheer panic. They had
stepped from the darkness as if each one of them was Blue Sighted, their greedy
passion for violence oozing through the air like pus from a sore.

She fumbled in the darkness, freeing her knife and sheath — not to
fight, but to hide it. It dropped to the ground and she wedged it into the tiny
fissure in the rock behind her. These men knew they faced a girl — a Blue Sight.
Their snarling laughter showed they did not believe in the illusion of empty rock
before them. She felt their appetites whetted for a kill — or perhaps, better, a
slow death. There was one exception, their captain. His orders were clasped
hard to the front of his mind, as if he might forget their importance.

They knew what she was! How could they have known?!

In another second they would start swinging their weapons. Through
blackness, fire or raging armies they were prepared to ignore their own senses
and wield blades in precise, practiced arcs. And even unseeing, their arching
patterns would slice her illusions and her body.

Down on one knee, hands atop her head, Elana trembled, letting her
darkness slide away. The captain wanted surrender; she wanted to live — for a
while yet. Di'nay was too close.

❄ ❄ ❄

Diana buried her face in the gritty mud, jamming her gloved fist to her
mouth. Silence — she choked on her silence. Her free hand clutched at the earth,
her fingers curling — digging deeply through the soil. The laughter shouted again,
and her body stiffened in rage. That was her lover, damn it! Didn't she have the
guts even to watch — not to leave her totally alone?!

Fierceness matched tears as she forced her gaze back — silently shouting
to Elana to survive as another booted foot smashed into her side. Just a little
longer until —

Until what? Her mind screamed. Until the decoder was done and the
gun shut down? Just what in Fates' Cellars did that help? There were twenty-odd
men out there! Amazons are human. We bleed red blood. We die too! Just how
would that help Elana? Frontal assault to victoriously die in unison? Or if you're
very lucky, in each others' arms? Think, woman!

But they were going to kill her!

Not quite. They dragged their bound and blindfolded captive to her feet, and slowly Diana realized there was much more to their purpose than the uncovering an odd intruder. The blindfold meant planning; the beating, too severe for merely gaining compliance, had been too short for permanent damage — again forethought.

Distraction?

Pain blurred all but the best of concentration. Yes! They had known of Elana's Blue Sight, and they were dutifully crippling her ability to use it. And dutifully enjoying each gesture.

Diana's teeth ground together savagely. Someone knew far too much. If she lived long enough to find who!

No! Her fist uncurled from the depths of the black soil. Who was responsible was secondary. Freeing Elana — and Garrison — was first order. But if someone was that well informed, there was the risk that she too was being tracked.

Yet there was no sign of a matching welcome on her side of the perimeter. She was well enough hidden that she would have seen something of their approach by now. Perhaps the lone Southern Trader myth was still the current belief?

Oh good Goddess how could she have been so stupid?!

They had never suspected Di'nay, Southern Trader of the Desert Peoples. It had been Elana all along. Nattersu's tale of a red horse was of Elana's bay, Leggings — not her own stallion. The patrol at Cellar's Gate must have carried word about her Blue Sight, so they had waited for their next ambush until the rocks would hide their presence. They had waited until she appeared in Maltar's land to try again.

Diana shivered, realizing an informer at the Keep must be very close to the Council in order to be tracking them so well — yet the pieces did not quite fit. Shouldn't they have known about her by this time? Unless that someone was a mala' perhaps? A bedfellow and slave with limited snatches of conversation to guess by with another master here that was piecing the whole puzzle together?

She would be that traitor's undoing!

But Diana's heart tore as the savage captors took Elana away. She closed her eyes against the half-dragged, half-stumbling image of her beloved, and her face pressed into the soil again as the sobs rose.

❋ ❋ ❋

Chapter Twelve

How many corners — how many stairs — how many hands bruised her body? She did not know. Elana lost count as she was slammed into the next wall — or thrown against the next step. If she kept their pace her feet were knocked out from beneath her. If she stumbled fists struck, causing her to fall. If she fell hard-leathered boots lifted her, commanding her forward — or spears prodded, ripping seams and skin with careless malice. And with each man's cuff or push she knew his perverted pleasure and felt his merciless amarin.

She would have cried, had there been time, but the pain and twisted commands came in rapid succession, and she was left with no time for thought. Behind the blindfold her eyes flashed white with the sharpness of blows as the emptiness of the stone corridors rang with tormenting laughter.

Then suddenly she staggered to a halt and was left standing. No shoving, no pulling — just left.

Hushed breathing — the rustling of cloth registered quickly in her mind as the blindfold was snatched from her eyes, twisting and almost snapping her neck.

Waves of stinging, aching pain rushed past her. Elana made no effort to keep her eyes closed. If the monsters were so stupid...!

A denseness wrapped the room. A heavy, black, almost fog-like humidity smothered her, quelling the barrage of sensation. And her power was shackled though she was not harmed by that shackling. Mother of All — a Seer?! Her eyes shut. Instinctively she shied, ducking her chin into her shoulder with the terror.

Think! Before it was too late — concentrate!

A spear shaft struck the backs of her knees. Arms still bound behind her, she went down with a gasp, landing heavily on her hip and shoulder. Her teeth snapped shut with a resounding clack as another boot swept into her ribs.

Concentrate! He must not learn anything. Think of the Mistress — of trainees running. Concentrate.

"Enough!"

Murmurs in the court hall died instantly. The jabbing toes and spears stopped.

Concentrate.

The pain made her dizzy as hands roughly pulled her back to her feet. That was good. That was fine. Use it — project it. Make him control it.

A handful of hair was yanked hard, blinding her with white again. Her eyes flew open at the captain's threatening amarin. She faced the summer court of the Maltar.

"I am here!" Elana barked harshly, arrogantly — despite it all. And she stared hard at the man upon the throne. The mute figure beside him shifted its attention to protect its master from her blazing blue gaze. "What is it you want?"

Beneath the crimson and gold tunic, a gruesome rasping noise grew to a shout of laughter. The Maltar was enjoying this new game. He had been sorely disappointed when he heard one lone Council spy had been sent, and that only a female. But perhaps — between her blue gift and her stubborn spirit — it would be amusing after all.

His laughter died as his dark eyes narrowed. He flicked a hand, and the captain released her hair; she almost fell — but not quite. The Maltar nodded approvingly, stroking the thin beard that outlined his jaw. She was not pretty by his standards, but he had never bedded a Seer. It would be an interesting experience — to know her disgust and fear, her debasement? — first hand. To know what this woman felt just as he triumphed? Yes — perhaps there would be advantages to this that he had not yet discovered. Aye, breaking her would be tedious, as it had been with the idiot beside him — that Blue Sighted male had taken nearly a full ten-day to lose its wits.

She would be no different. But afterwards — afterwards he would have breeding stock — and his fun. His voice rang smooth, an elegant tenor. "So what would she have us overlook, Seer?"

A trace of madness in that voice? Elana wondered while her concentration was held tight to her body's acute pain. Brutally, she threw it all at the Seer.

The elder swayed beside the throne, his breath shallow, his skin darkening.

"Well?"

"I do not read her, mi'Lord." His voice was weak and hoarse.

Elana sneered almost wickedly, using her anger at the men's violence. She sought strength from the tension of the legions that lined the stone walls...from the craven bloodlust of the Captain's guard...from the twisted desires of their ruler. Gathering every vile shadow that she could find, she flung them at him. Focused, magnified — she passed the raw savagery onto him. And the advantage was hers.

He was the Seer, she only a Blue Sight. Her powers were less, but her mind was still her own — her thoughts still hers to plan with — to attack with! Too long immersed, lost within his planet's tides, the Seer was a communicator of visions — a mere tool for his master! without the consciousness to plot, without the ability to defend his mind's boundaries. If the Maltar had any sense he would cut her down now — before she turned his precious counselor impotent for a monarc.

The Maltar's lip curled into an appreciative, satirical smile.

Pity and revulsion stirred within her, but Elana's concentration remained fixed. She continued. A black cloud hovered at the edges of her mind — watching. She would piece it together later, if there was a later.

The laughter of the Maltar rang out again. He could see that she twisted his fool well. Talented indeed but it would not save her. He felt his loins harden with the thought of her groveling insanity at their next meeting. "Do protect yourself, you witless bastard." His fingers snapped; the Seer blinked, breaking his direct contact with Elana and turning to the Maltar, who said, "Well?"

Hollow words rasped, "The pain...the beating. The woman uses it against me."

"I see you are not the only hapless idiot in my employ. Captain! Did I not order the woman bound and brought before me in good piece?"

No one looked at the man who stepped forward.

"Mind you," the Maltar continued softly, "a little bruising may often breed cooperation, but in this case your men have overstepped their boundaries."

The silence stretched.

"You are the elite of my guard, Captain! If my orders are not reliably executed under your command, where do you suggest I turn?"

The Captain had the wisdom to hold his tongue.

"The discipline in your ranks has broken, Captain! I am waiting to hear what you will do!" His breathing had quickened in the face of an implied snubbing. The Maltar writhed on his chair, black eyes glazing in a demented glare. "Captain?!"

"Yes, m'Lord!" He snapped to a straighter, more rigid pose. "Discipline has lapsed. The guilty will be dealt with. Obedience sharpened, m'Lord!"

The Maltar relaxed, a grimace half-hidden beneath his trembling hand. The stupidities of his militia were so unsettling; the need to assault this woman-spy had been gone when she was blindfolded. She was Blue Sight only until hooded; then she was no more than any other wench. Curse them! Carelessly they had provided her with the very weapon...and now? Now?! He would have to wait to discover the Council's tid-bits of suspicions and plots.

Or would he? His eyes narrowed curiously, roving the length of her figure. A twisted, sugar-sweet smile grew slowly as his long fingers tapped his chin. He leapt with a startling quickness.

Elana jumped as the vile face thrust close to hers. The Seer's blackness pressed the advantage as she ducked her head, eyes squeezing shut again. The blackness cracked across her shoulders, but the Captain's brutal fingers pulled her back by the nape of her neck, preventing her fall.

"Yesss...." The Maltar's hiss brought her eyes open again, but her resolve was steadied. The black cloud once again could only hover, waiting.

His eyes were shadowed by the Seer's dimness, a tempting bait for her to snatch at — so close. He grinned as he realized she would not play that game. Yes, she would mother a fine stock of Blue Sights for him.

His hand flicked and the Captain released her. The Maltar circled slowly.

"You are quite a catch. Bedfellow...blue eyes...Council prize...quite a catch." His smile carried a sickened, heady lust in it, and Elana's stomach cringed as she pushed the amarin of madness outward again.

"Don't feel too betrayed by my old friend there." He pointed idly at his Seer, pausing beside her and watching her unfocused gaze, waiting for it to waver. "He had very little to say about it, I assure you." The Maltar's words were slow, taunting. His gesture was lazy as he opened his hand and the Captain's dagger was laid in it. "You see, he was not merely faced with death — but with madness..."

This was not making sense. Elana felt her mouth go dry, despairing in her effort not to think — not to grasp at his amarin for understanding.

"...though the threat of death itself can be quite a persuasive thing..." The silver point danced before her nose. "...can it not?"

Anticipation rippled through the men behind her. A tremor began within the pit of her stomach as she felt her control slipping.

No! Throw it back! Make him control it! Make him absorb it!

"Death..." The dagger pressed flat against her cheek, and the king leered as she flinched. "...what is death? Hmmm?"

The blade scraped down over bone, grazing a reddened trail — a rough burn across dark skin. But he was not drawing blood, not quite yet. He chuckled, twisting the wicked point at the base of her throat. "Death is so very enticing to some..."

She caught her fear rising.

"...to some," he repeated, savoring the words. The blade withdrew a fraction of an inch. "But only to the very ignorant, don't you think? Because...there are so many ways to die."

Her legs shook beneath her, and she ground her teeth shut — pummeling that hovering blackness into retreat. Fear would be her tool. Not her master! She would die at his hand — yes! But she would die silent!

"Doubtless you wish a quick death here, hmm?" The knife snagged the top strands of her black knit bodice and flicked. The yarn sliced cleanly. "But truly — you may find dying a very, very slow thing indeed..."

A few more strands were cut.

The air was icy against her sweating skin. Kill and be done! Her mind shrieked.

"...a lifetime even."

No — it must be now! Despair mixed with fury.

She felt something snap inside and that black wall staggered back another inch.

"Note with our friend there...how very long a lifetime can be." The dagger paused, its inviting tip at her sternum...her breasts bared to its steel.

May the Old Mistress forgive her — Elana gulped for air and the Seer blinked, suddenly disconcerted for an instant.

She lunged at the blade.

But the knife turned away as he laughed, side-stepping her. The Captain jumped, his massive hands grabbing her shoulders. She twisted and her feet kicked, knocking his boots out from under him, and they fell together.

Her head cracked against the flagstones. Lungs gasped — and swallowed the Seer's blackness. The suffocating, airless void of nothingness tore into her mind but her scream died as her failing body carried her the last step beyond their reach.

The Maltar's screech pierced the chamber.

His face blackened in blistering fury as he rolled the captain's bulk from her. His nostrils flared at her stillness. "Bitch!" He kicked her unconscious form, then turned toward the Seer. The dagger flew, whisking past the Seer to strike his own throne. "Witless puppet! The Fates should lose your cellar key, old man! She was to be kept conscious! Imbecile!!"

He shouted, "Take her...!" The Captain started as the Maltar spun back to him. "...out of my sight. Now! — now!!"

Shaking with rage, the king went back to his chair as they scrambled to remove the limp figure to a prepared dungeon. A page tentatively offered him wine.

He downed the goblet and gestured for more. His breath steadied, but he finished the second as quickly as the first, flinging the empty chalice aside, and the boy scrambled after it. Very well, what had he lost?

Nothing.

The Maltar pursed his lips and stroked his beard. Truly nothing...all had witnessed this moron's Blue Sighted clumsiness. There was naught to blame himself for. No one with any sanity could slight him. It had been the Seer.

And as for the Council?

Bah. He settled back on his throne. Those old misers were so predictable he did not need to be told what they were doing. They weren't paying the ransom, that much had always been clear. So, in a ten-day he'd have the idle gossip of that bloody Keep but probably not much else. After all, she was a woman — a Blue Sight...she was a carrier of visions, not a thinker. The perfect sort to send as a spy, but of use for little else. So — he'd have what? Nothing at all?

Except, he would have the girl — a strong, young Seer with which to replace this dwindling fool — a woman, not an impotent male like the slave beside him. No, she would be a strong, young breeder of more Seers.

His dark gaze flickered across the silent old Seer. Yes, he would have much, much more than nothing.

❋ ❋ ❋

Elana awoke with a start, blinking in the utter darkness. Then memory rushed in, and she covered her face and head in her arms.

Concentrate!

Fierceness — defiance echoed about her.

But that was different.

She paused, lifting her head cautiously as she listened.

A trickling echo of falling water surrounded her. Cold crept into her, icy as it touched her clammy skin.

Of men — of Maltar — there was no feeling, no sound.

Her body uncurled slowly, mistrusting this calm.

There was no scent — no smell at all save for her body's own fear...and the cold.

Crouching low on hands and knees, she waited. But there was no blow to her back — no yank on her hair.

The stone beneath her palms felt gritty with fine sand, but there was no smell of must or mold. And no sound other than that of the chortling water.

Elana risked opening her eyes.

Gasping at the cruelty of utter oblivion, she curled up into a tight ball.

She shut her eyes, feeling the emptiness swallow her whole — driving down her throat. Cold claw-like fingers were reaching in — groping for her soul...a painful squeezing that wrapped around the racing heartbeats. It would crush the very life from her...!

And mercifully, consciousness left again...for a time.

❋ ❋ ❋

She woke herself crying, tears wetting her face and sobs shaking her body. Knowledge had risen unbidden even before she had completely returned. For a timeless moment, she cried.

Fingers rubbed the cold stones beneath her, careful in their fearful touch yet hoping to find mortar in those smooth cracks, and despairing when there was none.

And there was none. These ancient stones were made of bedrock that had never seen foliage to cradle as fossil or vegetable soap to scrub them clean. Cut and wedged together, they held by design, not mortar. Scoured by sand, they offered no food for the crawlers of the dark, damp nights, and the isolation was complete.

She knew that the water trickling in the emptiness would be as lifeless. It would spill from metal pipes, stemming from vats that boiled all life from the liquid. There would be no algae — no mildew. And there would be a metal basin somewhere, sunk into the rock, with more running water, a latrine that removed even the need for wooden buckets.

Tears subsided, fingers pushed aimlessly at the sparse grains of sand, and Elana prayed for death. But the Mother goes unheard in the very depths of the Fates' Cellars and in the living pit of a Seer's Tomb.

A Seer's Tomb — empty chambers devoid of the coursing rush of life, isolating the ones of Blue Sight. Elana had not thought any still existed. Legendary, they were almost forgotten in the oblivion of time.

Isolated them? For the first time in her entire life, she was utterly, completely — alone...forsaken by the Mother...forsaken even by the mildews!

The Maltar's laughing, jeering face rose before her mind's eye and a scream of terror tore from her throat. "Mother!"

Fingers clawed at her face. Fighting the hysteria — fighting the fear that washed through her body. The heels of her hands pressed hard into her eyes, forcing them shut, instinctively protecting her from loosing that swelling panic into this chamber.

Release that amarin of terror in here and it would echo to infinity...she would never be rid of it. It would make her mad.

Pain from the savage pressure against her eyes — from the bruises of her body — invaded her consciousness. Slowly, seeping in past the horror, pain demanded attention. Elana welcomed the distraction. She concentrated, gulping in that ice-like air as she finally allowed herself to breathe. Slowly, she turned her mind inward.

Her shoulders and shins would be black-and-blue, and the swatches of yellow-green across her breasts and ribs would hurt even more. The shafts of spears had been kinder than the soldiers' boots. Her right hip where she had fallen felt swollen, almost frozen to immobility. Her cheek burned from the scraping friction of his toying knife, but she could move some. Miraculously nothing was broken.

But then, it was her mind — her very identity that the Maltar wanted raped from her soul. Her body was only a secondary concern.

She swallowed hard, her mouth sour from tears and fear. The sound of that mocking water registered again, giving her yet another thing to focus upon. She gathered her courage; she was alive. She did not want to be, but she was. Death was no longer a choice. Now, there was only survival — or madness.

Elana opened her eyes bravely, feeling the darkness taunt her. Mother — she had never been so alone.

Anyone left in such total isolation would know madness given time; but a Blue Sight — a Blue Sight would snatch at the Maltar's shining face as he walked through those iron doors and bond irrevocably — as if to a Savior! And the Gift would be at that malicious Savior's disposal. The power of life's flowing cycles — the power of Aggar's fiber would be the Maltar's to command as the Sighted one took refuge in the Maltar's insanity. Aloneness would be banished, but that terrible insanity — forever; identity would be only in that insanity...a shuddering, horrible eternity.

No, Elana thought grimly. She was alone, but she was not his for the taking. The lifestone in her wrist throbbed faintly, and her hand clasped over the leather band in a desperate grip. Somehow, some way she was still connected to Di'nay. The stone was not like Blue Sight. Neither animate nor inanimate, it survived on either, thriving on both. These cold walls held no power over this bond.

No, hers was not a soul to be raped of its identity! She was Elana, Shadow of Council and Keep. Hers was not a mind to be bent! She was bound to Di'nay; the stone would destroy her before another usurped her chosen shadowmate!

She had a choice. Without Di'nay near her, she could be dead in a ten-day or less. If she could survive, mind intact until then, the Maltar would have nothing.

Nothing!

And if she could not? Then the Seer would rifle through her demented mind and they would learn of Di'nay...and they would begin searching.

She would not let that happen. Whole and sane, she would survive.

If not for the sake of escape, then for the sake of her beloved. She would not take Di'nay with her. She would not!

❋ ❋ ❋

Chapter Thirteen

Diana returned to camp at dawn, where the winged-cat was settled comfortably in front of their tent, a fowl limply held beneath its forepaws. But their breakfast went untouched. Diana barely greeted the creature before turning to break camp and bury the tattered tent remains. The eitteh grasped the urgency quickly; it took her longer to realize that the Blue Sighted One was part of the concern.

The eitteh growled a quiet warning and Diana looked up sharply. In the distance she heard voices and, hurrying, she stuffed the last of the gear into the underbrush. The Ma'naur River surged past them barely a dozen feet away; its steady whoosh hid the small noises of her task. But they did risk exposure if she dallied too long.

When she was done the patrols could stand beside the packs and would never see them. Diana's green satchel slid over her shoulder and settled as comfortably as if it were a quiver of arrows. Elana's cloak was also folded within. Her own cloak rustled with the sound of leaves as she donned it. The eitteh turned from its vigilance and padded close. "Come then," Diana whispered. Together the two slipped into the shadows of the great blackpines.

With an uncanny quickness, the animal discerned Diana's course for the river and urged her around patrolling troops in the foggy morn. Diana remembered Elana's comment that the eitteh were sentient and found herself glad of the company.

Perhaps there was not a clear path, but at least she was not to be alone in the madness of this desperate moment.

❋ ❋ ❋

Darkness shrieked with the silence, startling Elana into wakefulness. Time had no meaning here. Minutes might have been days or days, hours. Mother, please — she wanted only that the waiting be done.

Reluctantly, she rolled onto her back and stared at nothingness. The stone was cold beneath her bare shoulders and she shivered. The emptiness would be harder to fight if she became ill; humorlessly she almost laughed. She doubted if there was a single germ within the cell.

Besides — she stretched carefully, palms reaching out across the chilled floor — the cold kept the insanity at bay. Its insistent touch confined her mind to her body, just as these walls confined her body to this blackness.

Still, it was time to move again.

Gingerly she raised her knees and felt the muscles begin to protest. She tempered the stretching, and gradually, the knots loosened a bit. Mechanically she forced her body through the morning routine she had led the trainees in for so many seasons. Having no concept of time, she did this each wakening now. She knew from logic and lessons that she would be sleeping more from the shock and trauma than from the day's cycles, so she did not attempt to estimate a day's time. The exercise was only to distract. Yes, she needed to create structure in emptiness, to create mythical purpose even here in this emptiness.

Not entirely mythical, she reminded herself gently. There was reason to her movements. Her body would stay more flexible if she carefully worked out the stiffness. She would need her body's strength if she was to survive — or escape. She must be able to trust her abilities.

She stood, feeling unbalanced between the blackness and her soreness. But her feet held her, and the ringing in her head from earlier trials had faded. Cautiously, she continued her regimen.

The air seemed warm after the stone, and she thought the rock must be very thick to resist warming from her body's heat.

In the corner the rags of her knit undergarment lay discarded. It was a mixed blessing now, still glowing from the savage touch of her captors, mingled with the familiarity of her own body, though too shredded to don again after her washing. The soft leather of her breeches had been torn by a spear's point and the seam was unraveling, but they were still comfortingly warm. She had drawn strands from the knits to mend the torn waist seam and with her belt it promised to hold.

She had been surprised that they had not taken her boots from her, but then they were not the fashion most women would wear, and undoubtedly they would be too small for her captors. The men, too, did not strike her as the type to take an interest in a growing boy, if any were about to give boots to. They had left her with her leather lacings, and she might very well be able to make use of those.

Or perhaps...?

She looked again at the knits piled off to the side. The strands were soft but tenaciously spun. A dozen or so braided together might make a small rope...the size of a man's throat.

A bolt slid with an echoing clang, and she looked to where she knew the iron door to be. A blinding whiteness streaked through the doorjamb, and she covered her eyes with the sudden pain, dropping to a crouch as the door swung open with a violent bang.

Later she would remember two hulking figures; the torches they carried fueled to burn more fiercely than safety warranted. She would shred the bread they left, moisten it, washing as much of the Seer's touch — the Maltar's touch — from it as possible. How carefully coaxed in the ancient lore of Blue Sights this Maltar was.

She would remember their jeering coarseness as they threatened but never quite touched her before leaving again. Their errand was to bring the metal plate with the Seer's fresh baked bread. They sought only to intimidate, not to punish physically. Later she would understand that the Maltar had forbidden the touching; any physical contact would have prolonged her sanity within this dim tomb. The Maltar was not foolish enough to risk her inadvertently bonding with any other than himself.

But in the stinging brightness of their torches and the overwhelming assault of their amarin, she froze. After such emptiness, the onslaught was too great. Like a stunned animal, she hid her head, losing a true consciousness. Long after they had left she still lay curled, shivering in a bodily terror. Struggling, she refused to open her eyes...her only sane thought was not to loosen that horrifyingly helpless fear into this chamber. Somewhere, in the middle of that silent, inner terror, consciousness did leave her — as if the Mother had reached in gently and said, enough!

❋ ❋ ❋

Time passed much too slowly this day. Diana and her small companion skirted the Priory perimeter's woods, evading the patrols — avoiding confrontation, a thing neither of them did easily. Their temperaments were matched; revenge would have been sweet. But their purpose bid patience, so sword and claw remained sheathed.

They traveled lightly, both expert in this game of stealth, both well-versed in the forest's ways. But still the day dragged on. Plans formed, dissolved and re-wove in the depths of Diana's mind as they scouted the roads and defenses of the mountain stronghold. A plan began to unfold but impatience dictated another should be found; she did not want another day to pass. The thought of Elana in their power... But entry was not their only goal, and impatience must to be curbed...yes, perhaps there was a way.

❋ ❋ ❋

Elana sang softly as her fingers worked in the dimness. The cold seemed far away as she rocked in time to the music, and the faintest of smiles pulled at her lips. The words warmed her in a way the rough spun tunic never could; they were the songs of praise — of beginnings that Di'nay had sung that last morning to greet the rising sun.

The Old Mistress taught, "Have patience, and your foes will stumble."

Her jailors had erred in two ways on their last appearance. The Sergeant had dropped a tunic over her huddled figure with a nameless grunt, thinking she was unconscious. The other man had muttered something incoherently through a mouthful of his eventide meal. The Sergeant had snapped back that her food rations were not to be tampered with. But as Elana inwardly shuddered from the rising violence of their interactions, she had grasped much more as they turned to leave.

From their brief exchange above her, she had understood that they were to feed her twice a day. That was their first mistake. She now knew how to track time here.

Their second mistake was the life signs they brought and left her. They had taken care with the tunic to choose an old piece whose linen was faded. The fiber had almost lost any trace of the aging plant stems of its origin. The thing had been laundered last in the boiling kettles of the Priory's washers. But the tunic had lain untouched in wooden closets of its owner for too long; it had absorbed the steady pulse of blackwood. It helped now to warm her skin and to comfort her ache.

They had thought it necessary to clothe her better in order to ensure her survival. The Maltar wanted her alive, mindless but breathing, and he undoubtedly would have taken someone else's life if thwarted by carelessness — she wasn't supposed to die of hypothermia. So perhaps their risk was understandable. Yet they should have asked someone — someone with more grasp of this isolating torture. Then they would have sent one of the Seer's robes or blankets to her — something tainted with the power of the Maltar's amarin.

The one man's munching stupidity had compounded their error. The crisp fruit of his eventide meal had touched the air with a tangy scent, and carelessly seeds had fallen as he turned to leave, biting into the sweet meat. Another two steps of patience and he would have been beyond that doorway, and the precious bits would have meant nothing. But he had not waited and the seeds had remained within.

Three seeds. Above weapons, above keys...if she could have chosen a tool for survival, would she have been wise enough to choose these? But the Mother was heard even in the darkest of Fates' Cellars, and Her wisdom was infinitely vast.

The seeds were smaller than her thumbnail, but they held the essence of life itself. Irregular ovals of a woody texture, they shimmered a gold-white in the darkness, and suddenly the inky black dissolved. Dimly the interior of the circular chamber became visible, and Elana had felt her spirits lift. The pulsing chorus of life filled her, and she felt the terrors recede.

She worked now, braiding the thin, woolen strands from the knits into a more deadly type of string. It would not be much of a weapon against sword blades, but it would fit a man's neck in closer combat.

Her singing was almost inaudible, but silence was too barren. When she got the small seeds, her reasoning began to clear more quickly. Then the silence did not need to be so empty, so dependent on the monotonous trickle of the water.

She again practiced her Sororian and that led to the Songs of Helen. There were words she was still unsure of, and she fleetingly wished Di'nay were here to ask, but it was dangerous to have such wishes. She was learning to be careful for what she wished. She remembered once, at Melysa's, how she had wished for a chance to die before the end of this venture. She had thought that would be easier than sending Di'nay back to her people.

Easier? Here she had tried to die and failed. Her body's memory rekindled the cruel touch of the men — the evil of the Maltar's voice. She shut her eyes, closing out the feelings — sending them back to the locked corners of her mind. Her breathing did not want to be steadied. Her stomach wanted to be sick. But she would not deal with this now. If she lived to rejoin Di'nay, she would face the memories — face the insanity — the burning blackness that dove for her very soul. If she could ever rejoin Di'nay, there would be time to heal.

Time? Would there ever truly be the time? She would survive long enough to seek a way out of this chamber or long enough to die with her secrets, but did she expect escape from this room would mean freedom?

No, she would not think beyond leaving this room. And if she did leave it, she would not lead the Seer to Di'nay — she would not. Perhaps she could even lead them away.

❉ ❉ ❉

The eitteh growled faintly, tail slashing about Diana's ankles. An echo of retreating boots carried the length of the stone halls, and, cautiously, Diana peered around the corner. The winged-cat lay low to the ground between her feet. The rhythmic switch of its tail against her calf was steadying, Diana drew a slow breath. It was a nice reminder that she could trust this seemingly unguarded route. Twice they had come across sentries, and both times the eitteh had warned her of their approach. Despite her misgiving, she was beginning to trust this extra pair of ears.

The whole thing was going too smoothly. Either the Maltar had grown overconfident with his capture of a Council spy or this was, somehow, a trap.

Still, regardless of whether she was captured or not, his mechanical defense was at an end. She had reprogrammed the decoder to scramble the electrical circuit to overload the system. She had also traced the powerlines back to the solar generators and had the grim satisfaction of knowing that the technology was beyond their ability to rebuild once destroyed. Actually, it was surprising to find Garrison had used the solar batteries from his space cruiser since there was so little sun in this region. But the defense system used relatively little power compared to a cruiser.

It had been impossible to get into the solar-paneled greenhouses that held the batteries, but Diana had been close enough. Her malleable plastique compound was powerful enough to crumble a small mountain; it would certainly destroy batteries. She had placed explosives around the area and set them, she hoped, to go off shortly after the laser guns disintegrated. With luck, the men would assume the intruder was moving south to north. It might buy them a few moments' grace.

Something they would need, Diana admitted grimly, and she moved down the hall — the echoing steps finally gone. She had no illusions about Elana's abilities to travel quickly; she wasn't in the mood to entertain Garrison's limitations. She suspected since he had been so quickly cooperative with the Maltar, he might well resist leaving and he'd likely be useless on horseback in any case. It couldn't be helped. Horses and carts were about all that this Priory kept at hand, and carts did poorly without roads and were too slow.

The three beasts she had chosen had been sturdy, smaller creatures. There had been others in the grazing herd that certainly would have been swifter, but they would have been missed sooner too. Diana was gambling that these animals would not be particularly noticed or missed for some time. She supposed she should have risked stealing their tack as well, at least for Garrison, but there were limits to what could be done in a few hours.

Her gloved fingers tensed and flexed over the hilt of her bared sword. The glowing heat of the embedded lifestones was stronger than it had ever been before. Her palms sweated slightly. The corridor forked abruptly, so she ducked into a shadowy corner, alert for sounds from either direction.

Nothing came, and she inched ahead only to halt again.

Which way now?

Diana had been steadily working her way down ever since entering the main building of the fortress. Elana had said the dungeons were in the lower levels. It had seemed the most likely place to start her search. All she had was the hope that the warmth of the lifestone would be a guide. Now neither of these routes appeared to rise or descend. She guessed she was as deep as the foundations went.

So which way? She pulled off a glove for a moment, to feel the stone better.

The eitteh paced curiously across the yawning portals and, rumbling indecisively, sat down between the two. No help there.

✺ ✺ ✺

Elana blinked and moved her head slightly, trying to ward off the sudden dizziness. She stopped in her exercises and lowered herself to the floor, feeling her disorientation grow. The small seeds before her blurred, and she strained to clear the fuzziness. With a shallow breath she closed her eyes, rubbing her forehead. For a moment she thought the eitteh had been sitting there.

The dull rush and thud of her blood suddenly pounded through her ears and her chest felt tight. A sharp pain stabbed her heart, making her gasp, and finally she realized the strain of her body for what it was — the aching bond of the lifestone. But it was too soon, she thought desperately, and her fingers fumbled with the leather wristband. It was too soon! It had barely been more than a day — it couldn't — dear Mother don't let Di'nay be hurt!

The lacings yielded and the shimmering opal depths met her questioning eyes. The ruby-blue lines pulsed steadily, but the stone was growing hot.

Her vision blurred, and Elana saw a flash of silver in torches' light...then gone.

Think.

She tried to slow her breathing.

Think. The Mistress or Master would have said something about this. It was not an ending — the pulse was too steady. But it was hot — sizzling hot, like the day of bonding. The joining? The stone's power commanded her body.

She looked again and saw nothingness — not even the precious stone. Then suddenly the darkness lifted as if fingers uncurled from before her eyes, and she could see. The eitteh sat between two passageways and the torch light flickered brightly.

It was gone again, but the stone grew hotter, more demanding, and her neck ached with the pressure of blood that made her ears roar.

In some the Sight works through the stone, with the help of the lifestone, the Mistress had once said. Elana blinked again and wondered if it could be true even here. But it was so rare — so very rare.

She concentrated and forced her breathing to be even and deep. With blue eyes fixed on the glimmering white depths, she reached inward and sought Di'nay.

She saw the forked tunnels clearly outlined by a bright glow of blazing torches, and the gold body of the eitteh sitting almost immobile, only that subtle twitch of her tail in motion. Di'nay stood staring perplexed at the sword held before her — the shining blade flat upon her open palms. The green gloves seemed almost black in contrast to the silver-white of the metal. The heat of the sword sent shimmering waves through the air. The hilt was a white haze, coursing with ruby lines.

Elana realized suddenly that this sword — her father's gift — was the key to their newfound strength. She focused her attention on the paths ahead of Diana. She did not know the way from the grand hall above, but — the stones could find the way! Her hand closed as if to clasp the hilt of the sword — and the stones knew.

❋ ❋ ❋

The weapon swiveled in Di'nay's grasp; the hilt swinging towards the left corridor as if someone there was grasping it. Stunned, Di'nay balanced the weapon carefully in its new position, wary of the clattering noise that dropping it would cause. But the sudden jerk was not repeated. She looked into the depths of the passageway and again at the sword.

Tentatively she closed her gloved hands over the hilt and felt the pull beneath her fingers. Again it directed her to the left passage.

The eitteh rose with a rumble and padded a few steps down the hall, pausing when she realized the human was still standing.

Di'nay nodded with her decision then and reclasped her fingers about the hilt. She joined the winged-cat.

❊ ❊ ❊

The images faded, and released from their grip, Elana closed her eyes and remembered to breathe again. Di'nay was coming.

She had not thought — she had not expected the Amazon to seek her out. She had not thought of what Di'nay would do at all. All she had wanted was to protect Di'nay from the Seer's attention.

Those with the Blue Sight seldom unraveled the plots of others, she reminded herself. We see so much but do not understand. She felt guilty at crediting Di'nay with so little involvement. Partners — did that not mean each looked after the other? Did that not mean that they would work together?

Perhaps — Elana felt a warmth rise with her tears — perhaps she would truly see her love again

❊ ❊ ❊

Chapter Fourteen

Two men disappeared down the far passageway with a metallic plate of bread and unlit torches. Diana noted the remaining soldier was still half-asleep as he stared at his breakfast. A grumbling call came from a chamber off to the side, and the man at the table grunted something, pointing behind himself at the bubbling pot of breakfast porridge on the fire....

❊ ❊ ❊

Elana drew a steadying breath as that outer bolt began to slide. She squatted near the door, back against the wall, and the faint glimmer of the seeds urged her on. Then suddenly, the bolt jammed home again and muffled voices broke out in argument. She swallowed hard, fighting the knot of panic inside, and concentrated.

Across from the doorway, against the stone wall, the rags of her underknits sat in a heap, cradling one of the three seeds. From nothingness she could create nothing, but the glowing embers of life gave her much more to work with — enough even to discard the violence associated with those clothes. Beneath her blue touch the illusion grew, and the remnants became a huddled figure of an unconscious woman. Beside the doorjamb, another seed nestled between metal and stone — safely tucked where the careless foot would not crush it. But she breathed and the space between the two seedlings stretched. Another illusion, this one designed to draw her unwitting guards further into the room. The last seed lay securely folded between tunic and belt; this one she would carry with her.

Her palms felt damp; the newly woven rope was wrapped around each hand. She did not doubt that it would hold. It was her own strength that she was less sure of, but there was the chance that she would not have to test herself or her weapon....

❊ ❊ ❊

Diana waited a moment longer, but there was only one voice that came from the side room. She looked at the eitteh and slowly sank down to her knees. Across the room near the hallway that the two men had trudged down, there was wood stacked for the fire. Diana pointed. The eitteh rumbled so quietly that Diana felt it through the soles of her feet rather than heard it, and the animal slid off.

The fire burned brightly and torches lined the room, chasing away many of the darkened shadows with their flickering fingers, and the creature went soundlessly, slipping around the edges and across the open passage. Without a noise, the eitteh disappeared into the dark crevice behind the wood. She would slow the pair, if they returned to help.

Diana stepped forward, sword drawn.

Too much happened at once then...the man at the table glanced up at the sound of a returning guard in the far corridor and saw the Amazon just as the soldier appeared with an unlit torch in hand.

Green eyes sought Diana for an instant. As the voice from the chamber beyond materialized into a sergeant, the two acted as one.

With a cry Diana arched her blade and the eitteh lunged. The table heaved forward as the man fled the singing sword — as the torchbearer shrieked, claws opening his face. A grasping hand fell across a burning branch in the fire, and Diana jumped back from the flaming club, spinning as she met the sergeant's sword....

✳ ✳ ✳

Only one finally entered the cell. Elana breathed carefully, fixing her eyes on the far wall to keep from being blinded. Now it was her turn to pull the darkness into a cloak around her. The soldier walked in, his crackling laugh coming as he saw only the unconscious heap across the room. He took another step.

She came from behind, stepping between his legs to pull his ankle back. Her elbow drove into his kidneys. With a cry of pain and surprise he fell, torch and plate flying from his grasp. In an instant she was out. The bolt closed with a steely clang.

Dropping low she huddled against the iron door and listened. Usually there were two of them. Where was the other?

On the stone floor beside her lay a wisp of molding cloth — a torch scrape. And she had her answer. The other's torch had been too poorly made to kindle.

A dull thud came through the thick metal as fists pounded within. She ignored it. That was a Seer's Tomb...the door was too thick to allow much sound in — or out.

Elana turned to look and understood why there had been no light or sound passing through the door jamb. Directly in front of her cell stood a mammoth wall of the same ancient stone. It essentially blocked everything that might have seeped in through the cracks.

Cautiously then she edged about the barrier. She moved slowly because of the pain in her right hip and to let her eyes adjust to the torchlight. The light was not quite as bright as she had feared; the seeds' amarin had guarded against that too.

With a faltering step, she started down the prison's corridor....

❄ ❄ ❄

Metal rang as swords clashed. With a vicious swipe, Diana sent the sergeant staggering aside. She turned as the fellow covered in ash and burnt porridge rose from the hearth, fiery branch in hand. He rushed her. Striking downwards, Diana split the wood in an orange flash. She lunged. The man went to the floor with a death gasp.

Then she spun, ducking low. Her leg kicked out, seeking to trip the sergeant behind her as her sword pulled free. But he had backed off with a grunt, his knee only grazed.

The eitteh clung to the torch man's back. Her jaws sank deeper as the man rolled. The unlit torch clubbed the winged-cat's shoulders, but she remembered her mother's death. She kept her wings folded, throwing her weight behind their roll.

The cloak slowed Diana's arm and her boot slipped in the blood. The weight of the sergeant's sword sent her tripping over the body at her heels.

The sergeant's blade lifted high.

Only half-standing Diana pushed her sword up broadside in defense — a knife flew from behind...a gold flash streaked upwards. As one, dagger and tooth sank into flesh, and the sergeant fell. Beneath the sudden weight Diana stumbled again and dropped with him as the eitteh's great wings unfurled in her lunge upwards; the animal twisted and his neck broke all too easily.

She lay a second sandwiched between the dead soldiers, then gathered her breath and pushed the sergeant away. Diana raised herself to an elbow and looked towards the far passageway. She would know that warm, silent call anywhere. "I thought — I was suppose to save you this time?"

Elana smiled weakly from where she crouched against the wall. "And you have." She let the torchman's knife sheath drop with her black string.

Brown eyes shifted to the golden creature, and Diana tipped her head. "My thanks to you as well."

The animal ruffled its fur and yawned widely.

Diana moved to the side chamber, reappearing in a few moments with a long bow and a quiver of arrows.

"Sleeps only four," she muttered curtly, stepping across the bodies. "I don't expect any of these fellows will miss their things. Did you meet up with the fourth? He went down your way."

Elana nodded faintly. "He's locked in my cell."

Diana helped her to stand, noticing her deeply browned color.

Elana forced a cynical smile — she would cry if she did not. "They aren't very hospitable here."

Diana's eyes reflected her concern, but she respected the sarcasm. She knew only too well how much pain it could hide, and they were not yet safe.

Elana clung to Di'nay's arm, drinking in her lover's strength. She let herself sag a little. "Dearest Mother...I am so very glad you came."

Diana held her closer, a kiss brushing the soft, dark hair. "I'd not leave you."

Elana nodded, her cheek pressed against Di'nay's sleeve. She knew that now. With an effort she drew away and looked to the corridor where she had just come from. "I believe your pilot may be down there. The third door to the right."

"Third door?" Diana glanced anxiously at the passageway. Urgency was pressing, but she did not want to leave Elana either.

The younger woman nodded again, turning Di'nay and pushing her down the hall with, "I am not certain. But there was a — difference. Something very out of place. I think perhaps it is his alienness."

With a grunt Diana tried the wooden door before them; not surprisingly, it was locked and with an iron tumbler at that. So much for the metal-poor planet. She pulled open the portal's shutter but the dim light inside showed her nothing. Stepping back she asked, "Can you feel anything in there?"

"There is only one." The shadows glowed with weakened life. "He is not of Aggar. He's dressed much as Commander Bailey was — in synthetic."

"Garrison." Diana glanced about them, frowning at no sign of a key rack.

"The keys are with the soldier in my cell," Elana said quietly. She hesitated the barest of moments before adding, "I would rather not face him again."

"Is Garrison far enough in for me to safely hack through?"

"Yes," and Elana moved back.

Gripping the hilt with both hands Diana planted her feet...unfortunately, she had no more plastique with her, and the noise would bring other soldiers anyway. Her concentration focused and she swung.

The wood splintered with hot orange sparks. Another blow and smoldering chips flew. Again and the plank holding the lock was severed.

Well done, Symmum, Diana praised and brushed aside the dangling fragments. Her hand, protected by the glove, grabbed the ragged edge of the plank and tugged. With a single wrench the lock came away, the bolt sliding free from its stone hole.

She pulled the door open and felt her heart stir with pity. Suddenly Diana was not so certain this man had been capable of arranging the lasers' defense outside.

A frail man, perhaps a hundred and twenty pounds, knelt curled against the stone wall. Half-hidden by the straw that lined the cell floor, his slight frame could have as easily been a heap of rags. The white fieldsuit was tattered and grimy. His dark hair was straggly and unwashed. His beard was full. Seemingly mindless he was bent over, intent on the small twirling movements of his fingers. His eyes were wide and unfocused as he watched his hands.

"Pilots are usually thin," Diana muttered, fighting a rising nausea at the stench that drifted to her, "but not like this."

"It is the porridge," Elana said, attuned to Di'nay's revulsion. She pointed to the bowl that lay beside the door, tipped on its side. The cream on top had curdled long ago. She looked more closely then at this pilot. Surely he would not have let the food spoil if he'd been so hungry.

His fingers fumbled without purpose, and his gaze was unblinking.

"He is not wholly sane," she murmured and cautiously stepped into the chamber. The touch of the straw about her booted ankles was welcoming as she concentrated on Garrison. Elana's body absorbed the amarin's strength. A few feet in front of him Elana paused. Slowly she sank level with him, seeking his eyes.

Whiteness... sheets and sheets of empty white metal... grooves... tools... fine lines of metal string.... Color on whiteness... endless lines... fine adjustments... endless, endless colored lines....

Confused, Elana blinked and separated from him. The things had made no sense to her. His fiddling fingers went on in their empty task, and she watched curiously. Perhaps he was doing something with those metal lines of color?

"Di'nay." She only half turned, too sore to move her neck and too fascinated with those playing hands.

Diana came to her, taking the hand that Elana reached out to her.

Her blue eyes looked up then, seeking Di'nay's. "Do you know these things?"

A tension filled her first, and Diana realized how tightly Elana was controlling herself. Then images slipped by and suddenly left.

Elana dropped her gaze, fearful of sharing too much.

Diana frowned, understanding that something was not being shown to her, and she worried that that something was not merely from Garrison's thoughts. She held her tongue; they were not safe.

"Do you recognize any of it?" Elana prompted again.

"Some." Diana remembered the question. "It looks a bit like the electricians' shop at the base. That's what he's thinking about?"

"That is where he believes he is. Was it in such a place that he could have made use of laser guns?"

Diana's scowl deepened. Somehow the pieces were beginning to make sense. He had done such a thorough job on that defense system because he had not known this was Aggar. She nodded grimly at his hunched figure. "Can he travel?"

"His legs will move..." Elana had doubts about her own. Holding herself steady with Di'nay's hand, she managed to get to her feet. "...but he will not be hurried."

Elana turned to face Di'nay. "This is not merely a madness grown from isolation. He is under the Seer's touch, Di'nay, and this illusion is reality to him."

"A Seer? Here?!"

Elana nodded.

"But — " How did not matter, she reminded herself, and she spun, moving quickly to the door. "Fates' Jest! No wonder there were so few guards."

The eitteh sat outside watching for soldiers. Calmly she glanced over a shoulder as Diana emerged. Her ear flicked a greeting and she went back to her vigil.

"The Seer cannot see through stone," Elana assured Di'nay quickly. "Once the madness set in there did not need to be direct vision. The Seer will be in the open turrets above. You and I will remain unseen until we venture out beyond the stone."

"But how did I get by him?!" Diana rasped. "None of this makes any sense."

"You carry no surface clues of your foreignness. Perhaps he has been so concerned with me that he has not discovered you. I do not understand it, but he is very old and very, very abused. It is possible that his Sight has become so distorted that he has not recognized you. Or he sees you as a ordinary traveler not to be feared. I did not want to lead him to you, Di'nay. Through me, he may find you now."

"No doubt he will," Diana muttered. Her matter-of-factness was reassuring as Elana read her amarin — her Amazon wanted them together before all else.

None of this changed anything, Diana decided finally. Plans had been laid. They had about fifteen more minutes before the lasers blew, and then five before the batteries. She was counting on the confusion of the explosion for their escape. If they made it to the horses, they still might outrun followers before dawn found them at the river. It did suggest they should go downstream from there, however. Distance was going to be critical in the sort of race where a Seer might track them. They'd confiscate the ferry barge and cut her free; then even if they were tracked downriver they would make better time than those on horseback. And too it would delay the pursuit in crossing until Maltar's crew detoured to the next ferry.

"All right then." Diana slipped the quiver of arrows over Elana's head. Bending the bow to set the gut string, she explained, "I'll carry this fellow and you'll again have the dubious honor of protecting my back. I have horses waiting beyond the south guard gate where I came in. We'll cut through the trees and angle right back to the road. If we can make the ferry crossing before they catch us, there's hope."

"There is always hope." Elana smiled softly.

Diana paused, sharing the warmth of that smile with one of her own. Yes there was always that. She handed the bow to Elana and bent, heaving Garrison's slight form over her shoulder like a sack of grain; he was even lighter than she'd thought.

The eitteh eyed this new hindrance with suspicion, but she set off silently, leading them back to the gate.

They met no one on the way out. It was near dawn and those that had such early business were already up and moving about in the cold halls above. The others of the Priory were in bed still, intent only on snatching as many precious moments of sleep as possible. The same, single guard was still on duty as they returned to the entrance. Diana struck from behind. She couldn't wait for him to need the latrine this time around.

She nodded to Elana as the younger woman drew her cloak from the green satchel. It was going to be a cold, misty ride this morning.

East near the road, the explosion blew. Diana stepped clear of the shadowy entrance to watch. The master control and its stone housing were not visible at this distance, but the brilliant flare lit the eastern air like a sun going nova. The chain reaction started and the guns went in quick succession, metal casing, bursting like egg shells into a fiery orange.

Diana turned back to shoulder Garrison again and met Elana's astonished expression. "You think that's something, wait 'til the batteries go."

Elana blinked and said nothing. The power of the Empire was daunting.

They hurried across the open perimeter. The savage gray smoke and electrical stench mingled, thickening the morning mists and cloaking their passage. Within a dozen meters the guards scrambled and jostled in confusion. No one was quite certain what to do with the flaming machines.

The batteries went and the explosion shook the ground; the entire Priory was silhouetted in the blast. Neither woman paused this time as they reached the nervous horses, but Diana had chosen well. Long tried and true campaign animals these were, and even the unfamiliar scent of fused wires did not totally unsettle them. They had seen villages burnt and witnessed rioting battles. They only stirred uneasily at this — it was the men of the Priory who were taken by the raw panic.

"The Maltar may kill him for this." Elana spoke quietly, kneeing her horse around to join Di'nay's. Garrison was clutched firmly before her, in no state to ride by himself. The third horse they let go.

"Kill who?" Diana settled herself on her horse, feeling more secure with the bow back in her own hand.

"The Seer."

A gruff grunt came in return, "We could not be so lucky."

An arrow whizzed from nowhere and Elana ducked, her arm flinching as it grazed past. She spurred her horse as they heard a soldier cry, "Bu' I saw one! There I tell you! There!"

They rode hard, pushing the horses as fast as they dared through the fog and forest. The eitteh left them for the heights. Elana took the lead, keeping a tight rein on her Sight as well as her horse. The Seer would not find them from her own Sight's betrayal. He could hunt Garrison, but she would not inadvertently help him again.

They made the road and felt the horses steady with familiar ground underfoot, and the mounts found their second wind.

The boatman's shack was barely three leagues from the Priory's gates. Diana drew her sword as they thundered into his compound. Warned by the explosion and pounding hooves, the old warrior had readied himself for a battle. Sharp and quick the man's blade swung as she swept past the corner of his hut. He struck only air.

Diana wheeled to meet him. Silver and sparks flashed through the misty white as swords sang. But she had no mercy this morning, and with a cry her horse pushed forward and her blade bit deep. Gasping, the man folded and she pulled clear.

Elana rode grimly onto the barge. Diana dismounted in mid-stride to send the horse aboard alone. For an instant she slid into the brush beyond the boatman's shack. With packs in hand she reappeared, tossing them onto the barge.

She paused to take an oar — just in case — from the flat bottomed boat nearby. With a thrust the keel opened and the water began to seep in; Diana had no intentions of allowing anyone an easy pursuit. The mooring rope was severed by a flash of her blade. Hurrying she boarded, exchanging the oar for pole and, sheathing her sword, she turned to guide them off.

Elana watched silently, keeping her mount steady and centered with a hand lightly holding Di'nay's horse too. Garrison slumped against her, barely conscious even to his electronic world.

Di'nay dropped the pole on the deck with barely a clunk and stepped to the crank. The ropes protested with a wailing creak, but the barge moved into the current. Mid-way across Di'nay left the turnwheel and heaved the old, decrepit rudder off its rack. There were ironcast locks at either end of the barge, and Di'nay chose the southshore end. The rudder resisted slipping in, but a swift side kick joggled it down the last inch. She set the pin securely and turned to Elana.

The sudden release of Garrison's weight almost unhorsed her, and Elana stretched her back muscles with caution, wishing again that her right leg wasn't so stiff. Di'nay set Garrison down. He lay curled up and barely alive on the deck. Diana reached for her. Her feet prickled and nerves stung as she was forced to stand again. Di'nay let her cling an extra half-second. Then Elana nodded. "I'm all right."

"Can you handle the rudder?" Diana was not convinced Elana could even walk those few steps.

"Yes." It was a decisive answer.

Elana took her place and Diana drew her sword again. With a resounding thunk the rope that held them to shore was sliced on the north side of the crankcase. Quickly Diana grabbed for the loose end that snaked over the top. It pulled and she clenched her teeth, wrapping the piece around her gloved hand for a better grip.

The current tugged and the rope tightened, and gradually the barge began to swing downstream. For a brief moment Diana thought she was going to lose her hand, but she planted a foot against the crank and heaved. The extra inch came and an eddy caught the flat bottomed ferry, aiming them due west, down the Ma'naur. Diana released the rope with a sigh, and they were away.

Fingers flexing, she glanced apprehensively at the lifting fog. For the last four days it had hung on well through mid-morning. It was clearing earlier today.

"The Seer is raising the fog. He is looking for us," Elana said quietly, her voice falling flat in the dampened air. This dark haze her Sight saw was not as characteristic of the Maltar's lands as she had first thought when gazing across the wastelands to his shores. She now knew it for what it was: the cloaking cloud of a Seer hiding what his master bid hidden. She knew of such hazes only from apprentices' stories of foolery. After all, Seers were always Council's men...until now. It was little wonder that she had not recognized it as that blue spun power. For how many years had the Maltar schemed unwatched by the Council eyes?

"How is your arm?"

Elana nearly jumped. She looked down, gripping the dusty wood of the tiller with white-knuckled hands. It was frightening that she could be so easily startled. There were dangers in readjusting to this outside world. With an effort she steadied her breathing. There were so many swirling, tangled energies flowing around her that she found herself almost numb, and she wondered if this had been how it felt when she was a small child before she had learned to control her Sight. She resisted the impulse to reach out and absorb those flowing lines — that would be as good as setting up a signal fire for the Seer.

"What is wrong?" Diana prompted in a gentle voice. Carefully she knelt beside Elana, her dark eyes searching the averted face. She set her medical box aside and covered the tense, browned hand with her own. "Ona?"

"Wrong...?" Elana whispered faintly and then seemed to gather herself together. She turned to Di'nay. "My arm, I think." She shrugged sideways, glancing at the bloodied sleeve. "It's not bad, but — "

"I'll see to it," Diana reassured her, squeezing her hand lightly. "Yet there's more, isn't there? Can you tell me what it is?"

Blue eyes stared at their clasped hands, and Elana felt the hollowness in her stomach begin to churn. Tightly she clamped down the panic and stirring memories. "Not yet."

"You're safe for now." Diana spoke calmly, respectful of Elana's judgment even as she was concerned for her.

"Not safe enough yet." Elana looked up, her eyes caressing Di'nay's weathered face in a familiar search. "Give me time — and distance from this Seer."

Diana nodded and held her hand for a moment longer before turning to the arm. But her grimness had turned to a savage anger at this Maltar. Her fingers grasped the stained fabric, venting fury as she ripped it.

Elana gasped at the amarin.

Diana grabbed her shoulder to steady her. "Have I hurt you?!"

"No." Elana's dark braid shook with the denial as she pushed back the memory of men and ravaging malice. She smiled shakily. "It's been a rather eventful day."

Diana broke open the antiseptic and set to cleaning the wound. "This will make your arm a bit numb."

Elana nodded mutely.

From the corner of her eye Diana watched Elana. Everything about Elana urged her to gather this woman close and let her cry. But this was not some safely enclosed bathhouse, and a Seer was searching for them.

Elana said, "I counted the night before last as the eve they took me. Is that right? Or did I lose count?" All of a sudden it seemed important to know exactly how long they had held her.

"You're right," Diana murmured, grimly thinking how awful those nearly forty hours had seemed to her and the eitteh. "Where did they have you that you couldn't follow Aggar's cycles?"

"They call it a Seer's Tomb," Elana replied almost curtly. She drew another deep breath as Di'nay tied the bandage; there was so much she wanted — no, needed Di'nay to know, but she did not trust her own self control. "The walls are very thick, and even the door is stone."

Diana swallowed the ache in her throat and wished that her love had been spared that nightmare. Gently, she took Elana's small hand in hers. "Ona... I or Eitteh will always stay near. To remind you, you're not alone now."

The hand grasped hers gratefully, and Diana tightened her own grip.

"Where is our eitteh?" Elana asked then, glancing about the barge.

"Out hunting breakfast, I expect. Neither of us remembered to eat yesterday."

Elana shook off Di'nay's clasp. And for a brief instant, she was feeling better. "By the Mother's Hand, can't I even leave you for a day?"

Diana laughed and her spirits lifted. "Here." She pulled the cap off the flat little jar and shook a pair of tablets into Elana's free hand. "Take these. They prevent infections. It's a clean cut, but we don't need to take chances."

She peered critically at the friction burn along Elana's right cheekbone. "Does your face hurt badly?"

"No, it will be fine." The feel of cold steel crawled along her skin, eclipsing thought, and suddenly Elana could only stare at the tablets in her palm.

"You are not alone," Diana repeated softly.

"No..." She nodded shakily, fighting her sudden tears with a weak smile as those gentle words cut through the terror. "...I am not, am I."

Garrison was their most pressing problem, given not only his dubious mental state but his obviously alien appearance. His mind was so racked with the Seer's rape that it lay completely open to Elana now.

Diana took over the rudder and Elana quickly drew the information the Empire so urgently needed from him; the details of that distant assassination plot were plucked all too easily from his ravished mind. Then she gently sent him into a deeper darkness. They could not risk him regaining awareness while they still lay so near to the Seer. Even if Garrison only half woke, still too confused to understand what he was seeing, the Seer's eyes would discern enough that the Maltar would identify their route.

Then, while Elana guided the boat, Diana scrubbed the dungeon smell from his gaunt figure and trimmed his hair and beard. Her extra tunic and breeches hung too loosely on him, but they were a good deal better than the tattered shreds of his fieldsuit. She cut the feet from the remnants of her extra fieldsuit, the one the cucarii had torn, and once she'd managed to get a limp foot into each, she wrapped the rags from the discarded Priory tunic about them. The end result was not so odd for this planet. Slaves were often clad in their owner's older garments, and it was not uncommon for them to lack proper shoes; Garrison merely looked as if he'd tied his feet up in rags to keep them warm.

❋ ❋ ❋

The eitteh returned mid-morning, rumbling with well-fed good humor as she curled up against Elana's leg to doze. They stayed close to the towering cliffs and the sheltering shadows, the sun finally lifting clear of the plateau. Clouds began to gather and it seemed the Mother had not forgotten them.

Both women were pleased to see the storm warnings of the northern front. There would be a full day before it broke, but it was probably not the doings of Maltar's Seer since a storm would only obscure tracks and slow soldiers. Yet the Maltar dared not order his Seer to hold off this onslaught of winter; such an act would be certain to draw the attention of the Council Seers. It was a complex game this man played with the Council and Keep; he had gone undetected for years. Diana gambled that his shrewdness would not lapse now.

It was a long day in the slow way days will pass when so much is at risk and yet so little may be done. The current was swift and took them well past the broken ravine that they had followed from Melysa's to meet the river. Their first glimpse of the Ma'naur had been four days ago, and with luck this would be their last acquaintance with these black waters. But the farewell seemed to last an eternity.

Elana quieted the horses with promises of grass at nightfall and found herself to be only a little stiffer despite the ride. The stretching had helped after all. Dressed again in her own tunic and jerkin, with the eitteh curled close and Di'nay here, she found the waiting a relief after those hours in the blackness. In her pack she found the hunting knife Di'nay and the eitteh had retrieved for her, and she smiled at the memory of her first night with her Amazon. There were moments where she was as nearly content as conceivable, given the circumstances.

The river, however, was too exposed for Diana's comfort. She conceded that it was the best of the available options, but she did not like it. In mute frustration she set her mind to the work before her.

There was the problem of Diana's transmitter. Without the descrambler unit it was just a receiver. Without it, there was no way she could accurately key the base's frequencies. Her last contact had been with Cleis in Gronday, and it was unlikely that anyone was still there. Most probably even that channel had been lost due to the jostling of travel. She could not even reach Gronday.

"Commander Baily's people do not monitor all the frequencies?" Elana probed.

"Security monitors all the usual channels. However, they only randomly check in on the field channels unless something specific is scheduled, then they'll record it for files. Granted, it's a careless practice, but since your people have no use for this type of communication it never seemed to be much of a risk." Wearily Diana settled at her feet beside the rudder seat. "Our best chance will be to keep sending whenever possible. But sitting out in the open every night for the next ten-day does not sound very safe with this Seer searching. Also we do not know if the Maltar has the receiver from Garrison's ship. If he could get the laser working...."

Elana shook her head. "It is too dangerous. And there is no need for it. Even if your base cannot receive you, the Council will know to alert them."

She was beginning to expect that kind of remark, Diana realized. "Am I to understand from what you are saying that the Council monitors our transmissions?"

Elana nodded.

Diana wondered if that meant they had been listening even on her conversations with Cleis. She said, "But even when we dare transmit, why should the Council of Ten pass the information on to Thomas? Won't they just interpret our loss of contact with my base as another sign that they shouldn't interfere?"

Solemnly Elana reminded her, "Maltar has a Seer. The winds of the Mother stir strange sands. If he had not been discovered, the Maltar would eventually unseat the Council's balance — just as the assassin would unseat your Chairman. A Seer outside the Keep's walls is the Council's business. The Council's involvement in the journey will be well met — once the Council knows this Seer exists. They have little reason not to repay the aid and inform Commander Baily and the Terrans of the assassination and its details."

Elana placed a hand on her lover's shoulder. "They believe in balance, Di'nay."

"I begin to think, Elana, that your Council is somewhat like our Shekhina. On my planet there is relatively little technology compared to that of the Empire. On Shekhina, however — on our single moon — we have a very technologically sophisticated society. It is our bridge — our point of contact with the rest of the Empire; it is all they know of us. You seem to house all you need to protect your world, and yet you measure the use of such sciences — for use to Aggar — for use with the Empire. But both your Keep and my Shekhina must be in harmony with their world or it is for nothing."

"As I have said," Elana touched her friend's face, "in some ways we are not so very different."

With a calm peacefulness growing within her, Diana nodded. A smile softened her weariness as she turned her cheek to Elana's hand. "And each day, perhaps I come closer to remembering that."

✳ ✳ ✳

Part Three

Until the End

Chapter One

A gray dawn appeared as Diana climbed the trail from the stream bed where she had caught a string of fish and a plump pair of grubbers. They had taken a day here to hunt and prepare for the coming trek through the Wayward Path. There would be no food to be found in the depths of the mountain caverns, and despite their need for speed, it had been wise to call a halt.

Six days — had it only been six days back that they had left the Ma'naur to begin this trek south? The wind whipped at her ears and her breath was a frosty white. She quickened her pace up the side of the ravine.

Despite everything she had been through, Elana had guided them well. The ravine she had chosen at the Ma'naur had cut abruptly into that giant wall, and the rocky stream bed had been a tracker's worst dread. The black current too had been swift at that junction. It had been Fates' own Jest that they had managed the landing; then the waters had carried the barge west again. When it was eventually found, there would be no trace of where it had unloaded its passengers. It was almost possible that the soldiers would think they had cut the ferry free once they were across at the eastern crossing to prevent being followed. In any event, Diana had scrubbed the deck quickly before releasing the thing; she had not been about to confirm or deny that they traveled on horseback.

The wind grew stronger as she went higher, and thankfully Diana spied the shadowy entrance to their cave. She made a clicking noise with her tongue, calling to the eitteh on guard inside as she approached.

The long, low entry into the rock opened to a gaping cavern with endless tunnels. She walked down the sandy slope inside, not waiting for her eyes to adjust. A fire glowed, reminding her that she was cold. Snow may not have set in, but winter certainly had.

An unreadable green gaze followed her and Diana nodded to the eitteh. The creature blinked sedately. Comfortably enclosed by Elana's curled figure, its golden wings lay open, protectively covering much of the woman's body. It pleased them both that Elana still slept — the nightmares had finally begun to fade.

Diana brushed the ash back from the glowing embers stoking the fire. She would clean her catch while it burnt down to cooking coals. Needing the light, she regretfully went back to the windy entrance to work. It would be for the best. She'd not wake Elana and she had a good vantage point to watch for pursuers.

So far, they had seen no sign of tracking soldiers. The eitteh had brought news that there were riders scouting the easterly road and that there were more than the usual number of boats abroad on the Ma'naur. But no one had come far into the canyons — yet. It was not surprising, though. Elana had taken them deep into the winding passes and led them crisscrossing through the narrower, wet paths for two days before arriving in this sprawling, green ravine — a major tributary, spawned from the very foot of the Dual Peaks. Here traveling had grown easier and the game slightly more plentiful.

Tomorrow they would halt just beyond the Dual Peaks settlement, and the day after, if the Mother's Hand allowed, they would find the Wayward Path. She was not very excited about the venture. It would not be a far walk, but they no longer had the horses and so Garrison would need help.

Still, she thought as she paused in her work to look out across the small valley, it had been a good decision to leave the horses.

Yesterday while Diana was hunting, Elana and the eitteh had taken the animals downstream to a grassy pocket of canyons and left them there. Eventually, the Changlings would find them. But they would have been discovered immediately if loosened at the entrance to the Wayward Path. There were already enough people searching for the 'Council spies'.

The heavy overcast brought the scent of snow, and Diana felt her bones chill. Elana said that the Seers of the Keep were responsible for the thick clouds coming with the northern front. Even after the driving rains were gone they had not dissipated. It meant the Council had received Diana's transmission and, rather than searching for them with their Seers and inadvertently aiding the Maltar's Seer by locating Elana for him, this dimming blanket had been sent across the Wastelands and half of the Maltar's reign to hinder his search.

Diana looked upward with a sigh. She knew she should wake Elana. She would start the cooking herself. It wouldn't hurt them to suffer through one of her meals, if it let her beloved sleep.

The eitteh opened her emerald eyes as Diana withdrew from the entrance. She had been dozing while Diana could take the watch. She yawned and flipped her ears forward. Her hearing was acute enough to well warn them of any approaching. Diana smiled at her, mentally noting she'd offer the creature one of the roasted grubbers for breakfast; they were all tired of fish.

Between the two of them Elana had not been left alone since her escape. They found their habits matched well. When the eitteh took the hunt or the late night watch, Diana was always near Elana; when the Amazon went foraging or addressed Garrison's half-conscious needs, the eitteh stayed close. Their gentle protectiveness had not gone unnoticed by Elana; the young woman had not protested, but drew upon their strength, and her healing was hastened by their patient vigil.

Images crowded through Diana's mind unbidden, swimming impressions of soldiers and blackness that Elana had finally shared with her. Diana sighed tiredly and pinched the bridge of her nose. Elana had said that the Seers routinely schooled all trainees in the cruelties of men; just as the masters taught them how to avoid — or survive — the blows. Elana had always distanced herself from the Seers' lessons just as she did daily from others' experiences, and she said now that the practice had helped. True, she could no longer say to herself, "That is not my body. This is not happening to me." But she could say, "It is over now. This is a memory. I am safe." And she found it easier to sleep each day.

Diana respected her for the honesty and for the pain that she did not deny. At night when she woke shivering in a clammy sweat, Diana drew her near and whispered of gentler things and warmer places. She whispered in her Sisters' tongue and often of home where men were never known and where darkness did not come from locked doors. Then slowly, Elana's body would relax and her mind ease, and bit by bit she would drift back into a more peaceful sleep. Diana only wished that the bruises on her body could heal as quickly as her spirit seemed to be mending.

"Breakfast smells good." The faint murmur carried the sound of a smile in it.

"I promise only edible," Diana returned, looking up.

The eitteh moved with a stiff stretch and a yawn. She squinted with smug satisfaction as Elana scratched the top of the eitteh's head fondly. Then she rose and padded out to the sandy slope of the entrance. She looked hopefully for a little sun on the single, jutting rock. Unfortunately there was none, so she settled for the cool breeze. The golden winged-cat found shelters and caves a little too cramped for her tastes.

"Those are fresh," Elana said in surprise and sat up. "You've been out again?"

"I went before dawn. I didn't want to abuse the food stocks so soon."

"So, you do not trust me when I say there's enough to see us through?"

"It's my appetite that I don't trust," Diana corrected, delighting in their friendly banter. Again she thought how beautiful Elana's eyes were and how lovely her hair. She was so glad to have this woman safe.

"How — how is Garrison?" Elana asked haltingly.

Diana felt her stomach twist with guilt as she realized what Elana had read in her amarin. Anger surged through her, quickening her heart, and awkwardly Diana dropped her gaze to the fire. She was learning that since the beatings — the demanding threats, the isolation — Elana cringed at any touch tainted with powerful amarin. Anything of anger — anything hinting of strong amarin...passions of love so easily mimicked passions of another sort when mixed with the memories and the panic.

Diana drew a steadying breath and raised her eyes. "You once said you were not afraid of me, Ona. I am still me. I have not changed."

Elana swallowed, then nodded, uncomfortable, yet relieved at Di'nay's astuteness. "It is not you that I fear."

"I know." She half-heartedly smiled. "It takes a while...give yourself time."

"And you?" Elana looked to her hesitantly, she too caught by guilt. There was nothing on this world that she would want to deny Di'nay, and it hurt her to feel reluctance — uncertainty — at Di'nay's slightest desire. Had she not once felt proud to draw her Amazon's attentions? Did she still not find comfort and strength in the sleeping circle of her arms?

"I care for you," Diana reminded her softly, "for all of you. Do not mistake my caring for demands."

Her faltering smile grew stronger, and Elana nodded, feeling the intangible hug Di'nay wished her. There were many reasons why she loved this woman; this was just one of them.

❋ ❋ ❋

Chapter Two

Thomas Baily was a man who had risen, as did so many in the Terran militia, to a level above his dubious abilities. And so he found himself plagued by a hundred small decisions that weighed far too heavily upon his mind. As Commander of an Imperial Charlie-IV Base, his problems were further compounded because of his planetary isolation — or maybe that was to his advantage? After all, he might not be able to seek advice from others with more experience, but his superiors were seldom around to scrutinize his decisions either.

Until today.

But then there is always That Day, even on an infrequently toured base.

Thomas tried to reassure himself that the Assemblyman on this tour might not be coming to censor him. This thing about Garrison and the plot against the Chairman had been well enough handled — except for the Council of Ten's interference. But even that had turned to his advantage when the Amazon's field equipment failed.

Leaning back in his chair he smiled, a crooked finger stroking his moustache. It was inventive of his crew to use birds instead of transmitters to send messages. Somewhat quaint, but all the same, it was a marvelously creative solution.

His pride was short-lived, however. He remembered the other half of the Assemblyman's communiqué. "Coordinate arrangements for discharge and replacement of your three Amazons."

As Assemblyman and as the military governor for this quadrant, Haladay had top ranked security clearance for everything Thomas might or might not be doing. He was also cleared for dozens of projects beyond a commander's position. So Thomas Baily did not even hope that there had been a mistaken count. If Haladay said "three Amazons," then Aggar housed three Amazons...unless his own people had misfiled the transfer papers for that last one? But no, that was five years back — it would have been caught before this. The personal computer had nothing either, and everyone on payroll had to go through that department.

So now where was this younger n'Athena? What was her other name? Drat — intolerably rude of them to have so few surnames for so many. How they ever kept their records straight was beyond him.

The deskcom beeped and Thomas snapped, "What is it?"

There was a pause, then Samuel Weis' well-schooled tenor responded, "Cleis n'Athena is here, Commander."

"Then get her in here!" Bristling impatiently, Thomas snatched up his computer pen and frowned down at the glass console in his desk top.

"A poor habit," an insolent young voice announced, "taking your frustrations out on Samuel."

The pen slammed against the glass as Thomas half-rose from his chair. "You did send for me, didn't you?"

He reddened, his thin moustache twitching. Damn her. She knew something. And she was just waiting for him to fall flat on his face.

Cleis n'Athena did enjoy disrupting Thomas Baily's life. She had dealt with his bludgeoning incompetence for almost eight years now, and she only survived it by using a sarcastic antagonism.

"Want a drink?" He didn't even pause to pick up a second glass.

She refused to acknowledge the game and dropped her rather rangy frame into a chair sideways, a leg dangling over the arm and her back to Thomas. Cleis was a good deal younger than Diana, although not young for an Amazon. A single tour of ten Terran years was the typical duty assignment, and she had served more than eight (compared to Diana's twenty). Unfortunately she had spent all eight of them here with Thomas; it was one of the chief reasons she was accepting the early disability discharge. She'd been cut up once too many times, in the field — and in this office.

She brushed the shaggy hair from her eyes and with a finger flicked it free from her collar. She grinned at Thomas' grimace at her gesture. Her unruly hair was not at all regulation, but it was befitting her field assignments, so there was nothing he could do about it. His eyes disapprovingly evaluated her bulky sweater, tight fitting pants, and sandaled feet. They weren't regulation either, but she was off-duty .

He sat down still glowering at her, his drink already half gone.

"You wanted to know something about a third Amazon?" she asked carelessly.

"Who is she?" Thomas spat in frustration. This person was utterly infuriating.

"You tell me — "

"You arrogant little bitch! Don't play with me!"

"Since I'm a good half-foot taller than you and I'm not a canine, I'll assume you're being colorful." Her smile was unperturbed and her gray eyes were still laughing as they met his. "But should I also assume you still want me here?"

"I want to know who she is?!"

"She's a cultural supervisor, of course. We all are."

"I know her title!"

Her leg swung down and she leaned forward with her own show of impatience. "Then tell me who you're talking about. Diana, Elana or myself!"

"Elana!" His stomach churned at the matter-of-factness her voice carried. How the hell could he run a base properly if he didn't even know who was in the field?

"Ahh, yes," Cleis settled back in her chair, "the Assembly's special assignment."

He shifted uneasily with her words. Cleis fleetingly thought that this was being rather unfair to the man. But the thought didn't raise enough guilt to change anything, and the fact that this scene had been played over and over again throughout the Empire for the last thousand years only reassured her. He would survive.

He forced a little more calm into his manner. "Yes, exactly what do you know about it — about her?"

"About her assignment? Very little. She's been in the field without contact for about three years. She was to infiltrate some trading routes outside the three hundred mile mark that we've mapped to date. The Assembly contact muttered something about the locals never suspecting a woman so she went in alone as a woman."

"Wouldn't that be kind of difficult for one of you gals — on this planet, I mean." He'd been on the cutting edge of more Amazons' ire than he cared to remember. "The women here are — are so short."

Cleis decided not to take offense at that archaic word gal; it wasn't worth it. "I seem to remember Elana n'Sappho was much shorter than most. Smaller than you."

The man shifted uncomfortably. There was undoubtedly more in that remark than its face value. "You met her then?"

"Of course I — " Cleis halted in mid-sentence and suddenly leaned forward, feigning suspicion. "You don't know any of this, do you?"

He straightened defensively, but she rushed on before he could open his mouth. "Damn it, Thomas! Don't you ever read anything? You were only on Crigil III for two weeks! Do you realize she could get killed because you don't prioritize her calls? What happens if she needs to come in in a hurry?!"

He drew a slow breath and pointed out, "There hasn't been any message. She hasn't been in any trouble. Let's just calm down a bit, hmm?"

Cleis begrudgingly eased off her attack. No matter what his other faults were, he didn't actually want to see anyone hurt.

"My problem is," he cleared his throat a little, choosing his words carefully now, "that I can't find her records in Personnel."

"Probably because they aren't there," Cleis muttered.

"Do you know where they are then?" His voice was too sweet to be sincere.

"Since she's working directly out of Haladay's sub-committee, I'd suggest you look in his classifieds." Her voice was just as sweet as his.

"Good enough." The man's lips thinned with his irritation, but she was not going to get to him again. "You said her last name is not n'Athena?"

"No, it's n'Sappho."

"May I ask how you spell it?"

"S-a-p-p-h-o. It means...wise diplomat." She couldn't help that last bit.

"Very well." He rose politely, although it was obviously difficult, and offered his hand. "Thank you for your help."

Cleis ignored the gesture and the dismissal, crossing her arms in front of herself. "I received a personal communiqué from Haladay that he's arriving on the Belmont next week."

He swallowed uneasily at the mention of Haladay's name. "Yes, I know. He's requested you meet him at docking and shuttle him down privately."

"I assume you've no objections?"

A dozen or so, actually, but there wasn't much he could do about it. Haladay did not give orders to have them ignored. "Arrangements have been made. The shuttle craft will be waiting for you."

"I don't want a co-pilot."

"No, Haladay specified 'private.'" It was those types of specifications that kept him from transferring Cleis and every other Amazon off his base.

"I understand..." Cleis slowly got to her feet — hiding the fact that her third rib had just slipped out of place again, "...that Diana is working with a Council guide by the name of Elana?"

His moustache twitched with the realization that somewhere, somehow, he was being manipulated. He began to hate Haladay for engineering the whole thing.

"You know Diana contacted me a while back?" She didn't wait for his nod. "This Elana is Elana n'Sappho, isn't she? Did you or Haladay arrange that?"

He went pale as his ulcer kicked. With a sharp crack, he snapped the deskcom on and shouted for his secretary. "Weis! I want Haladay's discs!"

"All of them, sir?"

"The classifieds. Now!"

"Yes, Commander."

Thomas turned smugly to the Amazon before him. "I believe it's your day off. Do enjoy it."

"Never mind." Cleis met this dismissal with a sarcastic grin. She paused at the door. "I'll just ask Haladay about Elana."

His chin quivered as the door slipped shut. That — that bitch!

The console on his desk blinked and he sat down abruptly. Security codes punched in and his fingerprints matched, the computer began to scan for the appropriate files. He reached for the rest of his drink and downed it quickly. One day — somehow — he'd figure out how to get around those women. Or maybe he could just get transferred to a nice, neat job without their interfering tricks!

There it was — Elana n'Sappho.

The screen flipped by and he frowned. As usual no photos, no fingerprints — nothing at all conclusive. Bloody stupid system these Amazons kept. Always took three times as long to verify any of their special agents as it took to check on anybody else in the universe! But that girl of the Council's had had dark hair. Yes, it could have been black. And she'd been shorter than he — height could be right. He didn't remember her eyes.

But she'd spoken Common, and it might explain why she put herself so far away from him at the table. Idiot, he could have blown her cover. But when the hell did she sign on? He personally reviewed everybody's records as they came in. N'Athena had mentioned Crigil III?

He ran down her file to the assignment dates and her dispatch. Crigil III — the administrators' conferences. Yes, that was why n'Athena had met her and briefed her; he'd been gone for ten — no, twelve days that year. And he obviously hadn't checked his classifieds for updates. No, he winced — his stomach stabbing again with his most recent ulcer; it was like him to miss that sort of thing.

But three years was a dangerously long time to be solo, and if your base commander forgot about you, no one might ever remember. People died with that kind of carelessness, just as they died from breaking the safety regulations on fuel transfers. Damn...his stomach hurt, protesting both the liquor and his foolishness. He wanted to go back to a space barge — a simple refueling station. Diplomacy, field agents — military disputes were not what he wanted to be dealing with! Give him a good crew, decent flight controllers with a competent workshop and he could keep any supply line on schedule. But this, this was just useless chaos!

❋ ❋ ❋

Cleis locked the door behind her and slumped back against it. She forced the air into her lungs with shallow, even breaths and fought the pain. It was the first day in two weeks that she'd gone without her rib belt, and apparently it was still too soon. Carefully she stood upright again, concentrating on making the muscles in her torso and back relax. Her fingers prodded beneath her arm along the right side of her rib cage. There it was. She drove the heel of her hand sharply into her side and gasped, feeling the rib pop back into place. The pain felt as keen as it had the day the sword struck her broadside.

Gingerly she walked across her apartment to the bedroom and fetched the rib belt. The healer had shown her that trick and had warned her against swinging a sword again. The medical chief here had ordered her to report for surgery so that he could weld the two ribs into one unbendable piece. He had warned her that procrastinating might mean she would puncture a lung.

In the end, she had agreed to go home for the operation as soon as Diana's mission was done, and he had agreed not to take her off the active duty list until her ribs shifted out of alignment again. Thanks to the brace that wasn't happening as often as it might have, and as long as the healer's trick worked, she wasn't going to report it when it did.

She fastened the velcro under her arms and reached for her music discs. She had a dozen bottles of various pills to take for this pain — that was the Empire's medical community — but she preferred the music and a flat bed. The woodwinds swelled and lifted around her, the pain eased enough so that she didn't feel nauseous, and her hands felt less clammy. It would be all right. She could deal with this, and at home the witches would tend her. She did not trust those doctors of technology with their knives and lasers...not after dear Lynn's death. The hands of her Sisters would find the ways and follow the course of her body's life. If they decided to operate, she would not hesitate; but a body was not a machine to be soldered or pinned together on a whim — it was a shelter of life to be nurtured and supported. No, she preferred to let the crones n'Shea do the tending.

Her thoughts turned to her Sister as her body began to drift with the music. She wondered what had happened to Diana's transmitter and how badly this Garrison was injured. There had been no mention of Elana in that scribbled hawker's message that the Council had delivered to Thomas. With a brief prayer, Cleis hoped the woman was safe. Even without meeting her, Cleis could not help but extend the Sisterhood's bond to include her. The woman must be very special to have broken through the lonely wall of isolation that Diana had built in these last years.

Cleis did not regret the distance that had begun to separate her from Diana as much as she ached with knowing she could not heal the growing fatigue — the silent pain that was settling within her friend. It felt like a defeat of some kind. But Diana seldom seemed inadequate or incompetent, so Cleis truly did not understand the weariness. In the end she had merely decided that it was time for her friend to go home...time for her to remember that the Sisterhood was not a myth.

Yet now there was this Elana. A woman who made Diana n'Athena 'uncertain' of her own homebound date. Perhaps it had not only been the Sisterhood's shelter that Diana had grown to forget? Perhaps it had been their love as well?

Elana n'Sappho, what are you like? Cleis drew endless pictures of dark-haired, blue-eyed women through her mind. Are you truly blue-eyed? Perhaps you will be n'Shea...with the spells you weave about my friend's fragile heart. And only twenty-five...twenty-six years in age? A year or two behind myself, but many seasons behind my Sister. What kind of enchanting wisdom do you possess to open her weary eyes again?

And Elana n'Sappho, how kind is your heart? Will you protect this tender soul you have won and let her guide you to our home? Or will you taunt the whims of destiny and bind her to Aggar — forever banished in the guise of man from her neighbors...from her Sisters?

No — Cleis thought of all she had come to know of her friend — this young woman would know, just as she did, that Diana was bound to the Sisterhood more strongly than even Diana might grasp. No, Elana n'Sappho, you will know she is to go home, and I with my Sisters will do anything necessary to ensure that you may go too.

✿ ✿ ✿

Chapter Three

"She's been very restless today," Diana murmured, turning to look at the eitteh, who was pacing back and forth near the edges of the fire's light.

It was the first night they had not camped in the shelter of a cave or ledge, since the ravine was narrow and offered no access to its heights. The larger canyon had broken off earlier into dozens of smaller chasms, and they found themselves settling beside a trickling little stream in scattered brush. The winged cat found no comfort from the black shadows of the sandstone walls, and she growled her distaste.

"She cannot tell me anything directly," Elana answered quietly, kneeling beside Di'nay at the fire. "There is something that moves to the west, but it is not clearly a threat to us."

Diana's mouth thinned faintly. She glanced at Garrison's motionless body. Splitting defenses was not usually the best maneuver, but if they were attacked here odds were they would be killed or Garrison would have to be left behind. Neither proposition was attractive.

She reached for the long bow and stood. Sometimes there could be advantages in taking the offense.

Elana rose slowly. "Take Eitteh with you."

"You are certain?"

"Yes," Elana said decisively, "if you are not back by dawn, I'm coming after you."

The words hovered on her lips, but Diana didn't say them. She would have left Garrison to pursue Elana. It wasn't fair to demand Elana do differently.

Elana grasped her sleeve and the Amazon paused. She smiled and reached up to gently kiss Di'nay's cheek. "May the Mother ride your winds."

Diana nodded and hugged her quickly. "We won't be long."

The night swallowed them, their movements fading like the rustling of a breeze. She suddenly felt chilly, and Elana pulled her cloak more tightly about her. It was such a temptation to send her Sight out to decipher those distant shapes, but it would not do. She shivered again in the winter's coldness and turned abruptly to Garrison. If she was chilled, he would be near frozen.

❀ ❀ ❀

The night was an eerie mixture of blue-gray and inky black. The two moons had risen, but the overcast scattered their light. The twins were virtually unseen and yet the sky was aglow.

There were three of them, moving in and out of the shadows on the rocky trails on the upper plateau. The eitteh rumbled, drawing Diana's attention to the swirling black of horns ahead of the three. They were hunting a slender goat of some kind.

Diana clicked off the infra-red toggle and folded her binoculars away. The shimmer of metallic thread in their cloaks meant more than hunting. They were Maltar's men, and the only reason they had for being in this area was to find Elana and the Council's spirit, Garrison. It also meant that someone had guessed they might be seeking the Wayward Path. So far, hopefully, it was only a guess. If the Seer had managed more, there would have been a confrontation already.

Patiently, stealthily Diana worked her way up the steep trails. The eitteh stayed on foot and followed, cautious of the hungry hunters with their bows. They parted as the trail forked where the men before them had divided, attempting to corner the goat ahead. The eitteh bounded up the higher trail, and Diana drew her sword. The path twisted too much; she did not want to go around a rock and face a readied archer. In such close quarters her sword and the shaft of her bow would serve as better weapons.

She paused, pressed against the sandy rock as the sound of shuffling feet moved before her. The twist in the rock hid her, and she edged nearer.

The snarling of the eitteh and the scream of a man echoed through the night.

Hooves scrambled and the goat-like beast bolted. A shout rang out. Diana flattened herself into the wall just as the animal came charging past. Heavy boots hurried forward and Diana stepped out, sword singing.

His arrow and bow was halved. His gaunt frame stood rooted in fear, the skin browning beneath a neatly trimmed beard as he imagined goat had become man; no one could fight a Changling's magic. He twisted, groping for his sword as he began a retreat. With a scream of his own, he found he had stepped back into nothingness, and he tumbled from the edge.

She pressed herself into the stone and shadows again, listening. There was no sound of man or eitteh. Somewhere there lurked at least one more soldier. Diana prayed for all their sakes that the eitteh had been successful in her kill.

He met her, sword drawn, on the broader ledge ahead. The canyon echoed with their first blow. She dropped her bow, feeling the weight and skill of this man. Her blade swung and he met it well, stepping into the moons' light, and Diana realized he outweighed her by two — and all of that was muscle. He swung and she jumped aside with the clash. He outreached her too. Her strength more than matched, she warned herself to move slowly. He had the advantage of leverage with his height. Instinctively her feet tested the ground beneath them, hoping the footing was solid.

Silver flashed and she parried, orange fire sizzling the length of her blade, and suddenly she remembered her sword's lifestones. Perhaps they were more evenly matched than she'd thought!

"Changling Dog!" he snarled, a thick Ramains accent cutting his ragged breath. "None of your tricks will save you here!"

She side-stepped his swing and they squared off again.

Diana ducked and swung for his midrift. He dodged and backed away. He grinned and she heard a throaty growl. A piece of her mind noted he did not recognize her as Elana's companion; he too thought her to be some magical Changling. She counted them lucky — perhaps the Seer still did not know about her.

He swung, she blocked and recovered, attacking with an echoing cry. Their blades bounced apart with a splay of sparks, leaving his sword nicked. Two-handed she descended, pounding again and again in a flaming torrent of orange and blue, and he retreated a step, blocking blow for blow. The metal of his sword shivered fire with each contact, and his face grew grim as he felt his weapon cracking.

In desperation he lunged and she slid her blade against his, swirling the flat shaft around and deflecting the blade as hers drove true. With a grunt his body took the point, and they stared at each other. His sword dropped. She went to pull free, but with a savage growl the man hurdled himself forward into the steel. Snatching her cloak, his feet stumbled. Dying, he fell from the ledge — dragging Diana with him.

Falling, his grasp opened as the rock pounded against his hand and they separated. Something raked her thigh and Diana grabbed for anything! Gloved fingers tore into the soft sandstone...her toes driving hard. A half-dead, tenaciously clinging bush jutted out, and she held onto it for dear life.

❋ ❋ ❋

Elana stood with a silent cry on her lips. The night sounds blew undisturbed through the air, but her heart raced unchecked.

Di'nay!

She grabbed her crossbow and darts. Without a glance at Garrison she ran.

❀ ❀ ❀

Think a little now, Diana told herself. Below, use your feet, what's there?

Nothing. The rock slopes inward.

All right. Open your eyes. What's in front of you? Can't tell...bends around like the ledge above. The roots in her hands were thin and slick, but so far they weren't slipping. They weren't slipping. That was good. There was time to think.

To the right...what's behind to the right?

Her face scraped against the rock as she dared to turn, but her eyes made out nothing but blackness.

Blackness?

She peered harder. There should be gray light or a cliff immediately above to block out that light. A cliff might give her something to sit on.

Not quite from above, she realized. It was more of a hole than an outcrop. But it would do.

Slowly she shifted her weight, foot probing...seeking something for her boot to scuff into. Carefully, she found a niche for her toe, then a hand extended...the branch quivering as she let go. The rock crumbled beneath her searching hand, then held — a single fingerhold...and then another. Quarter inches...slivers of cracks...her crawling fingers found and held to them each...her boots slid, scrambling, and then balanced her weight on their very edges...and she moved. Time hung suspended...but she moved.

The shadows drew over her face. She felt the coldness more acutely. It was her imagination, she chided herself, and crept on. She had nothing to spare for ancient fears in this moment — it was merely cold...and she was nearer. It gets to be night and you expect it to get colder, the darkness means night and cold...fingers dug where there was no hold and instead, created one...it was going to be all right. This blackness meant safety...it was not like the other.

Her palm fell inward as ground opened, and the hole seemed like a cavern after the lifetime of nothingness she had been clinging to. She pulled herself forward and rolled inside, praying there were no cucarii-type creatures in the back. But the wind had carved this hole into the softest layers of the sandy stone, and it was not a sheltering place for bird or cucarii.

It was truly colder here. The wind whipped around the distant canyon wall and drove straight into the niche. Diana pulled her cloak up and folded her tall frame into the narrow box.

Her feet braced against the stone although her legs were bent almost in half. Her head had enough clearance only when she managed to scoot down onto her tailbone. But the rock was firm and the cloak took the bite out of the wind. She breathed and thanked the Goddess for all favors large and small.

❀ ❀ ❀

Diana shivered and woke. Without opening her eyes she knew where she was, and instinctively she resisted the urge to stretch. Her body had grown so stiff that she doubted it really would have helped anyway.

The wind whipped against her, and she rubbed the sleep out of her eyes.

Suddenly the breath caught in her throat — her stomach twisted in fright. Blackness...total blackness. With rising terror, her fingers dug into the rock around her.

Think. Breathe. The rocks twist — the shadows are thick. The moons are down — the sun will come...an hour or two, no more than that. Never more than that. This is Aggar...Aggar. Elana — Elana and eitteh will be searching. When it's light, they will come. The tension in her stomach, very slowly, began to ease. She clung to that thought — Elana will come.

And yet, this cramped, dark place was not so very different from that other. The haunting memories pressed forward again. She buried her face in her hands, feeling herself shiver. Not now, please!

The images faded, but the fear would not, and resigned, Diana tipped her head back against the rock. She gathered in a deep breath. She knew the best way with this horror was to walk through it — not deny it. It had been a long, long time since she'd been forced to face this fear so tangibly. She almost believed she'd forgotten how.

But it was only a memory. She had lived through the reality, and Oma Hanna had been right — she had proved she could live through much by that survival.

Her breathing became more even, and she let her eyes close. Her hand grasped the gritty edge as a reminder of the physical limits of her safety, and slowly Diana turned to face her childhood ghosts.

It had been a spring day. They were out riding, entertaining themselves as the adults worked. A fine, sunny day in a tall-grassed meadow where they had shared a picnic lunch.

Lunch? A feast. Estelle had outdone herself, but now she was busy cleaning dishware and packing away the wagon. The other adults, Ivory and her two colleagues from Shekhina moonbase, were off with their machines doing whatever adults did to test the ground.

Morgan and Teresa had begged to ride the horses. The two gentle giants had been as eager as the twelve-year-olds. And because they were well accustomed to the antics of these youngsters, Estelle had set them loose under the children's hands. How she had pleaded with Morgan to let her ride too. At barely four, the youngest of the three children there that day, Diana had so wanted to sit behind her cousin and canter through the yellow grass. Laughing Teresa had lifted her high upon that golden animal and told her to wrap her arms tightly around Morgan's waist.

Under the sunny sky they had raced and laughed, never thinking of the history of the place. A history of men mining...of drilling and careless markings. In the distance the women worked, tracing the old shafts, testing the ground to decide if the earth was rich enough to support crops. In the time before the

Sisters' settlement, ore barges had landed here, burning the soil acidic. The children were far from the areas that had been mined — so distant that Ivory was lost to their sight.

And then the horse stumbled. Not badly, but Diana's legs were too small to grip the broad back, and she lurched to the side, pulling Morgan with her.

The ground opened up beneath them with a terrible crack, and wood suddenly splintered. Beneath Morgan's weight, Diana was pushed into the ground and dropped into the darkness.

Screaming, Morgan rolled, clutching at the crumbling edge. But she was bigger and stronger and the hole too small for her. Teresa went for Estelle, and Diana remembered Morgan calling — frantically calling for her, and then there was nothing.

She woke stiff and in pain and realized she was twisted and unable to move. The darkness around her was thick, and she began to cry, but from somewhere she heard Terri's voice calling.

Terri and Moma too — somewhere. She cried out for them. Telling them she was here — and that she couldn't move.

"Listen to me, Diana!" Terri's voice cut through the four-year-old's frightened tears. And in that determined but loving tone she always used when Diana was to follow instructions, she demanded, "Diana, are you listening?"

"Yes...." It was a feeble answer.

"I can't hear you, Diana. Are you listening?"

She summoned up a little more energy and yelled, "Yes!"

"Do you remember how you wanted to do things like an Amazon, Diana?"

Voices mumbled above, and Diana found later that her mother had been protesting, but silence came again, and Terri's voice was back.

"Like an Amazon, Diana. Remember?"

"Yes!"

"Well, you've just started your first adventure, Darlin'. Can you be a brave little Amazon and help us get you through? Come on, I know you can do it."

"It's dark!" And darkness to a four-year-old can be more terrifying than all the laser guns Maltar would ever rejuvenate.

"I know it is, Diana. But you've got to do this. All right now?"

"Will I be a real Amazon?"

"You sure will be, Darlin'. And we'll celebrate it with cocoa and cream, how's that?"

"With strawberries?"

"Strawberries aren't in season, Honey." Her honesty was something that made Terri special — she never promised what couldn't be. Her niece had trusted that even then, especially then.

"Okay! Cocoa and cream."

"Good girl, Diana. I knew you would help. Now can you tell me what it's like where you are, Diana? Are you sitting or standing or what?"

With a frowning intensity, the child had concentrated on that. She felt the cold dirt around her, but there was no clammy feeling on her neck, and she tried to turn her head a little. Her foot could wiggle some too, but there was nothing around it. She sniffled some of her tears away, and she remembered Terri's stories of being out in space with no up or down. It must feel a little like this, not knowing where you were.

"Diana, are you still there?" It was her mother's voice, and the child responded to the panicky edge in it — she had heard it the night Teresa had been taken to the witches with her broken leg.

"I'm all right, Moma. I'm just thinking. Terri said Amazons are s'pose to think first."

"That's right, Honey," Terri's voice jumped in enthusiastically. "Can you think out loud now. So I can hear what you're saying?"

"My foot moves and my neck is cold. But there's no dirt on my neck."

"Are you sitting or what, Darlin'?"

"Kind'a."

"Describe it to me, Diana. Use your words. Where's the dirt?"

"All around me!"

"But not on your neck?"

"No. I'm crunched up. Moma! It hurts."

"I'm right here, Diana." Her mother's voice had grown stronger. Kate was not a woman prone to hysterics and her child needed her now. "Tell me where it hurts."

"All over. Real achy. It's so small here."

"I know its hard, Honey. But we're all here, and we're going to get you out. It's going to take a while, but we're coming."

"Diana?" Terri's voice reached through the darkness again. "Are you stuck where you are? Or are you sitting against a wall?"

"I'm stuck. I'm scared."

"Okay, it's okay to be scared. Amazons are scared all the time, but you have to keep thinking, all right? You can't let it stop you from thinking."

"All right."

"Good, Honey. You're doing good — " There was a loud rumbling noise above her then, and she couldn't hear if Terri was talking or not. The dirt around her began to shift, and she shrieked as she dropped another few feet. The sound above stopped abruptly.

"Diana!" Terri and her mother yelled frantically. "Diana!"

The pitter-pattering shower stopped, and she coughed a little. Terri said to think out loud. Tell her what was happening.

"The dirt's falling down!"

"Did you fall too, Diana?" And her voice seemed even further away.

"Yes. Yes!"

"Okay. It's okay. We've got a big machine up here, Diana. We were going to bring it closer to try and dig you out."

"But it's all coming down!"

"Is it still falling?! Diana, is the dirt still falling on top of you?"

It wasn't, she had realized. "No."

"Good. Okay...Diana, your moma is going to talk to you for a while, okay? I've got to go see Ivory about the machine now."

"Don't make it fall on me again! Please Terri...don't!"

"I won't, Sweetheart. I promise we'll try not to do that again, okay? You're still my brave young Amazon?"

"I'm thinking, Terri. Like you said to."

"Good girl."

"I'm proud of you, Diana." It was her mother's voice. "It's going to be a long wait now, Darling, but we're going to get to you. Do you want to hear a story or something?" Her mother had begun with her favorite tale and continued for hours. And then Estelle had come and she had heard of the ancient journeys of Huitaca and Awehai.

In and out of a cramped, cold sleep she had drifted. Always coming back when Terri's voice called and always remembering to listen — to think. Terri told her about mine shafts and air ducts and how they were digging another hole from the side to reach her — how they were going to look for the mine tunnel below her too. And then her mother's voice returned.

It didn't seem as though she had ever lived anywhere else, and her tummy ached with hunger.

Dirt fell from above again, and she felt the earth tremble as she slipped deeper. It seemed that the air smelled different after that, but the darkness stayed. That was the angled tunnel they had cut, Terri had told her years later. But she had been so deep that she was beneath the hard rock and to reach her they would have had to shake the walls around her closed. From that shaft, however, they could try to drop her some food and a light. Then maybe if they could see her better, they could plan the next step.

Earlier they had tried to drop her some food by rope, but it had not reached. Now from the side shaft a pair of nut bars were dropped, and then a fully glowing light bar.

The bumps had not hurt so much as the things found her, but the light had hurt her eyes. She had closed them, crying again, working a small fist closer to her face to rub the dirt away. The slight movement had loosened her suddenly, and with a startled scream she fell.

Dirt gave way to hard, smooth wall and her hands flayed out. The metal screeched beneath her fingernails as she slid. A corner bumped, and her body was falling free before a gritty floor slammed into her.

Everything had hurt with the sudden freedom and the sharp smack of the ground, but the food and the light bar followed her. If she had been less hungry, she would have stayed in a tearful heap, but the nut bars fell close, and she was so very, very hungry. Once she was munching, quietly huddled into a corner, things seemed a little less awful. With the light bar she could see the tunnel went in two directions like a hallway, and she could see the metal tracks on the floor. She knew metal and people went together, and she wondered if Terri's friends would be coming. Terri had said they were trying to find a tunnel that would come underneath her. Terri had said they would come get her from below through that tunnel. This must be it. They must be somewhere.

Another light bar descended with a shower of dirt, and she shied away from the falling debris. As the dusty hail tapered off, her curiosity began to stir again. She picked herself up and stiffly went over to the glowing tube.

A small square box was tied to the light bar, and she fumbled with the string to slide it free. It was not really a box at all. It was a compass like the one Terri had taken on her off-world travels. Morgan had a bigger one, but it didn't work as well as these, and the child grinned with delight. Amazons used this kind. Now she was a proper Amazon.

And Amazons always think.

She looked at the box carefully and saw the thick tape on the one side. She held it closer to the light and saw the big black mark on the tape. There was a little red line on the little piece of tape on the opposite side.

The needles twirled as her hands clumsily tipped the box to peer at the marks. She remembered Terri showing Morgan and her how to point the arrow at a tree or something and follow it. Morgan was a lot better, she remembered; she could use paper maps instead of trees, but Diana had been good for her age. Terri had said so.

There weren't any trees here, but there were those taped marks.

She held the small box close in front of her like Terri had taught her and turned all around until the black arrow matched the black tape mark. It pointed her right down the tunnel along the metal tracks. She picked up the extra light tube and, still munching on her nut bar, set out.

The walk had been terribly long. She had stopped and rested or slept when she got tired, but she always checked the box carefully as she began to walk again. Her mother would later tell her that it had been a much longer walk than she had even imagined, but in the end the child had come to a windy cliff entrance.

Very like this one. Diana sighed and opened her eyes to find the cold, clammy tension in her body lessened. She had come out at the ore dump station, although without the ancient cargo shuttles, there had been no way off the yawning ledge.

The adults had been frantically busy, and n'Sappho had finally recovered the mining records from the galactic trade union for those centuries before the Sisterhood's settlements. The summer's dawning sun had seen the helicopters launched in their search through the numerous cliffside entrances. As small as a four-year-old might be, and as grubby as her adventures had made her, the yellow of her coveralls had been a bright mote of hope against the dingy, beige rock.

Terri had cried as the 'copter swung around the cliff's bend and she sighted the sleeping little bundle on the cold ledge. Later she had explained how the woman in the side shaft had distinctly seen the light bar stop and then abruptly fall again before suddenly flashing silver and disappearing. It had been Terri's hope that it meant Diana had fallen past the metal casing at the end of the duct and that she was 'safely' in the mine tunnel itself. Hurriedly, Terri had snatched one of the field surveyor's compasses and taped her crude directions together.

Her mother's arms had never felt better than that night as Diana had been cuddled and soothed to sleep. Terri's cocoa and cream had never tasted so rich. Morgan had been one of those most happy to see her safe, and for the next several months, whenever the nightmares struck, her older cousin had been right there to hold her and wake her.

Her family had always been there; Diana breathed a slow deep breath and remembered their strong love and embrace. Thirty-seven hours she'd been lost...an unbelievable thirty-seven hours. Her eyes opened and she found Aggar's gray dawn beginning. Goddess, nearly forty hours she had survived that night. And now, she thought triumphantly, she had just dealt with two more tonight.

❄ ❄ ❄

Grimly, Elana knelt beside the body of the soldier. Di'nay's sword stood upright in the ground nearby. It made her shake to think what must have happened to part the Amazon from her weapon.

This was the second man she found, much larger than the first. The first had been slender and well groomed. Elana recognized him as the messenger who had struck the boy in the Keep's hall that night so long ago. But this one was large enough to have challenged even Di'nay's strength.

It was readily evident that the sword and its victim had fallen from the heights above. To some extent, it had been the power of the sword's lifestones that had drawn Elana to this place. Her eyes lifted to the craggy shapes above but dawn was not yet here, and the shadows were indecipherable unless she risked searching further with her Sight. She looked at the man before her again. The Seer would soon discover the deaths of these scouts. Her presence had been announced to some extent already.

Her wrist's stone would not have brought her here if Di'nay were not somewhere near too. The sword's stones did not have quite that much power over her. It worried her that the citteh had yet to find her as well. At least one of them should have returned.

Determinedly, Elana rose and looked above.

The winds howled, overwhelming her for a moment with the frosty, sleeping life of the distant mountains. Then slowly, the familiar touch of brush and hibernating animals that slept nearer here came to her.

Cold — not the air, but a feeling. Loneliness — fear...Di'nay? Worrying, Elana cast her Sight into the dark shadows, and a faint glow of life began to emerge. Yes, there — caught between the trail above and a sheered-off drop below...but she was very far away — much further than four hundred feet.

Quickly Elana searched above, tracing the routes taken by the soldiers and Di'nay by the shimmering afterglow of lifesigns. She took up the fallen sword and started for the foot of the trail. It was going to be a long climb.

❄ ❄ ❄

The sword drove deeply into the sandstone of the trail, and the length of rope dropped with a thud. Elana had stumbled across the hidden packs of the soldiers and had gratefully confiscated the rope they carried as standard gear.

Cautiously now she approached the edge of the ledge. The ground crumbled a little where the weight of the soldier had crashed over it, but the whole was fairly solid. She squatted low and peered through the gray overcast.

Her brow wrinkled as she searched below her, but the angle was steep.

"Di'nay!"

"Here!"

She could see her now. They were lucky. The line would reach.

"Wait! A rope is coming!"

Diana heaved a sigh. It was good to hear another voice. Then she smiled at herself; it was especially good to hear Elana's voice.

"Can you reach it?!"

"Yes!"

Diana would have reached it, if she'd had to jump. This nook was too cold and too cramped to tolerate any longer. The rope swayed in the wind and snaked almost in front of her. With an easy grab Diana caught it and called, "Is it secured?"

There was a second or two before, "Yes!"

Her muscles were stiff and protested as she began to pull herself up. The wind teased, snatching at her a little. But the rope was sturdy and she defied the swirling tug. Her toes scraped against rock, and despite her stiffness, it felt good to be moving again. She made the ledge and managed to drag herself over before collapsing.

Elana sat braced with her back against the wall and the rope wrapped around her waist, its tail end tied to the sword. Her smile was a mixture of weariness and gratitude. "It is good to see you in one piece."

Diana lifted a hand, still laying on her back. "Thank you for..." She gulped another breath of air and admitted, "I am so glad...you didn't wait 'til dawn."

"I heard you fall, I think," Elana murmured. "I could not wait after that."

"Thank the Mother you didn't."

I love you, Elana thought as Di'nay rolled and stood, stretching. The Amazon's brown eyes were warm as she looked at Elana then, and her grasp strong as she took Elana's hand. Yes, she was whole — with a silent prayer, Elana let Di'nay pull her to her feet. Her lover's arms were sheltering even as they trembled from the exertion, and Elana hugged her fiercely.

By the Mother's Hand, they would survive.

❈ ❈ ❈

The camp was quiet in the sheltering shadows of the narrow ravine. Garrison's body lay curled tightly, still well covered by the thermal blanket. The fire had died, and guiltily Elana realized she had left it burning in her haste to leave; they had been lucky.

The air stirred with a strange breeze, and startled, Elana spun about. Di'nay paused, her hand falling to her sword's hilt.

"Eitteh?" Elana whispered, suddenly whirling back towards Garrison.

A faint whine called out to them then, and they saw the flicker of golden ears behind Garrison's form. Diana winced as she recognized in the cry, the pain it carried.

The emerald eyes were glazed and focused poorly on her approaching companions. Her small frame was huddled against Garrison, seeking the warmth of the blanket and the protection of his shadow. Her wings were folded awkwardly, and Diana's heart twisted as she saw the knife slash along the animal's side.

Together the two knelt and gently Elana took the creature's gaze, easing the burning pain.

"I thought it strange she did not find me sooner," Elana murmured and carefully lifted a fine furred wing. "Di'nay, I need my medicine purse."

Diana hurried to fetch it.

The wound had bled slowly. It had not touched the muscles that supported her wings, Elana saw with relief. Instead the hind leg had been hurt. She might always be lame, Elana explained to the young animal; although she would fly unhindered. Melysa would be able to stitch the tendons together so that the leg might still carry some weight, but it had to be done soon. Elana apologized, but that kind of surgery was beyond her skills.

The golden cat rumbled reassuringly, rubbing her face against Elana's gentle hand.

"Can she make it to Melysa's alone?" Diana asked in concern. She owed much to this small one. She would not abandon her now.

Blue and emerald gazes locked and Elana said softly, "She says, yes."

"And you say?"

She hesitated and then nodded. "I believe so. The bandage will hold for a few hours, and the drug will keep the pain at bay for as long. It is not very far by flight. Yes, she will manage."

The long tail twitched, and Elana paused, concentrating. Blue eyes blinked and the two separated. Turning to Di'nay she smiled without much humor. "She reminds us that Mclysa is a hawker. If we wish to send word to the Council, she can take a message. You will not have to guess at their ability to receive it then."

"Dear friend," Diana lay a hand on the silken head, "we will miss you."

With a throaty growl, the eitteh tilted her head, urging Diana to rub the fur behind her ears. Then returning to sensibilities, the green eyes looked back to Elana.

Slowly Elana drew a breath; they needed to make decisions and break camp soon. The soldiers would be missed, and the Seer would be nearer to finding them.

"Did you use your Sight to find me?" Diana asked unexpectedly.

"Some. I was careful. I do not think he will know exactly where we are. But he may be close."

"Maltar is not stupid. If he knows we're in this area, he will know we seek the Wayward Path. There are no other neighboring routes."

"Truth."

"In the South Ridge, is there more than one entrance to the Path?"

"Two or three, depending on weather," Elana supplied. "But they are all near the mouth of the Black River."

"Most obvious route would be to retrieve our horses in Black Falls and ride east," Diana mumbled, thinking aloud. "Is there another way?"

"To the Keep?" Elana shook her head regretfully. "The River Road is the sole approach. Although we could always go through the forests...?"

"No, they'll be scouting the woods as thickly as the road, and we need the speed. The longer we're traveling now, the better the odds that they'll find us. If we went directly south after the Path, where is the next settlement? Is there some way to cut east below Black Falls?"

"There is a better way," Elana said suddenly. "At the mouth of the Black River there is a trader. He harbors boats and is always well stocked with supplies. And a day downstream at the village, Rotava, the Black River is joined by the Suiri — "

"The Suiri that runs through Gronday?" Diana asked quickly.

"The same. The Black River there is white water, but the current back up the Suiri is lazy, and it is not so very long a trip even if it is farther. It would take five days — at the most, maybe six."

Diana smiled. From Gronday it was a single day's hard ride, north to the Crossroad and on east into the Keep. Less than a ten-day totaled — once through the Path. And the horses she had stabled with Mattee were strong and quick.

"Will the Council send word to the base?" Diana asked.

"Very likely. What would you ask?"

"For Cleis — and our crew, an escort from Gronday." Using Melysa's hawks would give an added bonus of credibility to the Council too; Thomas would undoubtedly appreciate a note in her own handwriting. If Melysa delayed a day, it would also mean that the Council would not receive the message of their whereabouts until after they'd reached the caverns of the Path. That would reduce the risk of the Seers inadvertently lifting the clouds before the rocks protected them. Perhaps that gray ceiling would keep the Maltar's puppet from discovering the death of the scouts too soon.

Elana's voice drew Diana back from her thoughts and she noticed the woman's faint smile. "Perhaps the Council will add a few sword arms of their own. They owe you much for this Seer's identity."

Diana grinned and pulled the green satchel from her pack, seeking her writing pad. This mission might yet change the way Aggar and the Empire dealt with each other...or at least, how Sisterhood and Council did.

❋ ❋ ❋

Chapter Four

𝔇iana was gambling — gambling that the Maltar's Seer was having difficulty with the thick overcast sent by the Council — that the scouts would not be immediately missed. She was gambling that the Maltar would not risk igniting a border war with the Changlings by bringing a larger force into the territory, if he had other options. And he did have another — he could muster his Ramains' spy rings and attack his quarry as it emerged from the Southern Ridge. He had been shrewd enough to avoid detection by the Council's spies as well as the Council's Seers, and he was not one to ignore the advantage when it might be his. While it might insult the Ramains' King, it would be a negligible risk given the King's dependence on Maltar ore. It was to his favor to wait — she was gambling he would.

She was praying he would.

After the hellish night spent amongst the rocks, she had little left to give and even Garrison's skinny figure had grown into a heavy burden. She held no delusions about her abilities to travel far. By early afternoon she decided to take the risk of searching for shelter long before darkfall.

The cave was a welcoming place with black-and-orange runes painted on the smooth walls. Murals of animals and half-human, half-beast people lined the innermost curves — pictures of a celebration. Diana walked around the twisting walls, amazed at the detail the artists had managed even with such crude strokes.

Garrison was tended, and eventide finished, yet Diana's eyes still returned to the dancing images on the wall. A spring of sacred water centered the merriment, and creatures of wings and children of fine fur played with one another.

"They are the records of the Beginning." Elana's voice was so very quiet that the reverence she spoke with was almost lost. Di'nay looked at her sharply, but she only stared into her tea. Fascinated, Diana came to sit next to her and waited.

Her lips pursed slightly as Elana set her drink aside. She waved a hand at no wall in particular. "I had forgotten these were here — so near us."

Diana understood. This was another piece of Aggar that the Council would have wished kept from her as an Agent of the Empire. But the firelight and shadows called these images back to life. She wanted to know of this Beginning.

Elana spoke quietly. "Long before the Council...humans rose in the Kingdom of All. There were no animals, no people, just — everyone. None were better or worse.. There was food and peace for all...without strife or vindictiveness. Then there was an upheaval...the legend says it was the Fates. The historians said it was the shift in our land masses." She wet her lips. "The Council holds both as truth."

Diana nodded, understanding the Council's perception of Chance and Nature.

"The creatures of Aggar found themselves separated for a time. When they returned to the Spring of Life, they found themselves changed. At first, it did not matter. Their joy at reunion was great. Here — on these walls — you see that time of thanksgiving.

"There are other walls in other places, however." Elana drew a shaking breath. "They are not so pleasant.

"After a time the differences did begin to matter. Some became greedy of their specialness and would not share their abilities. Some became covetous of what they could not do — or did not have. And quarrels began to break out. Tribes of likened bodies drew together and trading — hunting...," she shuddered, "wars began.

"Gradually, the eitteh became the sole messengers between factions. The winged-cats would fly from place to place bringing news, and the men-cats would translate and placate — trading goods of one tribe with those of another...reminding each of common ground.

"In time, the humans became more clever with their hands and grew to despise counsel with the others. Others grew weary of unheard dialogues, turning inward more and more. Again, at each meeting, they would find themselves so changed that speech was less and less possible, until finally the fear of differences and dwindling resources banished the joy. Survival became the sole demand.

"Predators and prey became the way. Those bestial ancestors of humankind grew stronger as their ability to coerce and conquer others grew. Within their own kind, they began to separate, and one tribe rose that was never to be satisfied.

"In their greed, they sought out the eitteh, coveting its special intellect and flight. The eitteh — for so many generations the carrier of news, of barter — of bonding All into Oneness — still had the ability to understand the numerous others. Whether beast or bird or human, the eitteh could speak and sense meanings.

"It was the greed of that tribe which forced the eitteh to flee into the mountains for their freedom. When they stayed, they stayed as captives. The children of those forced joinings were not as blessed. Instead greed corrupted these descendants as it had corrupted their tribe, and, although they did indeed become half-man, half-beast, neither man or eitteh, the females were unable to fly, and communications were a mockery of the common tongue. Their speech became a conglomerate of all creatures' sound, intelligible to none. They were ostracized; even after generations, they still only manage elemental contact with other peoples. But they have a perfect mimicry of many creatures' tongues, although sense is poorly grasped."

"The Changlings?"

The dark head nodded, and Elana looked into the empty palms of her hands. "Superstition also tells of their abilities to change their shape to match the sound of the animal they make. It is a myth they do not chose to deny, although in truth it is only the sounds they can change."

"And the eitteh? Did they grow to distrust all men so much?"

"No." Elana shook her head in adamant denial. "Others feared the Changlings would succeed, and with such abilities of flight, speech, and the beginnings of tool-making, they feared the Changling tribes would grow too strong and too greedy. Humankind feared they would then be conquered and enslaved, just as they wished to rule countless of other creatures. The Changlings were swift and crafty, and they could not easily be defeated. And so the tribes tried to destroy the eitteh, thinking that without breeding stock the Changlings would fail."

Diana closed her eyes...to be the victim and hunted for that very victimization.

"So the eitteh fled. Only the very strongest, most savage of the men-cats could survive the constant battles and increasingly barren terrain of the mountains. For the most part, the winged-cats avoided the tribes and battles with their flight. They would bring food, scout and leave. But then they too became warriors, lest they lead the hunters to their mates. Yet gradually, their own males grew too barbarous for them, and they began to see less and less of them. Until eventually they evolved into an almost totally separatist society."

Diana's throat grew tight. The story was sounding cruelly familiar.

"All along the Changlings were growing less trusted, and the territories of the other tribes were growing more important to each for their own survival. Tools came. Borders were drawn. Distrust and greed mingled — this world is no different from so many others. Wars broke out — bitter, tribal-feuding — pure hatred spawning the fervor of real war. They had progressed past the petty, easily forgotten transgressions of earlier disputes. And from the icy tip of the Southern Continent across the deserts of the South, from the Plains of Ramains through the wastelands and timbered northern hills, deathwish of tribal furies reigned."

Elana trembled. This legend was very real to her. The later-born eyes of Seers gifted with out-of-time Sight had piece together Aggar's tragedy bit-by-bit, until it was known. The apprentices of the Keep had been tutored under that Blue Sight — passing on the history with such a vividness that none would ever forget.

In this place of forgotten artists and of dancing flames, Diana felt the loss of that once joyous unity. The blue touch of Elana's past — the past of her people — echoed mournfully through the empty cavern, and Diana knew the lesson as from a Seer.

"There were a handful of men and women in the White Stone Isles of Fire — the archipelagoes. They had little others could want, save safety from wars. Isolation produced differences once again. But this time, it bore those of mercy — those who remembered the Spring, and the first Blue Sight was born.

"It was many, many generations later that the Council finally formed, traveling to settle more centrally — choosing their place well for defense but never seeking to lash out. Not concerned with just one tribe — those of compassion with those of the Sight came to watch over Aggar. Their hands began to bring peace. Tribes grew less frantic over territories as the lands calmed under the Seers' touch and the Council's guidance. The mountains of the northwest became the Firecaps, while others — such as these ahead — ceased to explode and became dormant, sheltering walls. Floods and earth-wrenching storms quieted. The people grew to like this peace, and the Council encouraged trade over raiding. Then slowly, the balance grew, continues to grow — as the Council's watch goes on."

"In every life — on every planet," Diana said slowly, "there is much wasted. But perhaps Aggar is not as lost as many worlds."

"We almost destroyed ourselves. Then we remembered to find our place in the Mother's scheme. We are learning again to value that ideal of unity. Someday, perhaps, we will do both — think and value life."

Diana savored the beauty of the dark-haired woman before her and remembered the specialness of her being...that subtle meshing of both Wisdom and Sight. The magic drew her, and very softly, she kissed the cool smoothness of Elana's lips.

Blue eyes fluttered open as Diana withdrew, and Elana gazed at her, perplexed by the warmth and reassurance that her lover shared with her.

"Your people will do both. You are living proof that they will."

"You are my people now," Elana whispered and felt the tender love she held for this woman surge through her. "What we share, none of my Sight have ever known on this world."

"None of my Sisters have either."

It didn't matter how Di'nay spoke of her Sight. It didn't matter that this woman had not grasped how differently she treasured Elana's specialness or the freedom Elana had discovered under that unaccustomed acceptance. Nothing matters, Elana thought, if only she will look at me this way until the end of our time together.

Beneath the loving, brown gaze Elana drew near, seeking her lover's gentle mouth. Hands were soft and bodies warmed, and she knew the cherished touch of their loving again.

❋ ❋ ❋

Diana finished spoon-feeding Garrison and sighed. He was so helpless she couldn't help but pity him. Brushing hair from unseeing eyes, she said in Common, "Just one more day, Lieutenant. Goddess willing, you'll be free of this madness."

Or at least, she thought, standing and returning to the fire, he would be as free as the rest of them. He would be able to run and think and maybe even wield a weapon. Consciousness was necessary if he was to have a fighting chance of seeing the base again. Eventually, there would be a confrontation, and his only way to survive it was to be able to outrun or outfight them with Elana and herself. But Elana thought his mind must be protected until they were beyond the reach of the Maltar's Seer.

Slowly she finished washing the cookery and closing the packs. But her mind was on her absent companion, and worrying, Diana returned again and again to the mouth of the cave; her eyes searched for some sign of Elana's return. She did not know how long the woman had been gone.

When Diana had awakened, the first light of daybreak was appearing, but breakfast had already been prepared and was left warming near the fire. The Blue Sight had kept her from waking to the sounds of the cooking, Diana knew. It was a habit Elana had taken on early in their journey. Now it was not comforting, however. Since her imprisonment, Elana had not risen so early, and Diana fretted that she had caused some rift — some mistrust between them last night.

Time to heal, Elana had asked for — only the other night, and she had carelessly forgotten her lover's request. Their loving had been slow, unhurried...undirected; their closeness had been the only goal guiding them. She did not doubt the yielding softness nor the stirring caresses that Elana had shared. But even the gentlest of stroking could bring the harshest of memories forth by sheer comparison. Diana worried this morning's light had brought such images to Elana.

It was an added fear...as if the threats of the Maltar's scouts and neighboring Changlings were not enough.

A shadow caught her eye and she jumped, startled, to find Elana standing motionless just inside the cave.

"You are angry...?" In a shocked whisper, Elana's words could barely be heard.

"No!" Diana gasped — realizing her anxiety had become overwhelming. "No. Frightened! I did not know where you were. I — "

Her breath drew in again, and unsteadily Elana moved forward. She dropped her crossbow and shrugged off her cloak, still shaken by the intensity of their meeting. With a hand to her head she concentrated a moment, then straightened. "I didn't mean to worry you. I hoped to be back sooner. Forgive me."

"You're back — that's all that matters. Are you all right?"

Elana nodded wearily and came to Di'nay, wrapping her arms around the pensive woman. A strong grasp gathered her near, and Elana buried her face in the soft jerkin with a sigh.

"I was afraid something happened because of last night," Diana confessed.

"No." Elana shook her head and hugged tightly, feeling the fear of her beloved's amarin. "Last night was beautiful. Nothing was wrong with it."

Diana pulled away a little. "Yet something has happened."

"I've been scouting for the Path." She moved away, reaching for a waterskin. "This morning when I was down at the stream, I saw a messenger hawk above. I thought its errand might concern us, so I brought it down and confiscated its note before letting it continue on. I glimpsed its home roost.

"The message itself didn't concern us, but the bird was from a Changling's roost. Apparently its keeper coordinates supply shipments for the miners of the Wayward Path."

"Melysa was wrong then," Diana saw suddenly. "They have had time to shift to a new entrance."

Elana nodded, pausing to drink. She sat down as Di'nay came to kneel beside her in concern. "I am all right," Elana assured her quickly. "I'm just not as strong yet as I would like to be."

With a gentle finger Diana traced the faint rash of the friction burn on Elana's cheek. "Take your time."

She smiled wryly. "We do not have much of that, Di'nay. The bird was released not far from here, and it gave me a clear image of the place, so I went looking for it. We were very lucky last night that we stopped so early. Another two leagues and we would have crossed their camp."

Puzzled, Diana said, "I don't understand. The mountains are a good six or seven leagues out yet."

"The original dwellers of this cave lived in a labyrinth of tunnels between here and the mountains. The Changlings have stumbled across one which leads to the heart of the Path. They have found the richest vein of stones since their grandfathers' era, because this route leads them so deeply. It may also save us from going twenty to twenty-five leagues out of our way."

"You did not learn all of this from a bird," Diana challenged softly.

Shivering, Elana remembered the man-like beast that had fallen with her bolt. "I found their encampment. I chose a poor place to watch from. The Changling literally stumbled over me...there was — " she broke off, realizing she was about to make excuses. That wasn't right. It had become necessary — for survival...to protect Di'nay...to elude capture and a return to prisons and cruel hands.

"I panicked, I think," Elana admitted, finally. "Rationally, I know it was — it might have been necessary. But...I don't know. Just the thought of being taken again — "

"No," arms enclosed her and Diana held her fiercely, "it's all right. You did what needed to be done."

"He was a hunter...he will not be missed until darkfall," she mumbled almost incoherently. With a shuddering breath Elana clung to Di'nay then, fighting back a myriad of nightmares. The Amazon's strength surrounded her, keeping her safe. Still her voice wavered as Elana opened her eyes again. "I am so tired of death — and fear, Di'nay. I have never been afraid before...not like this."

Diana nodded, stroking her dark braided hair. "You're not alone," she murmured. "Dearest Elana, you're not alone. I know it's frightening."

"Oh, Mother!" Elana straightened suddenly, her eyes filled with alarm. "This entrance, Di'nay — it is leagues through the sandstone and bedrock before the Path proper is reached."

Black, dense tunnels, Diana realized. Her mouth grew grim. It appeared to be a day for confrontations.

Elana shivered as the amarin rose about Di'nay, and slowly, with more vigor, she shook her head in denial. "No — Di'nay, no! I cannot take you into—"

"Yes." Diana's voice was firm, and she met Elana's eyes fully. "You take me nowhere. I choose to go."

❋ ❋ ❋

It was evident why the Changlings were considered neither human nor animal, Diana thought. These half-people were slightly built; not one of them stood as high as four feet. They walked upright. Their mottled hide was as short-furred as any cat's and yet their movements were neither cat-like nor man-like, just odd.

Diana watched them closely as they moved between the camp and the mine, wondering how much more of their oddness was cloaked by the loose-fitted tunics and breeches. No boots, she noted, and then finally identified the strangeness of their motion. They stopped and paused frequently, as if to test the air for scent — or listen to the sudden whisper of a breeze. These creatures checked themselves in task...in walk — in everything they did. For a brief instant their attention was interrupted. And then, they would return to their work.

The battle of instinct and intellect — poorly combined, Diana mused and watched as a cinnamon-and-bronze creature paused, lifting its black, flattened nose to the breeze. Fur-tufted ears flickered against the side of its head; a black-nailed hand, raised palm opened. The distraction identified, the eyes looked to the path again and the creature resumed its walk.

"They are not as strong as humans," Elana whispered.

They were crouched in a rocky alcove about two hundred feet from the camp. There were twenty or thirty miners housed in the area, judging by the size of their compound.

"Ann, there is some reason they are so feared by the humans," Diana prodded quietly. "If it is not their strength, what then?"

"Their speed and cunning can be deadly. And they are united across the wastelands by their common shape, although as kin they have little real love for one another. They need few excuses to revenge even an imagined injury done to one of their kind by any human. And too, their eyesight is uncanny. Their ability with slingshots and long bows are dangerous threats. The strength of a man's sword arm is little help, if one is not close enough for combat."

Diana nodded, noticing again how the creatures stopped to test the air. "How sensitive are they to human scent?"

"They track very poorly," Elana assured her. "Fresh scents carried on the wind are the most accessible to them, but they are neither men-cat nor hunting cat. They cannot follow one scent imposed on another. They track by sight just as men do."

"There is no hope of winning passage from them by negotiation?" Diana ask rather wistfully.

"They will have been informed that the Maltar will pay well for our capture. No doubt that was part of the mission of those you fought. Our only if unlikely hope if they were to capture us is that they might go first to the Council for a better price."

"Are we too close?" Diana asked nervously, feeling the wind ripple around the narrow canyon's bend. Here there were only gusty drafts from the heights above.

"I will not let them sense us," Elana promised quietly. Di'nay's hand touched her shoulder briefly in thanks. That was strange, Elana thought as they retreated to where Garrison lay in the shadowy crevice...it was strange how well Di'nay appreciated the talents Elana herself took for granted. But then, Elana smiled, Di'nay was sometimes flattered but bemused by Elana's respect too.

"Oh, Dearest Mother," Diana groaned, collapsing into the small space. The thought of her aching shoulder supporting Garrison while she wielded a sword was not very realistic. She sighed. "We cannot fight our way onto the path."

Elana agreed, "The route to the Path is too long. They would too easily track us in the tunnels. If at all possible, we must slip by them undetected."

Diana sat up a little straighter, eyeing the encampment in the distance. "Did I see horses on the far side there?"

Elana nodded. "A scruffy lot. There are about ten saddle mounts and two dozen pack animals."

Their shelters were rough wood shanties, Diana noted.

"Are you thinking of a diversion?"

Diana's head tipped absent-mindedly. Abruptly she turned and dug into the side pocket of her pack, producing her box of emergency matches. It just might work!

❋ ❋ ❋

Carefully Diana peered out from behind the rocks. She glanced down at the crossbow in her hand, checking the set of the bolts. She wished for her long bow, but in this small space she could not stand up to use it.

Across the compound the horses stirred, and Diana squinted to see. A light swirl of the dust made it difficult to make out the corral, and she blinked. She should know better by now than to try to find Elana from such a distance. How many times had the woman simply appeared beside their campfire? She turned back to her watch, concentrating on the Changlings that lounged around the fire of their noon meal. Two sentries stood a little way off at the mine's entrance. They were fighting boredom with their dice.

She looked back to the horses. The dusty air seemed thicker nearer the corral. She did admire the woman's skill.

Behind the outhouse a thin trail of smoke from the small fire began. It crept skyward and then abruptly all trace of it vanished. Diana smiled with a grim satisfaction. The loosened horses might keep everyone's attention, but the 'careless pipe ashes' that Elana made them think had set the outhouse ablaze would prompt everyone's immediate action. One without the other would not insure that the sentries left their post. She hoped their curious habit of watching over their shoulders and checking the winds would reassure them that no one had gained entry.

Her sleeve was brushed and Diana gasped with a start.

"Me," Elana said softly. She remained half-crouched, her eyes unfocused as she stared toward the corral. "I cannot control the illusion or the stallion much longer."

"Let the fire start first," Diana reminded her gently, careful not to distract. "We want it to seem as if the horses panicked."

Ivory skin began to darken ever so slightly as amarin focused. Diana turned quickly back to the encampment.

"It's burning," Elana whispered.

"Let it go."

Flames licked out, suddenly bursting to the height of the shack. Dried timbers cracked, and with a yell the door was flung open. Breeches half-down, the figure raced from the smoking latrine, stumbling and rolling as he tripped on his clothes. And the entire camp jumped with the alarm.

"Now," Diana ordered.

The brown stallion rose with a piercing scream and the loosened rails clattered under his hooves. The herd moved as the animal reared again, and with a bound the brown lunged through the fallen fence.

The thundering hooves brought the camp into action. Buckets were snatched from hooks, and the stream splashed with feet. With a shout the captain brought the sentries in, and together the pair grabbed ropes for the animals.

Diana dropped the crossbow back into Elana's hands, and hoisted Garrison up and settled his weight over a shoulder. Elana glanced at her. She nodded ahead.

In a scrambling sprint they rounded the rocks. The noise around them seemed further away as they moved, and Diana fleetingly wondered if it was Elana's doing. But there was no more than a thought to spare. With a last gasp of open air, she dove into the tunnel. The scattered torches seemed too few but Diana refused to think. Her eyes were bent on following Elana's booted heels, and quickly they pressed forward.

Panic rose in her throat like poisoned bile. She fought it down.

These Changlings must have the night vision of an eitteh; the torches were set four and five hundred feet apart. Sweating, she wished the flashlight could be tucked into her belt, but they dare not risk it. Their footsteps seemed lost in the echoing blackness. She wondered how Elana was moving so confidently. But then she remembered that this tunnel was used often now, and there would be glowing life signs for Elana to see by.

Dear Goddess, just as long as Elana could see, she would follow. She swore it!

The path twisted and turned, sometimes dropping, sometimes climbing. Diana lost track of time, but didn't want to know how long an eternity she was to spend beneath the ground this trip, or how many leagues would pass under her feet. She needed to concentrate on walking, on keeping her tread soundless, on moving forward.

Her sweat went cold, making her skin shiver. She gritted her teeth. The weight of the pilot slipped some. She swallowed a curse and shifted him back.

"We'll rest soon."

Diana nodded awkwardly, disoriented by the disembodied voice. They had indeed come far.

A hand touched her arm gently, reassuringly. "I'm here, Di'nay."

Could she have forgotten, Elana was here? Her breathing steadied, and she forced a dry swallow. Surprised, she found the aching in her chest had eased.

"Yes, I'm here."

And finally, for the first time since she had decided to enter this ancient tunnel, Diana realized that she truly was not alone — that this time was different, and she knew she could make it.

In the darkness, Elana smiled at the silent victory. She was so very proud of her Amazon. Perhaps now, this ghost would finally know rest.

❋ ❋ ❋

Chapter Five

The whoosh of the vacuum seal filled the waiting area. With a grimace, Cleis tugged down her jacket and turned to face the V.I.P.'s privileged gate. She despised government officials, and the formality of her best dress uniform did nothing to ease her temper.

The airlock slid back, the boisterous laughter of the passengers announcing their arrival. Half a dozen military and civilian men emerged, still sharing their off-color anecdotes; Cleis clenched her teeth in silence. The male bastion of ribald humor had never been one of her favorites. She was not going to be a very tolerant escort if she had to deliver the lot of them to Thomas. Mentally she groaned at the thought of Baily's knowing grin as these idiots arrived.

With a mute sternness she stepped before the group. The men stopped, surprised at the appearance of a woman. A few nervous throats cleared and shoes scuffled as she turned so the insignia across her left shoulder became visible. An Amazon was not a person to be casually overlooked.

"Ah yes." An older man pushed his way forward. "You must be my shuttle captain. N'Athena, isn't it?"

Could this mild, balding gentleman be the same person that sent Thomas into shivering stupidity? Cleis did not show her surprise. With a military informality that few planets allowed, she refrained from saluting and stiffly extended her hand. "Assemblyman, Military Governor Balawick Haladay?"

Behind him the men stirred, disquieted at the seemingly disrespectful greeting. He grinned. "Hush there, boys." He winked conspiratorially at the young Amazon. "This is a n'Athena. Can't stand on high'n'protocol when we're around royalty now, can we?"

Backs straightened and a nod or two of apology were directed her way. Cleis fought to hide her smile.

"How soon can we be under way? My baggage is all right in here." He gestured with the pipe in his hand at an ancient leather briefcase.

"We can depart immediately, if you like."

"Splendid." He turned and shook hands with a few men, muttering instructions and last minute details. His quiet, cheerful manner bemused Cleis as he disentangled himself from the party quickly.

He was a renowned enough figure to be recognized by several of the militia corps as well as the lounging civilian travelers as they walked the length of the station. But with his quiet, smiling demeanor, Balawick Haladay merely waved his pipe or tipped his head in acknowledgement and continued on. A diplomat, Cleis decided as she admired his amiable ability to keep the people at bay. He was considerably less self-centered than most officials, she conceded — at least outwardly.

Cleis reminded herself that men usually came to be involved with the Sisterhood because of something in their pasts they needed to hide — something politically or personally so sordid that to have it come to the public's awareness would mean instant ruin. And always the closeted ghosts dealt with the traumatic abuse of women. No matter how pleasant Governor Haladay appeared, she needed to remember that somewhere — sometime he had been charged and found guilty by dey Sorormin and to this day was still held accountable.

As she waved him into the shuttle craft, he said, "I do apologize for the crassness of my companions." He followed her forward into the control cabin, quite matter-of-factly settling himself into the empty co-pilot's chair. "They've unfortunately had a very limited exposure to the Sisterhood out here. I admit, they are sorely lacking in basic manners. I do hope you didn't mind my little royalty ploy there. I assure you, I meant no offense. Nobility is about the closest concept they've got to your Sisters' shared esteem."

Cleis busied herself with her pre-flight check. Flattery and truth were too easily mixed, but she had to acknowledge that there was some truth to his words. By imperial standards, dey Sarormin did attempt to endow a 'royal status' on each of their daughters — those qualities of personal respect and treasured esteem. A pity, actually, that the Empire was so tied into ambitious values and hierarchy.

He did not seem to mind her lack of reply as he sighed and sank back into the deeply padded seat. His eyes were bright with an almost boyish pleasure as he pocketed his eternally unlit pipe and watched the console of lights and levers before him. "I do so love flight decks." Cleis could not help a small smile.

Launch and initial trajectory were accomplished smoothly. Her fingers flicked the autopilot on, and she triple-checked coordinates and their re-entry position.

The stars glittered. Cleis could see that he was enraptured by the velvety expanse; this majesty clearly touched his soul. It reassured her and confused her.

He pulled his wire-rimmed glasses free, cleaning them with his handkerchief. Cleis did not miss the hasty swipe across his eyes as he murmured, "Always takes me by surprise." The glasses awkwardly returned to their place, and he smiled. "Didn't mean to keep you waiting."

"No..." She couldn't prevent the warmth of reassurance from creeping into her voice. "...you didn't."

"Yes? Good then." He relaxed and cleared his throat. "I did want the opportunity to run over a few things with you. I realize I'm a poor partner for this sort of venture, but I'll do my best not to raise suspicions."

Cleis held her breath, suddenly mistrusting him again.

"The background Cara forwarded to me is all in place." He pulled his briefcase up, unsnapping the thick strap. His movements belied his age — quick, efficient and not in the least clumsy. She suspected the mind behind this pleasant exterior was no less clumsy.

"N'Sappho," he read triumphantly. "Elana n'Sappho — the papers are in order, and there shouldn't be any traceable connection. I had my personal secretary enter it all directly — after hours. He's quite reliable, and I pulled the entire thing up to double-check for holes before leaving. No one should be able to link her with any planet of origin save your own. Even if Baily gets suspicious, he won't find evidence to support anything out of the ordinary."

Her dark eyes narrowed. In a galactic border quadrant spies were generally numerous, and it was not all that unusual to forge entry documents or scramble assignment dates.

"Please now, don't take offense." His smile faded to an expression of gentle reassurance, and quietly he explained, "There have been several of these

requests passed across my desk in the last decade. I am not entirely blind to the
implications.

"What I need from you," he continued, pulling his pipe out now that
they were safely under way, "is an idea of what your Commander Baily is like.
I've never met the man personally. Is he apt to make trouble over this? Is he
going to buy the idea that this Sister has been down on Aggar for some three
years?"

The tension in her lower back eased. Fleetingly she was grateful for the
rib belt as she realized how tight the muscles had become. She didn't need to
shift that rib out here. "Thomas Baily is not overly creative, but he abides by the
regulations well enough."

"The man is obviously overwhelmed — beyond his competence," he
muttered, reading between her phrases well. "How nasty does he get?"

"He has a great respect for your authority."

Merriment lit his bespectacled eyes, coaxing half a smile from her. "I'll
try not to intimidate him too much."

They laughed together at that, and Cleis decided, against her better
judgment, that she liked this Balawick Haladay. "Actually, Thomas is already
nervous about your arrival. When I left him, he was pulling up your classifieds
on Elana."

"It seems as if he bought the three year story then?"

"Somewhat," she admitted, warily. "He has a habit of prioritizing the
depot functions and neglecting the cultural-political details."

"Dangerous habit so close to the edge." The Governor chewed
thoughtfully on his pipe. "I'll take a look at his files more closely when I get
home. I already have my suspicions. Garrison was right on schedule when he hit
this solar system. I think it a bit odd that he wasn't hauled in by the orbital crews
before he hit atmosphere."

Cleis shrugged noncommittally. As much as she detested Thomas, she
was not about to accuse him of something she had no knowledge about.

"What you're telling me is that Baily is too nervous about his own
efficiency to contradict anything that has my approval on it, even if he is
suspicious?"

"As it stands."

"How about you and — Diana n'Athena? What kind of relationship do
you supposedly have to this Elana n'Sappho?"

"I'm to have met her once. When she came down, I did an initial
orientation before she went out solo — "

"That was supposedly because Baily was on Crigil III, right?"

"Yes." He was prepared, Cleis thought. "At the moment, Diana is
working with her to bring Garrison in. I already accused Thomas of setting Elana
up with Diana intentionally — perhaps by your orders. Diana did not meet Elana
at orientation."

He nodded, clearly shifting facts and possibilities. "The story must be
plausible — and simple is usually best. I will admit I did not intentionally order
her to go after Garrison — that's too recent a development. Baily would expect to

have records of some sort of message relay. But I'll agree that she was supposed to get close to this Council of Ten here and to use her position to the best advantage of the Empire. It ought to be obvious even to a military man that after this escapade she'll need to come in. Her cover will be too shaky to risk further exposure."

Cleis nodded, pleased with his logic.

"She'll report to me for debriefing." He closed the file and locked it away. "Not to Baily — reasons classified. I'll mutter something about an information leak and have him update his security checks — that ought to distract him."

His cheerful smile returned. "I do hope your Sister n'Athena will include the pertinent details from this woman's experience in her own reports?"

"I'm sure she will...as always." They both knew Amazons were notoriously lax in recording details, even if equally notorious in accomplishing the impossible.

"I'll assure Baily that n'Sappho's report will be made out during her journey home and that my agent will rendezvous with her on Shekhina."

"Fair enough."

"No hope of that actually coming off, eh?"

She grinned. "Difficult to say."

"Didn't think so. Sometimes Cara surprises me with a concession, so I ask."

Cleis didn't know Cara personally, although she was undoubtedly the Sister charged with watching Haladay. That reminder disturbed her.

Haladay's smile faded. "I seldom see the woman. She's not so abused in having to keep track of me."

"No," Cleis felt her heart harden, "she wouldn't allow that from any man."

He suddenly looked much older as memories shadowed his eyes. "No, she wouldn't. I am eternally sorry others were not as strong."

Cleis was surprised and yet unyielding before his apparent remorse.

He tapped the edge of his pipe and sighed, drawing himself back. "I'm a bit different from your usual male recruit, you know."

Cleis said nothing.

He seemed to be speaking to the stars. "All my life I have worked for humanity. All my life I've stood beside the forgotten factions — always working to draw this vast Empire into a consciousness of its own interdependency. How desperately we need each other, how delicate the balance, how idiotic dominance and force!"

A dry, bitter laugh echoed. "And the boy I spawned...what did he become? The very epitome of all I fought. An insatiable, brutal youth who has crushed everything his hand touched."

He shook his head. "I will always carry my child's horrors as mine. I was too busy with my worldly concern to give him the emotional help he needed. We avoided and delayed and hoped he would grow beyond it all. He didn't.

"Covering for him — buying him out of trouble became a habit. If he hadn't died that night, I would have deserved every public accusation your Sisters threatened to heap upon us. Because of my neglect of the problem I am just as responsible for those women dying...and just as responsible for those he mistreated before that night. I was ignorant, but no less guilty. At some level, I knew he was capable of it — or it wouldn't have seemed so credible when your Sisters told me of his games...of his death."

His breath drew unevenly, but the hands that cradled the pipe were steady. "My son Dixon was dead. There was little that could done for those tormented other than knowing that, but there was much to be done to aid those still seeking safety. I was glad they suggested a way to make amends — of a sort. There will never be an end to the Dixons of this universe. But perhaps there will be an end to our blindness to their deeds."

Her hand squeezed his gently. But she held little hope.

Chapter Six

A faint smile softened the curve of Elana's mouth as she watched Di'nay's half-submerged figure. Eyes closed against the weariness of the march, her Amazon sat in the steaming mineral pool, absorbing the subtle peace of Aggar. The water rippled with foaming lines that seemed to mirror the shimmering, opal-like veins of the cavern walls. A muted florescence filled the endless winding chambers, and the steadying warmth of the hot spring was a tangible touch of the stone's cradle. The frothing waters were completely undrinkable; their mineral content was too high for human consumption. But the healing powers drew upon the strength of the raw lifestones, and Elana had watched the strained hunch of Di'nay's shoulders ease beneath the bubbling waters.

"Are you coming back in?"

Di'nay's eyes did not open, and Elana wondered again at the calm acceptance Di'nay had for her Sight. She drew near the pool's edge and finished her thought aloud. "The Mistress would be chastising me if I 'shouted' so at her."

"Oh? Are you so much gentler with me then?"

A whimsical expression brushed across her face as Elana sat, slipping her feet back into the steaming waters. "We have had our differences."

Diana laughed, remembering the cavern at Cellar's Gate. She came across the pool and, standing near, tugged on Elana's pale ankles. "Come in?"

"I don't need to." Her breath caught then as she felt Di'nay's gaze drift across her shoulders and breasts. Lovingly those brown eyes devoured her, searching for the vanquished bruises, and Elana realized the healing auras had reached into her own soul too. She felt nothing but warmth and desire at her Amazon's appraisal...and pride that she could still draw the wanting from her lover.

But need took a different form this time as Diana moved between Elana's strong thighs, wrapping her arms around Elana's waist. Her cheek pressed into the smoothness of her lover's stomach as the barest of sighs crossed her lips.

Tenderness swept through her as Elana held Di'nay near, relishing this rare show of vulnerability. She bent and kissed the damp, brown hair.

"Have I thanked you for yesterday?" The murmur was low and muffled.

Elana's hair, silky and clean, moved around them as she shook her head. "There is no need. You have done much the same for me."

"That doesn't lessen my gratitude," Diana returned, tightening her grasp briefly. "The fears were not as bad as when I was caught on the cliffs waiting for you —"

"You knew I would come, yes?"

A nod — satiny skin against satiny skin. "I did not doubt it. But the darkness and cramped space brought back other memories."

"Yes." Elana's touch was gentle on her face. "It felt as if you had gone very far away to a very isolated place."

Undisturbed, Diana nodded again; the balm of the raw lifestones had touched this too. "I had gone back to the mining accident of my childhood. But last night in the tunnels, it was different."

"You were not alone." Elana's quiet voice held no surprise.

Diana drew away a bit and looked up into the blue depths of her lover's eyes. "I realize you do not have to share your strength with me, Elana. I am grateful when you do." A slightly rueful smile lightened their exchange as their gazes shifted. "It seems I have rather abused your gift on this journey."

Elana laughed tenderly, pushing a stray hair back from Di'nay's forehead as she too thought of the cucarri. But Di'nay's eyes were compelling, searching her expression with an intensity that quieted Elana. With a single finger, she traced the faint lines of concentration at the corner of that silent mouth. "You must ask me the question, Di'nay. I cannot guess your meaning clearly enough."

"Will you tell me something?"

Di'nay's amarin was clutching desperately for honesty, and Elana watched her closely. "I have always answered what I could."

Di'nay absorbed that for a moment, and Elana added, "I will say if I cannot."

Finally — uncertainly, Diana asked, "Are you happy being with me?"

"Yes." It was a quiet, unfaltering response, but not enough, Elana sensed. She waited, needing to understand this strange mood before rushing in with assurances.

"Can you tell me why?"

Why? Elana's brow furrowed with her puzzlement.

The warmth of Diana's palms moved to grasp her waist, drawing Elana back from her confusion. "What is good for you in this? — our relationship."

"You are." Elana quickly grabbed Di'nay's wrists as the woman's frustration threatened to separate them. With a sudden motion she caught Di'nay's face between her hands, lifting the startled gaze to meet hers. Beneath the Sight Di'nay grew still. For an instant panic receded as Elana grasped the intent in her words. "You mean what do we share that is special to me?"

Diana felt disoriented as she nodded. She wondered if it was from the withdrawal of the soft blueness or the warm hands.

"Your respect...your..." Elana faltered. Di'nay had never spoken directly of love.

"The Mistress gave you as much."

"No...or perhaps it is the combination of respect with acceptance."

She felt Di'nay begin to withdraw. Elana realized these things were uncommon for the women of Aggar but not within the Sisterhood. Any one of Di'nay's House would grant her as much. She shook her head, finding words were difficult. "Yes, your Sisters would give some of this, but it is different."

With a sudden inspiration, Elana reminded her, "You have always said my Sight's call never irritates you. You speak of it as a gift. Would your Sisters be as completely at ease with me as a lover?"

Diana understood again how alienated this woman had often felt. But to her the gift was a part of Elana that she treasured dearly and would never wish to be deprived of.

"You are not merely my friend, Di'nay. You cherish me as I am. You support me when I falter. You praise me when I succeed. I am what I am meant to be when I am with you...that is your gift — your gentle strength that I draw upon."

Diana laid the back of her hand against Elana's cheek. "Thank you," she whispered. "I have worried about taking too much without giving anything in return."

"Have you forgotten Maltar's prisons? Or Colmar after the birthings? How can you say you have not given me anything?" And disbelief grew to anger — anger that Di'nay could so belittle her own worth. "How dare — how could you be so blind?"

"Not blind," Diana assured her simply. "Merely frightened."

That stopped her, and Elana felt the sharp pain of their parting descend. Di'nay's mouth moved to speak again, but Elana hushed her with trembling fingers — too quick for a sound to be uttered.

"No," Elana said gently. "At Melysa's I said I was not ready to lose you. It was no less true as I followed our bondstone to find you in the bluffs. It was true for you too as you searched the passages of the Priory — I will always be ashamed that I did not think of your coming until I saw you and Eitteh standing there undecided, staring at your sword. But that was death, Di'nay, and we would never be prepared to knowingly lose each other to death. Yet I am prepared to see you go...and I swear to you, I would not trade one day of what we share for anything. I would not change you. I would not change us."

"And if I chose not to leave?" Diana probed tentatively.

She was incredibly still. Then the saddest of smiles grew on her lips. She shook her head slowly, kindly. "You would always be welcomed, but...."

"But?"

"My world is not yours. You would wither and die here on Aggar, my dearest Di'nay. I would be no match for the isolation that would grow, and...," the pain was clear in her voice, "...I could not bear to watch you be destroyed like that."

Your world. Always the assumption of staying in your world. Why do you make it so hard to ask? Diana cried silently. Is it because you fear the questions so much? Is it because you truly fear a lifetime with me? Or do you hurt so much just thinking about leaving that you can't bear talking about it?

Elana's lips were warm as they touched hers, easing the choked tension that was threatening to bring them both to tears. Their bodies sought comfort in their unspoken love, and urgency usurped gentleness. With eyes closed, they ran from their words. Elana's legs clasped about Diana's back, her hand possessively slipping behind Diana's head, and the Amazon's arms wound high to bring Elana lower as she urged Elana's lips to part. Diana's frustrations — her vulnerability — felt raw and reflected in the unfamiliar height Elana's position gave her. Desperately she clung, surrendering her fears in blind trust, and Elana's legs tightened in response.

Breath turned ragged as wet mouths broke free to devour flushed faces. Skin browned and heated beneath urgent caresses, and gasping, Elana pulled Diana's mouth back to hers. Plunging, giving — igniting the very core of Diana's center, and the panicked fuse sizzled, flaming into white passion.

In this passion the fear evaporated and with it Diana's neediness, leaving a hunger to share, not to take. Her breath sighed as she drew Elana even deeper, and her hands loosened, finding the steam-moistened skin smoothed like silk beneath her fingers. Against her breasts she felt Elana's heart pound in response, and her palms stroked the long lines of legs and back. She used her body to caress the shuddering figure wrapped around her. As her fingers drifted into the small space between them — following the tensed, brown thigh — the hands that had imprisoned her face sought her shoulders.

With a gasp mouths tore apart as Elana arched suddenly, Diana's fingertips slipping into velvety places. A single arm encircled Elana, supporting her...holding her from escape...pressing her forward into those caressing fingers. And Diana's mouth found a taut, darkened nipple.

Frenzied, tormented ecstasy drove her, and Elana moaned at the swollen, aching sweetness. Fingers teased, tantalizing her even as Di'nay's lips coaxed shivering, silver trails from her breasts.

She shook with the intensity of her clamoring senses, and her hands pushed at the shoulders in their grasp. Pushed and separated the hot mouth from her breast, but she could not say if she had wanted that. And she groaned as the moist, long fingers began to slow. Her head shook, not knowing what she needed, and she felt Di'nay's arm loosen, allowing her to lie back and find the ground. Her legs trembled as Di'nay guided them from her waist to her shoulders, and suddenly frightened that her lover would step back beyond all reach, Elana's legs tightened convulsively, her hands groping blindly.

Words came...Sororian phrases. Hands met her hands. Lips turned to the fine hair along the inside of her thighs, and her legs eased their anxious clasp. The words drew her further on as always, and her body moved beyond that driving, shuddering need to a hot, blazing ache that seared the soles of her feet and steadied the beat of her heart.

A gentle trail of kisses was broken by teeth that lightly tugged on the fine hairs. Warm breath sank into thicker hair, and Elana's body was paralyzed. Lips lifted and words drifted to her. Her breathing started only to stop again at the softest touch of touches.

Dear Mother...she had not dreamed of this...and then she was rising, pushing into the sweetest stroking.

Diana moaned her name in pleasure and dove into the depths of her lover. She thought she might be lost forever in the honeydew scent and taste.

The trembling drew her by surprise, and Diana's tongue returned to the swollen bud, soothing...coaxing...in that last minute, drawing Elana higher beneath her stroking touch.

With a shuddering gasp Elana arched — her body quivering...strong, full waves that washed the tension from her muscles...thought from her mind. The tender tongue gentled as the caressing warmth within spread, filling her hollowed shell of tissue and bone.

Diana sighed, feeling the release in Elana's grasping hands. With a selfish tenderness, she buried herself in the sweet moistness.

Elana smiled, touching a hand to Di'nay's head. This was her love, dearest Mother. There was not a thing in this world she would deny Di'nay...with a sudden gasp her hand stiffened, silver-white flames licking out again. The gasp became a groan, and arching, she found herself pressing upwards, urging Di'nay's mouth to begin again.

No, there was nothing she would deny either of them.

❋ ❋ ❋

The world glowed with a diffuse light while dark blotches swirled recklessly. What sickening, complicated patterns, he thought. The pain in his head forced his eyes shut again; the black spots only became white ones and continued on their careless way. It must have been one hell of a crash.

A low voice murmured somewhere, and he heard footsteps approaching from his right. As a reflex his eyes flew open, turning towards the sound. The pain stabbed sharply and sent his body trembling. He caught a glimpse of a tall figure kneeling down, but then everything turned into a senseless whirl.

"If you can manage these, it will help your head." The words were in Common.

He forced himself to look again. The figure was oddly dressed in a loose-fitting shirt and an animal leather vest of some sort dyed in green. But the expression on the wind-tanned face was carefully neutral as the brown gaze peered at him. He closed his eyes a minute against the unaccustomed strain of using his vision and tried to think. He couldn't even clearly remember the quadrant he'd been in. This person spoke Common easily enough, but there was too little accent to identify a particular world or corporation. He wasn't even certain if he was dealing with a man or a woman.

"I am Diana n'Athena," the voice reached out to him again. "You are on Charlie IV, ATB.7-1000. Do you remember? Your ship was fleeing the border patrols and you were headed to the base. You were stationed here a while back."

"Aggar Planet," he muttered, wincing at the way the words pounded through his skull. "Priority Redfire — must talk to the Commander."

"It's been done." A hand moved beneath his head and lifted.

He accepted the pills and water that were pushed between his lips. Anything to lessen this splintering laser light in his head. But it was good to lie flat again.

"Thanks." It was a hoarse sound, he thought, but he was grateful. The ground seemed firmer under him after a moment, and the hand stayed, gripping his shoulder comfortingly.

The words slowly made sense to him then, and his eyes flickered open. He was surprised to find his vision clearer.

"Give the meds a few minutes to work before you try to move."

At last! he thought, then pulled his wits together. "Baily knows?"

"The Chairman probably knows by now too," Diana assured him.

"How...?" His voice seemed to be growing fainter, but he was confused. Who else had he been talking to? He couldn't remember.

"You've been out for a very long time," Diana explained, speaking slowly. "We are taking you back to base. Don't worry, you didn't say anything to anybody that made sense. The locals don't speak your language, remember?"

"Yeah, non-tech." He did remember. The tension in his stomach relaxed a bit, and he found exhaustion was overwhelming him.

The hand on his shoulder squeezed as his eyes slid shut. "Sleep now. You'll need it."

And as the pain receded he welcomed the calm.

❋ ❋ ❋

Elana looked at Garrison closely. He was lithe and well-built for all of his skinniness. Although he was somewhat shorter than Di'nay, he wasn't unusually small for a man of her planet. His dark hair was beginning to thin on top, and he had a beard that grew thick and straight. Save for his amarin and that beard, Elana thought he looked fairly typical for those in the Ramains.

He would be conscious in a few moments, she knew, and because of the healing powers of the raw lifestones, he would find himself in much stronger shape than he had upon his first wakening. She had agreed with Di'nay, however, that the less he knew of the happenings at the Priory, the less awkward it would be for everyone. Neither of them particularly wanted the Empire to know of the Blue Sight, and any reports mentioning the locals' dubious use of imperial technology would only stir suspicions of military rebellions. So Garrison would be told nothing of either. Enslaved and drugged to ensure compliance would be the story — anything else he would have to remember himself, and Elana knew that the effects of the Blue Sight would only allow him to recall the fantasy of his imperial workshop. And that would doubtless be remembered as awkward dreams.

She looked at him, smiling; he did not strike her as the type who would freely admit to having hallucinations. He was about fourteen or fifteen seasons, she guessed, much younger than Di'nay. But then they were nothing alike, if her brief glimpse into his mind had said anything. Egotistical, she remembered — quick, bright and very conscious of it. Well, she supposed those were qualities for a good spy — one had better stay a step ahead of others or one would tend to get hurt.

She sighed shortly and looked at the material in her hands. Her breeches had been exchanged for her skirt as she had decided to take the opportunity to mend the torn side seams. She was suddenly less certain about her choice. She glanced down the tunnel that led to the lava pits and wished Di'nay would hurry back. Sometimes her Amazon's curiosity was not well-timed. Aside from the fact that Garrison was a man and she was not feeling very comfortable in being alone with men in general, not since the beatings by Maltar's soldiers — she was not terribly certain that her Common was going to be sufficient, although she had been practicing with Di'nay these past few days. It only made matters worse that Garrison was an off-worlder; she had never particularly cared for off-worlders.

He was also an intruder. She well understood that the intimacy which she shared with Di'nay would have to change to accommodate this new person. That certainly did not predispose her to like him. It would have been nice, she thought wistfully, if he had been another Amazon.

"Hello there."

She turned to face him, absently noting that he had a pleasant smile despite the rather ragged growth of his beard.

He propped himself up on an elbow, his smile broadening into an appreciative grin as he took in the long, loose hair and her skirt. "Well, you certainly don't look like an n'Athena Amazon."

"Looks can be deceiving," Elana returned icily, taking up her sewing again. His amarin had been friendly enough, but his tone had carried an overconfidence she didn't like. It did not help that she would have been flattered and not insulted if he had mistaken her for one of the Sisterhood — and Di'nay had said not to tell him different. Still, they were going to spend a great deal of time together over the next ten-day. Reluctantly, she softened her tone. "If you'd like to try a bath, the hot springs will help the soreness. The water's no good for drinking, though, so be careful."

"Is there drink? And food?" His tone was polite but edged with gnawing desperation and Elana felt a guilty twinge. He was literally half-starved.

"There is only cold meat," she said gently, putting aside her mending. "Water is rationed." Elana lay the meat plate down beside him before uncapping the waterskin. "There are two more days of walking before we leave these rocks."

He accepted the half-cup gratefully. She left him her small dagger before moving back to her sewing.

"How many in 'we'?" Garrison asked as he clumsily bit into the dry meat.

"Three. You, I and Di'nay."

"And you are?"

"Elana."

"You have an unusual accent." He tried another bite, and decided this primitive stuff wasn't so bad at that. "You don't use Common much?"

She did look at him then, wondering why he was doing so much talking when all he was interested in was the food. "There are great number of other languages, Lieutenant. Why don't you simply enjoy your meal?"

"It's Paul, everyone calls me Paul. So, tell me, where's the Amazon?"

"Di'nay is out exploring."

"And you?"

He was deceptively shallow, Elana realized. Because he tended to think as nonchalantly as he spoke she found his auras did not indicate his curiosities well. But at this moment, she did not doubt that he cared more for himself than for most other things, including herself.

"I am trying to work." She lifted the garment as proof.

"No, about the Amazon. How'd you end up with her?"

"I am with her, if that is what you ask," she returned coldly. She had about as much intention of explaining the Council or Di'nay's background to him as she did of returning to Maltar's reign. But she had been right, he didn't actually care much one way or the other.

He looked regretfully at the rest of the meat before pushing it away. "Is there any soap? Don't suppose there's a chance you gals have a razor or a mirror around, is there?"

She looked at him sharply, concentrating — grasping for meaning around the unfamiliar words. But he was fingering his beard thoughtfully, and it didn't take much to realize what he wanted. "The knife will have to do," she answered slowly, setting aside the trousers again. "I believe we have a glass." She thought Di'nay's first aid kit had carried a smaller one.

"And soap?" He rose, wiping the little dagger clean on his thigh. He looked around the small scattering of supplies. "Oh, you've got a cake by the pool."

Elana handed him the mirror and he smiled charmingly, bowing slightly. "Thank you, Elana."

She returned his formality with a tip of her head, but found herself almost smiling. "You are welcome — Paul."

His brown eyes lit with delight at his name. He would get her to thaw out yet! There was absolutely no reason why they couldn't get along. After all, not all of the Empire's men were so bad — and it felt so good to be alive. He figured he could do just about anything — starting with a real bath. Now, if he could just have had a thick, polyvit steak and a beer — everything would have been perfect.

❋ ❋ ❋

Diana accepted the cup of tea from Paul as he joined her near the outskirts of the fire's light. The flickering shadows hid his clean-shaven face, but the stiffness of his gait attested to his soreness.

"It's been a hell of a long time since I've done the hand-to-hand stuff...for real, I mean." His tone was derisive, and as he sat down he sighed, disgusted with himself. "My clumsiness almost cost us."

A disbelieving grunt greeted him in return, and Diana sat up a little straighter against the rough-barked tree. Her eyes turned back to the night's depths as she reminded him, "It's like docking a shuttle. If you succeed, it was a good maneuver. If you don't, nothing much matters any more."

"You believe that?"

She took a long, slow breath and thought it over. The two scouts had only been one pair of dozens scouring the forested foothills of the South Ridge. Slipping past the lot of them undetected would have been possible only if Elana had used her Sight, but that would have alerted the old Seer to the fact that they were indeed out of the Path's stony depths. By tomorrow the hawker would have brought word and they would have been in even more trouble. So they had run a bluff — side-tracking east and then west again so that their trail looked as if it had originated in Black Falls and not in the heights of the Ridge. Then, rather than avoiding a party, they had taken the offensive. Like a batch of roaming thieves they had attacked, leaving the pair of soldiers unconscious while raiding their possessions. There had been relatively little bloodshed for a change. That had been a relief to both Elana and herself. They were growing more and more tired of death and intrigue.

She looked at the silent man in front of her again. And she remembered his adroit disarming of the soldier's knife. He had done well considering his lack of preparations. She smiled encouragingly. "Yes, I do believe it went fairly well. It was my fault in not warning you that the men of Aggar always carry hand daggers in addition to their hunting knives. You did well to throw him. I am sorry about your arm."

He shrugged, feeling better at her reassurance. He had in fact, felt clumsy only because of Diana's quickness in rescuing him. She'd dispatched the first man with amazing ease and then had not hesitated to knock the second unconscious as Paul wrestled with the soldier.

"Did Elana redress your wound for you?"

He flexed his arm. "Barely even hurts. She has a nice touch. I want to thank you for bailing me out with that guy." Paul examined a blistered hand intently. He had collected firewood this evening, and the hot, heavy wield of Diana's sword had not been much to his liking. "I mean, I am grateful and all."

Diana chuckled lightly. "It's been one of the lesser feats of this trip, believe me."

"Still," he swallowed awkwardly, "with Elana watching and everything—"

"She would have stepped in, if I'd not been able to," Diana pointed out quietly. "She's much more talented than you credit her."

"Well, sure — yeah. I mean — but the whole point to her hanging back was not to be recognized — her hair 'n all — right?"

Her eyes narrowed and Diana agreed, disquieted, "Right." Males, she thought tiredly, but she couldn't bring herself to be too upset. He had adjusted well. Being the odd man out was not a role that he was accustomed to. His openness in helping with camp chores without being asked and his seemingly respectful distance that allowed her to snatch a moment or two of Elana's time were points in his favor.

She said, "Don't feel too bad. She's not your typical guide."

"She is something special. You trained her well. You can tell just by the way she tracks through these woods."

"Not me," Diana corrected. It was odd to be sitting here discussing Elana with a Terran male!

"Oh." Paul looked at her in confusion, "I thought — never mind." He shook his head dubiously, not wanting to look like he was intruding despite his curiosity.

"Yes, she is well-trained," Diana amended. "Just not by me."

He nodded thoughtfully, his eyes drawn toward the figure in the firelight with hair a dark cloak hiding her face as she bent over her medicine purse. He was aware of the Amazon's silent scrutiny as he asked, trying to keep on the casual note, "Have you two been together long?"

"Long enough."

Her evasion was not lost. Paul looked back to his companion, his curiosity mounting. "She calls you something else — Di'nay?"

"It is the name I use here on Aggar. She happens to like it."

"Does she speak the local dialect then?"

Diana answered truthfully, "Elana is proficient in many languages. Without her, I might never have found you simply because of the language barriers."

It seemed, Paul thought, that they must be very newly partnered. Perhaps even just for this occasion? He looked out into the forests and commented, "I've noticed she seems less comfortable with Common."

Diana carefully chose her next words. "Little need to use it around here. And as with me, it is not her first tongue."

He jumped on that. "Your native language is hers too?"

"Actually we share several."

"That's good — nice, I mean." He didn't even know the names of the languages Amazons used — not many did. But he had never met an Amazon that looked anything remotely like Elana, and he found himself wondering if maybe she wasn't one. If the two of them had not been together long...anything was possible.

"We have a lot to do tomorrow," Diana reminded him quietly. She appreciated the way he seemed to respect the tacit limits she set, but was uneasy at his silences. Perhaps she was overly sensitive. It had been a long day for all of them.

"Yes." His grin was charming. "Sleep would be a good idea. Well, good-night Diana. Again — thanks."

"Save it 'til you see the base."

After he left Diana sighed and settled her cloak more securely around her. Above the early moon was rising and the silvery threads of her light began to lace down through the trees. A beautiful night for romance, she mused with a faint stir of disappointment. The garden at the Keep would be enchanting. She thought of standing beside the low wall, the moonlight shimmering across the forested depths below. She thought of standing there with her arms entwined about Elana as the two of them peacefully waited for the midnight moon to appear — time to be together without the press of the mission, of Maltar's men, and without the awkward, stumbling assumptions of their initial misunderstandings.

At the last, Diana laughed at herself. Did such assumptions ever really disappear? Or did they merely get exchanged for another set as you went along? Misunderstandings were part of love and life. Perhaps it was growing to handle them with some degree of trust that made love so sweet...then theirs was growing to be very sweet indeed.

❄ ❄ ❄

Chapter Seven

No!

The word rang through her mind. Gloved fingers clenched and mortar crumbled. Frustration hissed from her lips as Cleis jerked her hands away from the garden's wall. She trembled with anger, and with a curse, slapped her hands down hard on the gray stone.

No. Not a rider to spare — not a single horseman to send. No!

Council and Empire did not mix. How many times had she heard Thomas say that in her eight years here? How many times had she winced at that blind, prejudicial statement? But there was truth in the words to be sure. Too many centuries of mistrust — too many centuries of bitterness had passed, and cooperation was still never more than tentative.

Ann Nehna?! The Council had demanded a role in this venture! They — not the Empire — had assigned a Council guide. And now — now they blithely, calmly denied any further support. Didn't give a second thought about either woman!

"There are always alternatives to an aggressive stance."

She snapped around, cloak flying.

The dark robes of the Old Mistress rustled as her hands sank into hidden pockets, and having announced herself, the woman moved forward again. Her gray eyes serenely met Cleis' blazing gaze. The Mistress smiled.

"Meanwhile you allow your agent to be killed." She did not try to hide the sharpness in her voice. Cleis was not about to pretend she understood.

The old woman took a seat on the garden's stone bench. "Our agent — your agent — definitions are so vague."

"Death is not. Neither is the threat of it."

The elder nodded. "Sometimes quite true."

They faced each other in silence, the air stretched thin with the tension. Then, with a sigh, Cleis leaned back. The cold stones' solidity reminded her of the Goddess' stoic patience. This woman would not be here if her pleas had gone completely unheard. Perhaps it was again time to listen.

"I do not understand, Mistress," Cleis began in a softer voice, "why is it the Council cared so much that they sent a guide with Di'nay, and yet now they care so little to have her safe return?"

"It is not a question of concern for either woman," the old one answered quietly. "It is a question of diplomacy. You — and your commander — have come here to ask that we of the Keep use our influence to gather a force to ride to Gronday in preparation for battle."

"As escort," Cleis amended quickly. "We are not searching for battles of any kind. We need only to be able to defend ourselves if the need arises."

Levelly the gray eyes held hers. "In truth, Amazon?"

With a short sigh Cleis shook her head again. "I do not know."

"Fair enough." The Mistress shifted and offered Cleis the seat beside her.

The Amazon declined. She was too weary just yet to court peace.

"Your proposition has presented the Council with two difficulties. First, our role has always been one of mediation here on Aggar. We have always urged reform by mediation. We do not, by principle, ever leave the territory of this fortress with a military force. We tend to travel only in pairs or trios."

"Doesn't that place you a little beyond the mortal scheme of things?"

"Perhaps." The Mistress' tone was biting. "But it appears to have its advantages. There is only one Terran base."

Cleis nodded. "Granted."

"Even if we of the Council acknowledge raising your escort as a single incident, there are tribes who would not. We risk setting new precedents. The balance would be threatened. Power corrupts, as your people have often reminded us. Do you grasp the repercussions we might be courting?"

"Yes, there is more at stake here than three lives."

"If we do as you ask, we could appear to be a threat to the Terran Empire. Now we are considered harmless, despite our proximity to the galactic border and our ambivalent truce with the Empire. How will your Terran leaders take it if we can respond so quickly to this threat today? Might we not strike equally as quickly against your base at another time? Perhaps in a crucial time, when the Alliance is under attack? Perhaps we bide our time until the opportunity is ripe? Perhaps we await only the proper moment to drive you from our soil?"

"Why would you not?"

A dry chuckle came from the Mistress. "It would be foolishness on our part. At best, those across the borders would claim Aggar, and an intergalactic battle would begin all over again. At worst, either — or both — sides would annihilate life in this solar system. We have no wish for either outcome. We want to develop our cultures — our planet — within our own codes of ethics. We do not wish to adopt your problems along with your technology."

Cleis found herself agreeing even if it hurt to know Diana and her companions were still left unaided.

"But remember. There are always alternatives. There is the recourse of abandoning the River Road altogether...?"

"At what price?" Cleis snapped back, her temper flaming again. "What would Council spies gain with such a detour? If the scouts identify us, there are

leagues of undefendable tracks that would force us to outride them — if we can!
And then? Then they are led to the Unseen Wall! Treaty forbids we take any of
Aggar with us into the base. Yet you would have Diana ride into the base at full
gallop with men of Aggar driving behind? Just how long do you think it would
take for the another tribal lord of Aggar to come searching for the Terran base?
Then where would your precious balance be, Mistress? How would you curb the
jealousies and suspicions?"

A faint smile of amusement at the passions of youth hovered on the
thin lips of the old woman. "So you have not suggested such a plan to your
Commander?"

"Certainly not."

The Mistress came closer. "What would you advise him to do,
Amazon, now that you know the delicacy of all our positions?"

Cleis sighed. "I will tell him to withdraw the request."

"For what reason?"

"I will tell him we would not be able to trust our backs to such
comrades."

The elder nodded. She had no doubts the man would believe that
rationale. The Old Mistress turned to face the forested depths beyond the stone
wall, her hand sinking into the folds of her robe. "Send Commander Baily home
alone, Amazon. Travel to Gronday by horseback. Say it would be advantageous
to ride this route before you must defend it. That would be helpful, would it
not?"

Shrewdly Cleis' eyes narrowed. "It is always good to know the kind of
land one must race across."

"We could supply you with horse and gear. We have some very good
animals here, as you may know. There is one in particular that Elana — your
Amazon's shadow-guide — trained herself. You might like the mare...?"

"I'm certain I would."

"Perhaps too, you would find the road interesting from an instructors'
point of view." The Old Mistress raised her brows. "I understand that you have
trained a good many of the Commander's agents here on Aggar?"

"A few."

"Then I suggest you pay particular attention to the bridge crossing at the
gorge. It sits just this side of the river junction. It is a long morning's ride from
here — about a third of the way to Gronday."

"I believe I know of the place."

"Good." The Mistress nodded approvingly, walking away as she added,
"It is a common practice sight for my trainees — quite a good place to teach
defense strategies." She paused, glancing back. "A very good training ground,
don't you think?"

"Yes..." Cleis' heart was beginning to pound, "...a very good one."

A smile touched the lines of her face. The Mistress knew they
understood one another. She left the gardens to turn her attention to the Master.
Formalities were to be observed...but doubtless he would be as eager as she for
Elana's safe return. If she could gain his agreement to this 'training venture,' then

they would not need to consult other Council members. After all, 'teaching' was their sole responsibility and none could argue if they viewed this experience as an opportune training exercise. All the more defendable because, in truth, it was. She chuckled. It would be the Mother's own wind blowing.

❀ ❀ ❀

With a satisfied nod, Cleis turned from the edge of the narrow ravine and mounted the bay. The old woman had been right; this made a very defensible place.

She kneed the mare around and put a few paces between herself and the bridge. From this vantage point, it was obvious that a few well-trained swords would slow any group attempting to cross. Add a handful of archers at the side and a direct assault would never be successful.

The gorge was no more than eight or nine feet wide, but it was considerably deeper. And the jagged rocks of the river bed below were not inviting. A horseman would be foolish or desperate to attempt to jump the crossing. Although it was not an impossible feat in itself, the low border of rocks laid at the far edge was clearly an added deterrent. A horse would have to clear it as well as the chasm, and its rider could be cut down by sword or arrow long before the hind hooves would strike the earth. That left the bridge. Two could ride comfortably abreast, but not three. It was, Cleis judged, the perfect width for two sword arms to protect. And again, the shrub on this side had been cut well back, allowing an archer good sighting whereas cover and dim shadows were left for the Keep's defenders.

One might say it was a good training ground. The Mistress had probably never lost a defending recruit. It was doubtful, however, that the invading class had ever been so lucky.

She looked skyward at the shrill of a hawk. The sun was arching high, and determinedly she wheeled the blood bay around. There had been too much bickering with the Council this morning.

Her knees clamped tight, and the mare leapt forward into an easy canter. If she pushed, she could make the Crossroads Inn tonight; she could be in Gronday within a few hours of sunrise. That would be good. Stevens and the others would be coming in by darkfall tomorrow, and she wanted to talk to Mattee before they arrived. It was not often his Southern Borders had requested his family's help, but Mattee's father had not denied it when last asked. Although, Cleis sorely hoped it would not be needed.

❀ ❀ ❀

Chapter Eight

Elana and Paul were standing at the corner of the rough-hewn trader's post, waiting for Diana to emerge with the proprietor.

Stooping low to avoid the doorway's timber, Di'nay and a grizzled old trader stepped into the glaring, gray light of the morning. He squinted, ignoring the two of them, and pulled a twig from his mouth. He pointed it towards the river landing. "Got'em four monarc 'go. Good set in the water. Cuts nice'n clean line. One handles ar'right. Two best. Carries four'n parcels." He chewed on the stick for a moment and then started off towards the moored boats. "Show'm to yer."

Diana jerked a thumb over her shoulder at the open door. Garrison jumped at the elbow in his ribs, stepping back as Elana tried to steer him towards the doorway.

"Inside!" she hissed, and he stumbled in his hurried compliance.

Suppressing a sigh, Elana followed him in. Nonverbal cues were obviously not a part of his 'vocabulary.' Unfortunately, Garrison only knew Common. He was to appear to be a deaf and dumb slave; she winced to think of the added risk of exposure they were running, but it made sense, considering the soldiers were still looking for two, a Council Blue Sight and a scrawny Council Spirit.

The blackness within lifted as eyes adjusted. Elana breathed in the sweet scents of herb and stone grains. The place was much, much larger than the small exterior structure suggested as it was burrowed into the hillside; the thick, river-fed earth chilled the shelter almost to an iciness. Safe beneath the soil she sent her Sight searching. Like lost treasures to be caressed, she touched the food stocks and their sturdy life sources. Fondly her Sight went around stone and board to find the small burrowed creatures hidden in their slumbering, winter corners. The vibrant energy surged through her veins, and for the first time in what seemed a lifetime Elana drew the Mother's precious life into her, unhindered by fear of discovery.

A well-shaped, generously plump woman appeared from the depths of a storage tunnel. Elana turned quickly to Paul, her back to the approaching figure. "Do not notice her. Merely take the goods."

He gave the barest of nods as he continued to gaze over the top of Elana's head. She had to credit him with some acting ability .

With a tentative smile of her own, Elana greeted the trader's mala', but said nothing. As Di'nay's mala', a brief acknowledgement of one another was expected. But Garrison was an attending slave and a male — his post was not as favored as that of a servant, but his authority was certainly above these two women. Without consciously understanding these distinctions, Garrison was adopting the image well. A little too well, Elana thought fleetingly as the man absently accepted the soft hide boots. Two servants appeared from the back, arms laden with fresh supplies and extra blankets, and her concentration bent towards their amarin. The burly pair seemed to ignore them, hurrying outside to join the trader at the landing, but Elana felt something odd as they passed. Not quite completely ignored, she realized suddenly and glanced at Paul.

His cloak!

Her jaw clenched. The bearded man had recognized the cloak. Maltar's spies had come upriver in their hasty journey. It meant that the next scout back this way would be told of their visit. Or worse, if the price was handsome enough, the trader would send a runner out to find the commanding captain.

The mala' reappeared with a tray of steaming wine. She set the mugs and a plate of cheesebread down on one of the smaller tables near the spice shelves. With a shy glance at Garrison, she disappeared again.

Elana was amused. The woman was attracted to the Terran...if she only knew.

That Di'nay had arranged for Paul's boots and for their refreshments was worrisome — unusual behavior for most masters, although on longer journeys a slave's best behavior was often rewarded in small ways. Di'nay was using that custom now — a compromise between her personal integrity and the constraints of the situation.

The problem was that Elana had been identified as a Blue Sight at the Priory. If that had not happened they would not now be feigning this servitude. But traveling as a trio (instead of the expected twosome) had become a necessity, and in the end the wisdom of passing as the least significant of persons had seemed the safest since a wandering Council Blue Sight would not normally deign to be anything but a Seer's apprentice, certainly not a slave. Elana bit into the hot, tangy bread. Her Amazon would never be truly tolerant of any of Aggar's social roles.

After knowing Di'nay, she too would never be as matter-of-factly comfortable with Aggar's social structure. True, she had been raised to understand and even use the inequalities. The Council's unspoken goal was for differing status one day not to matter. She was no longer as tolerant of that 'one day' proposition.

She sighed inwardly. She had never felt the pride for Aggar which Di'nay had for the Sisterhood. Had she ever actually been complacent about Aggar's social order?

With a muffled exclamation Elana jumped from her seat, snatching the boot from Paul's grasp. His foreignness was acutely visible in his fumbling attempt to don the floppy, calf-laced boot. She cursed herself for their carelessness as she knelt, hiding his clumsiness with a show of humble servitude. Fates' Jest, couldn't he have at least waited until they were away?

"Thank you," he whispered as she finished one and reached for the other. "Awkward things, aren't they?" Why couldn't he keep quiet? All they needed was for his Common to be heard.

His good humor was not contagious; she merely jerked the leather laces tight. She was tempted to knot them too tight, but her common sense prevailed.

A shadow filled the entry way, and Elana felt Di'nay's anger flood the room. Fingers snapped in command and, obedient to her part, Elana rose quickly, stepping aside. Ducking her head guiltily, she let Di'nay pass and followed her to a side corner. Her guilt was not quite an act; a piece of her was ashamed at allowing herself to be manipulated into such an awkward position. Given her blue-sighted sensitivities, she might have noticed Garrison's intent earlier and warned him to wait.

"You are not his slave," Diana hissed. Her dark eyes scanned the room; she was mindful of listeners. But they were alone.

"Later, please!" Elana whispered, tight-lipped. She resented the need to explain at all, but she was not about to do it here.

Without loosing an iota of her fuming anger, Diana switched smoothly.

"The two loading our canoe are exceptionally nervous. Have you been close enough to them to get a sense of why?"

"Paul's cloak was recognized. They know we've met the scouts."

Diana drew her scattered thoughts together. They hadn't actually been identified yet because of the cloak — a certain amount of trail bartering or brawling was common for travelers — but they had become a suspicious crew.

Diana faced Elana. "Two possibilities — ignore them and hope they don't find anyone to talk with too soon — or bribe them. We could say we're on King's business. The Maltar isn't so very well liked in this region, is he?"

"Not much," Elana replied, but shook her head hesitantly.

"Nehna...?"

Elana smiled quickly, feeling Di'nay's annoyance evaporate. "It is best not to speak of the Maltar or the King. Any freeman this far from a settlement would not want to appear to be taking sides, if he wished to live long."

"Truth."

"You might identify yourself as a Council's man, Di'nay. They're not known to be particularly involved with border disputes, although they often have secrets."

"Would this trader be apt to hold silence then?"

"If paid well enough. In truth, he would probably assume we are not the twosome the scouts search for in any case. Unless he was directly asked about a Southern Trader with two slaves, he would not offer information."

"If we do nothing would he not embroider the tale and see if he could wheedle a price for news of the cloak...?" Diana was not surprised to find herself suspicious of the old trader. The last five years had taught her much about the men who chose to live on the obscure crossroads. Whether they kept tavern inns or trading posts, greed was a primary motivator. In a village or well-traveled crossway, their goods and services would have gotten reasonable prices and trustworthy silences — or patrons went elsewhere. In the vastness of the wilderness, however, they had no such competition and so they demanded whatever price they willed. This old trader had been no different in bartering for the boat's price, and Diana had no illusions about his ethics. But the Council was a different matter — and after hearing of the Beginnings, Diana could well understand why. The Council's role was something of a Savior to these people, and one did not lightly betray one's Savior.

"All right." Diana pulled her purse from her jerkin pocket. "Gather up Garrison and take a look at the supplies they all loaded. I'm not so certain everything's there. I'll go have another talk with our host."

❄ ❄ ❄

Elana winced as the hull skidded off another rock. With a bump they hit the foaming waters again. But they were through the rapids quickly enough — for now. Another stretch awaited them around the bend, and further on, in a league or two there was nastier white water. She looked at Garrison's slender back as he drove the paddle into the river again. She sighed; this is what happened when you gave an off-worlder a difficult task and no technology.

"Pull to shore!!" Di'nay's sharp order carried well over the river's rumble.

The Terran paused in mid-stroke, peering ahead at the shore line, then nodded. His paddle plunged downward, and Elana wondered at the odd twist of his wrist. It would appear that he used most of his energy doing nothing; but then she had guessed his inability was not solely due to prolonged imprisonment — despite his earlier words about boating skills.

The silence behind her was laced with fury. It was daunting even though it was directed elsewhere, and Elana simply made herself as small as possible amidst the bundled supplies. She was thankful that it had not been her incompetence that had guided them into the rocks so often. But then — she knew how to handle a boat.

The canoe scraped along the shallows, and Paul jumped out quickly, pulling them onto the brush-lined beach. One in his favor, Elana thought sourly. At least he wasn't afraid to get his feet wet. The grim set to his jaw, however, did not reassure her as she stepped from the boat. Confrontations weren't always productive, she knew — especially when Amazon temper and male ego were about to clash. But she was wiser than to try to interfere with this one.

"When was the last time you handled a boat?!" Diana shot, climbing out.

"Now we didn't do so badly," Paul offered in a forced, bantering sort of tone.

Wrong place to start, Elana noted and wandered off a few feet. The tension between the two was mounting with a gloomy force.

"We're damned lucky we didn't crack a seam!" Diana spat. "What in Goddess sight were you doing out there?!"

His mouth set, his back stiffened, and the Lieutenant met her gaze evenly. He was tired of playing second fiddle to this woman, but he was not going to give her the satisfaction of losing his temper either — let Elana see off-worlders were capable of civilized behavior despite what this one had shown her! With a tight-lipped restraint, he said, "I've been thoroughly checked out on all small water craft, n'Athena. Perhaps if the aft had been responding a little faster, we wouldn't have been in trouble."

The breath caught in Elana's throat.

Diana stood frozen. Her voice suddenly rang out. "Elana! Take the front."

Then the Amazon spun on her heel and disappeared into the forest. Diana hadn't trusted herself to step back into the boat. She didn't trust her tongue or her temper. Swiftly she put distance between the man and herself, swearing silently. Z'ki Sak, Diana — how ignorant could she be! She'd never even questioned his casual assurances before they left the dock. Not exactly an appropriate place, in front of the trader and servants, she remembered. But it was her job to get them back safely. She should have asked him sooner! Last night — or sometime. Blast it. Elana could have been hurt — she could have been drowned — what the hell had she been thinking? Had she been thinking at all?!

❋ ❋ ❋

Paul deposited an armload of firewood next to Elana, before he presented her with a handful of leafy greens. He'd barely spared Diana a word since the day's fiasco on the river, but his charming attentions had been unfaltering towards Elana. Trying to dodge her own jealousy, she thought; it was fortunate someone could tolerate him. She was finding it more and more difficult herself.

"I thought you used these in the tea the other night." Paul smiled graciously. "Was I right? Or have I threatened to poison us?"

Elana smiled vaguely; he knew he was right. "They are the same."

Diana turned her back to the two of them at Elana's faint smile. Games! How she hated his games.

From the corner of her eye, Elana saw Di'nay turn, and she felt her Amazon's withdrawal. Forcing a brighter face, she asked Paul, "Could you find us some dry kindling? This is going to be difficult to light."

He frowned, fingering the damp twigs and wood. "Don't know if there is any. It's been so wet."

And it hadn't helped anybody's temper. "Try the lower branches. They should be dryer than those on the ground."

"Good thought." He nodded seriously. "I suppose we'll need quite a lot — the wood will take its time catching."

Whatever, Elana thought, wishing he would just leave. But he was already tromping off into the woods. She breathed a sigh of relief when he had moved out of hearing range.

Their solitude heightened her awareness of Di'nay. Elana turned her blue gaze onto the bent figure that prowled through the packs. "What are you searching for?" Elana called softly, the gentle sound of her native tongue offering a peace that the harsh Common words could not have carried.

A sigh, a pause, and a reluctant lift of her head preceded the tired admission, "I've forgotten."

Elana laughed sympathetically and kneeled beside her lover. "It will come back to you in a little while."

Diana sighed and nodded. "I suppose so."

With a gentle hand Elana brushed the hair from Di'nay's face. She looks very tired, Elana thought. She looks almost as fatigued as she did that day in the garden. Did all Terrans make Amazons feel as battle-worn as Paul made Di'nay feel? The weariness in her lover worried her. "You are upset by more than his poor boating?"

"Ah yes." Diana drew a long breath. She certainly had been, hadn't she? "Part of it was my fault. I shouldn't have assumed so much. I should have asked him for more details that other night when we were planning."

"He said he could handle a canoe. What more should you have asked?"

"How well — how — ?" Diana grinned at herself, somewhat derisively. She had fallen for the old Terran line that it was her own fault when Garrison had been the one to err — to egotistically misrepresent himself with that small exaggeration.

Elana smiled too. "And I thought all Amazons were raised to be suspicious of men. At least enough not to feel responsible for their egos."

"Well, sometimes...when we've been off-world, we do tend to forget."

Still, Elana guessed — watching Di'nay, trying to unravel the knotted amarin — the man's carelessness had not been the sole worry. "Something changed between you two the other morning — after we attacked the two soldiers. Do you remember what it was?"

"No, before then." Diana shook her head, remembering only too well. "It was the evening after our scuffle."

Elana thought about that a moment. "He brought you some tea."

"Tea!" Diana dove into her pack. Triumphantly she pulled out a new parcel. "For us. I picked it up at the trading post — a change of taste for a night or two."

"You're not going to tell me what went on between you two, are you?"

Diana shook her head slowly, "No. It's just a feeling. Nothing happened. Nothing was said." Her gaze drifted out to the tumbling river waters. "It's mostly my own suspicions, that's all."

"You're instincts about situations — about men — are often valid." Elana's eyes bent to the small package in her hand. "Why do you doubt them now?"

Diana asked abruptly, "Are you comfortable with Paul?"

"Comfortable? I don't think I understand what you mean."

"Are you uncomfortable around him? Does he make you feel odd — ill at ease?"

"I...," she shrugged, "no more than any other off-worlder would, I suppose."

Diana's dark eyes turned to her sharply. "How do you mean?"

"In truth, I have rather low expectations for him. Every time he's polite enough to smile and say thank you, I am immensely impressed. A rather insulting way to credit him, I'm afraid."

They laughed together at that, and the smile that curved Di'nay's lips reminded Elana of how beautiful the woman could be when she was truly happy. A warmth spread through Elana that she still had the key to unlock that small corner of peace in her lover. "So tell me what has this to do with your ill feelings for the man?"

"Nothing and everything," Diana grinned. And she thought that actually there was nothing to be jealous about. "It is merely proof that I worry over much."

"A thing I have often accused you of!" Elana retorted sassily. And she smiled as she got to her feet as the forest noises announced the Terran's imminent return.

❄ ❄ ❄

"I haven't thanked you for such a wonderful dinner." Paul wrapped the extra blanket around his shoulders.

"Your fish," Elana reminded him, sparing him a smile. In the past two days, he'd been trying very hard not to irritate Di'nay.

Still it seemed to Elana that he was always either complimenting her or cross-examining Di'nay's decision, even though he was quick to apologize and withdraw at Di'nay's slightest annoyance. Too quick. Elana remembered her first impression of him, that he was shallow and self-centered. He was certainly charming, but charm only went so far.

She finished stirring the embers into the mud and set the heating unit on high, directing it toward Paul's huddled figure. The rain had grown a little steadier, and the friendly, crisp nip in the air had vanished shortly after they passed Rotava. It was a wet, frosty winter that was settling in, and Elana found only a small measure of comfort in the fact that the farmers would have plenty of water for their next growing season — provided the winter held to this pattern.

Beyond the sheltering tarp which they had brought from the trader, Di'nay's still figure sat on watch, huddled in the shadows of the silverpines. The Amazon's sword and bow were invisible in the lines of darkness. Her body was a black contour, blending with the shapes of the river and the night. Beyond her, the twin moons barely peeked through the overcast, graying the hushed waters of the Suiri. The river was a dull, uneven surface pocketed with little raindrops as the drizzle continued. Few hunters were abroad tonight, Elana guessed, and she only hoped that the human kind were not prowling either.

Paul broke into her thoughts. "Is there more tea?"

Elana waved at the single pot set to the side of the heater. "You're welcomed to the rest." Picking up her full cup, she quietly got to her feet to walk toward Diana.

"Where are you...?"

"Visiting.

"Di'nay?"

Diana was startled, then chagrined as she recognized the gentle voice as Elana's. "What brings you out in the rain?"

Elana smiled, moving forward again. "I have a cup of tea to share. Would you like some company?"

"If you don't mind the damp," Diana warned, pleased as she made room on the makeshift seat of her thermal blanket.

"I don't mind," Elana said, handing Di'nay the cup, then nestling close beneath her arm, and Di'nay's cloak wrapped about them both.

With a contented sigh, Diana swallowed a sip of the tea. She didn't care how cold it was or how many hours of watch she had left — Elana was near and the tea was warm. In that instant, she wanted nothing else.

"Are you ever going to tell me of your growing suspicions? They fairly shout from you. Garrison is pleasing you less and less, it would seem." Elana slipped a hand between the laces of Di'nay's jerkin. The softness of the breast and the warmth of the fieldsuit through the tunic made a welcoming nest for cold fingers.

Diana chuckled, "If you really want to know."

"I want to know."

With an awkward shrug, Diana admitted, "It is simple jealousy."

Elana answered with a scoffing laugh.

"An absurd idea, isn't it?"

"That I could be interested in a Terran male? It certainly is."

Diana shook her head quickly. "Not you. My impressions are of Paul. He seems attracted to you. He runs around like a poorly trained pup after a child."

"I have not done anything to encourage him," Elana assured her firmly. "He is building it all in his own little mind."

That had not been a denial. More seriously, Diana asked, "I'm not mistaken then? He is attracted to you?"

Elana snuggled against her lover's chest. "He is flattering his ego."

"In what way?"

"He is very intimidated by you, my dearest. And in his shallow soul he finds consolation only in my occasional smile."

Diana grinned, remembering several incidents. "When you thank him for gathering wood or warn him not to eat the spice leaf in the stew."

"And Mother forbid I should notice his exhaustion and ask for a respite!"

"You are more acutely aware of his frailties than I am," Diana murmured. After all, it was not her desire to drive him until he collapsed.

"I have the advantage of deciphering his amarin," Elana reminded her softly. "His fatigue is only too apparent. If he was less stubborn, he could call the halt himself."

"But then he would not be who he is."

Elana sighed. "Off-worlders do not seem so different from the people of Aggar. Foolishness is always foolish. The only difference is that technology allows even the frail and feeble-minded power enough to declare wars and murder people."

"Perhaps you are right." Diana's thoughts drifted back to Paul and her own misgivings and she hugged Elana quickly. "Are you comfortable with his attraction?"

"It does not disturb me. He is very polite...not at all intimidating."

"If he makes you uneasy in any way...?"

A teasing chuckle answered her as Elana kissed the place above Di'nay's heart. "I do not doubt your readiness, my fearless Amazon, and I do not think he will do anything I cannot handle. But thank you."

Her grasp tightened. Diana believed that too.

✵ ✵ ✵

They pressed on through their last night on the trail, pausing at the shore only long enough to eat. Time was short, perhaps too short. Diana only hoped Cleis would be in Gronday. Still wary of decisions to come, Diana sent them back to the river with regret. The hours left to Elana and herself were growing fewer.

The gloomy fog and drizzle of the wintry morning clung tenaciously to the river shores, and Diana welcomed its added cloaking. The current was a lazy flow here on the Suiri, and their boat slipped upstream with a quiet, quick speed. The added luxury of the gentle current had been the reason that Paul had been able to paddle too, and they had switched off positions every three or four hours so that each of them could have the chance to sleep.

Diana counted them fortunate so far. She planned to stay overnight at Mattee's since they would reach port around mid-afternoon. But she was still leery of this calm; she suspected they needed to be preparing for anything.

The rain thickened as the fog lifted, and Elana, wrapped in a blanket amidst the gear, nodded at the dim outline ahead. "The old cavalry's river fort." She pointed ahead, outlining the dilapidated stone walls that crept down to the edge of the forested beach. "It's been empty for about two hundred tenmoons — since the King moved them to Gronday."

"It means we're closer than we thought." It was still early afternoon.

Garrison's paddle paused as he demanded, "What'd she say?"

Elana wearily shifting back into Common. "Five leagues to the town."

He bobbed his head as if there had been some decision of great importance.

Elana sighed. She was immensely glad Di'nay did not speak this Common as a native tongue, because it was not in the least pleasant to listen to. And then another thought brought a mischievous smile to her lips — she wouldn't be surprised if Paul actually liked the sound of the language, poor man.

The mists closed in around them again, and Diana bent her concentration to her steady stroking. She was surprised at how anxious she had become and at how much she was hoping to find Cleis ahead.

Elana finished changing from her trousers into her skirt, when Diana suddenly noticed that the woman had turned in the process and was watching her mutely.

At her questioning amarin, Elana said, "Gronday is not the Council's Keep."

Astute observer, Diana admitted. "Part of me is beginning to equate Gronday with safety. But you're right. There are still many leagues to cover. I was just realizing how much I'm relying on Cleis and the others to help us."

"There is some benefit to a larger party at this point."

"They know by now we are not coming through Black Falls. They've probably known for several days."

Elana nodded. "If their captain is bright and ambitious, he will reason we've come upriver."

Diana's stomach tightened. "Let us hope he is tired and anticipating a pension."

"Perhaps Gronday will be a safe enough haven. Your friend will be there, I know it."

"Our friend perhaps?" Diana's paddle dipped and sculled in the gray waters. "The thought of meeting Cleis once disquieted you. Is it still so?"

Elana shook her head, freeing her hair from its braid. "I was much less certain of you — of us then."

Diana did not look at Elana. "What are you more certain of?"

The blue fire and scorching touch of those eyes reached her, holding Diana with a fierceness that stole the very breath from her throat. She gasped as the fleeting embrace receded, the power of Elana's emotions lingering —

tantalizing her body with memories of impassioned nights and softer words.
"You have an unfair advantage!" Diana chokes hoarsely.
Elana laughed, a sweet sound that drew Diana's smile.
Garrison's harsh Common interrupted them suddenly. "To the left!"
Elana spun forward in her seat as Diana looked to the port. The faint
lapping of river on wood drifted through the haze, and a barge appeared out of
the gloom. Dim figures moved along the flat deck, checking the ropes that
secured the cargo crates.

Bound for Rotava and further west, Diana thought. Neither boat
acknowledged the other, and the mists soon veiled them all again. But Diana
knew the crew had not been long out of harbor because they were still walking
the ties, looking for slackened lines. She turned her eyes ahead, peering for signs
of Gronday.

The noises of the city heralded their arrival before the docks became
visible. The low din of open carts and warehouse clatter grew slowly, although
the individual cries and gruff curses were barely distinguishable. Today the air
muffled the animals sounds from the wharfside liveries, and the fog parted just
enough to let them glimpse the sprawling buildings. Mammoth by Aggar's
standard and impressive after endless days spent in the forests, Gronday
dominated the river shore with an endless line of wooden walls.

A large city, Gronday was known for the crystal glass it produced and
the crafted furniture it created. It was home of the best mead in the Ramains
since silverpine bees were native, though grains were imported, since the soil
eroded too easily when the woodlands were cut back.

It was a place of pride for the Traders' Guild whose largest tannery was
housed in the southern quadrant, because those silverpines also sheltered
creatures with some of the finest pelts on the northern continent. It was a city
built on news and commerce and merchants' dreams. It was a testimony to the
great strides the people of this planet had made — just as Elana's independence
heralded a new step for the Blue Sight.

She was brought back to the present, guiding their small craft around
the cargo flats. Fishing boats were safely moored upstream at the eastern end of
the harbor.

Diana turned their canoe towards shore. Everything was shrouded and
quiet in this eastern sector. "I do believe they've built another dock."

"No, they haven't." Elana pointed to the L-shaped pier where a young
boy sat hunched over his fishing pole. "There — where Madt'dan is. They've
only added another few sections paralleling the shore."

Diana followed the line of her finger. "I see it now." She slid them
round the end of the pier, bringing them between the shore and that sheltering
arm.

The young boy's head snapped up. He pulled in his line as he
recognized Di'nay. Mattee's boy of six snatched up his bait jar and scampered
down the steps of the inner pier. He grinned and waved as the canoe cleared the
corner. He'd grown a good hand's breadth in the scant monarcs she'd been
gone.

The drag of Garrison's trailing paddle drew her attention. "He's a friend," Diana called softly in Common, and Paul nodded, lifting his paddle. They bumped the lower dock gently. There was not a single soul about save for young Madt'dan. With a somber expression the boy hurried to secure the lines, intent as any newly trained apprentice in making his knots.

Diana nodded at his proud work as she climbed out, and extended a single palm in greeting. "Well done, Tad Madt'dan. Well done."

Her clasp was strongly met for a twelve-year-old, but she could not play this formality to the end, and laughing, she hugged him.

The boy grinned, bursting with pride, although he was at an age where such displays usually caused him embarrassment. But Tad Di'nay was different, this was his Southern friend. "Father sent me to meet you," Madt'dan explained, only half-curiously eyeing Di'nay's two companions. "He has sent me each day to fish an' look for you."

"Is Tad Leist here then?"

He nodded officiously. "Aye, with your other southways folks. Father has them in your quarters an' those next to yours."

"Good." Diana drew a short breath, feeling better. But her sixth sense would not be quieted. Cautiously she scanned the pier above them. She drew him to where Paul bent, taking the gear as Elana passed things up from the boat. "This is Paul."

Still kneeling, Paul paused and looked at the two of them. Diana laid a hand on his shoulder and said, "Paul — he is working for me now. He does not speak your language. Can you help him with the supplies and bring these things up to the inn?"

The boy nodded solemnly. He'd not often been given charge of a servant; he was still too young for that. But Mattee had told him that Di'nay's mission this trip was very important and that they needed to be ready to help with anything.

"You must bring him by the back way," Diana explained quietly, glancing overhead again at the pier. "The packs come to the room but the other goes to the stables. And Tad'l, the fewer people you see, the better."

He nodded again, his thick hair falling into his eyes.

"Can I trust you with the bow and crossbow there?" Diana did not want to bring the weapons into the commons room. It might give too many people ideas on where the Southern Trader had been. She wanted to leave neither Paul nor weapons with the lad, but Mattee knew the ways of his city well, and it would have appeared odd if she had come in fully equipped and yet not been met — or if she had not left the unloading to Paul and the boy.

"I have always brought them safe to you!"

"In truth, you have." Diana ruffled his hair. She knew the pride he took in fetching her weapons from Mattee's arms' hold whenever she had need of them. "This time I will need them brought into the rooms, though — through the back way."

"But Father's rules are — "

"You ask him," Diana interrupted gently, strapping the black scabbard and sword to her waist. "He will be saying yes this one time. It's very important."

"I won't ask him in front of another."

"Good man." Diana clasped his shoulder and nodded to Elana to join her. "Now remember. Paul here does not understand your words. So be careful."

"Aye."

"He'll show you where to bring the gear," Diana said to Garrison in Common. "Let him take the weapons and try to stay out of sight. We'll see you at the tavern."

Paul nodded mutely and turned back to the unloading.

"At the inn," Madt'dan repeated and Diana nodded to him.

She turned and Elana fell into step, pulling her hood forward to hide her hair and eyes — as any proper mala' might do. And together they mounted the stairs for the pier top.

❋ ❋ ❋

Chapter Nine

She was amazed that she had never recognized the place as Gronday. After more than two tenmoons of images and dreams, Elana found the sprawling, two-story inn with its thatched roof as familiar to her as the Council's Keep. She smiled as Di'nay stooped beneath the low canopy of the door; Di'nay's Gronday home had become almost that to her too — home.

Inside, the commons opened off the foyer, the large tavern crowded with afternoon patrons. It was winter and trading had slackened off for the season. Days were growing too short and the weather too nasty for safe portage, so the winter habits of Gronday's residents had begun to set in. Every commons in the city would be comfortably filled by mid-afternoon now, and Mattee's inn was no different.

The smells of fresh bread and stew drifted through pipe smoke. Loud and cheerful, the folk were scattered about the long, worn tables. A pair of tavern maids, bare-footed and dressed in black skirts with colorful petticoats, wove their way in and out of the crowd with their trays of mead and meats. There was a huge fire blazing at the far end of the room, and Elana guessed the kitchen's bread ovens were behind the wall.

A movement — a piece of forest green disappearing through the kitchen hallway caught her attention. Startled, Elana snatched at her Sight. She dared not reach out to follow the fellow.

"Fates' Cellars, where's Mattee now?" The Amazon's mutter barely nudged its way into her awareness as Elana still searched the commons, her reply only half-conscious. "Back in the King's Seat, Di'nay."

"Truth, he would be this time of day." Diana strode down the short hall to the smaller pub. The King's Seat was reserved for the more elite guests.

There — by the amarin — Elana identified the vacated table near the fire. The two corner seats had been emptied. A single, broad-shouldered male sat hunched over his stein; Terran, she grasped quickly — although his sword-callused hands attested to a long acquaintance with this world. She pulled back, realizing her Sight was more focused than she wished. This inn was too open to safely chance that here.

His gaze casually roamed over her, half-hidden by the door post as she was, and then moved on. But he had seen her; it had probably been Di'nay's entrance that had sent his companions off to the back. She was relieved to know they were here, but also sad, realizing that their mission's end was indeed near.

A suggestive, somewhat lurid glance from a nearer patron registered. Hastily Elana stepped further back into the foyer, thought her response bothered her — not because her actions were suspicious, but because of how anxious she felt. No matter how much healing Di'nay and the lifestones guided, she was never going to react quite the same way to the intimidating behavior of a man.

Another amarin drew her attention, and Elana half-turned. Beyond the stair well, Di'nay stood staring at her with a brooding frown. It was as if she had never really seen Elana before; and disconcerted, Elana looked down. Her plain, belted tunic hung over the top of the calf-length skirt. Her boots were laced high, although the knots were hidden beneath the folds of the skirt. Her cloak was open, covering her hair below her nape. She wore nothing, in fact, that Di'nay had not seen her wear before, and questioningly she raised her eyes to the Amazon.

Di'nay shifted abruptly and turned, hand on her sword's hilt as Mattee emerged from the King's Seat. But Elana could not forget that disturbing scrutiny, and her fingers curled around the edges of her cloak. She wished she could risk deciphering those scowling amarin, though she doubted if it would help. When something was puzzling Di'nay, there was little to be learned from her amarin save that she was confused. Elana would simply have to wait until she could ask.

Diana unbelted her sword as she and Mattee spoke, with a casualness that Elana did not believe. At the entrance to the commons room she passed the weapon to the innkeeper. House rules in most of Gronday's taverns demanded that anything larger than a hunting knife be surrendered to the proprietor before service was rendered.

"Aye, Tad Leist is 'round here someplace, waiting for you," the burly man rumbled, and in a matter-of-fact fashion he greeted Elana with a nod. He had been raised with 'Southerners' such as Di'nay and their strange ways; so he gave it little thought that Di'nay would count this mala' as an almost full personage.

Diana drew her cape off slowly, careful not to shed water on her landlord. "Madt'dan said others have come as well?"

"Aye. All the regulars are here. Save the one — the scrawny, jumpy fella."

Diana nodded. Cedros, or Tad Ceders as he was locally known, was a naturally dusky-skinned Terran. The man had found the transition into Aggar more volatile than most, since the men of Aggar had always assumed his darker coloring was due to an excitable temper.

"So my boy did meet up with you?" Mattee was moving Di'nay toward the staircase. Elana thought this conversation rather odd given the tension between the two.

"He brings equipment and my manservant."

An eyebrow lifted. Neither Di'nay nor any of the Southerner's predecessors had ever had a man in their service. But a raised brow was as startled as Mattee would ever show. "Could put your fellow next to your quarters, in with your Southways men if they don't mind sharing with servants? Tad Leist is already staying in with you, as usual. I assume this one here will too?"

"That sounds fine." Diana mounted the stairs, her damp cloak brushing past Mattee's hulking frame.

"I'll send your man up when he's in."

Elana realized the innkeeper had just slid the long sword back into Di'nay's grasp. Her cloak had swallowed the black scabbard immediately.

An interesting arrangement, Elana thought as she hurried after Di'nay. Loyalty and absolutely no show of curiosity. It was clear that the generations of Amazons housed by Mattee's family had become more than mere boarders.

Upstairs, the dark paneled hall was gloomy. The fact that there were only two windowed alcoves in the whole length of the corridor did not help either, given the day's cloudiness. But the wood had a a well-oiled shine, and Elana breathed in the ancient strength, smiling. How many times had she watched Di'nay walk down this passage? The wood-slatted doors were not of the best fit, although they too were oiled and shiny. Elana remembered that last midnight vision with the torchlight squeezing through those boards. Again she felt the warmth of a homecoming.

Then, suddenly, she grasped Di'nay's hand before it touched the doorbolt. Today something else was visible through the cracks. Her Sight bristled at the faint amarin of another's presence beyond.

For a moment, Diana hesitated. With a decisive movement she threw back her cloak, freeing the scabbard, but she did not draw her sword. Although experience taught her to be cautious, she suspected she already knew who awaited them. She pushed the door open as a slender figure rose from tending the fire. With a lazy grin their guest turned, and Diana laughed softly as the woman teased, "Surprised?"

Diana shook her head, slipping easily into their cherished Sororian, "You are one of the more pleasant moments of this journey."

Cleis winced. "Then it has been a very long trip for you."

"It has been, my friend." Diana grabbed Cleis in a strong but careful hug.

"You're getting me wet," Cleis grumbled, disentangling herself long enough to toss the damp cloak and scabbard aside. Then with deep sigh, she pulled her friend near again. They parted as Elana shut the door, tears in their eyes as they stood with hands clasped, staring at each other.

"How mend your ribs, Daughter of Mothers?" Diana asked tenderly, swearing the younger Amazon to honesty as she did.

"Well enough to help you home. I can't tell you how worried I've been. I was expecting you day before yesterday."

"You always did underestimate travel time." The jest was a gentle one.

"Is this Elana?" Cleis asked, returning to the local dialect with a warmth in her voice that made her simple words a genuine welcome.

Elana peeled off her wet cloak and shook her hair free. Diana smiled, answering her friend, "Yes. Elana, Shadow of Council and Keep — my Sister, Cleis n'Athena."

"Shadow?" Cleis asked curiously as she grasped Elana's hands.

"Guide," Elana supplied, amused at herself for finding this woman to be young.

With a shock, Cleis suddenly realized how striking this woman was. Certainly by none of Aggar's standards was she a voluptuous beauty, but the subtle strength of her stance and the confidence of her returning scrutiny — these would lure any Sister to a second glance. The dark, swirling cloak of her hair was drawn back from an ivory-skinned face, and the startling ice blue of her eyes was dynamic.

Cleis' eyes narrowed faintly. Yes, undeniably blue — she had almost changed that description in her report to n'Sappho.

"Blue is rather rare here," Elana said quietly.

Cleis blushed, embarrassed at her staring. "I beg your patience — "

"I find no grudge," Elana assured her, adding to herself that she had been as guilty of staring as Cleis — perhaps more so as her gaze had been in feigned casualness. She liked this Amazon.

"Is there a chance that we can risk spending the night here?" Diana asked.

Cleis shrugged. "You must tell me. I sent Cedros scouting in Colmar, but he hasn't radioed anything back. He ought to be coming in himself late tonight, so I'd suggest waiting until then at least."

Elana felt the stab of pain that shot through Cleis as she settled on the hearth. "I admit," Cleis continued, "that I don't believe the official report that he offended the Maltar. What has this fellow Garrison done to warrant such a persistent chase?"

Di'nay pulled a chair away from the center table and joined Cleis by the fire.

Elana ruefully noted how hot the room was becoming. She bent over Di'nay's shoulder then to softly ask, "May I open the window? You've spoiled me with all the open air camping — "

"Oh no — a true wanderer!" Cleis moaned, but she was grinning too.

Elana caught the chilled shivers of both Amazons, and she smiled reassuringly. "I promise it will be only a very little bit."

"You will be sitting in the corner furthest from the fire and us," Diana protested, amazed at the cheerful camaraderie that was developing between her two friends. "No, open it as much as you like and come back to be comfortable."

"Comfortable? In this heat?" Elana's brow raised in skepticism.

While Elana opened the window Cleis asked, "Soroe...? The 'official story'...is there any more to it?"

Diana frowned. "Only generally. This Maltar is a nasty sort — "

"He is not wholly sane," Elana said quietly, settling herself on a footstool.

Cleis said somberly, "He'd see Garrison dead rather than with us and the Council?"

"Yes."

Cleis prodded, "Records aside, may I ask for the unofficial version?"

Diana drew a tired breath. "I am sure you understand that it is best for all if this does not go beyond this room."

Cleis nodded.

"Garrison is a tech engineer; under his supervision — or rather beyond his conscious control — he revamped some of the old imperial relics for the Maltar."

"How effectively?"

"An operational laser field."

Cleis shook her head. "Whew — not good. Do they know he's Terran?"

Elana said, "They think he is a Council spy."

"Well, small favors are blessings too."

Diana agreed. "They need him to repair the mess we left — and are desperate to prevent the Council from getting him."

"If they don't know he is Terran why aren't they assuming he's just one of many talented Council folk? Why pursue him as if he's a one-and-only?"

Fair enough question, Diana admitted to herself, and warily she looked at Elana. She did not want to share anything that her lover might find uncomfortable. And the Council had entrusted her with the Seers' secrets.

The silence stretched and Cleis too turned to the younger woman. This was something, she realized, that she might not be told.

"I am the other reason for their pursuit," Elana said finally, and it was a moment before she continued. "They were... dealing deviously with the Council of Ten. I — stumbled — onto their secret. They do not know that word has already been sent ahead to the Keep. They hope to stop us before the Council is informed. They know what both Garrison and I look like. We're not certain, but we hope they do not know of Di'nay's existence."

"Certainly they expect you to have found a hawker by now?" Cleis pressed.

"They would have been watching the usual roosts, and they have not seen us near any of them," Diana explained in a low, cautious tone. Silently she added a prayer for the eitteh's safety.

"Word was not sent by bird then?" Cleis read the reticence in Diana's dark gaze, but she probed, "The hawker's earlier message to Thomas said your radio was dead. I was back at the base, and the 'official story' on your transmitter is...?"

"Broken in transit. Not dead," Diana answered. "We used the descrambler in sabotaging the laser equipment. My channels were set for here."

"That means you were incredibly lucky and someone at the base caught your signal or...."

"No, the Council has the means to read radio signals," Elana said, ready to trust this new Amazon. Cleis nodded.

Then Elana watched them talk. So very much alike and yet not. Cleis n'Athena was warm and open, as unassuming as she was vibrantly alive. Her ribs forced her to be still, Elana realized. This woman was usually much more animated. Exhaustingly so, Elana granted, amused. If she had found Di'nay's amarin demanding, she shuddered to think how fatiguing this woman would have been on a more intimate basis. But as an acquaintance...as a friend, she was quite appealing.

No, attractive was a better word. Cleis was strong and attractive in that strength. Perhaps that was why she and Di'nay seemed so alike. But the wistful romanticism in Di'nay was not in the younger Amazon's character. Impatience...perhaps some margin of innocence, but there was no cynical overcloak to hide disillusionment here...no romantic soul to be nurtured and fired from within. Her gaze came back to her lover, and Elana smiled to herself. The protective cynicism was less a part of Di'nay now, and she found that pleased her.

Elana heard, "...at least, she has been known to," and started at Di'nay's teasing. She blushed a faint brown and automatically responded in the Sororian that Di'nay had been using, "Sorry, I was drifting."

Cleis leaned forward in her defense. "Don't be. You're doing just fine."

Elana laughed at that. "Am I?"

"I was just warning Cleis not to assume too much." Diana's gentle auras reached around Elana like a warm cloak. "She slipped into Sororian and I was telling her you follow it quite well — usually."

"Only when I listen," Elana amended, still smiling.

There was suddenly a tense undercurrent running between the other two women, and silence descended. Elana realized that Cleis was waiting, expecting something, and that Di'nay was unprepared for a discussion.

Deliberately redirecting them, Elana asked, "Would anyone be insulted if I suggested food? It has been rather a long while since we ate properly."

Diana was startled to find her stomach so empty. A peal of laughter rang from Cleis. "Let me guess," the younger Amazon teased, "you forgot mid-day?"

"We didn't do so very well for breakfast either," Elana retorted dryly.

"Would you join us?" Diana asked Cleis, feeling a stab of guilt.

"No, thanks just the same." Stiffly she pushed herself up from the hearthstones. "I'm well enough fed, and I need to follow up with Stevens. I sent him out the back way to find Madt'dan and Garrison — purely a precaution." She nodded at the wardrobe and cupboards against the far wall. "There's fresh bread and cheese in your larder, if you like. Or I can have Mattee send up something more substantial?"

"Anything he has," Diana agreed eagerly, and Cleis chuckled. She knew her friend's eating habits only too well. Diana said. "Make it enough for three. Garrison will need something too."

"All right — oh, I took the liberty of asking the Min to send up a hot bath."

Elana brightened with delight, and Cleis grinned again. "Good, I didn't mean to organize things too much."

"Rarely." Diana caught Cleis' hand as the woman passed her, causing her to pause for a moment. "Thank you for coming."

"There was never any doubt." Then with a nod to Elana, Cleis left them.

Quietly Elana came to stand behind Di'nay, her hands slipping under the damp jerkin. "She is a good friend."

Diana nodded, hugging the arms that wrapped about her so lovingly. She added, "So are you."

Elana kissed the top of Di'nay's head and released her, turning to the cupboard doors. Inhaling the sweet scents of the morning's baking, she opened the small door to the food stocks. Doubtless it had been this faint aura combined with Di'nay's hunger that had reminded her of food.

The wind rattled as rain began again. Quickly Diana went to the open window. With a bump one side was secured, and the other opened a bit more, adjusting so that the water wouldn't come in. She paused, her eyes following the line of the thatched roof just below her to the stables. She thought of her horses, especially of Kaing. Mattee had a good stable crew, so she was not worried about his feeding, but she hoped they had found time to exercise the stallion too.

A breeze swirled a bit and a fine spray blew into her face. It carried a fresh scent within its dampness, and Diana had to smile at herself. She had come to think of this place as a home of sorts. Elana had been right when she said Aggar was not in her life — in her heart — as her home truly was. But still, it was a part of her now. She slid her hand along the worn, polished wood of the window frame, marveling at how familiar this place was to her...much more so than the base itself.

The clack and shuffle of the cheese board and the cupboards made her turn. Mutely, Diana watched Elana. Familiar...it was a term that fit more than her own sense of homecoming here. She was silent as Elana filled the metal goblets with the diluted mead from a worn flask. And she wondered again about the Council's Seers and how much they knew of off-worlders. She remembered the illusive, defiant quality she had seen in Elana the day they met in the gardens. "I would like to work with you..." hadn't Elana said? But it had been a very personal statement. Diana had been left in no doubt that Elana had meant she wanted to work with her — Diana n'Athena. She had not simply been repeating a formality...she had cared enough to risk tradition by seeking her out before the Choosing. She had the Blue Sight, Elana had said, so she knew Diana well enough to want the honor. But that had not been all of it.

A dull ache caught in her throat as Diana looked at the young woman, slowly sorting pieces. The woman had known before their garden tryst. She had known of this Inn — well enough to know the King's Seat, the window at the end of her room — well enough to recognize Mattee's presence by his amarin alone — his son by name. And the cupboards here? Certainly she could find the food stocks by their auras, but the metal cups and such were not so visible to the Sight. Separately, each meant nothing. But together, there was too much for coincidence.

Elana had known from the beginning. As the Council had known of Garrison's mission, Elana had known of her.

Elana interrupted her thoughts quietly. "You're frowning at me."

The furrows between Diana's eyes deepened into a scowl as she left the window. What would it change? But her stomach felt constricted in a painful knot. She did not think it was from the discomfort of knowing she might have been spied upon...it felt far more unsettled than that. Some trust broken? There had been no promise...but there had been no sharing either.

Worried, Elana sat down as Di'nay neared. She had not seen this sort of displeasure directed at her since that night in Cellar's Gate.

Standing there, tracing the grain of the table with a finger, Diana wondered if she really wanted to ask. But not knowing would be worse. She slid into the seat. "How well do the Seers know Gronday?"

Elana felt the more personal accusation behind the question instantly. Di'nay's amarin had crystallized as she formed the words, and Elana felt the old defenses rise within herself. Inevitably her Sight came to make her an outsider. She had been a fool to think it could actually be different with Di'nay. And it hurt — that biting disappointment hurt. Her gaze fixed grimly on the chalice in her hands and she challenged flatly, "The Seers, Amazon? Or me?"

Too late Diana remembered how aggressive her words could sound when wrapped with the intensity of her amarin. She pinched the bridge of her nose, forcing a gentler calm on herself. Then she tried again. "How well do you know this inn? Did you learn of it from the Seers?"

"Well. And no, not from the Seers."

The silence hung between them, and suddenly Elana felt ashamed. The shift in Di'nay's amarin had been deliberate; her lover was trying not to find blame. Elana was reminded of how painful secrets could be — what would she have felt like if her treasured first memories of Di'nay had not been theirs to share? What would it have been like to find there were things Di'nay had known earlier, things that Di'nay had never spoken of? She would have felt suspicious — and used.

"Forgive me...it is difficult...." Elana swallowed hard, glancing away, shaken. "The Seers know this city well. I learned much of it from them, in the same manner as I learned of Colmar and the Priory. I would not be surprised if they knew something of Mattee and you in this place. His family has been respected here for many centuries. But they did not teach me of them — of you. I...stumbled across this...," her hand gestured to the room, "...for myself — in dreams and visions."

Diana considered that, feeling exposed...vulnerable. Then cautiously she asked, "Did you know of Cleis before — before we talked of her?"

Elana shook her head. "The Council spoke of two Amazons sent here by the Terrans, both with honorable reputations. But I did not know you were one of them. I knew nothing of Cleis — nor of any of your off-world associates." She understood. No one, in fact, had been shown to her who might have caused her to suspect Di'nay was an off-worlder...no one who might have stirred the amarin within Di'nay that would suggest she was an Amazon — that she was different. "Maryl was not known to me either."

A finger gently touched the black leather of her wristband, and almost bleakly, Elana stared at the open palm offered across the table. It cost Di'nay much to reach through her confusion. Suddenly — almost desperately — Elana grasped her hand. They were both different here; she needed to remember that. There was no better, no lesser — just different...merely inexplicably, complexly different.

"It hurts that..." Diana was still not looking at her. "...that you said nothing sooner." Startled, Elana realized Diana was blinking away tears. "Would you have ever said anything?"

It hurt Elana not to have an answer to that. She tightened her grasp, trembling. "I don't know. At first I said nothing because you were so leery of us working together — being together. I felt it was because of my Sight...because I am of Aggar and you are not."

Diana shook her head, the pain audible in her strangled words. "It wasn't you. I did not...I could not trust myself. It wasn't you."

"It was me that expected too much too soon," Elana corrected quietly, firmly. "Until the day we met, I did not know you as an Amazon — as an off-worlder, and yet I was not warned by that discovery. I should have realized I didn't know you — all of you. It should have reminded me not to assume you would come to feel as I did — as if you knew me too."

"A feeling I simply could not trust," Diana reminded her. Her brown eyes were still shadowed with tears as she looked at Elana. "What did you know of me?"

"Your strength, your compassion...some of your travels..." ...and, she thought, that I loved you and would follow you beyond the White Isles if you bid me. Elana shrugged helplessly. How did one put such dreamspun visions into words? "I knew — hoped — we would be brought together, but whether it would be by the Mother's Hand or Fates' Jest, I could not tell."

Diana drew a steadier breath. She wondered if she would have said anything to Elana had their positions been reversed. "How long did you — watch me?"

"I did not watch consciously," Elana murmured. "I would dream and you would be there...talking...riding. You would simply be there. Vision-stirred, we call it. Half asleep I would find myself beside you. I could not touch you — call to you. Each time I would stand beside the window and search, I could not find you. But you haunted my dreams and the dark pools of mountain streams. Only once, at the very end, did I stand on a mountain and call and have you come at my bidding. But even then I did not see you as an off-worlder. I could only see that this crisis drew nearer as you rode further away. Where you rode to, I could not see — that you lived in Gronday, I did not recognize." A wry little smile crossed her lips as she added, "I did say that we of the Blue Sight are poor at unraveling other's paths. The pieces were there, yet I could not puzzle them together."

"For how long?"

"Since your first night on Aggar."

Two-and-a-half seasons? For five years?! Diana balked at the idea.

"Less often in the beginning...more so in the end," Elana added softly.

Five years? Five years of influence...five years of waiting — wondering...and yet she had warned Diana of her right not to choose the Council's first candidate. Had Elana cared for her so much? Had she known of Diana's wish to stay uninvolved with life and return home — even then?

And as for herself?! Diana had had the audacity to suggest Elana was blithely submitting to the Council's wishes! A chuckle rose, and suddenly Diana found herself laughing.

At Elana's confusion, Diana squeezed her hand. "You never thought to tell me sooner?"

Elana shook her head, bemused at the relief and astonishment that held Di'nay.

"I accused you of wanting me because of the Council's directives. Did you not think five years might have changed my impressions, if only a little?"

Somberly Elana pointed out again, "I did not know you were an Amazon until the day we met."

Diana quieted. "Were you frightened then?"

"No." Elana remembered the morning they had ridden out from the Keep. "I thought — with you as an Amazon, I thought I was incredibly lucky. Still...," her voice dropped, "I was too young in your eyes, Di'nay. Would it have changed anything? Or would I have seemed to be a foolish romantic?"

She could not say, Diana admitted. There was much that she had not understood about the Sight — or about Elana. But she was thankful that Elana told her now, and she was sorry she had wasted so much time in the beginning. "I regret hurting you — mistrusting you. I wish it could have been different."

Elana took both of Diana's hands and smiled tenderly. "I have often said that I have no regrets. I would change nothing. When will you begin to believe me?"

When I stop hearing what I am afraid to hear, Diana thought a little desperately.

There was a rough banging at the door. Elana's shoulders slumped in relief, and she answered Di'nay's unspoken question. "It is Madt'dan and Garrison."

Servants arrived with tub and bath water as Di'nay was going out. With a grin Elana watched her sidestep the men — bread in one hand, mead in the other.

"Ought to know better then to try to eat and walk." Diana smiled across the room at her. But she managed a bite as she left in search of Cleis and their hot food.

Mattee's men were soon gone, and Paul turned a longing eye to the steaming wooden tub. He was drenched through to the skin, and without the benefit of a fieldsuit, he was chilled to his bones, a fact attested to by the bluish tinge of his lips.

"Why don't you get in?" Elana said sympathetically, handing him a chalice of mead. "You look like a drowned river rat."

She pulled the window closed, adding, "Di'nay has an extra fieldsuit here. Would you like to try one? The fit won't be very good, but it might help."

"Yes, thanks. It's nice — your taking care of me."

Elana hid her amusement as she turned the key in the lock and opened the trunk. "Di'nay wouldn't want you to go neglected, Paul."

"It's not Diana that interests me, Elana," Paul returned, stripping his wet tunic from his torso. "And I know you know that — "

In the kitchen, Cleis met Diana at the foot of the stairs. "Mattee wants to know if you want meat or fowl sent up?" She confiscated Diana's cup and helped herself before adding, "The bird is that stringy stuff that I know you don't like. But I wasn't certain of Elana?"

Given that lexion was the most popular roast in the region, it was a reasonable consideration, Diana admitted. But she sincerely hoped Elana didn't care for the bird. The fowl had a peculiar taste that tended to cling to one's breath. As much as she cared for Elana, Diana didn't fancy sleeping next to her, let alone kissing her, if she munched on the stuff.

"Suppose I'd better ask," Diana groaned, and Cleis laughed. Diana snatched the mead back with a dark scowl.

"You could always tell her you hate the things. She didn't strike me as stupid — "

"That is quite enough!" Diana growled and thrust the goblet back to the woman.

And Cleis' laughter followed her up the stairs.

"Please Paul, don't — " Elana shied away from the man, nervously laying the fieldsuit out on the bed.

"Don't what?" Disbelieving confusion and wounded pride hurried him forward.

She started at his quickness, shutting her eyes in panic. This was desperately wrong, but everything was moving too fast.

"Elana! Answer me!"

"I don't — Paul, I never meant..." She shook her head, fighting the sudden rising image of another aggressor. And then suddenly she was in another place and another time. "Di'nay!"

"Damn n'Athena!" Garrison rasped and spun her about.

"Please — " She pulled back, her head bent and eyes shut tight, but he wouldn't let her go. "Mother please!"

"Please to what?!" He shook her hard, trying to make sense. "You can't want her! I won't let you want her!" His mouth took hers with a vengeance.

But his assault softened to a coaxing, pleading caress...the hovering cloud of darkness did not press forward. Slowly the rigidity left Elana's body as the memories released her. This was frustration, not insanity, that held her now, and she felt her fists uncurl.

His hands loosened their ironlike grip on her wrists as she relaxed. But then, as Elana was gathering her strength to speak, Garrison was finally understanding her reluctance for the truth that it was...and he was withdrawing.

The door exploded with thunder. Fury of white hot amarin shook Elana as her eyes flew open, and Di'nay's hands tore Garrison's body from hers.

Footstool and woodbox cracked as the weight of the man was thrown.

"Monster!"

"No!" Elana moved as Di'nay's foot kicked the stool aside, splintering it against the far wall. But her words fell unheard as the Amazon heaved the man up and out again — crashing into the bedframe as he fell.

"Di'nay, no!"

"Selfish Terran carrion!" Her hands grabbed his shoulders. Fingers dug into muscle as she lifted, slamming him up into the wall, his feet dangling. "By what right?! She travels as Amazon!"

His head rolled half senseless as again she pounded. "Men die for less!"

"Di'nay — don't!"

"By what right?!" and her elbows came forward, his body crunching between her forearms and the wall. But she couldn't stomach the stench of his sweat and drew half-back, throwing him higher, screeching, "Answer me!!"

"Diana!!" The muscles were like sword's steel beneath her clutching fingers. "He did nothing!"

Sense hovered, almost penetrating the blood-red haze in her mind.

"Diana n'Athena! Nothing — he did nothing!"

Teeth clenched. The muscles in her neck strained as white as the knuckles in her hands. Dazed eyes sought Elana's pleading figure.

"Nothing...," and blueness flashed, washing through angry heat.

"Nothing — " Elana whispered, and slowly she let Di'nay see what had happened...see how Paul had been slowly, but finally, withdrawing. But then Di'nay knew she had not halted Paul's advance, and Elana didn't know if she would be the one to draw this frenzied rage — or if Paul would still be targeted.

Blank eyes turned, harsh in their blankness, to the man's limp form. His mouth was bleeding from hitting the corner of the woodbox; his hands clenched her wrists weakly. There was nothing he could do against an Amazon's strength — it was all he could do to breathe.

"I should break you in two for even trying," Diana hissed, but her words were hushed with the vise of control now. She dropped him to the floor and released him as soon as he could keep his feet beneath him. She stepped back, despising the feel of him. "Your room is next door. Use it."

He stumbled towards the door, halting as she barked his name. The fieldsuit was flung at him. As the door closed behind him, Diana felt the pit of her stomach retch. She turned from Elana in shame as she realized what she had been about to do. Trusted...she had betrayed that trust. Entrusted with Garrison's safety, and she had come within a breath of killing the man. Entrusted by Elana to respect their partnership — Elana's strength and judgment — and she had exploded past reason...past her own judgment. Never had she been so blinded by fury.

She had wanted to kill...to hurt him. She had wanted to maim him past recognition. And by what right had she been acting?

"Di'nay — "

Her body flinched at Elana's gentle call, and without a word she fled.

"Mae n'Pour! Diana, ann nehna?!!" Cleis sprang up from her seat at the kitchen table and grabbed Diana's arm to steady her. She had never seen her friend so white. "Soroe...nehna?"

"I'm all right," Diana muttered, too shaken to shrug off the hand.

"Like hell you are." Her eyes darted about the kitchen. Everyone was hurrying about. The Southerners had too long been a part of this household to be noticed in the rush of the kitchen work. "What happened?"

What indeed? She slumped against the doorframe. "I just threw Paul Garrison into a wall."

The breath hissed through Cleis' teeth. "Is he alive?"

"Probably. He walked to his room."

"Any reason?"

With a sarcastic drawl, she said, "Would you believe he propositioned Elana?"

"Elana... ?! But she travels as — I may kill him myself. Is she all right?"

"Much better than I am."

Cleis wasn't sure exactly what that meant, but she did know she needed to get Diana away from here.

"The food." Diana suddenly seemed to drift off somewhere else. "I didn't — "

"I'll deal with it." Cleis pulled her down off the staircase. "Why don't you go check on your horses. I'll be right out."

Confused, Diana shook her head. Garrison might be more seriously hurt than she'd explained. "Paul needs — "

"I'll see to it," Cleis insisted firmly. "I'll tend to everything. Now go. Go!" and she pushed her out the back door.

❀ ❀ ❀

"There you are," Cleis smiled rather cheerlessly and reached over the stall door to hand Diana a warm mug of mead. The big chestnut snorted and stomped a little as Cleis slid the door back. "It's all right, Kaing," she soothed and under her familiar voice, he quieted. "I'm only going to pull your friend here out of your box."

Diana sighed, forcing herself to rise, and Cleis pulled the door closed behind her.

"There's that sweet stack of hay back against the wall," Cleis suggested.

Diana wasn't ready to return to the inn, and the hay bin was familiar from long talks they'd shared in the past.

Cleis settled herself and the flask of mead into the piled straw. "I warn you, I have no intention of drinking you into a drunken stupor tonight. It's too cold and too wet and you've got a much warmer bed to crawl into than this old hayloft." It was a standing joke between them that they never drank much together — they talked too much.

Cleis got no answer. Diana merely stood there, gazing out the door into the night where the wind whistled and the drizzling downpour continued. Cleis drew a steadying breath then and prepared to wait. She knew Diana well enough to know the woman would say something when she was ready to.

"How's Garrison?" Diana asked finally.

Cleis shrugged. It was not something she was particularly worried about. "I sent up a bath, a platter of food, and Stevens to take care of him. Apparently he's not as badly marred as I'd feared."

"And Elana?"

"I sent food up — meat, no lexion, and some bread pudding. Not as good a fare as the Keep, I'll wager, but good enough. The Min took it up personally. She said the girl looked well and was bathing...she didn't appear to want much company." For a curious second, Cleis eyed her friend then. "I took you at your word when you said you were worse off. Should I go back and check on her myself?"

"No." Diana shook her head adamantly. After all, hadn't that been the problem from the beginning? Her assumption that Elana couldn't take care of herself?

Cleis swirled the mead in her cup. "Garrison didn't say anything about a scuffle with you. He told Stevens that he'd been pretty seriously hurt on the trip in."

Diana began to pace.

"So, are you going to tell me what happened?"

"Haven't I said?"

"Details," Cleis persisted, and, unrelenting, she added, "Preferably before this rain turns to ice, if you would."

That almost drew a smile.

"Are you going to walk through the whole story?"

"Probably — yes!" But they were grinning at each other.

"Nehna...?"

Diana drew a deep breath and shrugged. "He kissed her. I walked in and over-reacted. He stumbled out. I ran. What else do you want to know?"

Cleis scoffed, "Remind me never to ask you for a history lesson. Obviously there's something else! Diana, you don't go around beating people, despite your reputation as a short-tempered Southerner. I know that, remember? So why would he kiss her at all? Why would she let him? Why would a single kiss — we are talking about a single incident, aren't we?"

Diana nodded.

"Then why would a single kiss make you so furious that you try to crack his head open? Angry, yes. That I can understand. Angry enough to want to hurt him? That I can understand. But raging, furious madness? That's not you, Diana. You usually exasperate me with your patience for the male-kind. This is simply not in character. So what's missing?"

"That's part of it," Diana admitted, setting aside the mead. Self-pity was not helpful tonight.

"Part of what?" Cleis was on her feet, her own temper rising.

"Why I'm so shaken."

"Hey! This is me, remember?" Cleis caught her as Diana went to pace past again, and then more gently, she drew her Sister into a warm hug. Diana's arms slipped around her finally, careful of the injured ribs. Cleis' strength gave Diana a safe place to begin as the tears started.

When she was done, they found a kerchief and a cushioned seat in the hay. Wrapping an arm over her Sister's thigh, Diana laid her head in her friend's lap. And when she was ready, she began to talk. Without speaking of the Sight, she told Cleis much...of how for so long she had thought Elana too young...of how she had even left...of the Priory and her silent watch after the night they took Elana...of her lover's torment — the escape and some of the healing.

As she finished, Diana shuddered, again remembering her rage at Garrison and her shame in her actions. "But compared to the Priory, Cleis, Garrison was nothing."

"So Elana knew he was not threatening so much as he was merely being tactless?" Cleis asked.

"Yes." Diana sighed and sat up finally, wearily. "She understands him a bit better than I do. I think she tends not to take him quite so seriously."

"Are you — jealous of that?"

"Of him? I have always been a little jealous of his attentions to her. I know he finds her attractive. I'm sure that was part of the reason for my stupidity tonight."

Cleis ignored that last part. "And Elana? Did she seem attracted to him?"

"No, she has a rather low opinion of most Terrans, and he's done nothing to change that."

That sounded reasonably sister-like, Cleis admitted. But she was still puzzled. She tried a different tack. "What should you have done tonight?"

Uncomfortable, Diana shrugged again. "Interrupted and asked if she needed help? I don't know."

"Personally," Cleis shared, "I too would have stepped in a bit more forcefully than a mere question, Diana."

"But she's not Maryl — or anyone of Aggar, Cleis. She's...?"

"A Sister," Cleis supplied. "Whether formally indoctrinated or not."

"Yes! I had no right to go barging in assuming she's some helpless mala'—"

"So...you're thinking of her inexperience again? You're afraid you're not trusting her enough?"

"Maybe," Diana sighed. It didn't seem quite so plausible now that the words were spoken. Confusion whirled her reasoning into tangles. With frustration Diana shook her head almost helplessly. "Cleis — Elana was in no immediate danger. I had no right to interfere. She could have handled it — him. I know that. I do!"

"I'll agree that you shouldn't have thrown him about, Diana, but...." Her voice dropped low with conviction as she faced her Sister in the lantern light. "I do not agree that there was no danger."

In silence, Diana listened.

"Given her history at the Priory, given you know her history — you had every right to step in. You had no way of knowing if she could say no to him...no way to know if she was in shock — intimidated — or what. The very last thing you should have worried about was Elana not wanting the help."

That was right. Instinct had said to protect her. Why hadn't she trusted that? It didn't matter how old or how young a woman was — if she was about to be burned you pulled her to safety. Should she turn around and walk back into the flames, well, that was something else. But until you knew better, you acted first.

And Elana? Shadow of Council and Keep, a protector in her own right, wouldn't she — of all women?! Wouldn't she understand that? Hadn't it been Elana who'd come after Diana in spite of Diana's own rashness? Elana who had stood between Tartuk and death despite Diana's blindness?

"You're thinking good thoughts, I hope," Cleis finally pressed.

With a start, Diana glanced up at her friend. "Good or bad, you have reminded me of much, Soroe. Thank you."

"Meaning?"

"There are many ways to over-react."

"You think too much." Then she said soberly, "You spoke of Elana's recovery as you journeyed. Diana, what of your own?"

"My own?" The words echoed dully and she looked away.

"Yes, you. I have known you a long time, my friend. What you described tonight is something I would have expected to see that eve at the Priory — provided it had been viable. Have you been so busy with her healing...with this mission — that you've forgotten your own wounds?"

The total helplessness of that night...the taste of the soil in my mouth? How would I ever forget that? Diana cringed. And holding her as she wept in the caves, washing the bruises so gently...flinching as she moved from my own touch? How will I ever forget?

"Not forget," Elana's voice came back from those days and fearful nights, "but now it is done — over. It is time to go on. It is time to remember that I am safe."

Time to remember I am no longer helpless, Diana rejoined in her mind.

A hand gently touched her shoulder, and Diana reached up to catch it. "You are right, Cleis. Perhaps, after our work tomorrow, I can properly tend to myself as well." With a despairing sigh, she wondered how long it had been. She had spent a very long time in running, it seemed — from Maryl, from Elana...from herself. It was time to do more than go through the motions of caring for herself. She had to smile, thinking of Elana's tolerant amusement — eating regularly had never quite been the issue, had it?

"Perhaps you should begin sooner?" Cleis prompted softly.

"Yes." Her thoughts turned to Elana and where she was waiting above.

"You'll have the room to yourselves tonight," Cleis announced and poured herself a little more mead.

"You need to sleep," Diana protested. "You can't seriously expect to make that ride tomorrow on no rest."

"I'm expecting Cedros in from Colmar tonight, so the Min arranged for a cot by the kitchen fires." Cleis grinned wickedly. "I'll probably be a good deal warmer than you. No windows to open. And the oven's stoked up, readying for the morning's baking."

Diana got to her feet. "Thank you for the shoulder."

"My pleasure." Then, with honesty, "It's good to know that I'm still needed."

"Very," Diana murmured, catching Cleis' hand. "You always will be."

❋ ❋ ❋

Chapter Ten

As Diana slipped into the room a gentle touch of sorrow washed over her. She had not meant to worry her lover. In an instant it was gone. Elana was on her knees on the bed, clutching a pillow. Clad in a nightshirt of Diana's with her hair loose about her, she reminded Diana how beautiful she was. Diana shut the door quietly. The firelight flickered, chasing the shadows away from the room, but it could not chase the pensiveness from Elana's expression. "I owe you an apology," Diana murmured, drawing near the bed.

"For what...?" Elana whispered desperately. She dropped the pillow and curled her fingers about the polished footboard where Di'nay's restless hands played. "...For wanting me safe? For caring?"

Diana's fond smile softened the weathered planes of her face. "No, for losing my temper and not listening...for running. I didn't mean to worry you."

"I knew you were near...and safe." Then in a hushed, strained tone Elana pleaded, "What happened, Di'nay? I have never seen you so angry. I have seen you fight, argue...rave at your commander — at me. But this...?"

Diana was a little shaky admitting, "I don't think I've ever felt that way before."

Elana's hands folded over hers gently. "What happened?"

"I saw him with you — all I could think was that he shouldn't. He had no right."

Elana stared at her for a moment before saying, "He was not hurting me."

"I don't think that registered." Diana forced her voice to keep it from faltering. "I think I was — was back were I couldn't stop them from hurting you."

"You did stop them," Elana insisted softly, framing Di'nay's face with warm hands. "You stopped them by taking me out of the Priory. You and Eitteh stopped them by staying so near, always holding me to the present — to safety. You stopped them by chasing the nightmares away with your arms and your voice. You stopped them by touching...by caring...by giving me better memories to cling to. Don't you know that?"

Perhaps I don't, Diana thought, and then her eyes slid shut as Elana's hands pulled her near. Elana's lips were cool...tender in their seeking, and Diana felt a ragged shudder of relief move through her body.

A knock brought them apart; perplexed for a second they looked at each other. Then smiling, they turned to the door as the barrage began again. "Come!"

"Sorry to disturb you, Di."

"It's all right." Diana grinned, switching easily into Common. She gestured to the woman beside her. "Hal, have you met Elana? — this is Hal Jörges."

"Hello," Elana said, feeling her heart warm at this burly man's awkward respect. She recognized him from earlier as the Terran downstairs in the commons.

"How' you?" He bobbed his head quick with his greeting, then hurried onto business. "Cedros just got in."

"So early?" Diana frowned with concern. "Is he all right?"

"Yeah, just dogged tired. Seems we've got trouble. He would have sent word by radio, but apparently the satellite's out again — "

Diana glanced sharply at Elana, suspicious of the Council's tamperings. But the woman denied it with a quick shake of her head. "No, they wouldn't. Not after passing along your plea to Cleis."

Hal frowned, confused, but went on with, "Anyway, there's a party pulled into Colmar middle of last night. They're armed heavy, metal-tipped arrows. They're looking for anybody traveling with Southerners, and they're moving for the River Road. Boss said we should be ready to leave tonight — as soon as the commons quiet down some. Says we'll try to outrun them, unless you've got a better plan."

"Unfortunately, I don't. Together in about three hours then?"

"Thereabouts."

"We'll be ready."

Hal nodded again, looking at Elana, "Nice meetin' you." He slipped out of the room quickly, just opening the door enough to push his towering frame through. Elana had to smile. It was always odd to see someone so large become so flustered.

"You have to excuse Hal," Diana said. "He's the most unassuming man I've ever met, and he tends to be easily embarrassed."

"I noticed." Then Elana said, "Whose this 'boss'? Commander Baily?"

A scoffing laugh came. "No, Cleis is. She's been on Aggar for the longest. That makes her senior supervisor here."

"Senior?" Elana raised a brow. "What kind of youngster does that make you?"

"Brat!" Diana grabbed the pillow and tossed it back at her.

❋ ❋ ❋

Refortified with food, bath, and a bit of sleep, Diana felt much more prepared for their night's venture. She found herself almost looking forward to the ride. The rain had finally cleared, and, as she stood at the window overlooking the back court, she noticed that the twin moons had begun to peer through the clouds. It was a good sign. The Mother's wind would ride with them.

The others had slipped down the kitchen stairs, staggering their departure so as not to alert suspicious guests. Cedros had said Cleis guessed at least one or two of Maltar's men lurked somewhere in Gronday — the Southern Trader was a known resident of Mattee's. Diana chose her tried and true 'back door' over the squeaking floorboards, and she led Elana out over the kitchen roof to the stable's upper lofts.

Elana gave a cry of surprise. Cleis had brought Leggings from the Keep. With a friendly toss of her head, the bay recognized her favorite human. Diana smiled as the animal playfully pushed its head into Elana's chest.

Cleis had prepared well. They found all the animals saddled and readied with light supplies strapped behind. She had even planned for Garrison, Diana noted with approval — bringing a Terran-styled, bulky, stirruped saddle for the man, knowing he had had little experience riding. They might stand a chance now.

They left through Gronday's eastern gate unhindered. The guards opened the mammoth timber doors without comment. Diana wondered how much that had set Mattee back. She made a mental note; the next Amazon would increase the rent.

❋ ❋ ❋

The early moon had barely set when they made the crossroads, and the seven reined their mounts in to a quieter walk. Diana spoke with Cleis, and Elana moved ahead as their scout; it was time to lift this self-imposed ban. Let the Seer of Maltar know where she rode tonight. The waiting was done. By the time the hawker flew word, this chase would be over!

Bonds loosened, her Sight swept outward, filtering through the trees' great roots — gathering speed and force, flowing from limb to leaf to rustled brush. The vastness of the Mother's night stirred and woke with familiar things, and her strength grew as Leggings moved on.

Sentries...? There — with horses tethered in the wooded depths. The men were travel worn and warded off a night's sleep with hushed voices and a game of cards.

With the quietness of a ghost, Elana returned to Diana's party. In mute affirmation she met Di'nay's gaze and the sentries' scene passed between them; there were only two sentries to be deceived, and the distance they used to hide themselves would now be used against them. Unlike the ultra-sensitive Changlings, these sentries would be easily passed beneath the Sight's cloak.

Diana mutely acknowledged Elana's intentions, and the woman of Aggar again disappeared into the night. Cleis looked questioningly at her friend. Diana drew her sword. Mutely Cleis followed suit and signaled the three men to press more closely around Garrison's mount. Weapons drawn, in utter silence, they continued on.

The night's blackness seemed denser. The sound of their horses' hooves seemed to die — almost to be smothered — by the air's blackness. She saw no trace of the sentries or of Elana; they stayed in a tight formation.

Gradually, the clouds grew more defined. The half-sphere of the midnight moon drew visible. Wary, Diana looked above. Surely they were too close to the Counsel's Keep for Maltar's Seer to play his game tonight? The smothered feeling lifted more, and the noises of the forest slowly drifted back into her consciousness. Diana felt relieved. This was Elana's subtle touch.

She caught Cleis' glance as she sheathed her blade. The younger Amazon hesitated, then did the same. Diana had been dealing with these hunters for longer than she. Cleis did not doubt her judgment now.

They broke into a trot again, and after a time Elana cantered out of the darkness to join them. They were a good two hours from Gronday now. If they could hold this pace — trot, walk, rest and repeat — they would make the gorge bridge by mid-morning. If the Mistress kept her word, there would be no followers beyond that border. But as Elana had reminded them, the dawn would bring new sentries to relieve the old and their tracks at the crossroads would become visible in the daylight. That meant in two, maybe three hours, Maltar's men would be following...the difference should be enough. It was going to be a narrow margin.

At dawn they rested the horses as their steady rhythm demanded. Elana left the others to find herself a quieter place where the trees were more ancient. The smooth-barked pines drew her into the forest, their touch welcoming; at her request their whispering life rushed through the wooded leagues, seeking a helper.

From the branches above the wild hawk crashed downward. A piercing screech rang, and with a ruffled flutter the sharp talons dug into the silverpine's limb. The lower branches were all but bare of needles and twigs; the sunlight seldom found these places. But the golden eyes glimmered with the light from above as they turned their wide and glossy stare to the woman. Blue and gold matched, and the icy fire bonded them. It sprang with a short, protesting cry and rose, twisting and climbing between the thick upper branches. Then with a wild fluster of wings, it broke free, and the two were soaring above the Mother's land.

The red fingers of dawn stretched to touch the northern mountains where wooded slopes yielded to barren, wind-stripped snowy peaks that were splayed with dawn's rose and orange and where the air was sleek with dampness. The joy of wind and mountain heights danced as wings tucked. Together they rolled and banked and played...but thought formed and somberness settled. They circled and turned west, their sharp eyes following the crevice cut amidst the trees — the road of men. Beyond leagues to forked paths the winged quest sailed; where men lodged, the brown of mud was lost. A party of men astride well-muscled steeds was setting out to the East.

Elana blinked, releasing her wild friend to the morning's wind. Her fingers curled against the glossy green bark, drawing its strength as she steadied herself. She smiled then, stroking the giant in silent thanks before turning. They had gained two hours, no more. They would need to hurry.

✻ ✻ ✻

"Fifteen? How does she know?" Cleis demanded in hushed tones. She and Diana stood apart from the others, tightening the cinches of their horses in preparation for another ride. "Each time she returns she knows more. How?"

"She has a gift," Diana returned flatly. "Something like n'Shea." Diana swung up into the saddle. Then she paused before reining Kaing about, and her voice softened as she met Cleis' worried gaze. "Can we leave it at that, Soroe?" Cleis hesitated, then a smile broke. "Of course we can." Mounted, she turned with Diana to start them off.

✿ ✿ ✿

"I hate to quit so close. We've barely two leagues to go," Cleis mumbled as they found themselves dismounted again. "But the horses — "

"I know." Diana sighed. Gratefully she patted Kaing's sweaty neck; he had done well. She was thankful to the stableman that had kept him exercised too. But then, she should have known that Mattee would have allowed nothing less.

The men's laughter drew their attention, and Cleis hid her own humor. Neither Cedros, Jörges nor Stevens had let Garrison's stiff gait go unnoticed. He obviously was going to be a very sore fellow tonight. She sobered then — if there was tonight.

"Up!" Elana's voice sounded through the forest. Scrambling — sliding she dodged through the trees on the hillside above. "They come! Mount up!"

Jörges' strong hands seized the spindly form and near threw Garrison into the saddle. Cinches jerked, knees clamped and they broke — Leggings already in a run as Elana pulled herself up.

They prayed their mounts would last.

Cleis forced them to a slower canter, her heart pounding. They could not gallop the entire way; panic would not decide their fate. The gamble was that those behind had been pushing harder to make up the distance. She hoped that outweighed the extra leagues from Gronday that their own animals had traveled.

"They have lost two," Elana announced as she came along side of the Amazons. "They may lose one more because of their pace."

"Just so we do not," Diana said under her breath, but Elana grasped her concern.

"Paul..." Elana warned, "his legs already quiver from the exertion. His seat becomes more unsteady by the stride."

Cleis nodded and dropped back to warn Stevens and Jörges. They would hold him up by the elbows if they had to.

✿ ✿ ✿

With a shout from Elana the first arrow came. It arched wide, and in the back Cedros snatched his dagger free and flung it behind. Too fast to aim, it whistled into nothing, but the silver flashed, causing the horse to shy. Screaming the animal stumbled, rolling forward — its rider tumbling — a single rider, his horse the swiftest.

He heralded the thundering pack to come. Their horses jumped forward. With spirit their riders were proud of, the animals leveled low into the gallop.

Battle cries and arrows loosed. As the bend opened, hope lifted — the bridge!

Then suddenly Leggings was spinning aside and Diana was cursing. A cry wretched from behind and the Amazons glanced back to see Garrison bounce from the saddle — his horse smashing into Stevens'!

Kaing wheeled with a shrill whistle as Diana's blade came free. The stallion launched himself forward between soldiers and Terran. Silver flashed — white foam splayed as steel blade and stallion teeth bit deep. The sword swept wide — an arrow halved in mid-air as beneath it Elana bent in her saddle, dragging Garrison to her. Jörges was there too. Carrying him, they drove for the bridge.

Hooves beat across wood and the Keep's arrows loosed. Cleis rounded at the bridge as Stevens raced by. She kicked a soldier from his horse, her sword singing as it met another. An arrow unleashed, and she slumped, weapon dropping. Cedros snatched her arm — urging both their mounts across before she fell.

A call of Blue pulled Diana 'round, and Kaing leapt for the bridge. But a blood-curdling cry split the air and a Northerner came.

Arrows whisked from across the gorge and one found his shoulder. Her sword countered his as they galloped. Too late she saw him dead as she was pushed aside from the road. Gritting her teeth, she felt the great muscles of her stallion gather and she leaned forward with him. Reins tight to steady his head — sword flung wide for balance — they lunged into the air, and the jagged teeth of the river gorge below.

Trainees dove to the sides as the chestnut cleared the low wall and then they scrambled to send their arrows off, protecting her back. Sword arms swung, downing the three who tried the bridge crossing; and suddenly the remaining crew were reining back, swords slackening... bows lowering.

"You have come to our borders!" The robed figure of the Old Mistress appeared beside the bridge and young sword carriers.

"Our quarrel is not with you, Old One," the captain challenged. "Let us pass!"

"Your quarrel is against those we now protect," the booming voice of the Old Master proclaimed. He stood with the archers against the southern wall. "Would you challenge the Council's very Keep?!"

The horses shifted uneasily beneath the soldiers — witness to their riders' fears.

"You have come to our borders," the Mistress repeated. "You will not be given passage this day. Tell your master such, and he will understand it is over."

The captain hesitated, then with a disgusted grimace jammed his sword into its sheath. Curse the old woman! They all knew that much more than this journey was done — that his report would never be made. Any that carried this news to the Maltar would lose his head. With a wave of his hand he signaled the arms to be stowed, and still glaring at the robed figures, he pulled his horse around.

❊ ❊ ❊

What would have been a leisurely ride to the Keep became a grueling wagon trip. Their party had not gone as unscathed as Diana had hoped. Garrison had slipped from his mount after taking an arrow in his hip, and Cleis had been struck in the side. The extra protection of her rib belt had deflected the arrow, but the impact had badly dislocated a rib. Elana's Sight warned that a lung had been pierced.

The healers immobilized them both and packed them into one of the supply wagons before drugging them against the journey. Garrison would walk again, they assured Diana, but only the Terran surgeons could repair the damage well enough so that he would not limp. Paul jokingly told them limping wouldn't be so bad since it meant he'd never have to sit on a horse again, but Diana knew better than to take his humor so lightly. Agents such as he didn't keep their jobs if they were easily identifiable — a limp would retire him. She would get him to the base surgeons.

Cleis was a different case. She despised the imperial medical profession with a passion — her lover had died on an operating table. Diana knew the Chief Surgeon at the base. Indeed, she had served with him years past on assignment elsewhere, and she respected his abilities. If any could save the lung, he would. And he would respect their request that he do nothing but immediate needs. The House n'Shea would assume the rest of Cleis' care, provided the Amazon agreed to an immediate discharge. Somehow, Diana didn't think that was going to be a problem now.

In the end Hal Jörges and a young trainee drove the wagon as Elana and she tended the two in the back. The Master promised a hawk would be sent ahead, and the base would be notified. A shuttle would be there by the time they arrived at the Keep. But watching Cleis' drawn face made Diana wonder if it would be soon enough. She wiped the sweat from her friend's brow, her throat tightening. At what risk was she putting her Sister? A person could live with just one lung.

Elana's hand touched Diana's. "She would want this chance," Elana said. She remembered the vibrant energy of the young Amazon. To be forced to limit how far she ran or how hard she played would be a different kind of pain for this woman. Elana squeezed Di'nay's hand. "She has time. It will work."

Diana nodded gratefully. If the Goddess willed, it would.

❋ ❋ ❋

The shuttle seemed empty to Elana despite the tidy rows of a dozen or more seats. Metal, she though disgustedly. Metal and artificial air...but they were pressed for time, and she forced her attention back to their patients.

Behind another of the sliding doors, beds were set in the wall, and Elana recognized the red crosses that Di'nay's medicine box carried. Hal left them quickly to find the pilot in the cockpit, while, with practiced efficiency, Di'nay arranged the two in the beds. Under her quiet commands, Elana helped put life support systems in place before the man returned.

"We're set when you are, Di."

"Nearly — damn." She turned to Elana. "The tranquilizers — the drug we gave them on the way in. The surgeons will need to know what it is."

"I'll get it," Elana assured her, turning for the doorway.

"I'll call when ready," Diana told Hal, and he nodded, letting Elana pass before following her forward.

The trainee handed her the purse, and Elana sent him off with the wagon. The shuttle would only spook the horses while the craft was lifting off. She hit the door's button, ducking inside. The door sealed behind her; in mid-step, she froze.

The metal cavern of emptiness stretched about her. Unprepared, she found herself suspended in a synthetic world — devoid of wood or linen or any organic fixture. She faced a white abyss and felt herself falling.

A door slid open and someone said, "Elana?" Diana grabbed her, holding her upright as she searched the darkened face anxiously. "Elana?!"

Her skin felt clammy and her breath was forced through clenched teeth. As Di'nay's strength stole into her body, she realized this was not the emptiness of the Seer's Tomb. Scattered remnants of men and women lay in seat corners, in the dust trekked in by boots — even faintly in the odd taint of the air.

"Elana?"

Elana blinked as Di'nay shook her slightly and focused on the worried face before her. With a gasp she fell into her lover's arms.

And then as Diana looked at the white fiberglass and metal of these walls, she understood. Moaning, she tightened her clasp and buried her face in the dark curls. "Forgive me. I didn't know that your Sight — never would I ask...."

"I'm all right," Elana protested, shaking her head and pulling back a little. "I hadn't thought either. It's all right now."

"In truth?"

"Yes." She smiled then and felt Di'nay accept her reassurance reluctantly. But there were still other concerns to be tended. "Here. The drug you need. A pinch mixed with a few spoonfuls of water, nothing else."

"This and water?"

"Yes."

Diana's hands trembled as they took the parcel. The realization of their parting was finally sinking in. Her dark eyes searched Elana's solemn face quickly. "I'm not leaving forever, Elana. I will be back."

Elana shook her head slowly. "Do not say that, please."

"Why...? After Cleis and Garrison are tended and my reporting done, I will be back! I promise you."

Elana's tongue moistened her lips as she asked, "When?" Her blue eyes lifted to Di'nay's face. "I cannot promise that I will be here if — "

"How long?!" Diana demanded. "Why would they — the Council couldn't be so cruel! I'll only be a few days — a ten-day at the most."

A ten-day? Elana swallowed hard. "I cannot promise more than a ten-day."

"Before the ten-day then. I will be back." If it wasn't for Cleis she would stay and to hell with Thomas' regulations. But she needed to explain things to the surgeon — there would be papers to sign to release him from obligations...from — damn them! "I swear to you...please let it be enough?"

"I'll be here," and Elana felt the light begin to burn within her. No matter what it took, she would be here.

Their kiss was urgent, filled with promises of words spoken and unspoken and with fear of their separation. But the shuttle's engine hummed beneath their feet, reminding them of other duties, and they parted. Regretfully Elana stepped outside, and kept walking until she reached the edge of the courtyard. Then she turned.

The afternoon sun was breaking through the clouds as the ship whined, slowly rising with a swirling wind of exhaust. It looked very white and pristine in the sunlight as it nosed its way to the southeast. Her wrist throbbed with a sudden ache as the craft shot forward. She clasped her hand over the hidden lifestone and watched until the shining speck had been swallowed by the grayness of Aggar's horizon.

❀ ❀ ❀

Chapter Eleven

Elana rubbed the tired ache from her eyes and drew an icy breath. The garden's scent was lost in the air's chill, but the cold sting of the dawn's mist felt fresh and alive on her cheeks. She smiled softly at memories of a snowy morning — Di'nay standing on the trail at Cellar's Gate. Her Amazon had been irritated and exhausted that morning, not unlike she herself was today.

That was not quite truth. Her fatigue was very real, but she was not annoyed at anything nor anybody. She was frightened, but only a bit now and it was buried deeply — something she did not need to deal with as long as she acknowledged its presence. Her exasperation was more about physical limitation. Her body was restless and grew so easily wearied; that she kept forgetting her lack of stamina was creating this internal tension. No, it was not irritability, although if she was not careful, she tended to express it as such. It was more the exhaustion of separation.

Her blue gaze was drawn to the mountains beyond the garden walls — hidden by low, white clouds threatening to engulf the Keep with foggy tendrils. The whiteness made her think of the shuttle craft, and she sighed. The lifestone was not the reason for her regrets. She had never missed anyone as she now missed Di'nay.

Di'nay would be back, even if for only a brief stay. That knowledge would keep Elana strong until her last breath, if need be. Elana knew the value of Di'nay's promise to her lover. She would be back within the ten-day. It was a simple fact.

Almost as if it were happening in a dream, she felt the heavy door of the Keep open and swing closed again. It was an effort then to draw herself inside, but it wouldn't do to drift too far away.

"You are up and about early," the Mistress observed when Elana appeared at her door. "Would you join me for a cup of mulled wine? You must be fairly chilled."

That brought a smile and Elana nodded. In the past she and the Mistress had often begun the day quietly in the elder's room, sharing something hot.

The Old Mistress moved to the hearth, leaving Elana to shut the door.

After so much time with Di'nay, she found the overheated room almost pleasant. "I have tea also," the elder said, half-turning back. "Would you prefer that?"

"Yes, I would," Elana admitted, unclasping her cloak. She slipped off her ankle shoes, and then with a sigh she sank down onto a backless couch and tucked her feet up under her. "Is there any honey?"

The Mistress gave her an odd glance. "Certainly."

The mug was warm between her icy fingers, and contentedly, Elana settled down to let the brew cool. It was a good morning.

With a drink in hand the old woman stiffly seated herself across from Elana. In a habitual gesture she tasted her spiced wine, already knowing it was too hot, but it seemed there were some things one never learned. It was a long time before her gray eyes turned to Elana. "You were rarely given to sweets. Has your Amazon been teaching you new tastes? Or perhaps the bondstone wearies you?"

"The stone, I think. Honey — sweets — seem to help some." Candor had always been part of their relationship; she saw no reason to hide from that sharp gaze now.

"It has been known to help for a time," the Mistress said, nodding.

"It is the oddest feeling," Elana continued reflectively. "I am alert. I can still do almost anything, and yet there is this — weight. When I ignore it and insist, my body responds well. It seems that I run as fast and tumble as well as I ever have...?"

"You do," the elder confirmed.

"Yet beneath it, Mistress, I am exhausted. It is as if I could sleep for a ten-day."

"And then you find, you can barely sleep at all."

Elana said with a touch of a smile, "I had expected that, but for other reasons."

"You have grown to love this Amazon."

Elana had almost forgotten how good it was to talk with this woman — she had seen so little of the Mistress since her return four days ago. The Seers and scribes had been monopolizing her, although she had still supervised the trainees in their exercises each morning. But there had been no opportunity for the two simply to sit and talk. A sigh escaped her. She wished Di'nay could have grown to know this old friend. Elana felt her heart tug. "Her promise is to return within the ten-day."

"Will that be soon enough for you?"

"It is not a problem," Elana returned calmly.

The Mistress nodded slowly, seeing the quiet strength in the younger woman. It would not be a problem, not for this Shadow. "The scribes could not tell me if she is to leave you again or not?"

"I don't know. It is enough for me to know we will be able to say good-bye."

"You haven't told her then?"

"No, and I don't want it otherwise."

Silently the Mistress absorbed that. Then she asked, "Has your Amazon never spoken of staying? Or of you accompanying her off-world?"

"Once. We did not choose to face tomorrow until our task was done. There is the added difficulty involved, if we were to plan for my traveling off-world."

"Ah yes, this Charlie IV ruling." The elder frowned. "It's alarming to realize how careless we've grown in our off-worlder dealings."

"It was not the Council's doing then? The initial stipulations?"

"No, no." The Mistress shook her head. "The original decrees were the Empire's policies. It has always been assumed that none of us would have need — or desire to leave Aggar. The original Council agreed with the policies so the information was filed in the vaults as our decision."

"The Terrans have been here for nearly two hundred tenmoons, Mistress. That's a very long time to accumulate a great number of scattered details. It's inevitable that some of what we know is set aside."

The elder scoffed. "It does not excuse the risks imposed upon you."

"Nothing was imposed," Elana reminded her quietly, "except by the Mother's Hand. I could have chosen not to be the one to go."

"Truth. It is also truth that regulations often have little to do what can be done. If there is the desire, Elana, a way can always be found."

Memories softened her expression and Elana felt a faint smile upon her lips. "You forget you have made me into a Shadow, Mistress. I must always believe in finding the way where none is said to be."

The Old Mistress sighed and turned to other matters. "Would you like to know of this Seer and the Council's plans for the Maltar?"

"Yes, please." Elana looked up eagerly. "And Di'nay? I have not been able to fathom why Maltar's Seer did not know of her existence."

"Because he never saw her clearly. Your meeting with her in the gardens — yes, the scribes told me of that as well. Your meeting was surely guided by the Mother's Hand. You spoke some of the Sight and of the Seers. Your Amazon is of quick wit. She refused to deal with our own Seer later that day because of your words. Her amarin were clouded with an intensity that our best Seer could not decipher without meeting her eyes..."

Oh yes, Elana knew of that intensity, didn't she?

"...she patently refused all attempts to face him, and, in the end, the Council Master abandoned that effort. We agreed we would content ourselves in following you. Which the Seers did, as you expected."

"So they never connected directly with Di'nay." Elana understood. "Maltar's Seer saw me since he followed the edges of the Council's vision of me. Also he could not so easily find Di'nay because she is not Blue Sighted."

"Exactly." The Mistress nodded in satisfaction at her student's astuteness. "Whenever this Seer glimpsed your Amazon, he undoubtedly reported her as a green cloaked figure. Without direct information, he would never have discriminated between the two of you."

"And the Maltar was not adept enough to decipher the confused images." For a brief moment Elana remembered why she had fought so hard to avoid the Seer's fate — that inability to think — to interpret images — what terrible madness.

"For any Blue Sight it would have been difficult unraveling anything through your perceptions. You have always known Di'nay to be a woman, and so the brief glimpses this Seer had following you would be of a woman clad in green. Yet to any bystander your Amazon is a Southern Trader and a swordsman. I do not think it would have been possible for the Maltar to unravel such details unless he knew of the off-worlders and Amazons beforehand — a Blue Sight and an Amazon. No one else could have succeeded."

Elana nodded. She had thought much the same herself.

"Without your Sight you would not have threatened the Maltar and deceived this Seer — nor safely journeyed. You certainly would not have been able to guide your Amazon through the Priory's dungeons or into the Wayward Path."

"And if the off-worlders had not become involved," Elana added, "there would have been no quest that could have indicated this Seer existed. We literally needed the crisis to fall from the sky."

"Truth. Everything was so clouded beyond Maltar's borders that we would not have deciphered the imbalances until his scheming was well hatched into war. The necessity of an Amazon over other Terrans was plain from the beginning: the ethics of her Sisterhood hold the secrets of Aggar as sacred as her own. The Empire will not fear our inadvertent abuse of their antiquated machinery, nor will they learn of the ways of our Seers. Yes, you and your shadowmate have played your parts well, my child. I could not have imagined a game so intricately woven a tenmoon ago and yet there are none I would rather have sent to challenge the Fates."

"I am honored," Elana murmured, shy of such praise from her mentor.

"As well you should be...although," a wicked gleam touched her old eyes, "I am sure the Maltar would not offer you any laurels."

Elana smiled grimly.

"The Council is aware that this madman's family has held power undisputed for an inordinate amount of time."

"They took their throne a generation or two before the Imperial Invasion?"

The Mistress nodded. "It may be appropriate to see this changed."

"Is there a challenger already?" Elana asked. It shouldn't have surprised her, but knowing that the Seer was there, she had assumed that any threatening noble would be long dead by now.

"Two in particular. Fourth cousins to the Maltar and quietly secluded in the northern ice ranges. The younger is unerringly bright and the elder worships the ground the child walks upon — they are more like father and child than brothers — with ambitions well cloaked by patience and more honorable than many. It is time for that region to begin developing a conscience. An invitation for the Spring's Turning is being sent to them end of the monarc. If they accept, we will search amongst our trainees again."

"But what of the Maltar's Seer? Won't he learn of such an expedition?"

The lined face grew solemn, and the woman looked as old as her seasons. "He is dying, my child. The veil of blackness with which he once clouded Maltars' realms, the Seers of this Council have now folded back against him. He is nearly as isolated as if he were in a Tomb. He will not see the single moon rise again."

With pity...with revulsion, Elana shuddered. His death would release him to feel the Mother's winds as he could not while in the Maltar's chains, but the dying would be lonely. Though no lonelier than existing with the Maltar's insanity. Her breath steadied, and she looked back to the Mistress. "Who was he? He came from this Keep sometime in the past, did he not?"

The elder nodded. "All Blue Sights pass through these grounds. He was a senior apprentice when he left here. It was to be his last journey beyond these walls...he would have been fifteen in the monarc of his return."

"So old?" Elana breathed. Senior apprentices were seldom ten or twelve before their Sight's melding with Aggar's forces seduced them to the Seer's path.

"Occasionally," the Mistress reminded her, "there are apprentices that choose even as trainees to turn from the way of Shadows. As you chose not to become a Seer — they choose a more delicate balance. Ror'tay was such a man."

"It must have been a very difficult choice," Elana whispered. She knew the lure of that rushing flow of life...to be trained to catch such a temptress and then to deny the culmination? Surely that was to dance with fire and turn away?

"He found it less difficult than many — as your mother found her turning away."

Elana finally grasped the treasured amarin in the words. Astonishment echoed in her whisper, "Your husband! ...the one you thought murdered by the Maltar."

"As he was in the end," she pointed out wearily.

"What happened?"

The Mistress sighed. "He was sent to fetch a youth from Maltar's reign — a lost historian's apprentice — a typical journey for a Seer's apprentice. One of my best trainees went with him as guide. They were ambushed shortly after finding the boy, and word was sent that they had died...or rather, been executed for crimes against the realm. The Council's Seers could find nothing of them — absolutely nothing. Now we know that the depths of the Tomb prevented our Seers from finding him...just as it prevented you from reaching Aggar's life cycles.

"After a few days, they abandoned the search, and my daughter and I were left to mourn. We assumed that the three had been murdered within some windowless stone chamber — somewhere generally inaccessible to Seers. We never suspected how completely inaccessible."

A daughter? Since she had been a youngster, Elana had known the Mistress had unaccountably lost her husband to a whimsy of the Fates. It had never been openly discussed by any at the Keep, and she — who knew so much of respecting another's privacy — had not asked. But never had she suspected there'd been a child.

"Yet we were not so far deceived," the Mistress pointed out. "The younger two did die, and the man I had loved was gone. A Seer's Tomb rapes the soul from the body. He truly died that season. The battered husk that has cloaked the Maltar's realm all these seasons since has been a mindless reflection of that tyrant's plots. It is time for that aged shell to join his spirit. I do not mourn his passing now. Both my child and I eased our sorrow many, many seasons past.

"But," the Mistress drew a slow, deep breath before admitting, "the bitterness will be assuaged. The Maltar will never sit easily again. Even if this challenger we sponsor fails, courage will reach throughout the lands, and another will rise. That — and the Maltar's great plans will not come to be. He will not mold the Sight to his meddling ways. He will no longer swallow innocent people whole. No, my Ror'tay was not the seed for our destruction but rather the beginning of Maltar's downfall. There is irony in that handling." Her gaze drifted into a far place; there was peace in her eyes. "Yes, to the chagrin of the Fates, a balance grew from this situation."

As she spoke Elana felt the release of the other woman's weary, silent despair, and saw more clearly than ever before how the events of her life were interwoven with this woman's. Now that the Mistress' thoughts were of family — Elana grasped the familiar amarin they shared. Since her childhood she had seen these, but for the first time she recognized the pattern beneath the emotions and was stunned.

"Rai!"

The Old Mistress started, pulling herself abruptly back to the present. With a snort she stood and went to pour herself more hot wine.

But Elana was not daunted, and more loudly she repeated, "Rai?"

"What of her?" she snapped, and the clay jar smacked as it hit the hearthstones.

"My mother — "

"I know she's your mother. What do you think me, child? A fool?"

No, but she herself had been one. Elana had known someone in her family must have been gifted with the Sight, but she'd never given it much thought. Her parents had been trainees, their families left behind in unknown records. It was the way of the Keep.

"We both have work to do," the old woman rasped irritably. "Unless you choose not to lead the trainees through their paces this morning?"

"What? No, certainly I will." Elana rose hastily, slipping back into her shoes. There was really nothing else to be said, was there?

At the door, though, she paused to find her oldest friend still standing before the hearth. Elana was not concerned that the Mistress was ignoring her. As sometimes irascible as the seasons had been, they had spent them together. There would never be a charge of favoritism simply for the sake of blood in this Keep; she knew that...so did the Mistress and every Council member. Her respect for her young Ona had come from Elana's own character and from skill, but the Mistress' pride and her concern had been heightened in knowing that after so many generations, one of her family had finally become Shadow.

The Mistress half-turned, scowling at Elana's unmoving figure. Elana's pride deepened; it meant something to know she had earned this woman's respect. It also meant a great deal to know she had such a woman as a grandmother. "Thank you, Mistress — for everything."

The old lines softened, and for a moment, the Mistress was unguarded. Then with a crooked smile, she waved toward the door. "They will be waiting."

❊ ❊ ❊

Restlessly Elana pushed back the thick quilt. Sleep came so seldom now that she wondered why she even tried. Reluctantly she climbed from bed to dress. Warm tea and a little honey would be much more satisfying than this chilly chamber.

She grinned ruefully at herself as she reached for a fleece-lined jerkin. She was growing more and more like Di'nay each day in her need for hotter temperatures. The fire was stoked high and still she shivered. It was a small room, the one she and Di'nay had shared that first night. It should have felt sweltering hot by now.

Should it really? She chided herself. It was not her Amazon's influence; the lifestone was drawing heavily upon her body's reserves. Usually it was nurtured by the mingling energies of Di'nay and herself. Their proximity...their interactions fed its powers and linked it, as well as themselves, to the flowing circles of life around them. But that primary link was stretched too thin — too taut — by the distance. To maintain their bond the stone drew upon the most available life force now...Elana.

The grand hall was not quite empty at this moons-lit hour. Alone, a robed figure sat before the fire in an ornate, high-backed chair. A distant stare watched the leaping flames as his lax hands held a forgotten cup of mead.

She hesitated, yet Elana welcomed company. With a soft tread she descended. "You sit up late, Master," she murmured as she neared.

The Master shifted, pulling his gaze from the fire long enough to recognize her. With a grunt, he waved at the warming jar of sweet mead and the nearby footstool. "Come. Join me if you will."

The drink was hot and the cup chased the chill from her fingers. With a nearly contented sigh, she drew the stool towards the hearth and settled quietly.

His gaze turned, studying the bruised shadows beneath her sapphire eyes and the faint caramel tinge of her skin. He might have been amazed if any other had come to sit so calmly at his side after six days of emptiness, but Elana had never been like the others. He was proud of her decision to fight this waiting. Regardless of her Amazon's choices, if she was abandoned now there was hope that her body would be strong enough to manage the withdrawal. And if the Amazon did return — well, then that was reward enough.

But he had had a hand in raising Elana...and compassion stirred as he spoke. "You're finding it hard to sleep?"

"I manage a little. It is odd to be restless and yet weary."

He nodded slowly. "The weariness comes from the strain. The unsettled feeling — it is the stone's urging you to find your shadowmate."

"She will find me. I need only patience."

His smile was kindly. "That you have always had."

They sat in silence for a time, each accepting the other's solitude, companionship easing the isolation. As the flames danced and the wood popped, Elana felt peace envelope their stillness. Gradually a subtle awareness drifted between them.

A mild surprise took Elana as she recognized that in some way, each of their hearts was drawn to the same thought...to their would-be mates. "I did not know that you ever cared for her in such a way."

A corner of his mouth lifted in irony. "The Mistress? Oh yes, as Fates' Jest would have it. I thought it comfortably settled into oblivion, but I was mistaken."

"She does not return your affection?"

His bald head moved sadly. "No, her heart has always been irrevocably bound to Ror'tay. Your grandfather was quite a man. A dear friend of mine in days past. I am glad to know he finds peace tonight."

"He...he is gone?"

The Master nodded. "At darkfall." He raised his cup in salute. "May the Mother hold him near."

Elana felt a sadness stir. She knew nothing of the man, Ror'tay, this Seer now gone, except the fear she had felt while running from the Maltar that he was following her with his sight — and would discover Di'nay. She wondered if perhaps, somehow, he had recognized her, and whether the faintest of consciousness of who she was had stirred in him to thwart Maltar's decipherings. She would never know. Seers slipped into mindlessness sometimes, never to return. Yet for some pieces of life would touch them, and — for an instant — the individual would re-emerge.

"How do you feel — to know he was kin?" The old man broke into her thoughts with gentle concern. "It would make many bitter."

"I bear Maltar my grudge, not Ror'tay," Elana said icily. Her voice softened. "I could never hate one so mindless and abused. I will never know him as you did, Master. I feared him as I fear an ensnaring rope. But to be bitter? No. How can I hate a piece of rope? It is the one who knots and tightens the noose that is responsible. The Ror'tay I saw was a sorely worn and abused tool, no more."

"And as your kin?"

"I regret not knowing him as he was before. I regret my mother did not know her father." Elana shuddered as the memory of the Seer's Tomb returned. "As his granddaughter I am Sighted, as a Blue Sight I understand — as a prisoner in the Tomb I knew some of the horror he endured. If it were me, I would have been grateful to the one who ended those seasons of insanity — those eons of torture. I am even a little glad I could do that for him. Because he is of my blood, did I not owe him at least that much?"

He took her words in slowly. All she said was true. A painful wisdom for one so young. But no more painful than the loss Aggar would know when she departed. Whether Elana left this life or this world, the Council would sorely miss the path she could have shown them. He caught his thoughts — hadn't he

just been reassuring himself she might survive?
Reassuring? Or denying...?

✿ ✿ ✿

Chapter Twelve

$\mathcal{D}$rawing a deep breath, Diana thoughtfully looked at the comphone in her hand. Hal the shuttle pilot was still not answering; short of putting the base on Attack Alert, there was no way to reach him until ten o'clock since this was his day off. Another four hours. With grim resignation she set the receiver down. Thomas would be suspicious if she requested another shuttle pilot at this late date. With the transport she was supposed to be taking off-world waiting, everyone on duty would already be assigned...that would mean calling in a volunteer. By that time she knew it would be close to ten anyway.

And she could not ask Cleis to take her. Her friend would never say no to this sort of favor, but she was not sure that Cleis was even up to a short shuttle hop. She could not trade one of them for the other.

Diana dropped wearily into the desk chair. It seemed like hours had passed since she'd left the destroyed lab. But it had barely been sixty minutes. Her mind churned, refusing to acknowledge what she knew must be true. Her own ignorance — slowness — stunned her. There had been enough evidence, yet she had been too self-centered to see it. Or had Elana's gentle redirecting been at work?

She should have understood sooner. It was called lifebonding for a reason. She remembered Elana's vagueness when referring to her future. It had happened often enough, that elusive muttering. Why hadn't she heeded its importance?

Their menses had followed the same calendar, yet she had not really noticed. Women who worked or lived together often had the same cycles. But Elana was of Aggar; she should not have bled as frequently as Diana no matter how attuned their natural rhythms.

Diana remembered the way the ruby-blue lines shivered and pulsed into life at their bonding. It had been her own rhythms setting that flow into motion — her rhythms passed to Elana. The soothing tempo of Elana's heart beneath her ear as they lay together had been the tempo of her own heart. Not quite equal to the number of heartbeats, the sound had seemed familiar to her; the rhythms had slipped into matching measure with her own, like half-notes imposed upon quarter notes. Always in time, always together. It had seemed right to hold her and listen to that steady beat. Of course they had matched — the stone's power had matched them.

It had brought the two of them safely through so much, the power of that small stone. But their bonding had gone beyond the stone's ties and their minds had meshed with their bodies.

And what of their hearts?

She loved Elana, Diana knew. From too soon to this day, she loved her. Elana returned that love, but it took so much more to leave one's home and way of life.

Time... Diana mourned the empty days of their separation just as she feared they had been too many. In fifty-two hours now the transport would leave orbit, and Thomas expected the three of them to be on it. There would not be another for two months. Two months — only a monarc... it was not so very long. She could become ill with some mysterious thing or other. Or fall from a horse, perhaps? Yes, Thomas would believe that readily enough.

She did not — could not know — if Elana would want to leave this world. Grimly she thought of Elana's frozen form aboard the shuttle and wondered if the journey could even be risked. What would six months sealed within the artificial world of a spaceship do to a Blue Sight — and with her different metabolism? Then what of the two years of assimilation on Shekhina moonbase at home?

More immediately, what did eight days of separation do to one named Shadow?

She had said within a ten-day. Elana had promised she would be there. And yet the sword had lasted what? Seven... seven-and-a-half days?

"Have you been up all night?" Cleis' voice interrupted her, and Diana glanced up thankfully. This waiting was growing unbearable.

"No." Diana forced a smile. "And you? Why are you up so early? You're suppose to be resting."

"I am resting, and if that laser tech did his job properly, there's no reason I shouldn't be in here resting instead of in bed."

Diana chuckled, spinning her chair fully around as Cleis settled onto the couch. The 'laser tech' was the chief surgeon of the base.

"What time do you leave?"

Diana stretched her legs stiffly and crossed her ankles. "Tennish."

With a scoff, Cleis returned, "Hal is off-duty today. You'll need to wake him if you want to see her before mid-day."

"You're in an awful hurry to get rid of me," Diana observed dryly.

Cleis shrugged matter-of-factly but winced as her ribs protested. The hole in her lung might have been repaired, but there were still other things to be tended.

"Do you need the meds?" Diana asked in concern.

"No — " Exhaling slowly, Cleis felt the spasm slow. "I have no interest in being groggy for the next six months, thank you. I'd only end up addicted to the stuff."

A wry twist to Diana's smile added to her sarcasm as she said, "Unlikely. Much too fanatical."

"I refuse to answer that," Cleis said, but she was grinning.

They were silent a moment, and thoughtfulness drew across Diana's face. She pressed the bridge of her nose, refocusing her attention. "I'm sorry. I had forgotten you didn't know."

"Know what?"

"Earlier this morning, around five, there was an accident in the chem lab."

"Dearest Mother. Was anyone hurt?"

"No, no one at all. They can't quite figure out what happened. Apparently the transport just brought in some new supplies and they're guessing something was mislabeled and poorly packed. Whatever it was, they think, it made Lazarus' new acid compound critically unstable. Everything was fine when he left the lab around nine last night, but the alarms went off this morning. It was simply incredible...two square meters of equipment, cabinets — the wall and everything beyond it was gone."

"Gone? How do you mean gone? An explosion?"

"A very silent one. It disintegrated. Turned to powder and just fell away."

"Eieh — if they ever figure out what was mixed together, the arms people will have a field day."

"Maybe...," Diana mumbled. She remembered standing there, looking through the two-inch steel wall that sat gaping open like a cavern. It had been the south wall of the lab, and the field depot was housed beyond it. Her locker had dissolved along with the lab wall. Although Thomas had been very sympathetic in the few seconds he could spare from his general panic, his words had barely registered with her. She had only stood there, stunned at what she saw. There had been nothing left of cloth or steel; all that was left was a gray dust...and the stones from Symmum's sword.

In the commotion no one had noticed her sifting through the gray powder of her belongings. No one had seen as she lifted the murky white stones from the dust. Six imperfect ovals, so cool to the touch...once they had scorched her palms through the very gloves she wore. Unscathed by Lazarus' mysterious 'acid,' they merely lost all glimmer and pulse of color.

Wordlessly she had pocketed them and left the scientists to their speculations; she had her own pursuit. How could she have been so slow?

"Diana...?"

She glanced up at her name.

"I said, you're brooding again."

"Am I? Sorry." Her friend's words registered then, and curiously Diana looked back to her. "What do you mean 'again'?"

"Again. What does it usually mean? Somewhat frequently and recent, recurrent, repetitious...you know, again!" With a short, exasperated sigh, Cleis threw up a hand. "For the past week you've floated around here half here, half back at the Keep. When you're there, you're wistfully content. But here, you're brooding. When are you going to tell someone what you're fretting about?

"All right...," Cleis corrected herself quickly as Diana began to laugh, "all right. Me, I mean — tell me. Isn't it about time to?"

"It would seem so," Diana returned, wondering how her friend's patience ever extended to accept any of Diana's moodier moments. Cleis had the curiosity of a cat...but she had the strength and warmth of the feline, too. Perhaps, Diana decided, it was time to ask advice.

"I guess," Cleis began more somberly, "that there is a problem between you and Elana about immigrating. Am I right?"

How much to tell? Not the stone. But if it wasn't too late, was it possible?

Diana sighed and slumped forward, covering her face for a moment. It seemed to take forever to muster her wayward thoughts together. Why did her mind always seem so muddled when she thought of herself and Elana? The answer to that, she realized with sudden clarity, was that she needed to think with her heart a little more often. She dropped her hands and faced Cleis. "You remember me speaking of a gift she has that is similar to n'Shea?"

Cleis nodded.

"Elana's gift is much more strongly tied to the Goddess' world and herself with it. When she is isolated — separated from organic auras, it is...I can't explain it. But it's like drowning in a cold, black well."

"You're worrying about the trip then?"

"And about Shekhina...two years of screening, education — immigration procedures before she sees planetfall."

"That could be changed," Cleis reminded her. "Special Provisions exist for a reason. You could petition n'Sappho while we're still in transit. The hearings could be arranged for the day of arrival if need be."

"I know very little about the Provisions," Diana admitted. "I've only heard of those rejected."

The imperial agencies were eternally attempting to circumvent the Sisterhood's immigration process because none of their agents ever successfully completed it...either the women were discovered and denied entry or renounced their imperial duties and sought political asylum from n'Sappho. The result was that the Empire knew quite a lot about Shekhina, but very little about the Sisterhood itself.

"Do you think n'Sappho might consider such a visa?"

"My grandmother was admitted with one. They surely can't be that uncommon. Most simply, the need must be there, and your case is certainly legitimate enough. And even if they denied it, Diana, two years would not be in a complete vacuum. The greenhouses are open to all; there are quadrants where wood stuffs and linens are more frequently used than fiberfill and polysynthetics. I mean, look at what you're wearing." She waved to the bulky sweater of homespun beastie wool. "Wouldn't any of that help her?"

"Yes, of course, but walking around half-blinded for two years is a lot to ask of anyone's sanity, Cleis."

She had no answer to that, and yet Cleis would have sworn that Elana wouldn't be daunted by such a challenge.

"On the transport it would be much more difficult," Cleis began again, finally addressing the worst of the problems. "But there would be a way. If nothing else, you and I could ensure she was never left alone. It would not be easy, but perhaps it would be enough?"

"Yes...perhaps." Tiredly Diana sighed. Given a chance, it might work. "I have not talked to her yet about immigrating."

That didn't surprise Cleis. Matter-of-factly she said, "Then it's time to."

"If she decided to stay, I won't be going home," Diana added quietly.

She had not really thought to say that, but as the words came, she knew them to be true.

Finally she understood why Elana had not spoken of the dangers of their parting — she would not hold Diana to this world through pity. That made two of them, Diana thought, because she would not force Elana to leave Aggar merely because the companion she was bonded to was an off-worlder.

"You are serious," Cleis said, almost too upset to speak, "but are you certain?"

Elana had been right, Diana thought. I will never be prepared to lose her to death. "I am."

Cleis had never known the woman to break her word. The words Diana spoke echoed of such a pledge. The tears stung behind Cleis' eyes, and stiffly she rose to her feet. Her mouth felt like cotton, and her voice sounded dull to her own ears as she said, "Give me a minute to get ready. I'll fly you out."

Diana began to protest, but Cleis held out a hand to forestall it. "I'll be fine. I'll even check in with what's-his-name when I get back, if you like. But if there's a chance that you are to stay...at least a Sister should see you away."

Pain twisted through her heart as these words were said, but Diana was grateful...truly Cleis would never know just how grateful.

❀ ❀ ❀

Chapter Thirteen

"Do you think it wise to let her still work so with the others?"

The Old Mistress turned a stern eye to the Council Speaker. "There is more here than you appear to see." Below them was the practice field where Elana coached the younger trainees. They watched as a pair bent and leapt into a sprint.

Elana's voice carried in the wind as she urged them on. Satisfaction flickered across the old woman's face. "Do you see how they follow her every move — absorb her every word? There is not a single daydreamer or jester amongst the lot."

Elana squatted, placing someone's foot into a better position. None of those above could see what she was pointing at, but the trainees' concentration was evident as several began shuffling their feet into place and testing the new directive.

"They do seem inordinately respectful," the Council Speaker admitted. The young apprentice beside him nodded, and he realized the same awed attention held this lad as those below.

"She is the Shadow alone and yet returned," the Mistress said with pride. "She is the epitome of their dreams...their dreads. She is a Shadow separated from her companion and yet look — she moves, she speaks...she can still out-race the lot."

"Quite a feat...but she is dying, is she not Mistress?"

The woman frowned impatiently, "She wearies. She is bruised. Yes, she is a Shadow separated. But the myth — the fearful myth that without the shadowmate the Shadow is helpless falls! What do you see here? Weakness? Or strength?"

"She is an incredible young woman. I have never suspected otherwise. She was your finest student."

"Was...is. Look at her! See the living proof in her very motion! She is testimony to the essence of lifebonding and yet she dispels the ancient myths that even you fall prey to. Look! She walks with them, laughs, and yes — bests them at much of their own sport. Not useless without her shadowmate, Speaker, she is tangible evidence that Shadows move, think — act without their human's directive presence. She is creating a whole new generation of Shadows, now — as we speak!"

"But in two days — three maybe, she will be gone. What will they remember of her then? That she died gallantly, without fear?"

"No!" Exasperated, the Mistress drew a tight breath and tried again. "She is the strength of Shadow. They will remember that strength. When separated from their companions — in death or by distance — they will remember her walk...her words, and they will seek to imitate. Think of the countless we have lost because of the separations that might have been merely a five or six day ordeal? And yet their fear caused them to weaken — to lose hope, so they died before they could be reunited. None will be lost so easily now! Think of the missions that have failed because the companion fell before the quest was finished? Shadows will not yield so easily, and their task may yet be done before they follow their mate's death. She shows them how to live — to fight the weariness, and this they will remember.

"She breeds a new expectation — a new challenge into their souls. Separation will no longer mean despair. Disagreement with one's companion will no longer breed quite the intensity of fear it once has. They see the power of a Shadow in its own right — not merely as the companion's pawn."

The Speaker frowned. "Was this not always our intention?"

"Our ideal — yes. Realized? In truth, less often than we would hope; Elana's name will be remembered by those below. The students have their own litany of history, and she has become an intricate part of it. And not just among my trainees, Speaker. The young blue-sighted apprentices question if they should simply be Seers — or if there is more. Yes...these are subtle winds our Elana sets in motion, but long felt, I would wager."

He sighed, perplexed. "Don't you make more of it than it is? We've had Blue Sights turn Shadow before. We've had a few survive the separation...yes, maimed and confused, but they have survived. I don't see the difference here."

"The difference is she has returned whole! Whatever tomorrow brings, they will remember today! She has walked among them and shared their bread. She has faced the Maltar separate from her shadowmate, and her companion sought her — even as Shadow would seek. The difference is she has created our ideal and lived time enough to show it to them. She is not a tale embellished by teachers for learning, Speaker. She is flesh, and bears hope. Elana has been accepted — as lover — by her companion. Do you realize how each Sighted apprentice who dreams of being a Shadow is frightened by the thought of finding themselves bonded to one who despises the Blue Sight? She has not only found herself bonded to a tolerant companion, but to an off-worlder! And not merely accepted, but embraced. If such an unlikely match could succeed, then the forging of well-knit bonds with one of Aggar becomes so much more of a possibility."

He had to admit her reasoning explained the requests that had passed across his desk in these last few days. More of the Sighted apprentices were contemplating the change. The Council had been worried that too many Seers would grow to guard this Keep, but now it appeared that the Mother was finding her own use for these blue-sighted children... a finer use too. A handful of Seers could easily do the work of the Council and Keep. But the subtle interweaving of Blue Sight and ordinary people could alter Aggar's path in a way that would ensure the Mother's balance. Patience and time — perhaps they would find the Spring of Life.

The Council Master folded his hands into the sleeves of his robes. "Perhaps we should reconsider this tradition of ours — of not naming a Shadow to history."

The Mistress smiled. "The potential at this crossroads is great."

"At least — she might be named as the Blue Sighted Shadow. The first of many?"

"A nice, diplomatic compromise, Speaker... as always."

His dark eyes sparkled with the Old Mistress' teasing. For a moment, the man wondered, who had done the negotiating today?

❊ ❊ ❊

Elana shook her head. Left-footed, every one of them. She smiled tolerantly as the adolescents turned to walk back towards her — they were trying, and some were improving. So perhaps all was not in vain.

"Remember not to pull up until you are past the mark," she repeated at the next pair readied into a crouch. "If that mark were a snake, would you slow to bait it? Now... ready — off!

"No! Don't stand so fast — lean!"

"They do much better," Telias murmured, joining Elana at the starting marks.

"Do they?" Elana ruefully met the other's sapphire gaze. "Have I grown cynical? Or am I merely out of practice as instructor?"

"Neither. I don't know how you ever found the patience for us. It seems there is this magical day in which each foundling transforms into a well-coordinated candidate, but for some, I am hard pressed to imagine the date."

Elana laughed. She could well commiserate with Telias' frustrations, and she did not envy the honor Telias had been handed when the woman assumed the duties of the Eldest Prepared.

"But I did not come to supervisor races," Telias said. "The hawkers received a message from the wastelands this dawn."

"From the healer Melysa?" Elana prompted eagerly, thinking of the small eitteh she had sent to her charge.

"The same. She included news for you. Your eitteh is well and will be walking by spring. She has chosen to adopt the healer's caverns as home. Melysa thought you would like to know." Telias smiled gently, reading Elana's relief plainly. "You shared much with the winged one, did you not?"

Elana nodded. "We wouldn't have returned safely without her."

Almost wistfully, Telias sighed. "There are times I envy you your animal sense."

"And there are times I have envied you your lack of it," Elana retorted with a grin. "Life has enough responsibilities without seeking to add more."

"It certainly has," Telias agreed. With a comical frown she glanced about at the students, who were growing rather impatient. "I suppose I should take them from you. You've been out here several hours between the tumbling groups and this lot."

"I haven't minded," Elana admitted quietly. "It is a good way to pass the time."

Telias stared at her hard for a moment, then nodded. "You're looking better than you did at breakfast."

What Telias did not say was that "better" was still very poor indeed. Elana's hands trembled now, but working on running and tumbling maneuvers did not call attention to such tremors. Vying with the spoon and porridge had not been so graceful a task, however.

"What about a last sprint?!" Telias challenged lightly, raising her voice to draw the trainees into the bout. "A mass troop? Send them off to the bath house with something to feel good about?" Then her voice dropped to a murmur. "And send you off for a nap? I'll handle the endurance laps this afternoon."

Elana nodded, but teased, "You're so confident that these gangly scheafea will outdo me?"

Shouts of protest turned them both to the adolescents standing about them. And the trainees demanded their chance. "You were close yesterday, were you not, Sa'ran?" Elana smiled at the tallest boy.

"I was closer the day before!" a lithe, small woman of eight seasons interjected quickly. "One of us will have you today!"

"Will you indeed, Desl?" It was a jovial challenge that warmed Elana. On her first day back these trainees had been too frightened of tiring her to risk such a boast. She was pleased they were learning about speed — and about inner strengths.

"Enough!" Telias threw her hand high. "To the marks!"

The lifestone stabbed beneath her wristband, and Elana absently loosened the leather as she took her place.

The boy Sa'ran looked down at her as he jostled a little more elbow room from the pack. He grinned then. "Today — I will catch you!"

"Now..."

"Remember," Elana said, still the instructor, "run through the mark. Do not pull up... Ready..."

The stone throbbed again, and she blinked, looking downfield.
"...Off!"

Her toes pushed, her legs drove, and she felt her body leap forward through the heavy weight of her exhaustion. But the speed was there. Her stride lengthened and she moved a step in front of the others —

The stone flamed beneath her skin, and she slowed suddenly, unconscious of the trainees rushing by. Dazed, she stopped — and turned, lifting her leather-bound wrist. Facing the terraced hill and the Keep above, she suddenly realized what it was. With a cry she was off for the steps.

Telias turned around in concern. She glanced upwards, but she could make out nothing in the gloomy overcast. Then the shining ship dropped into view. Shouting, she darted for the stairs herself, and on the terrace above the Council members turned too.

The imperial shuttle was returning.

Elana took the steps two at a time, running across the stone terraces only to bound up the next staircase. With a speed that would have astounded her for any lesser reason, she raced over the last few levels and past the elders. Her hands snatched at the banister as she slammed to a breathless halt.

Nothing, she thought, had ever looked so beautiful as that white-and-gray craft settling into the courtyard below. Nothing — except the sight of the woman emerging from the portal.

Elana drank in the vision of Di'nay's tall figure dressed differently now — as a Sister. Her heart rose in her throat as Elana discovered she liked the fact that her Amazon could look like a woman. Soft kid boots bound her feet as white pants showed the strength of thighs and the soft curve of hips. The ruddy orange knit sweater was bulky, but it did not flatten her chest as the taut jerkin had, and Elana felt incredibly proud to know that this woman was here for her.

Diana set aside the small duffel bag and looked above to see Elana — and the straggling trainees of the Keep staring down at her. But her gaze sought only one, and with a wave of her hand she broke her lover's trance.

Elana rushed down the steps. Neither of them cared who was watching as she flung herself across the courtyard into Di'nay's arms.

Arms closed and lifted — as strong as she had remembered them. And lips kissed hers as desperately...as tenderly as she had dreamed. "You are here!" Diana rasped, her lips trailing across Elana's flushed cheek. "I was so afraid — "

"My dearest Di'nay!" and she pulled her lover's mouth back to hers, assuaging their grief in the best way she knew how. Finally, slowly, their breath drew in around their kiss, and Di'nay's arms loosened enough to let Elana's feet find the ground. Then tenderly their lips parted and eyes opened. Smiling, Elana breathed, "Yes, I am here...here as I promised."

"You are not well." Diana brushed the stray wisps of hair back from her face. In concern her fingers traced the bruised hollows beneath the sapphire eyes, and she felt the faint tremors in her lover's body. "You are not well at all."

"Nothing that seeing you won't cure," Elana teased joyfully. "I am all right, Di'nay. In truth, I am. Believe me. Now that you are here, I will be even better."

She did believe her. Diana knew that that was the trouble. Diana remembered a similar reassurance at Melysa's, and she recognized how often her lover had used such cryptic phrases. She felt her concern rise again. She had been blind.

"Diana?"

They turned to find Cleis standing in the doorway of the shuttle. She nodded faintly to Elana. "Tomorrow, this time?"

Tomorrow? Elana felt her throat close, and Di'nay quietly said, "Yes. Thank you..." and the door slid shut before Elana could decipher the pain in the younger Amazon's face. By the Mother's Hand, the woman had looked stricken.

Diana picked up her small bag. With an arm around Elana she steered them both back from the shuttle as the engine began to whine.

Tomorrow? Elana thought again, her heart thudding painfully, but she pushed the pain aside as the craft lifted. She would be thankful for any small time she could have with this woman; there was much that could happen within an evening's passing, was there not? She dared not even wish that hope into words, though, and as the shuttle disappeared, she turned Di'nay to greet the approaching elders.

"It is a great pleasure to meet you again, especially under better circumstances." The Council Speaker smiled brightly, extending his hands.

As the Amazon accepted the Speaker's greetings, Elana exchanged a smile with the Mistress. Stubbornness they both knew well in others — and in themselves.

"As Mistress here I welcome you to this Keep," the older woman said in her turn, but as Diana bent near she added softly, "It is good to see you again, young Amazon. How does your woman-friend?"

"Well, thank you, Mistress. She returns home in two days' time."

"I don't believe you've met Telias, our Eldest Prepared." The Council Speaker gestured at the young woman beside him.

Telias nodded hesitantly, daunted by the intensity of the woman's amarin.

"I am honored." Diana returned her nod politely, remembering another Eldest Prepared, reminded by the familiar way Telias' gaze danced across her face.

The Speaker's pleasant tenor directed her towards the curious throng of adolescents above on the patio and steps. "Telias and Elana have just been putting these youngsters through their paces."

"You must forgive them," the Mistress said, feigning annoyance. "They are the gangly ones of seven and nine tenmoons, and their manners are sorely lacking."

Diana grinned at the eager, inquiring faces and admitted, "There is nothing to forgive. They do no harm."

"If you like being a fish in a pond," the old woman scoffed. With a wave of her hand she snapped, "Telias! Find them something more suitable to do. Or I will!"

"Yes, Mistress." She nodded quickly to their guest and left.

The Mistress stepped forward with a mischievous glint in her eyes, and gently slipped a hand through the Speaker's arm. "These two need time to themselves. There is nothing so news-worthy that young Elana can't tell our guest of it later."

Diana half-bowed as the Mistress guided the Council Speaker away. And then her smile softened as her gaze returned to her lover.

"You look tired," Elana murmured, "and cold. How did you expect to survive in only a sweater? You – in the middle of winter?"

"I didn't count on standing here in the wind," Diana teased, gathering up her bag. "And you're not at all cold?"

"I've been quite warm working with the trainees, thank you. Come. Inside. Neither of us is going to last long out here." But the glowing warmth they were sharing had nothing to do with the weather.

"I've been worried about you," Diana murmured as they walked through the endless halls of the Keep.

"And I about you," Elana returned. "How is Cleis? She looked – strained."

"Her ribs still need tending, but she will wait for the care of the witches n'Shea."

"And her lung?"

"Mending well. You were right. There was time enough."

It was the same room they had shared before, but Diana realized she actually felt awkward as she set aside her bag. It was strange to stand here in white pants and knitted sweater, devoid of the Southern Trader's protective garb.

"Word about Eitteh came," Elana said as she snatched an armful of clothes from the bed. "She will walk by spring. She's taking up residence with Melysa."

"We spoiled her with cooked meats, do you think?"

"Very likely." Elana was suddenly nervous as she backed towards the door. She nodded at the empty hearth. "Would you start the fire? I – I'll only be a moment. After the running, I need a bath."

"Yes, certainly." Diana smiled reassuringly, a bit amused at the woman's stuttering. "Take your time. I'll be fine."

With a racing heart that had nothing to do with hurrying, Elana nodded and fled. Dear Mother, she had forgotten how beautiful Di'nay was. She was embarrassed that all she wanted in this world at this moment was to climb into bed and hold her.

Chapter Fourteen

Diana smiled fondly as she munched on a piece of bread and swirled hot tea around in its mug. Someday perhaps Elana would let her return the favor of simple tasks such as tending to the food.

"Good, they did not send the lexion," Elana noted happily, shutting the door behind her, her skirt swirling about her calves. "There are times I doubt that they ever listen to me."

Diana liked the way the blue weave of the tunic reflected in her lover's eyes. "I assume you told them to send the meat and cheese instead?"

Elana nodded, kneeling down on the other side of the footstool that held the tray. "I thought you'd prefer it. Lexion was distinctly missing on the platter at Mattee's."

Lovingly their gaze searched the other's face, delighting. Then the fire crackled, as eyes met.

"Have I told you how beautiful you are with your hair down?" Diana felt the warmth of Elana's blue touch and hugged her nearer, before she said, "Thank you."

Elana released Di'nay, biting her lip nervously. "The Speaker's apprentice stopped me in the corridor. He is asking again if we would join the Ten for mid-day meal. I told him no." She looked to Di'nay tentatively. "Was that right?"

With a long drawn out sigh, Diana felt the weight of the world return. She supposed it would be best, politically, to accept. After all, it was quite an honor.

"This is my home." Elana studied the tiny flowers tooled into her wristband. "You are my guest. You need do nothing here you'd rather not do."

"Nehna?" Diana grinned. "You've something you'd rather we do instead?"

Elana swallowed hard. A tentative smile began to play across her lips. "Left to me, Di'nay...I'd bolt the door." Her voice grew rich and low. "Lead you to bed...." Her eyes lifted boldly. "And never let you go."

Hunger and politics were obliterated in the heat of blue flame, and breathlessly Diana whispered, "The door is already bolted...."

❄ ❄ ❄

Diana was awakened by the crackling pop of a log disturbing the night's peace. The wood settled with a small splay of sparks, and dreamily she let her eyes slip closed again. Beneath her cheek, the satiny softness of Elana's stomach lured her to memories of their twilight hours. As she lay curled about her lover, Diana realized she was happier than she had ever been. It was the quiet sort of happiness that Elana had introduced into her life that she was cherishing — and not simply the feel of a lover's arms. It held the peace of a homecoming, and she recognized that it had been missing in her life for much longer than the scant years she had spent on Aggar.

With a tender touch Elana's fingers brushed through her hair, drawing a lazy smile from Diana. There was no need for words between them. Elana knew Diana was awake just as she knew that those blue eyes were watching her. Dear Goddess, there was a magic here that often wrapped their quiet moments. She prayed that she would never forget nor take this bond for granted.

With a deep-throated purr Diana unfolded her legs and hugged the precious woman beside her. Lovingly she pressed a kiss into the warm flesh.

Elana's lips moved in a smile as Di'nay muttered a favored phrase in her Sisters' tongue. She teased her lover gently, "Are you ever going to teach me those words?"

"Hmmm...," was all that Diana managed to say as she nestled closer.

Elana smiled again but with a sadness, her fingers still playing in Di'nay's hair. With all the Sororian Di'nay had taught her, none was the cherishing litany Diana murmured when they made love. Perhaps it did not matter because she knew the amarin behind the tender phrases, as Di'nay understood the touch of her Blue Sight. Still, one could wish for the words.

"Soroi n'ti Mee," Diana repeated quietly, and startled, the hand in her hair grew still. She pushed herself up on an elbow, looking at Elana, and very slowly, very distinctly said, "It means...love of my life."

Elana stared at her, barely able to hear the words through the silent power of Di'nay's amarin.

Unprompted, Diana formed the syllables again, "So-roy... na... teh... me...." Elana's lips followed in mute imitation. Her dark gaze did not waver as Diana murmured, "They are old words of my Sisters, from a poem Helen's child left to us:

Soroi n'ti Mee,
Love of my life...
Soroe n'ti Mau,
Friend of my heart...
z'Mee kumin Tau,
Join me in life...
be nor ret n'Kahn, tizmar sae?
Please stay, beyond the cruel dawn?"

Blue eyes slid shut as a tear slipped free, and Elana felt herself tremble beneath the love of Di'nay's gaze. It had been so long in coming. They had spent so much time in dreading.

"Kumin Tau... sae?"

And she nodded, thinking her heart would burst with Di'nay's tenderness. "Yes, I will join you, beloved shadowmate. Yes — "

Di'nay's arms slid around her shoulders as her lips, warm and sweet, kissed the tears from the corners of Elana's eyes. "I love you," Diana whispered. Her body shivered at the infinite gentleness that touched her as Elana's eyes opened to her. "I have forgotten why I feared to tell you. I cannot imagine a true enough reason to hold my silence. Forgive me for my slowness, but I do love you — so very much."

"As I love you...have always loved you," Elana returned. "I would follow you to the very stars if it were possible."

Diana shook her head. "No. Not follow — sae, choose. With your people or with my Sisters, I will be content, if only you will share my life. But you must choose — please?"

And because of the openness they shared beneath the blue touch, Elana suddenly knew that Di'nay had learned the meaning of the lifestone's bond.

Sadness and doubt stirred within her as Di'nay grasped that understanding too, and the gentle lips that brushed Elana's were not tinged with guilt nor pity, only with reassurance. A sigh released her pensiveness, and Di'nay's gaze was freed as beneath a coaxing kiss Elana's body melted.

"I love you, Elana," Diana repeated, drawing back finally to look at her again. "Could you dare risk such a journey in our metal ships? Would leaving Aggar be so terrible for you?"

"Leaving, no." She shook her head. "The journey is possible just as the seeds made the Seer's Tomb bearable. There are ways to prepare for that, but...."

Her hesitation drew Diana's fear and she said, "But?"

"The Empire would not permit me to come with you, would they? Is Aggar not a closed planet?"

"Closed for those of Aggar...," Diana said slowly, "...not to those of the Sisterhood. If you could, in truth, bear to leave, a way could be made for you — to pose as a Sister merely returning home. If you would dare...?"

"Dare?" Elana murmured, and her gaze drifted to a distant place. "What is a Shadow, my love, if not one given to such dares? For you, it would be home, but for me? Dearest Di'nay, it would be an adventure for a lifetime to come. Yet...," her doubts crept back and she looked to Di'nay, "...could the way be cleared soon enough for your leaving tomorrow?"

"If you choose it, yes!" And then with all sincerity Diana pressed, "Or choose to stay, Elana. There are still many places of this world that you have not seen. Choose and we will stay, and there will never be need of leaving at all."

"No, Di'nay." Elana's smile was gentle. "Aggar would not hold you well. The loving that you need is not here in these people. You have roots to be nurtured within your Sisterhood, my dearest love, and I will not cheat you of that."

"Do not cheat me of you," Diana pleaded hoarsely.

"Nor you me." Elana's arms possessively wrapped around Di'nay's neck. "If I join you, it must not be as friend."

"Joining as mate, sae?" Diana wanting that with all her heart. Then tenderly her fingers traced the fading shadows beneath Elana's eyes. "Never let me do this to you again, Ona, I beg of you. Please love me enough not to...?"

"We will love each other enough," Elana said quietly. "No more secrets, I vow."

"No more fears left unspoken," Diana added.

"Then take me home with you, Di'nay."

"Ti Soroi..." Diana murmured, drawing nearer.

"In truth," Elana declared, "my love...for always." Then slowly blueness eclipsed the world, and in their kiss they found the Mother's destiny was, after all, to be their own.

❋ ❋ ❋

Dictionary of Terms from Aggar

✵ amarin: The amarin is the essence of life, the empathic imprint of animate existence which results in a cumulative pattern of feelings, thoughts and reflexes. It is one's aura.

✵ blackpine: A valuable hardwood conifer with a black, barkless trunk and green-black needles which is common to Maltar's lands.

✵ Blue Sight: The Sight or Blue Gift is a sixth sense genetically linked to blue eyes; an awareness of and ability to manipulate life auras and amarin. The terms also refers to a person possessing the Blue Sight.

✵ boko: A food native to the Ramains, boko is a vegetable-meat paste wrapped in boiled leaves.

✵ bunt: A tall, stemmed grain which yields red-brown seedlings and whose husks are often used for animal fodder. The term also applies to the grayish flour produced from the seedlings.

✵ "By the Mother's Hand": (idiom) "Done with the Goddess' blessings."

✵ Changlings: Sentient half-human, half-feline beasts native to the Northern Continent, Changlings are a race of people known for their amoral selling and reselling of information. They are also miners of lifestones.

✵ commons: A Ramains' term for a tavern housed by an inn.

✵ Council of Ten: A collection of ten Masters and Mistresses educated in the history and humanity of Aggar who are guardians of the planet's integrity.

✵ cucarae: A small, extremely poisonous scavenger, this crustacean is found in the wastelands of both the Northern and Southern Continents.

✵ cucarii: A group or nest of cucarae.

✵ Desert Peoples: Also known as The Southerners, the Desert Peoples are loosely organized nomadic tribes native to the Southern Continent and renown for their distilled liquors and merchant ventures.

✵ dracoon: A governing marshal appointed by the Ramains' King.

✵ early moon: The first of the twin moons to rise on any given evening.

✵ eitteh: A sentient feline native to the Northern Continent. The term eitteh usually refers to the winged females of the species as males are never seen. See also winged-cats and men-cats.

✵ Eldest Prepared: These individuals are the best of the Shadow trainees at the Council's Keep and are the preferred choice for assignments and lifebonding. They also instruct the younger recruits.

✵ Fates, the: The male deities of evil mischief, the Fates are mystical rulers of the dark underworld. Their primary figures include Malice and Ambition while their secondary figures include War, Ire, Greed and others.

✵ Fates' Cellar: The legendary home of the Fates, Fates' Cellar is the mythical place where evil souls go after death to suffer in a punishing afterlife. Also known as hell.

✵ Fates' Jest: (idiom) A malicious turn of events attributed to the Fates.

✵ Firecaps: These intersecting, volcanic mountain ranges comprise the northeastern third of the Northern Continent. They are uninhabited and controlled by Seers in order to stabilize continental land masses.

❋　　grubber:　A generic term for ground rodents in the Northern Continent. Grubber generally refers to smallish, nasty-tempered mammals.

❋　　Jezebet:　Usually given to a woman, this title is bestowed upon someone who is a resident of the Council's Keep and is trained in the arts of lifebonding Shadowmates.

❋　　lexion:　A domesticated fowl common to farms of the Northern Continent which is raised for its meat.

❋　　lifestone:　An opal-like energy stone often found in limestone deposits in the Northern Continent and used by the Council in the practice of lifebonding Shadowmates.

❋　　mala':　A female slave or bond-servant of the Ramains whose duties are restricted to the household and the bedroom.

❋　　Maltar:　The ruling family of the northern half of the Northern Continent. The term may refer either to the ruling family member or the country itself.

❋　　men-cats:　The male of the eitteh species, these cat-like savages inhabit the mountain ranges on the Northern Continent.

❋　　mesta:　A thick-skinned, amber fruit with a tart, meaty pulp in the seed pods that is cultivated by farmers in the Northern Continent.

❋　　midnight moon:　The second of the twin moons to rise on any given night.

❋　　Min:　A generic title given to free-born women in the Ramains. It is comparable to the Terran term ma'am.

❋　　monarc:　A standard calendar division, roughly equivalent to a Terran month, which is comprised of four, ten-day periods.

❋　　Mother, the:　A nurturing female deity who is seen as the birthmother of the universe. Aggar's twin moons are associated with her watchful light.

❋　　pripper:　A small, tree-dwelling mammal known for its comical antics and bushy coat.

❋　　Ramains:　The southwestern third of the Northern Continent which is united beneath a liberal monarchy and shares a border with the Council's lands.

❋　　schaefea:　A hoofed scavenger of middle size native to the northern mountains. The schaefea has protruding tusks and venomous saliva glands.

❋　　Seers:　Those individuals gifted with the Blue Sight who are bound to Aggar's lifecycles and no longer capable of individual thoughts or actions. They are directed by the Council of Ten and are the crafters of Aggar's landscapes. Sometimes referred to as mystics.

❋　　silverwood:　A hardwood conifer with a smooth, silver-green bark and gray-green needles which is common to the Ramains foothills and mountain regions. Also called silverpine.

❋　　single moon:　The night at the end of each monarc in which only one of the twin moons is visible. Term is synonymous with monarc.

❋　　Tad:　Generic title given to free-born men in the Ramains which is similar to the Terran term sir.

❋　　ten-day:　A division of days within a monarc, roughly equivalent to a Terran week.

1000 Reasons You Might Think She Is My Lover. Erotica. Angela Costa. Romantic, rowdy, tasty and titillating. A red-hot, pocket-sized collection that will make you laugh, blush and... look for a lover.

ISBN 1-886383-21-9 $10.95

Fall Through the Sky. Future Fiction. Jennifer DiMarco. In this stand-alone sequel to the best-selling adventure *Escape to the Wind,* Tyger and her gang the Windriders discover incredible secrets and prepare to face the Patriarchy.

ISBN 1-886383-16-2 $12.95

At the Edge. Play. Jennifer DiMarco. You'll laugh out loud. You'll shout hallelujah. Therese Weaver is a poet who gives new meaning to the word "melodrama," and Daniel O'Donald is an HIV+ construction worker and activist. When these two women meet tectonic plates shift.

ISBN 1-886383-11-1 $9.95

Still Life with Buddy. Poetry. Lesléa Newman. A novel told in fifty-two poems, following the intense friendship of the female narrator and her best friend Buddy who dies of AIDS. A story of friendship, loss and undying love. Recipient of a National Endowment of the Arts grant.

ISBN 1-886383-27-8 $9.95

Sweet Dark Places. Poetry. Lesléa Newman. Exploring the places of anger and rage, fear and longing and most of all, the place of love in so many women readers. Less than two hundred copies left in print!

ISBN 0-939821-01-X $8.95

Love Me Like You Mean It. Poetry. Lesléa Newman. A collection rich with culture, memories, humor and spice, both sexy and powerful. These poems are touchstones to the vital transitions in a woman's life. Less than two hundred copies left in print!

ISBN 1-878533-14-2 $8.95

Children's Books
Books brought to you by Little Blue Works, Pride's children's division.

The Magical Child. Carol DiMarco and Connie Wurm. In the days of castles and kings, dragons and things, there lived a little girl named Angela Marie who was magic but didn't know it... yet! (Twenty-six pages. Ready-to-color.)

ISBN 1-886383-19-7 $10.95

The Best Thing. Jennifer Anna and Joey Marsocci. With help from a magical key to Ladybug Land, two sisters discover the best thing in the world — each other! (Sixty pages. Ready-to-color.)

ISBN 1-886383-26-X $12.95

Send check or money order to:
Pride Publications, Post Office Box 148, Radnor, Ohio 43066-0148

Matters of Pride

Pride Publications' books are available <u>to bookstores</u> through distributors (Alamo Square, Baker & Taylor, Bookpeople, Koen, Stilone/Bulldog, Turnaround) as well as direct for 50% off retail, payment due in ninety days and free shipping. Books and games are available <u>to readers</u> for retail price and free shipping.

Novels, Poetry and Plays

Books brought to you by Pride Publications, our cutting-edge division.

Annabel and I. Romantic Fantasy. Chris Anne Wolfe. Set on Chautauqua Lake, the tale of a love that transcends all time and all categories. Jenny-wren is from the 1980s but Annabel is from the 1890s. Features thirteen interior artplates by Chris Storm.

ISBN 1-886383-17-0 $10.95

Roses and Thorns: Beauty and the Beast Retold. Adult Fairytale. Chris Anne Wolfe. Magical, sensual retelling of Beauty and the Beast with two heroines. *From the Lion Fairytale Series,* #1. Features eight interior artplates by Lupa.

ISBN 1-886383-12-X $10.95

Fires of Aggar. Fantasy. Chris Anne Wolfe. In this second book in the *Aggar Series,* join Royal Marshal Gwyn of the Amazons of Aggar as she travels into danger to aid and protect Blue Sighted Llinolae, the ruler of Khirla, as the city is plagued with Terran raids.

ISBN 0-934678-58-8 $10.95

talking drums. Prose Poetry. Jan Bevilacqua. Poems of love, life, sex and empowerment. Exploring gender and butch/femme in our society today. Features fourteen artplates by Kateren Lopez.

ISBN 1-886383-13-8 $9.95

The White Bones of Truth. Future Fiction. Cris Newport. In a future where film stars are owned by the Studio and independence is illegal, revolution brews. A novel of rock 'n' roll, redemption and virtual reality. Features five interior artplates by Pride Publications.

ISBN 1-886383-15-4 $10.95

Sparks Might Fly. Fiction. Cris Newport. Pip Martin is a brilliant concert pianist, but when her passion for music becomes entangled with her passion for the seductive Corrinne, her heart and her life strike a dissonant cord. Her journey to back to her music and herself is the story of *Sparks Might Fly.*

ISBN 0-934678-61-8 $9.95

Queen's Champion: The Legend of Lancelot Retold. Adult Fairytale. Cris Newport. A classic and enticing retelling of Lancelot and Guinevere's love and the legend of Lancelot with a twist! *From the Lion Fairytale Series,* #2.

ISBN 1-886383-20-0 $11.95

Pride Publications
bringing light to the shadows
voice to the silence

Our History
Pride Publications was founded in 1989 by a circle of authors and artists. A publishing house dedicated to shedding light on misconceptions, challenging stereotypes and speaking for those not spoken for. A press created for the authors, artists and readers, not for profit. With several imprints and divisions, Pride publishes books in all genres by all kinds of authors, regardless of gender, orientation, race or age. We are always looking for new projects that are revolutionary in content. At Pride we believe that risk and diversity are part of life. We believe in opening eyes.

Our Facts
Pride Publications works with artists, authors looking for publishers, authors self-publishing who want help, and authors in need of agents. Authors published with Pride receive 10-15% of gross monies received and retain the rights to their books. Authors will also have say in all edits, artwork and promo done for their books.

Authors co-publishing with Pride's help pay only half of the paper costs. Pride pays for all other costs and offers all standard services including accounting, advertising, storage, tour planning, representation and international distribution. Authors receive 50% of all gross monies received.

Authors working with Pride literary agents will receive complete industry representation for 12% of gross royalties received.

Artists working with Pride novels receive advance payment for their art in addition to royalties on all two dozen products that will feature their art. Artists working with Pride children's books receive royalties equal to the author's.

Author submissions: Send complete manuscript, typed, single-sided, double-spaced on white paper. Resume and bio. Summary of entire manuscript. SASE for return of manuscript.

Artist submissions: Send five to ten color and black-and-white samples of artwork. Resume and bio. Cover letter discussing what types of projects you are interested in working on. SASE for response.

❋   Shekhina: The moon of Helen's second planet. This moon is home to Helen's high-tech base where diplomatic contacts between the dey Sorormin and the Galactic Terran Empire occur. It is also the home of the Immigration offices and the orientation/screening facilities for new Sisters. Historically, the term refers to an ancient Terran goddess of Judaic lore and sometimes connotes the divine image of a woman.

❋   sor: The noun meaning woman.

❋   soroe: The noun denoting friend or dear companion.

❋   soria: A noun meaning loved one, lover or beloved.

❋   Sororian: The woman-made language of the Sisterhood. The term derives its root meaning from the ancient Terran word which refers to sisters.

❋   Sorormin: A noun that is synonymous with the word Sisterhood.

❋   Sorormin, dey: The word which represents the proper name of The Sisterhood. The term also refers generally to the culture of women who settled on Helen's second planet. dey Sorormin are recognized members of the Senate in the Third Galactic Terran Empire.

❋   sueht: A past tense form of the verb to lose or to misplace.

❋   tau: A pronoun denoting me.

❋   ti: A word that indicates possession (my).

❋   tizmar: A verb which means to remain, to settle or to unite and/or join together.

❋   vu: A term meaning very little, a small amount.

❋   z': A term indicating for or with.

❋   "Z'ki Sak, Diana": (idiom) An expression of regret or disbelief which translates as "By your wits, Goddess."

❋ ❋ ❋

* mau: A noun meaning heart.

* mauen: The plural form of mau (hearts).

* mee: A noun which denotes life.

* minmee: A word meaning birth, minmee also carries the connotation of the sacred connection of life-giving or creating.

* n': This expression denotes possession. It is usually used to indicate an individual's House.

* n'Athena: One of the Seven Houses of dey Sorormin, members of this house are traditionally the guardians of the Sisterhood. The term also recalls a Terran goddess from ancient Greek lore.

* n'Awehai: One of the Seven Houses of dey Sorormin, members of this house are traditionally the builders and craftswomen of the Sisterhood. The term also recalls a Terran goddess of Iroquois (Native Northern American) lore.

* n'Hina: One of the Seven Houses of dey Sorormin, members of this house are traditionally the agricultural providers of the Sisterhood. The term also recalls a Terran goddess of Polynesian lore.

* n'Huitaca: One of the Seven Houses of dey Sorormin, members of this house are traditionally the treasurers of music and arts of the Sisterhood. The term also recalls a Terran goddess of Colombian Chibcha (Native Southern American) lore.

* n'Minona: One of the Seven Houses of dey Sorormin, members of this house are traditionally the historians and teachers of the Sisterhood. The term also recalls a Terran goddess of African Dahomey lore.

* n'Sappho: First House of the Seven Houses of dey Sorormin, members of this house traditionally make up the legislature and leadership of the Sisterhood. The term also recalls a Terran stateswoman of ancient Greek citizenship.

* n'Shea: One of the Seven Houses of dey Sorormin, members of this house are traditionally the healers and earthwitches of the Sisterhood. The term also recalls a Terran woman-deity and/or the white witches of ancient Irish lore.

* nehna: (idiom) A prompt for more information meaning and then, then it happened that or so then.

* nor: An word that indicates an event happened in the past.

* puor: An word meaning strength, stability or virtuousness.

* quinn: A word denoting peace, tranquility or the absence of violence.

* ret: A word meaning cruelty or harm.

* sae: Another term for please, this word denotes a request.

* sak: This word means intelligence or cleverness.

* shea: This noun refers to a healing witch from the House of n'Shea. A member of this house will frequently be one who is closely bound to nature. She may also be a mistress of love potions and possess the evil eye. See the term n'Shea.

* sheaz: A noun meaning the earth or world, this term may also refer to the components of a nurturing Earthmother Creator.

* **tenmoon season:** A period of time roughly the same as two Terran years. The name comes from the fact that ten single moon nights will occur during the time it takes for Aggar to complete one orbit around its sun.

* **torin:** An edible, broad-leafed fern commonly found in the wooded rangers of the Northern Continent.

* **twin moons:** Two planetoids orbiting around Aggar's globe. The term is also associated with the Mother's watchful care.

* **Unseen Wall:** An unidentified energy field which was ordered by the Council of Ten and is controlled by the Seers; the Unseen Wall comprises the border around the Terran Base Quadrant.

* **White Isles of Fire, the:** The group of volcanic islands off the eastern Firecaps of the Northern Continent. Sometimes called the Archipelago, it is the native homeland of the Council and the Seers.

* **Wine of Decisions:** A spiced wine containing a natural drug which prompts the visions of the Blue Sight.

* **winged-cats:** Generally used as another term for female eitteh.

Dictionary of Sororian Terms

* **ann:** (idiom) A word used to emphasize thoughts or ideas and function as a verbal exclamation point. Ann might also be translated as "Take note!" Other meanings include to be far away or distant.

* **beasties:** Large, hoofed mammals, these horned animals have copper-colored, wooly coats and are descended from the Highland Cattle of old Terra.

* **bin:** A preposition meaning between. Sometimes means to or from.

* **Cee:** A word that refers to the customs or ways of any given people.

* **corean:** A verb meaning to find precious, to treasure.

* **dey:** This word can be used as either an article as in "the" or a pronoun as in "we" or "our" and is meant to connote respect.

* **Feast of Helen:** This anniversary celebration of unity and independence marks the birth of the Sisterhood's firstborn child.

* **felan:** A verb form meaning using, doing or creating.

* **Helen:** This name refers to the Red star of dey Sorormin's solar system, the firstborn of dey Sorormin's original settlement and the leader of n'Sappho during early negotiations to retain Sorormin independence. The word means "light."

* **kahn:** A noun meaning sunrise or dawn.

* **kamak:** A verb which indicates something is brought to completion or finished. It may also be used in place of is made.

* **kau:** A pronoun referring to the second person singular (you).

* **ki:** A word indicating possession (yours).

* **kumin:** A verb meaning to join together.

* **m':** A preposition denoting as or of (from).

* **mae:** A word indicating that something is dear or precious.

* **"Mae n'Pour":** (idiom) An expression which means "Give me strength." This term is often used as a curse to express frustration or anger but can also be used as a genuine prayer to the Goddess.